DENYAH

BY

HYACINTH BROWN

Published 2006 by arima publishing

www.arimapublishing.com

ISBN 1 84549 083 5
ISBN 978-1-84549-083-6

Printed and bound in the United Kingdom

Typeset in Garamond 10.5/16

Swirl is an imprint of arima publishing.

arima publishing
ASK House, Northgate Avenue
Bury St Edmunds, Suffolk IP32 6BB
t: (+44) 01284 700321

www.arimapublishing.com

About the author

 Hyacinth Brown was born in St. Kitts, St. Peters Parish (West Indies) in 1938 and came to live in Birmingham, England 1958. Mother to eight children, 17 grandchildren and 15 great-grand. She is a highly regarded member of her local community. Hyacinth Brown a.k.a Nana has always had a strong passion for writing literature. While attending a writing school she won first prize for a top selling publisher in the short romance category. Although this is her first novel to be published there will be many more works in the pipeline, so sit back and enjoy.

Acknowledgments

First of all I would like to thank the Lord Almighty for giving me great strength and belief to complete this novel.

Thanks and gratitude to arima publishing and all personnel involved and a big thank you to my proof readers. I raise a glass to you all!

I would like to thank a dear departed friend and teacher, Mistress Santa Wilder who inspired me to write and seek publication. May she rest in peace?

Special thanks and appreciation to my granddaughter Treverlene and my youngest daughter Rita, who helped me to type and edit, right up to the very end, they never once complained even when I was being a nuisance.

Judith my eldest daughter that laughed at me, thanks the laugh is on you now!

My son in law Paul Douglas for being at hand whenever I had problems with my computer, which was continuous!

Sarah Green "my financial backer" who encouraged me to do it on my own!

Many thanks to my good friends Eulalie Glasgow, Oreta Rawlins, Mary Blackman, Dorrel Brown and Mavis Carty for encouragement, support and laughter.

To all my readers who have taken time out a big thanks you.

Last but not least, my family and others not mentioned (you all know who you are) Thanks for the support, motivation and a listening ear.

Peace and love to you all.

CHAPTER ONE

After a hard days work at Country National Bank, Denyah returns to her home in the Yardley area of Birmingham to find her husband, Wesley, lying comfortably on the black leather sofa. He is deep in conversation on his mobile phone. Denyah ignored him and carried on with her day to day chores of tidying the house. Wesley had been a Caribbean police officer and now worked for the police service. He is six foot two inches tall with chocolate coloured smooth skin and chiselled features. His body is perfectly cut in all the right places. Wesley is also known as a well-respected man of the community. On the other hand, Denyah kept herself to herself. She is a very attractive white woman with olive skin and striking features 5'11" with big brown eyes and full lips. The way that her clothes hug her body you cab see she is 'a perfect ten' with curves in all the right places. Denyah's job takes her from one bank branch to another, advising customers on the best way to invest money. However, her husband hates her job and has often told her to leave so she can look after his daughter Paris. Paris is the child of Wesley's previous relationship. Her mother was an alcoholic and later started taking harder drugs. Wesley took his daughter and asked Denyah to care for her. It's now ten years since he and Denyah got married.

Stepping back a little, Denyah had Paris from six months. As soon as Paris turned three, Denyah took her to nursery, so that she could go to work. At three thirty she would finish work and drive to get Paris before the nursery closed at four. Paris is now nine years old and Denyah's husband continues to insist she give up her job to look after his daughter. But Denyah has told him she will divorce him if he carries on asking her to give up her job.

One Tuesday afternoon Denyah returned home from work with migraine to find her husband in bed with her sister Fay. After she confronted him, she ended up in City hospital with three cracked ribs and a broken arm. At the hospital, she lied to the doctors and police saying she had been mugged and beaten up by a hooded man. When the police asked her if she could identify her attacker, she told them it was too dark and happened so quickly. The policewomen took her statement but didn't believe her. Before the two policewomen left the hospital, the taller and prettiest one said, "Mrs Davis, while taking your statement, I could clearly see you're shielding someone. You might have your reasons, but I think you're protecting the one that has done this to you. Please Mrs Davis, be sensible and tell us before they hurt you worse and you mightn't be able to tell."

Denyah closed her eyes painfully. Within her, she wanted to tell the police it was her husband who'd beaten her up but she turned her back on them as she was feeling sorrier for her husband than for herself. The nurse that was present at the time the policewomen questioned Denyah, asked the police to come back another time, but Denyah said, "My answer isn't going to change. I don't know who's done this to me." The young policewoman touched Denyah's shoulder, smiled then they both left with her college.

"Mrs Davis. I have a strong feeling you won't see them again." the nurse said. Denyah stayed still with her back towards the nurse. The nurse, touched, said, "Well Mrs Davis I think you have your reason but I would have told the police what's happened if I were you. The nurse closed her eyes and quickly opened them and brushed downwards the back of Denyah's hair and left.

Denyah spent over three weeks in hospital, and then stayed with her mother so that she could rest for a bit longer. Two weeks later she decided it was time to go home.

Even though Denyah wasn't quite well, she did some work from home to help her boss out as he was behind with piles of work. Five weeks later Denyah returned to work. The Friday was her thirty second birthday. Her boss remembered it was her birthday and how kind she was, always helping him out. He ordered flowers and a box of Black Magic chocolates to be sent to the bank for her.

When the young man arrived at the bank with the flowers and chocolates, he went to the counter and asked for Mrs Denyah Davis. But Denyah was at another branch.

"I'm Gail Henry, a friend of Mrs Davis. I would be happy to sign for them. I will make sure she receives them as soon as she gets back."

"Well Mr Handsome, it's your choice." Gail told him.

He smiled and took his seat on a chair holding the carrier bag and decided to wait.

Gail smiled as their eyes met. As he waited for twenty minutes for Denyah to come, Gail said to him: "Well, Mr Deep blue eyes handsome, if you would like to keep hot in your seat, I'm sure you'll only have to wait for the next three hours as she's working elsewhere for the day." Gail

"You're joking aren't you?" The man asked smiling.

"I wish I was." Gail said.

The young man got out of his seat and walked to the counter and said. "Mrs Henry, I had strict order to deliver this bag to Mrs Davis only."

"Look here Mr Blue eyes. I don't know about you but I've other customers to serve. So you can either sit and wait or leave what ever you have for Mrs Davis with me!"

The young man gave Gail the gift bag but demanded a receipt after giving her the flowers and the chocolates.

"Very wise choice my young handsome blue eyes. By the way, how do you know my name?'

"You're wearing it." He said.

Gail smiled and asked. Have you a girlfriend?"

"Yes, we would be getting hitched in four months time."

"Luck for some." Gail said. The young man smiled looking Gail in her eyes.

After Gail gave the delivery man a receipt for the items, he said "Thanks," and left After Gail watched him disappeared out the door, she smiled, read the card and then tossed the flowers and the chocolates on the floor at her feet to served a customer. After, she ruffed up the carrier bag and took it in the back room of the bank behind and tossed it behind some cardboard boxes in the cupboard, saying to herself "Denyah, you don't know how much I hate you. Every man that comes into this bank wanted to be served by you." After Gail finished work she took the flowers and chocolates and drove to the Mrs Evelyn's house as she picked the bag up, she said angrily. "Bitch:" and rest in beside her on the seat to look in her car mirror, fixed the front of her long plaited hair to the left side of her face and put lipstick on. She smiled as she took up the nice gold-coloured carrier bag with the Black-Magic chocolate. She got out her car carrying the bag, walked to Mrs Evelyn's door and rang the doorbell with a dirty grin on her face. Mrs Evelyn answered looked as though she just come from under the sun bed as she was wearing a white house coat with dark glasses and a towel wrapped round her head.

"Hello Mrs Evelyn."

"Gail, what are you doing here?"

"Mrs Evelyn, your husband sent these to Denyah three hours ago."

"So why have you got them?"

"Well I signed for them and when I saw that your husband sent them, I thought you should know. That's why I brought them to you."

"Tell me Gail, was it out of jealousy that you thought I should know that my husband gave these presents to Denyah?"

"No…no…of course not, but I do think your husband and Mrs Davis are having an affair, and it's only right that you know."

"So Gail, why do you think I want to know?"

"Well if I was married and my husband were having affair, I would like to know. However, your husband takes her to lunch regular and when they're not out for lunch they're penned up together in a room. You should see them like two little playing kittens."

"Well Gail, I've heard enough. I do hope you don't mind if I don't ask you in?" Mrs Evelyn said as she instantly showed distress on her white pale looking face. As Gail got nearer to the door, Mrs Evelyn took the flowers and chocolates from her and then flung her door shut in Gail's face.

Gail smiled and walked to her car and before she got into her car, she turned and face Mrs Evelyn house and said "Hard face bitch!

Mrs Evelyn took the flowers and chocolates into the garbage cupboard and threw them into her bin, spat on the bag and slammed the lid down saying when that son-of-a-bitch of my husband comes home he would be in there with you where he belong."

"Well done Gail." she said to herself as she got back in her car smiling and huffed breathlessly. Meanwhile, Mrs Evelyn took a glass and savagely tossed it at her husband's photo, shattering it. She then hurried to her room to get dressed and rushed out of her house, slammed the door shut' and set out in her car to see Denyah's husband. At this time Gail was still sitting in her car with her face stiffed vex like wondering if she done the right thing. As she slapped her face hard, she huffed and said, "Silly Gail, what have you got yourself into. Denyah I do hate you but not as much as that wrinkling hard faced bitch Mrs Evelyn. Are well, what has done, is done:" She said and drove away.

Meanwhile, Mrs Evelyn just knocked on Denyah's door. Wesley answered the door and looked firmly into Mrs Evelyn's eyes and said "What ever you're selling I'm not interested."

"Mr Davis, I'm not here to sell you anything I just want you to hear me out. I'm Mrs Evelyn. My husband is a bank manager and your wife worked in his back sometimes. Please Mr Davis. I'm not here to cause trouble." She said as Wesley looked down at her.

"Well come in and let me hear what you have to say." Wesley said and moved himself inside his house and invited Mrs Evelyn in but didn't offer her a seat. Standing facing Wesley while he sat, he looked up at her to hear what she has to say.

"Mr Davis, one of the bank staff brought to me flowers and a box of chocolate and told me they were from my husband to your wife."

"So what is that prove Mrs Evelyn? Wesley asked smiling.

Mr Davis, I believed my husband and your wife are having an affair."

"Pardon me Mrs Evelyn if I by pass this one. By the look of you, I can imagine what your husband look like. Your husband sent flowers and chocolates to my wife, I'm sure there's a perfect reason.

"Mr Davis, would you think I would come to you if I wasn't sure about my husband and your wife having an affair?"

"Are you sure of that?" Wesley asked her.

"Well, would you send expensive flowers and chocolates to a female you weren't sleeping with?" Mrs Evelyn asked.

Wesley did not reply. Instead he rubbed his forehead and got up looking deep in thought as Mrs Evelyn stared at him.

"You can leave now! I'll deal with my wife when she gets home. But I'm sure we'll find we have it wrong." Wesley said taking the lead from the living room to the front door and opened the door.

Mrs Evelyn was going to speak, but Wesley looked at her and pointed outside, saying. "I want you to leave and never come here again!" After he watched her get walked out the gate and into the car, he flung the front door shut and angrily said, "Bitch!" Then he poured himself a large amount of whiskey, gulped it down and smashed the glass against the wall in a temper he then fell back on the sofa exhaling deeply. He drank mouthfuls of whiskey from the bottle until he fell asleep sitting up with the opened bottle of whiskey resting by the right side of his head.

One hour later, Denyah walked into the house to find him stretched out on the sofa with half a bottle of whiskey resting by the side of his head, dried-up blood on his left hand and broken glass on her front room wooden floor. "Wesley" she called as she shook him to wake up. He opened his left eye and leaned his head on to the side looking up at her. "What happened honey?" she asked him. He opened his eyes and stared at her. She smiled, and as she went to touch his hand, he kicked her away and said, "Fuck off and leave me alone" he stood up and pushed her away.

"What's the matter with you Wesley?" she asked him.

"Do you want me to tell you what you already fucking know?" he grunted angrily.

"Wesley, why are you treating me so badly, when all I've done is loved you. Is it so hard for you to show me a fraction of respect even though you don't love me, Wesley, even though you rape me most of the time, I haven't run from you. I don't like what you're doing to me. But you're my husband. I married you for better or worse. But the time will come when I can't take anymore" Denyah said as she walked towards the kitchen.

Wesley followed behind her, swung her to face him and knocked her down with a hard backhanded slap to the side of her head. "You only walk away from me when I throw you out. You leave before I finish talking to you, and I will break every bone in your body. You don't move until I say you can go! Now, get the fuck out of my sight"

Tears came in her eyes as she vacuumed up the pieces of glass while he sat and watched. After she finished, he got up, looked at her, grinned scornfully and then pushed her making it hard for her to keep her balance. He then slapped her across her face again. She covered her face and backed away she then muttered, "What have I done?"

"You've been sleeping around"

"That's not fair. I've never looked at another man since I've been with you and you're a fine one to talk" Denyah said defending herself.

"What?" Wesley asked in surprise.

"Fay! My sister, you've been sleeping around with her for years along with all those other women. And never once have I questioned you about them. "

"Denyah, your sister is more of a woman than you'll ever be. Just look at you! You make me sick!" he said and grinned. She looked hard at him and left the room crying.

He followed behind her with the half of a bottle of whiskey in his hand and pulled her to face him. She became frightened and knelt down at his feet holding onto his legs begging him, "Please don't hurt me anymore."

He looked down at her and smiled in a patronizing manner he asked. "Do you want some whiskey?" she shook her head to say no, he put his foot in her face pushed her on her back and walked away laughing. She got up shivering with fear and walked into the kitchen and started peeling potatoes. He left her feeling frightened, she was trembling so much it took her a long time to peeled one potato. He walked into the kitchen and slapped her bottom then walked out laughing.

Even though she shivered in disgust, she managed to cooked dinner in spite of her fearfulness. As they sat down at the dinner table Paris refused to eat.

"What's the matter Paris?" she asked her.

"I don't like you cooking!" she cried.

"You don't have to eat it, if you don't want to honey," her father said and offered to take her to a restaurant. Paris smiled as she left the table to get her and her father's coat. Wesley laughed as he got up out of his seat and left with his daughter.

The next morning was Saturday. Wesley took Paris shopping while Denyah went to the hairdressers. On her way home she bumped into her husband's sister, Lisa, standing outside the Iceland supermarket with two shopping bags filled with groceries. The bags were heavy and Erdington high street was so busy with shoppers and so many reckless drivers showing off their new cars blasting out the latest hip-hop tunes over the sound of the heavy rain. Denyah suggested they could they could share a taxi home.

"Thanks Den, I was waiting for my husband but it doesn't look like he's coming"

"That's the trouble with most men, they're so unreliable. Always forget what they're supposed to be doing" Denyah said as she took one of Lisa's shopping bags.

"What're you doing here spending all your money?"

"Oh no, I just come from getting my hair my done"

"Have you changed your hairdressers?"

"Yes, ever since I saw Wesley stalking me"

"My brother does not deserve you" Lisa said smiling. "Shall we go somewhere for a hot drink?" Lisa asked.

"Sure, but what if Richard comes for you"

"I hope he does and waits for as long as I have"

"Well then, where would you like to go?" Denyah asked,

"Anywhere I can get a drink" Lisa replied.

"Have you got anything planned for tonight, I've been invited to a party?"

"Who's?" Denyah asked.

"Joan and Austin they both are my friends. Their engagement party is tonight. It starts at ten."

"Yeah," Denyah said. "I could do with letting my hair down."

"Good, I'll call for you about nine" Lisa said. "I will tell Claire if she's coming, to get us about eight."

"How is Claire anyway?" Denyah asked.

"Well the latest I heard was Marcus had left her and he's now living with Grace."

"Well, she hasn't told me and I have no intention of prying into her and Marcus's business. Besides, if she had wanted to tell me, she would have done so."

"True."

Lisa phoned for a taxi. When it arrived they got in, she told the driver to take them to a nice restaurant to get lunch. "At your service Madams, how does China town sound?"

"Great."

He drove towards town and stopped outside the hotel. The driver turned around, "eight pounds please" Lisa gave him ten pounds and told him to keep the change.

"Thanks" he said and drove off. They walked towards a white painted restaurant; Lisa stopped and said smiling, "This looks like a nice place" she looked at Denyah before they entered and took a seat facing the window overlooking more restaurants, a hotel, confectionary shops and the Bull Ring shopping centre.

While Denyah sat flicking through the menu she noticed Lisa was very quiet she looked up at her and said "I don't think we should be here if you want us to leave I'll pay for a taxi home" Denyah asked her.

"No Den, we're here to have lunch and lunch we shall have."

"You're alright - Richard will understand but as for Wesley I don't think he will."

"Don't worry about my wicked brother, I will tell him I asked you to accompany me."

While they talked a waitress walked over and asked if they were ready to place an order. Lisa looked up and said no, the waitress stood still for a moment looking in Lisa's face before saying "Don't I know you?" Staring into her eyes she said "Of course, you're Lisa Davis. We went to the same drama classes at least fifteen years ago. Am I right?"

"Hold on, remind me of your name." Lisa said interestedly.

"Cindy, Cindy Miller." Cindy said.

"Oh yes, that's right, has it been that long." Lisa laughed.

"Time flies." Cindy said.

"We had some good times together. Didn't we?" Lisa asked.

"Yeah, we sure did. Do you remember Pat Lewis? How we used to call her greasy head - she was in here a few minutes ago too?" Cindy said giggling.

"Cindy, you were the one who nicknamed her greasy head."

"I know Lisa. But she was scruffy looking and unattractive at that. Anyway, she's now Lady Warner. She married a very wealthy man and they have two children together. Life for her has really moved on, anyway who's your friend?" Cindy asked.

"My brother's wife, - Denyah." Lisa said looking at Denyah.

"Pleased to meet you Denyah, forgive me for yapping on. It's just that I haven't seen my friend Lisa in years. One more day and I would have completely forgotten her. I'm Cindy."

"Cindy it's a pleasure meeting you." Denyah said smiling.

Cindy and Lisa burst out laughing and embraced each other while Denyah watch both of them with interest. Then as silence was stored between them, Denyah smiled and said.

"Can we have two glasses of coke with chicken rice and salad, please Cindy?"

"Sure." Cindy said as she rested her right hand on Lisa's shoulder and looked at Denyah smiling.

"I'll be right back." Cindy said as she walked to the drinks bar and passed the food order to the cook. Suddenly a very tall handsome good looking tanned man walked over

to Cindy. She spoke to him and then he walked away. He was smiling as he walked over to Denyah and Lisa's table. He stopped and looked directly into Denyah's eyes.

"Who are you?" Lisa asked him. "Hi I'm Eugene. Cindy's married to my cousin. She told me that you and her go way back so I thought I'd come and introduce myself." "Oh well, I'm Lisa and this is my sister-in-law Denyah. You can sit down if you like" "Thanks, I will" Eugene said as he sat facing Denyah. He smiled then touched Denyah's right shoe with his. Denyah quickly moved her foot and lowered her head gazing on the table. "Your brother's lucky" he said. Denyah sat listening while they spoke about her as if she wasn't there. "So, what about you Eugene, what do you do?" Lisa asked.

"Well like I said, Cindy and I have known each other for a long time. But I haven't seen her for years, as I've been in Canada working. But for now, I'm here for at least one year or for good."

Denyah was anxious to hear what his job was, but he didn't say. Throughout his conversation with Lisa, he kept staring at Denyah. She tried her hardest not to look at him as she knew Lisa was watching her.

Cindy returned with the drinks and then the food. Denyah picked up her glass and took a sip then placed the glass on the table. Eugene then picked up her drink and sipped from her glass. Lisa and Cindy looked at each other and then at him. As Denyah stood up to walk away, he asked her, "Are you leaving us?"

"No. I'm going to the ladies" Denyah said.

"Why, don't you like my aftershave?" he asked giggling.

"It's not your aftershave I don't like, it's your attitude. Besides, I didn't think I needed consent to use a public toilet" Denyah replied with a straight face.

"No you don't, you can go where you like" he said as he winked at her.

When Denyah got into the ladies, she looked at herself in the toilet mirror and imagined Eugene was kissing and hugging her. After a moment of thought, she shook her head and sighed blissfully. She then noticed her make-up was looking very pale from the rain but she left it as she didn't want Lisa or Eugene to think she had done it for him.

Denyah then went into a cubicle and again thought deeply of Eugene. She felt a tingling sensation that tears came to her eyes and the feeling of love sparked through her like fire crackers as she slithered her fingers over her breasts and downwards to her vagina. She then closed her eyes thinking of him. Before she left she took a long look at herself in the mirror, washed her hands, dried her eyes and returned to the table to see Lisa sitting alone and her plate practically clean.

"Your food must be cold now." Lisa said.

"I'm not that hungry anyway." Denyah told Lisa glancing around the room to see if she could see Eugene.

"He's gone Denyah. He said he might see you some other time." Lisa said smiling.

"Thank God for that! Have you checked the time Lisa?" Denyah asked.

Lisa looked on her wrist watch before saying "Oh no, Richard is going to kill me when I get home."

After Lisa and Denyah put their coats on and were ready to leave, Lisa went and told Cindy that they were leaving and they wanted to pay their bill. "Your bills have been paid by a secret admirer." Cindy said and smiled. Then she asked Lisa and Denyah to wait while she signed out. As Lisa and Denyah waited, Cindy gave them another cold drink then removed her apron and cap. She phoned her husband telling him, "I met a

friend that I haven't seen for years she's with her sister-in-law and I am giving them a lift home." Cindy's husband was okay about that. "That's fine honey." he said.

Cindy returned to Lisa and Denyah, "Well girls, I'm going to give you a lift home And save you having to wait for a taxi."

Denyah and Lisa got out of their seats and walked with Cindy out of the restaurant to the car park. Denyah sat in the back and took Lisa's shopping bags and put them on the seat beside her while Lisa sat in the front. Cindy took the scenic route home, she took them though Smethwick showing them some hotels and restaurants that Eugene owned. After Cindy drove them around, she took a short cut and ended up passing a small old unused burial ground that sits on a hill. Denyah looked back at the little old demolished church. She shivered as she felt a strong stream of coolness run through her body with the thought of Wesley killing her if she tried to leave him. To prevent her burning eyes from weeping, she thought deeply of Eugene, she smiled meekly. When they were past the burial ground and her body feeling returned to normal, she told them about the strange feelings she'd experienced. Cindy smiled.

"Well," said Lisa. "Maybe you were thinking of that gorgeous specimen and you know who I'm on about!" Lisa giggled as she looked back at Denyah.

"Lisa, if I didn't know you better, I would say that you're trying to put ideas in my head about other men." Denyah said smiling and then turned to look out the window at the skies thinking of Eugene until she got to Lisa's house in Yardley.

Cindy stopped at Lisa's house first and said, "Oh yeah Lisa, do you remember Joan and Austin?"

"Yeah of course, I'm going to their engagement party tonight, why do you ask?"

"I was gonna tell you the same thing. Well I'll see you there then."

"Yeah, I'll see you later then" Cindy said as she helped Lisa take her shopping to her door before she drove on to Denyah's a short distance away. Cindy walked Denyah to her door. As Wesley heard laughing coming from outside, he went and waited in the doorway. Denyah opened the door with her key and invited Cindy in to meet him and her step-daughter Paris, Wesley moved into the living room as Denyah and Cindy walked into the hall. Denyah thought Wesley was ignorant and rude the way he'd looked at her and Cindy but she still took Cindy into meet her husband Wesley. Shamefully Denyah eyes met Cindy as they met Wesley drinking whiskey from the bottle.

"Wesley, this is Cindy. Cindy this is my husband Wesley and my stepdaughter Paris." Denyah said looking in shame.

Cindy smiled and stretched her hand out to Wesley, but he turned his back on her and belched rudely and got up and walked into the kitchen. Denyah looked at Cindy with tears in her eyes. Cindy forced a laugh. Wesley walked out the kitchen with the bottle of whiskey and went to sit in the living room dining room.

"Would you like a drink?" Denyah asked Cindy.

"No thanks." Cindy replied smiling when she saw Denyah's face was covered with tears. Just to break the embarrassment Cindy leaned towards Denyah and whispered.

"How would you like me to set you up with the best mannered man?" Denyah smiled and Cindy said. "I only just got to know you, and I know you're suffering."

"Are you sure you don't want that drink?" she asked Cindy again and smiled but Cindy saw that Denyah was tense.

"No thank you Denyah. I'm really okay." Cindy replied turning towards the door. But before showing Cindy out, Cindy shouted "Goodbye Wesley." But Wesley didn't answer.

Cindy smiled and left. Denyah walked out behind following her to the car. But before Cindy got into her car, she hugged Denyah, and touched her hand sympathetically and looked at her. Denyah's eyes filled with tears. "By the way Denyah, here's my phone number. You need another friend to talk to, please give me a call."

"Thanks Lisa, I will. Drive carefully."

"I will. By the way, tell Lisa if she needs a lift to the party, give me a call!"

"I think Claire's taking us Lisa said. But I'll pass you message on to her anyway." Denyah said.

"Goodbye Denyah" Cindy said and gave Denyah a card with her mobile number on and remaindered her "Don't forget to call if you need an urgent friend."

"Thanks." Denyah said and watched until the car was out of sight. As she walked back to the house, her heart began to pound. She hesitated before going inside. Timidly she walked in the living room and saw Paris sitting on her father's lap. She looked at Paris and her father before sitting on the sofa. While looking at him, he gave her such a hideous look that she got up and walked into the kitchen to start cooking the dinner. But when she lifted the lid off the roasting dish to put the lamb chops she had seasoned before, she saw they were cooked and only the burnt seasoning remained in the roasting dish. She looked in another covered dish on the cooker expecting to find her dinner but it was empty. She then looked in the oven, to find nothing.

"Why don't you try the plate on the table sweetheart?" he told her. She walked over to the table and removed the cover off the plate to see one raw carrot and two slices of bread decorated with some dead bugs. He sat at the table and laughed aloud and exploded fart after fart with his bottom half lifted off the chair. When he saw Denyah burst into tears, he almost choked with laugher at this time Paris was in her bedroom playing with her dolls.

"What's the matter darling?" he asked still laughing hysterically and then hoisted his right leg and farted again. "You don't like your dinner? After all the trouble I went through?" His laughing sounded louder as it echoed through the house. His face expression then changed you could see he was angry; he got up and walked over to Denyah and slapped her around her face then walked out the room. Paris came down on time to saw him slapped Denyah again. As Denyah felt the spot he hit her, Paris held her hand and said, "Mom, I'm sorry dad hurt you." When Denyah saw her little innocent face dropped looking sorry, she hugged her and said. "I'm okay honey." Paris smiled and then took the plate up, carried it into the kitchen and threw it into the bin and walked into the front room and saw her father sleeping on the sofa. She then walked back into the kitchen and hugged Denyah tightly and kissed her cheek. "I'm sorry mom," she said crying. Denyah assured her she was okay.

CHAPTER TWO

Six thirty that same evening, Denyah was on her way up the stairs to go to the bathroom when the phone started ringing. She jumped nervously and turned staring at the phone. After the phone was ringing for a while she raced down to the bottom of the stairs to answer it, and as she was about to pick it up, Wesley stared at her. As they both stood listening to the phone, she reached for the handset but he lent forward and snatched the phone from under her hand. She looked at him as he answered.

"Hello,"

"May I speak to Denyah please" Eugene asked. Wesley looked wildly at her and extremely hard as he asked. "Why do you want to speak to my wife?"

As Denyah was standing near to him, she recognised Eugene's voice as he said, "We met earlier. Will you tell her Eugene called?"

"Who the hell is Eugene? Well, whoever you are, you're welcome to the bitch!" he said rudely and slammed the phone down and looked at her. She ran into the kitchen out of fear. He walked in after her and asked. "Who's Eugene?"

"He met me and Lisa in the restaurant while we were having lunch." Denyah answered nervously.

"How did he get my number? Are you fucking him?" she shook her head. He raised his fist to punch her in her face, but dropped his hand when he noticed Paris staring at him.

As Denyah looked at him in fear, he said, "Let me put it this way, is he fucking you? And did you give him my telephone number?"

"I don't know how he got our number. I didn't give it to him. I honestly don't know how he got the number. And no, I'm not having an affair with him or anyone. Wesley, I'm telling you the truth."

He looked at her in a funny way like he didn't believe her. Then he put his hand around her throat choking her. But as he saw Paris crying, he took his hands from around Denyah's throat as she was coughing repeatedly. "I'll end your life one day."

Paris looked at him and asked. "Why do you want to hurt mommy?"

"Honey, I wouldn't hurt your mommy." Paris ran to her room crying and fell asleep on the bed.

A couple of hours later Denyah went upstairs to Paris's room and saw her sleeping. She spread a sheet over her and then went to her room to sort her clothes out. After she sorted her clothes out, she took them into the bathroom with her and hung them on the towel rail and got into the bath. Slithering under the soft scented foam warm water she inhaled deeply feeling good. And as Eugene came into her head she covered her face and thought of him getting into the bath with her and as they were kissing in a passion of love making. As her thought was her and Eugene was coming to climax, her husband kicked the door open for real disturbing her day dream. He had his hands behind his back and a cold grin on his face. But for some reason her fear was invisible. He knelt down at her head and brought his hands from behind his back and ranged the gun to her head. She sat up with her knees under her chin and stared into his eyes. She said nothing. But at this moment she felt her throat close tight.

"I will ask you once more, where did you meet your friend Eugene?"

Trembling, she said. "Wesley, I told you before Lisa and I was having a drink at Cindy's restaurant and she introduced him to us. She's married to his cousin. Wesley, why are you treating me like this?" she asked him.

"Because you deserve it, you're a slag!"

"That's not fair. You took me away from my family. There was no man before you and I've been faithful throughout our marriage. I go to work and put up with all sorts of shit from my bank manager's wife and now I have to come home to hear this from you. I only met Eugene once." she said in tears.

"Do you ever think sometimes that your sister should have been my wife and not you, Well, I wondered all the time why I didn't married your sister and have you for a punch bag." he said.

The tears rolled down Denyah's face, she his hurtful words penetrated through her like a sharp knife. Felling dirty and crying, she heaved back her choking as her own saliva accumulated. Wesley watched her then he left the bathroom laughing. She got out the bath and dried herself quickly as she wanted to get out of the house and as far away from him as possible. She put on her low cut black Versace dress that came just above her knees. The size ten dressed hugged her body perfectly. Her black Dolce and Gabbana high heeled sandals that wrapped up her leg and tied just below where the dress ended, you could just about see her big hoop gold earrings behind her hair which was pressed straight but flicked at the end and she smelt of Glow. She walked out the bathroom and saw that Wesley was leaning on the door frame. She didn't say anything as she didn't want to start him off again. She just walked into the bedroom took her handbag off the bed and left. She walked around the corner to Lisa's house. As she got by the front door the spotlight came on. Lisa's husband Richard looked out the window and then opened the front door.

"Hello Denyah, you look nice!" he said smiling.

"Thanks" Denyah said as she walked inside the house."

"She's upstairs - go up" he said as he shouted up to Lisa that Denyah was on her way up. When Denyah got upstairs Lisa was just finishing her makeup.

"What time are you leaving for the party?" Richard asked.

"Are you trying to get rid of us?" Lisa asked him as she slowly twirled herself around and then took a sip of port from Denyah's glass and then gave her the remainder. "Finish your drink Den. Our lift will be here anytime now." Just then a car pulled up. Denyah looked at the clock and got up out of her seat. Lisa walked over to Richard and kissed him on his lips. Richard whispered softly to her "I love you." Lisa smiled. Richard walked over to the drinks bar and took from it a bottle of champagne. He looked at Denyah and smiled then said; "We shall drink to our first baby." he looked proud and happy.

"Are you having a baby?" Denyah asked smiling.

"Oh Den. I'm so sorry you had to hear this way. I only found out this morning after taking a pregnancy test. You're going to be an Aunt. We'll have to go shopping for baby clothes."

"Lisa, that's excellent news for both you and Richard. Congratulations." Just then the telephone started ringing. Richard answered it. He looked at Denyah and said. "It's for you Den, it's Wesley." She smiled and took the phone. "Hello," she hesitated.

Wesley belched rudely down the phone and laughed. "You remember what I told you, a clever police could kill his wife and get away with it. Oh, I do love you and I must admit, you're very beautiful but don't let it get to your head. Do you love me," he asked her laughing.

Denyah swallowed deeply then softly answered coldly, "Yes." and put the phone down. Lisa's mobile rang. "Hello." She said.

"It's Claire. Is Denyah with you?"

"Yes she is and we're ready and waiting." Lisa said.

"Well girls, Cindy sent me to get you. I'm outside your gate" Claire said and turned music on in her car.

Before Lisa and Denyah left the house, Lisa kissed her husband Richard goodbye. Walking to the car, Richard followed behind. As they were getting into the car, he said. Smiling "You take care honey, and you too Den."

"We will honey." And Lisa kissed him again to assure him she would be alright. He said "hello." to Claire, "drive carefully."

"Thanks." Claire said and she drove away to go the party. On their way, Denyah kept quiet listening to Lisa telling Claire the good news about her having her first baby. Later Claire looked back at Denyah and said, Den, you're very quiet. Is anything wrong?"

"No, nothing really, I was thinking about leaving my daughter alone."

"Den, you left your daughter alone?" Claire asked concerned.

"No- no, she's with her father but I hate leaving her."

"Relax honey. Paris would be alright with her father. Just remember you need some happiness in your life." Lisa said.

Claire looked on her wrist watch and said "Hey girls, we're a little early for the party, do you want to go for a drive first?"

"Sure," Denyah said. "I can do with a long think to take some pressure off my mind."

Claire set out driving down Parkers main road which stretched about two miles to a turning off Meldrew Road and drove a quarter of a mile on and then came across a dark green jeep that was parked near the edge of a lonely road under a big tree surrounded by tall thick green twined twigs. The jeep door was flung wide open showing a young dark skinned woman with a white middle-aged man having sex. The woman was practically naked and her feet were dangling outside the opened jeep door while the man's jeans were below his legs with his bottom exposed. Claire and Lisa laughed whilst Denyah kept silent. Claire drove until they came to some shops - they were prettily decorated with Christmas lights. Most of the shops showed that they were open until midnight. There were a few beggars, begging at side of the road as well as in doorways. A couple of beggars were curled up in blankets sitting in the corner of shop doorway, one playing his guitar. As they drove on to Wall Street, a tall dark policeman diverted them onto Farm Road. "There must have been an accident earlier as there were a couple of cars badly smashed." Claire said.

Denyah still sat quietly while Lisa told Claire all her good news about her baby. "Girls, we're in for one hell of a night." Claire parked outside the house.

"Come on, let's go in girls!" Claire said. Denyah stalled. "Come on Denyah, lets go inside you'll soon forget all your troubles."

"I hope so," she said with a cute smile on her face and got out the car and walked between Claire and Lisa and knocked on the door. A middle aged clear skinned woman answered the door smiling and said "Come right in." Then they were greeted with glasses of ice cold champagne and crunchy buttered puff twisted pastry rolls. "I hope you enjoy the rest of the evening." She said while taking their coats and carried them into one of the guest rooms, and then locked the door each time she entered for security until the guests were ready to leave and wanted their belongings.

Denyah couldn't help but stare at the engaged couple when she saw them with their arms around each other's waists. As Claire stood watching Denyah staring at the engagement couples, she walked over to her but before Claire spoke, Denyah whispered into her ears. "Look at them. They both seem so much in love."

"Yes Denyah, they are." Claire replied smiling.

Denyah smiled then sank deeply in thought over Eugene. Claire then handed her another glass of champagne and said, "Snap out of your day dream, Den, Have some fun and enjoy yourself. Come on let's go and get some food."

Denyah took a sip and followed Claire to the food table. After they filled their plates, they went to look for Lisa and found her mingling with some of the guests and Cindy. As Denyah was eating, Eugene passed his hand over her shoulder and took one of the small sausage rolls off her plate. She looked up and saw Eugene standing over her eating the sausage roll. Lisa and Cindy came in time to see Eugene take another sausage roll from Denyah's plate. She smiled and then whispered in Denyah's ear. "He's really handsome and good looking. And I'm sure he would respect you more than my brother."

"I'm a married woman and I love my husband." Denyah replied. Lisa smiled and said jokingly. "If you don't want this gorgeous looking Angel, you just pass him on to me."

At this time Eugene was looking at Denyah with a smirk on his face. Then a love song began to play. Eugene took her hand and led her into the crowded room where everyone was dancing. She felt his erection as they were dancing closely, she tried to pull herself away but he held her more closely to him. As he looked on her face, she showed embarrassment and rested her head on his shoulder with her eyes glued the floor. The words of the song were so beautiful and powerful that he held her so passionately then he carried his lips to hers and kissed her. Still feeling his erection made her feel uncomfortable - she wanted the CD to end so that he would let her go. But as he held on to her so delicately but firmed, she felt deep love for him that sent a warm sensation all over her body. When the CD stopped she broke away from him and took Lisa with her into the toilet room. "Lisa your brother hasn't made love to me for almost eight months except when he raped me repeatedly. He treats me and uses me like a call girl when his woman is on her period and he needs a release, he would just take me without my consent and he never kisses me. He would always look distant, and face somewhere in the room when he's having sex with me. Lisa I still love your brother but I know he don't love me or want me. You knew it is my sister Fay he loves and wants as he has told you so many times."

"I'm sorry D. I didn't know it was that bad." Lisa's mobile phone rang but then cut off. "It was Richard but the reception isn't very good. I'm gonna go outside and see what he wants. Are you going to be okay?"

"Yeah I'm okay." Denyah said then tears came in her eyes

After Denyah washed her hands, she took a good look at herself in the mirror. She dried her eyes to see an attractive young woman who came up behind her and tapped her on her shoulder. She faced the woman and asked her, "Do I know you?"

"No. You don't fucking know me." The woman said in anger, "and I don't think you would want to know me either. You keep your fucking hands off my man." Denyah was so shocked she froze.

"Keep your hands of my man!" the woman repeated. "If you so as much as look at him again, it's going to be you and me! Do you understand me?" the woman bluntly

said. Then she turned and looked in the mirror, fixed her hair and her make-up then left the toilet and went back to the dance floor. "I wish I could crawl down the toilet and wait for someone to flush me." Denyah said softly to herself. Eventually, she left the toilet and faced Eugene. He smiled saying "I bet it was an excuse to get away from me?" He then reached out to touch her hand but she quickly moved and told him. "Please leave me alone and I don't want anything more do with you." Eugene looked at her in wonder wanting to know what she was talking about and why she had suddenly turned against him.

"I really want to be with you Denyah." He said and closed his eyes as if he was feeling pain. Then as she turned and walked away he held on to her hands. She looked hard at him.

"Please Denyah don't turn me away." He pleaded as his eyes became moistened with tears. At this time heads turned and looked at him holding on to Denyah's hands before he dropped on his knees.

Denyah wiped her tears dry and pulled her hands away and tried to walk past him, but he raised himself up quickly and blocked her way with his body and then tried to kiss her. During this time, the woman who'd slapped Denyah stood in the middle of the dance floor and was watching her and Eugene with eagle eyes.

"I want you Denyah." Eugene said so softly to her as he held her in his arms and tried to kiss her again. Tearfully she pushed him away. "Damn-you Denyah! I fell in love with you." he shouted.

She faced him, "I want you to leave me alone." she told him.

"I would if you tell me you don't love me," he said looking hurt.

Instead, she turned her back on him with tears running down her face. He twirled her facing him and went down on his knees again while the guests watched. "I don't care if you're married. I want you to be my wife." Tears came in his eyes as he held on to her hands. She slapped his face so that he would let go, but instead, he pulled her down to his level and kissed her. Her face looked worried - she felt cheap and dirty and concerned about being seriously warned by his woman, and that the news was bound to reach her husband. Crying heavily, she pulled herself away and then ran to find Lisa, Cindy and Claire. She found them talking to some of the guests in the living room. As she tries to tell them what Eugene's woman did to her Austin beautiful middle aged mother came and stood between then and touching Denyah's face saying. "As you were admiring my son and her bride to be living room, I was admiring your beauty. You're a very beautiful lady. My name is Dana Robson." she said.

"Well thank you Mrs Robson." Denyah said. Mrs Robson held Denyah's hand and led her away from Lisa, Claire and Cindy and into the room where the food is, "I went to speak to my friends over what a friend woman said to me, but the beauty of your son's living room won me over that it has left me forgot what she went to tell them."

"Let me give you a tour around the house." Mrs Robson said and she showed Denyah all five bedroom and around. Denyah eyes widened to the beautifully furnished rooms that it left her speechless and almost breathless. She stood in the middle of Robson's room for a few minutes admiring the beautiful of the room. The beautiful picture of the engagement couple that sat on the gold mantel look like fireplace captured her attention. Then her eyes travelled and stopped on the Robson .family photos that hung proudly on the tall soft blue painted partition. Even though the night had became bitterly cold, the enormous room was feeling comfortably and warm. With the dimmed soft blue lights penetrating the large painted vessel that hung proudly on the partition,

Denyah got closed to the painted vessel   and while she was admiring the vessel, she was distracted by Joan the engagement lady. Denyah and Mrs Robson left the room and returned downstairs into the living room. Mrs Robson asked to be excused and left. Denyah turned to look at Lisa, but didn't bother to say anything to her or Claire. She left the room and found a seat in the dining room with some of the guests. After awhile she went outside for fresh air and to be by herself as she was still feeling hurt. After sitting alone for at least an hour in the dew and bitter mid-night breeze, she returned to the party again shivering.

"Where the hell did you go Den honey?" Claire asked her huffily.

"I've been out side for fresh air." she replied.

"I was looking for you, I asked where you were and someone said you left. Lisa, Cindy and I were upset and worried as you hadn't told either of us where you were. We were worried over you. Denyah, the next time you decide to walk out on us, please tell us. Will you?" Claire said.

"Well, I'm here now. I was feeling a bit overcrowded so I went out for fresh air." Denyah said and closed her eyes then opened her eyes to see Eugene coming towards her.

"Eugene just had an argument with his troublesome ex-girlfriend for something that she'd done to you. Are you okay Den?" Claire asked looking concerned. "By the way, he also had another girlfriend named Chardonnay before he'd finished with that troublesome black bitch that slapped you." And as Lisa looked at Claire, she said, "Lisa my friend, I didn't mean this to sound offensive." Lisa smiled and Claire went on to saying. "Chardonnay was pregnant when Eugene left her for some reason. He went back to be with her for the sake of the child. Then he left her again when she told him the child wasn't his. Two years later I heard Chardonnay became a call girl. Since then, I heard nothing more about her or that bitch that slapped you. Until now the bitch came on the scene and attacked you. She was the reason why Eugene and Chardonnay split. Her name is Rena. I also believed she's the reason why Chardonnay had a nervous breakdown before she went into prostitution after she gave Chardonnay a bad beating and a gash to her face warning her to keep away from Eugene. That bitch even threatened Chardonnay's mother several times and said that she must tell her daughter to leave Eugene alone and that Eugene is her man and they're serious about getting married. When the bitch found out Chardonnay was pregnant, she gave Chardonnay such a bad beating that she'd had a miscarriage. So I was told. If it wasn't for an Afro-Caribbean woman who was walking passed the main Post Office in Town and saw that bitch beating and kicking Chardonnay all over her body and stopped her by fighting her off with her umbrella, she might have killed Chardonnay if that woman hasn't saw Chardonnay bleeding and phoned on her mobile for an ambulance. However, the kind woman left before the ambulance arrived as she didn't want to be identified. Onlookers told the paramedics they saw two black women leave the scene. Poor scared Chardonnay had told both Paramedics and the police she was attacked by someone she didn't know only because she was scared of that wicked bitch Rena. On her way to the hospital, Chardonnay gave birth but the poor little thing didn't survive as she was five months pregnant. It was a baby girl. That bitch Rena got off home free. I also heard that bitch was selling herself as well when Eugene warned her he would kill her if she gets in his way".

"Who was selling herself?" Denyah asked interestedly.

"The bitch that hit you," Claire said. "Her and Chardonnay, his two exes had turned out to be hookers. So you can see the effect they had on Eugene. But I think you're the sweet ripe strawberry Eugene was so longingly looking for. Please Den. I haven't seen Eugene cry before over any women until now. Denyah, from what I heard of your ill mannered husband, please give Eugene the chance to care for you that you truly deserve."

"How long ago did Rena and Eugene finish?" Denyah asked showing tears.

"About eight months, I was there when she and Eugene were arguing. Eugene had made it clear to both her and Chardonnay he doesn't want either of them. Chardonnay walked away peacefully, but that bitch Rena won't let him loose. Eugene took out a restraining order on her to leave him alone. The last I heard of her, she got engaged a month later to some other pimp whom I don't know. Since then, Eugene has hardly had time to date other women as the family business took him different places around the world."

Denyah turned to walk away when she heard Cindy saying, "Eugene is in love with you. He's very wealthy, young and handsome. He and his family own hundreds of supermarkets and other business here and in other countries. His father is a high court judge. Den, you deserved to be with Eugene and not with that horrible husband."

Claire nodded her head smiling then said, "Cindy told you the truth. But something is still bothering my thought about the child you and your husband share."

Denyah stared hard at Cindy without saying a word. Cindy inhaled deeply looking at her. Then smiling she asked, "Will you see him Denyah? Or at least pass a message on to him to let him know where he stands."

At this time, Claire was standing near Cindy and looking into Denyah's eyes.

"I don't know Cindy. I really don't know what to do right now. I must admit that I have feelings for Eugene. But I just can't give up my marriage and my daughter just like that. I still love my husband in spite of his ruthlessness." Denyah said before she walked away in deep thoughts and in tears.

At this stage Denyah was confused over whether to leave her husband to be with Eugene. But as she was standing in one corner of the dance room listening to Pamela Maynard's hot tune playing (Hear my cry oh lord) as the words penetrated her heart and thoughts keep running through her head, she ran into Eugene's arms and closed her tearful eyes in the power of feeling strong love for him. Then as another love song was playing by Charlene Davis (Stealing love) Eugene couldn't help kissing her as they were dancing. After she parted away from Eugene, Lisa went to her and said, "Den, if I were you, I wouldn't go home after I leave from here. I would go to my mothers as you know if Wesley knows about you and Eugene, he might hurt you terribly."

"Lisa, I know you mean well, but I will be going home when I'm ready." Denyah said.

"Denyah, you know how ruthlessly cruel my brother is and to top it all, he's very jealous of you. I saw him slap you after seeing you speak to a man." Lisa said.

"Well, he had it wrong Lisa. My husband trusts me completely." Denyah said.

"I'm sure he does to put you in hospital every six weeks. Wake up Den. I love my brother but not what he's doing to you. I'm concerned about you and he might hear about you and Eugene as I said. And if I know my brother well, he might ask one of his women to stay with Paris, and he may be hiding somewhere looking at you. " Lisa then looked hard into Denyah's eyes and shook her head ferociously.

Denyah looked at Lisa before she said. "Look Lisa, I know you mean good for me - but running from my home and my husband, it would only makes matters worse." Lisa looked up to the ceiling before she looked at her again and said, "Look Den, I'm only giving you advice. I mean, you're more than welcome to stay at my house until you're sure my evil brother will not lash out on you for staying out until the early morning, I'm sure by now some interfering brute has told him about you and Eugene."

"Thanks again Lisa, I know you wish the best for me. But no thanks; when I leave here I will be going home. Besides, the party is now coming to an end. Lisa, as I said, you're a good friend and a Sister-In-Law, but please don't ask me again to sleep anywhere else but in my own house and in my bed."

"Okay Denyah, if that's what you want, I will not bother you anymore. But I still think you should go to your mother's or stay at my house for a few days as Wesley might be still furious." Lisa said looking worried and walked away. Denyah followed her, "Please Lisa, don't worry about me. And don't look as though you're carrying the world on your shoulders with me sitting on top. Cheer up my friend and give me one of your beautiful smiles" Denyah said. Lisa smiled faintly, but still looking worried.

"Now come on let's enjoy the time we have left at this party." Denyah said as she grabbed Lisa by the hand and led her into dancing room where they danced together a couple of times until the DJ announced the party's over.

Joan and Austin thanked them all for attending their engagement party.

It was a misty and very cold Sunday morning, about four thirty, when the remaining guests were leaving the party. Denyah, Claire, Cindy and Lisa were the last to be leaving and as Denyah was scared of going home to face her husband, not knowing what she's up against, her face pictured with fear. Eugene had left with a long and romantic kiss from Denyah.

"Den, I know you're scared. Your face tells me." Lisa said.

"Of course I'm scared, but I have to go home and faced my devious husband and get over what he's intending to do to me." Denyah whispered to Lisa and Claire. Then she crossed the room to the engaged couple and thanked them for a lovely time before she hugged Clara and said goodbye before she and Lisa left Claire with Cindy for Cindy to take them homes.

Cindy dropped Lisa off at her gate and watched her got into her house, then carried on to Denyah's house. Denyah invited her in for coffee, but as Cindy remembered how ill-mannered Wesley was to her, she said smiling, "another time Den," she watched Denyah walked to her front door and take her key out her hand bag then open the porch door. Denyah looked back at her and waved goodbye. She smiled and then droved away.

As Denyah turned her key in the front door, sweat covered her face and left her feeling very scared. She opened the door, walked in and switched the lights on to see her husband sitting on the sofa looking drunk. She could see about a quarter of whiskey left in the bottle before he put the bottle to his mouth and gulped some down. He got up and staggered over the other side of the room to where she was standing. "Wesley, I'm sorry to come home at this time. But I had to wait for my lift" she said nervously.

"You mean you had to wait until your man rolled off you. I trusted you to go to the party, and you had to rush between his legs. Denyah you're nothing but a slapped whore."

"Please Wesley, why are you behaving in this way, I love only you and I can't help or prevent people loving me. I was with friends and your sister all night."

"Of course you were with them, for them to witness your man went down on his knees and proposed to you. Tell me this, my precious whore, what shall I do with you" Wesley asked Denyah and watching her with half closed eyes.

"You're drunk Wesley. And you're fumigating me with your alcoholic breath. I'm going to take a shower to wash the smell off me." Denyah said.

As Denyah walked passed him, he grabbed her right hand and then hit her hard across her face. She pushed him away and ran into the bathroom. He laughed saying, "You're not running to the bathroom to get away from me. You're running to wash the semen off you" he then straightened himself up and pushed the bathroom door opened and staring in her eyes showing her that he hated her. He hit her again with the back of his hand splitting her lower lip before pulling her out the bathroom and dragged her downstairs into the living room and tossing her across the room where she fell against the wall unit hitting her back and her shoulder. As she screamed out, he ranged his gun at her head and said telling her. "Shut your mouth before I send a bullet down your throat." She was so petrified that she didn't make another sound - shivering terribly. As he was looking at her and her shivering slowed, she tried to crawl behind the sofa but he pulled her by her long hair and tossed her in the middle of the room and laughed. Pointing his gun to her head, she tried again to get away, but as he had had the advantage over her holding on to her hair, she eased in to him as she knew that there was no way she could have escaped from him.

"I've a good idea to deal with whores like you" he said sliding the gun from between her breasts downward to her vagina and said. "Paw:" and looking seriously mean at her. She screamed out and knelt at his feet in fright and begging him, "Please don't hurt me anymore"

He looked down at her then kicked her on her bosom pushing her on her back.

"I love you Wesley," she said crying as she looked up to him.

He grabbed her by the hand and pulled her up from off her knees saying disgustingly, "Prove to me you love me only and not that fucking creep you had on his knees saying he loves you."

"Wesley, what should I do to prove I love you," she asked him easing to him in pain as he had her hair pulling and her face pressing towards his fly.

"I want you to suck me for the first time!" he told her slipping his hand down his pyjamas and brought out his penis. As he straightened himself to relax and smiling with her hair in his hand, she gave him a hard punch to his balls. He spun around like a spinning top and then folded up with pain before he fell on his knees with his hands between his legs. While he was on his knees groaning, she kicked him hard in the mouth busting his lips. Blood spouted heavily. She ran into the kitchen, grabbed a vegetable knife and got back to him saying, "You touch me again, and I would send this knife straight through you heart."

"You fucking dirty bitch! He groaned and as she walked away, he fired a bullet at the ceiling just to frighten her. She stood still in fright and frozen where she stood. He straightened himself standing up and went and slapped her face twice and pulled the knife from her laughing even though he received a small gash in the palm of his hand.

"Why didn't you fucking shoot me and get it over with." she told him.

"Shut up!" he shouted as he squeezed her bleeding mouth opened and forced the gun almost down her throat before pulling the trigger making her semi-faint that she fell but conscious she was.

"The next time I pulled the trigger, it will be loaded." He said as he stood over her and burst out laughing when he saw urine coming from her. Still laughing he loaded his gun with two bullets, then said, "Now sweetheart, you carry on messing with other men and you will soon be parted from all men. So you make sure I'm the only man in your life. And please darling, don't ever look at me like I'm the guilty one. As you well know, a man is entitled to as much women but a wife should have only one husband and should respect him. You just hurt me. But I can live through that and I forgive you for acting on instinct. But, never ever raised your hand or your feet on me again, for if you do, believe me, you will be very sorry." he spat blood on her face and ripped her dress off and wiped blood from his lips on the dress and tossed it to her face.

She screamed out crying while he carried on laughing. Then seriously, he fixed his face and looked at her again before he said, "Since you still love me, I'll let you live for a while as you will suit my needs when I want to explore and my girlfriend is not available or menstruating. Still, as you come cheap and free and my daughter needs you, you can stay here. But remember, I hold the key to your heart." he then kissed her bleeding lips and told her. "Go clean you self up". By this time, his lips were bleeding too. As she went to go the bathroom, he dialled some numbers to his friend Finch. When Finch answered the phone, "Hello", Wesley laughed.

"Wesley, what's so funny?" Finch asked with confused expression on his face.

"Finch, Wesley speaking."

"I know it's you Wesley, what can I do for you?" Officer Finch asked.

"Finch mate, I have a little thing going on here. She's a regular call girl when my wife isn't at home. And I would be more than grateful if you would pass on words to our best mate Tom and you both meet me at my house in twenty minutes." Wesley said.

"Well, I'll give Tom a call and we'll be there." Finch said and smiled then looked down on his crutch saying, "Finch piper, you might be in for a rough ride." He laughed and then made a phone call to Tom telling him "Wesley would like to see us both at his house in twenty minutes."

After Wesley spoke to his workmate Finch, he rushed into the bathroom as he thought Denyah was naked. But when he saw she was dressed, he madly tore her clothes off and roughly pushed her down on the bathroom floor, and raped her in her back-passage out of spite. All through his horrible forcing up her, she was crying blue murder and feeling terrible pain. As he ejaculated and pulled out of her, he saw she was bleeding. With no remorse, he proudly said "That's what happens to dirty whoring wives." He grinned proudly and showered the blood off her with cold water from the shower then said, "We wouldn't want to mess my mates, would we?"

He dragged her into the spare room and tossed her on the bed, gagged her mouth with a pair of her silk stockings, blindfolded her eyes with one of her silk scarves and said, "After your fancy man knows what you are, he will left you to the dogs." he squeezed her face and kissed her forehead and quietly left the room. When she no longer felt his presence, she began fighting hard by trying to free herself, but he sneaked into the room again and knocked her faced down on the bed and made it more difficult to loosen the tied knot as she had got weak fighting with the slippery knot he made.

He bound her hands together with another pair of her silk stockings, then when he was about to leave the room, he looked back at her and said. "Oh, I forgot to tie your pretty feet to the bedstead as my mates would like to see you in full view before they decide how to take you". As he tried to tie her feet to the foot of the bedstead, she kicked him in the mouth and opening the wound causing his lips to bleed again. Angrily he punched her unconscious with a hard blow to her temple and said "You bitch! I warned you if you hurt me again, you'll be sorry" she became powerless lying flat on her back. He roughly spread her feet apart, tied them separately to the foot of the bedstead, moved the sheet off the bed and left her naked and did not even have the decency to cover her with one of the sheets. After he spat on her, he went downstairs and waited in the living room for his mates to come. As she came around and found her husband had tied her feet to the bedstead, she started struggling to free herself, but twisting and wrangling she found it was useless as she was only making it harder and tightening the binding on her hands and to her feet causing them to bruise and become painfully swollen. Her hands became very painful and looked as if they were ready to burst bleeding, she lay still groaning as she was feeling horrible pain. Then as she heard her husband bouncing up the stairs and laughing, she lay still in fright and pain. He walked into the room and stood over her and watched her tears moisten her blindfold. "Too late for tears my sweet loving whore" he said, then running his fingers downwards between her breasts to her vagina, he slapped her legs and left leaving her crying her eyes out as well as feeling disgusted and humiliated. Outside the door he stood laughing. Then after a couple of seconds he spouted whiskey out his mouth on the floor and closed door with a bang. From behind the door, she heard him saying "Denyah you're the cheapest whore I've fucked in the arse. And you're so distasteful. Still, as you come free and cheap, you ease my burning dick."

While he was standing outside the door and slurping whiskey from the bottle, he shouted "Den my whore you will be having two clients. I hope they enjoy you as I didn't."

He laughed walking down the stairs to hearing the doorbell ringing. He went and opened the door. "Come in mates "he said to Officers Tom and Finch. Officers Tom and Finch walked in the house, Wesley closed the door with a bang that Denyah heard when the front door opened and then slammed shut. Again she was trying desperately hard to get free, but it was just making her tired and frustrated. It was only then she realised that her daughter Paris wasn't at home.

Wesley took his two friends into his living room where they finished a full bottle of whiskey between the three of them - after he led them upstairs and into the room to his wife for them to have sex with her. As Finch watched Wesley standing outside the opened door draining the dripping whiskey out of the bottle, he eyed Wesley as saw Denyah's beautiful slim and naked body ready and waiting for him to enjoy. Wesley was shaking nervously with his left eye half closed and only wearing his black silk boxer shorts with his penis dangling over the fly hole and his head leaning on the right side, and showing a wicked fearful grin on his face that would scare any vicious animals out of their skin. As Finch edged nearer to Denyah's bed, he looked back at Wesley to see his head leaning on the right side with scowled eyebrows and giggling while swinging the empty whiskey bottle forward and backward. As his eyes clashed with Finch's, he asked Finch. "Mate would you like the whore on her knees or on her back?"

"Anyway suits me!" Finch replied zipping down his trousers and pressed down on the edge of the bed.

Denyah shuddered with fear as she felt Finch crawling up the bed. His breathing into her face had caused her to heave. He slapped her naked bottom and kissed the back of her neck. Then looking again at Wesley outside the wide opened door, he said sneering "Wesley, you really do know how to pick the very beautiful whores."

"Just get on with it:" Wesley snarled. Then he went on to say, "Just let us know when you finish" Wesley then turned to leave, but looking back at his wife Denyah, he held the door handle to close it, but he went on to say, "Queen of whores, you're looking so radiant. I want you to send my mates away feeling very happy" his laughing was irritating to Finch and Denyah's ears. He then closed the door leaving his wife Denyah and his mate Finch in the bedroom. Denyah mumbled through her blind fold and gagged mouth "Please don't hurt me" shaking her head thoroughly. Even though Finch was tipsy, he slackened the gag from Denyah's mouth so that he would hear what she was saying more clearly. "Please don't hurt me. Wesley's my husband and he's doing this to me out of jealousy. He's accusing me of being unfaithful when he is sleeping with one of my sisters. Please, I've done nothing wrong. Like he's hurting me, so he would hurt you to shut you up." After Denyah convinces Finch, Finch rolled off her back. Denyah sighed with relief and thanked Finch several times for not doing what her husband asked. By this time Finch was coming to his senses and getting sober. As he was listening to Denyah telling him "Thanks" for not raping her…. Finch madly burst out saying "Shut your mouth before I change my mind" Then Finch went on to say "Wesley told me you like a rough stiff fuck from behind. He also told me you put yourself above the other whore's that's why you nickname is Queen of the whores. Your husband must have really hated you to turn you into a whore."

"That's true. He hated me for loving him but he's in love with my sister." Denyah said shivering and crying.

"I told you to shut your mouth; it's in your best interest to do so." Finch said

A few minutes later, he rolled over Denyah and got up. Leaving the room, he looked back at Denyah saying "You just remember if Wesley found out I lied to him, it's not only your life would be ended, it would be mine too. Just act just as if I had you."

Just then Wesley's other friend Tom staggered into the bed-room to see Finch zipping up his trousers in pretence.

"Come on lets leave her." Finch said to his mate Tom.

"No, I want my turn" Tom rudely replied and starting to zip down his trousers.

"Well, I've just used the last rubber I had and who knows what she got. But it's up to you!" Finch said. "I would hate for you to pass on to your wife what she don't want" Tom smiled and untied Denyah's hand before he left the room with Finch. Just then the room went quiet. She could hear their footsteps going down the stairs. In agony she patted between her bruised thighs and as her hands smeared with the disgusting and messy feeling from her husband's semen she heaved and let out vomit on the bed. And her eyes felt like they were burning up, and a throbbing pain going on rapidly in her back-passage and vagina by having the roughest sex from her husband throughout their time together.

Wesley rushed into the room laughing. She cried asking him "Why do you hate me so much that you spitefully had sex in my back passage and then had your mates hurting me. You have hurt me bitterly. I begged you to stop hurting me. Why do you hate me so much Wesley, why?" He watched snot dripping from her nose before he said.

"This is what you get by cheating with other men," he climbed on her and raped her again. She cried out in pain. Officer Finch couldn't bear to hear her squealing. As he got up to go and know why she was squealing so horrifyingly, Officer Tom said "Leave her Finch"

"I can't, she sounded like he's murdering her and she needs our help." Officer Finch said.

"Look Finch, Wesley's not an easy person to get on with. We just sit tight till he come down and let us out" Officer Tom said. But worrying over what Wesley's doing to her Finch said "He might be hurting her. We would be as guilty as him if he hurt or killed her and did nothing".

"We should have not come here Tom. That woman he called us to have sex with, she is his wife. He accused her of being unfaithful when he's the one that is fucking his sister. Tom, Wesley is jealous of his wife. He's in love with her and at the same time, he's hurting her. Tom, how low can he get?" Officer Finch tears showed as Officer Tom looked hard in his face.

"I'm going to do what I can to stop him hurting his wife." Officer Finch insisted.

"Look Finch, I don't want my family to hear about this. So would you cool it and wait on Wesley to come down."

Officer Finch took his seat and dropped his head on his lap with his hand covered his face and breathed out deeply while they waited on Wesley to see them out.

After Wesley raped his wife Denyah, he left the room leaving her crying. His abusing her left her feeling discomfort and full of hate towards him. He went to the bathroom and had a wash and shouted down to his mates. "I'll be down soon. Help your selves to drinks." Again he entered into the room to be with Denyah and sat on the bed beside her. She'd felt sickness ejecting from her stomach that caused her to vomit all over the bed and on her chest. She turned her face away in disgust as Wesley alcoholic breath was choking her but the more she was gasping for breath, the stronger his alcoholic breath was parching deeply up her nostrils causing her to heave rapidly. Hatefully he slapped her face even though she was choking on her vomit. She got out of bed and was going to the toilet when he stretched his right foot out and she fell at his feet. Timidly she looked up at him as she was kneeling at his right foot crying. Sneering, he looked down at her and spouted from his mouth some whiskey into her face before pushing her over with his right foot then telling her "That's how husbands treat a whoring wife!"

She said nothing except crying and in the knowledge she's defenceless against him. Timidly, she dragged herself in one corner of the room begging him not to hurt her anymore.

As he laughed at her, she said, "I do love you Wesley". She cried, pulled herself up and went and sat beside him. He got up off the bed and looked hard at her. "Please Wesley, I've done nothing wrong."

Arrogantly he jumped on to the bed and sent her flying to the floor and after kicked her in her back and telling her "I know my mates haven't enjoyed you. But you'd done the job of cooling them off" he then put on the television and turned it up loud to cover her crying. A few minutes later he urinated on her and sprinkled the half bottle of whiskey over her and flamed his cigarette lighter to set her alight. Very frightening she pulled towards him holding on to his feet. He shook her off and moved to his mini cabinet for a full bottle of whiskey. As she saw her chance to escape she ran to the bathroom and locked herself in and got under the shower. He kicked the bathroom door hard. She almost jumped out of her skin but went under the shower. After spending

sometime scrubbing herself, Wesley went and saw his mates out and went back up to Denyah and stood at the bathroom giggling. As Denyah thought she still wasn't clean enough, she exchanged the soft scrubbing brush for the hard one. But the more she scrubbed, the more unclean she felt. And so, she scrubbed and scrubbed between her thighs with a scrubbing brush until between her thighs became tender and bled. Even though she saw blood coming from her, she was still scrubbing herself from head to her toes but mostly between her thighs and legs. Wesley, her husband knocked at the door saying "No matter how long you stay under the shower, you will still be filthy" His irritating laughing was penetrating her ears so she turned up the shower to maximum - boiling the water. As she was showering under the boiling shower, crying bitterly while scrubbing herself hard, she went into dizziness and she barely heard when her husband slammed the front door shut and left. Still crying and scrubbing between her legs and thighs, she fainted under the boiling shower.

A few minutes later Lisa called to see her.

After Lisa knocked at her door several times and had no reply, she let herself in with the key Wesley had given to her. She stood at the foot of the stairs calling "Denyah, where are you?" As Denyah did not answer, Lisa walked up to the stairs and repeatedly calling. "Denyah, Denyah, Denyah- where are you?" But still there was no reply.

"Den, where are you?" Lisa shouted again standing on the stairs. Then hearing the shower gushing, she run to the bathroom door and call "Den," but still Denyah didn't answer. Lisa banged hard on the bathroom door again and several times after but all she could hear was the gushing water from the shower.

"Denyah," Lisa called twice and banged hard on the bathroom door. "Denyah, it's me, Lisa, open the door, I know you're in there. Open the door."

As Denyah didn't open the door Lisa tried to force the door open by using her shoulder. But it was impossible for Lisa to force open the bathroom door. Minutes later, Lisa was feeling heavy pain in her left side and her tummy followed by what felt like a flush of discharge gushing from her and saturating her panties. Lisa was scared and quickly went to Mr Welch, one of Denyah's neighbours, telling him that she thinks Denyah has locked herself into the bathroom and that she needs his help. Mr Welch left his wife in bed and quickly followed Lisa into Denyah's house and up to the bathroom. "The shower is definitely running" Mr Welch faced Lisa and said before busting the door flying with a heavy pounce with his strong shoulder, calling "Mrs Davis". But as he got no answer and the bathroom was thick with steam, he brushed away the steam that clouded his eyes and wiped some built up steam from his face. He couldn't see clearly in the bathroom as thick steam took over and was hindering him and Lisa seeing clearly. As the steam subsided, forcing its way out the door, Lisa could see Denyah stretched out under the steaming shower lying face down. "Oh my God, Denyah-" Lisa cried out and dived down hauling Denyah free from under the steaming shower and not thinking about the danger to her pregnancy. Mr Welch fully opened the bathroom window and turned the shower off before he carefully fixed Denyah under the shower again and slowly set the shower to trickle cold water over her while Lisa phoned for the ambulance. After Lisa returned to the bathroom and when she looked at Denyah she cried out. "She looked badly scalded and she's unconscious." Mr Welch said. As Denyah was naked Lisa rushed into the kitchen and bought cling film and covered Denyah before spreading a sheet over her. Mr Welch nodded his head but as tears came in his eyes, he dried them quickly and shook his head remorsefully.

"Mrs Sandwell, you stay with her while I go and get more cling film from my house if needed." Mr Welch said.

Lisa shook her head crying and kneeling over Denyah under the trickling cold shower. Lisa spread cling film delicately over Denyah's scald and as she watched Denyah lying so calmly, she burst out into loud crying saying, "Wesley, what have you done to my friend?"

Mr Welch returned with a large role of cling film but as Denyah was lying so peaceful he leave her alone then hugged Lisa around her shoulders and trying to comfort her as she was crying. "We've done our best for Mrs Davis. The cold water over her would help cool her burning scalds." He said.

Mr Welch went to his home and said to his wife "I'd taken your cling film but I brought it back."

"I know," she said, "I watched you taking the roll of Cling film. What did you want it for?"

"Honey, you get back in bed." Mr Welch said. But as Mrs Welch looked at him, he said. "I thought Mrs Davis had needed it as she got badly scalded."

"Poor Mrs Davis," Mrs Welch said and got dressed and went with her husband to help Denyah in any way she can. She was shocked when she saw Denyah lying under the cold trickling shower with at least forty percent blisters to her body. Tears came into Mrs Welch eyes. Gently and carefully she spread more cling film over Denyah's burns that Lisa had not been able to cover. She then looked closer on Denyah's body and saw how badly scalded she was. She dried her tears with the hem of her night- dress. "How on earth can this happen to such a lovely lady like Mrs Davis. Ah, that husband of hers gives me the shivers anytime I see him and especially how he treated his poor wife. Only God knows why she put up with a louse like him after beating her so often and having affairs even with her sister and other women. Well, if what has happened to her doesn't wake her up, God knows whatever will" Mrs Welch spoke her mind regardless even though Lisa was there. Then Mrs Welch went on to say, "Miss Lisa, I know what I just said about your brother must have hurt you, but I spoke the truth. Mrs Davis should get well away from you brother and take her daughter with her."

"That's enough Maude" her husband said. "It's up to Mrs Davis what she wants to do with her life. Right now, all we should be concerned with is getting Mrs Davis to a hospital"

Lisa, Mrs and Mr Welch carefully turned Denyah on her left side that was not scalded so badly in order that the cold water reached her scalds on the right side and elsewhere that was badly scalded. Mr Welch made sure Denyah was as comfortable as possible while they waited for the ambulance to arrive. Mr and Mrs Welch waited in the living room while Lisa stood watching over Denyah crying. The ambulance arrived very quickly. Mrs Welch answered the door to the two Paramedics and told them Mrs Davis was upstairs in the shower room and badly scalded. Briskly both Paramedics rushed upstairs to the shower to see Denyah stretched out on her left side under the sprinkling cold shower. The heavy built good looking short red beard Paramedic shook his head when he see Denyah with at least forty percent burns to her body, especially on her legs and thighs. Delicately the slimmed tall and handsome Paramedics injected Denyah with morphine to ease her pain and then carefully removed the cling film and sprayed her blistering burns with liquid then covered her with a special sheet before they carefully carried her into the ambulance.

Lisa thanked Mr and Mrs Welch in assisting her helping Denyah.

"That's ok Miss Lisa. Mrs Davis is a lovely lady. Just let us know how she is" Mrs Welch said.

Lisa smiled then turned to climb into the ambulance with help from the heavily built red beard Paramedic. As she sat looking at Mrs Welch standing by the ambulance door, she said "Mrs Welch, please don't tell Mr Davis about Mrs Davis."

"Don't worry Mrs Sandwall. Mr Davis would never hear anything from me. I hope Mrs Davis would be fine."

Lisa smiled and moved nearer to Denyah. The heavy built Paramedic sat with Denyah and Lisa talking on the radio to the hospital and writing down notes from Lisa while his young baby faced mate was driving. Cause the road was clear that early Sunday morning, it took the Paramedics fifteen minutes to get to the Hospital. One of the Paramedic said to Lisa "Mrs Davis you stay good and please see a doctor before you leave and let them check you out to know if the baby is alright as you told me you have a flush."

"Thanks I will." Lisa said. Then the paramedic gave Denyah over to the doctors where they rushed her to the Burns Unit. When Denyah regained consciousness, she was in so much pain that they had to give her another injection and pain relief every four hours. Lisa was allowed to see her for five minutes as the injection had an effect on her to make her sleep. Lisa was also told that Denyah wasn't allowed to have any visitors for the first two days as her legs had to be spread apart with only a special sheet covering her. After Lisa left the hospital, she went to see Denyah's neighbours Mr and Mrs Welch and told them Denyah would be all right but she has had forty five percent burns and not seventy as she had feared.

"I wondered if she slipped." Mrs Welch commented then said, "Thank God, she isn't worse than I thought. Miss Sandwell, what do you think happened to Mrs Davis?"

"Mrs Welch, the truth is. I'm not very sure what happened." Lisa said.

"Well when you visit her, would you please pass on my husband and I sincere regards?" Mrs Welch said.

Lisa nodded her head smiling. "I will certainly do, and I thanked you and your kind husband again for assisting me in helping her. I'm really grateful. And thanks again to both you and Mr Welch for your help." Lisa said to Mrs Welch and left.

As Lisa walked into her house, she met her husband Richard with the phone in his hand. "Where were you? I phoned you at Denyah's and got no answer."

"That's because no one was there." Lisa said harshly and showing Richard how upset she was. Richard put the phone down, looked hard into her eyes and saw her tension.

Softly he asked her, "Where were you honey?" Lisa hugged him as tears built up in her eyes saying, "I was at the Hospital with Denyah. She has forty five per cent burns to her body. I don't know what had happened, but she's in a very bad state and she's not allowed to have any visitors for at least a couple of days." Richards looked at Lisa in disbelief. Lisa tears dropped heavily as she said "I'm sure my brother had something to do with her being hurt."

"Well, we don't know the fact so just wait until she tells you" Richard said comforting Lisa. "Oh Richard, as I was pulling Denyah from under the boiling shower, I had a flush of discharge but the doctor check me out after I told her and she said. I and the baby are fine."

"Thank God.' Richard said.

Three days later Lisa went to visit Denyah. "You had me worried" Lisa told her. Denyah smiled.

"How are you?" Lisa asked looking worried as she pulled up a seat near to the bed.

"Well, I'm not going anywhere for now." Denyah replied smiling. Lisa was looking sad, as if it was her fault.

"Don't look so serious." Denyah said smiling. Lisa let out a giggle.

"Are you feeling okay? Is there anything I can get you?" Lisa asked.

"I'm okay Lisa." Denyah said.

"Denyah, I'm really sorry that this has happened to you. Do you want to tell me what happened?" Lisa asked and looking deep in Denyah's eyes.

"Lisa, there's nothing to tell." Denyah said.

Denyah looked into Lisa's face and saw anxiety.

"Look Denyah, when are you going to stop hiding behind your lies? I know that what happened had something to do with my brother and you should hate him for that"

"Lisa, I don't hate anyone. Just remember you're talking about my husband. Even though he's your brother, I don't want you to come between my husband and me. I would deal with my husband when I'm ready and in my own way. Now can we change the subject?" Denyah said frustrated by all the questions.

"Sure, if that's what you want." Lisa said.

"Anyway, how's Paris?" Denyah asked.

Lisa smiled as she tried to avoid answering Denyah. Instead, she asked. "Where can I get a hot drink?"

"You'll have to ask the nurse" Denyah said. Then asked Lisa again, "How's Paris?"

Again Lisa didn't reply, her eyes looked distant and her face caved with pity. Denyah then realised that something was wrong.

"What's wrong Lisa?" Denyah begged her to tell. Lisa got up and looked sadly at Denyah then faced the window overlooking the hospital ground and car park before she stretched upright and took in a deep breath. Lisa facing Denyah again, she smiled covering her mouth with her left hand. Again she took a deep breath, raising her high heeled shoes off the floor. By this time Denyah was silent except when she felt pain and let out a soft groan. As Lisa heard Denyah groaning, she moved closer to the window and stared at the old red painted pub that stood across the road. All this time Denyah was staring at her hoping whatever Lisa told her wasn't as painful as her burns. Eventually Lisa twisted away from the window and faced Denyah again smiling before walking over to Denyah's bed and sat down on the chair. Lisa had realized the depth of pain Denyah was in as she saw her look away in tears groaning. Lisa flicked a few strands of hair off Denyah's forehead and then said, "Honey, I can tell by your face you're feeling pain. I don't want to cause you anymore. But there's no point in me hiding anything from you. I mean you're going to find out anyway" she then took Denyah's hand into hers and barely smiled. Denyah nodded her head.

"You know I'm here for you" Lisa said trying to comfort her.

"I know that Lisa" Denyah replied smiling even though she was in pain.

"You look so tired!" Lisa said as she tried to change the subject.

"I know. I haven't slept for the past two nights. I just can't get comfortable. Lisa what were you going to tell me?" Denyah asked her.

Lisa sighed deeply and then said, "Denyah, Wesley took your clothes to your mother's and told her he caught you in his bed with his two mates. I think your mother believed him. She gave your clothes to the Salvation Army. I'm so sorry Den."

"Well how's Paris" Denyah asked, looking worried.

"He took her to one of his women's house, Bonnie Lee. You know who I mean. He also told me I'm not allowed to see Paris again if I see you. I'm sorry Denyah." Lisa said.

"It's not your fault" Denyah said feeling hurt and some how managing to hide her tears as she kept quiet and staring up at the ceiling.

"I saw Eugene earlier. He said he was going to come and see you" Lisa said hoping that it would cheer Denyah up a bit.

"I don't really want to see him" Denyah replied, "How does he know I'm here anyway?"

"He came to see me this morning after Claire gave him my address. I told him you were in here because he was asking for you. I hope you don't mind."

"Did he not know I was here before you told him?" Denyah asked.

"No! He said he was going to see you at your house." Lisa said.

"Is he mad? I told him I'm married and have a daughter. What is he playing at?" Denyah said angrily.

"Look Den, he's just trying to be friendly. I mean not every husband would get angry because a male friend came to visit his wife. Eugene cares for you a lot; you'll be a fool not to see him" Lisa said.

"Lisa, I am married to you brother!" Denyah said.

"Don't remind me Den. My brother is a devious bastard. He'll never change. Only god knows why you stayed with him when he's treating you like a rag doll and trampling all over you" Lisa said trying to hold back her tears.

"Lisa when I get out of here I'm going to find somewhere else to live. I want to make something of my life. It seems like I have no family now and my husband…Well, I needn't comment on him. I just don't want what had happened to me and your brother to come between us. Promise me, it won't." Denyah said.

"You know I don't like what Wesley is doing to you. Nobody should have to go through this. You're always welcome to stay with Richard and me for as long as you need too."

"Thanks, Lisa how did I get here?" Denyah asked looking puzzled.

"I phoned you a couple of times and got no reply. Then I saw Wesley outside talking to Richard, I asked him how you were after having so much champagne at the party. He told me to go round and find out for myself and ask you about your men visitors and that he was late for work. What he said frightened me. So, as soon as he drove off, I rushed over to see you. I rang the doorbell a few times and got no reply, so I let myself in with the key you and Wesley gave me. I found you lying under the steaming shower unconscious after you must have slipped and were badly scalded. I called the ambulance and they brought you here. Oh, Mr and Mrs Welch, your neighbours assisted me in helping you. I didn't tell Wesley anything. He doesn't know you're here and I asked your neighbours not to tell him. I only told Eugene. Den, I know my brother had something to do with you being here. You can deny it all you like, but I know better, he's a mischievous bastard" Lisa said and then looked at her wrist watch before she got up and said before turning to leave, "I have to go now. I'll be back though" she looked at Denyah and smiled then leaned forward and kissed her on the forehead and as she turned to leave Denyah said, "Thank you for everything Lisa. I'm really grateful."

Lisa smiled, waved goodbye and Denyah watched her walked out of her sight.

CHAPTER THREE

A few minutes after Lisa had left a nurse went and gave Denyah her medication for the pain then a second nurse helped Denyah into the chair while she changed her bed sheets.

"How's the pain now Mrs Davis?" The nurse asked as she gave Denyah the medication asked taking her temperature.

"Still pretty painful, but I feel a lot better than when I first came in. I'm mostly feeling the pain at the back of my head and my legs." Denyah said. The nurse smiled and helped Denyah back into bed after taking her temperature. And asked." Have you had a goodnight's sleep last night?"

"Not really nurse, "I'm feeling very rundown as the pain made it hard for me to get comfortable. I really hate complaining, but the pain is getting worse between my thighs." Tears began to roll down her face.

"I'll be right back" the nurse said. She then hurried away to find a doctor.

Moments later a doctor arrived, he stood by Denyah's bed looking at the nurse as she slipped two tiny tablets on Denyah's tongue from a small medicine glass followed by a drink of water. "You will soon be alright Mrs Davis." the nurse said.

"The pain should start to ease." The doctor said.

"Try and get some sleep Mrs Davis." the nurse said then left to go to another patient two beds away.

Two hours later the nurse returned. By then Denyah was awake and was reading a crime novel. 'The Glass Bowl.'

"How's the pain, Mrs Davis?" the nurse asked.

"I'm hardly feeling any pain since you gave me the tablets. Thank you" Denyah replied smiling.

"I'm glad you're feeling better." the nurse said as she fixed her pillows, "Do you need anything before I leave?" the nurse asked.

"No thank you nurse." Denyah replied.

"Well I'll see you after dinner." the nurse said and then left.

A black woman patient that was in the second bed on the other side went to Denyah and greeted her with a warm hello and a charming smile.

"Hello," Denyah returned the compliment.

"Well dear. I'm Ivy. I was listening to your groaning so much last night and I was feeling so sorry for you. However, you looked so much better and more at ease."

"Thank you very much Ivy. I'm feeling much better. I'm Denyah."

Ivy sat on Denyah's bed and said. "You know I was admitted two hours before you. You must have been very careless to have hurt yourself like that." as Denyah looked hard at Ivy, Ivy smiled.

"Yeah, I guess you can say that. What about you Ivy? Is it carelessness why you are here?" Denyah asked.

Ivy laughed before saying to Denyah "Actually, I'm here because of my husband's jealousness. See that woman in fifth bed, and wearing blue pyjamas, her husband is a drug addict. He fractured her left jaw, broke four of her ribs and her left arm, all because she didn't give him enough money to buy drugs. To look at her husband, you wouldn't think he's capable to hurt anyone. His white handsome young face gave out the wrong signal - as if he'd walked on eggshell but would never crush it. If she hadn't told me he was the one that done that to her, I would have thought she was beaten up by a thug.

Her husband is tall and blonde, I would say he's about five foot, eleven to six foot tall and he's very good looking with little scattered freckles on his face, not to mention his exquisite bright grey cat like eyes and a nice medium build. Both her and her husband are thirty four and have been lovers since they were nineteen, she told me. Well, that's the trouble with mixed raced marriages. No offence to you Denyah."

"None taken, I'm married to a black man myself. In fact he's the reason why I'm here too."

"Yes I know. I heard from a little white dove that your husband's black and he's a copper."

"Ivy, I'm thinking of going into writing. I'm sure you would give me all the information I need to start my novel" Denyah joked.

Ivy laughed, "I have heard someone said if he wanted to write a book he only had to go to the post office, banks, doctors surgeries, supermarkets, hospital and chemists and he'll gather all the information he required to write it" Ivy said.

"I strongly agree with that man whoever he is." Reply Denyah.

Ivy smiled contentedly before she said "However, my husband beat me up almost every week for nine years. When he got tired of beating me, he found a younger woman and moved her into my home. I was left with nothing. He got the house and everything that went with it. I suppose him being a solicitor the law was more on his side as he knew all the right strings to pull" Ivy explained to Denyah.

Denyah was feeling sorrier for Ivy than for herself. Denyah and Ivy eventually became good friends; they even exchanged their mobile numbers. Denyah gave to Ivy her mothers address, hoping that her mother would soften when she told her what happened and that her mother would take her in to her home so that she could stay in contact with her hospital friend Ivy that she came to like very much. Ivy reminded her of an old friend she once had and loved. But unfortunately, that friend had died in car accident.

As Denyah was deep in thought, Ivy took her left hand into hers and said, "Denyah, I really like you and I'm very sorry how your friend died."

"I like you too Ivy. You're good fun and easy to get on with." Denyah said

Ivy smiled as she asked Denyah, "Do you want to know something else?"

"Okay Ivy, you have my attention,"

"Well," said Ivy, "the woman in fourth bed stabbed her husband to death and I don't blame her. Even though he put her in here, her husband has come off the worst." Ivy laughed as Denyah watched her. Ivy raised her eyebrows while she was speaking about the patient in bed four to Denyah. Then as the patient fixed her eyes on her, she waved to the patient in guilt, giving the patient suspicious feelings she was talking about her.

Throughout the time Ivy was telling Denyah what the patient had told her, the patient was looking at them with discomforting feelings as she sensed that they were talking about her, and, especially when she saw Ivy pointing her finger directly at her. The patient put her unclosed magazine on her locker, got in to bed and turned her back on Denyah and Ivy.

"I think she suspected we were talking about her," Denyah said.

"Don't worry about her, she's a lovely person to get on with," said Ivy.

The patient could not help turning her head to look at Denyah and Ivy. Ivy waved to her smiling, but she turned her head quickly facing the other side of the room and pulled the sheets up to her shoulders.

Denyah smiled as Ivy went on to say, "However, the case between her and her husband were dismissed on the grounds of cruelty and adultery. And for some other reason which is unspeakable to talk about and I don't wish to mention to you. Well, I suppose it's only fair for the jury to find her not guilty. After all, he forced her to sell herself to keep his drug habit going. Now she's free of him. The good-for-nothing bastard, ah, some gain by their wickedness and others lose. Well Denyah, I hope you sleep well tonight" Ivy said as she got up off Denyah's bed to go to hers.

"And you too Ivy. I hope you sleep well" Denyah said.

As Denyah and Ivy became friends Ivy shared her fruit and drinks with Denyah as Denyah had no visitors. And poor Denyah cried most nights in silence after the lights had dimmed.

Two weeks later on Tuesday afternoon, Lisa went to the hospital to visit Denyah. Denyah had noticed that Lisa did not look like her normal self and she could tell that something had happened as tears clouded Lisa's eyes before she looked up to the ceiling. Denyah didn't bother asking Lisa what was the matter. She lay quietly in bed waiting until Lisa was ready to tell her whatever it was. After Denyah took Lisa's hand into hers, Lisa looked into Denyah's face and said, "Den, you know that I care about you and there's nothing I would let come between us. Not even my brother, your husband."

"Okay Lisa, I understand our valued friendship. But what is so wrong that you came here for me to see you with flowing tears and can't tell me why."

"Den, Wesley is telling everyone that you have left him and Paris to be with Eugene. I went to see him and I asked him why would you walk out on him after thirteen years, he said you told him that you are no longer in love with him. So you've left him for another man. I didn't want to hear anymore of what he had to say, so I told him I'm late to do my shopping. He then smiled and saw me out of his house."

After Lisa spoke to Denyah, she left. For the rest of the evening Denyah were feeling disgusted and so alone that she hardly had a good night's sleep. The following morning she wouldn't eat, drink or speak to any of the patients. Not even Ivy who's she got friendly with. She had just about managed to answer a few questions to the doctors and nurses. Apart from that, she just lay in bed in thought over what her husband was telling people. She couldn't believe her husband would sink so low as to feed people with lies about her in spite of what he'd done to put her in hospital.

After an evening of hard thinking, she fell into deep sleep and only woke up when nurse James' tapped her on her shoulder saying, "Mrs Davis, I'm sorry to wake you from your sleep. But it's time for medication."

"Thank you nurse, I was so tired." Denyah said and took the tablets and water off the nurse.

After Denyah swallowed her tablets, Nurse James took the empty glass off her, fixed her pillows, and said good night before she left.

The next morning six o'clock nurse Baker woke Denyah up. "I'm sorry to wake you Mrs Davis. I would like for you to take these tablets after I take your temperature." Nurse Baker then told her. "The doctor wants you to have an x-ray. Are you feeling much pain?" nurse Baker asked.

"Not so much since the doctors changed my tablets." Denyah said.

The nurse smiled then said to Denyah. "The doctor will be here around about ten. I think he would like to have a word with you."

A few minutes after the nurse Baker checked Denyah's chart and took her temperature. Doctor Hill came to Denyah and said. "Mrs Davis, I would like to have a look at your scars?"

Nurse Baker drew the screen around Denyah and waited while Doctor Hill put his surgical gloves on and examined what scars Denyah had especially those on the lower part of her tummy, legs and between her thighs. After Doctor Hill examined Denyah, his smiling showed things were satisfactory. He then said to Nurse Baker, "I would like Mrs Davis to have her burns X-rayed and then return with them to me please. Thank you Nurse Baker." Doctor Hill said as he puts Denyah's medical charts in the holder on the foot of her bedstead.

Eleven fifteen that morning, Nurse Baker and Nurse Grant wheeled Denyah into the X-rays room for her to be X-rayed. After ten minutes, Denyah X-rays were completed. Nurse Baker took the four X-rays of different parts of Denyah where she had most scalded and took them to doctor Hill. After Doctor Hill studied the four X-rays carefully, he went to Denyah and said "Mrs Davis, you might need a skin graft on the upper part of you left leg, thighs and the lower part of your tummy. But possibly your skin might grow naturally by itself in a couple of months. Still, some skin returned immensely and looking glorified while some is folded or defective and needs some surgery. Well Mrs Davis, we'll see what you gain from nature in a couple of months before we do anything." Smiling nicely, he said, "You seem to have healing flesh."

"Thank you Doctor Hill." Denyah said as she saw his name on the badge pinned to his suit jacket.

Nurse Baker smiled as Doctor Hill gave Denyah a bright smile before he left.

By dinner time Denyah was feeling a lot better. She ate all her dinner.

Six o'clock in the evening, Eugene entered the ward. Denyah was so surprised to see him that her throat suddenly went dry and felt as if there was a lump in it. She broke out in a cold sweat and she was left with a fearful feeling. Eugene walked towards her smiling with a giant box of Cadburys milk chocolates and a bunch of white lilies. When he got by her bed he pulled forward a chair and kissed her forehead.

"How are you," he asked.

"Could be better," Denyah replied.

"I'm sorry about what happened to you, why you do this to yourself?" he asked.

"I just lost control while I was under the shower. I was tipsy. I must have slipped and knocked myself unconscious. Please forgive me for slapping you at the party, it was a misunderstanding."

"I forgave you before you did it. It took me a little while to figure out why, but I understand. I would have done the same if I was in that situation. I'd love for us to be more than just friends."

"Eugene, I'm married" Denyah told him.

"Is that what you call a marriage," he asked sarcastically. "Where will you be staying when you leave here," he went on to ask.

"I'll find somewhere." Denyah said.

"Do you have any money?" he asked her.

"Yes, Eugene I will find a place to stay. Yes I am married and yes I do have money. Is there anything else you would like to know?"

"Yes actually, do you have a job to go back to? I was told your so called husband told your boss you no longer needed your job. Your last pay cheque was sent to your mother's house with your P45"

Denyah stared at Eugene in disbelief before asking him. "How come you know so much?"

"Your sister Blanche told Lisa and Lisa told me. Would you like me to take you out of here? You can go to a private hospital."

"No Eugene, I like it here, the nurses, doctors and patients are all very good to me."

As Eugene stared at her, tears came into her eyes. "Go on take a good look at me. I'm scalded all over" As tears streamed down her face she whispered to him. "I do like you but…"

"But what," he asked inquisitively.

"I don't want you to get hurt! My husband is ruthless. You don't know him, the more he hurts people the better he feels" Eugene turned his face away and then faced her again to see her crying. She looked away. A few minutes passed before she reached for a tissue. He took her hands into his, kissed them slowly and then wiped away her tears with his fingers.

"I would love to be with someone like you. But I don't want you to get hurt. So far you're the only friend I think I have. Eugene, I really feel as though I can trust you." she said.

"I understand what you're saying Den. But I want to be there for you. I don't want you to shut me out" he told her as tears slid down his face. She turned her face away. At this time nurse James was looking at them both. Nurse James couldn't help herself feeling a little discomfort for Denyah even though she didn't know the real reason for her turning away from Eugene. Nurse James, thinking remorsefully, and feeling deeply concern for Denyah, she thought it must be Eugene upsetting her. Nurse James was not thinking she might be doing the wrong thing and make things worst. Nurse James left her desk and went to them telling Eugene, "I'm sorry to disturb you. But visiting time finished ten minutes ago."

Eugene got up out of his seat, kissed the back of Denyah's neck, before telling her, " I 'm in love with you Den but I'll get over this and for both our sake, it best we don't see you again." sadly he left. She watched him walking down the long corridor until he'd disappeared from her sight.

"I didn't mean to disturb you Mrs Davis. But watching you turn away…"

"He's just a friend" Denyah interrupted Nurse James, as she didn't want to hear whatever she had to say. Nurse James sat at the edge of Denyah's bed, smiled and looked deeply in to her eyes and said, "Your friend seemed very concerned about you. He's also very good looking."

"Yes, I know." Denyah replied. "But I don't think he'll be coming to see me again"

Eugene was the last to leave the ward. Shortly after, supper was served but Denyah had found it hard to even swallow hers. As the auxiliary nurse saw the uneaten food on Denyah's bed table, she looked Denyah in the eyes and asked,

"Are you not hungry Mrs Davis?" Denyah shook her head. The auxiliary nurse looked on at her with sorrow before she took the food and pudding away. After the nurse left, Denyah faced the partition in tears while the other patients settled down for sleeping. Nurse James turned the bright ward lights off and then wished her patients a goodnight before she left.

That night Wesley went to visit his sister Lisa and brother-in-law Richard. He cried before telling them, "I came home from work the Friday night before you and Den went to the party and caught Denyah in bed with one of my work mates" Wesley cried hard as Lisa and Richard looked at him in disbelief. After Wesley finished telling his story he got up and walked towards the door smiling and stood facing the door with that cunning smile on his face.

"What are you going to do now?" Richard asked Wesley.

Wesley wiped his smile off before turning and faced Lisa and Richard.

"Are you going to stop her from seeing Paris?" Richard went on to ask him.

"Yes, I have to. I don't want my daughter to be growing up like her" Wesley replied.

Lisa huffed and shook her head.

"Goodbye then" Lisa said trying to hurry him out her house. He left in tears. Lisa then turned to her husband Richards and say, "A bad liar, always changes his lies. He told me a different lie before. I didn't know I would come to hate my brother so much."

When Wesley got home, he laughed and threw his keys on the table and flung himself on the settee. "I won" he said as he laughed aloud. He then called his fiancée Bonnie Lee to come downstairs to him from upstairs. At the speed she ran down the stairs to him, she missed a step and twisted her right ankle and went down on her knees. Scornfully he looked down on her before he said, "Get me a glass of whiskey!" she looked up to him, "Give me a couple of minutes to get on my feet." she said feeling her ankle and groaning.

"Get your arse up and fetch me a bottle of whiskey!" he demanded.

Bonnie raised herself up quickly and hopped away into the kitchen and brought to him a full bottle of his favourite whiskey and a glass. He dragged the bottle out of her hand and went to lie down on the settee and gulped down about a quarter from the bottle, and tossed the glass hitting Bonnie on her back. Bonnie faced him, he widened his eyes to her with a mean looked. As she stood watching him, he told her "Make me a sandwich! And be quick!" she did not move as her ankle was painful. "Get your arse in the kitchen and bring me a cheese and tomato sandwich and make sure you slice the tomatoes thin and not like you're feeding hogs. Now get moving" he demanded.

"Make it your damn self" she told him. "You don't want a wife. Or a mistress, you want a servant! You should have kept your wife! She was a good servant to you" Bonnie told him holding her painful ankle.

Wesley got off the settee in bad temper and kicked the coffee table out of his way, smashing the glass. Furiously he pulled Bonnie by her long red hair into him and thumped her on the mouth, blood poured from her lips like a burst pipe. Even though she was bleeding, he beat her up badly then tossed her across the room, she fell and gashing her forehead on one of the coffee table legs. She spat blood out on his living room cream rug. He walked over to her and kicked her out of his front door. She fell face down. As his neighbours Rachael and Mrs Welch saw what he'd done to Bonnie, they rushed out of their houses to help her. Shamefully Bonnie looked up at Mrs Welch and Rachael as she wiped blood from her lips. Crying, she managed to barely get up off of her knees as she had a sprained ankle, but she fought hard to straighten herself up on her sprained and painful ankle and staggered away in pain then fell about seven feet away on the pavement.

As Mrs Welch and Rachael rushed to help Bonnie, Wesley told them "Get back into your blasted houses and mind your damn business" But neither, Rachael or Mrs Welch paid him any attention at first, until he rudely said to them "You two get your arses back into your houses and stay there."

"You're so disrespectful for an officer of the Law" Mrs Welch told him.

He stared at Mrs Welch and then at Rachael swinging his gun in his left hand as he's left handed and the three quarter bottle of whiskey in his right hand. Mrs Welch and Rachael stood looking frightened and watching each other. He blasted out to them "Get your asses back in your house before I lock both of you up" As Rachael is a regular drug taker and had drugs tucked away in her bra, she became paranoid as Wesley turned and faced her. Grinning lightly, Rachael faced Mrs Welch, to say, "I best take my black arse in my house as I've my five year old daughter to take to school every morning and to take care of and especially as she has no dad. You could stay and let him lock you up and then your husband might find another woman to look after him. However, I think the bitch deserved what she got messing with married men such as him and to think that he treated his lovely wife worst than a piece of dog meat. Mrs Welch, that man's nothing but a maggot in lump of stale shit! Add to that he's so disrespectful. The one I am sorry for, is his wife, she's too good for a maggot such as him. Mrs Welch, like me, I think you should take your white face in your house and shut your door. As I said, I have no respect for that son-of-a-bitch as he has none for us. Just because he's a police officer, he thinks he can get away with his wicked doings" Rachael said.

Mrs Welch and Rachael went in their houses and Mrs Welch hurried to her kitchen window and watched Bonnie struggled to steady on her feet but she fell sideways. "Poor girl" Mrs Welch said, as Bonnie was struggling to get up but pitched forward and barely could balance on her feet. She stooped low and sprawled around her ankle and then slowly stretching upright with both her hands folded around her bosom and curved over as she's in pain. Before she walked away, she spat blood out. She then took her time to look back before slowly hopping on her good foot and dragging her sprained foot. The minute she got home, she soaked her sprained ankle in hot vinegar water then treated her sprained ankle with deep-heat ointment then took a couple of pain killers tablets and went to bed crying.

The following morning before Wesley left for work Bonnie went to his house and knocked on his door. He answered the door wearing his pyjama trousers,

"What the hell you came knocking on my door for," he asked her.

"Wesley, I'm begging you to take me back."

Wesley said nothing but gave her a dirty look and kicked the door shut in her face, then went and sat down at the kitchen table and shelled a boiled egg.

Bonnie banged at his door constantly. He got up and fixed his face furiously and threw the egg in the sink in temper and went and opened the door. He looked at her intensely and said, "You knock at my fucking door one more time I will put a bullet up your arse." Bonnie cried, "Please Wesley, I love you." she said. He looked down on her to see her wearing a broad bandage around her ankle. Angrily he flung the door closed almost hitting her face. He then turned up his Hi-fi to maximum so that he would not hear her voice. After Bonnie was crying for some time, she rubbed her lips and opened the cut that it starting to bleed again. She spat blood out on his doorstep and left crying. She then went to stay with her friend Gina as she and her mother has had arguments over how Wesley had treated her.

Later that day, she went to her mother's, packed her clothes, and said to her mother "I'm moving out."

"Where would you go?" her mother asked.

"I will be staying with a friend" she said.

"Are you sure you want to do this Bonnie?" her mother asked.

"Yes. I have too, sooner or later. So, I decided now is the right time" Bonnie said rudely and frustratingly to her mother.

"Well, if you choose to go and live with that rotten good-for-nothing man, it's your life you'll be wasting. If he can abuse his lovely wife and treated her like doormat, I'm so sorry for you. Bonnie, wake up girl, I haven't seen him beat you. But I know he's done this to you. You can hardly walk and look how he bust up you lips. At least stay until your feeling better"

"No mom, I'm moving in with a friend."

"Okay, but when things turn sour between you and your friend don't come begging me to take you back."

"Mother, doesn't it ever occur to you, that I hated living here with you and that scrounger man you bring in on us, I would rather take Wesley's blows than stay here!" Bonnie said outrageously.

Her mother slapped her face and said, "If that's the way you feel, take your belongings and get out of my way." Bonnie broke down crying on her mother's shoulder. "Mom, I should have listened to you when you told me Wesley's no good but I can't live here with that man you bring into our home. He tried to fondle my breast more than once and I threatened him, I would kill him if he touches me again in that way."

Bonnie mother was so angry that she said to Bonnie "you're a devious liar. I don't believe you. Mario wouldn't do that to any of you. And as for listening to me about that wicked Wesley, you listened alright, but you still ignored me when I asked you to leave that wicked Wesley alone. As I told you, his wife is a very lovely and decent good looking young lady, and if he could treat her like a doormat, you meant nothing to him. So every time he thinks of his wife, he'll beat your arse. Another thing, if he bedded his wife's sister in front of her and doesn't give a damn, tell me what sort of a man is he" Just take your belonging and get out of my sight!"

Bonnie looked hard at her mother and left in rage with her clothes to go and stay with her friend Gina and leaving her mother door wide open. Her sister Lacy closed the door and said to her mother, "Mom, I don't think Bonnie was lying. Mario has done the same to me, but I cut him with a knife on his hand."

Bonnie and Lacy mother then believed Mario tried it on with her daughters and so she packed Mario clothes and told him to leave. He puts up a strong fight saying "No, I will not" But when she told him she'd call in the police, he quickly took his belongings and went to his mother's as he had been in trouble with the law for selling drugs and raping his ex wife's daughter.

Meanwhile, before Bonnie knocked on Gina's door, she dried her tears. Gina opened her door and smiled as she saw Bonnie. "Can I come in?" Bonnie asked her. Gina moved away from the door and said "remember it's only for a short time you would be staying here"

"What ever you say Gina, and how do you know I want to stay?"

Gina smiled and said, "Bonnie, you don't bring your suitcase with you just to say hello. You know your room. The one you always have when you sleep over or you in trouble"

"Thanks Gina."

"Don't thank me Bonnie. You will be paying me rent."

The next day, Thursday morning, eleven o'clock, Denyah phoned Lisa and said "I really miss seeing your smile. So why haven't you been to see me for the past three weeks?"

Lisa paused and faced the piled up used dishes in the kitchen sink and went dumb struck and silent before breathing heavily into the phone receiver saying "Richard told me not to see you anymore and that I should stay away from you. I asked him why, and he said Wesley told him he caught you in his bed with his mates and you were drunk. I've never seen Richard so angry before. In fact, he became furious when I told him I couldn't make him a promise not to see you and it had caused an argument between us. Den, I'm sorry for not coming to see you and I apologise. But I don't think I should see you anymore as I have to obey my husband" After Lisa spoke to Denyah she took a couple of plates from the sink and smashed them on the kitchen floor out of anger before she cried and went and had a lie down as she had developed a migraine. Later Richard came home from work and found the smashed plates on the kitchen floor and scattered blood stains on the rim of the sink unit and on the kitchen floor. He opened the living room door calling "Lisa" in fright then as she wasn't there he ran upstairs calling "Lisa, Lisa," then quickly burst their bedroom door opened to see her lying on her right side and blood on her pillow from a gash on her right thumb. He shook her lightly waking her up. "Are you okay?" he asked her panicking.

"Yes, I think so, why do you ask?"

"I saw the sink piled with dirty dishes and broken plates on the floor mixed with blood. Oh God, you'd put the wind up me after seeing the state of the kitchen, I thought you were hurt."

Lisa lied and told him the plates slipped out of her hand as she went dizzy.

"I want you to rest honey. Let me have a look at your finger."

"Why?" Lisa asked.

"You must have cut it while picking up some of the broken plates." Richard said

Lisa looked at her hands and saw a small gash below her thumb and said. "I didn't even know I received a cut." said Lisa.

"Would you like some tea or anything?" Richard asked her.

"No Richard, I just would like to rest" Lisa said.

"Okay honey, I'll be in the kitchen cleaning up, you need anything, give me a call" Richard said.

Meanwhile, Denyah was lying in bed and crying softly over what Lisa told her. That evening Ivy asked her "Why doesn't anyone come to visit you anymore?"

Denyah replied. "Because I have asked my friend Lisa not to tell anyone I'm here, as I don't want my husband to know."

"Very wise Denyah. Anyway, you will be going home in a couple of days. Lucky you to be spending Christmas with family, just think of me, when you're stuffing yourself with turkey dinner and whatever follow." Ivy said.

Denyah smiled, but she couldn't get settled throughout her remaining time staying in the hospital as she became bothered by losing her dearest friend Lisa.

Two days before Christmas Eve, Denyah was discharged from hospital. She phoned her mother and asked her to bring her some clothes but her mother put the phone down on her. She then realized her husband had got to her mother as well. She sat on her bed distraught and cried thinking where would she get some clothes to wear out of the hospital and where would she be staying. She then phoned her younger sister Blanch and asked her to borrow a dress from their cousin Dixie for her to wear out of the hospital as they both wear size twelve. Blanch phoned Dixie and asked Dixie if she could borrow some of her clothes for Denyah as she has nothing to wear out of the hospital.

"Sure Blanch, she could borrow one of my dresses. Would she need anything else?" Dixie asked.

"Yes, Dixie, she needs underclothes and a pair of shoes."

"Well, you come and get some money to buy what Den needs" Dixie told Blanch. By the way, what's wrong with her, and why were mom and I not told?"

"Dixie she was badly scalded. That's all I can tell you" Blanch said.

"How did she get scalded" Dixie asked.

"Leave it Dixie. If you don't want to lend her the dress, I understand" Blanch said.

By this time Blanch mother was listening in on the conversation, she pulled the phone from Blanch's hand and told Dixie Denyah doesn't need any dresses. Blanches mother then put the phone down and faced Blanch and told her "I want you to keep well away from Denyah."

"Why mother, what has my sister done so wrong for you to warn me to keep away from her?"

"Denyah is my daughter but she's also bad news. How could she have slept with Wesley's two mates, How could she?"

"Mother, if you believed those lies about your own daughter, you're not the mother I believed in" Blanch told her mother and start crying as she saw no way to help Denyah.

After Denyah had a phone call from Blanch saying "Mom told Dixie not to lend you her clothes." Denyah went to the toilet and cried before she went to her bed looking so very sad and alone that nurse James asked her what was wrong. At first she told Nurse James she was okay but then burst out crying. Nurse James drew the screen around her before putting her arms around her to assure her she's not on her own. "I want to help you Mrs Davis. If you let me" Nurse James told her.

"I've nowhere to stay when I leave here. I don't even have any clothes to wear out" Nurse James looked at her in a sympathetic way and said "Don't worry about anything. I would like to be one of your friends" Denyah hugged her and said thanks.

"You try and get a goodnight sleep and do not worry. As you didn't eat your dinner, would you like a hot cup of milk and biscuits?" Nurse James asked her.

"Yes please" Denyah said.

"Well, I'll see what I can do for you Mrs Davis. You just try and relax. And after work, I would be happy to get you some clothes."

Denyah smiled and said "Thank you, and as I'm your friend, would you please call me Denyah or Den."

Nurse's James smiled and left to return with a cup of hot milk and biscuits for her. "Thank you so much" Denyah told her.

"Thank me later after I take you home" Nurse James said smiling. Denyah smiled back. Nurse James left her drinking her milk and went to attend to her others patients. Denyah was surprised but was very grateful to have had a great friend like Nurse James. Later that day, Nurse James took to her what she needed to wear out of the hospital saying, "We might have a little problem. I chose size 12 as I forgot to ask you."

Denyah was so lost for words that her tears came flooding down her face.

"As I said, you can thank me properly when I take you home" Nurse James told her.

Denyah went to the bathroom and got dressed. She then took one last look around the ward and said goodbye to ward friends and hugged Ivy before she left with Nurse James by her side.

As Denyah and Nurse James drove home, Denyah looked Nurse James in her eyes and asked her, "Why are you being so nice to me?"

"I'm a nurse, that's my job. Besides, we all have to help each other every once in awhile. It wasn't that bad being with me. Was it?" Nurse James asked smiling.

"Nar, I suppose not!" Denyah said jokingly, smiling, and feeling at ease.

"That is how I like to see you, smiling" Nurse James said as she opened her front door. "Well Mrs Davis, I mean Denyah. From here on, you will be in my care. Before I start the cooking, would you like a soft drink?"

"That would be nice" Denyah replied smiling. Nurse James opened two cans of iced cold sodas and gave one to Denyah. They both drank deeply showing how thirsty they were. After drinking most of their sodas, their belches had turned into jokes and laughter. Nurse James then phoned her hospital boss asking if she could have the rest of the day off work. "Certainly" her boss said. Then goes on to say "Nurse James, you're a good and a reliable worker. Take care of your patient and I will see you a week on Monday morning at eight o'clock" Nurse James thanked her boss and went in thinking that she must have known about Denyah staying with her.

"Nurse James, are you still there?" still in thought, Nurse James answered "Yes, Doctor Collins, I'm here and thanks for giving me time off" and they both hung up. Nurse James stood over Denyah and said "Even though we are short staffed there were no questions asked. My boss just told me she'll see me next Monday morning at eight. So my dear friend Mrs Denyah Davis, let's enjoy the rest of the week" Nurse James smiled happily and pressed off her mobile phone. After she remembered she had no bread, milk or much food, she decided to go shopping at One Stop at Perry Bar while Denyah was resting in her bedroom.

Before Nurse James left to do her shopping for food and clothes for Denyah, she said to Denyah, "Well my room is next to yours. You need anything during the night, give me a hard shake if I'm sleeping" Nurse James showed Denyah where everything was kept including telling her that her two bed roomed flat was a gift from David her fiancée. Nurse James then left in her car to do her shopping and then she returned two hours later with her shopping to last her and Denyah for at least two weeks including clothes, shoes and make-up that would suit Denyah as Denyah is white and she is of mixed race and thought her make-up might be too dark for Denyah.

"Thanks, thank you for everything nurse James." Denyah said as tears filled her eyes.

"Please call me Louise" Nurse James said smiling "Would you like us to go and have a drink at my local pub later, or, if you prefer to stay in, I've bought us a couple bottles of wine?"

"Do you mind if I skip going to the pub as I really doesn't feel up to it?"

"That's okay" Nurse James replied. "We stay at home and have a good time". Just before Nurse James started to cook dinner, she made cheese and tomato sandwiches for her and Denyah followed by ice-cream with freshly mixed chopped fruits and coffee. As Denyah hadn't finished her coffee, Nurse James took it that she didn't like the strong coffee.

And so Nurse James asked her "Can I get you anything to drink while the dinner is cooking?"

"Yes please, a cold drink would be nice" Denyah said. Nurse James poured Denyah a cold drink of fruit juice in a tall green glass and passed it to her.

"Thank you, Louise." Denyah said.

Nurse James smiled and went back to finish cooking the dinner. After, they both sat at the table eating and drinking, Nurse James had a couple glasses of port while Denyah drank cold milk as she was taking her medication. They both were very happy laughing and telling each other funny jokes. Besides that, they'd spent a quiet, friendly enjoyable and very happy Christmas dancing to CDs and watching TV in the late evening before going to bed.

CHAPTER FOUR

Boxing Day was also a quiet and happy day for them as it became the real beginning of their friendship and living together. It was so joyful for both of them to stay up watching TV each night.

The following week New Years Eve night it was again a joyous time at night to hear the bell rings out. 'Happy New Year' Denyah and Nurse James embraced and kissed each other on their faces and wished each other Happy New Year. By this time they celebrated the Old Year drinking, eating and playing music. They went to bed about three o'clock New Year morning. As they got up late, they skipped breakfast and had lunch, then supper at six thirty in the evening with snacks and cake between the meals. Late in the evening nurse James couldn't help herself saying, "Well, Denyah my friend, Happy New Year."

"Happy New Year Louise and thanks you from the bottom of my heart for your kindness and being the friend I've so wanted" Denyah said and began crying.

"Louise sat beside her, saying, "aye, this is a day of celebration and not to be in tears" Nurse Louise then put her arms around Denyah's shoulder, shook her slightly, got up and tied the white table cloth around her head saying as she smiled, "Denyah would you marry me?"

Denyah burst into laughter and said joking "Yes Louise, I'll marry you." Denyah then dried her eyes, and burst into laughter again.

"That's how I want to see you Den, be happy my friend. Den, I have few friends, but you're the only one I hitched on to right away. Den I love you. You're exceptional."

"I love you too Louise, for your kindness, your sense of humour, and for you" Denyah said. Louise smiled as she saw Denyah smiled.

"I do really love you Louise James."

Louise smiled and kissed Denyah on her left cheek.

New Year Day was very special to them both.

On the second of January, Wednesday evening, Denyah and Nurse James were sitting at the table having tea and almond cake while watching TV. The news was of no interest to them until Denyah heard that two men had been found dead with their throats slit in different cars on Long Grass Road about fifteen yards away from each other. As Denyah listened with interest, the newscaster announced the dead men found were Officers Finch Lomott and Tom Bailey. The police announced on the TV, Officer Tom Bailey was also knifed in the back of his neck as well as his throat. As for Officer Finch Lomott, he was badly mutilated as well as his throat being slit. The news left Denyah feeling sickened. She had a strong feeling that her husband had summoned both of them to be there and then murdered them as it was raining heavily that night and as hardly anyone walked that road as it only contained buildings for demolition and long wild tall twigs stood on that road, and as well that it was known as a lover's spot.

Even though Denyah has had strong feelings that her husband has murdered Officers Finch Lomott and Tom Bailey, there was no way of her proving that her husband had murdered them.

She told Nurse James what her husband had done to her and that she strongly believed that her husband is responsible for the deaths of Officers Tom Bailey and Finch Lomott. She then asked Nurse James not to tell anyone that she was staying at her home, nurse James promised.

One week later, Friday at twelve thirty, Officers Finch's funeral service was held in St Vincent Church in Nechells although he had lived in Sutton. After the service, his family had him cremated privately with only immediate family and after, the mourners had a meal at the Gold Link restaurant. Also Officer Bailey was buried two days later at Witton Cemetery at one thirty. Denyah didn't attend any of the funerals as she didn't want to be seen by her husband or any member of her and her husband's family or friends. But she was very much upset over the death of both Officers and especially Officer Finch who had respected her by not have sex with her as her husband had wanted him to do. She cried as she thought Officer Finch was good to her that time.

One week later Saturday afternoon, Nurse James met Denyah's friend Claire in the Birmingham Bullring market while shopping. As they got talking, Nurse James accidentally said to Claire "Denyah is staying with me until she finds somewhere."

"Oh, I was wondering where she got to after her ill mannered husband threw her out of her home. Well, give her my best wishes. And thanks for telling me. Well, goodbye Louise"

"Goodbye Claire."

After Claire left Nurse James, she phoned Lisa and told her that Denyah was out of hospital and is staying with a Nurse named Louise James. Lisa told her husband and asked him not to tell Wesley. But somehow, the news travelled back to Wesley and he found out where Nurse James lived. Nurse James later realized she shouldn't have told Claire that Denyah was staying with her. So, as soon as Nurse James got home, she said to Denyah "I bumped into your friend Claire and I accidentally told her you're staying with me" Denyah looked at her in disbelief then said, "I've asked you not to tell anyone I'm staying here. I'm trying to protect us from that vicious husband I've married. I'm very grateful for all you've done for me. But I have to get well away from here before he comes looking for me."

"I'm so sorry Den, I forgot you warned me. It just slipped out" Nurse James said sympathetically. Denyah hugged Nurse James and said, "I do not want any harm come to you. I love you for your kindness and for you. You became more than a friend to me. But to protect you, I've got to go even though I don't want to."

Much later that evening, Nurse James's two friends knocked at her door. Both Nurse James and Denyah jumped up out of their seat looking very tense and looking at the door. A louder knock came on the door again. But before Nurse James answered, she put the chain across the door and asked "Who's it?"

"Oh it's me, Randy and Stephanie." Said Randy

Again Denyah looked at Nurse James in relief and sat down while Nurse James opened the door to let her friends in. Before her friends took their seats, she introduced them to Denyah.

"We went to visit a friend in your area, and as we heard you were on leave, we call to say hello" Randy said.

Denyah looked hard at Nurse James in wonder before Nurse James offered her friends a glass port and a slice of her left over Christmas cake. Then as Nurse James and her friends chattered, Denyah listened with interest but she said nothing unless when she being asked questions. After Randy and Stephanie spent sometime with Nurse James and Denyah and were ready to leave, they both hugged Nurse James and said goodbye to her and Denyah. Nurse James showed them out and put the chain on the door for safety as well as locking the door from the inside.

Denyah looked Nurse James in her eyes. She smiled and said "Don't worry Den we can trust them not to say anything."

"I hope you're right" Denyah said feeling uneasy. "But how did they know you're on leave?" Denyah asked.

"We'll be alright Den, so don't worry. They visit me often. Maybe it was just a chance they took. How about some hot cocoa before we go to sleep?"

"Yes please" Denyah replied smiling.

"You know what… I'm glad we became friends" Nurse James said.

"Me too" Denyah replied smiling.

The following week, Monday morning Nurse James got up early and cooked breakfast. She went to Denyah's room as she heard her coughing.

"I've a tickling throat." Denyah said.

"Your breakfast is in the oven when you're ready. Would you like some cough medicine Den? "

"What time is it?" she asked turning on her right to face Nurse James.

"It's only six o'clock. It's much too early for you to get up. You finish your beauty sleep. As I heard you cough, I came to tell you I've left your breakfast in the oven" Nurse James said smiling. Then as she turned to leave, she said, "I'll see you when I get back from work" But before she left to go to work, she took the cough medicine to Denyah and said, "I would like to see you take some before I leave." Denyah looked up at her. "Come on, open those beautiful lips and swallow" Nurse James told her as she carried the measured cough medicine to her lips. Denyah shook her head smiling and opened her mouth. Nurse James drained the medicine in her mouth, then, they both laughed. "That wasn't too hard to swallow was it Den,"

"Not really, but you being more of a friend than my nurse, I wouldn't want to impose too much on you as you have more than your hands full."

"Den, I enjoy looking after you" Nurse James said and kissed Denyah on her face. "I'll see you later, Oh I left you ten pounds on the kitchen counter in case you need a paper or a bar of chocolate." Nurse James left to go to work.

As Denyah heard the front door shut, she drank some water after swallowing her tablets, pulled the quilt up to her shoulders and went back to sleep.

Nine o'clock that morning she got out of bed had her shower and her breakfast then removed from the breakfast area to the living room where she settled down to relax and listen to some Jim Reeves greatest hits.

Three o'clock she started peeling the vegetables to cook for dinner as Nurse James was on double shift. As she peeled the last potatoes, a loud bang came on the door; she left the kitchen and stared at the door nervously holding a turnip and a knife in her hand. The knock came a second time but much louder. Nervously she opened the door trembling to see a dark skinned policeman and a white policewoman standing at the door. She stood at the doorway in shock.

"Are you related to Nurse Louise James?" The policewoman asked.

"Just a friend, she letting me stayed here until I find a place." Denyah said

"Can we come in?" The Policewoman asked.

"Yes, of course. I forgot my manners." Denyah said as she moved away from the door and said to the two officers, "Please come in" As both police walked in the living room, Denyah said "I'm Denyah Davis" she swallowed saliva deeply and said, "Louise-I meant Nurse James went to work this morning. Why Officers, is there something wrong?" Denyah asked looking very worried. The policewoman took a deep breath just as the policeman stepped forward with his hat in his hand and said, "We found her body at the foot of Hockley old cemetery in her car about a mile away from City Hospital. She was raped and then strangled."

"Are you sure it was Nurse James's body you found?" Denyah asked as tears built up in her eyes.

"We're quite sure Mrs Davis. Her body has being identified by Doctor Roberts. I'm very sorry" The policeman said.

"No, No. Not Louise" Denyah cried. "She was the only loyal friend I had - poor Louise, she didn't deserve to die. Her boyfriend is away spending time with family. He won't be back for another two days. Louise told me."

"Have you any idea who could have done this to her?" The policeman asked.

"I think it was my husband who murdered her!" Denyah told them crying.

"Your husband, why do say that Mrs Davis?" The policewoman asked very concern.

"Because he's is a violent man. He'll hurt anyone who tries to help me" Denyah said as the policewoman looked hard at her.

"Mrs Davis, just because your husband may have shown a little violence towards you, you can't just accuse him of murder." the policeman said.

"Can't I" Denyah said under her breath but loud enough for them to hear.

"Are you trying to tell us something? I mean if you know for sure that your husband is behind this, please tell us." The policewoman said thinking. As she spoke, she led Denyah to the sofa and introduced herself as Officer Moore and then she introduced her colleague as Officer Roberts. Just as she was about to ask Denyah if they could sit down, Denyah offered them a seat.

"Can I offer you a drink?" Denyah asked.

"A cold drink would be nice" The policeman said.

"The same for me please" the Policewoman said. Denyah went into the kitchen and took two cans of Pepsi out the fridge, opened them and poured them into two cleaned glasses and gave one each to them.

"Thank you." They both said placing the glasses down on the coffee table.

As Denyah watched the officers drinking, she was contemplating whether she should tell them what her husband had done to her. But she couldn't stop thinking about Nurse James. She then plucked up courage and told them what her husband had done to her. Both officers were shocked and disgusted. And then when she told them that her husband is a police officer, they both looked at each other. The Policeman finished his drink and he and his college both got up and told Denyah they would get back in contact with her. Denyah nodded her head then both officers walked towards the door. Before Denyah showed them out, the policewoman faced Denyah and said "Thank you for your time and information Mrs Davis" The Policewoman then smiled while Denyah held a serious face.

As soon as the officers got out the door they both looked at each other in thought.

"Do you think what she said is true?" The policewoman asked.

"We'll soon find out! She sounded very serious." The policeman said.

"She sure did as her face showed" The policewoman replied.

Denyah watched as the police officers left in their car. She closed the door and lay on the settee crying.

Two days later, Nurse James fiancée returned home and heard the bad news. He went to see Denyah; she told him everything about her husband and what Nurse James had done for her. He understood and felt sorry for both Denyah and his fiancée Nurse James. Denyah broke down in tears. He took her into his arms. "She will be greatly missed by us all" he said. Then he went on to tell Denyah about their wedding plans and then tears came in his eyes. "If only I was here. I left a message on the answering machine, but I don't think she got it"

"Why do you think that?" Denyah asked.

"She always wiped the messages off. But this time she hadn't. I left a message on my machine explaining I'd to go to London and see my son in hospital after I left my parents" he wiped his tears dry with both his hands.

"Did she know you spent Christmas with your son?" Denyah asked.

"No, it wasn't planned. It was a spur of the moment thing. His mother phoned me on my mobile to tell me that he was in hospital getting his tonsils removed."

"How old is your son?" asked Denyah.

"He's six. Louise and I had him spend Christmas and Easter with us last year. He adored Louise. She loved him so much Denyah. He would have to know she's no longer here" David said.

"How about your son's mother, would you try and get back with her?"

"No Denyah, we both have moved on, she is with someone now and ready to give birth. I'm supporting my son monthly and I saw him on a regular basis."

"I'm happy for you David" Denyah said.

However, Denyah tried finishing the dinner, but the thought of Nurse James being murdered kept floating around in her head. The dinner burnt and it was uneatable. Nurse James's fiancée' David ordered a take-away. While they both picked at their dinners, Denyah told him that she was frightened of her husband and that her family doesn't really talk to her anymore because he lied and told them he caught her in our bed with his mates. "And yet, they're talking to my sister although she slept with him."

"Well, can't you ask his mates to tell your family your husband lied to them?" David said to Denyah.

"They were both murdered. Police discovered their bodies in their own cars mutilated and their throats slit. They were both police like my husband."

"Your husband sounds like a dangerous man. Have you any plans to move on?" David asked.

"I've nowhere to go, but I know it's best for me to leave here."

"Look Denyah, you're welcome to stay here for as long as you like." David told her.

"Thank you, but I don't think that's a good idea" Denyah said.

"Have you got any money?" he asked.

"No," Denyah replied. "I and Wesley had a joint account. When I called the bank from the hospital to get some money I was told there was only two pounds and thirty three pence left in our account. Oh David what am I going to do. I do not have anything."

David gave her two hundred pounds and a cheque for one thousand pounds.

"I can't accept this cheque!" Denyah said looking very shocked.

"It's a loan, until you can afford to pay me back. But if you change your mind you can always stay here. I brought this flat for Louise eight months ago for an engagement present. Or if you would like to move on, I could help you find a place."

"Oh David, I'm sorry." Denyah said as she rubbed her forehead. "I wouldn't want to put you to any trouble. Look what happened to my friend. The only decent friend I had."

"Well we can't bring her back, but I'm sure she would have liked for us both to be happy. She was that kind of person; she always wanted the best for everyone." David said smiling. Denyah agreed with him. Then David gave her his phone number and address and told her anytime she was in need of anything even a friend, she could always call on him. They hugged and David wished her goodnight and left.

Denyah spent two more weeks nervously at the flat. During that time, David phoned her to make sure she was alright.

A week later Denyah moved out to rent flat and settled down in a quiet area outside of town and was fortunate to get a job as a dinner lady at an all girls' school in the area. But as one of the girl's mothers recognised her she left that job and got another working as a secretary for a small warehouse firm in Bilston. One month later she also gave up her furnished rented flat and took up board in a run down leaking one room flat in Erdington for five weeks. On the sixth week on Friday morning she went to a Spar Shop to buy bread and milk when she heard the shop owner in conversation with a middle aged black woman saying. "It's a shame old Mrs Carter has no living relatives to care for her and it's more of a shame she's living in such a big house all by herself with so much land surrounding" Denyah said nothing but her eyes fixed on the shop owner's face. Denyah then said in her head, 'I wouldn't mind a job looking after Mrs Carter!"

Denyah pretended to look for what she thought the shop owner might not have to delay time until the customer had left the shop. Then straight to the point she said to the shop owner, "I couldn't help myself from overhearing you say to the woman that was just in the shop that an old woman is in need of a carer."

"Yes, that is so. Why, you interested? She's about eighty something and a bit miserable to get on with. So I heard. Mind you, I also heard if she doesn't like you, she wouldn't open her door to you. So many people she refused before she even opened the door. However, you might soften her stone hard heart as you look like a nice person who seems to care. I myself sent three young ladies in turn to work for her, but she didn't even give them the time of day. Still, if you're still interested and would like to try, I will write out her address" The shop owner said as she began to write the address down on a brown paper bag.

"Thank you so much" Denyah said as she took the paper bag. Smiling, Denyah said, "I'm really grateful, thanks again."

"Well, let's hope you have better luck than the others. However, all the best"
"Cheers," Denyah said as she turned to walk out the shop. But before leaving she looked around and said "I don't believe in luck, only faith. That comes close to God. Apart from his messengers and angels like you!"

The shopkeeper smiled.

The next morning Denyah went to Mrs Carter. As she walked up the garden path she took several long steps to overstep the wildly grown weeds covering the garden path. The house set in a quarter of acre in a secluded area of Nechells with the nearest neighbour living some distance away. Mrs Carter's house was very old and looked as though nobody lived in it. The iron frames surrounding the windows and doors were rusty and some bricks to the front of the house looked loosed with spy holes and cracks. The nets in the windows were very dusty and discoloured; the curtains downstairs were slightly parted so you could just about glimpse her sitting in a rocking chair in front of the window. Nevertheless, this didn't put Denyah off; she still went up to the door and knocked. Mrs Carter looked at Denyah from behind the curtain before she got up slowly and opened the door smiling. Before Denyah could say anything, Mrs Carter said, "I know why you're here. Yes, I need a helper, there's certain things I can't do because of my old age. So would you like to work for me? However, if you do, I wouldn't have it any other way. You have to live here with me"

"Mrs Carter, I would love to have the job and even more I would love to live here" Denyah said looking around at the neglected house.

"Well, that's settled. The quicker you move in, the quicker we'll get to know each other" Mrs Carter said.

"One thing, don't you want to carry out a check on me first." Denyah asked smiling.

"Naturally, I would like to know your name, whatever else would fall into place after. So the job is yours if you want it and you wouldn't mind helping an old woman change her clothes sometimes?"

"Can I ask you question? Mrs Carter?" Denyah said.

"Of course, ask what you wish." Mrs Carter said with her eyes fixed on Denyah.

"I would like to know, why has no one worked for you?"

"I don't like their faces. But you, you're exceptional. The minute I saw you, I knew you were the right person and still I'm waiting to hear…what is your name?"

"Oh, I'm sorry; my name is Denyah, Denyah Davis. Would it be alright if I move in sometime next week?"

"Yes, of course. But why not now, it would be much better all round and why continue to pay rent at your old place when your room here will be free" Mrs Carter explained.

Denyah smiled and wiped dust from the old fashioned brown settee with her paper handkerchief before she sat.

Mrs Carter smiled, and said "When you move in, you can do the dusting"

Three days later Denyah moved in with Mrs Carter. She worked hard to make the place looked tidy but she told Mrs Carter much work needed to be done to the house.

"What's this Denyah, are you telling me my home is not up to standard?"

"No, not at all, I'm letting you know it needs fixing. I don't wish to take over and tell you what to do, but from my room I could see halfway around the world through so many holes."

Mrs Carter chuckled away in laughter that brought Denyah to laugh as well. "You know what Denyah, I've become like an old match box and you're a live match that's ready to explore. I really do like you Denyah. Where were you before now?"

"Dreaming sweet dreams about you?" Denyah said nicely and joking.

Mrs Carter laughed so much and was feeling so happy since Denyah moved in with her that she said to Denyah, "You find the builder and I'll find the money."

Two months later, Mrs Carter and Denyah's friendship grew very strong. Denyah cared so much about Mrs Carter, and Mrs Carter loved Denyah's company. Denyah phoned David and told him how she was getting on, and where she is staying. David visited her once a week, mostly week-ends to make sure she was okay.

As time went by, Mrs Carter told Denyah she was African born and her husband was Canadian and they were in the jewellery business. But he passed away some time ago and left her with all his wealth and she has no family to share it with.

"I hope you stay with me. After my death you might inherit all I have."

"Mrs Carter, I haven't come here to grab what you have."

"I know that Denyah, I know."

Denyah spent three weeks doing Mrs Carter's garden until she was satisfied and proud. The tall hedges that were there and hiding the sunlight was gone and the sun glittered through the rooms. The view was very clear and the garden path began to show again. But she needed someone to maintain the gardens. A week later Denyah phoned the shopkeeper and thanked her then asking her if she knows of anyone who might need a gardening job.

"Yes, I know a fine young man named Ryan. He had done gardening jobs for me and some people. Shall I send him to you?" said the shopkeeper.

"Yes please. I would so appreciate it." replied Denyah.

"Please leave it with me Mrs Davis." The shopkeeper said.

The next morning when Ryan went to stock some cases for the shopkeeper, she asked him if he would like a job working in a garden. "It might be a big job."

"Yes. I wouldn't mind having a go." Ryan said. After he stocked the back of her shop with the boxes, the shopkeeper paid him with some extra money for a taxi and sent him to see Denyah and giving him the address. Denyah interviewed him then took him around the front and back gardens and told him she would need a fulltime gardener, one that would like to live in.

Ryan scratched both sides his head with his two hands as Denyah waited on him for an answer. Then Mrs Carter spoke to Denyah saying, "Denyah, I know you're trying to get the gardens to look nice and I really appreciate it. Since my husband passed away fifteen years ago I haven't been out there."

"Has nobody been to see you since your husband passed away?" Denyah asked.

"Yes, a few of my friends came now and again but no more. I suppose now we're all old and feeble we've lost touch of each other. Why do you ask?"

"It must have been lonely for you with no relatives or friends visiting" Denyah said.

"Yes, it was at first, but you get used to it" Mrs Carter said. Denyah smiled.

Then after Mrs Carter spoke, Ryan said, "It would be a pleasure to work in your garden and to live in."

"Well, that's settled. Denyah why don't we take the young man into the kitchen, and treats us both to a nice hot cup of cocoa."

"Sure Mrs Carter. Ryan would you like some cocoa? Denyah asked him and said, "I'm Denyah and old mother here is Mrs Carter."

"Well, you knew my name already. However, I'm Ryan Taylor." Mrs Carter took the lead. Denyah and Ryan followed slowly behind and into the kitchen.

"Well Ryan, I and old mother Carter would have cocoa, but the choice is yours, cocoa, coffee, tea, or what ever you wish" Denyah said.

"Would you mind if I have a cold beer," Ryan asked.

"A cold beer you shall have brother," Denyah said. And from the fridge she took a bottle of beer, and as she reached for the opener, Ryan prized the bottle opened with his teeth. Denyah smiled and gave him a clean tall glass. "Thanks." he said and put the glass on the table and drank deeply from the bottle.

"You have strong white teeth." Denyah said.

He smiled. Denyah made him a cheese sandwich and told him, "Never drink beer without your cheese sandwich."

Straight off Denyah saw kindness in his face and asked him to move in straight away or soon as he's ready.

"Well, I would try working for awhile and see how it turns out before I decided" he said.

"Okay, well take this twenty pounds and I'll see you in the morning." Denyah told him.

"Goodbye Denyah, goodbye Mrs Carter" Ryan said and Denyah walked him as far as the gate. Denyah hugged him and said, "I'll see you tomorrow."

Ryan's white face went cherry red with embarrassment as his clothes were looking tatty and his fingernails were filthy. But as he turned the corner to catch his bus, he smiled thinking of Denyah, how kind and nice she was. Denyah thought about him as well, as she saw kindness and friendliness in his face and had the impression he was above a gardener. However, she closed the gate and went to be with Mrs Cater.

"He looked well mannerly. I like him." Mrs Carter said.

"I like him too" Denyah said as she was brushing Mrs Carter's hair.

"Your hands are so relaxing. Denyah, I'm very happy with you being here. You're a real gem, kind and genuine. Denyah, there's a grey safe in my bedroom behind a safety door it contains some jewellery that my husband gave to me when I was in my late thirties. I have not worn any of them since he died. They're now yours as I have no further use for them. The number to the safe is w, 2, 7, 3A left, 5 9 right and 4t centre. My husband even made the clock face on the safe. Have you got the numbers down?"

"Yes, Mrs Carter. But I'm sure there are some you can wear."

"Maybe so, but I used to wear my jewellery as part of my clothes - that's why I have no further use for them as I have outgrown what is vanity. I'm now looking for my heavenly treasure. As I said, what I now own, they're yours. Why don't you call me Grand? I've always wanted someone to call me by that name. Well, child, I'm starving. I can almost taste those mouth watering lamb chops."

"Well Grand, I hope you can devour one thick and tender lamb chop with plenty of freshly cooked vegetables and rich gravy. You just sit where you are, I'll fetch our tea" Denyah said before leaving to get the dinner, Denyah kissed Mrs Carter on her forehead.

Three days after Ryan worked in the gardens.

"For the short time you've been here, you've treated me like I'm someone special. You're very well mannered and you've brought so much laughter and happiness back into my life. I think you are so beautiful inside and outside and your friends David and Ryan are so nice too. Both you and Ryan have worked so hard in the garden to make it look beautiful. I'm glad you gave Ryan the job and a room. But there's something strange about him, not bad, just strange. Well whatever it is, we'll soon find out. I'm also glad you took him when he wanted somewhere to live. You both are like my very own children I didn't have."

"Yes, he is like a loving son to you and brother to me." Denyah replied. "I was so glad when he called saying the shopkeeper told him we need a gardener. Well mom as you said, whatever's in him will soon bud out. All the same, I like him very much as a brother."

After dinner, Mrs Carter had her nap while Denyah sat looking at the jewellery.

That same day, during the evening David went to see Denyah and told her that he went to the police and they told him that they can't find any evidence concerning Nurse Louise James murder and that the case has been left open.

"Oh David, I'm one hundred percent sure my husband is the one that murdered our Louise"

"Being sure is one thing, but proving it is another. As the police said, you just can't accuse your husband without solid proof. There's nothing more I would like than for Louise's murderer to be brought to justice. Right now, I haven't a clue. Anyway, would you like to have dinner tonight at the Ibis Hotel?"

"Oh David, I would have loved to, but I just ate, about an hour ago."

"How about tomorrow night" David asked.

"Maybe, but right now I'm a little tired."

"Okay Denyah, I'm going to go now, I'll give you a ring first thing in the morning"

"No need. I will have dinner with you tomorrow night. Did you say eight?

Make sure you're on time!" Denyah said. "I'll starve myself for that dinner"

"I'll see you tomorrow night, goodbye" he said and then left.

Denyah closed the door behind David as he left. She smiled and went to put the jewellery back in the safe. Then she and Mrs Carter had a cup of cocoa before going to bed and before Ryan gets home.

The following morning before Denyah got out of bed she phoned David and told him how wonderful Mrs Carter is to her and that even if she wanted to move on she couldn't. David was happy to hear her say that. He smiled enchantingly and was really looking forwards to having dinner with her.

Seven o'clock that night, David called at Mrs Carter's home for Denyah. Denyah was hesitating on whether or not she should go to dinner with him, as she didn't want to leave Mrs Carter on her own. She thought Ryan would be home before she left with David. But Ryan phoned to say he's having a drink with a long time friend. David understood, but Mrs Carter insisted that they should go to have that dinner.

While they were having dinner, Mrs Carter was rushed into hospital with a severe heart attack. Straight after dinner, David took Denyah home. Before going into the house she knew something was wrong as all the lights were on, and the front door was partly opened. Denyah ran inside calling Grand but got no reply. She ran back down the path to David's car, short of breath she leaned against David's car and told him, "Mrs Carter has gone and Ryan hasn't come home."

"What do you mean she's gone?" David asked.

"She's not inside. She's gone. Where could she be, look at the time ten past eleven," Denyah said as tears ran down her face.

"Just take it easy Denyah; I'm sure nothing has happened to her." David said trying to calm her down.

"Take it easy! Yeah you're right I mean she could have gone to that late night café for dinner, midnight shopping, or a rave even. She's nearly ninety!" Denyah said sarcastically.

"Come on Den, please calm down."

"Something's wrong David, I know there is."

Denyah and David walked into the house. David sat down while Denyah paced up and down the long and wide corridor. The telephone rang. Denyah quickly answered it.

"Hello, is this Mrs Davis?" The voice said over the phone.

"Yes, who's speaking?" Denyah asked looking very puzzled.

"I'm Doctor Evens. Mrs Carter was brought in two hours ago, she had a heart attack."

"Is she all right, which hospital." Denyah asked. As tears built up in her eyes, the doctor went on to say, "The Heartland I'm sorry Mrs Davis, she died about five minutes ago." Denyah went extremely quiet before she dropped the phone and stood crying.

"She's dead David, she's dead" David walked over to her and told her, "Come on, let's go to the hospital. We'll phone from there to let Ryan know."

As soon as Denyah and David got to the hospital they both got out of the car. Denyah walked over to the desk still crying, she told the receptionist her name and why she was there. A nurse took her and David to see Mrs Carter before she was taken to the morgue. Denyah cried holding her hand. "Mom I'm so very sorry" David gave her his shoulder to cry on. The nurse left her and David for a few minutes to grieve before David walked her out the ward.

"Mrs Davis, I'm so sorry you've lost you mother. The Doctors worked hard to save her, but there was no hope." David closed his eyes painfully as he thought if he hadn't taken Denyah to dinner, Mrs Carter might still be alive. "Oh Den, only if I knew she was sick."

"Don't take it too hard David - I did not know she would have had a heart attack. Why has this had to happen to me! Two great friends, whom I love and became my sister and mother, have gone." Denyah cried.

David hugged her as she phoned Ryan from the hospital on her mobile phone but he wasn't at home.

"I'm sorry Den, would you like me to stay with you tonight?" David asked.

"Yes please, if you don't mind."

After Denyah and David left the hospital, David drove to his flat to collect some of his clothes. Before he got out his car, he looked hard at Denyah and saw how stressed her face looked. "Would you like to come in for a hot drink?" he asked her. She shook her head with tears in her eyes. "Well, I'll only be gone for a couple of minutes. You sit in the car and please don't stress yourself" Denyah just barely smiled. David hurried into his flat and quickly out with his overnight sack and drove Denyah to her home and stayed the night with her.

As Denyah couldn't sleep, she heard when Ryan walked in. She wrapped her gown around her and went down stairs to him crying. "What's the matter Den," he asked and went on to say, "I will kill that husband you married."

"Ryan, mom died last night. She was rushed into the Heartland hospital with a severe heart attack. David and I phoned from the hospital to let you know, but you were out."

Tears came into Ryan's eyes. "I blame myself for not being there for her."

"Ryan, neither of us are to blame. We did not know mom would have a heart attack. She insisted that I should go and have dinner with David. He's now sleeping in one of the rooms. I needed a friend last night and he was there for me."

Ryan cried, "When you most needed me, I wasn't there."

Denyah hugged him, "We will be okay Ryan. We have to keep strong for mom."

Denyah gave Ryan a paper tissue to wipe his tears. "I'll have to thank David" he said.

CHAPTER FIVE

The next morning Denyah spoke a lot of Mrs Carter, she told David that Mrs Carter seemed very fit and that she can't believe that she was gone.

One week later, Friday at ten o'clock in the morning, Denyah, David, Ryan, the shopkeeper and about twenty other mourners attended Mrs Carter's funeral service in a Methodist Church not too far away from their home. Then they moved on to have her body cremated privately at Yardley crematorium. After, David took them to the Wing Yip restaurant to have a meal. David, Denyah and Ryan thanked the mourners for their support. After everyone had left, David took Denyah and Ryan home and he made sure Denyah was alright before he took himself to his home. That night before he went to bed, he phoned Denyah and Ryan to make sure they were okay.

It took a while before Denyah got over the loss of yet another great friend. Time went by and Denyah cut her hair short to try and hide her identity. But she and David kept in touch with each other by 'phone as well as David visiting her.

Two months later, a solicitor came to see Denyah and Ryan. He asked them how long they knew Mrs Carter.

"Eleven months" Denyah replied. Then she asked him "Would you like a drink?"

"Yes please, a cold one if possible." As Denyah went to get his drink, he said. "Excuse my manners, and then introduced him "I'm Mr Rogers, Mrs Carter's solicitor."

"Please to meet you" Denyah said as she passed him his drink.

"How about a brandy," Mr Rogers said pointing at the brandy on the old wooden bar.

"Of course" Denyah said as she reached for the bottle. Just as she passed the poured out brandy to the solicitor, he said smiling with his right leg over the left.

"I meant for both of you!"

Denyah was looking very confused, as she looked at Ryan and didn't know whether he was trying to be funny or just polite in a sarcastic way. Before Denyah could say anything, the solicitor told her she and Ryan has one hundred and eighty four million pounds locked away in the bank. Denyah could not believe what he said.

As he pulled a pen out of his suit pocket and said, "I just need you both to sign these papers to say I've seen you and you understand the terms."

"Are you sure Mrs Carter doesn't have any living relatives?" Denyah asked.

"I'm quite sure Mrs Davis. Even if she did, they wouldn't be entitled to a penny" the solicitor replied. The money was left to you and Mr Ryan Taylor. Ninety two million each and everything else was left to you Mrs Davis. Mrs Davis and Mr Taylor I would like you both to sign please."

Denyah and Ryan signed the papers and then Denyah walked the solicitor to the door. The solicitor and Ryan shook hands. "Thank you very much Sir" Ryan said.

"Here's my card, if you need to get in contact. You and Mrs Davis will be sent a letter so you both can come down and put everything into your accounts. Oh, and the house has been left to you Mrs Davis and the guest house to Mr Taylor."

Denyah just about caught her breath before saying, "Thank you very much" The solicitor nodded his head, smiled and left. Denyah got back to Ryan and told him "He seems a nice person. I would like to keep him as our solicitor as he was moms for a long time. What you think Ryan?"

"I see no reason why he shouldn't. Yes Den, he would be our solicitor."

The next morning Denyah applied for a job in a police station canteen only to prove her husband had murder her friend Nurse James. She got the job and hoped and prayed that nobody knew who she was.

Four months had passed since Denyah had her job working in the police canteen. While she was there she got the opportunity to dig up information about her late friend Nurse James's death. But her husband didn't seem to link in anyway.

One Friday afternoon after work, she arranged to have dinner with Ryan, but forgot and doubled booked with David. However, she still went out but booked a table for three. While sitting at the table, she opened her heart to David. She told him all about her husband and Eugene. She then went on to say,-

"I never let my husband go anywhere without money in his pocket. The way he's treated me it's unbelievable. He told me it was my sister he'd wanted and not me. Well, he proved what he said. Denyah sighed as tears came in her eyes. She lifted her eyes to the ceiling and dried her eyes then looked at David smiling then went on telling him: One day after work, I went home to find them both in bed naked and then he refused to eat from me. He also accused me of having affairs with my bank boss and Eugene. So he kept on raping me with insults so vicious I was ashamed to look at myself in the mirror. However, I went to a friend's engagement party and after I returned home he beat me. Well, that didn't satisfy him, so he squeezed my mouth open, shoved his gun almost down my throat and pulled the trigger knowing that the gun was empty. Obviously, I didn't know until he did it. My heart almost flew out my mouth out of fright. Still, that wasn't enough. He raped me again and one time in my back passage, while he was doing this, he was saying, that how a husband deals with his whoring wife. I hadn't felt pain like that even though the scalds were bad. My husband raping me in that way was cruel. The pain was like a razor stuck into me. This had happened the same morning he invited his friends to bed me. However, he then blindfolded my eyes, phoned his two mates to come round our home, stripped me naked, forced me over on my tummy, sat on my back while he bound my hands to the bedstead head, jerked my head backwards while he gagged my mouth and with the intention that his two friends should have sex with me. He gave me a hard thump on my bottom before he left and leaving the door wide opened. Then the next I've had experienced is when one of his friends sat on the bed and slapped my bottom. I shivered coldly followed by the worse sickening feeling. I cried through my blindfold - that convinced his friend that I'm not that sort of a person he thought I was. Amazingly, one of his mates was decent enough to convince his other mate not to do what my husband wanted. Well, they pretended they had sex with me. I was so relieved when they left the room. A few minutes later, I heard footsteps come into the room. The next that happened I was kicked off the bed. It was only when he spoke I knew it was my husband. He left me feeling so dirty after he and his friends walked their hands all over me that I went under the boiling shower to scrub myself clean, that's when I must have fainted and fell unconscious; Lisa, his sister found me and called an ambulance where I was rushed to the hospital. But needless to say, my husband managed to convince my family, my boss, Eugene, his family and the few friends I had, he told them he has proof that I had prostituted myself to his mates. Well, they all have bitterly turned against me. That is when your fiancée Nurse James helped me."

At the time when Denyah was opening her heart to David, Ryan was listening in shock and he couldn't help but speak out as he was so hurt by what Denyah's husband has done to her, "The bastard should be put away for a long time. However, I think I may be able to help you to get rid of most of your scars. You were so kind to me when I called for the job. You treated me with kindness. All I have now is because of you, after working in your garden a few weeks I told you I was a doctor and you insisted I should pick up where I left off. Besides, you never once doubted me."

Ryan pulled his chair closer and sat beside Denyah. Smiling, Denyah held Ryan by his left hand as she looked into David's eyes before she told him, "When I first knew Ryan he was so thin. Now, look at him, he's looking so different. He has changed so much. I was looking for a gardener and the shopkeeper sent him to me. He looked at me so hard that I couldn't turn him down for the job. I asked him to live in if he wanted the job, his facial expression suddenly brightened. He was in shock and at the same time, he looking so happy. But he took his time moving in after two weeks." Denyah reminisced to David.

"Yeah, I remember that. Well a lot has happened to me too that I haven't spoken to you about and would like to get over quickly" Ryan said to Denyah.

Denyah went dead serious while David said to Ryan, "Well I'll like to hear what you have to say" As Ryan straightened his tie, tears build up in his eyes. Denyah gave him a tissue to wipe his face. After he done so, he began to say,

"After I graduated I got a job as a doctor working in a hospital doing mostly surgery and other job which I don't want to name. However, one Friday night my two mates and I were going to a doctor's dance. We picked three nurses up and went for a spin. On our way, we finished a couple bottles of scotch between us. We then ended up in a lonely place where people make love. Then we went to a club and were drinking vodka chased with brandy. We were all feeling merry, I guess. On our way back to the doctor's dance the car overturned. One of my mates was driving. As I was sitting in the back seat, I managed to pull myself clear and one of my mates but both his legs were broken. When I went back to help the others, one of the nurses neck was broken and as I was trying to pull one of my other mates clear, I could feel the car rolling, he was trapped and needed more than my help to free him while the others lay drunk. I found a rock and I tracked the slipping wheel thinking it would be safe. Soon as I left the car to go and get help, the car plunged about twenty to thirty feet down a ditch and burst into flames. Since that night I never worked as a doctor again. My mate I'd rescued didn't make it as he was bleeding internally and very heavily.

Denyah and David stared at Ryan dumbfounded by the horrific experience he had been through. Ryan's eyes then began to fill with tears again.

"I am very sorry to hear that. It was only a year ago when you were working for me, you were so happy then. And all that time you were carrying a burning torch. You poor thing, even though you had graduated to be a doctor; you took the job of a gardener" Denyah said and took the back of his hand to her lips and kissed it. Saying "mother Carter was so right when she said, there was something strange about you. She said nothing bad. Just strange, I only wish she'd known about you before she died. She loved you so much Ryan. You too David, she spoke so much about both of you. I miss her so much. Ryan, do you think you can work as a doctor again?"

Ryan smiled over his tears as he said "Things have really taken a bad turn since back then. I don't think I could ever work in any hospital again. I am still seeing flashes of my friends in my mind. Working as a doctor again, would only bring back strong memories. That's why I couldn't."

"Ryan, we all have memories, but some memories haunt us worst than others. I'm sure you've got over the worse, but mine is just beginning with the worst yet to come" Denyah said. Then she went on to say, "Oh David I hope you remember Ryan, the mysterious gardener I adopted for my brother; the one you've only had the privilege to speak with a couple of times. Even so, I do hope you and him will get on well."

David laughed, "So tell me Ryan, what it is you're hiding brother?" he asked.

"Ask Denyah" Ryan said smiling.

"What do you mean by ask Denyah, you are never at home to be meeting any of my friends, but now you've got all this free time, I hope David would get the privilege of meeting you regularly" Denyah said. Then she went on to say. "That night when David slept at our house, you came home late. You only got to meet him as he stayed on for me."

"Anyway, Ryan it's nice to have a strong conversation with you after all this time." David said comforting him with a friendly handshake.

Denyah and David continued with their conversation leaving Ryan sitting at the table in thought.

"Does Eugene know what your husband did to you?" David asked.

"Yes. He knew. But I haven't told him the full truth." Denyah said.

"Who's Eugene?" Ryan interrupted.

Denyah didn't give an answer instead she said, "Why don't you two boys let me take you out for a drink tomorrow night. It's so marvellous having two handsome men called brothers. It's also nice the way things worked out. I had no brother, and now I have gained two. If this is not faith well what is?"

"Denyah we both admire you, you are a lovely and a very considerate lady and we would like to take you anywhere your heart desires." Ryan said.

"Naturally, anything for my new sister as well as a great friend of my past fiancée," David said.

That night, David and Ryan took Denyah out for a drink and then for a long drive to Birmingham airport and then take her home. She thanked them both with a kiss on their cheek and a hug for giving her a lovely time before David drove himself home.

The following morning Denyah phoned Lisa and told her how happy she was last night after having a drink with two special friends she admired as brothers.

"I'm very happy for you Denyah. You could do with some happiness after what you been through." Lisa said.

"Yeah, you're right there!"

"Anyway Den, I'm sorry to cut you short but I'm a bit busy at the moment. I'm packing for a holiday in France. But I'm sure we'll catch up when I get back." Lisa said.

"It's okay for some, isn't it? Well, we'll meet up for a coffee when you get back and I'll fill you in on the gossip." Denyah said and both her, and Lisa hung up the phone.

One late Saturday afternoon Eugene rang Denyah's door bell, she answered the door knowing it was Eugene as he made a kind of music sound ringing the bell. Denyah invited him up to her room. As he got on the landing, he met Ryan coming out of the bath with a towel around him. Jealously he asked Denyah "Who's this? And what he's doing here?"

Denyah explained. "His name is Ryan and he was the gardener. He was homeless and we took him in, Mother Carter and I, he has been living here for almost a year. After I found out he's a decent lad I kept him on. Eugene, Ryan's a lovely kind lad and you'll get to like him as well. Just give him a chance. He rates me as his sister and I love him as a brother."

Eugene smiled,

A month later Ryan, David and Eugene friendship grew closer, they were like brothers. They spent many nights out drinking as well as in Denyah's house playing cards and have good times. Eugene had practically moved in, and was spending at least five nights a week with Denyah.

Two weeks later Lisa arrived back from France, she arranged to meet Denyah for breakfast at Cindy's restaurant the Friday morning at ten 'o' clock. Lisa arrived first and Denyah arrived shortly after. They both ordered bacon and eggs for breakfast and a black coffee. Over breakfast Denyah asked, "How is Paris?"

"Paris is fine. But she missus you very much: What my brother done to you, it's unforgivable. If there's anyway you and him can come to an agreement only for Paris's sake I would be so glad."

"Lisa, you can forget what I think you're thinking. I love Paris and I would be so happy to have her living with me. But Wesley made it clear to me that he didn't want me and that it should have been my sister Fay he should have married. I love him but what feelings I had for him he destroyed when he started raping and abused me. Anyway, how's my nephew?"

"Oh Den, he's growing so fast, and he's greedy as well" Denyah laughed then Lisa.

Just then Eugene and Ryan walked over to Denyah and Lisa's table.

"I have bumped in to an old long time friend I'd never thought I would see again." Ryan said.

"One of your old girlfriends," asked Denyah.

Ryan smiled but didn't answer. Denyah then treated him to a cold soda and a salami cob of his choice. Before he had finished eating, Eugene told him he was ready to go. Denyah looked up at Eugene as he took up her coffee and sipped some and then blew her a kiss and left with Ryan. Lisa smiled "Den, he's so very handsome."

They both are." Denyah said.

"Lisa, you have a very handsome husband too, Richard is lovely. You should be happy."

"Den, I'm very happy. And I'm in love with him." Lisa said.

"I'm very happy for you Lisa my friend."

"Den, would you like a strong drink?"

"Thanks, but no thank you Lisa. You shouldn't drink either as you're breast feeding" Denyah said.

Lisa smiled, "Den, if you'd fallen out with me, I wouldn't know what I would do."

"The same goes for me Lisa. Anyway I hope our friendship's solid."

"Of course Den, we have been friends for over ten years and we have a lovely niece and daughter between us and that makes us family. Den, I love you."

"I love you too Lisa."

An hour later Ryan came back with a brand new car that Eugene bought him. His white face showed happiness all over. He dangled the key in front of Denyah's face and then said, "When you're ready, I'll take both of you home."

Eugene then came over and said, "He can't be a doctor without wheels. However, Denyah, you told me you love him like a brother, so, I'm treating him like he's my brother-in-law. Tomorrow we'll search for a couple of gardeners."

"Thank you Eugene" Denyah said while Lisa watched Eugene with affection.

Denyah was more than happy to have heard Eugene was treating Ryan so good, that she gave him a tight hug and said "Thanks for treating Ryan so nicely."

Ryan then joked and said, "The time will come when I pay you both back by delivering my niece or nephew."

"I don't think so. The last thing I will want is my brother to look into me."

"Don't worry sis, when the pain hits you, you wouldn't think of me as a brother but as your doctor" Denyah and Lisa laughed heartily while Ryan and Eugene stayed silent. Still laughing Lisa then said, "Ryan, you're so awful."

"Well ladies, if you're ready to go home, I'm your chauffeur" After Denyah and Lisa said goodbye to Cindy they left with Ryan for him to take them home. That night Eugene was late coming home. Denyah were very worried that something bad might have happened to him. As she lay in bed thinking, she became so restless that she phoned Lisa and asked her if Wesley was at his home. "Yes, he was at home all day up until now as we only just spoke on the phone. Why do you ask?"

"No reason" Denyah said as she heard Eugene's voice. "Lisa, I'll call you tomorrow" she hung up the phone. Lisa shrugged her shoulder in wonder and put the phone down.

After Eugene ate his supper, he said, "Den, I'm still starving" he then went and made himself a cheese sandwich and finished it off with a can of beer and then went and had a shower while he left Denyah writing letters to her friends she has in Canada and Wales when she was working at the bank. Just as Eugene walked into the room wearing a towel wrapped around him, the phone rang. Denyah answered the phone saying but the phone was banged down. She got nervous and became suspicious that it might have been her husband who had phoned. She put away her pen and the unwritten letters as Eugene asked "Who was that on the phone?"

"Oh, it was Lisa, thanking me for her breakfast this morning. As you know we had breakfast at Cindy's restaurant."

"Oh," Eugene said in wonder.

The phone began to ring again. But at this time Eugene and Ryan was playing blackjack. Nervously Denyah answered the phone and heard heavy breathing coming through. She hung up. "Who is that now it's nearly midnight" Eugene asked throwing down the king of clubs on Ryan queen of hearts. He then looked at Denyah for her to tell him who the caller was. But she answered "Wrong number" and smiled.

The following morning while Ryan was admiring his new car, Denyah joined him. "She's fabulous" said Denyah.

"She's more than that, she's part of my life and I love her second to you. From the time the sale representative let me take her for a spin I knew she was right for me. But I didn't know I would be the owner. Speaking of owners what about those stones, have you had them valued?"

"No not yet Ryan, I'm going to have them valued today. Come on let's go and have breakfast" Denyah said. Over breakfast, Denyah asked Ryan "Have you told Eugene about the money mom has left us?"

"I tried to, but he said, good for us and he still would like to buy me a car of my choice as a family gift. I think I even mentioned that our share is about ninety two Mil. He'd looked pleased and not surprised. I told him before he bought me the car."

"Well, I'm glad you told him. He really wanted to buy you the car." Denyah said.

After breakfast, Ryan drove Denyah in to town to see a jeweller maker, Denyah waited in turn for attention. "Yes Madam, can I help you?" The sales representative asked.

"I brought in some stones to have them valued." Denyah said.

"May I see them please?" The sale representative asked.

"Of course you can, but I rather pass them to one that will recognise the value of them." Denyah told him.

"May I ask you your name?" The sale representative asked politely.

"Denyah Davis."

"Mrs Davis, would you please give me a second to get the right person?" The sale representative asked and then left and bought with her a nicely shaped nearly grey beard attached to a middle aged white and chubby built man about five feet five inches tall and told him, "this is Mrs Davis, she would like you to take a look at some stones she's just brought in to have them valued."

"Nice to meet you Mrs Davis, I understand you have some stones you would like me to take a look at. May I have a look please? Oh, this is one of my shops. I am Fred Saunders" he said with a nice smile.

Denyah passed on the sealed brown enveloped to him. As he felt the size of what's in the envelope, he quickly opened it and had a look to see three pieces of rubies six large uncut diamonds and three black pearls shaped like pears. The jewellery maker stared hard at the rubies, diamonds and especially the black pearls. As he was rolling them in the palm of his hand for a good minute before he asked Denyah, "Have I heard you right saying you have brought these items to have them valued?"

"That's correct Sir. I would like to know just how much they are worth. That is if you wouldn't mind telling me."

"Oh not at all," the jewellery maker said still staring mostly at the diamonds and black pearls looking excitedly serious and interested. After he had a good look at the jewels, he beckoned a heavy built man to come and take a look. As the man took the jewellery in his hand, he swallowed deeply his saliva as he wiped away built-up sweat off his forehead and then backed away to his working counter which was about five yards away in a corner showing a bright spot light and his table almost overcrowded with what looking like scraps from jewelleries. He hurriedly swept some of the scraps to one side with his hand and examined each piece of the jewellery extremely carefully under the spotlights and something looking like a magnifying glass he'd hooked over his eyes. As he's finished examined the stones, he looked back and looked hard at Denyah and looking sternly. Denyah smiled. He wiped more sweat off his face before he left his seat and as he was walking towards Denyah he was rolling the jewels in his hand as he was staring at them as if he couldn't believe his eyes. Smiling and looking contently, he was still rolling each pieces of jewellery slowly and carefully in the palms of his hand and had a hard long look at them before he called another man and said "Here - you're the expert, you have a look at these nine beauties and especially these exquisite slim black ladies, (meaning the black pearls). His boss anxiously took the stones smiling as he watched his employee. "What are these? Golf balls," his boss joked grinning.

"Just take a good look at what you're holding boss" His employer said looking hard at him.

As his boss rolled the jewels out of the bag into his hand, his eyes widened and his mouth parted open then wiping the sudden sweat from over his eyes, he said, "Good Lord, where have these came from? I haven't handled riches like these in a long time."

"This lady has brought them to be valued" The jewellery maker said.

His boss lifted up his head to look at Denyah and then fixed his eyes again on the jewelleries smiling. Then he asked Denyah "Where did you get these?"

"Why? Have you heard they were stolen?"

"Oh no nothing like that. I asked, as they're so beautiful. And that they are the size of golf balls. With these exquisite beauties, you can buy a quarter of this town. However, if you decided to sell, will you please let me know and give us first choice? And as for the pearls, they worth many millions alone, these pearls are very rare and maybe the only kind in the world."

"Well I'll have to speak with my husband and my brother first."

"Well if you do, decide to sell any, would you please consider giving me first choice? That's if you're going to sell."

"Certainly Sir, I shall keep you in mind. But I'm only here to find out the value of these jewels and you haven't told me the full value yet."

"Oh yes of course. Well, those six beautiful diamonds are worth at least thirty five to forty and a half million. And the rubies, I'll say around fifteen to twenty, as for the pearls, well, they're in a class of their own. Would you mind me asking you your name?"

"Denyah, Denyah Davis."

"Yes of course, you've told me. Miss or Mrs,"

"Mrs,"

"Mrs Davis, would you please take one of my cards and if you do decide to sell, as I asked, please gives me a call."

"Thanks for a second card and I will give you first choice and many thanks for your time Sir and goodbye."

Denyah left the jewellery shop looking very happy and pleased with herself. She told herself as she held the bag with the jewelleries to her bosom "if you precious beauties are worth this much, your other fifteen precious sisters and eleven brothers must be priceless" (Meaning, fifteen uncut diamonds and eleven rubies and countless gold and silver, and so many other jewels) Denyah then got into her car and drove herself home. She met Ryan in the garden working. She gave him a lovely smile and a tight hug and said to him "I no longer want you to work in this garden anymore unless I ask you to. And don't argue with me your big sister. I had words with Dr Harris last week and he said he would be interested to see you and to offer you a surgeon job as you told me that what you most wanted to do. So you better get use to being that surgeon doctor again. And thanks for lending me your car. You didn't have to take a taxi home you know," Denyah said.

Ryan white face suddenly turned cheerfully bright red before he said. "Sis, you surely are looking after me. And you're one of the most remarkable ladies in this world. Sis, I do love you so much."

"By the way Mr Ryan Taylor, this has call for a toast to welcome you back in the medical world. I would be happy to take you out for dinner Saturday night. So get ready! You have two days to invite your girlfriend if you want. Oh our three rubies and six golf balls diamonds and a string of black pearls plus three others were estimated to be worth eighty, to one hundred and a half Million, brother, there's a true and living God and we've to thank him to lead us to mother Carter. And for what we have achieved from her. Everything shall be shared between us equally. Except getting into the same bed! Denyah joked.

Ryan's face went disconcerted as he forced a smile. Then said thanks Sis."

Denyah laughed saying, "I was only joking bros. You should have seen your face."

Both Denyah and Ryan burst into laughter. "Ryan, I must go and thank my friend the shopkeeper. She is the one that help me to meet mom."

"She's a nice lady, I should pay her a visit at least from time to time to know how she's getting on" Ryan said.

Later on that night when Eugene and Ryan were playing cards, Denyah asked, "Don't you two never tired of playing cards?"

"No, after I whoop your brother, I would be up to play a different game with you" Eugene told Denyah and he laughed.

"Don't you worry sis, when I finish with your husband, I don't think he'll have any strength to walk up those stairs." Ryan said winning another game making five wins to Eugene one.

Denyah laughed saying "I'm going to have my bath. Bros let me know tomorrow how many times you whoop him."

As Denyah relaxed in her bath with a flannel over her face, Eugene peeled his clothes off outside the bathroom before he sneaked into the bathroom, and quickly got into the bath with Denyah and removed the flannel off her face. "What are you doing in my bath?" she asked him. He smiled saying. "Haven't I have any right to share a bath with the love of my life?"

"I just want to have a quiet bath." Denyah said.

"Me too honey, with you." Then he carried his mouth over her left breast nipple. With quick reaction she elbowed him in the chest and jumped out of the bath like a fish jumped out of a pond.

"What the hell is the matter with you?" Eugene asked her.

She stared at him without saying a word. Then she realized what she had done. She got into the bath again and hugged him.

"Tell me the truth Den what did your husband do to you, and what did really happen? That each time I got near you, you grew tense and vicious towards me. You tell me, or I'll walk out on you and you'll never see me again even though I love you with all my heart. The choice is yours Den." Eugene said very seriously.

Tears came into Denyah's eyes, she opened her mouth to speak but the words wouldn't come out.

"Take your time my darling but the truth is very important to me. Mother told me she told you to leave me alone and that you're trouble. If I have to choose between you and mother, I would like it should be you."

"Please Denyah don't make this difficult for me. Please tell me what your husband done to you."

"Okay Eugene, here's the truth. After I left the engagement party, Claire took Lisa and me home. She dropped Lisa off then me. I opened the door and walked in. Wesley was sitting on the settee. A full bottle of whiskey was standing at his feet and one to his mouth half full. He looked tipsy, our eyes clashed, I turned to walk away when he pulled me by my hair and twisted me facing him. He slapped my face extremely hard three times with the back of his hand I think and busting my lips then squeezed my mouth opened and forced his gun halfway down my throat before pulling the trigger but as he knew the gun was empty, he laughed hilariously as urine trickling down my legs. I was so petrified. If I had a weak heart, I mightn't be here to tell you my life story." Denyah reached for piece of toilet tissue and wiped the dribbling snot from her nose as she was crying so much. She then inhaled deeply as she went on to say "I pulled away from him and tried to run, he grabbed me by my hair again and tore all of my clothes off, flung me to the floor and raped me and he even went into my back passage then spat on my face showing me a scornful grin. He dragged me by the phone, pinned me down with one foot on my tummy while he made a phone call to some one and asked him to bring his friend to our home before he dragged me upstairs and into the spare bedroom. Anyway, before his arrivals arrived, he gagged my mouth, blindfolded my eyes and bounded my hands to the bed post then I heard him leaving the room. I then heard footsteps on the stairs coming up and then coming into the room and stopping at the foot of my bed. I then heard laughing coming from the two men, one of them said. "Wesley told him you're a first class prostitute and that you come here on a regular basis when his wife is at work." The next thing is when I felt a hard slap on my bottom followed by heavy weight on my back and hot heavy breathing on my neck. I shook my head several times to let him know that I wasn't a prostitute as Wesley told them. As he noticed my blindfold was badly moistened he rolled off me and said to his friend something here is not right. He asked his friend to leave me by telling him I didn't smell nice but it is up to him if he wants to get what his wife wouldn't want. I thanked them both in my heart as I was still gagged. I then heard when they opened the door and left. After, I heard footsteps come in to my room again and stopped by the foot of the bed, I think. Then Wesley said your sweet man is now welcome to you. Meaning you, he then went on, but then again, he commented, when he knows about you the great whore, I doubt if he would ever want to see you again. After telling me this, he shoved me off the bed, sprayed whiskey from his mouth on me and ignited his lighter to light me in a mock way before he untied my hands. I cried hating myself as I went under the shower and turned on the hot water to maximum to scrub the disgusting filth off me. I remembered scrubbing my legs and between my thighs with a hard brush until they bled. Then I must've passed out. I didn't remember going in to an ambulance until sometime after when I woke up in the hospital."

While Eugene was listening to Denyah, his mouth opened and looked shock. He got out the bath and kicked the linen basket then faced Denyah with a stream of tears running down his face. He said nothing. He got in the bath and hugged her close to his naked hairy chest. She hugged him tightly around his neck and lay back taking him with her. "I love you so much" she told him and widened her legs and gave in to him and they had sex. "I should have been the one to comfort you" Eugene told her and carried her to her bedroom then went a made tea for her, Ryan and him. Ten minutes later before Ryan left to go to work, he said "I'll see you tomorrow Eugene."

"Okay my friend, and ease up on those nurses." Eugene joked

"To tell you the truth, I haven't got time, not for even the most beautiful one." Ryan said.

Eugene smiled and said, "Well, Den and I would see you in the morning" Eugene said and as Ryan left, Eugene turned all lights off and joined Denyah in bed. As they both settled down to sleep, she asked him "Do you mind Ryan living here? Or should I ask him to move in the guest house?"

"Don't be silly, he's a decent bloke and he's a good companion for you. Beside, you both became family and I also like the bloke. "

Seven o'clock the next morning, Ryan came home from his night shift and went straight to his room, kicked his shoes off and fell asleep on top of his quilt in his clothes as he was dog tired but he still managed to get up at nine thirty and cook breakfast for him and Denyah as she was sleeping and Eugene had left. Ten o'clock he had breakfast and took up a glass of orange juice to Denyah as she was resting after Eugene went to work.

"Thank you Ryan, I was so tired that I had to slip back in bed. I haven't even brushed my teeth yet. I should be cooking you breakfast" she said.

"So you haven't had breakfast then?"

"No not yet. I'm starting to feel hungry."

"Well sis you're in luck." Ryan said and went downstairs and returned with breakfast for her. She rested her breakfast on the side table to go and brush her teeth when the phone rang. She looked at the number, but did not recognise it, so she left the phone ringing until it stopped. After she brushed her teeth she slipped back into bed and ate her breakfast and put the tray on her dressing table. An hour later a knock came on her bedroom door. "Come in" she said.

Ryan walked in and took the tray and said, "Den, you're going to have a good rest today. I'm going to cook us lunch as well. And David phoned to say he will see you this Sunday"

"Thanks for telling me. About cooking lunch, I'm no longer tired or feeling sick. Besides, don't you need your sleep as you will be working tonight?"

"Well, if you want me to take up being a doctor again, I'll have to start somewhere. And that means starting with you, my favourite sister and patient. So sis, you'll have to do as I say. However, I'm off work until Sunday morning seven thirty."

"Okay Ryan, I'll stay in bed. But only for a few more hours, and I'll cook supper as you would be cooking lunch."

"It's a deal Sis."

"Where's Eugene?" she asked.

"He's at work. He asked me to look after you until he comes home. He said he would be home for four o'clock with our dinner."

"Well, he's phoned to say he was on his way home. I wondered what happened" Denyah asked.

Ryan smiled and opened the window in her room to let in fresh air before he went into the garden to rake up some weeds and burned them. As Denyah looked at him from her window she shouted to him. "Get out! I thought I told you never to work in the garden again as it is too much for you and being in a full time job."

"I would be okay Den. I'm only pulling out some overgrown weeds."

Denyah smiled and closed the window before she phoned the shopkeeper and asking her if she know of any gardener looking for work, or if she could help her to find a couple of gardeners.

The shopkeeper was happy to hear from her and to help. So she said "I'll see what I can do Mrs Davis. As a matter of fact, I know a couple of friends that are looking for that kind of work. Give me your phone number, and I'll get back to you. That's if you don't mind"

"Thanks" said Denyah. "And I don't mind giving you my phone number."

"Please give me a second dear to reach for a pen" The shopkeeper said, as she reached on her till and got a pen and envelope. "Okay, Mrs Davis,"

Denyah gave her house telephone number and her mobile number.

"Mrs Davis, I hope you'll be happy with both of them. You need them both, don't you?"

"Yea, oh yes, I can do with them both. And thank you for all you've done for me Mrs Jordan."

"Mrs Davis, please call me Ella as I've the feeling we'll be friends."

"Well, in that case, please call me Denyah."

"Denyah I was meaning to ask you, would you mind working for me, just part time, about two hours?"

"Ella, I would really like to help you out but there's some friendly faces that I would want to see. However, if you're that desperate, I can ask one of my faithful and reliable friends to work for you."

"Denyah, I would be so happy. I hope she would like to live with me, as I'm on my own. I did not bear any children and my husband passed away with Parkinson disease fourteen years ago.

"Oh Ella, I'm so sorry. However, as I said, I have a good friend that needs a job and maybe a home. However, I think she would be ideal for the job as she used to work in shops."

"Well Denyah, I would be looking forward to see your friend soon. Good bye Denyah."

"Goodbye Ella."

Two days later, Ella phoned Denyah to say, "I got in touch with two nice and reliable gardeners. They seemed happy and desperate, but they would need your address. Would it be okay if I give it to them? However, they both are in their early sixties and have been out of work for some time. Gardening was their job at the Flowers Fountain but was made redundant when the firm they were working for sold. However, they are best friends and used to work together doing gardening work for years. Their names are Sonny and Aungus."

Denyah gave the shopkeeper permission to pass on her address to the gardeners. The following morning both gardeners went to see Denyah. After speaking to her, they were both delighted with their wages and hours of working.

After the gardeners left, the telephone rung, Denyah answered the phone to hear an aggravating high pitched voice penetrating into her ears. She put down the phone quickly and went to her bedroom. She didn't say anything to Ryan but he'd noticed that she didn't look herself so he kept on asking "Are you okay?" But Denyah avoided answering him by saying "My eyes wouldn't keep open as they felt so heavy" she then went and lay across her bed and was listening to a CD 'You say it all over' sung by Jim Reeves. Ryan got the message that she didn't wish to speak. He smiled and left.

At the same time, Wesley was listening to one of Jim Reeves CD 'Last night was the worst night' He cried as he drank whiskey with Denyah on his mind and holding their marriage photo to his chest.

Twelve o'clock that afternoon, Ryan made chicken sandwiches and hot milk as they would be having a good solid meal with Eugene later. Three o'clock the same afternoon, Denyah said to Ryan "I'm feeling much better."

"I'm happy to hear that. Now eat. By the way, the two gardeners came to see you"

"Yes, I saw them this morning. I wonder why they came back. Why didn't you wake me?"

"It's alright sis, I told them they can start next Monday at nine. Morning of course, and they can choose any three days to work that suited them. I also told them their wages would be one hundred and sixty pounds each. The same amount you'd started me off with. If it's too much, I'll pay the difference."

"That's okay Ryan. I offered them fifteen pounds less. I think from now on, you should handle most of ours affairs. Ryan, you're the only family I think I have apart from my friend David, my sister Blanch and my stepdaughter Paris."

"What about Eugene?" Ryan asked.

"Well him too. Maybe, to tell you the truth Ryan, I'm not so sure if he would want me after hearing the lies my husband is spreading about me. His mother hates me. Come to think of it, I once heard my husband say she has no children."

Ryan interrupted, "What are you talking about? Of course she has children and Eugene is one of them. Maybe your husband said this to cause contention between you and the one man that you love so much."

"Ryan, I do love Eugene. But I don't think I could compete with his mother"

"Yes, I guess you're right. I guess also if you love someone it's worth fighting for. Win or lose" Ryan said.

"You know what, you're right brother. I love Eugene and I will let no one stand in my way. He's the man I want to spend the rest of my life with so that he can watch me going in to painful labour having his children. I also love you too Ryan as a brother and David as my bosom friend or a brother."

"I love you too sis."

Ten minutes later, Eugene entered in the kitchen with take away food. He met Ryan speaking with Denyah and he said "My mind told me I'll meet you home so I brought one extra. By the way, how come you're not out with your girlfriend?"

Denyah laughed. Ryan took a container of food and began to eat while Eugene pulled Denyah into him and kissed her before they both ate. After they all ate, Eugene and Ryan had a couple bottles of beers and then played dominos this time while Denyah walked into the living room and phoned Lisa to ask her how Paris was and that she would like to see Paris.

Lisa was happy to hear Denyah's voice. "Den, I would help you to get Paris. She needs you more than ever. Since you've left Wesley has got worse. He seemed to be drunk so often that it's interfering with his job. Every time I have been to see him, he's playing Jim Rees CD either I can't stop loving you, or Am I losing you and I'm falling to pieces. Paris is wearing filthy clothes and her hair looks untidy. She is crying for you. You'll have to find a way to get her from that good- for- nothing father of hers."

"Saying that Lisa, do you think Wesley would move aside and let me take his daughter?"

"Den, Paris is your daughter too. You were the one that took care of her since she was five months old, and that makes you her mother and a damn good one at that. Anyway, would it be alright if I bring her one of these days to visit you?"

"Lisa, you know it would be alright. Nothing would please me more than to see her. Anyway, it's hurting me so much not knowing if she's okay and especially hearing her father is living on bottles of whiskey. I have to go and iron some shirts for Ryan, goodbye Lisa" Denyah shortened her conversation as tears came into her eyes over Paris.

"Goodbye Den, and say hello to both Eugene and Ryan for me. Well take care."

Denyah felt hurt so much that she put the phone down and cried asking herself why is Wesley hated her so much.

However, Denyah struggled and did the ironing between her crying before she had her shower and went to bed. As Eugene saw her sleeping he joined her without disturbing her. Early the following morning he waken her with a kiss on her face then said, "Oh God, I love you" he then put his muscular arms around her slender shoulder and kissed her passionately before he got out of bed and cooked her breakfast. Then on his way upstairs to call her, she came out of her room wearing silk pale blue pyjamas and looking down over the landing on him while he was on his way up to let her know breakfast was ready, he smiled and said jokingly, "don't tempt me" she smiled, and said, "I'm not tempting you. I'm inviting you into our bed."

"I think you should put on something that is much thicker. I think we might have one more guest for breakfast besides Ryan. I think it's a she!" Eugene said

"How do you know this?" Denyah asked.

"I saw her last night. I think she stayed last night with your brother. She looks a nice girl" Eugene said.

Denyah had a quick shower, changed into some clothes and then went to have breakfast into the dining room. Eugene teasingly put three plates on the table as he looked at Ryan smiling. Ryan put another plate on the table and said smiling, "I had a friend stayed over last night."

Denyah smiled as she looked in to Eugene's face. Then Ryan said, "You know what Sis, you're the loveliest sister in the world. You've also made me the happiest brother ever."

"You mean the happiest doctor. Remember you have to see Doctor Harris tomorrow at ten. That's if you would want to work on the surgeon team."

Suddenly, Ryan's girlfriend walked downstairs wearing one of his shirts and showing a spotty light blue and mixed deep blue silk G string panties. She sat at the table and openly she asked Denyah, "Can I borrow a bra and one of your tops, I was wearing a strapless top last night and it's a bit too cold to put it back on."

Eugene looked into Ryan's eyes and smiled as he saw Ryan's girlfriend G string showing plainly. Ryan smiled and shrugged his shoulders. Denyah asked her up and into her bedroom and showed her to the dressing table drawers filled with underclothes and told her help herself. From one of the drawers she took out four sets of selected bras and panties, she then looked in the wardrobe and took from it a beige jumper then went to Ryan's bedroom. From Ryan's room she called Denyah and asked her. "Which one do you think Ryan would like" Denyah watched her smiling as if she'd just won the lottery and holding a bra and panties in each hand.

Denyah looked hard at her before saying, "I think you should ask him. But before, I should take a quick shower if I were you."

"But they are all beautiful and new. Why do you buy so many, do you think I should wear this pale blue one after I have showered?"

"Why don't you wear the one of your choice?"

"They're all my choice. You don't mind me taking them."

"No not at all. Why don't you go have a quick shower and then come and have breakfast, I'll keep it hot for you. As for me, I should go and have mine before it gets cold?" Denyah said.

"Denyah thanks for the clothes and for making me feel comfortable."

"Well, I glad you feel that way. Hurry taking that shower and come down" Denyah said before she went to breakfast.

After Ryan's girlfriend had her shower, she was sitting at the breakfast table. While they were eating, she lifted the jumper to her neck and said "It feels so soft against my skin" Then she faced Denyah and asked "you sure that I could keep all sister?"

"Yes, you can have them. Now can we have breakfast in peace?"

"Sure, my name is Meleta. I have been seeing Ryan for about five days and he said I can move in with him and that you won't mind. You look so different, are you really brother and sister?" she asked in her giggling West Indian accent. "What I meant, you two looked nothing alike in features. Even though you both white, I could see no resemblance."

"Well Meleta, It's a long story which I wouldn't wish to go in to now. Come on, I'm starving."

Denyah got up and looked at Ryan. Eugene moved from the breakfast table as he saw sadness on Denyah's face. Denyah looked at Meleta and shook her head and walked away out of the dining room.

Eugene went after Denyah and said "Come on honey, come finish your breakfast" he led her into the dining room and said "sit down honey, I'm sure she never meant it that way."

As Denyah and Eugene sat, they watched Meleta dividing small sections of her scrambled eggs on the plate before she ate. Then giggling, she forked a section into her mouth, as her giggling was prolonged, some scrambled eggs dribbled out of her mouth. Surprisingly, she got up and lifted her jumper to show her bra a second time and then asked Ryan, "Do you like lace" Eugene turned his face away smiling while Denyah kept a straight face. Ryan grabbed her by her hand and led her away from the table and said to her "I expected you to have more respect for yourself and for others. What you just did was totally out of order and damn right rude. And be careful what you say to my sister from now on. Even if I tell you how Denyah and I became sister and brother, you still wouldn't understand. Denyah is and would be miles in front you or any women. So if you want to be with me, don't push your luck. Even though I came to love you, Denyah is very special to me and you can imagine what I mean."

"I'm sorry Ryan, it was only meant to be a joke. It won't happen again."

"You're absolutely right! It won't. If you would like to finish your breakfast I would take you home after."

"Oh Ryan, can't you let me stay here until tomorrow. Your sister seems to be very nice and I'm sure she wouldn't mind me staying another night. And believe me I'm very sorry I upset her. I would apologise to her. "

"Well, I'll see what I can do, and if we have to see each other again, I'll do the right thing by asking the family if it's okay for you to visit. I must be honest with you, when I sneaked you in here last night I thought it would be a one night stand. But it turned out to be ------ I really do like you and I would like to see more of you, and, maybe you could spend many nights with me if you show respect" Ryan laughed. Then they both returned to the table and she apologized to Denyah and Eugene telling them, "I am sorry for exposing my body so rudely."

Then Meleta asked Denyah and Eugene, "Would it be alright to spend another night? And Denyah, I'm really sorry to upset you. I do feel ashamed." Meleta said.

Eugene and Ryan walked away. Denyah hesitated for a few seconds before she said "I accept your apology and I suppose you can stay another night" Then Denyah asked her, "Have you discussed this with Ryan?"

"Yes. He said he'll have to speak to you first" Meleta said.

"Well in that case, you may stay until you're ready to leave giving respect. Or there's a guest house Ryan owns, maybe you would like to stay in it for a while."

"Thank you so much Denyah. But I would rather stay with you. Would it be okay to heat my breakfast, I'm starving."

"Sure you can" Denyah said.

Meleta heated her breakfast in the microwave and ate to a finish then offered to wash the used dishes.

"We use the dishwasher." Denyah said.

Meleta packed them into the dishwasher to wash. Soon as they finished, Meleta put them into the cupboard.

It was so amazing for Eugene and Ryan to have heard happy laughing coming from Denyah that Eugene said to Ryan, "I haven't heard Den laughing so happy in a long time. I think they are good for each other. She has brought some happiness in Den's life today. Remind me Ryan, how did you meet her?" Eugene asked interestedly.

"Standing outside the City Hospital two weeks ago one Sunday early morning, I think she was waiting on someone at that time. She told me she's a secretary and working at the Hospital and it was her day off. So I invited her for a drink last night and you know the rest" Ryan smiled after telling Eugene.

"I'm glad for you mate" said Eugene nodding his head and smiling before he said "Well I should be going to work now. I'll see you later mate."

He then went to Denyah and kissed her and said goodbye to her and Meleta then left to go to work. As he sat behind his big mahogany desk staring at him and Denyah's photo that they'd took together when they were in Blackpool, his secretary knocked on his door. Putting down the photo, he said "Come in" The secretary walked up to him and put some typed letters on his desk and asked him "Please sign these" Looking up to the young black secretary with smile, he asked. "What am I signing?"

"These are the forms to order the goods and some letters to send to customers you asked me to do Mr Lake." The secretary said.

"Oh yes of course" Eugene said and signed the forms and letters then passed them back to his secretary.

"Thanks," she said politely and she left with the signed letters and forms to be sent out to customers and merchants around the country, Wales and Scotland. Then he suddenly remembered that he had to be at another one of his restaurants to meet a Mr Wong. But before he rushed away, he gave advice to his secretary that she must phone his merchants giving her individual sheets setting out what he needed such as food, jewellery, perfumes, plants, lumbers and so many more for his hotels, restaurants and shops.

Later that day, Denyah and Ryan called at the Hospital to see Doctor Harris about the surgeon job he'd promised to give to Ryan as that is what Ryan most wanted.

While Doctor Harris was looking at Denyah with so much admiration he smiled to Ryan, saying, "The job is yours my good lad. You may start working the following Monday, I'm afraid it has got to be nights for at least a couple of weeks as we are so much short of night doctors. Saying that, you might be asked to work sooner, if so, would that be okay?"

"Sure Doctor Harris. I'm very pleased. Thank you Sir" Ryan replied shaking his hand.

"Drop the doctor and Sir. Just Harris will do. I'm sure we'll get on well together. Your sister owes me a dinner. Let's keep your starting job next Monday. But you may be called sooner." Doctor Harris said looking at Denyah and smiling.

"That would be fine" Denyah said smiling. "About the dinner,"

"Oh and I'm also looking forward to meet that handsome young man of yours and you too Ryan if you are not working by then to have a drink together. Well Denyah nice to see you again."

"Well goodbye Doctor Harris and give my regards to the wife."

"Goodbye Denyah" Doctor Harris said smiling."

Doctor Harris shook Ryan's hand and watched him and Denyah leave before he went back on the ward.

Denyah and Ryan went home to meet Meleta dusting the furniture. "I've done the vacuuming for you while you were out."

"Thank you," said Denyah while Ryan smiled.

The day was really enjoyable for Denyah as Meleta made her housework much lighter by helping her and preparing a nice chicken salad lunch for Denyah, herself and Ryan.

Later that evening Eugene phoned Denyah to say he wouldn't be able to make it home that night. Denyah told him it was okay. As she realized he sounded upset she didn't question him.

When Ryan saw the sad look on Denyah's face he offered to take her and his girlfriend Meleta to the pictures. Denyah accepted and she, Meleta and Ryan went to the pictures to see Final Destination. After they returned from the cinema they had light snacks then Denyah showered and went to bed leaving Ryan and his girlfriend in the living room playing cards.

Early the next morning Denyah heard the front door open and then closed followed by laughing from Ryan and Meleta but as they walked passed her door, they went immensely silent then Denyah heard laughing again coming from the bathroom.

Later in the morning just before breakfast, David phoned Denyah to say he wouldn't be able to make it over the weekend as promised as he has to be somewhere urgently. Denyah understood but before she could say anything, David said to her, "Denyah I might as well tell you. I've met someone a couple of weeks ago. I like her very much and I asked her out to dinner this weekend and she said yes. I would bring her with me next weekend when I visit you if that's okay."

"I'm happy for you David. So I'm looking forward to see both of you next weekend then."

"Thanks Denyah for giving me opportunity to bring my girlfriend to your home next week."

"David, neither you nor your girlfriend need an invitation to visit me. My door is always open to you both. David I could never forget the kindness you've given me and I still got your key to your flat and I do hope you still have mine. If anytime you should visit me and I'm not at home, feel free and let yourself in. You became like family" Denyah said.

"Bet your bottom dollar I have your key," said David in high spirit and gleaming smile. And Den, I'm feeling so happy to have heard you said I'm family."

"Next weekend then," said Denyah.

"Denyah, to put your mind at rest, it doesn't matter how many girlfriends I may have, I would always carry deep love for my Louise. Even if I get married, I will still carry love in my heart for her as part of my heart is a pocket for her."

"Me too," Denyah said "Thanks to her she has brought us closer to be even more than friends. However, I'm looking forward to see you and your girlfriend soon. And please take the money that I owed to you."

"Please Den, don't insult me. The only way I knew you would have taken the money was to tell you it was a loan. So, please don't bring that up again. Den, you became more than a friend to me. Beside, I wouldn't want Louise to beat me in my sleep to have taken the money back from you" David laughed, so did Denyah.

"David, I can afford to give you the money back. I have inherited millions. Mrs Carter made Ryan and me her heirs."

"Den my precious. I'm happy for both you and Ryan. But my answer, I don't want a penny back. All I want of you is your friendship or a sister of you. I want nothing more."

Denyah faced Ryan and his girlfriend Meleta as she put the phone down saying, "That was David. He phoned to say he will see me next weekend" Denyah said nothing more to Ryan. She went to her room leaving Ryan and Meleta cooking lunch.

Denyah enjoyed her lunch again and complimented Ryan and Meleta on their delicious cooking. It didn't take Denyah long to get to like Meleta. And she began to call Meleta Mrs Taylor as joke. That at one time Ryan said with straight face, "Den, her name is Meleta. The wife I would have, she's got to be worthy of my name" Ryan then smiled and walked away leaving Meleta looking embarrassed and feeling disappointed over what he'd said. As Denyah looked at Ryan tears built up in Meleta's eyes.

"Well, I know now where my place is" said Meleta calmly.

"Meleta, Cheer up honey, you would be the one he's going to walk down the Aisle and kiss you in the presence of us all" Denyah said trying to cheer Meleta up.

Meleta smiled lightly as she tried to hide her embarrassment. Ryan came down stairs and said, "I would see you two later" Turning to leave, Denyah asked him" Where you off to now?"

"To have a quiet drink" he said and left in his car.

"Come on Meleta. Let's get up to my room." Denyah said taking the lead with Meleta following behind. As they marched into the bedroom, "Denyah said to her again. "My brother is only testing you. As I told you, you would be the one he'll end with" Meleta's smile was brighter as she took her seat on Denyah's bed. Denyah took a gold chain with a black pearl shaped pear pendant from her safe and hooked it around Meleta's neck. "This is my first gift to welcome you as my friend and sister-in-law."

Meleta got up and kissed Denyah on her left cheek with tears and said. "Thanks" Then her tears fall heavily down her face. "Aye, come on, stop crying. It's a matter of time when he would say, "Meleta honey, will you marry me? And you will replied yes my darling, I thought you'd never ask," Meleta and Denyah laughed happily.

Meleta dried her eyes and then she and Denyah went downstairs drinking one of Eugene's special bottles of red wine and dancing to some CDs then dropped off to sleep head and tail in the same settee leaving a love song disc playing. Some time later, Eugene and Ryan walked in and saw them both flagged out in the settee and a draining of wine left in the bottle. Eugene watched them for a little while before he kissed Denyah on her lips and breathed out softly on her neck waking her and then realized Denyah and

Meleta drank one of his special wines. He looked hard at the bottle and smiled shaking his head.

"How long you two been home?" Denyah asked.

"Long enough for me and Ryan to listen to the disc finish and turned the stereo off. You two must have had an interesting day - why you wanted to get drunk drinking one of my bottles of special wine" Eugene said smiling.

Denyah got up lazily and stretched upwards and hugged Eugene saying, "Honey, I'm sorry about your wine. I'd no idea the wine was special to you."

"Honey, the wine was not that special. It was only worth five hundred pounds,"

"Eugene, I'm very sorry. I actually thought it was just an eight pound bottle of wine." Denyah said.

"Don't worry over that honey. To me, you're priceless."

"Honey, I have a headache, I must have drank too much wine" Denyah said before she marched into the kitchen for strong black coffee for her and Meleta as Meleta was out cold drinking too much wine as well. After Denyah returned with two cups of black coffee, she then shook Meleta waking her, "Here drink this." she told Meleta.

"Oh my head, no, not another drop of that stuff again" Meleta said leaning on one side looking ready to drop off to sleep again. Denyah whispered in her ears saying, "Ryan and Eugene are here" Meleta widened her eyes in surprised and said, "Was Ryan ashamed of me being drunk?"

Denyah laughed, "If Ryan was. So was Eugene ashamed of me. But thank to you my friend. I haven't enjoyed myself since my dearest friend Nurse James died. Bless her. I loved her so much" Denyah tears dropped. "Here, I made us black coffee and I'll let you into a secret" Denyah said to Meleta and burst into laughter saying. "We just drank one of Eugene's five hundred pound bottles of wine." Denyah burst into laughter again. Meleta laughed too then took a mouthful of coffee and spouted the coffee out of her mouth saying, "How much coffee have you put in this cup. Are you trying to poison me?"

"Meleta, all you have to do is to march into the kitchen and dilute your coffee by adding boiling water." Denyah told her.

Later that evening, Eugene and Ryan took Denyah and Meleta out for a meal but not to any of his hotels or his restaurants but to the Ibis hotel in China Town.

After Meleta spent another day with Denyah and Denyah got to like her even more and told her that she would be a good companion spending some time with her and that she was thinking, maybe it would be a good idea to let her move in with Ryan as they asked, and, especially knowing that when she'd needed help, Nurse James was there for her. As Denyah looked deep in thought, Meleta said to her, "I think this house is so big for you and Ryan"

"So I noticed." Denyah replied.

"It needs some fixing." Meleta said.

"So I noticed too?" Denyah replied sharp and smiling.

Meleta faced her and said "I know when I'm not wanted and I should keep my opinion to myself."

"No Meleta, please sit down. I never meant to sound rude."

Meleta smiled as she took her seat next to Denyah on the settee.

"Have you a family?" Denyah asked.

"Yes," Meleta replied" I have one sister but she stole my boyfriend from me. So I beat her up and my mother and father threw me out with nothing! Not even a second change of clothes. I was sleeping here and there with friends for the past three weeks. I did go back and asked them to take me in but they closed the door in my face. That was after my sister spat on my face. I'm now looking for somewhere to live as I sometimes have restless nights of sleeping with friends and their noisy children. Sometimes I'm so tired that I fall asleep on my desk while working. Anyway, let me tell you how I found out about my sister and my boyfriend. I left to go to church one Sunday morning with my mother and dad. As my tights were torn and clearly showed, I went home to change them. As I got in the house, I could hear laughing coming from my room. I went to my room and there I saw my sister on top of my boyfriend. They both were so shocked that they said nothing and seemed to be stuck like dogs. I pulled her off him whipped her arse until she bled and begged me not to beat her anymore. They were both naked. As for my boyfriend, I got so mad that I gave him a souvenir to carry with him all times, a big gashes on his forehead with one of dad's bottle of beer. You should have seen him jumping up and down with mixture of blood and beer running down his white face. And as I aimed to hit him with a second bottle of beer, he ran out of the house naked and over the fence he jumped like a racing horse and down Cricket Road he was running like the wind and wearing no shoes and as I stood in the road watching him, he never one time looked back. I heard later police picked him up. Well, you should have seen me looking in our fence to see if his balls had burst off between the fence railings" Denyah and Meleta burst into laughter. Then Meleta continue saying, "I took his clothes in the back garden and set alight to them and after went for my sister again and I did whooped her arse again that she ran to our next door neighbour Mrs Simmons for rescue. I then went to church leaving her in Mrs Simmons house hiding. I told mother what happened but it was pointless. Well, I had my satisfaction. First I was feeling great but later I'd felt so sick and disgusted that I didn't want to be in that house and on that bed again."

"So you have been sleeping rough?" Denyah asked.

"Yes Denyah, but only with girlfriends, you know with so many diseases going around, us ladies have to be very careful. So if you're concerned about your brother's safety, you need not be. Your brother is the second boyfriend I've had and he will be the last if he wants me." Meleta said calmly and happy,

"I'm glad to hear that." Denyah said.

"So that means I can stay here for a while," Meleta asked.

"Sure, of course you can stay until you decide to move on or if you care to stay in the guest house." Denyah said.

"Oh I thank you so much Den," Meleta said charmingly. "I rather beg a hitch up here."

"I'll prepare a room for you" Denyah told her.

"Do you mind my sleeping with Ryan?"

"No not at all. That's yours and Ryan's business."

"Denyah, I think I'm in love with your brother. He's the one I would like to settle down with and have his children." Meleta said soundly and proudly.

"Does Ryan feel the same about you?" Denyah asked.

"I think he does. But don't admit he's feeling the same" Meleta said and went on to asked Denyah "Have you any children?"

"Yes, I have an eight year old daughter Paris" Then as Denyah felt guilty, she said "The truth is, he's not my birth child. She's my ex-husband's."

"Where is she?" Meleta asked interestedly.

"She is living with her father." Denyah answered.

"Why don't you take her to live with you?" Meleta asked looking very concerned.

"I might have to fight him in court for access as I was told by his sister he's not looking after her properly, but I have to get this house fixed first. Especially that she's not my birth child. You know how Social Service works. Homes have to be to their expectation."

"Sure I understand. I also understand that your ex' a drunken as well. So I think you'll stand a good chance of getting Paris." Meleta said "Well, I better go and see what Ryan's doing."

Ten minutes later Ryan went to Denyah and asked her, "Do you mind Meleta staying here until she finds a place?"

"No, not at all, truthfully, I'm happy for her company. She can stay for as long as she likes."

"Thanks Den, oh I had a letter from Doctor Harris this morning asking me to start working in the theatre this Thursday night instead of next week."

"I'm so happy for you Ryan" Denyah told him and then planted a kiss on his face.

"How about a drink to thank you properly for everything good that happened to me, you've made this possible for me sis" Ryan said.

"No not me. God has made this happen for us. However, I can do with a cold drink after Meleta and I finished off a bottle of wine" Denyah said.

Ryan left and returned with three glasses of iced coke for Denyah, Meleta and himself while Eugene had scotch. Denyah raised her glass and said. "To you brother. I love you." she then kissed him on his cheek.

"I love you with all my heart Ryan honey" Meleta said. Then she raised her glass and said "All the best on your new job honey."

Ryan raised his glass and kissed Denyah and Meleta and said "I love you two special ladies that came into my life. Thanks Sis. Without you, I don't think it would be possible for me to be a doctor again. When I needed help, you gave it to me. I thank God for people like you. I also would like to thank Eugene in person. But he just left in his car." Ryan turned his face away then turned facing Denyah showing a nice smile but at the same time, his eyes looked moistened as if he has been crying.

When Denyah looked at him, he said, "Sis, I'm emotionally grateful." Denyah hugged him. He smiled. "That's the way I like to see you. Be happy as I am for you." By this time Meleta was watching him and Denyah. Denyah walked away. He hooked his arms around Meleta's waist and kissed her with feelings. As Denyah watched them she smiled. Ryan and Meleta walked up to her with their arms around each others and smiling then Ryan said "I would like to take my two most loved and pretty ladies out to dinner some time if you accept."

"We'll love that" Meleta said looking at Denyah.

"As Doctor Harris asked me to work this Thursday night, I have three days left to take us four for a meal, we three and Eugene."

"Okay, I will pass on your message to Eugene. By the way, how come you would be working on your surgeon job this quick? I thought you told me you would be starting on the wards and then two weeks after in the theatre."

"Well you see sis, I went into town to buy a couple of shirts. On my way out of town and heading for home I saw a woman got knock down by a car. I pulled up near to the curb, stopped my car and rushed to her. She was bleeding heavily from her mouth, leg and the left side of her head. Also, her left leg was broken in two parts and the bone showed. I've done my best to hold the bone in place and I taped and then bandaged her broken leg with one of my new shirts and practically set her bone in place with my belt to support the bones intact and taped her wounded head to slow down the bleeding while we waited for the ambulance. Then I kept talking to her, but I could seen her slipping into unconsciousness and the only thing I could of do to keep her conscious, was to press my thumb against her wounded head. I know at that time it was cruel, but I'd no other choice. Well, the ambulance arrived quickly enough, but I left the paramedics with not much to do except hooking her up to a monitor and injected her with morphine to ease the pain. I gave my name to the paramedics and told them I used to work as a doctor. The next thing I knew, a Doctor Finn called to see me and told me Doctor Harris told him I would be happy to start working in the theatre. He asked me to work tonight but I told him that I would like to start working next Monday as they're short of doctors and that I have already arranged to take my sister and my girlfriend to dinner. So he said okay, but as I saw on his face how desperate he'd looked, I told him I could start Thursday night. Den, you should have seen the relief on his face. So he told me, he's looking to see me at work Thursday night. He even gave me the key to my locker and told me it contains my overall. Oh here's my badge that bears my name. I even told him why I'd quit being a doctor. He was unaware but very understanding and said only a doctor would have done a professional job on the patient and he thanked me greatly. I also told him I was feeling nervous as it was a long time since I carried out such work. But he told me it's only natural. The he went on to say, I've done a good job and so efficiently, he was well satisfied and I am one of the Surgeons he was looking for. Then he asked how I manage to keep the patient from going into unconsciousness."

"Well, I told him, I learned a life saving technique from my Godfather who was a doctor but never registered on the doctors list. Den, I haven't heard such hearty laughing in a long while. Oh yes of course until Meleta made you laugh!"

"Oh Ryan, I'm really happy for you. I also meant to tell you last week, we'll have to move into a rented house for a while until our home and the guest house is fixed. Eugene has spoken to one of his friends and he said we can move in to one of his guest houses anytime when we're ready. So I think we should move in; in about two weeks. Would that be okay?"

"If we move out in two weeks, how long do you think our place would take to fix?"

"Ryan, the truth is, I really don't know. With the whole house needs fixing, it might take at least one to two months, maybe a bit longer as we're going to add on a conservatory and enlarge the kitchen. Your girlfriend can move in permanently after everything is sorted."

"Thanks sis, but I was thinking of buying a place for myself as me and Meleta are serious. Den, I love her. Would you mind if I live somewhere else?"

"Don't be silly, I'm so happy for you. Besides, we all need privacy sometimes. But when you buy your house, you best give me a key" Denyah then hugged him and Meleta and said to them, "when you two get married, please take care of each other. Meleta, wasn't I right about my brother marrying you?"

"Denyah, you're the best, and I love you. I love Ryan so much. In fact, I'm in love with him. I want to have all my children with him" Meleta said in happy mood.

"By the way Den, are you still going to try and get Paris?" Meleta asked.

"Yes, yes of course I want her to be with me" Denyah said.

"Well, you can turn the guest house into a playroom for her." Ryan said.

"Are you sure about this Ryan?" Denyah asked.

"Sure, of course I'm sure. If I'm going to buy Meleta and me a home somewhere, I wouldn't need a guest house, would I?" Ryan asked.

"No, I suppose not. However, thank you. I'm sure Paris would love her play house" Denyah said and she thanks Ryan again.

"However, do you two fancy coming to a club tomorrow night with me?" Ryan asked Meleta and Denyah.

"No thanks" Denyah said. "You can take Meleta if she wants. I really don't want to become the gooseberry. Besides, I would want to spend sometime with Eugene. Oh Ryan, I have something for you."

"What is it Den," Ryan asked anxiously.

Denyah smiled and gave him a cheque for Ninety two millions pounds saying, "This is for you. Part of the inheritance our foster mom has left to us. The house has been left to me and some jewellery. There're some men watches, cuff links, and bracelets. They're yours to do with what you will. With mine, I will split the jewellery with who deserved it. However, you're entitled to half of the uncut stones. Oh I do hope you'll share your jewellery with Eugene, Richards and David. Oh, would you mind giving me one of your wrist watches to give to my brother-in-law when he comes from Canada, if that's okay with you?"

"Sis, you don't need to ask, you take what you like for him." Ryan said.

"Ryan, I need just a watch, a pair of cuff links and a bracelet. Ryan, why don't I let you give them to him when he comes?"

"Sure sis, I would be happy to do that." Ryan said.

"Well Meleta, I would give you part of the ladies jewellery too. You both really don't need to look for a place now. There are seven bedrooms in this house, but it's up to you if you're ready to move out. Besides, I and Meleta are getting on so well together. Meleta I came to like you very much. And I'm going to do what I said, share everything with you Ryan right down the middle including the uncut jewelleries."

"You do no such thing Den. You have given me more than you should. If it weren't for you, I would be still scraping and scanning rotten food from off streets and dirty rubbish bins, as well as stacking boxes in different shops. Well, as for staying here for a while longer I think I could put up with that." Ryan said teasing.

"Cheeky," Denyah replied smiling.

"Why don't we make it a double wedding Denyah? You and Eugene, me and Ryan" Meleta said seriously.

"Meleta, I'm still married to a very vicious and jealous husband." Denyah said looking very distressed.

"Divorce him! I know nothing about him, but I know if he was treating you right you wouldn't have left him. You are so beautiful and in everything else. I'm sure most men would be happy falling at your feet. Is your husband so blind and stupid that he couldn't see that he had a beautiful and loving wife? Your husband needs help as he's deranged and also, he needs a damn good beating knocking his senses back into him" Meleta said frowning.

"Anyway he wouldn't just give up on me like that. I think he wants to make me suffer. Really suffer" Denyah said as if she didn't care.

"He sounds like a jerk to me." Meleta said.

"Believe me, he's the greatest of them all." Denyah replied smiling.

The door bell ring, Denyah got up out of her seat to answer the door while Ryan and Meleta sat on the three seat settee almost in tangles.

Denyah opened the door. "I'm Sonny. The gardener, we met earlier." he said.

"Oh yes of course, please come in Sonny." Denyah said and she moved from the door to let him in. As Sonny walked in, Ryan got up and in respect, shook his hand saying, "I'm Ryan, Mrs Davis's brother."

"Hello Sonny." Meleta said with a lovely smile.

"Hello fine lady." Sonny greeted Meleta nicely before he turned and faced Denyah and asked her "Am I too early to start working Mrs Davis?"

"No Sonny, you start as early as you like and please call me Denyah as I know we'll be friends. Breakfast would be ready in about one hour" Denyah said.

"Thank you Mrs Davis, but I had a bowl of hot and tasty porridge before I came. I would like to start working now if you don't mind. And thank-you too Mr Ryan."

"Just Ryan, I hope we will be good friends too." Ryan said.

"I would like that Ryan" Sonny said then he said to Denyah again and asked, "Is it too early to start working?"

"No not at all, you go ahead, and Sonny, you can eat your meals here every day including breakfast and I'm Denyah to you without the Mrs or Miss. Just call me Denyah" Denyah said.

"Yes Denyah. You're a very good woman." Sonny said.

"Well, I try to be" Denyah said.

"Well Sonny, I hope we'll be good friends too." Meleta said.

"I hope so Meleta. I'm happy to meet you too." Sonny said.

While Sonny was just starting to work, Aungus the other gardener walked up to him and said, "Sonny I will take the bottom while you do the top."

Just then Denyah went to them and said, "I do hope both of you would get on well together. I need a nice lawn at the front with flowers surrounding and vegetables in the back garden if possible. Well, I shall leave it up to both of you. Do you both have a family?"

"Yes, I have a wife, and a daughter who vanished to somewhere and left behind three grandchildren for me and the wife to look after." Sonny said. Then he went on to say. "The children's mother is alive somewhere but I don't know where."

Then Aungus said "My wife is not in the best of health at the moment. Still, we both are taking care of our two six and seven years old granddaughters. Their mother and father died in a motorbike accident on their way home from a friend two years ago Christmas Eve night. I meant two years ago Christmas Eve night." Aungus smiled hoping to hide his sadness which had clearly shown.

"I'm very sorry to hear that from both of you. You know what, I think I should pay you well; I will start you both off with two fifty for three days in each week." Denyah told Sonny and Aungus.

Aungus and Sonny looked at each other in surprise and then thanked Denyah with smiles of happiness.

"Well, I'm happy you're both pleased with your wages. If there's anything you should need, or, if I could help in any way, please feel free to come to me or my brother Ryan. I'll see you both later. By the way Aungus, how old are your grandchildren?"

"Tammy nine and Chelsea seven, they both live with my wife and me."

"I would like to meet them" Said Denyah "Oh, lunch would be at twelve thirty."

"Denyah, you said we only have to work three days a week. So why should you be paying us this much plus meals?" Aungus asked looking puzzled.

"Because I believe you both will do a very a good job and you both have family to take care of. Please Aungus, no more questions over any payment. I feel you both would be well worth your salary" Denyah said smiling then before she left, Aungus and Sonny thanked her again so gratefully that tears showed into Aungus' eyes.

After Aungus and Sonny had lunch, Denyah told them to have tomorrow off as it was Friday, even though it was their first week working. She gave them full pay plus a tin of biscuits and sweet each for their grandchildren.

CHAPTER SIX

Monday morning the following week, Denyah gave Sonny and Aungus overalls, safety boots and gloves to work in. As time went by Denyah got to like both Aungus and Sonny like a father. And in turn they adore her not as their employee but as their daughter. She would treat them with either cold beers or iced-tea after lunch and would send presents for Sonny and Aungus' grandchildren regularly.

One Saturday afternoon, Denyah, Eugene, Ryan and Meleta had packed away the furniture so that the workmen could carry out the work on their home the following week. Most of the furniture was sent to a specialist to be face-lifted as it was looking tatty, while the others were secured in two rooms and covered to avoid damaging. The next Sunday morning, Denyah and her family moved into their borrowed furnished house from a best friend of Eugene's for at least a couple of months until their home and the guest house was repaired with the addition of a big gym with all the latest equipment, a conservatory and a child's play room.

Within six weeks, Denyah's house and the guest house was completely refurbished and were equipped with exquisite furniture and it looked magnificent and beautiful inside and outside with a manicured lawn.

The following Sunday evening Denyah, Eugene, Ryan and Meleta went for a drive around town and then ended up at Birmingham Airport admiring the fantastic view and watching people boarding planes and jetting off to their destinations as well as home comers landing.

"Would anyone like a drink?" Eugene asked.

"Yes please" Meleta said happily.

"We'll all would go and have a drink" Denyah said. And so Denyah, Meleta, Eugene and Ryan went into the bar.

As Denyah and Meleta waited for Eugene and Ryan in the sitting area to bring their drinks, two young good looking white women rushed passed them almost bringing down Meleta. As Meleta make a grab at the youngest woman, Denyah grabbed Meleta's hand and said, "Leave them."

Meleta looked at Denyah and said, "I just like to fist them in their mouth to teach them manners."

"Let's go to the ladies" Said Denyah as she saw how vexed Meleta was.

Meleta smiled before she went to the ladies with Denyah. Denyah and Meleta returned from the ladies to see the two women sitting in their seats at their table with Eugene and Ryan laughing and chatting. As Denyah and Meleta stood waiting for their seats, the youngest woman looked up at them smiling. Meleta said nothing except pulled her up out of her seat and tossed her on the floor and sat down. Shamefully the older woman got up and she and her companion went and sat at empty table facing Denyah and Meleta. Meleta gave them the V sign and then kissed Ryan. The youngest women snarled at her malignantly before turning her back on them.

Denyah then noticed blood was showing on the seat of the youngest women pale blue trousers but she said nothing. Meleta saw Denyah's eyes fixed on the woman and asked Denyah, "What are you looking at?"

Denyah whispered in her ears "The younger women looks like she's having her period"

"How do you know?" Meleta asked.

"Blood on the seat of her trousers," Denyah said.

"Aye," replied Meleta staring on the woman's trousers.

"Shush-," Denyah whispered in Meleta's ears. "We wouldn't want Eugene and Ryan to see. Would we?" Denyah asked.

Meleta shook her head no, but stared at the blood spreading on the back of the woman's trousers before she burst out laughing while Denyah kept seriously calm so as not to draw Eugene or Ryan's attention. Denyah asked to excuse her and went to the woman and whispered in her ears, "You should go the ladies and tidy yourself."

"And why should I need to be tidy?" the young woman asked.

"Because you're bleeding, I think you're having your period, can't you feel?" Denyah asked her.

The woman felt her trousers and blood smeared her hand. Shamefully she looked up at Denyah and said "Thanks for telling me. Believe me or not, I hadn't felt I was losing or feeling wet. But I'd felt funny and now ashamed."

Then the older woman softly said to Denyah, "I jokingly sat on your husband's lap and he rudely pushed me away. Both your husband and your brother are the most two handsome men here. Your husband even told me you won't approve of me sitting on his lap."

"That is because he's very choosy. And he's also right. I don't like sharing" Denyah said.

"I wasn't trying to steal him away from you, you know, especially having a beautiful wife like you. I could understand why he pushed me away" the older woman said laughing.

Denyah smiled before she said, "The truth is my friend. If you'd appeal to my husband's eyes and not displaying yourself like flying cockroach, he would treat you with respect. Then again, any woman who has respect wouldn't flaunt herself on men they'd met for the first time. And as for you my young friend, I think you should really go and change your trousers before you saturate the chair."

"You sound just like me. I like straight forward people. By the way, my name is Grace." The youngest woman said and my friend's Gene."

"I'm Denyah, and my sister-in-laws name is Meleta, my husband's Eugene and my brother's Ryan. However, would you two like to join us after you get back from the ladies? So, that we could introduce ourselves formally," Denyah asked.

Gene smiled as she left closely behind her friend Grace to hide her bloodied trousers. Shortly after, the older woman returned. Then about five minutes later, the young woman showed up wearing her black tassel scarf tied around her waist fitting her like a skirt to substitute for her blood stained trousers that she'd put in the bin. As she stood at Denyah's table, Denyah looked up at her. She whispered into Denyah's ears saying, "I always carried extra pieces of cloths in case of emergency as now."

Denyah smiled then asked Eugene to fetch a couple of chairs from the table nearest to theirs so that the two women would join them. After the older woman swallowed down at least five vodkas chased with Babycham, she began to giggle and then whispered in Denyah's ears "It looks like me and my friend Gene are out of luck as the most two handsome men here are counted for. Are you sure you and your sister-in-law wouldn't mind us sitting at your table?"

"Of course not, just relax Gene. You'll find Meleta and me less aggressive now that we're getting to know each other. So enjoy yourself. However, Grace, Gene, please meet my husband Eugene and my brother Ryan, Meleta's husband."

Ryan looked at Denyah mighty funny and then smiled faintly.

After Gene and Grace formerly introduced themselves, Eugene and Ryan brought drinks for them every time. As Grace was getting tipsy, she was making a fool of herself by hugging and kissing Denyah and singing to her "I'm in love with you girl." her friend Gene became embarrassed and told her Grace "Stop making a fool of your self and start behaving like a lady."

"There's nothing wrong in telling someone how they feel about them. Is it?" Grace asked.

Eugene looked Denyah in her eyes as he made a little gesture by moving over to the end of his chair and smiled brightly.

Denyah hit him lightly on the side of his head and said jokingly, "if, from now, you don't behave yourself, I might just do a turning" Eugene smiled as he pressed the palms of his hands together in a praying form and said, "There's only you for me my darling, but if you should ever decide to turn the other way, will you please put me to sleep with one of your poison kisses,"

Ryan looked at Eugene and then at Denyah. Shaking his head slowly, he said "I wish I could understand the parables of you two."

After Grace and Gene got very friendly with Denyah and her family, Gene said to Denyah and Meleta, "when we leave here, we would be going to one of our friend's party. Would both of you like to come with us?"

"No! I don't think we'll fit in." Said Meleta.

"Why don't you ask your husbands and hear what they have to say." Grace said.

"I agree" Gene said. "Look, we wouldn't steal your husbands. I'm sure they wouldn't want us."

"Ok," said Meleta. "But only if they agreed, then we'll have to go home and get changed."

Denyah looked at Meleta and smiled as she knew that Meleta has no clothes to change into except lending her some of her clothes as they're size twelve. Denyah and Meleta asked Eugene and Ryan if it was okay for them to go with their new friends Gene and Grace to the party in Sparkbrook. At first Eugene told Denyah he didn't like the idea. Then he changed his mind saying "yes, I think you could do with a little enjoyment, but, your brother and I would be coming."

"Then you can - let's go home" Denyah told him.

"Have you ladies driven here?" Eugene asked.

"No, we came by taxi." Gene said.

"Well you two ladies finish your drinks then you can come home with us before we go to the party" Eugene told Grace and Gene.

"Have you enough room for Gene and me?" Grace asked.

"Sure, I've a people carrier." Eugene said smiling.

Gene drank her last bit of vodka and she and her friend Grace left with Denyah, Eugene, Ryan and Meleta to Denyah's home.

As everyone got out the car, Denyah sighed, oh what a relief. I was beginning to believe I was a little bug squashed between three elephants."

"Cheeky," said Meleta laughing.

Meleta quickly took a shower and borrowed some of Denyah's clothes and dressed similar to Denyah in light and pale blue trousers suit, black see-through black vest and black high heeled shoes while Denyah wore a cream trouser suit, brown vest and brown shoes. Eugene and Ryan were dressed similar in pale grey trousers and black long sleeved satin shirts and black shoes as the night was warm. Denyah also gave Gene her new lovely grey trousers suit, new panties and tam pox to wear at the party.

"Denyah, Meleta, Grace and Gene looked cool and attractive.

"I just wish it was the other way around. I wish you and Eugene were brothers and sisters. Then I might have just got lucky with him. Ah well, I would just have to settle to be a friends to the four of you" Grace said happily.

"You always get straight to the point don't you Grace?" Denyah said.

"Now who wants a drink before we leave?" Ryan asked.

"Well, I wouldn't say no to vodka if you have one." Gene said.

"I wouldn't say no to a scotch or brandy either." Grace said.

After everyone had their chosen drinks, David and his fiancée turned up. "We seemed to have come at the wrong time" David said.

"No, not at all, David my friend, you're welcome here at anytime. Only we've decided to go to a house party with our two friends Grace and Gene on the spur of the moment. They invited us to a party, would you both like to join us?" Denyah asked.

"As we have nowhere particular to go, we came to spend some time with you. Anyway I would like you to meet my girlfriend Tracy."

"Nice to meet you Tracy, I'm Denyah, my sister-in-law Meleta and Gene, and Grace, my just met friends, my brother Ryan and my fiancées Eugene. Oh, Meleta and Ryan are engaged to be married."

"Do you want a drink David and Tracy?" Eugene asked.

"Just a small scotch please," David said.

"Tracy."

"No thank you. Eugene."

"Well David the scotch is right at your hand. Help your self." Eugene said.

David poured a drink from a bottle of scotch in a glass and swallowed all at once and rubbed his hands together, got on his feet and was ready to leave with the others to go to the party.

"Well, if you're ready to go to that party, let's get going." Grace said.

Ryan and Meleta went with David and Tracy while Grace and Gene went with Denyah and Eugene.

On their way to the party, Denyah was thinking over what Ryan had told her about his friends being killed. But she smiled to show Eugene she was feeling happy.

As they got to the party, they were told "It's a bottle party. No bottle, no entry!" A well built black man said as he guarded the door way with his body. Eugene left Denyah and friends to go and get some drinks. After, he returned with a crate of twenty four bottled beers and three bottles of whiskey. Denyah shook her head smiling when she saw Eugene with the drinks. Everyone got out of their parked car. Ryan looked into Eugene's eyes and smiled saying, "mate, you bought drinks for the whole party."

"These drinks make up for those who haven't brought any. Come on lets go in." Eugene said.

"And you think if anyone comes without a bottle, they would be let in? Mate, they would be turned away like us. We might be luckier than them getting a bottle." Ryan said.

As Eugene and Ryan got to the door with the drinks, Eugene rang the door bell and a lovely tall and slim mixed race young woman answered the door. As she saw the drinks, she smiled chewing, chewing gum and drew to one side and let Eugene and his companions walking in with the crate of beers and the whiskies. The doorman took the crate of beers and the three two litre bottle of whiskies from Eugene and Ryan and placed them on the long table with the other drinks. "Oh" asked the doorman, "How many are you?"

"Eight of us" Eugene answered. Then he went on to say, "Five beautiful ladies and three Sons-of-a-guns:" Eugene said.

The doorman laughed heartily and said, "My friend, I like you."

"I like you too" Eugene said. "I can do with someone as you."

"Why, what your business then?" The doorman asked.

"I'm in trading" Eugene told him and smiled.

"Why don't you give me a call sometime?" Eugene told him and gave him one of his cards with both his home and mobile numbers.

The doorman looked deeply on the card, smiled and put it in his shirt pocket and looking mighty hard at Denyah with the most enchanting smile.

"This lady's my wife mate." Eugene told him.

"Well, sorry to look on your rose so hard, but my eyes couldn't help looking at the most beautiful women. However, my name is Selvin but my friends called me Sil."

"I'm Eugene. I'm looking forward to hear from you."

"Well, Eugene a warm welcome to you and your friends. Enjoy yourself and you're free to serve yourself to food and drinks. And I would give you that call" the heavy built handsome black doorman said and then disappeared into another room.

The doorman was heavily built with a well fit and good-looking body, about six feet tall, very good-looking, dark but not very black, smooth looking skin, clean shaved head, beautiful white set teeth with a silver tooth at the top row on the right side that glitters under his lovely smile.

Eugene poured whiskey for himself and a glass of orange juice for Denyah. He passed the juice to Denyah and said. "Juice for you my precious" Then Meleta poured whiskey mixed with soda for her again, and sneaked away before Ryan saw her. Denyah took another sip of whiskey from Meleta's glass and as she saw Eugene coming towards her, she done the same, rushed a chewing gum in her mouth and swallowed some juice. David had whiskey while his girlfriend Tracy had a glass of sherry. Gene and Grace had whiskey so did Ryan and David. All eight of them moved into the dance room. But as the music was great and everyone was getting down to the beat, the room went hot and overcrowded with people. Denyah and Tracy stood in a corner watching the dancers. Meleta went to Denyah and said, "Come on Den, you didn't come to be a corner post, did you? Come on let's dance."

"I'll dance when I'm ready Meleta" Denyah said. Meleta smiled and then moved to Tracy saying, "Come on Tracy let's dance."

"Cool it Meleta, I would dance when I'm ready" Tracy told her. By this time, Eugene, Ryan, David, Gene and Grace were really getting down to the beat of the music with other women.

Eugene surprised Denyah as he was dancing sexy to Stealing Love by the fire drawing most of the women doing dirty dancing in reggae. Denyah stood in a corner watching her man Eugene, her brother Ryan and their friends attracting the women as they dancing dirty. As Eugene caught Denyah watching him hard, he gave her the eye and blew her a kiss. Denyah smiled giving Eugene his freedom with the women as she knows none of them meant anything to him. As Tracy saw jealousy on Denyah's face, she danced with Denyah in a corner near to the door to keep cool as it became overcrowded and too hot and the music was blasting. Denyah, Tracy and Meleta decided to go outside for fresh air leaving Eugene, Ryan, David, Grace, and Gene to enjoying themselves. As Gene and Ryan were dancing, she slipped her hand down Ryan's trousers and was fondling his penis until he ejaculated in her hand. Ryan quickly went to the bathroom and had a quick wash. When he returned, he told Eugene what had happened. "You should have taken her to the bathroom man," Eugene said laughing.

"No way, would I fuck her. I should have stopped her putting her hand down my trousers, but after feeling the geyser rise stiffed, well, I just had to shoot. Anyway, I love Meleta too much to lose her over tramps like her" Ryan said to Eugene then went on to say. "Anyway, why don't you take her to the toilet?"

"No way mate," Eugene said.

As the party was getting hot with dirty dancing, memory came freshly to Ryan as he sunk in thought of the time he and friends went to the doctor's party and the heavy price they had paid for heavy drinking.

At this time of Ryan's drinking, flashes of his friends accident was racing through his mind. The whiskey he poured out to drink, he left it on the table and had a bottle of super malt instead as he'd had two whiskeys before.

"Very sensible brother" Denyah told Ryan as she saw him drinking the super malt. By this time Meleta had served herself some brandy and she kissed Ryan before she went outside for fresh air again.

As Meleta, Tracy and Denyah heard the soft music they got back inside to be with Eugene, Ryan and David. Denyah was really enjoying herself dancing so that she Meleta and Tracy attracted a few good looking men who had wanted to dance with them. At this time, Eugene was standing next to Grace and Gene when Gene said "Denyah's so beautiful. No wonder she is attracting so many handsome men" Gene faced Eugene saying. "You will have to be careful someone doesn't take her from you. I would put her on leash if I were you. I myself fell in love with her as I like to act both ways." Gene said.

"You can swing your hook mate," Eugene told her.

"Oh what I meant, I like women but I love my men more" Gene said smiling. "We can go into the toilet and do a quickie. Denyah don't have to know." Gene whispered in his ears.

"If you're a bitch on heat plenty of bulls in here. All you have to do is to choose one to fulfil your need. My wife is all I need" Eugene told Gene.

As Denyah was dancing with a dark and tall handsome guy, he said softly to her, "I'm a doctor and I live in West Bromwich. My name is Glennis Morgan. Are you here on your own?" he asked Denyah interestedly.

"No, I'm here with friends and fiancée. Actually I'm here as friends invited us. And it's the first time I came to a house party" Denyah told him.

"Well, I have dated married women. I would really like to get to know you and who knows where it might lead" Glennis said.

"How do you know I'm married?" Denyah asked him.

"I can tell by your ring" he said.

"Well Doctor Glennis, you certainly don't beat around the bush and I don't think anything would lead between us except my husband who is standing right over there by the sound system and he owns all of me and we're so much in love. Now if you would slacken your hold from around my waist, I would be very grateful." Denyah said.

Doctor Glennis smiled and moved his hands from around her waist and danced with her decently. After the CD had stopped playing, Denyah tried to get away from him but he held on to her hand and didn't want to let go until Eugene told him, "I believe this dance is mine." And so as the DJ played a love song, ironically, Doctor Glennis smiled and as he and Gene's eyes clashed, he went and danced with her.

As Eugene and Denyah were dancing, she said to him. "This has brought back memories of when we were dancing at my friends Joan and Austin's engagement party." Then as she rested her head on his shoulder he kissed her. At this time, Doctor Glennis was looking hard at them even though he was dancing with Gene.

As Eugene caught Doctor Glennis looking hard on Denyah, he said, "Den, your fancy man is looking hard at me and showing jealousness."

"Eugene, I thought you were my fancy man." she said then went on to say. "He is a doctor and he works at the Hospital in West Bromwich and his name Glennis Morgan."

"Well honey, one doctor in the family is enough." Eugene said and held Denyah tightly to him. By then the room was so hot and well overcrowded that he and Denyah went outside for fresh air.

They both were surprised to see a young white man and a black women leaning against the back of the house having sex. Denyah walked away and as she saw Eugene watching, she held his hand and led him back into the house to dance.

"Why do people do things like that, their behaviour's disgusting!" Denyah said to Eugene as they dance.

"They're enjoying themselves." Eugene said smiling.

"They're vulgar and disrespectful." Denyah said.

"I still said they were enjoying themselves." Eugene said.

"Lucky I'm here as you might be doing the same." Denyah said.

"Den honey, I want only you to spend the rest of my life with."

"So you said Eugene, so you said." Denyah replied in a foul mood.

A few minutes later a friend of the woman outside went and whispered into the wife's husband's ears telling him, " Your friend is outside knocking off your wife" The husband, stopped dancing and hurried out of the house to see his best friend and his wife leaning against the back of the party house having sex. He stood in shock looking at them and listening to the aggravating noise they both were making before they exploded.

The husband aggressively pulled his friend off his wife and knocking him down with double heavy punches to his chest and head. His friend struggled up on his feet and ran away and quickly got into his car and drive off in a high speed.

As the husband was getting into his car to go after him, a black man said to him, "Look mate, it's not worth you chasing after him and you might meet with an accident or get killed for a wife that is unfaithful."

"That bastard is supposed to be my best friend and all this time he was laughing at me and fucking my wife" the husband said crying.

As some partygoers looked on, the adultery wife's husband said. "The deceitful bastard run away and left my wife with her thong down to her ankles. He then turned to his wife and asked her "How can you both do this to me?"

His wife faced him and said. "Grant I wanted to hurt you. But not like this even though I knew you were having affair with my best friend Ashia."

"Windy, why didn't you leave me when you found out I was having affair. Or confront me," the husband said.

"I'm so sorry I didn't know what I was doing as I was feeling tipsy and your friend came on to me strongly" his wife cried.

"Why do you have to fuck with my best friend? How long this was going on? And why do you have to humiliate me like this! Haven't you any shame Windy!" he asked his wife crying and then said. "You let everyone see how big your pussy is,"

"Yes I have shame, but not for you. I stop loving you since you slept with one of my friends. And yes, if you must know, your friend was fucking me from five months ago the same time you were fucking my friend" his wife proudly said.

At this time plenty of the partygoers were outside listening to the husband and his wife.

The husband was so hurt that he stabbed his wife in her tummy and her right side with his penknife and then sped away in his car searching to find his deceitful friend and leaving his wife bleeding and unconscious on the cold tiled yard gasping for breath.

A young woman who was smoking outside ran into the house screaming, "A husband stabbed his wife and she needs a doctor! Would some one help! She's bleeding to death" The young white woman yelled at the crowd, "Help, help, a woman has been stabbed. Are there any doctors or nurses here? There's a woman badly wounded and lying outside in a pool of blood."

Ryan rushed outside and saw the wounded wife lying in a pool of blood on the cold yard ground. Quickly he examined the woman's stabbed wound and found out the wound to her left side was deep but was slanting and the one to her tummy was about three inches long. Ryan raced to his car and took a reel of electrical tape and using it to help to slow down the woman's blood from flowing. Then as a young woman saw Ryan needed help, she ran into the house again and raised a second alarm shouting "Would someone come and help Doctor Ryan as the woman needs urgent attendance as she is still bleeding badly."

Doctor Glennis was in a dark corner in the dance room snuggling with Gene and drinking a bottle of beer, David touched him on his shoulder and telling him, "Ryan needs your help outside to help a woman that been stabbed."

Doctor Glennis rushed the half bottle of beer into David's hand and he rushed out the dance room and went to Ryan, "I need your help Glennis" Doctor Ryan told him.

Doctor Glennis quickly backed off his black dog collar jacket and assisted Doctor Ryan in attending the woman but after they managed to tape her stabbed wounds they found she has a gash behind her left ears and that was heavily bleeding too. They also managed to control the bleeding.

Doctor Ryan said to Doctor Glennis, "She has lost plenty of blood sp that we almost lose her. Thanks mate for helping. We'll have to get her into hospital fast as she's slipping away and she needs blood."

"I agree with you Ryan, it's my job as well mate, so let's get moving and no need for you to thank me. I believed we both had done what we can" Doctor Glennis said putting on his jacket. He then went on saying "However, if it wasn't for the gluey tape and bandage you carried in your car, only God knows whether or not we could have saved her. Still, I'm not so sure if she is having internal bleeding" Eugene and David rushed out to see if there's anything they can do, but Doctor Glennis said "I need to wash the blood off my hands, but each second tick it precious to the woman. Ryan and I done everything possible" After Ryan washed the blood off his hands, he said to Eugene,

"Well, with no time to lose, I best go and get my car so that we could rush our patient to a hospital" Ryan told Doctor Glennis as he eyed Eugene.

But Doctor Glennis hurried away to get his car instead and drive back to the house and stopped his car in the middle of the road. David and Eugene assisted Ryan in helping the patient very carefully in the backseat of the car. After, Ryan got in and sat at the back and rested the patient's head on his lap and trying to comfort her by talking to her to keep her awake. Ryan was watching her wounds very carefully as he was trying to hold her steady by not stretching or burst the tape to erupt the wounds. As Doctor Glennis was speeding the badly wounded woman to the City hospital and through every stop light, a police car had just drive off the next road just in time to see their car race through the traffic lights. The white policeman looked hard on his dark policeman and then sounded his siren.

"Glennis, the police must have seen us driving through the stop light." Doctor Ryan said.

"Look Ryan, we had no choice. The patient here is touch and go." Doctor Glennis said.

As the police siren was still sounding, Doctor Ryan asked Doctor Glennis to stop and explain, but Doctor Glennis said, "We stop and lose the patient, can you live with that? For I certainly couldn't, I know we broke the law but it's a case of life and death. We have no choice" Doctor Glennis said.

"Glen, I don't want to be breaking the law, but as you said, we have no choice and I see what you mean" Doctor Ryan said lifting the patient eye lid and feeling her pulse.

As the police car was racing far behind Doctor Glennis's car and sounding his siren, Doctor Glennis said to Doctor Ryan to try and steady the patient while I drive faster."

"Look Glen, I wanted no hassle from those Bobbies. We still have a few minutes to get to the hospital. It's better to slow down and let them know the reason for driving through the stoplight?" Doctor Ryan said. "Besides, I think she will be okay."

"Ryan we'll be fine. The police want us they come to the hospital" Glennis said.

"Glennis, shut up! We're broke the law driving through every stop lights." Doctor Ryan said.

"Of course I know, but do we have a choice?" Doctor Glennis asked.

"I guess not," Doctor Ryan said.

As the doctors drove through the last stop lights, the police car was right behind their car. But Doctors Ryan and Glennis had to be very careful of not speeding too fast to upset the patient. As they made their turning into the hospital gate, the police closed in on them. Both polices looked hard at each other. Doctor Glennis drove in front the hospital main door and stopped. He then flew his car door opened and rushed out and into the hospital demanding to see a Doctor and quick. Saying to the nurse he saw, "I'm Doctor Glennis and we have a patient that's badly wounded and lost plenty of blood and needed urgent attendance."

The nurse ordered two porters to attend Doctor Glennis in taking a trolley bed to Doctor Glennis car to fetch the patient and then she hurried down the long corridor to find a doctor to assist the patient.

The police officers drove into the hospital gate and parked their car on the far side facing the main door and got out of their car and walked over to Doctors Ryan and Glennis. "Why didn't you stop your car?" the dark policeman asked.

"You both ignored the warnings all the way and broke every law in the book by driving through every stoplight. Do you realise in doing so, you might have injured or killed someone" the white policeman said.

"We had no choice mate. There was a badly wounded patient needed urgent attendance" Doctor Glennis said as he was looking at the porters.

The white police sounded out m...m...m and gave Doctor Ryan a ticket for speeding. Doctor Glennis pulled the ticket out of Doctor Ryan's hand, tore it into pieces and flung it in the police face and said, "Now fuck off."

"We're sorry mate. I know we were breaking the law, but to save a patient life, we'd to do what we'd to do. But at the same time, we were careful not to cause any disturbance or accident. As I was the driver, I would take full responsibility" Doctor Ryan's said knowing Doctor Glennis was the driver. But to make thing easier, he lied to prevent Doctor Glennis causes more trouble with the police.

Immediately Doctor Blanchett rushed up to the patient and as he saw the patch of blood, he helped in wheeling the trolley into the theatre with two other doctors, one of whom was a black female and the other was a white male. Doctors Ryan and Glennis sat in the waiting room wanting to hear how the patient was. After an hour a tan-skinned nurse reported to Doctors Glennis and Ryan telling them, the patient was groaning heavily with pain, but the doctors are doing their best on her" Doctor Ryan smiled. Then a mixed race female nurse came to them and asked. "Would you both like some coffee?"

"Yes please, strong and black, no sugar" Doctors Ryan said.

"Just a little milk for me please, I want my coffee to look like you." Glennis joked. The nurse smiled as she left and then returned with the two cups coffee. As she gave Doctor Glennis his coffee, he eyed her smiling, she smiled back. Then she moved to Ryan smiling and looking him in his eyes as she gave him his coffee. But he made a gesture saying "I should phone my fiancée and let her know I would be home soon."

The nurse smile dimmed and she moved to Doctor Glennis again saying "It's over an hour, you'll soon hear how your patient's doing."

She then walked away and Doctor Glennis walked with her and they both stopped walking and faced each other. "Are you married?" he asked her.

"No" she replied smiling "I have no time to look after husbands." she said.

"Would it be okay to see you sometimes?" he asked her.

"Are you serious, or are you being polite?" she asked him.

"I'm very serious. Like you, I have no time to be serious with women, but I really like you and I would like to know you better. What you say, would you have dinner with me next Saturday?" he asked her.

"Well, I would see." she said.

"Don't strain yourself. Just forget I ask you." Glennis said with a straight face.

"Yes, Of course, I would be happy to have dinner with you. What time would you call for me?" she asked.

"Seven. Where shall I call for you?" he asked.

She wrote her address and mobile number and gave it to him. Then as her pen dropped from her hand, they both bent down to pick it up and with their lips almost met, he smiled and picked the pen up and gave it to her. "Thanks," she told him, and he walked back to be with Ryan. She then went away smiling.

While he and Ryan waited in the waiting room to hear the result of the woman's condition. Ryan questioned him. "Did you ask her for a date?"

"Yes, I asked her out to dinner next Saturday." He said and then laughed.

"What so funny Glennis?" Ryan asked.

"I forgot to ask her name." he said.

"Well, you have her address and her phone number, her name would follow after. Do you really like her, or she's another name that would add to your list?" Ryan asked.

"I do like her. Maybe she's the woman I would make my wife" he said.

"She's pretty and looked intelligent and I would like her as a friend" Ryan said.

"Why, does she remind you of Meleta?"

"Yes, in a way, but I'm afraid Meleta is the only woman for me" Ryan said

Just then a very good looking tall dark skin doctor went to Doctors Ryan and Glennis and said, "I'm happy to let you know that the patient will be okay, thanks to the first class work that someone has done on her. We also managed to control the internal bleeding."

"We're both happy to hear that, especially after she'd lost plenty of blood." Ryan said.

"Oh, I'm Glennis and my friend is Ryan. It was us who'd probably help saved the patient by taping her wounds." Glennis said.

"Believe me pals. The patient is very lucky to be alive. One inch deeper reaching her kidney, she might have not survive. Not to mention the amount of blood she'd lost. She will need at least six pints of blood. You fellows were very clever to have glued her wounds so carefully and so professionally. I'm sure I couldn't have done a better job. Thanks for saving her life. Tell me, where have you gentlemen learnt to do this fine work?"

"Sorry doctor, we didn't formally address our nature of work. We both are doctors. I'm Glennis Morgan" Glennis said. And I'm Ryan Taylor." Ryan said. "We must leave now as the patient's now okay and in the best of hands" Ryan said. And he and Doctor Glennis' shook hands with the white female doctor and said "goodbye," And as they walked out of the hospital and walking towards their car, they see the white male police officer leaning against their car and the black male police standing by the police car also waiting. Ryan and Glennis mirrored in each others eyes and smiled and walked on and stood by their car. But before they got in their car, the white police said. "Why didn't you stop and tell us. However, the ticket was a mistake. I will explain to my superior. Goodbye doctors, I do hope if we should meet again, it would be on friendly basis." the white police said.

"I would like that officer and goodbye to you officers, and thank-you very much for withdrawing the ticket," Ryan said to them.

The officers smiled and left as Doctors Ryan and Glennis got in their car and drove away.

Meanwhile, as police swarmed on the party house, party goers were driving away and only leaving those who lived in the house and few guests that were too drunk and couldn't run and those living near by.

Police asked the owners of the house to tell them what had happened, but both husband and wife said they saw nothing or knew of anything that went on outside the house until someone alarmed everyone that a husband stabbed his wife outside the house. The doorman also gave the same statement as the owners of the house.

"Well, Mr and Mrs Bartlett, as from now, your home would not be accessible to use for your convenience. In other words, there would be no more party to be held at this address at anytime as you would be prosecuted. However, have you a license to have parties?" the police asked.

"I don't think keeping a party now and then and invited friends would need a licence" the wife said calmly as the husband stayed at the back and kept silent.

"Well, you would be hearing from us soon. And as I said, no more parties from here onwards. Good morning," the officer said and left.

The same two police officers went to the hospital and took a statement from the wounded wife. In her statement, she said, "My husband stabbed me because I was outside speaking to one of his men friend. Maybe he saw me kissed his friend on his cheek and probably got jealous and acted impulsively and stabbed me. I'm glad his friend ran off as he might have stabbed him too. I can't say that I blame his friend to run away. My husband is very vicious, and it's time I stopped defending him and taking his abuse."

At the time the police were taking statement from the wounded wife, the police looked doubtfully that she was telling the truth. At one time, the taller police looked on at his mate and smiled and then said to the wounded wife, "I would like you to sign your statement after I read it back to you. Do you understand Mrs Morton?"

She nodded saying "Yes, I understand" then tears came into her eyes.

After the black police read back the statement to the wife in the presence of her attendant doctor and his white police colleague, he asked her to sign her statement.

Before she signed the statement, she lifted her head up to look at her doctor. Her doctor nodded his head to signal her to sign the statement. As she was signing her hand trembled and her face perspired with fear.

Both police officers thanked her and left with her written and signed statement.

Some hours later, the police went to her husband house and read him his rights before they arrested him for grievous bodily harm to her.

As the party was stopped by two different policemen, they asked for anyone who knew what happened to come forward but as no one went forward, the police ordered the few remaining people to clear the premises.

While Denyah was moving towards the door, one of the police officers saw her. He went to her, "Mrs Davis," he said smiling.

Denyah recognised him and said, "Hello Officer Dailey." The officer smiled before asking her. "What are you doing here Mrs Davis?"

"I was invited by friends. But it has turned out to be, that I came at the wrong time and the wrong place." Denyah said.

The officer smiled saying, "Mrs Davis we all deserve a little happiness now and then. By the way, we're still working on your nurse friend's case. However, we'll get in touch, soon as we know anything."

"Thanks officer," Denyah said.

"Goodbye Mrs Davis" The officer said and walked back to his other officers leaving Denyah feeling sickened and disgusted that it's nearly a year since her nurse friend had been murdered, and still nothing had been heard about her friend. Coldly she frowned and went to Eugene and took the car keys out of his pocket. "Now what are you going to do with my keys?" Eugene asked.

"I'm driving you home as you were drinking too much." she told him.

"Let's go home and have our own party. You must invite our friends to our house" Eugene said feeling high.

"Okay Eugene," Denyah said and then invited her friends to her home where they had their own party until two thirty early in the morning.

After the party, David and his fiancée took Gene and Grace to their homes then he and his fiancée drive on to his home.

"I can do with some black coffee. Do you want some David?" His fiancée asked him.

"No thank-you. All I want is a good long sleep. Oh Tracy honey, if I'm still sleeping by nine' o' clock, would you call Peter and tell him to leave it until tomorrow. His number is in my diary on my dressing table."

"What to leave until tomorrow David? Are you seeing another woman?"

"Don't be silly sweetheart. I only have strength for you. Now why don't you come to bed Tracy honey?"

"After I have my coffee, then I might, or take myself home" Tracy said angrily.

After she drank her coffee, she joined David in bed and tickled him. He faced her saying, "Stop it Louise and let me sleep" he then buried his face into the pillow and as he realized he called his fiancée Louise. "Oh no, I'm sorry Tracy. It was a slip of my tongue calling you Louise. I'm so sorry" he said smiling.

Tracy got annoyed and poked him in his left side asking him. "What did you call me? My name is Tracy and not Louise like your dead woman! You're still in love with her, aren't you? Well, as from now, I don't think that I would want to be with you as I know just where I would always be, second behind your dead fiancée! This is not the first time you've called me by that name, and I'm sick to hell of you up to my stomach!"

"Oh Tracy, I'm sorry, it's just that I'm feeling so tired and the death of her is haunting me. I did love her and I just can't forget her overnight. Come here, you know that I love you and would love to marry you if you would have me."

"David, it's almost a year since your damn Louise is dead. As for marring me, I think you should ask your Louise first."

"Tracy, I did, and she said the sooner I marry you, the happier she would be to move on" David said smiling and peeling back the quilt for her to get in bed.

Suddenly there was a bright smile came on her face, showing happiness that she jumped into bed and into his arms and began kissing his lips like there would never be a next time to kiss him again.

"Aye, take it easy Tracy, if you don't want to send me over to Louise." He joked.

"David, you go to hell with her." Tracy said outrageously as she jumped out of his arms and walked towards the bedroom door and stopped with her back towards him and in tears.

"Tracy honey, I was just joking. I know that you could never get enough of me. But, if you would book an appointment, I'll see what I can do for you when my tired body produces energy" David laughed.

"David Beeches, I give up on you. I think it best for me to get out of here before I really send you to your dead lover" Tracy said angrily as she flung the door wide opened in anger. She faced him saying, "Have you made a mistake loving me?"

"Tracy, why do you ask that?" David asked.

"Because my name is not Louise:"

"How can you be so jealous of a dead woman? Yes, as I said, I did love Louise, but she's no longer alive. Now I'm with you because I'm in love with you. If you don't set your childishness aside, we might as well call it a day, and kiss goodbye."

Tracy turned and faced David in tears, saying, "David, you're so right. I'm acting like a spoilt child. After all, I should thank my lucky stars that Louise is not here. Mind-you, I'm so sorry she was murdered. I really am" she said then slapped David's bottom smiled and pulled his trousers off before she turned the lights off and jumped into bed and made love then they both dropped off to sleep.

Meanwhile, as Ryan was on his way to the toilet, he met Eugene coming out,

"So you really are a doctor. By the way, how is your patient?" Eugene asked

"She has lost plenty of blood, but she's now stable." Ryan said.

"Well, I'll be damned. You're really a true doctor." Eugene said again smiling and in a charming manner.

"Yes, I think I am and it's a long story my friend. Believe me, without my precious sister Den, I wouldn't have ever been heard of again." Ryan told Eugene showing gratitude all over his face.

As Meleta heard Ryan's voice, she rushed out of his room and into his arms and kissed him in the presence of Eugene. Eugene smiled looking at them.

"Are you jealous Eugene, maybe if you be nice to Denyah, you might just be lucky getting a kiss from her." Meleta said smiling.

Denyah was woken up by the laughing and talking coming from Ryan and Eugene. She flung a gown on and came out of her room to see Eugene watching Meleta and Ryan on the landing kissing. As she watched them she smiled, then she realized how much Meleta and Ryan are in love. Still smiling, she took Eugene by the hand and they went back to bed leaving Meleta in Ryan's arms on the landing and kissing.

Next morning over breakfast, Ryan talked of his reinstatement working as a surgeon. As it was so painful to speak of, he cut short his story and told Eugene and Meleta it was Denyah that had made it possible for him to be that caring doctor again. As tears came into his eyes, he softly blew his nostrils in his white handkerchief then he cried. Denyah gave him her shoulder to cry on and said, "Ryan, please stop your crying. I wouldn't have you crying on my shoulders anymore. You're a very good doctor and a loving son and brother to our adopted mother and to me, and we love you. That's why God has guided you in the right direction so that you would have a second chance as he'd guided me also that I could live my life again. My dad once told me, Wesley might lust after my sister Fay, but no matter how much he bedded her, he would see my face in hers as he's in love with me. Dad was so right about that bastard husband of mine. He was so in love with me that he treated me worst than a hunter would treat a vicious animal. So you see Ryan, all of us have a task to go through, whether it would be good or bad. But it is God who rules the world and faith is the master of our destiny."

Meleta and Eugene listened to Denyah with interest as she spoke to Ryan. They said nothing but looked remorseful. Eugene, gently touched Denyah on her shoulder before he went into the kitchen to get a glass of water for Ryan. Denyah followed behind him leaving Ryan and Meleta both in tears as they were hugging each other. Before Eugene and Denyah joined Meleta and Ryan again, Ryan asked Meleta "Will you marry me?"

Meleta lowered her head as she answered, "Ryan, you know I will marry you this minute. Oh yes of course Ryan darling, I would marry you." she said proudly and happily flinging her arms around his neck.

Ryan deep blue eyes sparkled with happiness as though he had chosen a wife from a thousand women. He became so happy, he went into the kitchen and broke the news to Denyah and Eugene telling them, "I just asked Meleta to be my wife and she accepted. So we decided to get married soon."

Denyah went to Meleta and hugged her and said, "Meleta, are you sure you want to marry my brother?"

"Den, it's the first time I have ever been sure and serious in my life about the man I loved. I love Ryan and we both are absolutely sure about each other" Meleta said.

"I know now how much you love my brother but I would like for both of you to do the right thing, and not rush into marriage and regret later as I did." Denyah said.

"Denyah, you're married for ten years. I'm sure you were in love with your husband" Meleta said.

Denyah then faced Meleta and told her "Yes, I was in love with my ex-husband. But not anymore, he killed the love I had for him a long time ago. However, you and Ryan have my blessing. If that's what you both want, to get married, just let me know when."

"Well nothing finalised yet sis. But you would be right in the middle." Ryan said and hugged Denyah. Meleta also hugged Denyah and told her, "I don't know how to love Ryan anymore." Tears came into her eyes.

Denyah hugged her.

She dried her tears before she said. "Den, you were so right when you said I would be the woman your brother would marry."

Denyah smiled saying, "I remember telling you Meleta."

The following Saturday evening while Glennis was on his way to get his nurse friend, he phoned before he got to her house saying, "I'm on my way."

"I'm also ready and waiting." she told him. He smiled and rang off. Ten minutes later he got to her house. As he sat in his car, he smiled and then he got out and went and rings her door bell. The nurse's mother answered the door.

"Good evening." He said.

"Well good evening young man." Kelly's mother said.

"I came to take your daughter to dinner." Glennis said.

"Well you better come in" she told him. He walked in smiling.

The Nurse's mother smiled also and she took him into the dining room to meet her husband where he was having his tea. Glennis introduced himself.

"Pleasure to meet you, Glennis," The husband said and introduced himself as Kelly's dad. "Mom, please don't wait up for me." the nurse said.

"Kelly, you know I won't be feeling okay until you're safely in the house." her mother said.

"Mother, this is Doctor Glennis."

"Well I'm glad to know you Doctor Glennis but please take care of my only daughter"

"I will." Glennis said.

"I'm Kayla." Kelly mother said.

"Well Kayla, it's so pleasant meeting you." Glennis said. Then he shook Nurse Kelly's father's hand.

"Oh, I'm Calvin." Her father said smiling.

"Well Glennis, I'm ready if you are?" Kelly said.

"Well nice meeting you both, Kayla and Calvin. Glennis and Nurse Kelly left in his car to go and have dinner at the Savoy Hotel where he had booked for them to have dinner. The music was nice and the dinner was great. After dinner, Glennis took Nurse Kelly to her home and thanking her for having dinner with him and asked her out again to dinner.

After that second time they had dinner, they became lovers.

Nurse Kelly mother and dad got to like Glennis very much that they invited him to many dinners the following Sunday when Kelly was off not working.

After dinner, Glennis joked saying to Kelly; I can see the resemblance between you, your mother and father."

"Yes, my father is black and her mother white." Kelly laughed while Glennis kept serious. "Come on Glennis, where's your sense of humour." Glennis smiled before his smiled turned into laughter. Late that evening Glennis said good night and left.

Five weeks later, Glennis asked Kelly to move in with him. She told her parents and her parents asked Glennis to move into their four bedroom house instead. The following day, Glennis then told Ryan, but Ryan advised him, "Mate, I think you should get to know Kelly first as you only just met her. But it's up to you if you're serious about her and want to move in the family house."

Doctor Glennis smiled but said nothing then looked hard into Ryan's eyes. Ryan shrugged his shoulders smiling then said, "It's up to you mate if you want to move in with her.

Two days later, Meleta and Ryan announced they are getting married on the twenty first of July which was two months away. Denyah was delighted with the news and she phoned Lisa, Cindy and Claire and told them Ryan and Meleta were engaged to be married in July.

Lisa was also happy to have heard the good news and told Denyah to keep her up to date about the wedding.

It was also Ryan's first week working nights at the Heartlands Hospital on the accident and emergency ward. His first week working nights was interesting as he was out of practice, but he coped well and he enjoyed working amongst some brilliant surgeons and nurses, and getting to know the patients he worked on.

The Saturday morning after Ryan signed off from his night shift, he went to see Glennis at his flat.

After Ryan spoke to Glennis, he phoned the City Hospital to ask how his patient was doing. As the nurse hesitated on telling him, he said to her, she was brought in by me and another doctor four days ago with stab wounds."

"Are you a relative" Nurse Julie asked.

"I'm Doctor Ryan Taylor, I and Doctor Glennis brought her in with stabbed wounds as I have just stated to you."

"Oh, that's correct. She's stable and is now off the critical list. Did you say that you're a doctor?" Nurse Julie asked.

"Yes, that's correct." Ryan answered "Anyhow, thanks for letting me know and please give her my regards."

"Thanks for phoning Doctor Taylor, and I will pass on your message to her."

Nurse Julie said and hung up the phone.

Ryan smiled and said goodbye to his friend Doctor Glennis.

"Ryan before you leave, you remember Nurse Kelly?" Glennis asked him.

"No, I can't say I do. Ryan joked. Of course I remembered her, anyway, what happened between you and her?"

"Ryan I love her. I also met her mother and father and we're engaged"

"So you got to know her name after all" Ryan asked.

"Yes Ryan. She would be Mrs Kelly Morgan soon. I love her. I really do."

"So were all your other women?" Ryan said.

"Believe Ryan, I hadn't felt the same to any of them. But being with Kelly, I felt so affectionate and different and I know it is love I feel for her. But I'm not in a hurry to move in to her mother's home. I want when we're married we would be living in our own home. Ryan I'm also sure she's a virgin. Ryan, I would like to take care of her."

Ryan smiled and said. "Good for you mate" Then drove home and broke the news to Meleta and Denyah that the stabbed wife is now off the critical list. Denyah and Meleta were happy to hear that.

"Would you like your breakfast now or after you get some sleep?" Meleta asked him.

"Just some coffee for now and I'll have something to eat later after I get some sleep as I can hardly keep my eyes open." Ryan said.

"Okay, you won't mind me going out to do some shopping with Denyah" Meleta asked him.

"Not at all, you go do your shopping and later this evening we go hunting for house" Ryan told her.

"Well, you don't mind me asking you for some money?" Meleta asked him.

"Of course not sweetheart, would three hundred do?" he asked.

"That's much too much Ryan honey. But thanks. Oh Ryan, would you like me to bring you something back?" she asked him.

"Only you my love, well you and Den have a nice day." he said.

"Oh we will Ryan. We will, and thanks again for the money." she said.

"You're very welcome sweetheart" he said to Meleta before she and Denyah set out for shopping.

That Saturday night it was Ryan's night off. On the Saturday afternoon when Meleta returned from shopping, she gave Ryan bottle of expensive and nice smelling after shave labelled Boss, "I had no idea I smelt high." Ryan joked.

Meleta laughed, "I think you deserved the best as it is your money I spent. I also love you so much that I want to have your baby." she said teasing.

"How do you fancy going house hunting now?" he asked her.

"Just let me catch my breath then we leave aye," Meleta said happily.

Before Ryan and Meleta set out for house hunting, Meleta said, "Denyah, Ryan asked me to go and look on some houses that are on sale. Would you like to come?"

"No, you and Ryan carry on, if I can, I might catch up with you both later" Denyah told her.

Ryan and Meleta left in their car and ended up on the outskirts Edgbaston on Broad Street where they saw some newly built detached four and five bedroom houses. They stopped and had a look at the sale board. As Meleta was writing down notes and phone numbers of some houses, a middle-aged black woman opened her front door and said to Meleta. "Love I don't think you can afford to buy any of these houses around here. So many people have tried to buy a house here, but because of the price, they have to change their minds. However, good luck in buying one. Even though my husband and I are head teachers, we just about managed to come up with the deposit to buy ours. Well, as I said, I wish both of you well. You are married aren't you?"

"No, but I soon will be" Meleta said proudly.

The woman pursed her lips and closed her door. Meleta and Ryan laughed. "Typical black woman," said Ryan.

"Aye, remember I'm the same" Meleta said laughing.

"When it comes to you honey, I'm colour blind," Ryan said in good spirit.

Meleta laughed. Then says "She seems like a busy neighbourhood watchdog to warn everybody off that comes to look at these houses."

"She's more like an inquisitive rattle snake" Ryan said and then went on to say "Well honey, as we are not married, we won't fit in here according to the snake woman. I don't think we would be welcome around here unless we get married. However, here comes Denyah and Eugene."

After Eugene and Denyah caught up with Ryan and Meleta, Ryan asked Eugene "Would you buy a house in this area?"

"No, I don't think so. Then again, if the neighbours are as nice as they seem to be peering from behind their curtains, as Mrs busy body is doing now, I would definitely go for that one facing her just to torment her. But my choice would be buying one of those five bedroom houses at the top of the Street. I had a look in couple of them last Tuesday and I like the double garage, iron railings, fence and gates" Eugene said. He then paused with a nice smile.

"Oh, I accompanied a friend. He is looking for a bigger house" Eugene smiled looking at Ryan in a peculiar way.

"Come out with it Eugene, ask or tell me what you want" Ryan said.

"And what makes you think I have something to ask or tell you?" Eugene replied smiling.

"Because I've recognised that smile" Ryan said.

"Okay Ryan, I know it's none of my business but where would you get the money from to buy a house in this part? A newly built four or five bedroom cost at least four to five hundred and twenty thousands" Eugene asked interestingly

"He came into some money Eugene" Denyah said.

"Like the money I gave to you Den?"

"No Eugene, like millions - he told you that Mrs Carter has left more than one hundred and eighty four millions pounds between Ryan and me, as well, as jewellery, bonds and her insurance. I also get the house and Ryan got the guest house but he gave that to me as a play house for Paris. Eugene, I can buy my freedom from Wesley. I will pay him to divorce me. And I should have let you know before now. I'm sorry that I failed to be honest to you. But as you didn't take Ryan serious when he told you about his inheritance, I was choosing the right time to tell you he told you the truth"

"Okay honey, I forgive you in delaying telling me about your inheritance. But as for that by-passed husband of yours, you would do no such thing by giving him one penny. That filthy bastard, don't deserve not even a look from you. You'll get your divorce from him one way or the other including your daughter Paris. And about the money that you and Ryan had inherited, wasn't there any living relative Mrs Carter has?"

"No Eugene, I was told she has no living relatives. She had a brother but he died in a pick-up truck accident when he was nineteen. He was her only relative. She told me. However, Ryan and I are the only relatives as far as my adopted mother were concerned when she was alive. Not even a child she had, she told me. I didn't even realize she was worth millions. Well, she made Ryan and I her heirs. So Ryan and I would have an equal share of everything she has left to us. Except the house if he moved out. However, I'm going to give you one million from my share. Eugene, if you'd known Ryan inherited so much money would you still bought him the car?"

"Denyah, I don't need your money. And yes, I would have bought him the car."

"Well don't you think it would be wise to put some money into a trust for Paris' future, rather than to give your money to that rotten bastard ex-husband?"

"I will do that tomorrow plus my share of the diamonds that I will leave to Paris and any other kids I may have, if I'm so lucky to have any, when they at least eighteen or twenty one. As for selling any of the jewellery, I won't." Denyah said.

"I think you should have them valued before putting them into trust."

"I did, I had three of the rubies and six diamonds and a string of black pearls plus three others valued last week. The six diamonds would be worth seventeen millions and a half or more, and the three rubies worth sixteen to twenty millions. As for the black pearls, they're in a class of their own. Eugene there is twenty more pieces of them for me and the same for Ryan. I am even told by the jeweller if I'm selling, I must give him the opportunity but I don't think that I want to sell any of mine now." "Wise girl, Den." Eugene said.

CHAPTER SEVEN

Five weeks later, Ryan and Meleta bought a five bedroom house in the Harborne area. The living room was enormous the dining room also large with a good size kitchen that holds a double oven cooker, a large double door fridge freezer, dish washer and a dining area and a division for a laundry room, a play room for kids. After three weeks, Meleta and Ryan had the whole house extended and added a double garage, a medium bedroom and a second playing area up stairs for children as well a walking wardrobe. But the play area would not be finished for another two or three weeks.

After the house was repaired and additions on to the front and back, it was big and roomy with yard room to build at least another house. But a month later Ryan told Meleta he's thinking of building a guesthouse. Ryan also took Denyah and Eugene to have a look at the house after he had it improved. "I think you have done well mate, and you still have enough yard room to build a guesthouse. Anyway, what makes you buy this one, when there're so many houses on the market for sale?" Eugene asked Ryan.

"Eugene, you were so right mate about those new houses that are on the market - how they're paper thin. However, I like this four bedrooms detached house. It has class, and I really like the arched doors and the high ceilings. Besides, it's Meleta's choice. Den, you wouldn't mind Meleta and me squatting in your home for a month or two until the repairing is fully complete as Meleta wants to add a playing area?"

"Ryan, not because you're moving out, you still have the right to live here. So, never ask again, just come home at any time" Denyah said to Ryan.

"Anyway, Den, Meleta and I only like to stay for a little while, while the workmen tie up the loose ends and finishing the play area. I trust it won't be for too long. I wanted our house to be up to standard before my gorgeous wife and I moved in. I'm sure it won't be too long" Ryan said.

Ryan and Meleta gave up their rented one bedroom flat and moved in with Denyah as Denyah's house was finished being repaired.

"Well," said Ryan, "I would not think that this old box would have turned out to be a shining mirror. Mom must be smiling down on us."

"Well my dear brother, mom would like you and me to spend happy time in this house to keep her memory alive" Denyah said with happy feelings.

After the late Mrs Carter's house was restored again to look almost new with an addition of playing area and the whole house nicely painted and decorated, Meleta, Ryan and Eugene were so amazed to see the late Mrs Carter's tatty mansion reformed back to its full glory and looking spectacular in and outside. Amazingly, Denyah had the old mahogany furniture transformed to look new. "The old lady must be here smiling and looking on us four." Ryan said again as he was so full with joy.

"After all, Denyah, you're not only a beautiful woman but a saviour. Girlfriend, you have earned everything you got" Meleta said.

"Except the ex-husband I left behind" Denyah joked and they laughed.

Eugene and Ryan tossed whiskey as Denyah and Meleta had snowballs to celebrate their future as family.

"Really," Ryan said, "Just look at our mom's house. It looks brand new, spacious and lovely and fresh. Just look at the rooms, the workmen have altered every room to make them much nicer and roomier. Even the rusted iron frames doors and windows had been replaced with the best double glazing and dark mahogany frames."

Ryan and Meleta were fascinated by the new conservatory and the arched doors that had added class to the house to separate the dining and living room from the kitchen plus an eating area. Smiling, Meleta faced Ryan and said, "honey, we should take Denyah's idea and recycle our home - even though we have arched doors of course, but we should add to our home a new a conservatory and an eating area since we added a baby room and another bathroom. We should also build a second shower room. The conservatory would make our house look beautiful - and a patio door at the back!" Meleta said and sat on Ryan's knees.

"Would that make you happy my sweet," Ryan asked her.

She kissed him and said "Yes" as she faced Denyah and said, "Den, I think we should go shopping tomorrow for plants and furniture for your conservatory. Just look at your gardens front and back. Everywhere looks so beautiful and cheerful. That's how I would want mine to be" Meleta kissed Ryan again and then she went on to say "Oh Ryan" she then inhaled deeply before she went on to say, "We shall have the conservatory to look just like Denyah's" Suddenly her mouth partly opened as she faced him again and said, "Ryan".... and stopped showing sad expression on her face.

"Meleta, what are going to tell me now?" he asked her with interest.

She faced him and threw her arms around his neck and said "Honey, you're going to be a father" she faced Denyah, and said, "Den, you would soon be an Aunt, I'm seven weeks pregnant. I saw my doctor this morning. Denyah, I'm so happy. Den, I'm not being ungrateful but the sooner Ryan and I moved in our own home the happier I would be. As this would be a new beginning for me and Ryan to be living together as a real family."

Ryan looked hard at Denyah smiling without saying anything. Then he turned and looked hard and long at Meleta with a mixture of sadness and happiness.

Denyah said "Ryan please don't look so sad. She is right. Just let me know when your house has been completely repaired and you're ready to move in. Oh, the sooner you get married the better as Meleta wouldn't want her pregnancy to show in her wedding dress. " Denyah smiled then went on to say, "well, we'll have to live apart one day, but even so, we'll still get under one another's feet as we're family. Meleta, I'm so happy it's you my brother is going to marry."

Ryan smiled and then hugged Denyah with love.

Two weeks later, Tuesday night, Ryan and Meleta moved in to their new home. Meleta gave Denyah one of her house keys as she has one of Denyah's.

"Den, my home's completed, so you let yourself in at anytime. And I'm inviting you and few lady friends to have a drink and to celebrate my new home. "

"Well thank-you Meleta."

The following Saturday afternoon, Meleta invited Denyah, Lisa, Claire, Cindy, Gene, Grace, Tracy and Kelly to her house to have a drink, rice and curry mutton. As they walk into Meleta's house, their mouths opened, except Denyah's. "Meleta, you must have won plenty of money to have a home like this." Grace said.

Meleta showed them around her house and Claire jumped on Meleta's bed and said "Meleta, if ever your man is in need of another woman, I'm free, single and disengaged."

Meleta laughed and took them downstairs into the dining room for food and drinks. And then they dance to some tune.

Much later that evening they hugged and kiss Meleta goodbye and went home.

As Ryan got home from work, he met Meleta cleaning the kitchen. "Had you a party?" he asked her smiling.

I invited Denyah and some friends to have a drink and a meal. I left you some food. I couldn't tell you as it weren't a planned party. Honey, they loved our home and I love you."

A week later, Meleta bought wedding invitations to give to friends and family but changed her mind.

Two weeks later, Meleta and Ryan went and got married at the Town Registry Office. As soon as she and Ryan got home, she phoned Denyah and told her that she and Ryan would like to see her and Eugene at the Ibis Hotel at seven 'o'clock. Meleta also phoned Gene, Grace, Tracy and invited them to dinner at the hotel. A little later she phoned Lisa, Doctor Glennis and his girlfriend Kelly, Claire, Cindy and all the husbands but didn't get them. Later she phoned them again and invited them to meet her at the hotel at seven 'o'clock. When they all turned up at the hotel for dinner, buckets with iced bottles champagne were awaiting them. Then, as a love song was playing (I want to wake up with you.) the hotel room went silent and the guests remained still for a brief moment before Ryan said to them "Meleta and I got married ten 'o'clock this morning at the Town Registry Office."

"You what," Denyah asked.

"Sis, I should have let you know before. Please forgive me."

"Honey, I'm happy for both you and Meleta and I think you both have done the right thing." Denyah told him.

"Thanks sis, I invited all of you my family and friends here to celebrate with my wife and I on this evening our wedding day." Ryan said.

After that song finished played, the manager announced Mr and Mrs Ryan and Meleta Taylor were married this morning."

Then Ryan stood up and announced. "I and the lady I'm in love with are now married."

Denyah stood up and said, "I wasn't at all surprised as I once heard Meleta said she would like to have a quiet marriage. But at the same time, I thought she would make me her chief bridesmaid." Laughter came from all.

Ryan went and said to the manager. "I would like you to serve each table with two bottles of champagne and food for all tonight and no charge to any customers."

"No charge? Are you sure about this Mr Taylor?"

"I'm quite sure Sir," Ryan said and he made out a cheque for one hundred thousand pounds and gave it to the hotel manager asking. "Will this amount cover drinks and meals for everyone that comes here tonight?"

The manager took the cheque and looked long and hard at it then a smile broke out on his face as he had a second look at the cheque again in somewhat of a trance and said, "Mr Taylor, you over-paid me."

"Let's say we became friends. You never know when my wife will turn down her pot on me and I may have to come to you with my begging bowl for a meal." Ryan said.

"Mr Taylor, please call me Dennis. And I would really like you and the wife to come and have a meal and drink at anytime. And I would be happy for us to be friends Mr Taylor."

"Please call me Ryan." Ryan said and went and sat by his wife Meleta.

The manager then announced free drinks and food for everyone with compliments from the newly weds, Mr, Mrs Ryan Taylor." And he ordered his staff to put on each table two bottles of champagne.

Everyone stood in respect leaving Ryan and Meleta sitting. They raised their glasses of champagne as they wish the married couple the best and a very happy and long life together. Ryan and Meleta got up and raised their glasses champagne.

Over dinner, Meleta showed off her beautiful diamond and sapphire heart shaped wedding ring that was engraved with her and Ryan's initials M.R.T. signifying Meleta Ryan Taylor. After they had dinner, they left the hotel and finished the evening having a party at Denyah's in honour of Meleta and Ryan being married and expecting their first baby and Ryan to start his job as a doctor again the following Wednesday night. As Ryan thought of Mrs Carter, he burst into crying and hugging her photo to his chest before he kissed her face and rested it on the glass unit.

Early Sunday morning, Denyah had morning sickness but she said nothing to anyone, not even the father of her baby.

One week later, Tuesday morning she went to see her doctor. After a thorough examination, her doctor smiled and said "Mrs Davis, your morning sickness is caused by your little precious. In other words, you're now six weeks pregnant." Denyah was left speechless and stunned by the news of her pregnancy after losing her first baby from her ex-husband nearly nine years ago when he pushed her down the stairs and thereafter hoping for another, which had never happened.

While her doctor was writing out the prescription, she were looking hard at Denyah over her turtle framed glasses what was more under her turned-up white nose rather than resting on her nose. Smiling, she gave Denyah the written prescription and said, "Mrs Davis, if the morning sickness goes on for more than three weeks would you make an appointment to see me? However, I do think you need to take one of these iron tablets every day and if the morning sickness stopped before six weeks, I still would like to see you. And please do take the tablets as you're a bit on the anaemic side. Oh, on your next visit, would you please bring me a sample of urine."

She then gave Denyah a small see-through plastic vial. Denyah thanked her doctor, smiled and left. She stopped at the pharmacy and got her tablets and drove home to meet her fiancée. Eugene having breakfast but still she did not tell him she's pregnant. He noticed the down hearted look on her face and asked her, "What did the doctor say honey?" she looked deeply at him with a stiff upper lip and then faced Ryan and said "So you brought a lovely five bedroom house just twenty minutes drive away from me."

"Yes Den, so that we can be near to each other. Besides, you and Meleta can see one another as often as you like. I bought her a car too so she has no excuse not to come and visit" Ryan said to Denyah.

Two weeks later, the Wednesday morning, Denyah picked up a letter that was addressed to Eugene. That evening, as soon as Eugene got home she gave the letter to him. He looked at her for a few seconds before he went into the dining room and opened the enveloped to find a wedding invitation from his friends Austin and Joan stating "for you only". Denyah shortly followed behind him as she had suspected that it was an invitation from Joan and Austin as Lisa had hers two days before. Eugene turned and looked at her. Smiling, he slipped the invitation into his jacket pocket then faced her.

She watched him and waited for him to tell her about the invitation but he said nothing. Neither did she ask him who had sent him a letter at her address.

A week later, he asked her to take his suit to the dry cleaners as Meleta had accidentally spilt red wine on the front of his jacket while showing Ryan and telling him Eugene had bought the suit a week ago to wear to Austin and Joan's wedding.

The next day he reminded Denyah to take his suit to the dry cleaners to have the wine stain removed.

Denyah asked him, "Why do you want the suit to be cleaned when you only bought it a week ago,"

"Den, if you remember, Meleta had accidentally spilt red wine on the jacket when I showed it to Ryan and at the same time she was proudly showing off her wedding ring to you lot when her glass dropped from her hand."

"Oh yes, I remember" she said.

The next morning before she took the suit to the dry cleaners she went through his pockets to move what was there. She found the invitation from Austin and Joan stating, Eugene only. Even though the invitation stated Eugene only, she waited patiently on him to tell her, but he said nothing to her, and this had left her feeling sickened and disgusted knowing that she trusted and love him so much. Although she gave him the envelope, he never did tell her about the invitation.

Four weeks before the wedding, he still hadn't said anything to her about the invitation. And she didn't let him know that she knew. Tears came into her eyes when she thought he wasn't any better than her ex-husband.

As Austin and Joan wedding day drew closer and had one week left for them to get married, Lisa phoned her asking her, "Are you going to the wedding or the reception?"

"Who's wedding?" she asked Lisa coldly.

"Come off it Denyah, you knew Joan and Austin would be getting married in four days Saturday, and an invitation was sent to you and Eugene by Joan and Austin. Beside, Eugene is Austin's best man."

"Lisa, I'm sorry I have to tell you that I won't be going to either." Denyah said.

"What do you mean?" Lisa asked.

"As I said, I wasn't invited to the wedding or the reception. So please do not mention any of this to me again. The invitation stated to Eugene only. The bride-to-be has made it clear that she doesn't want me at her wedding."

"Denyah, I don't know what to say." Lisa said sadly.

"Well I do! So please, don't ask me again." said Denyah and hung up.

Two days left before Joan and Austin's wedding on the eighteen of October at two thirty the Saturday afternoon at St Michael's Church.

Lisa phoned Denyah again. "Den," she said very sympathetically "I know you told me you don't want me to speak to you again about Joan's wedding. But please hear me out…" Denyah was just about to put the phone down.

"Please Den; I would like you to come with me to the reception just to keep my company" Lisa begged her.

Denyah sighed, "Lisa, I have already told you the reason why I'm not going. So which part you do not understand. Ryan and Meleta were also invited so you would have more than enough company to assist you. Beside, your husband would be with you. Now, if you would excuse me, I have some work in my garden that urgently needs to be done. Good bye Lisa and have a good time and please do not get drunk" Denyah hung up. Lisa shook her head sadly and put her phone down after Denyah hung up.

Eleven thirty Friday morning, Lisa phoned Denyah and asked her, "Would you like to go with me to the hairdressers?"

"Yes, of course Lisa, I would be happy to go with you to the hair dressers" Denyah said and went with her, but Denyah refused to have her hair done even though Lisa had offered to pay for her.

"Denyah, you know that you are my best friend no matter what."

"Yes Lisa, I know." Denyah said as she and Lisa walked out of the hairdressers and headed to the Asda restaurant where they had a meal and coffee. As they were eating, Lisa said, "I think I saw your mother and your sister Blanch yesterday afternoon in The Bull Ring doing shopping. I didn't think they saw me as the place was crowded with shoppers."

"Lisa you won't believe - she wanted to see me. After what she has done to me, I wondered why the change of heart?" Denyah said.

"Maybe she came to her senses and felt ashamed about the way she treated you" Lisa said.

"Or maybe she wants to tell me off some more. Well, whatever her reason, she won't hurt me anymore than she already has." Denyah said.

"That's the way to think Den." Lisa said laughing.

All of a sudden, Lisa eyes filled with tears as she said to Denyah, "You took me back as your friend and as your family. I didn't give up on you, you know, but I was frightened that if I had you at my home again, it might so easy for Wesley to hurt you. However, I'm going to help you to get Paris away from him. He doesn't deserve to have you or her. I couldn't believe what he has done to you. Even though he's my brother, I shall never forgive him for what he has done to you and he almost split us up. He's one devious son of a bitch. Mother, I don't mean to slag you down. But you gave birth to a mischievous lousy no good for nothing brother. And believe me Denyah, as I said, I shall never forget or forgive him for the evil doings that he has done to you. My husband feels even worse than me. He feels so hurt and so ashamed by how he put us against you that he cried. How could my brother trick his mates into having sex with you, and then convince Richard and me that you were having affairs. Den, he is my brother, but also a rotten evil animal."

"It's now behind me Lisa, you can tell Richard that my husbands mates didn't had sex with me as my ex-husband had wanted. When they saw me crying they were softened and changed their minds."

"So Wesley thought they had sex with you?"

"Yes Lisa. But let's not rake over the past. You just remember to tell Richard I still love him and he's forgiven and he owes to me a big hug and I will be seeing him when I'm ready"

"You're coming to the reception with me aren't you Den?"

"Lisa, I would love to go with you. But I had a phone call from the bride herself telling me she doesn't want me at her wedding."

"Why? I surely don't think that she means that." Lisa said.

"You asked why, well I am the greatest whore of all women and she thinks I might steal her husband. Oh well, my husband made sure he warned everyone about me. I'm also sure my husband told Joan his two mates bedded me, one of them is her Uncle. My ex-husband gave them proof of that too. Even you had believed him. But I thank the good lord you'd woken up to see your brother's lies. Anyway, as I said to you before, you go and have a good time. Then you can tell me everything. Eugene will be there, he is Austin's best man. So, with him there and the rest of the family, you won't be short of company." Denyah said to Lisa.

"Please Denyah, come with me. When we get there, I will explain to Joan what had happened, besides, Paris will be there. I'm sure Joan would have a change of heart and as for Paris, she would be more than happy to see you."

"Ok Lisa, I'll come but don't be too surprised if the door shuts in my face. Lisa, why don't you let me have your baby until you get back instead," Denyah said.

"Oh no, my friend Kate will be looking after the baby. Are you trying to avoid coming with me to the reception?"

"No Lisa, I'm just being cautious about not getting kicked out the door. But since you insisted I should come with you, I will."

"Thanks Denyah, I will call for you about five. Don't freeze up on me when I call."

"Alright Lisa, I will come only to prove to you that Joan wouldn't want me at her wedding or at her home."

Two thirty Saturday afternoon, Joan and Austin were married. One hour later after guests said their speeches the table were opened to a sit down dinner and after everyone had eaten, Eugene went to Denyah's home to get changed out of his cream suit. Denyah watched him change into a nice pale blue three piece suit, brown silk long sleeved shirt, blue and brown stripe tie and brown shoes. He then faced Denyah and asked her "How do I look sweetheart?"

"You looked ravenous honey. You looked absolutely great and your blue suit picks out the handsome look in your sexy sea blue eyes." Denyah said to Eugene.

He smiled broadly then asked, "You're coming aren't you Den?"

"I don't think so Eugene. And you look absolutely great. Get out of here before I trick you into coming into bed with me and then give you a powerful sleeping sex dose." Denyah joked.

Eugene laughed and then asked "Why don't you want to come with me sweet heart?"

"Because you had the invitation for six weeks and you didn't tell me. So I know that my place is in the dog kennel amongst the dogs."

"Den honey, it wasn't like that at all. I simple forgot to tell you."

"Oh no Eugene, you didn't forget. As a matter of fact, I had a friendly phone call from the bride herself, telling me she doesn't want me at her wedding. So please spare me the embarrassment and go without me. Like her, you already knew why she scorned me. If you have forgotten, let me refresh your memory - I'm greatest whore of a bitch in Birmingham. Eugene, the invitation was meant for you only. So don't you pretend that you want me to come with you! So, just go back to your wedding and leave me alone. I wouldn't want you to be ashamed of me. " Denyah was so very upset that tears came in her eyes.

Eugene stood to attention and astounded looking hard at her before he said, "Denyah honey, you're the woman I have and want."

Denyah said nothing but looked at his face then walked out of the house in tears and went into her back garden to look at her spouted cabbages and tomatoes to avoid him asking her to accompany him again. While she was pulling out weeds from amongst the vegetables, Ryan went to her and touched her on her shoulder. She stood up, turned and looked at him. He smiled.

"Ryan, you looked stunning in that blue three piece suit and your matching black silk dog collar shirt and black shoes" Denyah told Ryan. He smiled at the compliment.

"Denyah, I would like you to come with me and Meleta. I will wait on you until you're ready." Ryan said.

Denyah smiled and said "Ryan you looked so handsome. You take your beautiful wife and both of you go and enjoy yourselves"

Denyah beginning pulling out weeds again,

"Please Denyah, stopped pulling the weeds and come with us." Ryan said calmly.

Denyah smiled before she walked out the garden with Ryan by her side. They both looked hard at each other for at least a couple of seconds without saying a word. Then Denyah smiled and said to him, "You looked absolutely fabulous Ryan" she then kissed him on his right cheek. He smiled and hugged her before he walked off to meet his wife Meleta as she was walking towards him and Denyah. Denyah brushed some dirt off of her hands and met Meleta by the border of the lower part of the garden. "Meleta, you're very beautiful and you're looking great." Denyah said.

"You're coming aren't you Den?" Meleta asked her showing deep concern.

"I'll catch up with you later. Lisa's giving me a lift" Denyah told her so not to delay them.

"Okay Den and don't be too long. I'll see you later then," said Meleta and then she left with her husband Ryan to go to the wedding party. Eugene looked at Denyah in wonder and guilt of course, as he stood close to Ryan.

"You better be off also, otherwise you may lose your seat next to your precious bride and groom. Remember you're best man." Denyah told Eugene as she held a straight face.

Eugene stared her in the face as she hesitated to hug him as he was hugging her. As she made him felt uneasy, he loosened his arms from around her waist and walked away. She stood staring at him and feeling so much love for him that tears came into her eyes. Quickly, she ran into his arms and kissed his lips. His face brightened with a smile before he kissed her passionately with deep love feeling. She also felt over powered with love for him and didn't want to let him loose. As she barely loosed her hands from around his neck, he said to her, "If I don't see you at the reception by seven, I'm coming to get you."

She smiled, he kissed her again. Telling her, "I love you so much." he then walked away smiling.

"You go and have a good time and remember I love you very much. So please, don't worry about me. Just don't fall in love with any other women." she told him.

He faced her and smiled as she reassured him with happiness and made him feel comfortable. He walked back to her and kissed her and then left smiling. She watched him open his car door. He turned facing her and blew her a kiss before he got in his car and drove away with Ryan and Meleta following behind in their car and leaving her standing and watching until their cars had disappeared out of her sight.

She smiled and she went back into the garden to pull out more weeds from amongst the vegetables until it was four thirty when she left the garden and went and got ready. Nervously, she looked at the wall clock and then at the telephone before she put the T.V on and poured herself a glass of red wine and sat down on the settee to watch a romantic film. At the interesting part of the film, the doorbell rung so loud that it frightened her and she turned the TV off. As she sat in wonder and listening to the doorbell ringing, she raced down a full glass of wine - some had dribbled down the front of her cream trouser suit jacket because she was so nervous and her hands were shaking. Suddenly, the bell went quiet and after a couple of seconds, then came a loud bang on the door followed by a long aggravating sound of the door bell as if their finger was stuck on the bell. The doorbell had had sounded so aggravating that she jumped out of her seat in fright and stood frozen looking at the door. As she went weak because of the harrowing revolting sound, she built up courage and was going to answer the door when her high heeled shoe got stuck on one of Eugene's empty beer cans so she pitched forward and hitting her right foot on the coffee table leg, knocking over the opened bottle of wine from off the table and onto her new cream rug. "Shit!" she said and picked the bottle up put it on the coffee table and hopping to the door trembling on her painful right foot. Nervously, she fixed the chain to the door for protection before asking. "Who is there?"

"It's me Lisa. We have a party to go to. Remember?"

Denyah smiled and quickly removed the chain and opened the door.

"Haven't you got dressed yet?" Lisa asked.

"I didn't give you my address. I only give you my phone number. So how did you find me?"

"Denyah don't look so worried, I got your address from your sister Blanch. But don't worry, she asked me not to tell anyone else where you live. Your address is secret with me. Not even my husband I will tell. Now take off that sad looking mask and put the one on that always showed your beauty."

Denyah smiled,

"That's the mask I like to see you in." Lisa said.

"Thanks Lisa, I appreciate your friendship. I heard Richard has lost his job. If you should find it difficult for money, I would like to help. That's if you would want me too."

"Right now I could do with at least seven hundred pounds to bring the mortgage up to date" Lisa said as she and Denyah were walking into the living room.

"Den, were you having a fight with your cashmere rug?" Lisa asked.

"Oh, as I was going to answer the door, my foot hit the table and the bottle fell."

And the wine's run on the rug. Seven hundred pounds you said you want to bring your mortgage up to date?" Denyah asked.

"Denyah I'm just as crazy as you to tell you that I need money when you might be worse off than me. And don't you go and ask Eugene to lend us any money."

"Lisa my dear, I wouldn't do such thing, I've came in to a good amount of money. I might even have much more than Eugene has,"

"Please Den, don't make me laugh, especially now that I'm pregnant again and I always get hiccups when I laugh. Den I should have protected myself from having another baby so quickly"

"Lisa my friend, having another baby is not a crime. You should consider you're well blessed. However, I have inherited over ninety million pounds in cash plus much more in bonds, shares, insurance and jewellery from my adopted mother Mrs Carter. Oh, Ryan has inherited the same except this house has been left to me by her. And you know who I have to thank for all this? My evil husband who is your brother, so you see Lisa, good always conquers evil eventually. After my nurse friend had been murdered, I was looking for somewhere to live. And a very kind lady directed me to Mrs Carter who needed a carer. Well, Mrs Carter seemed to have liked me from the first time she saw me. I got to like her too. She asked me to live with her and so I did as she'd no living relatives, except, Ryan and me who she adopted as her son and daughter. Ryan has also inherited half of the one hundred and eighty four million pounds in cash. Plus the guest house, but he signed the guest house over to me as a play house for Paris. If you're wondering why he had a share in the fortune when we only employed him as a gardener, well, to cut a long story short, he hadn't a permanent home so we took him in as I found out he was sleeping rough in scrapped vehicles after he left work. The old lady was very happy when I took him in and offered him a home. As time went by, she got to like him as much as I did. Then I found out he used to be a doctor but gave up his position when two of his friends were killed in a car accident. Well, if you really would like my help, I'm just a phone call away or twenty minutes drive."

"Denyah, if I didn't know you, I would say you're pulling the wool over my eyes" Lisa said but still wasn't too sure about Denyah telling her the truth.

As Denyah saw the smirking smile on Lisa's face, she said, "Okay Lisa, you don't believe me? Come with me, I've something to show you."

Lisa looked hard on Denyah's face, smiled and shook her head then followed behind her up the stairs and into her bedroom. Denyah faced her and said "You know that I would never lie to you" she then carefully slid the late Mrs Carter's photo away from in front of the large twenty six inches wide and thirty two inches long silver gilt clock face built into her bedroom partition. She opened the safe showing Lisa the jewellery, certificates of saving bonds, insurance receipt from her solicitor and the bank statement of her inherited millions. Lisa could hardly believe her eyes. She sat on the edge of the bed and looking like she was wound in spider's web. With penetrating staring eyes fastened on the safe, while Denyah stood looking on at her. After Lisa had a good look at Denyah's inherited fortune, she looked up at Denyah and said, "I'm so sorry I have doubted you. But it was all too much for me to take in. I should have trusted you as I know you are very honest, but hearing this from you, it sounded like a fairy tale. I shall never doubt you again." Lisa replaced the jewellery and the certificates in the compartments of the safe as she found them and closed the safe door and then said "Denyah, you best lock the safe."

She then turned to leave as Denyah reached to lock the safe. "Lisa, you don't have to leave. I trusted you completely." After Denyah locked the safe, she slide Mrs Carter's photo in front the safe as it was before and then faced Lisa to see her with her mouth wide opened. Smiling, she hooked a double string of pears and mixed rubies on a diamond chain around Lisa's neck and a matching bracelet on her right wrist then hoisted her chin for her to close her mouth.

"You really can help us." Lisa said smiling.

"That's what I told you" Denyah said.

"Den, even though you're wealthy, I really can't accept this necklace. It must be worth quite a lot"

"Yes, it is. But what is a small gift to give a true friend- as well as that, you are my family. They only cost one hundred and sixty seven thousand and you are well worth it Lisa"

"Denyah, I'll get back to you with my answer as soon as I speak to Richard. However, you're still coming with me to the reception aren't you?" Lisa asked.

"I'm sorry that I have to say no. I can't." Denyah said.

"Why can't you Den?" Lisa asked sadly.

"Because I've already told you why the bride does not want me at her house and I'm not going where I'm not wanted. So please go and don't stay too long with your answer, and kiss Paris for me will you? Also, don't drown my nephew with to much champagne." Denyah said and touched Lisa's pregnant tummy.

Lisa smiled, "I might have a sip, nothing more, however, Den, about your nurse friend, maybe my brother had something to do with her death, but sadly I can't prove a damn thing. If I find out anything that will put him away I'll let you know and the police know. He's my brother and I love him but you have to draw the line somewhere, and especially how he's treated you. Look Den, will you please come with me and even the slightest remark about you, we'll leave."

"Okay Lisa, I'll go with you to the reception sine you begged me. But as you said, the slightest remarks about me, I will be home as quick as lightening."

Denyah changed into a light blue trouser suit that complimented a white silk shirt and white high heeled shoes and matching white hand bag. "Well, Lisa here I am. I decided to go to the reception with you,"

"Denyah you really are very beautiful. Core, you looked like fifty million dollars, you'll have every men head turned to look at you. Your earrings, necklace, wristwatch and bracelets are exquisite. I love the white daisies bracelet and earrings. Are they white gold?" Lisa asked.

"They are diamonds." Denyah answered.

"I'm sure they cost a fortune" Lisa said.

"About three million pounds or more, I haven't had them valued, but my adopted mom said they were worth three millions fifteen years ago. She and her husband had owned an expensive jewellery shop. But after her husband had passed away, she sold the shop and with some of the jewellery but kept most of the very expensive jewelleries. Now they're become mine" Denyah said.

"You deserved the best Den. You're a kind and lovely person. My brother doesn't deserve you. Now shall we get going to that reception before everyone leaves?" Lisa said anxiously.

Denyah smiled. But before she left with Lisa, she made out a cheque for ten thousand pounds to the bride and groom for a wedding gift. Before she and Lisa left the house, she double checked and made sure she'd left everything in place and the windows and doors locked. On their way to the reception, she asked Lisa to stop at the newspaper shop for her to buy a wedding card.

"You don't have to take her a card. I'm taking her a gift from both of us." Lisa told Denyah.

"Please stop the car Lisa. I rather give her a gift of my own." Denyah said.

Lisa stopped the car to let Denyah go and buy the card, after she bought the card and signed it and then put the cheque in it made out to Mr, Mrs Joan Austin Malden and sealed it before she got back into the car. "Can I read it?" Lisa asked.

"Oh, I've sealed it." Denyah said.

"That's ok," Lisa replied smiling.

Just before they arrived at the reception, Lisa had notice the frightful tension on Denyah's face. Lisa took one hand off the steering wheel to touch Denyah's hand and then said "Cheer up sweetie, as I have already told you, when we get there all eyes will turn on you because you will be the beauty amongst the beasts." Denyah smiled.

"That's the way I like to see you." Lisa said.

As they got to the house they both were welcomed with champagne outside before they went inside to meet the newlyweds. While Lisa went and congratulated the bride and groom, Denyah stayed unseen behind while some of the guests listened to the bride's father making his speech. Then as some of the guests were mingling, the bride saw Denyah and she left her husband and went over to her and looked seriously hard at her without saying one word. Denyah smiled and took the card out to her handbag and outstretched the card to give it to her, but she turned to walk away.

"Please Joan. I know I shouldn't be here, but Lisa begged me too come."

"Lisa's deadly wrong to beg you. You're not welcome here. So you can turn your face where your back is and leave!"

"I understand and I would leave. But please take this card."

"Take you and your card out of here before I use force." Joan said persisting.

"Please Joan, what have I done to you for you to hate me so much? I would feel so much better after I left if you would only take the card." Denyah begged the newly wed bride almost to tears to take the card.

"Okay!" Joan said. And she savagely pulled the card from Denyah's hand and tore it in half and tossed it into Denyah's face followed by the champagne she had in her glass. Denyah wiped most of the champagne off of her face with her hand as she stood in shock and looking ashamed.

"Now get out of my house. Now," Joan bawled for everyone to hear.

The room went dead silent. At that time Lisa had just walked into the house after speaking to friends. As she spoke to Denyah, she noticed Denyah's eyes were filled with tears and her face and hair saturated as well as the front of trouser suit was dripping wet.

"What's the matter Den?" she asked looking annoyed, but Denyah ran out of the house. Lisa looked hard at Joan then followed behind Denyah and begged her to wait. By this time, Eugene, Ryan and wife Meleta, David and his fiancé, Richard Glennis and his girlfriend Kelly were outside socializing amongst some of the guests. Meleta saw Denyah running down the path with Lisa behind. Straight away Meleta knew something was wrong and she told Eugene "I just saw Denyah running away with Lisa behind her." Eugene stared at Meleta in disbelieve then he set out running down the road to see Denyah and Lisa far beyond. As he saw Denyah flag down a white van driver to stop, he signalled the driver to drive on. The mixed race driver stopped and said. "Jump in lady." Denyah looked back at Eugene crying and told the driver "Thanks for stopping. But my problem is not with him. You can go now please."

"Are you sure lady?" the driver asked looking concerned.

"Yes, he's my partner and he really cares about me."

"Okay then, but if we run into each other again, you'll have to buy me a drink" The driver said and smiled. Denyah nodded her head and he drove away with a suspicious feeling.

As Denyah tried to run off, Eugene grabbed her by the hand.

"Let me go. Let me go please, she cried. I should not have come here. Why did I let you all convince me to come where I wouldn't be welcome?"

"Would you like to tell me what happened?" Eugene asked.

"I just want to go home" Denyah cried. "I didn't know Joan and your mother had hated me so much. Please Eugene, take me home and then if you don't want to see me again I will understand."

Meleta went to Ryan and told him, "I think Denyah is in some kind of trouble. She was running away with Lisa running behind her but Eugene is with her now."

Ryan asked Meleta to excuse him while he went to find out what had happened. As he confronted Denyah and saw her crying, he asked, "What's the matter Den?"

She hugged him while Eugene waited and watched. Ryan dried her eyes with one of his handkerchiefs and kissed her forehead. She smiled vaguely and rested her head on his shoulder still in tears. "Come on sis you're much stronger than this to cry over an idiot that's not worth it. You let out anymore tears and you'll let them think they won. Would you like to tell Eugene and me why you are crying?"

She shook her head and said, "I just would like to go home."

"Something must've made her cry." Ryan faced Eugene and said.

Minutes later Lisa went to tell Eugene and Ryan, "The bride told her she wasn't welcome and she told her to get out of her house. I also believe she threw drink in her face" Eugene looked at Lisa in disbelief then tears came in his eyes. "Now you're crying" Denyah said smiling. Eugene smiled and dried his tears then said, "Den, I would like you to come with me. I just want to hear from Joan why she told you to get out her house and why she insulted you by throwing her drink in your face. "

Then tears came into Lisa's eyes as she hugged Denyah. Loosening her hands from around Denyah's shoulder, she said, "I'm so sorry Den, I should have listened to you. But I'm glad you came. Now I know how much she hates you and so she will hate me when I give her a mouthful. Thanks to my vicious brother who has fixed it for you to be hated by us."

Eugene beckoned Lisa to keep quiet and said to "Denyah you are coming into that house with me whether you like it or not."

"Please Eugene I don't want to go back into Joan's house. Going in her house again would only make matters worse and I will only be insulted and that would make your mother laugh at me again. All I want is to go home. Please Eugene, take me home. I've tried to tell you, Ryan and Lisa that she was certain about not inviting me. But none of you would take me seriously. Well I hope the three of you are satisfied that I came and that I was humiliated and laughed at. If you don't want to take me home. I'll take a taxi."

"I only want you to come in with me for a minute. Den,"

"Eugene if I go back into Joan's house, she would only insult me again. She has scorned me and tossed champagne in my face. I have also tried to tell you that she'd phoned me and told me that I wasn't invited to her wedding. Oh God! What have I done for her to hate me so much? My husband has put me into these people's hands and they'd have tossed me into the depths of hell!" Denyah said as she closed her eyes and then opening them to look at Eugene still in tears but dried her tears again.

"As I said," said Eugene, "I only want you in there for a minute and you're going into that house to face that bitch even if I have to carry you. Then we go home."

As Denyah made a couple of steps in the direction of Joan's house, tears filled her eyes as she hesitated. Walking to the door she breathed in deeply and hesitated again. Eugene and Ryan held each of her arms and walked her inside the house. There was a sudden silence and everyone's head turned with their eyes fixed on the three of them. As Denyah lowered her head, Eugene raised her chin up to lift her head. David and his fiancée went and stood with Denyah, Eugene and Ryan. Then Lisa walked in and joined them. Richard went and stood by his Lisa, then Eugene's friend Cindy and her husband Frank, Claire, Glennis and his girlfriend and some more of Eugene's friends including Denyah's friend Ivy and another that she hadn't seen for a long time. They all stood together in the middle of the room. Then Denyah's long time friend Bernice hugged her and said, "I have only just arrived and I've heard what the bride of a bitch has done to you. I felt like forcing my fist down her filthy throat."

Eugene walked Denyah to Joan's table and asked her, "What has Denyah done to you for you to hate her that much and insult her by almost drowning her with champagne."

Joan said softly, "Her husband told me he caught her with his mates in his bed. One of them was my Uncle and he was murdered and now left two children behind under the age of thirteen. I'd loved my Uncle very much."

"And I love this woman very much." said Eugene " he then faced his mother and said "And as for you mother, I was told how happy you'd looked applauding when the bride told my fiancée to get out of her house and almost drowned her with champagne. Now this speech is dedicated to those of you who hated this lovely lady now standing by my side. I'm sure most of you know Mr Wesley Davis who is her husband and a police officer who always cowardly hiding behind his badge. Well, he has fooled us all and weaved us into a sleeping web.

But I've woke up and rose above the surface of his trap to see what a louse he is and what he has done to this lovely lady. Just look at you all, you all looked as though you've just came back from a losing battle."

Ryan, David and Bernice laughed and Bernice applauded Eugene while everyone stayed in silent with eyes glued to the floor and others looking shameful. "Now I'm glad everyone here is going through a patch of silence except those of us that love and cared about this beautiful lady. I like your silence! Now what I have to say to all who hated my fiancée, will only take me a minute. I suppose everyone knows by now that this beautiful woman that stands besides me has been wrongly labelled as one of the greatest whores of all women. But I love her and would always even if I saw a man jump off her. Well, where was I? Oh yes, as I was saying, her vicious husband has labelled her a great harlot. How was that? Her jealous husband made sure of that. One Saturday afternoon she returned home from shopping to be beaten by her husband and being accused of being unfaithful. And for a second time that Saturday night after going home from this brides' engagement party." Eugene turned and looked at everybody with anger, then turned and fixed his eyes on the bride and went on to say. "Well, this lovely lady went home from this bride's party to see her husband drinking heavily. He accused her of seeing other men so he set up a secret camera and then invited over two of his mates after he blindfolded, gagged and bound his beautiful wife's hands to the bedstead. But God was with this precious lady when she made a sign to let his mates know she wasn't that sort of person. And that's when his two mates realized that her blindfold was moistened with tears and with a sign of mercy they pretended that they had sex with her and that's not all, this high and mighty police husband had done to her, the one that you all admired and believe so much in. Well, he shoved an unloaded gun down her throat then forcing her to eat a slice of bread decorated with dead fleas on her return from her hair dressers after he spitefully eat and binned what food was left. Luckily for her, her daughter was there and took the bread to the bin. Oh how I wonder why his two mates ended up being murdered just like a very dear nurse friend that tried to help this woman. As for me I almost lost her for being a damn fool, don't you get the picture we're all being used by her husband, but I thank God I have woken up and regained my senses and risen above this evil. Well, if you're looking for that wicked husband of hers for a confession, we're well behind time as he has sneaked out a couple of minutes ago as he knows the truth has come to an end."

Eugene faced his mother and looked at her with hate. "Now as for you mother dear, I have just chosen this precious lady to be my bride. Thanks for your silence. Now you all can get back to your happy party while I take my beautiful lady out of this shit hole to breathe in fresh air. Oh one other thing, here is Denyah's scars, a souvenir from her loving husband because he were so jealous and couldn't bear the thought that she's more successful than him" Eugene then persuaded Denyah to show her scars to the guests.

The tearful bride left her table and went to Denyah, "I'm so sorry that I've failed to recognize the lies Wesley has told me and to insult you on the account of my weakness. Denyah, will you please forgive me?"

"Joan, I have forgiven all of you for crucifying me without giving me the chance to defend myself. My husband has put me into a straw basket on the road to hell and you and your kind had lit the fire to burn me. But as I'm not guilty, the fire had failed to burn. Now as Eugene said, I have to get out of this shit and hell hole before I suffocate."

"Please Denyah, don't go. Please sit with me" Joan said and then kneeled down at Denyah's feet holding on to her hands. Eugene looked hard into Denyah's face as he waited on her for her decision as to whether she wants to stay at the reception or to leave with him. Denyah looked down at Joan and pulled her hands away. She took a glass of champagne from Bernice and made to toss it into the bride's face and then said. "Doing the same to you would only bring me down to your level. I'm too much of a lady to do that."

Lisa laughed and said "Joan, I honestly though you were a decent lady. But you're nobody and that means you're nothing but filth. I forgive myself dirtying my clothes by coming here to see nothing!"

Joan's husband listened and then looked at her and shook his head hopelessly and in shame. Denyah left with Eugene feeling pleased within that she had won. Her brother Ryan and wife, and friends walked out the wedding party behind Denyah and Eugene and went to Denyah's home where they had their party and Eugene and David went to one of his hotels for food and drinks to take to the house.

CHAPTER EIGHT

That Sunday morning when Denyah got up, she gave Eugene the tightest hug ever, and said to him "Thanks for supporting me yesterday."

"That's okay my darling" he said. "If only you knew how much I love you."

Later, Eugene's mother phoned Denyah and asked for forgiveness and that she and her family would be coming for dinner. Denyah were so shocked that she didn't reply immediately.

"Are you there Denyah?" she asked.

"Yes Mrs Lake, I'm here. Do you really want to come for dinner, or to have a real go at me?"

"Denyah, I know the bond between me and my son is very weak and as he said he would choose you over me anytime. So please don't see me as your enemy anymore, I want to make up with you both. Now can I and my family come to dinner, say about four o'clock? And that friend of yours that you didn't see for a long while until yesterday, I gave her your phone number. I believe her name is Bernice. Do you mind?"

"No Mrs Lake, I don't mind you giving Bernice my phone number at all. She's one of the most decent people I've known."

"So will you please have us to dinner?"

"Yes Mrs Lake, you and the family would be most welcome."

"Well, we'll be there about four thirty then. And thank you Denyah." Mrs Lake said and she hung up.

Denyah went and told Eugene that his mother had just phoned her said, she and the rest of the family would be coming to dinner about four thirty. Eugene wasn't too happy to have to see his mother, but Denyah asked him to put his bitterness aside and see what happened. Eugene smiled and pulled her in bed and they made love.

"Well, it is now ten o'clock and I must go and prepared the dinner otherwise, I will not hear the last from your devious mother. Don't tell her I called her that." Denyah laughed.

"Wake me when the bitch of a witch arrives." said Eugene and pulled the sheets over his head.

Denyah went and showered and then went and start the cooking. While she was seasoning the joint of beef, Meleta joined her in stuffing the chicken. After the beef and the chicken were in the oven, Denyah said. "Meleta, we should cook breakfast as the beef and the chicken are in the oven. Then after breakfast we prepared the potatoes for roasting."

"Would you like me to cook the rice?" Meleta asked.

"Yes please Meleta, just about two pounds, as we would be doing more roast and baked potatoes and vegetables. But first I would like breakfast. I don't suppose Ryan is awake?" Denyah asked.

"No, and I don't think he'll wake for hours. So, I will only cook breakfast for us two." Meleta said.

"I think we better cook for the four of us. And guess who phoned me and invited herself to dinner?" Denyah said.

"Lisa?" Meleta asked guessing.

"Mrs Lake, Eugene's mother." Denyah said and burst into laughter.

"That bitch has got the cheek of the devil. I would tell her where to get off." Meleta said. "Oh I hate that woman for treat you so badly."

"Meleta, I hate her more than you do. But sometimes we have to let things pass and rise above."

"I still wouldn't let her into my house again. That woman is poison. Have you told Eugene that she's coming?" Meleta asked.

"Yes and he thinks the same as you. Now let me help with the breakfast as I'm starving." Denyah said.

"You can butter the toasts and set the plates while I make the scrambled eggs. The bacon is grilled and the coffee is brewing. Here comes our two men one behind the other." Meleta said as Eugene was just behind Ryan.

"Eugene, do you have to come to breakfast wearing pyjamas?" Denyah asked him then told him "You best go and get out of those pyjamas after you've eaten."

"Why?" he asked "I'm not going anywhere."

"I know, but your family would be here in about two hours, I told you your mother phoned to say they all are coming to dinner."

"Oh no, I thought you were joking. I was just about to invite you into bed again after I'd finish eating."

"Well Mr Eugene Lake, you're flat out of luck. Knowing that mother of yours, she might be here before the time she'd stated. So, no more bed for you my darling, until tonight. So as soon as you finish eating, would you please have your shower and put some clothes on?"

"If I change out of my pyjamas, what will you give me?" Eugene asked smiling and teasing.

"That... you'll find out later when you've changed." Denyah said looking contented.

After Eugene had breakfast, he went and had his shower and changed into dark trousers and a cream long sleeved shirt and a pair of slip-on brown shoes. "That's much nicer. Now you looked like that handsome man I fell in love with and his name is Eugene Lake - do you know him?" Denyah joked.

"Give me a kiss. Then I'll tell you." Eugene said smiling.

As Ryan and Meleta had slept the night at Denyah's, Eugene and Denyah lent them some of their clothes.

Three o' clock that Sunday afternoon, Denyah and Meleta finished cooking the dinner, prepared the salad and then put a couple bottles of white wine to chill as well as fresh carrot and orange juice.

"Well Denyah my friend, your lovely guest's dinner is now ready to be eaten, so I really think Ryan and I will be leaving soon." Meleta said.

"Please, Meleta, I'm so glad you and Ryan stayed with us last night. And I would be so happy if you both would stay tonight. Or at least until Eugene family have come and gone."

"Denyah, I don't mind spending another night with you, but facing that old cow, gives me the shivers" Meleta said and went on to say, "Ryan should be home in his bed as he is on early mornings. As that cow of a mother-in-law who would be here soon, I better go and wake Ryan."

"Let him sleep Meleta" Denyah said. "He must have been very tired to go back to bed. After working nights and was up at the crack of dawn no wonder he went back to bed. Meleta, I would really be grateful if you and Ryan stay here until Eugene family arrive and left. Please say you would."

"Okay Den, we'll stay. But only until that wicked woman and her family comes and leaves. By the way, I was meaning to ask you how did you and Ryan meet and claimed to be family really?"

"Okay Meleta, to put that little brain of yours at ease, I should tell you again for the fifth time, after moving in with Mrs Carter, and having long overgrown weeds in the gardens and the pathway, I managed to get rid of most but as the garden is so big, we did needed a gardener. So, I asked the shopkeeper the one who had helped me, to help me again to find a gardener, and she came up with Ryan. Then much later on, I found out Ryan wasn't a gardener but a doctor. As Ryan and I got to know each other, he told me why he gave up being a doctor and so, the old lady said Ryan and I could pass as brother and sister. So it came that we both love and respected each other. Our love for each other is very special and deeper than lovers, so if you're wondering why we aren't the other way around, you need not worry. But I'm telling you never hurt him for if you do you'll have to answer to me."

"I will never hurt Ryan. He makes me feel a real woman and I really do love him" Meleta said.

"You don't know how happy I am to hear you said that." Denyah said.

Just then a hard knock came on the door. "Shall I open the door?"

"Yes please Meleta." Denyah replied.

Meleta went to answer the door, but before she did, she brushed her hair behind her ears and looked back at Denyah smiling. Denyah beckoned her to open the door after hearing a second knock. Eugene mother and his dad stood at the door smiling. "Oh please come in Mr and Mrs Lake" Meleta told them as she moved aside to let them into the house and then lead them into the living room and asked them to have a seat. Mr Lake took his seat, but his wife stood in the middle of the room and had a good look at what the room was contained. "Mmmm…"She sounded. Her husband looked up at her, "For God sake sit down woman! Don't you know it's not very nice to stare at what other people have?"

"Can't I admire my son's house? This should have been his and Yvonne's, home." Mrs Lake said with envy.

"Tell me something that I don't know. Do you really hate Denyah that bad to keep on dragging up the past? Well, woman I feel really sorry for you. And why do you have to drag Yvonne in to it when you know she was the one that cheated on our son. Just rest it woman! Denyah is a decent lady. And I'm happy she's the wife our son has chosen." Mr Lake said.

"I despise her." Mrs Lake snapped.

"So why have you come into her home?" Mr Lake asked his wife with a stoned look.

"I came to make peace with my son. Is that so wrong?" she asked.

"Yes! The way you're going about this you best be careful you don't lose him all together. For I honestly don't think he would choose you over Denyah. And needless to say I saw how much he's in love with her."

"Have it your way my dear, but nothing that you've said would make me chose that woman over Yvonne. I'm not saying this because she is married to someone else, I simply don't want my son to get hurt or killed by her husband."

Eugene entered the room to see his mother and father. "Hello mother, dad," Eugene said.

"Hello son" His dad got on his feet and shook his hand while his mother kissed him on his cheek.

"You gave a lovely speech yesterday at Joan and Austin wedding that left everyone in surprise......"

'Good on you son" Mr Lake said.

"Stop right there mother, I'd said what I'd to say yesterday. And yesterday is thousand of miles behind us and I don't wish for you to say anything more but to treat Denyah with respect as she truly deserves. And please, I would appreciate if you would leave the past behind as you already know she is and will be the love of my life and she's the woman I'll marry and would like to spend the rest of my life with."

"Son, I came here to make a personal apology to you. I'm sorry that I didn't have even the common sense to know when I'd been taken for a ride. I was such a fool. How could I have been so stupid, so blind and cruel? "

"Mother, I think you should apologise to Denyah and not me."

Just then, Ryan walked into the room. "Hello Mr and Mrs Lake." he greeted them.

"Hello Ryan, we're here for dinner and for me to apologise to the lady of the house for being rude to her last night."

"Mrs Lake, some of us learnt about the wrong thing first. You were only protecting your son from under the claws of my cruel sister. But the only thing I didn't agree with, you were the only one that applauded when my sister were turned away and then almost drown in champagne by the bride. It's so shocking to know one brain is small as yours and can carry so much hatred for someone as beautiful as the lady your son would marry. Now if you would please excuse me." Ryan said and left the room leaving Mr Lake's eyes on his wife.

Denyah entered into the room and said "Mr and Mrs Lake, dinner is now ready. Would you please come with me?"

As Denyah was about to lead them into the dining room, Mrs Lake said, "Denyah, may I please have a word with you?"

"Certainly," said Denyah and took a seat. Mr Lake then left the room and went into the dining room to be with his son Eugene and Denyah's brother Ryan and his wife Meleta.

Mrs Lake smiled before she said, "Denyah, I was totally out of order at the wedding. Please accept my apology."

"Mrs Lake, I've forgiven all of you that were under my ex-husband's spell." Denyah said as she saw a guilty expression come on Mrs Lake's face. "Come on please, Mrs Lake, let's join the others in the dining room." Denyah told Mrs Lake and took the lead into the dining room to be with the others. The food was already on the table. As everyone took turn serving themselves the door bell rang.

"Those must be my children" said Mrs Lake examining one of the silver forks before she wiped it with one of her white handkerchief she took from her hand bag. Her husband looked hard at her and showing on his face embarrassment as he looked at Meleta. Meleta shrugged her shoulder and showed a fake smile.

Mrs Lake stared Meleta in her face saying "One should be very careful about what goes in to their mouth."

"I couldn't agree with you more Mrs Lake. After you finish with that fork, I'm sure the bin would like to swallow it." Meleta said seriously calm.

Mr Lake laughed heartily and Denyah got up smiling to go into the kitchen to get the trifle. But as the door bell rang, she went and answered the door but before she did, she burst into laughter over what Meleta said to Mrs Lake.

After Denyah opened the door to Eugene's good-looking brothers and their sister, she said naming each of them, "You must be Patrick, Ray, Carl and Jenny."

"You're absolutely right." Said Jenny and I'm starving after inhaling the smell of your cooking."

"I'm Denyah. It's a pleasure to have the four of you here. Please come in."

"Denyah, you really are beautiful as my brother Eugene said." Jenny said smiling.

"Thank you Jenny but I'm not half as beautiful as you" said Denyah as she walked them in to the dining room and asked them to take their seats at the eighteen seat specially made dark-brown mahogany table and high backed exquisite chairs, then she introduced her adopted brother Ryan and his wife Meleta to Mr and Mrs Lake and their sons Patrick, Raymond, Carlton and daughter Jenny.

Ryan shook hands with Eugene's three brothers and kissed Jenny on the back of her right hand then said, "I'm glad meeting all of you."

Then Meleta said, "I'm happy to have the pleasure of meeting all of you. Well, my friends, I don't know for you, but I'm starving. So let's eat."

"I haven't seeing such nice looking food in a long time like what's on this table" Ray said smiling.

"Well thank you Sir," Said Denyah to Raymond. "My sister-in-law has done most of the cooking. I do hope the food tastes as pleasant as it is appealing to your eyes. Mr Lake, would you be so kind and bless the food for us please?" Denyah asked him.

"Certainly" Mr Lake said and stood up respectfully. But before he blessed the food, his sons Carl took one of the chicken legs up and bit it. Mrs Lake looked hard at him.

After Mr Lake blessed the food, they all began to eat. Over dinner Carl said, "The food tastes as lovely as you ladies looked."

"That's enough!" Mrs Lake said rudely and got up out of her seat.

"What's the matter with you woman! Your son simply saying thanks in his own way. And I respected him for that." Mr Lake said. Then as Eugene watched his mother, she showed him a smile and sat and began eating. After she finish eating and used the napkin to clean her lips, she rudely tossed the dirty napkin on the remaining vegetables that was left in the silver rim glass bowl. Meleta looked at her. Smiling with what she done, she went into the lounge and then returned to the table almost immediately in a huff and looking at Jenny saying. "And as for you Jenny, I hope you no longer let my vegetables go to waste anymore when I put them on your plate." Every one looked at her.

"Mother if you cooked you vegetable like Denyah's I would eat them. But your vegetable tasted like unsweetened porridge. And you know what I think of you mother, you're rude, selfish and a riotous bitch! Sometimes I wondered if you are really my mother."

"Jenny! That's enough" her brother Patrick said. "What's happening to this family?"

"Jenny," Mrs Lake called.

"I don't wish to hear what you have to say. You made everything around you smell foul" Jenny told her mother and left to be with Denyah.

Mr Lake asked to be excused and went after his wife. And as he saw Jenny looking so upset, he knew his wife has caused it. He then approached his wife and said, "Woman, what the hell is the matter with you! From you been here you're acting like a bear with a sore head. Why did you really come if you despise your son's fiancée so much? You're forgetting that it was the Yvonne you so much like and rated that had affairs with other men while Eugene was away working. So please tell me, what Denyah has done to you to hate her so much? Is it because she's everything of lady than you will ever be? Well, if that what's worrying you, I'm sure she won't hold it against you. But if you're jealous of her loving your son, then I pity you as you give me the feeling you want your sons for yourself."

"How dare you speak to me like that, if he wants to marry that trash he can - but without my blessing. Now I should get back into the dining room to be with my children." Mrs Lake said to her husband.

"Speaking of children, what have you said to Jenny to upset her?" her husband asked.

"I simply told her I hope she eats her vegetables when I cook as she has just devoured Denyah's." Mrs Lake said.

"Maybe if you cook the vegetables the way Denyah's cooked hers, she might do you the favour of eating them. In fact, I too might eat for instance." Mr Lake said.

Mrs Lake got vexed and left fuming, leaving her husband standing in the middle of the lounge. As she headed for the dining room, her husband followed behind her, by this time everyone was moving into the lounge leaving Denyah in the dining room clearing the table.

"Can I help?" Ray asked her.

"I can manage" she told him taking a handful of plates off the table.

"Let me help" Ray insisted and he took a handful of plates from her and took them into the kitchen while she carry the left over food and put it in the fridge except the mixed vegetables that Mrs Lake flung her used napkin on. Denyah returned to the table for the vegetables and binned them - then she went to the sink and washed her hands.

"Would you like me to help washing the dishes?" Ray offered.

"No thank you Ray. My sister-in-law would help later by putting them in the dishwasher to be washed. Let's get back in the lounge to the others." Denyah told him.

Ray looked hard at her smiling and then said "Eugene is a very lucky man; I wish I'd saw you first."

Denyah smile and told him "Well, your brother saw me first and he's the one I am in love with and always will."

"You have put that strongly across but only time will tell" said Ray and left the kitchen smiling. Denyah smiled also and went and joined the others in the lounge where they were having coffee, cake and hot custard.

"Any one would like more coffee, tea or something stronger?" Denyah asked.

"I wouldn't say no to a drop of scotch please Denyah." Mr Lake said looking at the drinks display glass unit.

"Well the bar is right at your hand Mr Lake. Please help your self." Denyah said.

Denyah was felling very happy to know the rest of Eugene's family had appreciated her even though his mother had a different opinion about her. But that didn't put off Denyah from trying to get on with her. As time went on and Mrs Lake had a few scotches, she opened up to Denyah saying "Denyah, I do like your home. The dining room is enormous to hold a very big table with eighteen chairs. Denyah you have a lovely home."

"Thank you Mrs Lake, what the room contained, they were Mrs Carter's and it's the first time I have used the room since she died but I had them face-lifted." Denyah said and she showed Mr Lake and his family all over the house including the guesthouse, and around the gardens.

"I simply love your conservatory Denyah. It's so much you." Mr Lake said smiling. Denyah looked at him in wonder.

"You're as beautiful as your conservatory. I really love it." Mr Lake said.

Denyah looked at Mr Lake and smiled while Mrs Lake watched her with a scowling face with her lips pushed out.

Denyah smiled as she shook her head after seeing her face. Mr Lake looked at her, smiled and hugged Denyah around her shoulder as they walking out the house. Denyah walked them around the large front and back yard and gardens.

Before Denyah led them into the house again, Mrs Lake said. "Denyah I must hand it to you. You really are a fine young lady and I seemed to have miss-judged you. You've the whole house and as well as around the place looking spectacular. I liked the way the architect redesigned the living room in pale yellow and grey with the gilt matching drink bar that holds at least four hundred bottles of wines not to mention the lovely wall unit, even your kitchen flooring is quilted and soft. Denyah, would you mind telling me where you bought your living room settees? I would like to have the same. I do like your pale grey high back settees. Denyah they're the most exquisite settees I've seen with gilded gold bindings surrounding the seats. Denyah I'm glad Eugene is with you."

Denyah looked shocked at the thought of what Mrs Lake said to her.

"Shall we get back inside with the others Mrs Lake" Denyah asked. "By the way, Mrs Lake, I designed the settees myself and then had them privately made. Now shall we go inside? Since your husband has left us?"

"Oh yes, before they think we murdered each other."

"And why would they think that Mrs Lake?"

"My husband thought that I hated you."

"And do you Mrs Lake?"

"Well, I did at first, but now I believe we'll get on well. Oh before I forget. I would like for you and Eugene to come to dinner next Saturday afternoon."

"Thanks you Mrs Lake, I will tell Eugene."

Mrs Lake was just about to hug Denyah but Denyah walked away smiling and whispered, "Bitch!"

Denyah then led Mrs Lake into the house smiling. Eugene raised his eyebrows at Denyah in surprise. Denyah made a signal with her finger on her lips meaning to tell him keep quiet.

Then Mrs Lake went to Eugene and said "I think Denyah will make a good wife. And I was wrong to misjudge her."

"Mother, am I hearing you right? However, whatever you think, it doesn't matter as you have no say in me and my Denyah's lives."

Denyah didn't hear what Eugene mother said to him, but she'd noticed how she was admiring the living room as a contented embrace printed on her pale white high cheeked face. Her bushy eyebrows rose intensely as she widened her deep sea blue eyes to admire Denyah's living room. Eagerly her eyes were wandering all over the room. Denyah walked over to her saying "Mrs Lake, I couldn't help myself from noticing the way you've admiring my living room. I have spent a lot of money to have my home looked like this."

"I thought you and my son shared this home."

"Yes of course, I wouldn't have it any other way. Your son and I love each other."

"This means you would get your divorced and married my son?"

"I don't see why not, when I get my divorce and marry your son, you will be the first to know Mrs Lake." Denyah told her.

Mrs Lake turned her face away from Denyah and fixed her eyes on the display wall unit. She then left Denyah standing and walked over to the glass shelves unit and picked up a beautiful crystal figure of a beautiful curved lady.

Denyah looked at her as she held the figure with the most affectionate care and smiling before Denyah walked over to her and said. "She'd beautiful. Isn't she?"

"Yes. She's the most beautiful figure I have ever seen." Mrs Lake said and turned and faced Denyah, "She's is a beautiful figure. Even the platform beneath her feet is exquisite. Emerald green, it looks like" she said smiling and then stands it back in its place on the third shelf and carefully closed the doors. Once again she faced Denyah and said," I must admit, you're in a class of your own. I even like the built in big forty two inch TV and high fidelity system. It suits the big room."

"Come to think of it Mrs Lake, I've never noticed the quality of the crystal figure until you drew it to my attention. When Eugene heard Denyah speak of the crystal, his eyes were fixed fascinating and examining the crystal figure. He then realized the figure wasn't crystal but diamond with green emerald eyes and foot stool was ruby but he said nothing to attract anyone's attention. After some time went by, Eugene was still thinking of the figure and asked Denyah, "Did you say Mr and Mrs Carter were in the jewellery business?"

"Yes Eugene, they were. Why do you ask after I told you more than once? How did you think I come to have so much expensive jewellery and uncut stones? I have even told you what she's left for Ryan and me. Eugene, I saw how your mother has taken a fancy to the crystal figure, shall I gave it to her as a piece offering?"

"No! She's my mother, but the truth is, you're a good person to let her into your home after the way she treated you. If I were you, I'll keep her at a distance. For all I know, she may be putting on a fake pretence. Dad is so loving and honest compared to her. Sometimes I wonder if she's really my mother. And do you remember telling me, how choosey Mrs Carter was to have any one working for her?"

"Yes Eugene, I do remember telling you. Why have you brought this up Eugene?" Denyah asked.

"I came to understand why she didn't want any one around her that she didn't like. Den, the old lady loved you and Ryan. You both are very lucky. As for that woman called my mother, she is a nasty piece of work." Eugene said.

"I don't think she can help it Eugene. You know some mothers are very jealous of their son's girlfriends. Just don't ask me why as I haven't the answer." Denyah said and she and Eugene went into the living room to be with everyone again.

As Eugene was about to speak to his dad, Meleta interrupted, by asking, Mr Lake, "Do you enjoy your job being a judge?"

"Well, Meleta sometimes. And sometimes I have some bad days of course, especially when I have a difficult case. But the people I'm most sorry for, is the juries who find it hard to come to a conclusion." Mr Lake said smiling.

"Well I understand, but have you ever imposed the death penalty?" Meleta asked interestedly.

"Meleta, that's enough!" Denyah said.

"Denyah, I was tempted to ask him. That's why I did." Meleta said smiling.

"It's been sometime since we had dinner, so if we should go into the dining room, supper would be served. Or, if you prefer to have supper in here, I'll be happy to bring it to you." Denyah said to all.

"We'll have supper in the dining room" Jenny said looking at Ryan. Then everyone moved into the dining room for supper. Everyone took their seats at the table except Denyah as she went in the kitchen to take the supper to the table. While bringing the supper from the kitchen, Ray went and helped her. As Eugene watched her and his brother Ray with interest and as she stood at the table, Eugene said to her. "Sit down honey." And he took over from her and went and took the remaining food to the table and then took his seat next to her. At this time, Ray's eyes were all over her so much that Eugene had noticed. She looked at Eugene and then Ray then asked her brother Ryan to fetch the iced champagne from the fridge.

Ryan popped the bottle of champagne and filled the glasses while they all each in turn filled their plates with steaming buttered lobsters, creamed potatoes, salads and garlic bread followed by ice cream or left over Christmas steamed pudding and custard of their choice.

"This lobster tastes great, did you two prepare it?" Jenny asked.

"No, my cook did, her name is Mrs Brown. She will be here tomorrow." Denyah said.

"Ryan, would you put some more lobsters on my plate please, it tastes so good that I can't help myself having some more." Jenny said smiling.

As Ryan was doing her the honour of putting more lobster on her plate, she was sprawling her hand over his and looking deeply into his eyes. Meleta raised her glass and said jealously, "I might as well tell the happy news to every one here. Ryan and I will be having our first baby this summer. Denyah you will be an Aunt for a third time."

"Congratulations to you Ryan and to you Meleta and to your first born" Eugene said taking a drink of his champagne. Ryan smiled and sipped his champagne then said "I am very lucky to have a beautiful wife and to be a happy dad."

Jenny looked at Meleta shamefully and took her hand away from Ryan's. At this time Eugene was watching her and smiling.

After supper, everyone moved into the living room again to drink brandy and eat cashew nuts. Eugene played a few soft CDs before he and Ryan disappeared for at least one hour. After Denyah gave up searching in and out the house to find both Eugene and Ryan, they walked into the living room smiling. "Ryan and I went to the liquor store to buy some beer." Eugene said.

As every one were enjoying themselves dancing and having fun. Denyah was sitting and looking at them. As she got up and opened the window to let in air, the room became cooler with the breeze blowing. Then Mr Lake went to her and asked. "May I have this dance with you miss Denyah?"

"Yes of course Mr Lake." Denyah said and she danced with him. At this time Ray was looking at hard at her dancing with his father as her eyes met his, he winked his eyes and smiled. Then as the CD stopped and 'When would I see you again' was playing, Ray went to her and asking her to dance with him, she said. "No." And to each time he went to her. He got angry told her. "I want you Denyah!"

Denyah looked hard at him and left the room and went into the kitchen. He followed behind her without her knowing until she felt his warm breath on the back of her neck and looked back and saw him smiling. "Why are you following me?" she asked him. "I fell in love with you and I want you regardless. And I know you want me too."

"Ray, I love your brother and I with him so would you please leave me and go pester someone else?"

"Denyah, I want to be near you. Eugene doesn't deserve you."

"And you are?" Denyah asked.

"Yes I am." Ray said.

Denyah left the kitchen to go in her bedroom as she was feeling tired. But she stood on the landing in thought facing her bedroom door. Ray crept up behind her holding a bottle of brandy in one hand and two glasses with ice in the other. "I brought us a drink." he said. She looked in his eyes telling him, "I don't want a drink."

"Come on Den, "I know you want a drink?" he said.

"Ray, I don't want any alcohol to drink and I wish you would go and bother someone else."

"Denyah, just what are you afraid of? I won't swallow you. All I want of you is to love me as I love you."

"Please Ray, will you leave me alone?" Denyah asked him and opened her bedroom door and walked in. Ray followed behind her and smiled. "Ray, I don't want any more to drink. Will you please leave my room?" she told him.

"You're so beautiful." he said as he pulled her into his arms and kissed her.

She slapped his face and said, "Don't you realize or even care that I'm in love and live with your brother and we share the same bed?"

"My brother and I are two different people. I need you more than he does. I love you the moment I saw you."

"I love Eugene." she said.

"But I believe you love me more." he said.

"No Ray, I do like you, but I don't love you. What I feel for Eugene is love."

"Did Eugene tell you he was engaged to be married?"

"If you meant to that Yvonne, yes, he told me they were engaged four years ago before he met me. He also told me he caught her in his bed with another man that's why they finished. Is there's anything else you would like to fill me in with Ray?"

"No, only to let you know that I love you and I want you. Den, I would marry you this minute."

"Well Ray, you've a very long wait. And I will always refuse you."

"Don't worry Denyah I'm a very patient man."

"Ray, will you please take the bottles into the living room before someone comes looking for us."

"Sure." he said and left with the bottles.

As Ray put the bottles on the coffee table, Meleta left the room and met Denyah at the bottom of the stairs. "I was wondering where you got to." Meleta said,

"I was just heading into the kitchen to fetch a bucket of ice and more cashew nuts" Denyah said.

"Denyah, I watched Ray - it's like he's tormenting you. Remember, he's one of Eugene's brothers, and nothing would please his mother more than for Eugene to walk out on you" Meleta said with deep concern with Jenny standing behind her and breathing heavily on her neck. Meleta looked back at Jenny and asked her, "If you're looking for my husband, he's not here."

"I've come to say I'm sorry for the way I have behaved. I don't know what had come over me, I shouldn't have behaved so disrespectful and I'm sorry. I also didn't know Ryan is your husband."

"Ok Jenny, I forgive you. But in future just keep your distance and your hands off him"

"Just drop it Meleta. She has already apologised to you." Denyah said.

"Ok, I will not mention any of this again providing she doesn't give me any cause." Meleta said then turned and face Jenny and said, "I'm sorry to gabble on over my husband. You and I should be making friends and not enemies. However, I do hope the silly misunderstanding wouldn't come between us. Now let's get into the living room and have a drink."

"Yes" Denyah said. "I'm glad you two see sense - that no man worth worrying over. Now we better get back to Mr and Mrs Lake before they came looking for us."

Meleta took a bottle of whiskey from the cupboard and asked Denyah and Jenny "Are you coming?"

"We might as well" Jenny said and turned to follow Meleta while Denyah was still sitting at the dining table. "Are you not coming Denyah? Meleta asked.

"You two carry on, I be with you shortly." Denyah told them.

"Denyah, are you afraid to be in the same room with that old dried up prune faced witch?" Jenny asked Denyah and laughed out. Then she went on to say,

"I sometime wonder if she's my mother." she then had a small amount of whiskey drowned with lemonade and sipped some.

"Come on Den. Don't let the dried up prune think she won. Let's join Jenny." Meleta said.

"Meleta, with a situation such as this, there's no winner. All I want is too stayed well away from that woman" Denyah smiled, got up and followed behind Jenny and Meleta in to the lounge. "Any one for a drink," Meleta asked.

"I'll have a brandy this time as I don't care much for whiskey." Jenny said.

"What about you Den," Meleta asked.

"Nothing for me thank you Meleta."

Denyah left Meleta and Eugene's family in the lounge drinking whiskey and brandy while she went to do the washing up from the supper by hand, dried them and put them into the cupboard.

Mrs Brown walked into the kitchen to see Denyah putting away the dishes. "Honey, why didn't you use the dishwasher?"

"Mom it much quicker washing the dishes by hands. I think I better sit down as I'm feeling exhausted." Denyah said.

Mrs Brown leaned her head on the left side saying "You're doing too much honey and you should slow down."

"Denyah smiled and sat at the kitchen table drinking a cold soda. As she swallowed the last of the soda, she heard laughing followed by the loud shutting of her front door. She raised her head up in thought that must be Eugene and Ryan. As she was getting up, Mrs Brown said, "You rest honey."

Mrs Brown left and soon as she walked in the hallway to see Eugene and Ryan stood facing her with smiles. Mrs Brown smiled back before she went to be with Denyah and said. "Honey, it is Eugene and Ryan."

"Well, at least Eugene's came home to be with his family before they went off home." Denyah said. Then she asked Mrs Brown "You want a slice of cake mom?"

"Not tonight honey," Mrs Brown said as she sat facing Denyah drinking tea while Denyah eating cake with her tea.

After Denyah finished eating her cake and was getting up, she heard laughing coming from Eugene and Ryan. She sat down again when Eugene showed himself to her smiling.

"What are you smiling about?" she asked him. But before he answered, Ryan walked into the kitchen and faced her smiling as well. Then when she heard laughing in the hallway, she went to see who it was. To her surprised, there were Doctor Glennis, his fiancée Kelly and three other women one white, two black. Mrs Brown looked at Eugene, shook her head smiling.

"Where are you two coming from?" Denyah asked Ryan. Ryan and Eugene faced her smiling then Ryan said. "We went to have a pint and met Doctor Glennis, his fiancée and his friends."

"Eugene, would you please come with me up to the bedroom? I want to speak to you" Denyah said.

"Den, I know why you want me up the bedroom" Eugene said and followed behind her up to their bedroom. She sat on the bed while he stood and watching her as she asked,

"Who are those women?"

"Oh, they were with Doctor Glennis and after having a couple of pints, Ryan and I invited them to our home to have a drink. One of them is his fiancée."

"Eugene, I don't believe you, you've deliberately went to look for those women. Have you no respect for your parents."

"Denyah, I swear to you that they're Doctor Glennis' friends. Anyway, it's nice for you to have a few honest friends after what you been through."

"How can I forget, when you and the others had believed Wesley and always reminded me."

"Denyah, you're not been fair. Yes, I admitted he'd had me fooled at first, then after seeing a tape of you and those men, what was I to believe. Den, I told you how sorry I was to find out the sorrowful lies your ex fed to me."

As Denyah tears slithered down her face, he took her into his arms and kissed her saying, "Look I will go and ask them to leave." Eugene said

"Eugene before you does that. I would like have a word with my brother." Denyah said.

And she and Eugene went into the kitchen to meet Ryan smiling broadly. As she watched Ryan hard, he asked. "What?"

"I haven't said a word yet." She replied.

"Denyah, Eugene and me asked them to be here." Ryan said smiling.

"Ryan, you and Eugene are becoming two of a kind. I trusted you both to be decent and you both brought pickup women into our homes."

"Den, I am not lying to you. They're my friend's friends and his fiancée."

"Okay Ryan, I hope your wife will take this as lightly as I am." Denyah said.

She then went to the bathroom and washed her face, before she went downstairs into the kitchen again. As she walked passed Eugene, he lightly slapped her bottom and joked saying "I'll be back soon with more girls." As he and Ryan hurried away out the house again. Denyah smiled and shook her head.

"Where are those two off too now?" Meleta asked Denyah.

"I've no idea." Denyah said smiling then she escorted Doctor Glennis and his three lady friends into the living room to meet Eugene's family. She then introduced Doctor Glennis and his friends to Eugene's family and in turn they said their names.

At this time Meleta ran out after her husband Ryan and Eugene asking, "Where are you two going now and leaving your guests?"

"We're going to buy some fried chicken and booze." Eugene faced her saying,

"Eugene, there's plenty of booze in the house." she said.

"Meleta, get back in the house please." Ryan told her.

Eugene smiled and he and Ryan left in Ryan's car and returned home within twenty minutes later with three buckets of Kentucky fried chicken with fries, two cases of beers and six bottles of whiskey, brandy and martini. Denyah looked at Eugene and shook her head smiling and then Eugene took her into the hallway and said, "Den honey, please try and relax and enjoy yourself, if you want them to leave, I will tell them to. Just remember that I love you and all I want is for you to be happy. So just say the word and your true love would obey."

"I forgive you this time, let's go into the living room and join them. Then you can introduce me to your lady friends." Denyah said to Eugene then they both joined the others in the living room to see everyone eating chicken and drinking. The young woman introduced herself saying, "I'm Francis." She wore natural make-up and her long wavy red hair met her shoulders, her beautiful curved slim figure complimented her brown eyes, her long legs which shows her height about five foot eight inches tall and she weighed about nine stones. Then another young woman giggled as she said, "I'm Paula." Paula had looked mix raced, very good looking with deep dimples in both cheeks when smiling or laughing she had a lovely smile and showing her two sets of pearly white glittering teeth, her greyish eyes are penetrated and beautiful. Her short cropped wavy hair and an attractive figure which is about a size eight and her breast sizes seemed to be thirty two to thirty two as her nipples had looked firm under her see through blouse. After she had a few whiskies, she unbuttoned her short waist black jacket to show her pointed breast nipples through her red knitted blouse. Mr Lake became embarrassed and he held his head down with his eyes still fixed on her bosom as she was sitting facing him.

As Mrs Lake saw his eyes fixed on Paula's breasts, and the sweat on his forehead, she slapped him lightly across his face and told him. "Keep your eyes off her and remember who you are."

Mr Lake gave Paula a pleasant smile before he faced his wife saying, "We'll soon have to make tracks."

Then another two young ladies stayed in their seats and introduced themselves saying, "I'm Ida and my friend is Edna" Ida was also dark skin and could have well been a model like her sister, but preferred to entertain and sing to guests in pubs and night clubs.

"By the way, I'm Kelly. I'm a nurse and Doctor Glennis fiancée." The mixed race beauty said.

Edna was white and she worked as dentists assistant. These four young women are very attractive, but Paula was sharp and looked glamorously powerful like lit dynamite and especially she looked like Eugene's type.

Denyah approached Eugene and Ryan and asked jokingly "Have you hand picked you four girlfriends? Leaving out Kelly as I know she's doctor Glennis' fiancée. They're very beautiful and they all seem to have manners I must admit. I do like them, but I do hope you and Ryan are not taking Meleta and me for fools. Eugene, if at anytime you don't want to be with me anymore, please, do not to keep me in limbo."

"Den you're the only woman in my life that I want, and to have my children. I'm in love with you Den and as I said, if you want them to leave, just say the word and they will be gone. However, thanks for making Glennis's fiancée welcome."

"Oh Eugene, I got paranoid over nothing. It's only because I love you so much. Let's get back to our friends and enjoy ourselves." Denyah said walking back to go in the living room.

As everyone was enjoying themselves dancing and drinking, Denyah was more than happy to see Paula keeping Ray very busy dancing, in conversation and entertaining. It was a long while since Denyah enjoyed herself. But she noticed how tired Mr Lake's eyes looked, so she told Eugene it's time his mother and father went home. Eugene agreed after seeing his father's eyes looking half closed and so he told his three brothers and his sister to take their mother and father home, but his three brothers said, "Dad is capable of driving himself and mother home" Mr Lake heard Eugene arguing with his brothers so he asked them what the argument was about."

"I asked Ray, Patrick and Carl to take you and mom home, and them refused." said Eugene.

"You have more than enough room for your mother and me to sleep the night. But I'm capable to drive us home. In fact, I believe my bed is calling for me. I should ask Denyah for a cold drink of water and then make tracks" his father said.

Eugene walked with his father into the kitchen and waited for him as he said,

"Denyah my dear, I thank you gratefully for a lovely time. I have enjoyed the nice food and your company. Thanks you so much, but it is high time me and the Mrs should be in bed. So my dear, here is where I must wish you goodnight."

"Oh Mr Lake, before you leave I have something to show you" Denyah said.

"It must be now my dear or you'll have to show me next time."

Denyah took him and Mrs Lake into her bedroom and showed them her inherited precious stones and jewellery and then after she showed then around the other six bedrooms, two bathrooms, shower room and a private lounge which had a corner switch to activate an under floor heated swimming pool to relax and have a drink after night soak.

Mrs Lake eyes widened as she stared at her husband in surprise.

"Well Denyah, you have an exquisite home and I'm happy my son has chosen you. You're one of the most beautiful and loving people I've known. I'm very happy to have you as my daughter-in-law."

"Well thank you Mr Lake." Denyah said.

"Denyah, please call me Lewis." Mr Lake said.

"Tell me Denyah, have you come into some money, or, is it my son's money you used for your luxurious pleasure?" Mrs Lake asked fuming, then went on to say, "Eugene must really love you for him to almost bankrupt our business, to keep you happy."

"Mrs Lake, will you never give up? Why must everything that comes out of your mouth smell like shit! To put your mind at ease, I have inherited what I have from a very kind and loving lady who was very wealthy. I hadn't one penny from your son to put into this house. I don't need his money, I love him and not for his money. As I said, I fell in love with your son Mrs Lake, and thanks for telling me Eugene is near to bankruptcy. But I am so sure you have got it wrong." Denyah told her.

"How long you and my son been together?" she asked.

"About the same time you and my ex plot against me." Denyah said.

"Are you pregnant?" Mrs Lake asked.

"I don't think I am" Denyah said looking confused. "And if I am, it's nothing to do with you" Denyah told her knowing she's happily pregnant.

"You know what Denyah, I think you're really is in love with my son and not for his money" Mrs Lake said and she kissed Denyah on her face and said "Thanks for welcoming me and my family into your home and I'm looking forward for you and Eugene having dinner at my home next week Saturday. Say five as I like my food to digest before I go to bed. And Denyah, I will not take no for an answer. And you know what; I think I would get to like you very much and get to know you well. Oh your brother and his wife will be very much welcome to come with you and Eugene to dinner. Well, I must get the family and go home."

Denyah smiled and said, "Of course Mrs Lake. Ryan and Meleta would be delighted to come with Eugene and me."

Denyah led Mr and Mrs Lake downstairs and into the living room.

"Come on children, say goodnight and let's leave." Mrs Lake said.

"Why, can't we spend the night here mother?" Jenny asked sadly.

"No Jenny, we only came for a visit and we have overstayed, besides, it is improper to dump ourselves on Denyah. There will be other times when we'll arrange to spend a night. Right now we have to get home. Please go and fetch your brothers."

"Oh mother," Said Jenny.

"Please Jenny, Denyah seems to be a nice person, but she doesn't have eyes in the back of her head to watch you, and I'm not sure that I can trust you to behave. And remember Curt told you he will be at our house for nine o'clock after work. Now will you go and tell your brothers we're ready to leave?"

Jenny went and told her brothers her mother was ready to go home. Ray went to his mother and said "I'm not ready to go home mother but maybe Patrick or Carl would take you, dad and Jenny home."

"Okay Ray," Mrs Lake said, "Jenny will take your father and I home. I know you and your brothers don't want to leave just yet, but I have faith in the three of you to behave and don't give Denyah any trouble. Now come along Jenny, I think it is going to rain" Mrs Lake said walking out of the door with Jenny, Eugene, Denyah, and her husband behind.

"Mother, there are five bedrooms available and Dad doesn't have to go to work tomorrow. Why don't you and dad stay the night?"

"Eugene, I didn't come to sleep. Besides, you know that your father has a weak heart and he's on medication that's why we have to be home and I will also need time to get to know Denyah and to get used to her. I don't want to impose or rush things and spoil the friendship Denyah and I just developed."

"Well Mom, you take care and look after dad and the minute you get home, let us know you all got home safe" Eugene said to his mother and then kissed her and his sister on the cheeks and shook his father's hand before they get into their car. Jenny get into the driver's seat, buckled up her seat belt, and said, "Denyah, I thank you very much for a wonderful time and to have me in your home."

"Jenny you're welcome at anytime, and remember, you don't need an invitation to come to our home." Denyah said.

"Thanks" Jenny said and she drove away while Eugene watched them go. Suddenly, it began to rain.

Denyah rushed into the house leaving Eugene standing at the gate and looking at his family car until they were out of sight. As the rain poured down heavier, he rushed into the doorway and brushed the rain off his shirt and out of his hair before he took Denyah into his arms and kissed her.

"You're soaking wet. You need to change your clothes." she told him.

"I think you're right. Would you like to come with me and watch me change?" he asked her smiling.

"You'll be much quicker by yourself. You go and hurry back to be with your guests." Denyah said smiling too.

Eugene smiled then he hurried off up stairs and got changed and then returned downstairs into a pair of dark grey trousers, black long sleeved silk shirt and black slip on shoes. "You looked so handsome and cool that I hardly recognise you. So honey, I don't think I would let you out of my sight. And with your beard shaved clean, you looked much younger" Denyah said.

"I shaved off my beard" he said smiling. "Don't I look much nicer without it Den?"

"You've look different and more handsome and your deep dimple chin shows more clearly" Denyah looked hard at him before she said, "With your beard off, you look more like your brother Ray."

"Do you like me for your new man?" he asked smiling and joking.

"Mm…Yes and no" she said looking at Ray.

"What do you mean, by mm… yes and no?" he asked.

"Well, I'd love your red beard, and no, you shouldn't have shaved clean. You should have only lightened your beard." she said.

"I was going to waste my shaved beard in the bin, but you could transplant them to make your pasture fluffier so I would be landing on soft ground. I will even do the job of transplanting my wasted beard you know where for you just for a kiss." he joked.

Denyah laughed, saying, "I think I love you too much."

As she and Eugene were dancing, he kissed her a couple of times while Ray watched. As Ray eyes met her, she began to smile and rested her head on Eugene's shoulder. Just before the disc finished, Ray pinched her on her bottom and made her jump. "What's the matter?" Eugene asked. "Someone bumped into me" she told him.

By this time Ray stood behind Eugene and looking at her, as she looked at him, he moistened his lips with his tongue mischievously before he kissed Paula out of jealousy and then wiped his lips with his handkerchief. Denyah shook her head in disgust. She walked away from Eugene and went and sat near to the door. As the music start to play again, Ray went to her and whispered. "I have to settle for second best as I have to cool my burning pipe some where. The kiss meant nothing. I love you Denyah. "

Denyah said nothing but breathed in deeply and left him standing as she went into the kitchen only to stare at the fridge freezer. Rubbing her forehead she smiled. But with her back turned to the half closed door, she didn't see him coming. Suddenly the door flung opened and Ray walked in saying "I've only came for a drink of water."

"There's some in the fridge or from the pipe. Take your pick." Denyah told him and she turned to walk out of the kitchen, he twirled her around and kissed her. She pulled herself away then asked, "What the hell do you think you're doing. If you have any respect for your brother, you wouldn't be trying to hurt him by trying to drive a wedge between him and me" she said.

"You're so wrong Denyah, Eugene is doing that all by himself by fooling with these women he bring into your home. He's my brother but he's also a snake in grass" Ray said and tried to kiss Denyah again but she slapped his face and said "You stay well away from me! What if Eugene had seen you kiss me! How do you think he would feel?"

"Maybe relieved, so if you're afraid that he sees me kiss you, you need not worry."

"And what exactly are you trying to tell me Ray? And where is Eugene." Denyah asked concerned.

"You should know. Isn't he the love of your life?" Ray said smiling. "I've told you if you're worried that he would see us, don't be! He may be making love to one of his girlfriends right now." Ray said maliciously and laughed.

Furiously Denyah lashed out on him saying "You're a liar and a damn good one at that."

"Well, to prove me a damn good liar, why don't you get upstairs into one of your spare bedroom and then you'll find out if I'm a liar or not. Try the lemon painted room." Ray said then smiled.

Denyah made a wry face before taking her anger out by biting a chicken leg and then tossed the remainder in the bin in temper.

"Just look at your face Denyah, worry fright written all over it. Well, to put your mind at ease, and your thoughts at peace, you should go and see if I lied to you." Ray said teasingly with his cunning smile as he was pointing his fingers upwards towards the lemon painted bedroom.

As Denyah looked hard at him, and saw the aggravating smile on his face, she got so vexed with him that it became impossible for her to be in the same room with him as the suspense was too much. She swallowed some wine, stare him in his face before slapping him and said, "Ray, you're so devious as well as being a shrink. If you're trying to split Eugene and I up, it won't work!"

Ray smiled, felt the spot on his face where she slapped him. She looked hard at him and walked into the dining room. He followed her and touched her. She raised her hand to slap him again, but he caught her hand and kissed her with feeling.

Ryan saw him kiss Denyah.

"Be careful mate, it could have been Eugene that saw you." Ryan said to him.

Denyah looked at Ryan and then rushed passed Ray and almost knocking him over as he stood at the door. After he'd regained his balance, he followed her to the bottom of the stairs and stood watching her as she hurried upstairs and stood at the painted lemon bedroom door and looking hard at it. As she heard Ray whistle, she looked back at him to see him smiling and pointing at the door. Sadly she shook her head with frightful bad feeling over what he'd told her. While thinking, she widened her eyes and staring at the door. She stared painfully at the door that became almost transparent to her in a fit, thinking that Ray had told her the truth. She then mumbled to herself, "How would I bring myself to tell the man I love so much I'm no longer want him."

As Eugene and Paula were racing in her thought, she was thinking deeply that they might be in bed having sex. Tears came in her eyes as strong suspicion build up in her thought and especially that she couldn't get over what Ray had told her about Eugene in her lemon bedroom having sex with one of his women. She dried her tears and turned to walk down the stairs but Ray was still standing at the bottom of the stairs with a wide grin on his face and a bottle of beer in his hand. Of course she didn't want to believe Ray, but not seeing Eugene for at least half an hour made her think Ray was telling the truth. As Ray was watching her and smiling, she got so nervous that her hand starting trembling as she made to open the bedroom door. Deep in her thoughts, she believed she could trust Eugene not to commit adultery. Again, she turned around to walk back downstairs when she heard laughing coming from the yellow bedroom. She gently turned the door handle and opened the door quietly to see Paula and Eugene in bed well snug up underneath her blue satin sheets that she was given to her as a birthday present by Lisa. She couldn't believe her eyes even though she was watching them as they both were covered from heads to their toes.

As they were so much entwined and enjoying each other, they didn't even hear the door opened or when she entered in to the room. She stood at the door in darkness watching them having sex and making groaning noises. When she had enough of watching them, she left in anger and leaving the door opened and then stood outside behind the door in tears as she felt badly hurt and humiliated. Even then, neither, Eugene or Paula had heard the door open and were aware of being watched. As Eugene and Paula were still making love noises, she was still standing at the door listening. She caught Ray watching her. She went to her room and bawled her eyes out. Because she cried so much, her eyes and nose became so tender that instead of her wiping them, she sniffed up really hard and let her tears flow and fell on her bosom. Idiotically, she got out bed, went downstairs, got the champagne bucket of ice, filled it up with water, burst into the room without hesitation and threw the bucket of ice cold water over them then switched on the light. Eugene and Paula jumped up in fright. As she then turned her back to leave the room, Eugene said with a twist of his tongue. "Den, I didn't know what I was doing."

Denyah threw the ice bucket at his head and cut him over his left ear and ran out the room crying.

Ten minutes later, Eugene walked into their bedroom with blood dripping on his clothes "Den, I'm so sorry and so ashamed. Please forgive me. I never meant to hurt you."

"But you did Eugene. You were so snuggled up enjoying yourself that you didn't even heard when I entered the room and watching you and Paula having sex. I would like to know from you Eugene. Which one of us you find most enjoyable?" Denyah asked him furiously.

"Den honey, I tried hard to control my lustful feeling. But thinking so hard of you, I had an erection and knowing Paula was willing, I went along. Den, doing this to you, left me feeling sickened. Please forgive me. I beg of you. Please don't hate me. Den, I lost control after having too much scotch and I'm so very sorry."

"Of course you lost control by drinking too much whiskey, so why couldn't you go to the toilet and release yourself. But you chose the other way. How do you think I would have felt when I found out? However, as your brother Ray said, you're a snake in grass and you only want to release yourself and you did just that."

"I am sorry Den. As I told you, I didn't know what I was doing as I was pissed."

"Oh I understand, you didn't know what you were doing, you just fell over and your dick fell into her being you were pissed" Denyah said sympathetically and in tears.

"Den don't be like that, I was very tipsy, frail and maybe foolish."

"So that makes it okay that the man I would want to spend the rest of my life with uses his dick like a biro pen on what women come his way, and I should just accept your apology."

"No….No…..Yeah…" Eugene whispered.

"Well I don't accept, I can't believe what you've done, all day I've been proving to your parents how suited and in love we are and you go and do this…Well, well done, Eugene you've really proved how much you love me!" Denyah clapped her hands and walked off and went to bed leaving him and Paula to attend to his cut.

After he had done so and changed his clothes, he went downstairs with a plaster over his left ear to be with his brothers. Ray was laughing seeing him with the plaster. Doctor Glennis took Paula and friends to their homes.

Just as Eugene poured himself a strong drink the telephone started to ring, he answered "Hello," But he could have hardly hear what was said as the music was playing loud and his brothers were talking and laughing too loud as well. "Bros, I'm going to take this call in the hall. When you hear my voice, will you put the phone down?"

"Sure." Ray said smiling.

As Eugene suspected it was he that told Denyah about him and Paula, Eugene gave him a sly smile and he went into the hallway to answer the phone.

"Hello," he answered.

"Eugene, I just wanted you and Denyah to know we got home safely and as your brothers may be still be drinking, please don't let them drive home tonight."

"Please don't worry about them mother. They will be okay and I'm happy that the three of you are now home and safe. Well, mother you look after yourself and dad, and goodnight."

"Goodnight Eugene" her mother said and hung up. Eugene then went to be with his guests.

As the night went on, Eugene decided to go to bed as he was feeling very tired and tipsy. He said "goodnight" to his brothers, Ryan and Meleta before he went back upstairs to turn the bedroom door handle to his and Denyah bedroom and find the door was locked. He banged on the door several times, calling Denyah but she did not respond to his calling.

"Please my darling Denyah let me in, I'm really sorry." he said.

"It's too late for apologies." she said.

"She meant nothing to me, she's nothing compared to you" he said.

"I know that, but you've only just realised." she said.

"I'm sorry, please let me." he said. He begged softly as he saw Ray watching him. "Beg harder bro, her heart might soften, that's if she really loves you."

"Ray, shut your big gap and get lost" Eugene told him. Then as Ray went in the living room to be with his other two brothers, Eugene begged Denyah "Open the door."

"No, Eugene" she said in bed laughing before she got out of bed and opened the door to find him on his knees leaning against the door in tears. "Go on then, beg me to take you back" she said staring down at him in repulsion. Eugene stayed on his knees and begged, "Please Denyah, I'm sorry and I love you so much. I'd be nothing without you. Please Denyah, please."

"Okay Eugene, that's enough." she then closed and locked the door leaving him on his knees and went to bed. Eugene stayed there in shock for a few minutes in disbelief that she didn't let him in. He then plucked up the courage to knock the door again, "Don't bother," she shouted. "I've heard you pathetic apology and I'm not impressed, but still, I accept."

"Oh thank you," he said in relief. "I promise I will never do anything like this again." he said

"Don't get too happy, you're still not coming in here."

"Oh Denyah…" he said sadly but he stopped himself saying anything else and walked off into the spare bedroom he had made love to Paula in and slept on the couch.

134

CHAPTER NINE

Very early the following, Denyah was the first to get up. She walked lazily into the front room and took a long hard look at the cluttered and untidy room and walked out into the kitchen and made herself some black coffee. While drinking her coffee, Ray walked in the kitchen wearing a pair of Eugene's pyjamas and a smile on his face. Denyah got up. "No, don't get up on the account of me. I came to make some coffee but since you already made a pot, you don't mind if I have some?" he asked.

"No, help yourself." Denyah said.

Ray poured himself a cup of coffee, looked into Denyah's face smiling and then left. Denyah left behind him with a cup of coffee and went to her room to finish drinking her coffee. Later on that morning she was the first to use the shower and got dressed while everyone else was in bed. She decided to cook breakfast, but as she saw Ray heading for the kitchen, she went and tidied the living room. Ray made breakfast and took some to her. She looked at him before taking the plate. "Look Denyah about last night, I shouldn't have said anything, but I thought you should know the truth about the man you love so much. Even though he's my brother, you deserved to know the truth" Ray said.

"Yes! I saw them, but I don't own him. He's an adult and free as you men are accustoms to say." Denyah said.

"Those days are long gone Denyah. I know you're not married to him. But I also think you deserved full respect from him. Added to that, he brought women into your home and had sex with one. I would have never done what he has done to you if you were my woman"

"Well I can never be your woman, so lets forget everything yes?"

"You still love him after he'd disrespected you, and had sex in your home with another woman? Are you so stupid Den, or you so much in love that you afraid of losing him if you confront him?"

"No Ray, I'm not afraid of him. Yes, I love your brother. No women would make me leave him. Most of us women are still twined in bandages from our husbands with busted lips for speaking the truth. But your brother loves and respects me and I don't think he would ever hit me. So you see Ray, I do believe Eugene loves me, and our love was lost for a very long time. He made a big mistake having a woman in our house and I don't think he would do anything like that again. And believe me, before he has any affairs again, I'll take full control over him." Denyah told Ray.

"What about you ex-husband, did you love him as you love my brother?"

"I was in love with him. But he was in love with my sister."

"Why didn't you fight to save your marriage Denyah?"

"Ray, you can't fight or predict destiny. It doesn't matter how hard or how long you go on fighting, you would come to a bad end or good. And I came to a bad end." Denyah said. "My sister and other women won. But for your brother, I would fight on until my strength failed me to keep him."

"Denyah, I'm sorry that you husband deceitful to you. You're beautiful, intelligent, in good health and wealthy. You can have any man your heart desires including me:" Ray said smiling.

"Ray my dear, right now my heart only desires Eugene and I'm not sure if he really wants me for what he did to me, or how long his love will last for me. But as I've just told you, I'll fight the woman that comes between Eugene and me with my dying breath.

Don't think because I let Paula off lightly, I'm a coward. I never knew that after my ex treated me so wickedly, I could love any man again. But Eugene and I is am item. I also think Eugene and I sharing our hearts is positive and there's no negative side to it."

"I think Eugene's love will go on for you until the end of time. Now what he did at Joan and Austin's wedding, I could never in a hundred years pluck up courage and defend my woman the way he did. What he did last night was a desperate release for lust. I shouldn't have told you but I was jealous of my own brother after seeing him with the most beautiful woman my heart is yearning for. I love you Denyah but I now realize nothing would come of us. Now eat your breakfast before it goes completely cold and turns to jelly." Ray said.

"You must know I might be your sister-in-law." Denyah said.

Ray flared out in laughter. Denyah laughed also and began eating her breakfast while Ray took over the cleaning. When she'd finished eating, and was about to do some more cleaning, Ray told her to rest while he finish off the cleaning. She refused at first, but gave in to Ray when he insisted. She sat and watched him cleaned the room brilliantly. "Now my lovely sister-in-law, you have a beautiful room again, still, not as beautiful as you." Ray said.

Denyah smiled, got up out of her seat and kissed him on his face then said "Thanks for cleaning the room. You've done a brilliant job, thank you."

"Denyah, I'm really sorry. I almost caused you and my brother to split up because of my selfishness and jealousy."

"Ray shut up! If another woman doesn't fall for my man, he isn't much of a man."

"That's the way to be girl,"

Then the door bell rang. Ray answered the door to see Paula standing at the door with her head low and looking shameful. "Can I come in? I'd like to speak to Denyah about what I did last night. She took me into her home and treated me nice and with respect, and I paid her by luring her husband into bed. I'm here to tell her how sorry I am and to ask for forgiveness."

Ray drew back from the door and asked Paula to come in and he led her to as far as the kitchen door and told her to wait while he went and told Denyah "Paula would like to see you." He said to Denyah.

"Tell Paula I don't wish to see her now or ever." Denyah said. Ray smiled. Then Denyah changed her mind and said, "Eugene is as guilty as her. In fact I will see her. If I can forgive my sister for sleeping with my husband, I can forgive Paula who is not a relative. Tell her I would see her Ray."

Ray looked shocked as he deeply looked into Denyah's face before he walked away and met Paula outside the kitchen door. He then looked hard at her and as he saw she could do with a cup of coffee, he told her to go into the kitchen and help herself to some. He walked out of the house and around the back garden while Paula went into the kitchen and poured herself a cup of coffee before she went and joined Denyah in the living room. As she looked Denyah in the face, tears build up in her eyes as said, "Denyah, I wouldn't lift my hands to defend myself if you scratch my eyes out. What I did with your husband last night in your bed was cruel and disrespectful and I'm ashamed and very sorry and I'm asking you please forgive me for what I've done and for hurting you."

"Paula, what you and Eugene did in my bed last night was despicable and was well out of order. You came into my home and I treated you with respect even though I didn't know you. And you respect me in return by sleeping with my fiancée. Have you no shame and respect for yourself. You only met my fiancée last night and already you jump in bed with him. So tell me, what will men think about you? What sort of signals are you sending out to men about us women? That we're private prostitutes or secret whores, you know what Paula, I'm too much of a lady to watch you in my bed and in my house sleeping with the man I am going to marry one day. Instead I prefer to cool you down with ice water. Still we are women and none of us are perfect. Yes, I saw Eugene and I fell in love but I didn't jump into bed with him at first sight. It took me four months before I gave myself to him. Now if you have any decency left in you, you'll never breathe a word to any one about what happened. If you do, I'll crush every bone in your body and pay a private doctor to use your body for experiments." Denyah warned Paula.

"Look Denyah, I'm very sorry. I had too many drink last night and I lost control, I deserve a whipping and I don't blame you for being angry, but Eugene he's the most decent man I've came across" Paula said. "And I took advantage of him while he was pissed. It was I that carried my self to him Denyah."

"He can't be the most decent man if he'd end up in bed with someone he didn't know" Denyah said, then went on to say, "to me he'd acted like a Pitt Bull that served a bitch on heat. And a man that drunk would not be able to have sex. Eugene had known exactly what he was doing."

"Denyah, must you be so bitter towards me, I'm so sorry to sleep with your fiancée, but it happened only because I was tipsy, it won't happen again."

"You damn right, it would never happen again. You just keep your paws off my man; I don't even want to see you look at him again. As you said, what is done is done, I'm sure we can become good friends providing you don't fuck around with him again." Denyah said.

"I would really like us to be friends and also I would like to get to know Ray better, I saw how he looked at me. And yet, from the way he was hovering around you last night, he seems to be in love with you. Make him know that I like him would you?" Paula said smirking. "By the way, is there any chicken left from last night? I'm so hungry. I haven't come to beg for food. I came to make things right with you and to let you know how much I cared for Ray." Paula said

"I think we've a bucket that never been touched in the fridge. You may help yourself and as for telling Ray you're falling head over heels for him, you can tell him yourself as he's still here." Denyah said.

As soon as Paula heated two pieces of chicken, Edna and Ida walked into the kitchen looking happy as kittens. Edna inhaled deeply, rising her bare footed heels off the floor saying "Denyah, I thank you very much for a good night sleep. It was ages since I slept in a comfortable bed. Thank you again and there's any chance of me staying another night?" she asked pitifully. ......Denyah ignored her question.

"Well," Edna said smiling and rubbing her belly. "Denyah I don't mean to be a pest, but I'm really starving. What's for breakfast?"

Denyah looked hard at her then said, "Help yourself to whatever is there in the fridge. Now if you would excuse me. I have better things to do than to stand here with you and decide what's for breakfast" Edna sent out a long yawn before she turned and looked at Paula to see a wide smirk on her face.

"And what are you smirking about? I thought you'd left last night." Edna said.

"I did. But I'm back. And Edna, if you want breakfast, you make it yourself. Denyah didn't know any of us. She was kind to take us into her home and gave us five star treatments. And if that's not enough, you're asking her what is for breakfast? She's not our servant or running a café."

"Paula, I only asked for something to eat. Not to go to bed with her fiancée as you've done." Edna said.

"Look here both of you, I'm fed-up with your abusive lunges and your attitude towards each other and in my home. I don't want any of you to drag my fiancée through the mud with you. If we are to become friends, let's us start off decently by respecting each other. Maybe I'd made a big mistake letting you all sleep in my home." Denyah told them. Paula faced Denyah with sadness on her face and then closed her eyes in shame for a few seconds before she took her small black handbag up from off the settee and after turned towards the front door.

"Paula, I didn't mean to be cruel. I'm sorry" Edna said covering her mouth with her left hand.

Paula stepped forward towards the front door in tears and trying to choke back her cry. Denyah went and held her hand. Nervously she turned and faced Denyah saying "I did leave but I came back early this morning before you were up so that to tell you how sorry I am and so ashamed."

Denyah put her arms around her shoulder and said, "Paula, I would like you to stay. You've make a very bad mistake by going to bed with my fiancée. I'm sure it won't happen again and as I can see through you, I'm sure we would become good friends. However, the amount of times you've apologised to me, I know you mean you're sorry. So, if you really love Ray as you said, go after him before someone else does."

Paula looked deep into Denyah's face and nodded her head and then walked into the kitchen with Denyah. Denyah offered her a glass of port and then asked her to take a seat at the table while Edna and her friend Ida watched with jealous eyes.

As the time was approaching twelve mid-day and was nearly lunch time, Denyah said to Edna, you can heat up a couple pieces of chicken for you and your friends with some salads I've made and put in the fridge. Then as soon the rain stops, I think you and your friends should make tracks."

"Can't we please stay for another night? There are four empty bed rooms that haven't been used." Edna said.

"I don't think I want you to stay another night and you have really done your home work by telling me what I have in my home. You shouldn't have been here in the first place as I don't really know anything about any of you. My fiancée brought you all into my home and I was kind enough to let you stayed the night. I don't need an overcrowded house or a hotel; I need to have my home to myself again." Denyah said fuming.

Meleta walked into the kitchen and looked at Denyah and asked, "What's going on here, have I missed something? Ryan and I would be going home after the rain stops" Meleta said.

"Meleta, do you have to go home today?" Denyah asked.

"Yes Den, Ryan's going to work tonight." Meleta said calmly.

"Oh dear, I forgot he's on nights. Will I see you at the weekend?"

"Den I can't promise you, I'll phone to let you know. About your friends, how long would they be staying?" Meleta asked.

"I told them they should leave after the rain stops." Denyah. said.

"Denyah, I don't see any harm in they spending some time with you as they mightn't have anything better to do. Besides, with them around, it will make it so much harder for Wesley to fish around your house again - knowing that you are not alone will made him think someone is living with you beside Eugene. So he might keep away" Meleta said very caringly.

"What makes you say that Meleta?" Denyah asked looking worried.

"Denyah, I thought I saw Wesley sitting in his car a short distance away from your home last night. However, I wasn't quite sure it was him as it was dark and raining and as he was dressed all in black. Probably he saw me looking at him from the bedroom window and he drove away. I hadn't said anything to you because, as I said, I wasn't sure it was him and I didn't want to frighten or bother you" Meleta said and seemed to be thinking.

"When was all this?" Denyah asked.

"That was yesterday late evening about seven o'clock when it was raining heavy" Meleta said.

"I too had noticed a man sitting in his car on the other side of the road but as I don't know anyone around here, it didn't bother me." Edna said.

Denyah told Edna, Carol, Paula, Ida and Francis they could spend another night. The four of them were very pleased - they thanked Denyah. But Ida said, she would have liked to spend the night as well but she's a nurse and was on night duty.

"By the way, Denyah, I just remembered, Doctor Glennis and his missus asked me to thank you for them as when they left you were absent. Oh, David phoned to say he and Tracy would see you next Sunday lunch time." Meleta said.

Even though it was ten-thirty, it was dark during to heavy rain, thunder and lightening. Denyah showed her four guests the room they would sleep in and she gave each of them one of her nightdresses or pyjamas to sleep in and fresh towels to use. As the evening was getting colder and darker and it was still raining hard, Meleta decided to stay the night and asked Ryan to stay with her and told him he can go to work from there as he had some of his clothes left at Denyah's.

It was okay with Ryan to spend more time with Denyah and this had made her very happy. Paula and Carol shared a room Francis and Edna shared another while Meleta and Ryan slept in their favourite room.

Paula and Meleta cooked breakfast that morning. After they'd eaten, Ryan told Meleta she could spend the remaining week with Denyah but he would like to go home after work to write out some medical reports. And that he would take her home the Friday afternoon after work as it would be his night off again.

"Ok," Meleta told him. That Tuesday night Ryan and Meleta slept at Denyah's, as it's his night off he went home the Wednesday morning leaving Meleta to spend the day at Denyah's.

Thursday morning as he signed out from his night shift, he thought if he should go to Denyah and take Meleta home, or, go home to be by himself. After a brief thought, he decided and went to his home after work. From his home, he phoned Meleta in the evening to know if she okay. As he and Meleta chatted, she asked him, "What are you having for dinner honey?"

"Beans on toast topped with a fried egg and a steaming cup of cream coffee with an apple or an orange for desert which ever I decide. And I miss you honey." he said.

"You meant you miss your food honey," Meleta said

"Absolutely, but I do miss you more my sweet." Ryan told her.

Meleta sounded him a long kiss down the phone and hung up.

Later that night Eugene got home, he explained to Denyah, saying. "I went to see mother and my dad after work and it was raining so heavy that I could hardly see to drive - mother asked me to stay, but as I would miss you so much, I had to say no to her and come home to be with the love of my life."

"Eugene, call me a fool if you must, but I've let the girls staying another night as they asked" Denyah said looking into his eyes smiling.

"Oh, Denyah, that's kind of you" Eugene told her.

"So you don't mind then?" she asked him.

"Oh no, not at all, it's time you made some friends." he said smiling.

The next morning, Eugene's brother Carl and Edna was coiled up in Denyah's settee in the living room kissing, while Patrick and Ida were walking around the front garden admiring the beautiful flowers. As Denyah was looking at them, Paula went to her, saying, "Denyah, look at my ring that Ray gave to me. He took it off his small finger and slipped on to mine and asked me to go to the pictures with him this Saturday night. Denyah, I do like him a lot. In fact, I think I'm falling in love with him. Denyah, can I come and see you again?" Paula asked.

"Yes Paula, you and Ray can visit me at any time." Denyah said and hugged her.

"Denyah, how well do you know Ray?" she asked.

"To tell you the truth Paula, Sunday night was the first time I got to know him well. I think he's okay. The one you have to be careful of is his mother. But if you and Ray decide to make a go of getting together, try not to let his mother squeeze in. That woman seems to think no women is good enough for her sons. I had to fight her for her to back off and leave me and Eugene alone." Denyah told Paula.

"Denyah, would you mind if I spend the rest of the week with you?"

"Paula, I honestly think it is best you went home. I need some space for me and Eugene. You can come and spend sometime here next week if you like. Why don't you ask Ray if you could visit him, he has a nice flat and he's the manager of one of the family hotels, so if you love him and want him, jump in his skin quickly girl,"

"You know what Denyah, you're so right. And thanks for the advice." Paula said.

Later that day after lunch, Patrick and Carl thanked Denyah for looking after them and then they left with Francis, Carol and Edna.

Ray and Paula were ready to leave when the phone rang; Denyah answered the phone as Ray and Paula looked at her. "Give me a minute." Denyah told Paula.

Paula walked away into Ray's arms and began to kiss him. Denyah was looking at them while she was holding the phone to her ear.

"Denyah, is that you?" Lisa asked.

"Yes Lisa honey, it's me. Have you and Richard decided about that loan? You know you only have to say yes and it would be right in your hands."

"Den, thanks, just let me get back to you after I have spoken to Richard." Lisa said then went on to say "Denyah, I was so happy to have heard the way Eugene defended you. And as for that brother of mine, I wish he was there to listen to a real good man that loves you."

"That's where you're wrong Lisa. Wesley was there hiding behind some of the guests but sneaked out quietly when he heard Eugene speak out" Denyah said. Then Denyah said again with relief, "Lisa I saw him with Paris. The poor child is looking undernourished and the state of her was appalling. Her clothes were clean, but she looked scruffy. I so wanted to take her home with me, but he fled away and took her with him. Lisa, would you please give me a few minutes to get back to you. I was just about to say goodbye to one of Eugene's brothers and his girlfriend before they left."

"Okay Den, don't take too long." Lisa said.

Denyah put the phone down then said goodbye to Ray and Paula gave them a hug, and watched them leave. Shortly after she phoned Lisa, Lisa quickly answered the phone as she knew it was Denyah.

"Denyah, Richard and I are wondering if you would ever forgive him for believing what Wesley said about you. Denyah, Richard was acting on what my rotten bastard brother had told him. Poor Richard was in tears when he learnt of the wicked lies that my brother fed him about you having sex with his mates in his bed. You know how Richard is easy to convince. Den, I haven't blamed Richard, I blamed Wesley for the wicked lies he told about you." Lisa shivered as she paused.

"Lisa, you've told me that before. You tell Richard from me that he's not the only one that fell into my devious husband's trap of lies. Tell him I'm glad he has found out what Wesley is like. Anyway, I'm glad that Eugene has brought the truth to light." Denyah told Lisa.

"Denyah right now you have me drowning in tears and I thank you from the bottom of my heart to forgive Richard so easily. He's so ashamed of himself even to the extent of when I'm speaking to you over the phone he left the room. You don't know how relieved he will be when I tell him you've forgiven him. Den you're a true friend."

"Lisa, the bad things that has happened between Wesley and me, I would never forsake you. I class you as family. So, just because Wesley and I split that doesn't mean you and I have split too. Lisa I want us to remain family. Is Richard there?"

Before Lisa could say yes, she looked back at Richard, he signalled her to say no but. Lisa wasn't too happy lying to Denyah lies, so she beckoned him to come to the phone but he shook his head to say no. After a long pause from Lisa, over the phone, Denyah suspected that Richard didn't want to speak to her at that moment. Smiling, she said to Lisa, "You remember to tell Richard in spite of everything, I still love him and I'm inviting both of you to my home next month to have a drink on my thirty-fourth birthday."

"We'll be there, and I'll get back to you about the loan. I do need it but as Richard is still feeling shame it has became hard for him to say yes" Lisa said.

"How about you taking the money and paid up the mortgage without Richard knowing."

"I felt very tempted to take the money, but it would be dishonest and I wouldn't want to do anything disloyal behind Richard's back." Lisa said.

"Anyway, please discuss the loan with Richard and I'll phone you again and kiss Paris for me. Tell her that I love her and I'm longing to hug her, goodbye Lisa." Denyah said.

Just before Denyah put the phone down, Lisa said quickly, "Denyah I'll get back to you later."

"Okay Lisa, I'll be waiting for your call to tell me how Paris is doing and about the Loan." Denyah then put the phone down and smiled.

CHAPTER TEN

Very early the next morning, Denyah was debating if she should do the ironing or the washing as it was raining heavily and darkness covered set in and bringing thunder and lightening. As the rain pours down harder, Denyah looked at the baskets of unwashed clothes and those to be ironed and smiled then said, "Well Denyah honey, as rain hadn't stopped since the day before and you brought in your friends thunder and lightening this' my day of rest. She looked hard at the baskets of washed clothes and then at the dirty ones again. Smiling she took the ironing board and iron out of the cupboard and set them up to do the ironing. After drinking a cop of tea and start ironing one of Eugene's shirts, a hard knocked came on the door before it was opened and shut. As she was alone, she got frightened and dropped the iron as her hands and face instantly saturated with sweat following by slight shivers.

Mrs Brown stood at the bottom stairs and shouted. "Mrs Davis, it's me Mrs Brown. I've let myself in as I thought you might be having a lay in and I didn't want to disturb you."

Denyah smiled. "I'm in the washroom" She said feeling at ease and wiping the built-up sweat off her face.

As Mrs Brown stood in the doorway of the washroom, she took her coat off and shaking the rain off, and then she brushed the rain out of her hair and dried her face before she walked into the kitchen to have a cup of tea that Denyah had just made.

As Mrs Brown was sneezing too often, Denyah went to her, "Mrs Brown you shouldn't have come to work to day and especially as it's raining so heavily. You're soaked from head to toes and you're trembling terribly, Mrs Brown, are you crying?" Denyah asked as she thought she'd saw tears running down her face even though her face was washed with rain. Mrs Brown dried her eyes and forced a smile but as Denyah looked hard on her face, she hugged Denyah and cried out.

Mrs Brown "What's wrong?" Denyah asked, sympathetically.

"My Jimmy is dead. He died last night in the hospital." she cried. "He had prostate cancer." she cried out.

"Would you like me to take you home?" Denyah asked.

"I prefer to be here at this time, if you wouldn't mind." she said mournfully.

"Of course, I want you to be here Mrs Brown. Is there anything you would like me to do?" Denyah asked, being very understanding.

"I would like to rest" Mrs Brown said softly.

Just then Eugene's brother Patrick called in to see Denyah and saw Mrs Brown in tears.

"Her husband died last night" Denyah told Patrick.

"I'm so sorry to know" Patrick said and he gave Mrs Brown one of Denyah's paper handkerchief. Mrs Brown dried her eyes, blew her nose and swallowed some tea. Sitting in her wet clothes, Patrick asked Denyah, "Can you find some dry clothes for Mrs Brown to wear?"

"Sure, Patrick, where's my sense of humour. I would take her up stairs and find her something to wear" Denyah said.

Patrick smiled and poured himself some tea.

"Mrs Brown would you like to come with me upstairs?" Denyah asked her,

Mrs Brown followed upstairs behind Denyah into the late Mrs Carter's room. Denyah opened the wardrobe and asked Mrs Brown to take what she needed as most of the clothes were brand new with the labels. Mrs Brown looked at the clothes and said, "Any one would do. I just need to get out of these wet clothes."

"Well Mrs Brown, as I said take your pick. I had them all cleaned as mom would like them to go out to charity and most of them she'd never wore. Oh there're some new under clothes in the top two draws in the wardrobe" Denyah told Mrs Brown.

Mrs Brown had looked sad as she took a plain blue frock and underclothes that had never been worn and were still sealed in their wrappers. "Would you mind if I change in your bathroom?" Mrs Brown asked.

"Of course you can, I'll be doing some washing later so you could put your clothes in the wash and I'll be downstairs when you're finish. But I think you should take a warm radox bath to help you relax" Denyah told Mrs Brown as she walked out the bathroom leaving her.

Outside the bathroom, Denyah looked sadly hard at the door with a sad feeling for Mrs Brown then went and turned off the iron before she went downstairs to meet Patrick drinking brandy.

"Why are you still here Patrick?" Denyah asked him.

"I was with Ida last night and as you're not living far from her, I came here before I went home. And I also came to thank you for bringing me and Ida together as well as I brought you this little present as a token of friendship." he handed over the little red velvet box to Denyah. "Thanks." she said and she opened the box to find a lovely gold chain. Smiling, she took the chain from the box, held it up to look at it and turned her back to Patrick and asked him to hook it around her neck. As Patrick was hooking the chain, his hands were trembling as he was feeling nervous and uneasy about hooking the chain around her neck. "I could feel your hands trembling. If you can't hook the chain on me, I will ask Eugene." Denyah told him.

Patrick smiled and just about managed to hook the chain around her neck. "Thank you." Denyah told him then moved and sat on one of the dining room chair.

Mrs Brown came downstairs and joined Denyah and Patrick in the kitchen and sat on a chair and said, "Mrs Davis, I'm so sorry to bring my trouble to you. I couldn't help myself crying. I had no one except my Jimmy, and now he's gone" Mrs Brown rolled her bright brown eyes and then covered her brown round shaped face with the palms of her hands and sniffed up.

"You're not on your own Mrs Brown." Denyah said and went and hugged her saying "Eugene and I would like to help you through your bereavement. Can I ask you a personal question?"

"Please do Mrs Davis. What would you like to know? " Mrs Brown asked softly

"Do you own your home?" Denyah asked. Then said "Please Mrs Brown, you do not have to answer if you don't want."

"No Mrs Davis. It's rented."

"Would you like Eugene and me to take care of the funeral Mrs Brown?" Denyah asked.

"No Mrs Davis. I'm sure you've got your hands full of your own problems. I'll just have to give my Jimmy's body over to the government as I haven't got much money."

"You'll do no such thing. My Sister-in-law and I would come with you and help you to make all the arrangements. Then after, you can use my place to have refreshments. You don't have to worry about a thing. Would you like to stay here until the funeral is over" Denyah asked Mrs Brown.

Mrs Brown replied tearfully, "If it's not too much of a burden."

"Of course, it would not be. I want to help you right through the end. I know how much pain you're going through. We cannot bring your husband to life but we can help you to ease your burden. Please say you would stay here. At least until your husband is buried."

"Tell me this Mrs Davis, why do you want a sixty four years old woman as me, to thread around your feet all of the time." Mrs Brown asked.

"Mrs Brown, you don't look a bit older than fifty and you so full of life. Not to mention you shining black head of hair with just a few scattered greys. Besides, my daughter Paris will be coming to live with me very soon and I am pregnant. You'll be so helpful to us as well as a good companion. However, please keep my pregnancy to yourself until I'm ready to tell the world" Denyah said feeling great for herself and remorseful for Mrs Brown.

"Are you sure you're pregnant?" Mrs Brown asked.

"I think I am, I was having morning sickness for the past two weeks and the last time I had my period was seven weeks ago plus my doctors told me I'm about six weeks pregnant. That's two weeks since. Paris and my baby would need a nanny and I think you would be so right for them."

"Just let me make my mind up." Mrs Brown said getting up out of her seat. "Well I think it's time I start doing some work." she said.

"You'll do nothing of the sort. You just seat yourself down and leave whatever work to me and Meleta. However, there's hardly anything to do. Anyway, this is Patrick my fiancées brother. Patrick, you know Mrs Brown, my home helper."

"It's a pleasure to know you Mrs Brown" Patrick said then he asked her, "Can I get you a drink?"

"Yes please, another cup of tea blended with a little whiskey would be nice."

"Can I get you anything Denyah?" Patrick asked.

"Yes please, I'll have a cup of tea as well without the whiskey" Denyah said.

Patrick made two cups of tea and put one each on the table in front of Mrs Brown and Denyah. Denyah then reached for two slices of vanilla cake and gave one to Mrs Brown and kept one. Patrick reached for the whiskey. "Forget the whiskey please Patrick. The vanilla slice would be nice with the tea" Mrs Brown said.

"Where's my cake?" Patrick asked laughing

"Patrick, help your self. I'm not with it this morning" Denyah said.

Patrick helped himself to a slice of cake and a beer and took his seat next to Mrs Brown and left after he finished.

Later that afternoon Eugene walked in the house looking as happy as if he'd just won a fortune. Denyah thought as he was looking so happy, she would approach him and tell him Mrs Brown's husband had passed away and then ask him if it's okay for Mrs Brown to move in with them for a while until the burial of Mrs Brown's husband is over.

"Sure, I don't see any harm in her staying here. She will be good company for you when I'm out" Eugene said smiling from ear to ear.

Denyah were so happy to have heard him say Mrs Brown would be good company and she rewarded him with a passionate kiss before she went and asked Mrs Brown to follow her again upstairs and show her, the room where she would be living in.

"Are you sure Mrs Davis?" Mrs Brown asked surprised.

"Of course, I'm sure. And please call me Denyah. Oh how I hate to be called Mrs Davis now. I can't wait for my divorce to be finalized. This is your room for however long you would like to stay Mrs Brown."

"Denyah I am so very grateful for everything you've done for me. What have I got to give to you in return but to load you down with problem?" Mrs Brown said.

"You would be giving me more than enough by living with me and keeping me company." Denyah said smiling and holding Mrs Brown's hand.

"I would be so pleased to stay until my husband is buried. Not to live. I'm sorry Denyah I wouldn't want to throw my burden on to you. You're a lovely person, but your hands are full with your own problems. What if I took ill - you see Denyah, I wouldn't want you to have any regrets from taking on my problems as well."

"Look here Mrs Brown, you told me to call you Deloris. I will, but not until you say you will move in here. I would really like to know you're comfortable and I would like to be that daughter you'd so wanted. So please let me be her and don't worry. Our problems, we'll share. All I wish is for you to come and live here with me and Eugene after the funeral. Please say yes."

"Okay Denyah, I will give it a go. And Denyah thanks again. But truly, I really don't know why you want to burden yourself with me."

"Stop it now Deloris Brown! I want to hear no more about this. So get used to me as your adopted daughter and a friend. The sooner you move in with Eugene and me, the happier I would be. There may be times when you and I would accept a little backlash from each other as mother and daughter would." Denyah said as she watched Mrs Brown admiring her bedroom.

Mrs Brown faced Denyah and say, "I think I would like to live here. Already I'm feeling so comfortable here. What can I say except to give you a big hug and say thank you my dear. And don't think I misheard what you said about backlash. "

Both Denyah and Mrs Brown laughed. Then Mrs Brown hugged her again and said. "Thank you my sweet Denyah for rating me so highly."

"Well you take all the time you need to get used to your new home. Lunch will be ready in the next half hour."

Mrs Brown nodded her partly grey head in understanding. Denyah smiled and left her admiring her new bedroom while she went downstairs and into the living room to see Eugene drinking a can of soda. He tried to hide the serious look on his face by smiling, but Denyah knew he was worried over something as he had such frightful look over his smile.

"What's the matter with you now Eugene?" Denyah asked him.

"I'm not sure" he answered looking worried then said, "I'm sorry Denyah. I felt within myself creepy as though something bad is going to happen or has already happened"

"Like what honey?" Denyah asked him calmly.

"How the hell would I know?" he said very stressed and looking confused. After staring in Denyah's face for short while, he turned his back on her. Facing her again, he said "I'm so sorry Den, but I had a nervous shock like something dreadful has happened or is going to happen. Den, I had felt the same when my first girlfriend drowned in a boat accident. She was pregnant but I didn't know until her doctor told me."

"Oh Eugene, I'm so sorry to hear that" Denyah said and asked "So Yvonne wasn't your first girlfriend?"

Eugene shook his head and looking directly in Denyah's eyes. Denyah sympathetically held his hand and said, "Do you want to tell me about your girlfriend and the accident?"

"Den even if I tell you, you can't bring her back. I loved her so much that sometimes I used to have nightmares about her and my baby. She was having our child and she was living in Canada. I sometimes wished she was here. But she can't, can she," Eugene said unaware how much he was hurting Denyah. But Denyah understood the pain he was going through and took his hand in to hers. But he pulled his hands away from hers and he sank into a cold blot of sadness staring at her. Denyah turned away from him and she went to give Mrs Brown her lunch and then went in the washroom and cried softly before she went into the back garden and plucked a white rose that late Mrs Carter had loved so much.

Mrs Brown stood by the kitchen window and watched her, wondering if she had gone deranged as she was watering the plants and seemed like she was talking to them as she could see her lips moving.

But Denyah was saying to the plants, "I'm preparing myself for the worst that I might lose the only man I love. However, as the saying goes, easy come and easy gone and for some the best is only for a short time as love cannot be measured."

Just then, Ryan had just come to see her watering the plants. He shook his head before going to her. But as she saw him coming towards her, she lowered the water hose and went to meet him.

"I just saw Eugene drive off like someone was chasing him. Is everything okay between you and him?" Ryan asked.

"Ryan, I really don't know. Eugene is acting really strange all of a sudden. I think he's still in love with his dead girlfriend. She was having his baby, but sadly she drowned."

"Den, I'm very sorry to hear that. Poor Eugene" Ryan said. "But what brought this on?" Ryan asked.

"Ryan, I think I'm pregnant." Denyah said sadly.

"Telling him you're having his baby, must have brought back strong memories" Ryan said.

"But I didn't tell him." Denyah said.

"How far gone are you then" Ryan asked.

"About eight weeks. Maybe nine," Denyah said.

"Are you sure you didn't tell him?" Ryan asked.

"Yes, I'm sure and now I'm so scared to tell him I am pregnant. Ryan, what if he doesn't want to know." Denyah said nervously.

"Don't be silly, if you're sure you're pregnant, you should tell him. That would bring him closer to you. Den, your upsetting would upset the baby too. I wouldn't want you or my niece or my nephew to be affected in any way. So you tell Eugene you're carrying his baby. The sooner you tell him, the better." Ryan said.

As Ryan hugged Denyah around her shoulder, she said "I will tell him about the baby. But not until I'm sure he wants to share in our lives."

"Whether he wants your child or not, you have to tell him. Beside, I have the gut feeling he would jump over the moon. Sis, he may have loved his girlfriend, but you're exceptional and the apple of his eye." Ryan said.

"I don't have to tell him anything until I'm sure he really wants us. Loving me and not wanting the baby, I wouldn't want him to be near me. Ryan, you know how much I love him. Why is he acting so differently, when he takes me into his arms and shows me how much he loves me, only then I will tell him I'm carrying his baby: As for you, I would very much appreciate if you keep my pregnancy between us until I'm ready to let him know: " Denyah said.

"Okay Sis, but seeing you watering the garden while it was raining made me think you were going out of your mind" Ryan said smiling then went on to say, "Hey, give your favourite brother one of your beautiful smiles."

Vaguely Denyah smiled and turned to go into the kitchen to have lunch. "Would you like some?" she asked Ryan.

"Sure Sis, you don't know how much I'm starving" Ryan said walking at her side into the kitchen.

"Seeing you smile again, it makes my appetite greater. This is the way I like to see you. How would you like me to take you out for a meal later as I won't be working tonight? I'll let you choose where we should go for a meal."

"I'm sorry Ryan. I wouldn't want to leave Mrs Brown on her own as it wouldn't be proper and what about Meleta? Wouldn't she would like to come too?" Denyah asked.

"Believe me, I would only like to take my one and only favourite sister out for a meal but as I realize it might cause ill feeling if Meleta knows, then I'll phone her and ask her to buy us four curries and bring them here. Or, all four of us could go to a restaurant of your choice. If you prefer for Meleta to bring us the curry, I will call her and ask her to. As I said, I would be happy to take the four of us out to dinner Saturday evening to one of the best restaurants - your choice. Say seven o'clock, my treat as it would be my night off too" Ryan said.

"I would settle for a curry later." Denyah said.

"Then rice and curry we'll have." Ryan said.

After lunch, Ryan phoned Meleta and asked her to buy four curries and rice and bring the food to Denyah's house for five o'clock. "Ok," Meleta told him and hung up.

"Oh Ryan before I forget, Eugene's mom invited us to dinner this Saturday evening."

"Den, I don't fancy going. I would go only if you're going and only to please you" Ryan said.

"I won't be going. I'll find some excuse by tonight as Mrs Brown is staying here." Denyah said.

Ryan smiled.

Four thirty in the afternoon Meleta bought the four curries and rice and took them to Denyah as Ryan asked her to. "What's going on Denyah? Why has Ryan asked me to bring food?"

"Meleta there's nothing going on. I didn't feel like cooking, that's why Ryan asked you to bring the curries for the four of us." Denyah said.

"Who are the four" Meleta asked interestedly.

"Well, you and your husband, I and Mrs Brown." Denyah said.

Meleta said nothing more but put the carrier bag on the table with the curries and went upstairs to Ryan where he was resting in his room. "The rice and curry is on the kitchen table" Meleta told him.

"Thanks" he said then told her he was tired and he needed to sleep. But Meleta argued with him telling him "If it was Jenny Lake your eyes would be wide opened. I don't know why I bothered to come here. Ryan, I'm your wife and I love you and I'm having your child. But you appear as if you don't want to be near me anymore" Meleta said angrily and smashed the glass that he was drinking from on the floor beside his feet and cutting him with some of the flying splinters on his right leg.

"What's the matter with you Meleta? I came to see my sister, and as I was feeling tired, I saw no harm in taking a rest in my sister's home. If I'd realized taking a rest here would offend you, I would have drive home and might meet with an accident from over tiredness by crashing my car. Or even get killed. Is that what you want honey! Haven't I been treating you right, Meleta? You're the only woman I want in my bed and I love you. So don't ever link another woman to me. Now please let me get some sleep as I have had a very hard night at work and I'm still very tired." Ryan said smiling.

Meleta kicked the bed and went downstairs and said to Denyah, "You know what Denyah, I think after us women have been sampled by our men they seemed not to want us after. Why did he marry me? He should have chosen one of his white women."

"Now Meleta your being paranoid Ryan is deeply in love with you. By the way, what is this all about? And the little show you had put on last week Sunday telling every one you're pregnant, is that true? And least of all, please keep your complex remarks to yourself" Denyah told her.

"Yes Denyah, I'm eleven weeks pregnant. I'm also sorry to use racist remarks if it sounded like that. Den, you're the last person I would want to hurt" Meleta said nearly in tears.

"Have you told Ryan that you're truly having his child and how far you are?"

"Yes, I've told him and he's happy. However, what about you Denyah, have you told Eugene you're having his baby?"

"No not yet." Denyah answered.

"Den, I don't believe you haven't told him." Meleta said after seeing the uncertain look on Denyah face. Meleta then went on to say "Like you Denyah, I'm truly pregnant and the difference between us two is, Ryan is very happy and over the moon to know we're having a baby. Ops, here I go again. Den, what is happening to me these days? I'm just widening away from you and my husband, instead of drawing closer." Meleta smiled.

Denyah tongue suddenly went twisted as she found the words were difficult to speak out but as time crept on, she and Meleta forgot about their anger and patched up their differences and carried on as normal loving friends.

Five o'clock Ryan woke up, Mrs Brown heated the four curries and rice for the four of them. After they'd eaten, Denyah managed to persuade Mrs Brown to join her, Meleta, and Ryan in playing Black-Jack for at least an hour just to keep her mind off her late husband and to be happy and especially because she was crying so much.

Denyah was feeling very happy to hear Mrs Brown laughing especially when she won each time. Much later as it became very dark, Ryan and Meleta decided to stay the night. Mrs Brown treated the four of them with a glass of port, tea and ham sandwiches before going to bed.

As they were enjoying themselves having snacks, the door bell rang; Mrs Brown looked at Denyah before going and answering the door. As Mrs Brown walked to the door, she looked back at Denyah. Denyah shook her head for Mrs Brown not to open the door. Mrs Brown beckoned her, by showing her palm of her hand to say it would be okay. Then Mrs Brown secured the chain across the door and asked, "Who is it?"

"It's me Ray, I was with Paula earlier but she had to go to work. So I came here as its raining and I haven't got my car."

Mrs Brown moved the chain and opened the door to let Ray in. "You're soaked right through. You should ask Denyah to lend you some of your brother's clothes. I don't suppose you would be going home tonight?" Mrs Brown asked him as rain was pouring down heavily.

"That's if Denyah doesn't mind me staying here. I can't find my flat keys and I lent Paula my car been she was late for work. I don't suppose you could give me something to eat," Ray asked.

"Young man, you're in luck, we have some curry left" Mrs Brown told him.

"Curry would be fine." Ray said smiling. And Denyah gave him a pair of Eugene's pyjamas after he'd eaten, he had a shower. Denyah put his clothes to wash, dried them in the drier, ironed them and took them to him before he went to bed. "Thanks you so much Den," he said sniggering.

"What so funny Ray? You think I'm a fool don't you,"

"Den, my laughing is only meant to be the way things turned out to be. You're a lovely lady. And I was full of joy when you let my brother beg for forgiveness, not knowing in the least that the woman my brother bed would have turned out to be the one I've ended up with. Life is so full of surprises, don't you think so Den?"

"Ray, I really don't want to hear anymore of what went on last Sunday if you don't mind" Denyah said.

"I understand" Ray replied still giggling.

"Ray, grow-up!" Denyah told him.

It was bedtime and everyone said goodnight and went to their rooms. As Denyah knew Eugene might not be home that night, she'd locked her bedroom door in fear of his brother Ray.

During mid morning, Meleta and Ryan were arguing so loudly that they woke everyone. Denyah went to Ryan and Meleta and asked. "Why are you fighting? Mrs Brown and I need our sleep"

Denyah looked on the bedroom clock and saw the time was twenty minutes past four. She frowned as she was so vexed and went back to bed and sat up and hissed her teeth. Then as the house was silent again, she put out her lights, pulled the sheet up to her bosom, turned on her side and was trying to get some sleep. Then as she heard the sound of shattering glass, her eyes opened. "That's it!" Denyah said and got out of bed, switched on the lights, wrapped her dressing gown over her pyjamas and went downstairs to hear Meleta and Ryan arguing. "What's the hell is the matter with you two, your arguments sounded terrible. If you haven't got any respect for me and Ray, remember Mrs Brown needs her sleep as she has to be up early to go sort out her husband's funeral. However, what's going on with you two?" Denyah asked looking very angry.

"Why don't you ask your loving brother" Meleta said.

Denyah turned and looked at Ryan, "I'm sorry sis, go back to bed. You'll never hear another sound from us."

"You're damn right, any more noise from you two, I'll have to ask you to leave" Denyah said. Then as she turned to leave, she saw on the floor one of Mrs Carter's framed photo and splinters of glass. She took the photo up and said, "Look what you two have done to mom's photo."

"It was an accident Denyah. I'll have it reframed later." Meleta said.

Denyah placed the broken photo on the side table before she asked Meleta "Are you alright?" Meleta nodded her head then tears starting running down her face. Denyah was just about to ask her why she is crying, when Ryan said "She's accusing me of having affairs. I can't even find time for myself never mind having other women."

"Meleta, Ryan would never cheat on you. But you're doing a good job by driving him into another woman's arms. You best wake up and hold on to him for there are many women out there who would be glad to scrape him up away from you. Ryan is very honest and a decent person and, I not saying this because he's my brother. Now, if it's okay with both of you, I'll like to finish my sleep" Denyah said and went to finish her sleep without hearing another sound.

Seven thirty that Saturday morning, Eugene tumbled in the house and went straight to bed wearing his clothes with his feet dangling over the side of the bed. Denyah smiled and turned her back on him as she saw him in his shoes. Eight o'clock the morning, as he turned reaching to feel for Denyah, but she was sitting at her dressing table. "I had a hectic time last night. It's the last time I would sleep at my mother's" he said yawning.

"Well it's time for me to get downstairs. When should I wake you?" Denyah asked him.

"Never" Eugene said tiredly.

"So you won't be going to the funeral then? As I can see you're dog tired to jump in bed with your shoes on" Denyah asked him.

"Den, just let me get a couple of hours sleep then I will be as right as rain" Eugene said.

"Okay" she told him as she leaned over him to kiss him on his forehead. He smiled and slapped her bottom lightly then pulled her on top of him laughing. "No, not now, you should have come home last night." she smiled as she left the room and went and started breakfast.

One hour before the funeral, twelve thirty, Denyah phoned her friend Cindy at her restaurant to make sure everything was in order as the mourners would be having their meal after the funeral.

"Don't worry Den, everything is in order." Cindy told her.

Denyah put the phone down and went and got dressed and woke Eugene up. Telling him, "you have to wake up sleepy head. It's time to have your shower and get dressed and have some breakfast"

"What time is it honey?" he asked.

"Half past eleven. We have to be at the Church for twelve thirty" Denyah told him.

He got up raced to have his shower, got dressed, half ate his breakfast before the three hired family cars arrived followed by the mauve draped two black horses and carriage with a white gentleman driver dressed in white suit with mauve sash draping from one shoulder crossed meeting his waist and white cap trimmed with mauve sash.

The late Mr Brown's casket was also covered with a velvet mauve flag. Even though it was a funeral, it was also the talk amongst the mourners, and most of all Mrs Brown, as she was in shock and tears because she was only looking for an ordinary hearse and a simple funeral with cake, sandwiches, biscuits and tea refreshments after her husband's funeral.

Denyah smiled to see Mrs Brown looking comfortable. Both Denyah and Mrs Brown sat at the back in one of the front family cars while Eugene sat in the front with the driver behind the horse and carriage. As Denyah held Mrs Brown hand to comfort her, Mrs Brown dried her tears and whispered to Denyah, "Why have you gone to such an extreme when all I ever wanted was a simple funeral for my dear departed husband followed by tea and cake after?"

"Please don't worry Mom, I know what you meant by a simple funeral, but I think your husband deserved to be sent off in the way he deserved. Mom, you are my family now, so you just cry to your heart's content" Denyah said then looked back to see Meleta, Ryan, and Carl in second hired car followed by Ray, Paula and Patrick in the third hired car with Jenny and Curt following behind the rest of the family and also friends in their own cars as well a hired luxury white fifty two seats coach that Eugene hired for those that hadn't had a car and wanted to go to Mr Brown's funeral to paid their respects.

After Mrs Brown husband was buried, the mourners went to Cindy's, one of Eugene's restaurants, for meals and drinks. Cindy puts on a good variety of food and drinks. Every table was decorated with at least four bottles of red wines, whiskey and brandy including cartons of orange and fruit juices and self served meals of their choices and pints of beer.

As darkness beginning to set in, Eugene made arrangement with the coach driver to take the mourners to their gates and saw them into their homes before he left as some mourners were tipsy.

Eugene took Denyah and Mrs Brown home and went back to the restaurant to make sure Cindy and her staffs were okay but as he met his cousin Frank, Cindy's husband, and seeing the place was looking spectacularly clean he had a drink of scotch with Frank before he went home.

"Eugene, some of the bottles were taken away" Frank told him.

"That's okay mate. They deserved a drink before going to bed. My wife, mom and I are very pleased to have seen so many people turned out to pay their respect. Well, cousin, you take care. I'll say goodnight to Cindy and staff then I'll be off home" Eugene said.

Eugene went and thanked Cindy and staff and gave his seven staff two hundred pounds each and a thank you. And for Cindy, he gave her a deed with her name on as his partner in the restaurant she worked in and left. After Cindy read the deed, because of the speed she went to catch him outside of the restaurant before he left in his car, she twisted her ankle. Then as Eugene was getting into his car, she called to him. "Eugene" he turned to look at her then went to meet her.

She hugged him. As he knew her reason to come to him, he said, "You been working for me for years and you've been very honest. So, as you're family, I think you deserved a little extra income. So you won't be working for me alone, but for yourself as well"

"Eugene, I don't know what to say" Cindy said.

"Say nothing" Eugene told her smiling.

"Thank-you and tell Denyah I'll see her soon."

Cindy kissed Eugene on his face and hopped in to her restaurant smiling even though she was feeling pain. As she went to her husband with smile, he asked "Why are you looking so happy?"

"Eugene signed over half the restaurant to me. Frank honey, do you know what this means? We can afford to have a baby now. Here, take a look honey, Eugene Lake and Cindy Lake is the owner. It might come a time when he would give it to me outright" Cindy said to her husband.

"I'm happy for you honey" Frank said and hugged Cindy followed by a long passionate kiss.

Meleta and Ryan said goodnight to Cindy and Frank and left to give Richard a lift home as Richard's wife Lisa had left earlier because of a head ache.

That same night as Denyah and Eugene settled down in bed, he turned his back to her.

"Eugene, I am pregnant" she told him. Eugene immediately faced her with a bright smile and asked interestingly, "Do you know how many months?"

"Well" she said, "I'm not sure for certain. But I think I'm about eight or nine weeks. I hope he not as stubborn and hot headed like his father."

Eugene's face lit up with excitement. Denyah began counting her fingers slowly teasing him and smoothing one of his hands over her tummy, saying, "I think I'm eight to nine weeks now. Maybe ten, I was having morning sickness for the past five weeks."

"Oh Den my love, I'm now the happiest father to be. Why didn't you tell me? Will you marry me?" Eugene asked her. Then said, "No more gardening for you sweetheart, as I wouldn't want anything happen to you and my baby."

Denyah hugged him and said, "Oh yes, I shall marry you as soon as my divorce is finalized. Mr Eugene Lake I love you so much that I can't wait to be Mrs Denyah Lake. What would you like honey, a son or a daughter?" she asked him looking very happy and radiant.

"It doesn't matter my darling. I will love him or her, as I love you. From now on I'm going to take the very best care of you and my baby" he told her with a nice smile.

"Our baby" Denyah said hugging him around his neck.

That night they both slept happily as Denyah slept in his arms practically the night.

The next morning at the breakfast table Mrs Brown broke down crying. Eugene and Denyah comforted her and encouraged her to eat part of her breakfast. "What would have become of me without your support," Mrs Brown asked.

"Please don't think about that, Eugene and I, we were very happy to help." Denyah said.

"You haven't only helped me. You both have given me the best memory to keep for the remaining of my life by sending my husband to the next world like he was a millionaire. I can never repay both of you." Mrs Brown said still in tears.

Denyah hugged her, "you're paying us back by living here with us. We are your family now" Denyah said.

"That's correct." said Eugene, being supportive of Denyah.

One month later, Mrs Brown gave up her rented flat and moved in with Denyah. Denyah made her feeling so comfortable that she began to take Denyah as her daughter and especially when they go shopping together and Denyah would address her as mom. Mrs Brown couldn't be feeling happier or more important to be called mom.

After Mrs Brown lived with Denyah for almost four months, they both acted like mother and daughter. Denyah would call her Mother even in the home or anywhere. Even to when Denyah attended the antenatal, Mrs Brown would accompany her. They both became attracted to each other and share that motherly and daughterly love as well as sharing the house work and with Ray's girlfriend Paula helping out regularly as Denyah was pregnant.

CHAPTER ELEVEN

Three months later, Eugene placed a diamond ring on Denyah's finger above her diamond and sapphire marriage ring the late Mrs Carter had given to her. "This ring was my first adopted mothers. She told Eugene after he slipped his ring on her finger. "Mom slipped her ring on my finger one Sunday when I was brushing her hair. She also slipped her husband's on to Ryan's finger and blessed us both with a kiss and said we're her children and also we become very special to her as the son and daughter she were so longing for. This ring is so very special to me Eugene, Ryan and I are also an item. But as brother and sister, I came to love Ryan so much - in a different way to how I love you of course." Denyah said so calmly. Eugene smiled.

"I know that honey, and I won't have it any other way either." Eugene said.

Amazingly he took her hand into his and blessed both rings with a passionate kiss saying "Oh God, I love you so much."

Denyah smiled happily before she carried her lips to his lips and kissed him then said, "I could never love you more than I do now." she then took her wedding ring off and tossed it into her waste paper bin smiling before Eugene took her and Mrs Brown to have a celebration dinner at the Hilton hotel where they wouldn't be disturbed by customers who knew him.

Over dinner, Eugene noticed her wedding wing was no longer on her finger. As she realized he was looking for her wedding ring, she smiled and said," I've no further need for any other ring but yours and mom's," then she proudly out-stretched her fingers smiling, then as Mrs Brown caught on to what she meant, she slowly hid her hand under the table cloth.

"You don't have to put your hand away honey. It's time you move on from that wicked husband's name you're still carrying. Well, I'll leave you two to finish your dinner while I go and pay the ladies a visit" As Mrs Brown moved from the table, Eugene asked, Denyah, "What's happened to your wedding ring sweet heart? Will you get rid of my ring if our marriage doesn't work out?"

"No honey, our marriage would last for our love for each other is solid. We may quarrel and fight, but I don't think we'll ever part as we're deeply in love with each other and soon having a very special link to join us permanently that we will be so tightly packed" Denyah said.

"Honestly Den, what have you done with your married ring?"

"Eugene, I got rid of it as I no longer have any cause to wear it. As mom said, it's time I move on. Beside, I hate to be call Mrs Davis anymore."

Eugene smiled and kissed the back of the hand that has his and the late Mrs Carter's rings on. Mrs Brown returned from the ladies to see Denyah's hand to Eugene's lips. As Mrs Brown took her seat, she was beginning to feel a little uneasy sitting at the table as she saw they were looking deeply into each others eyes. Mrs Brown got up and said, "I think my bed is calling me."

"I think mine is calling me too." Denyah said smiling as she held Mrs Brown's hand and leaving the soft music playing - when I fall in love it would be for ever.

Eugene paid the bill and left a generous tip for the waiter and they left.

Before they got in their car, he took Denyah's hand into his and said "Honey, you know that I love you very much and that you're the only woman I want."

"I hope so Eugene. And you better not fool with any others otherwise you won't be let off so lightly as before" Denyah said looking radiant.

Mrs Brown smiled.

As they got home, Mrs Brown took to them steaming crumbled apple pie and custard as they sat in the living room. She put one each in front of them and said, "I am afraid it's apple crumble and custard as we haven't had any for a very long time."

"Apple crumble and custard is fine mom. Thank you" Denyah said.

"Thank you" Eugene said and as Denyah and Eugene started eating, Mrs Brown smiled and went into the kitchen to eat hers while she left them into the living room watching TV and Denyah rested her feet on his legs.

After they eaten their deserts, Eugene went to the Red Lion Pub where he met his friends to have a drink even though it was twenty after nine. After having two pints and three whiskies, he went to one of his hotels (The Yellow Floss) to sort out some business with the manager. From his hotel, he phoned and told Denyah. "I'm at one of my hotels and I might be late getting home."

"That's okay" she told him. And they both hung up and while walking with the manager, he bumped in to an old school friend. As they both mirrored into each others eyes, his friend widened his eyes and said. "My, oh my, Eugene Lake, man, I haven't seen you in about twenty years or so. So tell me where were you hiding pal?"

"I was here and there in different places but I think I'm now settled here." Eugene said.

"Well you please excuse me." The manager asked.

"Yes of course," Eugene said. And the manager left smiling.

"Well Dean, it's certainly a lifetime since we saw each other. Have you a family?"

"Sure, the wife is sitting at the far table by the window." Dean said pointing and we have three children, two daughters and a son. The oldest daughter is fourteen. Here is my card, give me a call sometime."

Eugene took the card and said. "I will and said good night." And as he turned to leave Dean invited him to meet his wife. "Well Eugene, please meet my lovely wife Coreen." Coreen outstretched her hand to Eugene smiling and he kissed the back of her hand saying,' It is a pleasure to meet you Mrs Leemore."

"Please call me Coreen." She said then asked, "Would you like to take a seat?"

Eugene looked on his wrist watch and before he said anything, Dean said, "Please Eugene, I insist you have a glass of champagne with the wife and me." Coreen smiled looking into Eugene's face.

"Okay, just one glass of champagne." Eugene said only to please Coreen and he took his seat. Dean served him with a glass of champagne. He sipped slowly and put the glass down. "Drink up mate, you sipped like my wife." Eugene smiled and drank the champagne at one go and said, "I have to be home."

"Please my friend, spend a little more time with us as I haven't seen you in a long time. Tell me are you married?"

"Well, is good as that. My fiancée and I are living together and we have tow daughters."

"Well Eugene, I hope I'll get the pleasure to meet her."

"I would like that Dean." Eugene said and after drinking four glasses champagne, he got up and said, "I really have to get home." He said goodnight to Coreen and Dean walked with him to the hotel door. "Well goodnight Dean." Eugene said.

Dean smiled and said, "I married my wife because I fell in love with her. I know she's of different race, but I couldn't love her more than I do now."

"Dean, your wife is very beautiful and I must say, you're a very lucky man."

"You can say that again mate, All I owed she has made it possible. Her father died and left her some insurance money and she invested it by making cakes and selling it to shops and from there, she set me up selling cars and now I owned five different showrooms. Anyway, I won't keep you any longer but I would like to know about you when we catch up again." Dean said. Eugene smiled and left. Dean returned to his wife and said. "Eugene and I went to the same high school and we left together. From there, we haven't sight each other until now."

"He's very handsome." Coreen said.

"Well, that's enough about my old time friend. And pay more attention to your loving husband. Me." Dean said giggling.

"Honey, I only have eyes for you." Coreen said and said. "Well, I really thing we should get home so the baby sitter can go home."

Dean paid the bill and he and his wife left.

Mid morning, Eugene staggered in the house well boozed-up. He flung himself onto the settee where he slept until the sunlight on the window penetrated his face and woke him up. Looking at his wristwatch he saw the time was twenty past nine. He got up, had a shower and then rushed out the house while Mrs Brown was cooking him his breakfast.

He checked in at one of his other hotels (The Red Fox Hotel) where he had his breakfast. Sitting and listening to soft music, he reached in his jacket pocket for a pen to sign documents he should have signed three days before to give to his bank. After he'd signed the documents and sealed them, he returned them to his jacket pocket again to take to the bank the following day which was the dead-line. As Cynthia the waitress stood in front of him, serving his black coffee, he stared in her face like he was stung by the toast he'd swallowed.

"What the matter Mr Lake. Was something wrong with your breakfast?" she asked him.

"No, oh no, Cynthia the breakfast's fine. Just that I have in my jacket pocket a letter for my fiancée from the hospital three days ago and forgot to give it to her." As he reached in his pocket and took the letter out, and looked at it, he smiled.

"Mr Lake, would you like to call her and let her know?" Cynthia asked.

"Call who?" he asked looking at the envelope.

"You said you wanted to call your fiancée Mr Lake, to let her know about the letter." Cynthia said

"No Cynthia, it would be okay taking the letter to her. Would you pass on these signed documents to Mr Woods for me, and thank you Cynthia:"

"My pleasure Mr Lake," Cynthia said and left with the signed and sealed documents in a large brown envelope. As she was taking the envelope to Mr Woods the hotel manager for him to take to the bank, Mr Lewis the bank manager showed up and before he took his seat, Mr Woods went to him smiling. He walked away with Mr Woods and stopped between five tables and said to Mr Woods. "I'm here with a client. I don't want my wife to know about this."

Mr Woods smiled, "I understand Mr Lewis. By the way, I only received this envelope from Mr Lake stating tomorrow is the deadline for the enclosed documents. Would you mind taking them?"

"Certainly Mr Woods, I'll see they get to the right place straight away and Mr Woods, not a word to my Missus to say you saw me dining with a woman."

"I understand Mr Lewis." Mr Woods said.

Mr Lewis went to his table and sat facing the lovely young fare skinned beauty. As he carried his lips to the beautiful young woman, a young black woman took their photo and run out of the hotel smiling. Eugene run to catch her and as she was going into her car, Eugene grabbed the camera from her hand and said, "Don't you know is rude to blackmail anyone?"

"What's it you to?" she asked.

"Nothing, but other people were kissing, why didn't you snap them?"

"Why don't you give me my camera back and fuck off." she said.

Eugene took the reel out of her camera and gave her the camera telling her. "If I caught you taking photos again with the intent to blackmail, the police would know about you."

"Fuck you." she told him and as he was going into his car, she tossed her camera to his windscreen smashing it. He smiled still getting into his car, but she kicked him on his bottom. He turned and looked at her, "Arsehole." she shouted.

"Look, take yourself somewhere." he said.

She pushed him onto his car and kissed him then backed away smiling.

"It wouldn't work with me. I have too much at stake to let a silly tramp such as you bring me down. If I want to explode, I would rather use a bottle." Eugene told her. And as he was taking his car keys out of his jacket pocket, one of his business cards dropped. She waited until he drove away and picked it up to see his name and his telephone numbers on the card. She smiled telling herself I got you where I want you Mr Eugene Lake. She then drove away. Eugene stopped at some distance away from his hotel, looked at his windscreen and smiled. Thinking of the young black woman, he turned his car around and drove to his hotel and went in to find her but as he didn't see her, he was leaving when Mr Wood walked up to him and said, "I gave your envelope to Mr Lewis. He's having breakfast right now."

"Thanks Mr Woods. I appreciate it. Did you want to see me Mr Woods? I got your message yesterday and seeing you earlier, I'd completely forgotten."

"Oh yes Mr Lake. I was meaning to ask you to do me the favour of lending me a thousand pounds. I need the money to get my daughter a few medical books as she will be going to University in two weeks."

Eugene smiled and took his cheque book out of his pocket and made out a cheque for five thousand pounds and gave it to Mr Woods.

Mr Woods said thanks and looked on the cheque to see five thousand pounds. "Mr Lake, thank you but I haven't asked for this amount."

"I know Mr Woods. Would that be enough to get your daughter the books she needs?"

"Yes, of course Mr Lake, it would buy her what book she needs. And my sincere thanks to you. You don't know how happy you will make my daughter when I gave her this."

"Well Mr Woods, if I can help again in any way, I would be happy to help. Give your daughter my regards and the best of luck to her with her medical studies. Well, I'll see you Mr Woods."

"Good bye, Mr Lake and I'll make sure you get every penny back."

"Mr Woods, the money is a gift to you and your daughter. I wish her well."

"Thank you Mr Lake, God bless you and your family." Mr Woods said and as Eugene saw tears in his eyes, he shook Mr Wood's hand and left.

Shortly after, Mr Woods ran out the hotel and caught him before he left in his car. "Mr Lake, I had a call from Mr Evens Saturday morning telling me you're three days late with the documents but as I told you, Mr Lewis said he would take care of that."

"Thank you Mr Woods, I'm sorry to put you through this. But I believe we still have two days left to seal the deal. Please let Mr Lewis know that the documents must reach Mr Evens today."

"Yes of course Mr Lake. I'm sure Mr Lewis would deliver the documents in person." Mr Woods said and left.

Eugene then phone Denyah on his mobile. Mrs Brown picked the phone up but before she could answer, Eugene said, "Denyah honey."

"Is that you Eugene," Mrs Brown asked.

"Yes, Mrs Brown. Can I speak to Den please?" Eugene asked.

"I'm afraid she had just left with Lisa and Meleta to go and see her friend Bernice and after, I think they would be going shopping she told me." Mrs Brown said.

"That okay, I'll call her on her mobile." Eugene said.

"Is anything wrong Mr Eugene?" Mrs Brown asked.

"No, not at all, I only wanted to tell her I have a letter for her from the hospital that I picked up on my way out going to work last week Thursday morning and I forgot to give it to her. Mom, I'll see you later. And I hope you don't mind me calling you mom out of respect," Eugene asked smiling.

"Not at all, Mr Eugene, I love that. You and Denyah are looking after me so nicely that I wonder if I had children would they be treating me as well. Anyway, I'll pass on your message to Denyah as soon as she comes home, just in case you don't reach her. " Mrs Brown said.

"Thanks mom. And no more Mr, you can call me son or Eugene."

"Okay Eugene and good bye." Mrs Brown said smiling and looking very happy. As she was leaving the room, her eyes caught Denyah and Eugene's photo they'd taken together. She took the photo up, looked hard on them and kissed them both and put the photo back and went to do the cooking.

Late afternoon as Denyah got home, Mrs Brown told her what Eugene said about the letter from the hospital.

"Thanks." Denyah said and she gave Mrs Brown a slice of iced cake that Meleta had sent for her.

"Thank you, but I'm so full, I would save it for tea tomorrow. Denyah you're an angel, you treated everyone so nicely and with respect. My heart was full with joy when Aungus cried telling me a week ago you were looking after him and his family very well. Like me, you gave him and his family a decent way of living."

"Mom, I've made a promise to Aungus that I will help him to take care of his grandchildren. And if the worst comes and he no longer can take care of his family, I would"

"Denyah, as I said, you're a good heart." Mrs Brown said.

"I visited his wife and the grandchildren a few times. I've make a promise to Aungus that they will be alright. I've even tried to get him and his family to move into the guest house for a while, but his wife said they would rather live where they are. Listen to me rambling on about people's business. By the way would you like a hot drink?" Denyah asked.

"I would go and make us some cocoa and would you like lamb chops, roast potatoes, fresh cooked carrots, cabbage and thick tasty gravy." Mrs Brown asked.

"Mom, it's nearly bed time."

"I'm talking of tomorrow as I have to be at my church meeting for two thirty. I would like to cook early."

"Lamb chops are my favourite" Denyah said. "Lamb chops would be nice. Cook a couple extra for Eugene."

"Naturally, apart from that, Eugene phoned and said to call him the minute you get in and you had another call earlier from another man. He sounded strange and drunk.

"Who sounded strange and drunk?" Denyah asked interestedly.

"The man, he was mumbling something P… oh yes, Paris needs you. And that he knows where you live and he's coming to take you home and that's a promise. He really sounded strange. Ah!" Mrs Brown said and frowned vigorously.

Denyah suspected that it must have been her ex-husband made that call, so she phoned Lisa and asked her. "Have you given Wesley my number?"

"No Denyah, I made you a promise that I will never give your phone number to anyone including my husband Richard. Why do you ask?"

Denyah explained "After I got home, mom told me a man had phoned to say Paris needed me and he's coming to take me home. Lisa will you see or phone Wesley and ask him not to phone my home again and to leave me alone?"

"Okay Den, I shall see him later, what the hell does he think he is doing. When he had you, he treated you like shit! And now he won't leave you alone. Denyah I'd wanted to tell you this before now, from when you left Wesley, he's taking it out on Paris. He beats her often and telling her it's her fault that you left him. You'll have to get Paris away from him before he hurts her real bad. Paris is not happy. And she shows signs of anxiety and that makes me worried. She's far too young to experience bad happenings and to be unhappy. Den, Wesley seems not to care for her anymore. All he does now is drowning his sorrows in bottles of whiskey everyday. You should see him now. He's looking so haggard that not even your sister Fay or his other mistress will he let into his house to clean it. And as for me, each time I went to see Paris he would send her to her room using bad language. Den, I'm really living in fear of what he might do to Paris. Den, I can't keep up with him, especially as I'm pregnant and have my son Tylo to take care of. Richard told me, the further I keep away from him the better as he doesn't want our baby to be in distress or harm. Den, even though Wesley is my brother, and I love him, I also hate him for what he's done to you and for the way he's treating my poor defenceless little niece. All I'm asking of you is to try and get her away from him. Believe me Den, I so afraid that he might do great harm to her. The way he's treating her, it's interfering with her school work. Her teacher sent letters to him stating Paris is always sleeping and not doing her work. But he doesn't seem to care. "

As Denyah listened to Lisa with interest, tears came into her eyes and she sniffs up. Lisa asked her, "Are you crying?"

Denyah closed her eyes hurtfully and then opening her eyes to say, "Lisa, I'm sorry for what he's doing to Paris. But as she is his daughter and I was only her stepmother, I have no power over him. And this means he can do whatever he wants with her if you let him. Lisa, Paris is your Niece, you have more power to fight for her and get her than I have. I am sure you can prove to the court or to the Social Services that her father is ill treating her. So I suggest you should do something about getting her away from him for her sake"

"Den, I wouldn't know where to start." Lisa said.

"Lisa, as I have just told you, you can start by going to the Welfare Service or take him to court. I'm out of Wesley's life for good. Besides, Paris has never liked me. She told me so many times. And that she only loves Fay and Bonnie her father's mistresses, so you see Lisa, there's not much I can do."

"Please Den I know you don't mean what you said. I also know you love Paris like your own child. Please Den, Paris needs you. If I didn't have to answer to God, I would send my brother out of this world with a strong dose of poison. And going to the Welfare and telling them how her father is treating her, they would only put the poor child into care."

As Denyah remained silent, Lisa said. "Okay, Den, if you wish the child dead by her evil father, you're doing the right thing by turning your back and letting her die slowly by the abuse of her evil father. He's killing her by the minute Denyah. You were very lucky to get away from him. But I can't say the same for Paris as she's only a defenceless frightened little girl who desperately needs you her mother whom doesn't care about her? Denyah, Wesley is here now to see Richard. Would you like to have a word with him about Paris?"

"No, oh no Lisa, that man is the last person I would want to speak to. Hearing his name mentioned makes me want to vomit." Denyah told Lisa.

And as Wesley heard Lisa say "Den," he snatched the phone out of her hand and said "Denyah please don't hang up."

Floods of tears came from Denyah's eyes as she asked him, "What do you want from me Wesley? You and your daughter didn't want to have anything to do with me. You both had made that clear. Now that I'm out of your life, why can't you leave me alone, I'm getting on with my live, why can't you. I want nothing to do with you. I want you to leave me alone!"

"Darling, I'm regretting all the wrong I've done you. You were my wife, my love and my all and I was too damn stupid to realize until now. Sweetheart Paris and I miss you so much and knowing you're out there in someone's bed is tearing me apart. Den my only love, please come home. If not for me, please come home to Paris. She needs you my sweet love. I know you still hate me, but I deserved that and I would live with that" Wesley said in tears. He then went on, "I played our tune every day (I can't stop loving you) do you remember how often we used to dance to this, our song, Den, my sweet love, please come home and please forgive me for all the wrong I've done you. I shall never hurt you again. And I wouldn't blame you for hating me."

"I don't hate you Wesley, I did but not anymore. Also the love I had for you has died. I feel sorry for a sickening devious cunning mongoose like you. If you really want me to have Paris, with all my heart I will have her. And all I badly wanted from you is divorce" Denyah told Wesley.

"You want my daughter you come home where you belong with us!" Wesley said rudely to Denyah "You're still my wife and I will never give you a divorce."

"As you said, Paris is your daughter and not mine. I don't give a damn what you do with her. Also I don't care a damn about you. Just leave me alone!" Denyah told him as she was trembling in fear and knowing that she really loved Paris and cared about her and that Wesley might hurt her just to get her come home.

As he heard the unpleasant turn in Denyah's voice over the phone, he smiled, saying "So, if I hurt our daughter you will not care? With you out of our lives we have nothing to go on living for." Wesley said in a threatening and angry voice.

"No Wesley, wait," Denyah said closing her eyes as she swallowed the built up saliva and then inhaled deeply before she said. "I don't mind having you as a friend, but you must be fair about us - we could never be husband and wife again as everything has changed for us. We can share Paris."

"Denyah my darling, I want you to come home." he said demandingly.

"Wesley, I'm having a baby."

"I am prepared to be the father. Just say you'll come home. At least come and see our daughter. She's so missing you. Den, I realise now, I nothing without you."

Denyah thought deeply as Paris was in her mind. Crying softly with one hand covering her mouth and the other holding the phone to her ear, she hesitated and just whispered, "I would like to see Paris."

"So, shall I come and get you? Just tell me when and the time. And I'll be there like lightning. Say about eight." Wesley said.

"Not tonight Wesley, I've too many people here and I'll be missed" Denyah said sadly between her tears.

"Oh yes of course, I heard you always have a full house. By the way, I heard you took over your housemaid husband's funeral. How thoughtful. Well, I'm a reasonable husband. Let's leave the time until tomorrow, I'll say the same time; I'm sure you could lie to your lover by telling him you need to spend some time with a friend. Then you could phone him from our home and tell him you're back with me your husband and your daughter."

As Denyah breathe out in lamentation. Wesley blew a couple of kisses down the phone. Denyah shivered in disgust and put the phone down. By this time, she had no idea that Eugene was standing behind the half closed door and was listening to every word she'd said. Turning sadly and in tears, she faced him and froze in shock.

"How long were you standing there?" Denyah asked him and looking guilty.

"Long enough to know something's bothering you" Eugene said looking deep in her eyes. Quickly, she pinned her eyes to the floor to escaped his look, he smiled intently, hugged her around her shoulders, "Denyah, look at me and tell me that it wasn't your husband you were talking to and who'd just upset you." Eugene said very calmly.

Denyah walked a couple steps from him. Then as her legs seemed to go weak and almost fell, he caught her in his arms. She looked deeply into his eyes with her glittered lips parted and in silence.

"Wasn't that Wesley?" he asked interestedly.

She nodded her head yes.

"Den, Wesley and your sister Fay were at the funeral, but they stayed at the back in the church. Lisa pointed them out to me as they both stood in the background. I suppose you didn't see Claire and Joan either."

"No Eugene, I can't say that I did - were at the hotel too.?"

"Den, if they were, I didn't see them."

"Well, you knew that Ryan did take me home on the account of my headache." Denyah said. Then she went on to say "Wesley and Joan have the nerve of the devil to be there where they were not welcome. As for that Joan she has a short wire joined to her evil brain, how dare she came to my family funeral."

"Den, I haven't heard you said anything about your husband, he's worst than Joan. Remember, he's the one that spreads the wicked lies about you."

Meleta intervened to say, "Well, I did see them at the hotel and many more of you so called friends such as, Grace, Gene, Dr Glennis and his fiancée Kelly. And so many more that I wouldn't wish to mention."

"We'll, I invited Grace, Gene and Dr Glennis and his fiancée to lunch next Sunday. I hope you and mother Brown and Eugene will be able to come. I also invited David, Tracy, Lisa and Richard. However, Den, you should have been there to see your ex's eyes wandering in searching for you. I was glad when you weren't there. Anyway, I'm sure you've bypassed him. So if you have one friend left, that must be me" Meleta said and smiled.

Eugene walked away looking confused and vexed leaving Denyah and Meleta facing each other as they stood in silence. As Meleta seemed to be tipsy, she was unable to balance on her feet and then fell bottom down on the special made ten seats curved pale blue settee.

Denyah gently helped Meleta up to Ryan's bedroom and help her out of her suit leaving her in her slip and panties.

"Where's my husband." Meleta asked rudely getting up but fell backward on the bed again as she was so trying hard to get out of bed.

"Meleta, please try and get some rest. You have had too much to drink" Denyah helped her back in bed and told her, "Ryan would be with you soon." Denyah stayed with her for a few minutes and as she saw her lying quietly, she turned the lights off and left the room. Outside the door she looked at Meleta, closed the door and went down stairs to be with Eugene to see him disappearing out of the front door. She rushed out of the house barefooted to go after him, but she saw him getting to his car and driving away. Sadly she got into the house to hear Meleta calling her name.

She didn't answer to Meleta at first, but when Meleta called her a second time, she rushed up to her and said, "Meleta, I'm here, would you like me to make you some coffee or tea?"

Meleta giggled, I would like you to bring me my husband." she shouted as she tried to get up and fell backward on the bed.

"Meleta, try and get some sleep before you hurt yourself and the baby." Denyah said.

"Den,"

"Yes, Meleta,"

Meleta giggled again before she said slurring her words, "I'm still puzzled at how you and my husband became brother and sister. Are you quite sure you haven't slept with him? I want the whole world to know how much my husband and I are in love and we're having our first baby. So if you're hiding behind this brotherly love, you can tell me the truth of what happened before my time with him" Meleta laughed until her laughing turned into crying.

At this time, Denyah eyes filled up with tears at feeling so hurt by Meleta accusing her of sleeping with her adopted brother Ryan.

"Meleta, I'm not staying here listening to you accusing me of been a whore. When you're feeling better, I would like you to leave."

"Den, I know there are certain secrets we have to hide, and I wouldn't blame you for doing that. But you can tell me the truth. I swear that I would never tell anyone if you tell me. Have you slept with my husband? I mean before my time." Meleta giggled again. "Please Den, you can tell me" she said with her right eye closed while the left eyes half closed. "Come on Denyah, are you going to tell me about you and my husband?" Meleta asked.

"Tell you what Meleta?" Denyah said furiously.

"Did you sleep with my husband Denyah?" Meleta asked.

"Oh my God." Denyah said standing facing Meleta as tears falling heavily down her face.

"Meleta how can you think so low of me, I knew my husband had poisoned my friends and family minds about me, but apart from that, I thought you were a true friend to me. Maybe I'm guilty of your husband loving me for whom I am, a sister. But I'm not a whore and the truth to you is I think I'm one hundred steps above you. I've never slept with my husband or Eugene the first time we met. I was married before I gave myself to my husband and that took nearly five months. Eugene, it took me four months. They are the only two men that have breathed in my face. And certainly, I wouldn't open my legs for any man that came my way. Meleta, I'm sorry for the way you felt. It's best we end our friendship and keep well away from each other. You of all people would think so nasty of me. But hear this! You'll never keep Ryan and me apart."

"Denyah, I went too far with you and I'm so sorry. Please don't tell Ryan. As I know he would choose you over me. Are you willing to tell me about how you became relatives?" Meleta giggled again in her childish way.

"Have you listened to yourself how you're hurting me? Meleta you're hurting me so much by insulted me and also accused me of sleeping with one of the most decent men I chose to be my brother. You may be tipsy but you're not fooling me. You damn well had this cooked up in you mind and all this time I thought you were my friend. I'm glad I found out what you are, and you're no better than my devious husband or Joan. I'm not rushing you to leave, but I hope when you leave here, it would be the last I see of you." Denyah said really looking hurt as she watched Meleta in disbelief.

"My sweet Jesus, what have I said, Denyah I was out of order. How can I hurt you and embarrass you after all what you've done for Ryan and me. And knowing you were the one that told Ryan to marry me. Denyah I'm begging you please don't tell Ryan what I said to you" Once again Meleta said and cried and sat up in bed with her hands covered her face. "Denyah, I have really hurt you. Haven't I?" Meleta asked again.

Denyah only looked at Meleta and went to her room in tears and laid across her bed as she thought of Eugene. Then Wesley and others came in her mind saying that she was unfaithful and a bad wife. She cried hard and tears fell heavily on her pillar. "What have I done so wrong to be hated by my own." she asked herself before Eugene walked into the room and left as he thought she were sleeping as she was lying face down and didn't make a move or say anything.

Eugene made himself a corned beef sandwich before he went to the pub to have a couple of pints with his brother Patrick and as he asked Patrick to collect his car from the garage as he had a new windscreen fitted.

Patrick gave him his car keys and asked him, "Did you have an accident with your car screen?"

"Yes, a young beauty shattered the screen with her camera."

"Eugene I don't understand."

"She made a pass at me and when I refused her she got furious and butchered my car windscreen so I had to have it fixed before Den finds out." Eugene said.

"Was she pretty?" Patrick asked.

"Patrick, she's like dynamite but I can't afford to lose Den as I'm so much in love with her. Any other women would be a cooling vessel." Eugene said smirking.

"So tell me brother, would you refuse her if you come across her and she's willing?"

"I did. But a second time, I don't know." Eugene said. And he and Patrick left the pub in separate cars.

After Eugene returned home, two hours later, he met Denyah still in bed face up but sleeping. As he saw the cover was down to her waist and her breast showing, he pulled the cover up to her shoulder and kissed her forehead softly before he went into the kitchen for coffee and after went to another of his hotels called. 'Sugar Apple.'

After leaving his hotel and on his way home, the young woman phoned him. "Who's this?" he asked.

"The bitch you told you would rather to use a bottle."

"How did you get my number?" Eugene asked her.

"Never mind, I want you to meet me in an hour. I would be waiting for you in the Mild Stone."

Eugene returned home, took some clothes and went to the Mild Stone to see the black and beautiful young lady. As Eugene walked towards her she smiled. "Why did you phone me?" Eugene asked her.

"I fallen love with you."

"I'm married and I don't love you."

"You don't have to love me to go bed with me?" she said.

"Who are you? Are you a call girl?"

"In a way but only for you, are you going to buy me a drink?"

Eugene took some money from his wallet and tossed it on the table in front of her and turned to leave when she said, "I'm a model and my name is Kalor. I don't need your money, I need you."

"Well Kalor, let me go home and ask my wife if I should bed you and if she says it's okay, I'll get back to you." Eugene said and left leaving the money on the table. She took the money up and slipped it all in the charity tin that was on the counter and left. "Mr Eugene Lake, you won the first round, but I will win in the end" she smiled looking at his card.

By this time he went to spend sometime with his parents as his dad had taken ill. Denyah was okay with that when he phoned and told her.

After one week went by and Denyah didn't hear from him, she phoned him, but he refused to take her calls and to speak to her.

After she'd phoned him so many times and left messages and he didn't return her call, she became confused and feeling rejected and thinking that he no longer loves her. Smiling, she said to herself. "Denyah, girl, pick yourself up and move on. You have God, an adopted mother again and a brother who loves you."

Another week had passed and still she hadn't heard from him or seen him. She felt bad and sickened but she resolved to get on with her life as she thought may be he had heard Meleta asking her if she had bedded her adopted brother Ryan. Or, he'd heard what she said to her ex-husband and thought she still had feelings for him.

This had made Mrs Brown was very upset and feeling concerned for Denyah that she blamed Meleta and Eugene for upsetting her.

After two more days went by and Denyah still hadn't heard from Eugene, she phoned Wesley and asked him to pick her up in China Town car park. He was so happy that he told her "I would be your foot stool for ever."

"Wesley, my only reason is to see Paris. I've no intention of living with you again." Denyah said.

"Den honey, we'll talk when I see you." he said

After Denyah spoke to Wesley, he was very happy. He danced with the kitchen mop to one of Jim Reeves discs (HAVE I TOLD YOU LATELY THAT I LOVE YOU.) As the disc finished, he phoned his sister Lisa and told her Denyah would be coming back to him and Paris.

Lisa turned and looked at her husband in disbelief then faced her brother Wesley and said, "Wesley, I'm sure you have it wrong."

Wesley banged the phone down in anger and sat staring at their marriage photo that hung on the partition over the three seat cream settee.

Just before Denyah went to meet Wesley, she made one last phone call to Eugene, but still he didn't answer or returned her call. In a huff she grabbed her black shoulder strap bag, kissed Mrs Brown on her face and told her she would be home in about an hour. As Mrs Brown saw the unhappy look on her face, Mrs Brown closed her eyes in fearing she might be going back to her wicked husband as she heard her speaking of Paris to him on the phone. Mrs Brown looked hard at her as if it was the last time she would be seeing her. "Mom, I will be okay. Stop looking so worried. I'm really will be okay and I will be home in the next two hours. I love you."

"I love you too Denyah." Mrs Brown said "Den honey, please hurry home."

"Mom, will you please lock the door after I've gone?"

"Yes, of course," Mrs Brown said and patted Denyah on her shoulder then went on to say, " I don't want to know what's going on between you and Eugene, but he's a fool to treat you like he don't care anymore. I'm not going to question you over where you're going, all I'm asking of you is to be careful and to take care of yourself and our little precious you're carrying. Would you like to leave any phone number so that I can reach you just in case Eugene phone or comes home and would want to speak to you?"

"Mom, I really don't feel he might come home tonight. Besides, I won't be gone for long. Here this is my mobile number if you should need me. For you only if you should need me before I get home" Denyah said and gave Mrs Brown one of her cards with her mobile number and reminded her to lock the door while she was on her way out.

Mrs Brown watched her drive her car out of the garage before she locked the door and went and made herself some tea.

As Denyah sat in her car in thought over Mrs Brown and leaving her by herself as she'd left her late Mrs Carter, she got out the car and stood thinking before she got back in and started the car on and off as she was debating whether she should go to see her ex-husband or not. Deep in thought, she rested her forehead on the steering wheel in desperation thinking about Eugene. Smiling, she lifted her head from the steering wheel, lay back with her head resting on the back of her seat and wiped her eyes dry as instant tears filled them. She turned the key into the ignition again. As the car started, she turned it off again as she was still thinking over Eugene. "Shit!" she said feeling so hurt and so used that she cried. She left the car again to get into her house, but changed her mind and stood outside her gate where she phoned Eugene again, but still he didn't answer. She phoned him again but this time, he turned off his mobile phone. Angrily, she walked to her front door and as she was just about to take her key out of her hand bag to let herself into her house, Mrs Brown turned the lights off in the living room. Smiling she dropped the key in her handbag and walked to her car. In thought, she turned back to get in to her house once again but as she open the front door with her key, she found it has been chained. Sadly, she returned to her car and after thinking for a brief moment, she drove away. On her way to her ex-husband, she phoned Mrs Brown and asked her if she was okay,

"Yes Den, I'm okay, are you honey?" Mrs Brown asked her. Then said, "Oh would you give me a call on your way home, so I would move the chain from the door,"

"Yes mom, I will call you, and I'm fine. I'll see you later." Denyah said smiling senselessly. She drove in to China Town car park and parked up her car and bought a ticket for eight hours. Leaving the car park, her ex-husband was on time to pick her up. Playing a gentleman, he got out of his car, and opened the front car door smiling. She got in, he gently closed the door and rushed around getting in the drivers seat. Before he drove off, he looked hard and longingly at her with moistened eyes. He then removed from her eyes her dark glasses and stared into her eyes. He smiled, "I see you still have that sparkle in your beautiful blue eyes. Do you still love me?" he laughed. She made no reply and pulled away her glasses and put them on. He looked hard on her again and drove away with such a lustful smile and went on to say "Honey, you really don't need to be wearing those dark glasses. Denyah my love, I'm really missing you."

"Well, I don't miss you." she replied as she looked at him like she would look at shit, scornfully.

As he caught her watching him with hatred, he meekly said, "I know you hate me honey, my mother always said, you never miss the water until the well goes dry. What was I doing to drive you into another mans arms?" he looked at her as he placed one hand on her leg, while the other one was on the steering wheel. She closed her legs closely with her hands supporting them in a tight hold as if they were going to fall off and then eased near towards the door as she was feeling dirty and sickened of the thought of him touching her. As he saw her face quiver, he cunningly looked at her with a smirking smile and moving his hand upward to her breasts while his other hand remained on the steering wheel. As she looked at him, she heaved and twisted away from him.

"Are you feeling sick? Honey," he asked.

She turned and looked outside the window ignoring him.

"Would you like me to stop for you to sick-up outside honey?" he asked

She didn't answer, but as he smiled, she mumbled, even though, you clothes are clean, you are still riddled with the disgusting smell of alcohol." she then inhaled in perfume scent from her handkerchief and wound down the window to let in fresh air.

He drove on looking at her until he got to his gate. "We're home now my sweet." he said as he was parking his car at his gate. As he did so, he got out and opened the car door for her to get out. Smiling, he made to hold her hand to help her out of the car, but she glided away from him and got out. As they both walked towards his front door, she turned her face away as she shivered coldly. "Honey, we're now home" he said proudly as he opened the door with his key and flung it opened. With a melodramatic smile, he beckoned her to walk in as he stood to one side to let her in before he entered inside behind her and closed the door still smiling.

"I so wanted to carry you into our house like a baby." he said with the same idiotic smile. She looked at him with such hate, that if hate could have killed him, he would have died.

Before she took her seat, he led her by her hand into the kitchen, then to the window and said "Just have a look at our garden my darling, even the flowers are pining for you."

He then left the kitchen and within a few minutes he returned with a half bottle of whiskey and asked, "Shall we move into the lounge my darling?"

She quickly walked passed him and stopped in the hallway looking in the mirror with such a sad look on her face as she said "Denyah I thought you were sensible enough not to let the evil man con you into coming here." she sighed regretfully then Wesley approached her saying "Now you're home sweetheart, please try and relax." Then as they moved into the living room, he said. "As you can see, the whole place is pining for you. I hardly done any work as I myself was losing my marbles over you not being here. But as from now, things would be back to normal. Yes, I would gain respect again with you being here Mrs Davis. My love, I'm sure our daughter would be so happy when we break the good news to her. Well, as I know you were coming, I let her spend some time away."

"Wesley, I'm only here because you promised to give Paris to me."

"Den, my darling, this was the only way I would have get you here." he said and hugged her.

She struggled free and began to cry as she realized her ex had conned her into getting her at his home. As she was having a look around the living room, he said to her. "You see honey I hardly had time to look after the place. But with you here, I'm sure the place would look like it used to be. This means our home would return to its full glory."

"Where's Paris?" she asked him coldly and frightened.

"When you told me you were coming, I took her to her Godmother's for the night. You're staying tonight, aren't you darling?"

"I don't think so Wesley. I'm here because you told me to come and fetch Paris as she wants to live with me, and that you cannot look after her properly."

"Den my sweetheart, I never meant for her to live anywhere but here in your home. This is always your home. I had to cheat you a little for you to come back here to your home where you belong." Wesley said.

"So, where is Fay and the rest of your women, aren't they good enough to take care of Paris and to look after your house? Wesley you disgust me." Denyah said looking at so many empty whiskey bottles lying everywhere on the living room floor and in the corners.

"I only want you Den, a real lady, not sluts or bitches like your sister and the others. You're the only woman I would let touch my daughter. Our daughter, no one else! Not even my sister Lisa would I let have her, would you like me to order us some food before we go to bed? Or would you rather have a light snack? "

"Wesley, I haven't come to sleep; besides, I didn't bring a night dress. Wesley, I'm only here for Paris."

"Well, if you're worrying over something to sleep in, you have no problem. I'm sure you'll find one of your night dresses somewhere in your wardrobe. Or like old times, we can sleep naked. Alternatively, you can use a pair of my pyjamas." Wesley said touching her. She shivered coldly as she had a displeased look on her face.

"Is me touching you making you feeling sick? Honey, your face indicated that me touching you is making you feeling discomfort."

Denyah smirked at him before turning her face away, he said "I could see the expression on your face" he smiled then poured himself some whiskey and moved facing her and smiled showing her how happy he is.

Suddenly rain poured down so hard that it brought on instant darkness. He stared into her eyes and said, "Den honey, doesn't the heavy rain bring back sweet memories sweetheart, I remember times like this you used to fly into my arms until the rain, thunder and lightening passed. Don't you remember sweetheart and how we use to kiss and make love as we listened to the falling rain, oh darling, how romantic those times were."

"Please Wesley, I don't wish to be reminded. Those days I was in love with you."

"And now you're not?" Wesley rudely interrupted to ask "So you're telling me you hate me? Just listen to our record I played all the time you were away - I'm falling to pieces by Jim Reeves." he said then he began to sing with the disc.

"No Wesley, I don't hate you anymore. And you falling to pieces, you brought this on yourself" I just would like to go home as I have an old lady living with me and I'm not feeling good leaving her on her own. I can come back another time to get Paris." Denyah said.

"If you're worrying that I would try and make love to you, you need not worry. I won't even touch you without your consent. Of course, I so wanted to make love to you. But not until you come to me" Wesley said passionately.

Denyah closed her eyes with sickening feelings that she'd felt cheated and trapped. In desperation she used her eyes scanning for somewhere to escape. By this time he was watching her and smiling as her face was showing tension and fright.

As she heard the door bell, she jumped nervously in her seat and looked at him. He got up out of his seat saying, "Who the hell might that be to disturb us. I expected no one!" he said very angrily, pounding the whiskey bottle on the table and looking at her. She raised her shoulder in wonder before he looked on the wall clock to see the time was twenty to nine. He swallowed some whiskey and threw the glass against the partition shattering it to pieces and causing her to jump almost out of her skin with fright. "I'm sorry honey if I frightened you, but, I wish the hell, who ever that is, would leave us alone." he barked.

"Why don't you open the door and see who it is." she told him.

"Den my love, I expect no one but you." he said.

"I should still go and see who it is." Denyah said longing to run out of the door as soon as he opened it.

However, as he had his hand on the door handle, he was been smart in standing at the door holding the latch and watching Denyah as she was watching him. "Well, I must admit," Denyah said softly, "I gave you less credit than you deserved. You evil bastard,"

He opened the door asking "Who is it?"

As he hadn't seen anyone, he closed the door and returned to Denyah. A hard knock came on the door again. He looked at Denyah saying, "Who the fuck is taunting me?" he got up and went to the door again. But before he answered the door, he whispered to Denyah, you sit and don't move. He reached for his gun then smiled before he went and answered the door to see it was Fay. He stood at the door watching her, and then asked her, "What the hell are you doing here? And what do you want?" he asked her.

"Just let me in." Fay said trying to force herself in to the house. "Go home." he told her barring the door entrance with his right foot and the door partly opened as he was holding the latch firmly.

"I'm soaked down to my toes, and still it is raining heavy. So why can't I come into my own home? I live here since Denyah left you. You're a right bastard! No wondered my sister left you for another man, and a real man who cherished and knows how to love her." Fay said angrily.

"Get the hell away from my home!" he shouted to her. And as he went to close the door, he almost broke her right foot as she had her foot inside the door.

"I'm asking you one more time to leave." he said showing anger.

"I'm not going anywhere. I live here and I want to get into my house to change out of my wet clothes" Fay said angrily.

Wesley got so furiously angry that he hit her across her face and ranged his gun at her head saying, "I want you to go away and never fucking knock my door again."

"Why should I go away, I fucking live here too, have you got one of your sluts in there, that's why you don't want me coming into my house?"

"Fay, you are the only slut here as well as a cooling pot to fulfil my needs of cooling off when I need to release. I'm sure you know what I mean. But the truth is Fay, those times are long past, and I have no further use for you. So take you narrow arse off my premises and stay off!" Wesley told Fay and slammed the door shut with a bang that Denyah jumped with fright.

He got back to Denyah and said, "It's one of my dogs returned to get a bone but I haven't none." he grinned.

Fay knocked on the door again. Angrily, he tossed the half bottle of whiskey against the door and it shattered to pieces. Madly, he opened the door and said, "I asked you to go away and leave me alone. But you refused." he looked hard at her then pushed her with full strength sending her to the ground on her back and then flung the door shut with a loud bang making Denyah jump again. He faced Denyah saying, "It's one of my long time bitches that wouldn't leave me alone even though I gave her the push."

Constantly Fay was knocking on his door crying and shouting, "You no good bastard!" she then picked up one of the garden stone and threw it through the front room window breaking one of the glass panels in the door and then shouted "Bastard!" Denyah jumped to her feet out of fear and said, "I'll take a taxi home."

"Shut up! That was your fucking sister that threw a brick through my window. I'm going to break her fucking neck! Now get ready for bed" he rudely shouted to Denyah and then kissed her forehead before he cleaned up the broken glass from off of the wooden floor. Denyah ran to the bathroom heaving repeatedly until she'd vomited. Then as he heard her heaving and sounding like she was choking, he ran upstairs to her and asked "Are you feeling sick honey?"

With her head lowered over the toilet she nodded her head before she replied softly, "I haven't been feeling well lately,"

"So why have you come tonight? I would have waited until you're feeling better. You have only had to phone and explain." he said standing over her.

"I'll be okay. I just want to be on my own for a while." she said.

But at this time, Fay was outside the gate crying and swearing to the top of her voice. "You fucking bastard." Passers by were taking notice of her, as well as they were listening to her abusive languages. Mrs Welch, and few neighbours went to her and asked her to keep her noise down and her abusive language, but she told them to piss off. Mrs Welch went to her and said nicely, "Fay, why don't you go home honey?"

"I'm fucking home but the bastard won't let me into my home. So where am I supposed to go." she said under the bright light that came from the spot lights of the neighbours and Wesley's.

Mrs Welch said nothing more and went into her house leaving her at Wesley's gate.

Neighbours were looking at her and listening from behind their windows to see her running from Wesley as he chased her with his gun and fired a shoot high above her head to frighten her. At this time, Wesley locked the door from outside to keep Denyah in.

However Fay ran to four houses away and knocked on the door shouting. "Help-help, help me! He's going to kill me with his gun."

Catherine opened her door. Fay run into her house and quickly shut the door. "Help me, he's going to shoot me!" she cried holding on tightly to Catherine's boyfriend and screaming repeatedly. "Wesley tried to kill me.'

"Who is going to kill you?" he asked her over and over, but all she does was screaming "He's going to kill me."

During her hysterical behaviour, Catherine slapped her face to get her to stop crying and asked her again. "Who is going to kill you Fay?"

"Wesley, he fired a bullet at me." Fay yells.

"Look here Fay, that man you should stay well clear of. Why don't you find yourself a decent fellow?" Catherine told her.

As Catherine boyfriend didn't hear Fay, he asked Fay, "who did you say is going to kill you?"

"Wesley." Fay replied crying with snot and tears dripping on her bosom. And then went on to say "I know he has another woman in his house that's why he won't let me into the house."

"Fay, that man is bad news. Why don't you leave him alone and go home. Listen to me child, if he has no respect for your sister how on God's earth would he have for you. Have you no shame! Look how he treated your sister and tried to put the world against her, Fay, you need to leave that animal well alone and try to be friends with your sister. Would you like some tea?" Catherine asked her.

"No. I'm going to ask him to take me back." Fay said.

"Well, I think you're a damn little fool! You go to that man's place again and you need help, don't come knocking on my door again" Catherine told Fay.

But Fay just wouldn't listen and she left sobbing and went back and knocked on Wesley's door. By this time Wesley forced Denyah upstairs into his bedroom then asked her "Would you like something to eat?"

"No," Denyah said even though she was a bit hungry.

He turn his hi-fi on and injected one of Jim Reeves disc to play (Tears on my pillow, pain in my heart, you on my mind) He then went downstairs and turned the lights off and after took up with him a bottle of champagne and two glasses. He filled a glass with champagne and gave it to Denyah. She barely took it and smiled vaguely. "Drink up honey" he told her. "There's plenty more. I want you to feel real good." he smiled.

As he sat with Denyah in bed, Fay threw another stone through the front door, shattering the top part of the glass door. He jumped out of bed quickly, shackled Denyah's right hand to the bedstead head before he ran down stairs, opened the door and ran out the house wearing a bright blue short pyjamas pants and a pale blue vest. Fay ran off as she saw him, but he chased after her and caught her and gave her a bad beating busting her lips and blocking up her eyes then dragged her by her long hair from nearly at the end of his street, into his house and tossed her into the living room and kicked her all over her body. As she begged him for mercy, he laughed. "Who is the bastard now?" he asked looking down on her as she curled up hopelessly on her left side and crying out in pain with blood dripping from her lips.

Noises from her and Wesley disturbed Denyah as she was trying to wriggle her hand out of the shackle. Eventually, she got the shackle opened with her finger nail clip. Quietly she tiptoed leaving the bedroom and went and stood on the landing looking down to see her sisters face covered in blood.

As she saw her ex-husband beating her sister, she turned away. Fay cried out in agony from the blows she was receiving from Wesley. Denyah closed her eyes painfully like she was feeling her sister's pain. She moved into the bedroom again as it was all too distraught for her looking at her ex-husband beating her sister. She dried her crying eyes and said. "Why has my sister had to bed my evil husband when the world is full of so many lovely men" Strong hatred races through her mind towards her ex-husband. Then she told herself "Oh, there's no man on God's earth I've bitterly hated so much as my devious husband Wesley for inviting his two mates to have sex with me and then raped and murdered the only decent friend I've had and loved so much and raped me repeatedly and accused me of being unfaithful. Oh God! What am I doing here?"

As she thought strongly of her nurse friend, she was imagining they were dancing together as they had done on Christmas day. A sentimental smile came on her face before her thought went travelling to the morgue to identify her.

As Wesley stood at the bottom of the stairs looking up at her standing on the landing, he grinned sordidly before he tossed Fay to the floor again, savagely ripped her knickers off and cruelly raped her.

As Fay was fighting him to get him off of her, he roughly turned her on her tummy and forced his penis up her back passage out of hate. "No Wesley" she cried hard. "Stop! You're hurting me" But the harder she cried, the more he was forcing up her. She managed to bite his hand. Angrily he pushed her face down on the floor before he punched her in the back of her neck that she was stifling and choking on her vomit. As he ejaculated in her, she hardly had strength to move. At this time, he was pointing his gun at Denyah telling her not to interfere. As she was standing on the landing and looking down on them, she felt frightful and a sickened feeling took her over, she cried, knowing that there's was nothing she could have done to help her sister Fay even if she'd wanted too as Wesley had his gun holding her off.

As bad thoughts race through her mind, she thought of how spitefully Fay had hurt her by sleeping with her ex-husband when there were so many other men she could have had.

Denyah couldn't stop her self saying. "Sister Fay, this is pay back girl, as us mother always said, you lie down with dog, you wake up with flees. Wesley became a dog with thousand of flees bedded within him."

More hatred races in Denyah's mind again as she went into deep thinking, then, said, "Fay, you deserved what you got by regularly sleeping with the most worthless man. But fear not Mr Brute Wesley, your payment will come to you also."

Then as Denyah looked at Fay, she told herself, "Why should I help her when she didn't care a damn about hurting me, or who knows about her and my husband sleeping together?"

Still Denyah cried with her sister like she was feeling her pain as well as was feeling deeply sorry for her seeing the way her heartless ex-husband was penetrating up her back passage as he were carrying out some kind of cult revenge. Fay raised her head to look at Denyah with blood dripping from her lips. The sight of blood triggered off Denyah to be heaving so heavily that she ran to the bathroom to wash her face and swilled her mouth out. As she did so, she looked into the bathroom mirror and asked herself once more, "How could I be as damn stupid to fall into Wesley's slippery cage of lies and filth. What has made him turned into one of the most deadly poisonous serpents I wonder?"

Wesley touched her. She shuddered away from him saying. "Don't touch me!" he laughed then turned and looked at Fay saying, "You no longer appeal to me." he then shovelled up her torn knickers with the mouth of his gun and flung it into her face saying "Take your rancid arse and get out of my house!" Fay cried. "Please Wesley, let me stay the night. I have nowhere else to go and especially it's pouring down with rain. Please Wesley. You've hurt me so much that I can hardly walk. I'm begging you let me stay tonight."

"No," he shouted. "Get the fuck out of my house before I kick you out!" And he raised his gun to hit her. She moved towards the door with her hand covering her face. He opened the door for her to leave but she held on to his hands. He pulled away from her and bending her right hand behind her back then said, "I no longer enjoy you. My wife has come back to me and she's the only woman I want in my life onward."

"Would you think Denyah would want you after you invited your mates to fuck her and raped her nurse friend and then murdered her?" Fay asked him.

By this time Denyah were leaning over the landing rails listening and looking down at them as they moved into the passage.

Fay happened to be running up the stairs when she saw Denyah looking down at her. She went belligerent and said to Wesley. "That's why you don't want me here because the wife you so despised came back to you! She doesn't love you as much as I do. And Paris hates her. Wesley, don't you see we belong with each other?" she then looked up and faced Denyah as hate and tears covered her face. She flung one of her shoes at Denyah missing her head and bawled out at her. "You don't belong here anymore! Why won't you fucking leave us alone and get back to your rich man!"

"You know what Fay, you're so right! I was here because Wesley tricked me by telling me to come and fetch Paris. I couldn't agree with you more. You and Wesley deserve each other. You both resemble a two headed scorpion that has one body, slippery and nasty! Why don't you join the love of your life in his bath to wash the semen out of your backside while he's trying to wash his alcoholic odour out of him! With the seaman smell on you and his alcoholic breath, you both have nothing on a skunk. In fact, you both are a mixture of shit and sperm"

As what Denyah said to Fay had hurt her, she slapped Denyah's face. Denyah gave her a hard thump to her chest knocking her down. She got up, held on to Denyah and cried. "I'm sorry I hit you. You should hate me for hurting you" Fay told her.

"Fay, I could never hate you as much as I hated Wesley for what he's doing to us, you should hate him too. You're young and beautiful and I can help you to go forward if you let me. Look at what he's doing to us. What he just did to you. Fay, it's a matter of time until he would hurt you real bad so that you won't be any use to yourself. What I saw he's done to you, it was appalling. He's done worse to me. Do you think I came back to him? Fay, I'm here because he asked me to come and fetch Paris. But I should be wiser to his game. Fay why lower yourself over someone like Wesley?" Denyah said. Then as she saw her chance to escape out of her ex-husband Wesley's house, she tried opening the door but found it was locked from the inside. At this time Wesley was having a shower. Fay forced the front door lock open and told Denyah, "Go!" Denyah watched her with pity. "Get going now!" she told Denyah again. "Come with me" Denyah begged her.

But Fay smiled and then pushed Denyah out of the door and locked it. Denyah ran all the way until she'd disappeared out of the cul-de-sac and called a taxi on her mobile phone that took her to her parked car in China Town car park. Resting her forehead against the steering wheel, she cried and then phoned Mrs Brown telling her "I'm on my way home."

Mrs Brown moved the chain from the door and Denyah drove herself home to find Mrs Brown lying on one of the settees in living room waiting for her. "I am sorry mom to stay out this late" she rushed up to her bedroom and then downstairs again.

"If you're looking for that lovely Eugene, he still hasn't come home. Den honey, he will come home. He loves you too much to keep away. You get some sleep and he will be home soon, I promise." Mrs Brown said.

Denyah smiled and went and had a good long scrub with antiseptic soap in a scented foam bath before she went to bed with a glass of strong black rum coffee.

Meanwhile, as Wesley finished his shower, he had a large amount of whiskey before he staggered into bedroom hoping to be with Denyah, but found Fay instead. "What the hell you're doing in my bed. And where's my fucking wife?" he asked in temper.

Fay laughed and said. "Your wife is my sister and I will not let you hurt her anymore. We hurt her enough. What happened to your speech? Oh, I forget to tell you that I doctored your whiskey so that you would not be able to fight me. And Wesley, here's a gift from me" Fay told him and emptied the bullet from his gun and tossed them into the toilet. She then waited until he passed out before she shoved one of his pot handles up his arse and left it there. "Mi," he groaned as he felt pain. Fay laughed triumphantly and said. "At least I left your pot under your arse to fetch your fucking shit. That's more than what you done for me. You evil bastard, I hope you fall and the handle brake off up your arse." she laughed to her heart content even though she was in pain. And she left, leaving his front door wide open.

Mid-morning, Wesley was woken up by the howling wind and heavy rain to feel strong pain up his backside. He was so shocked to have felt his pots under his bottom and the handle stuck up his arse. With a strong pull he pulled the pot and the handle come flying out with a mixture of excrement and blood. The horrifying pain he was in, he called in his doctor and told him. "I was drugged by one of my whores and she pushed the pot handle up me."

His doctor laughed and said "Mr Davis, you were very luckily the pot handle hadn't broke off in you." The doctor giggled then asked. "Was the handle a substitute?" His doctor found it funny and burst into laughter then gave him prescription for two sets of Antibiotic ointments and penicillin tablets. "Mr Davis, you should take two tablets every four hours and the tube of cream, to be used three times a day in and around the bruised area using a surgical glove and the ten capsules to push up the back passage every night for ten nights. Well, you should be okay in about eight days. Oh drink plenty of prune juice to help you make passing excrement easier. Good morning Mr Davis."

And as the doctor was leaving, he smiled again and said, "Please take the real thing next time."

"Doc, would you keep this between us" Wesley lowered his head feeling shame.

"Don't worry Mr Davis, like you, I swear to secrecy." his doctor said and left smiling from ear to ear until he got in his car he burst into laughter and drove away to his home. Even when he walked in his home he was still in laughter.

"What so funny." his wife asked him.

"Miriam you don't want to know. Will you wake me about nine o'clock, I'm working in the surgery this morning and I have to be there at ten." the doctor said.

CHAPTER TWELVE

Very early the next morning Wesley was so much in pain up his back passage that he called his doctor to come to him again as he couldn't walk properly. "Doc," he said, the pain in my back passage is crucial but I don't want to go to a hospital."

"I understand." his doctor said, "I will prescribe some stronger tablets. But if the pain continues, I'm afraid you'll have to go to the hospital in case of internal injuries. As the pot end had a knot and might cause some damage. However, I'm putting you on an extra seven days course of tablets one each night and one morning after food and seven days dissolvable capsules. You push one up the back passage each morning, but still use the first course as I prescribed. Let's hope these tablets work. Mr Davis. Please carry on using the ointment as well, three times a day." The doctor gave Wesley a prescription for his medication and left him groaning.

At this time Denyah became very restless and jumped out of bed and had a mid-morning shower and went back to bed thinking about Eugene and crying softly so as not to wake Mrs Brown.

After she'd had a long and silent cry, she went to the bathroom washed her face, and, out of boredom she took herself into the kitchen and made four cups of black coffee one after another and only took a couple sips from each cup and leaving the unfinished cups of coffee on the table.

When she looked at the cups of wasted coffee, she closed her eyes and thought of Eugene. Then in anger, she wilfully knocked the partly full cups of coffee off the table breaking the mug and bringing tears into her eyes, then burst out crying.

After Denyah cried for about ten minutes, she dropped off to sleep on the table with her head resting on her folded arms and with thoughts of Eugene on her mind.

Much later that morning, she was woken up by the bright sunlight beaming through the glass window and penetrating her face. Ah-ah- she yawned lazily and her eyes came close to tears again as she thought of Eugene again but with a strong feeling that he might be making a mistake loving her.

A little while after, she couldn't help but burst crying again. She got up from the table and went to her bedroom, got dressed and went downstairs again and starting cooking breakfast for her and Mrs Brown but found it difficult to finish cooking breakfast.

While she was cooking breakfast, she stretched upright and inhaling the smell from the bacon. She smiled thinking of how Eugene liked the way she cooked his bacon. Then sadly she sunk into thought of sadness over him again knowing he's not been at home for days. Eventually she smiled and then beginning crying over the lucky escape she had from her ex-husband last night.

"Thanks to my sister Fay being there at the right time" she whispered looking up to the kitchen ceiling and whispering again. "Thank you Fay, even though you're a bitch." Then as she heard Mrs Brown singing 'Morning is Broken' she stopped crying and quickly dried her tears.

By this time Mrs Brown was on her way to have her shower. Later Mrs Brown went into the kitchen and met Denyah sitting at the table. As Mrs Brown looked at her, her tears beginning streaming down her face again, "What's the matter sweetheart?" Mrs Brown asked.

She shook her head to indicate nothing.

"Come on honey, no one is crying for nothing. You can tell me. Remember we promised to share our problems with each other no matter how small or large" Mrs Brown said sympathetically.

Denyah then smiled and used both her hands to wipe her tears dry.

Mrs Brown looked at her and finished the toasting.

As Mrs Brown and Denyah sat at the table eating, Mrs Brown was looking at her cockeyed and she could see how troubled Denyah had looked and was picking at her breakfast, she asked Denyah.

"Would you like me to make you some porridge honey,"

Denyah shook her head.

"Shall I put your breakfast in the oven for later?" Mrs Brown asked her,

She shook her head again.

Mrs Brown wasn't feeling comfortable knowing Denyah was suffering in some way and didn't want to share her problem with her. So Mrs Brown left mostly all her breakfast and said, 'I'm not as hungry as I thought." Denyah watched her carry her breakfast and put it into the oven and then cleared the table and the broken cups off the floor. As Mrs Brown looked up at her, she burst out crying. Mrs Brown raised herself up, put the pieces of cups on the table and hugged her saying, "You know that I love you and I'll give my life to save you if needed be."

Denyah nodded her head.

"Would you like to tell me why you were crying?" Mrs Brown asked looking sad.

"Oh mom, how could I be so stupid to believe Wesley when he asked me to come and fetch Paris. Mom, I almost got raped by him. If it wasn't for Fay coming there, he would have take advantage of me."

"That rotten good for nothing, I think you should let Eugene know before he turns him against you. So where was Paris?" Mrs Brown asked.

"I think she was at his Cousin Valerie's. That what I heard Fay say," Denyah answered then she drew back looking sad and cold.

As the phone started ringing, Denyah jumped nervously staring at the ringing phone. Mrs Brown looked hard in her face before she got up to go and answer the phone. "Let it ring mom. That must be Wesley." she said. Mrs Brown watched her and listening to phone until it stopped ringing.

Mrs Brown shook her head in despair and then continuing picking up the pieces of broken cups and then as she was about to vacuum the splinters up the phone started ringing again. Denyah got up to answer the phone, but instead she stood over the phone staring down at it. Mrs Brown looked in her eyes and signalled her to answer the phone. She smiled looking at Mrs Brown and then answered the phone, "Hello,"

"Denyah, its Lisa." Lisa said.

Denyah sighed and looking relieved - she showed Mrs Brown a smile to assure her she was alright. Mrs Brown wrapped the broken cups into a thick brown carrier bag and then put it outside in the rubbish bag. She then vacuumed up the splinters that were on the kitchen floor.

"Oh hello Lisa,"

"Denyah, are you alright?"

"Yes Lisa, of course I'm alright. Anyway, what do you want?"

"Can't I phone you my friend without wanting something? I phoned you because you're my best friend and hearing you went to see my evil brother, I was concerned for you. That's why I phoned to know if you are alright."

"Lisa, I'm sorry if I sounded harsh, yes, I went to see Wesley as he'd wanted to speak to me about letting Paris come to live with me."

"Den, I'm happy to hear so, but please be very careful with that man."

"Lisa, that man is your brother."

"Please don't remind Den. However, I would be very careful if I were you. Wesley is like a cock snake that would spray deadly poison on his victims from a distance and then devour them. However, I'm glad to know you're alright. Give my love to Mrs Brown and I'll see you soon."

"Goodbye Lisa."

Lisa put her phone down. Denyah smiled and put her phone on the receiver and looked at the clock to see it was just ten minutes after nine o'clock. After she emptied the coffee pot in the sink, she heated the breakfasts then took both into the dining room and they ate to a finish.

Later she went to her room and fell asleep.

Lunch time, Mrs Brown opened Denyah's bedroom door very quietly and saw her sleeping on top of the bed sheets face up. Mrs Brown smiled and covered her with a fresh sheet and left the room as quietly as she had entered. Outside the room, she closed the door so carefully so as not to disturb Denyah's sleep. "Poor sweet thing, you must have been so tired to sleep so soundly" Mrs Brown said smiling as she was going down stairs to the kitchen to see to the lunch for Aungus and Sonny the gardeners. After she did so, she went and told Aungus and Sonny lunch was ready.

Both Aungus and Sonny left the allotment to wash their hands before they sat down to have lunch. As Mrs Brown sat and talked to them, Sonny asked, "Are you not eating Mrs Brown?"

"I've ate a late breakfast. And I'm not really hungry. Denyah and I will have an early dinner. Well, I have to leave you two while I go and see if Denyah needs anything. When you finish your lunch, please leave the plates on the table and if you need more drink, please help yourselves to what ever you like from the fridge."

"Okay Mrs Brown and thanks for lunch." Aungus said.

"I thank you also Mrs Brown." Sonny said.

Mrs Brown smiled, left and went and had a look in on Denyah but found her sitting up in bed and deep in thought. "I came to ask if you would like some tea or anything to eat. I came before, but you were sleeping." Mrs Brown said.

"No mom. Did you cover me?" Denyah asked.

"Yes honey, you hardly had any clothes on, so I put a sheet over you. Are you coming down with the flu honey?" Mrs Brown asked, very concerned.

"I don't think so; maybe my pregnancy has a strong hold on me. I've been having morning sickness from five weeks ago. I was so hot that I stripped. Mom, is Eugene downstairs?" Denyah asked.

"No Den, he hasn't come home yet. Is everything okay with you two?"

"I hope so mom." Denyah said sadly.

"Well, his dad has had a bad heart condition for some time. I've heard Eugene telling his brothers Ray and Patrick last Wednesday. Den, he might be spending some time with his family and taking his father's illness hard. But at least he could have let you know." Mrs Brown said.

"I hope you're right mom. But if he is, why couldn't he let me know. Still, I hope you're right." Denyah said.

"Of course, I'm right Den. You'll see that he's spending some time with his parents helping out as his father is not well." Mrs Brown said and reassured Denyah everything would be alright.

"I'm very sorry to hear his father's sick" Denyah said.

"Well, I suppose he didn't want to worry you." Mrs Brown said smiling.

"Any phone calls for me, mom?" Denyah asked.

"Oh yes, Lisa phoned about an hour ago, but I didn't wake you" Mrs Brown said.

"Thanks mom, I best call her then," Denyah said and she phoned Lisa, saying, "Lisa, it's me Denyah. I got your message just now."

"Denyah, Wesley told Richard you came to see him last night and you are thinking of coming back to him and Paris."

Denyah sighed deeply before she said "Lisa, before you say anything more, please hear me out."

"I'm waiting." Lisa said, as she waited patiently on the other end of the phone to hear what Denyah had to say. Both Lisa and Denyah sighed then Lisa sent sounds of deep exhalation then said "Den, I only hope you know what you're doing. Eugene is a lovely person and I'll hate to know he left you on the account of my devious brother. Just tell me I've heard wrong and that you're not going back to my brother." Lisa said like she was ready to cry.

"Lisa it's true that I went to see Wesley. But the truth is. I only went to Wesley's on behalf of Paris as I told you before. He phoned and asked me to have Paris last night and said that he cannot cope with her anymore. When I told him I wasn't coming to his home, he said the best way out for him and Paris is a very strong dose of poison. And that her death would be on my conscience. Lisa he frightened me as though he meant what he said by the tone of his voice. This is why I went to see him to get Paris. And because you told me he beats Paris all the time. This is another reason why I went to strike a deal with Wesley to get Paris."

Before Denyah said any more, Lisa cut in saying "Yes it's true. He would beat that child especially when he's drunk, and blame her for you leaving him as if it's her fault. Denyah, he fractured her right hand three weeks ago, but the poor frightened child blamed her fracture on a fall. I think Wesley is the cause. And one evening when you promised Wesley you would see him, and you didn't turn up for some reason, he beat Paris so badly that he had to keep her at home for two days from school as she was badly bruised to her arms and neck. He's treating Paris badly. I'm so frightened for her. I asked her several times to tell me how she comes to fracture her hand. But she always said she fell." Lisa began to cry. As Denyah heard sound of crying coming from Lisa, Denyah said. "Lisa. I know Wesley has hurt Paris. Paris refused to eat my cooking many times, so I told her I would leave her and her daddy. Now he's blaming her for my leaving him. Imagine a little nine year old frightened child. All I wanted is to have Paris away from him for good. And to put your mind at ease Lisa, I will never go back to Wesley. Never, but I'll get Paris away from him somehow."

"Denyah I'm glad. However, Paris is with me. Richard caught Wesley beating her last Sunday and that caused him and Richard to almost have a fight. Richard also suspected that Paris's fractured had something to do with him. As always, Wesley is a cunning bastard, he even called Richard white trash and that I'm a black whore to marry him. Please Denyah, don't you worry too much over Paris, Richard and I won't let anymore harm come to her. You'll have Paris, but we'll have to go about this in the right way. Paris is much happier with me now. But she's crying for you. She also has a friend named Kasha and she is the same age as Paris. Paris doesn't even want to see her father now. All she wants is for you to come and take her home. She loves you very much Den, you'll have to let Eugene help you to get her and believe me Den, you should push forward for your divorce to come through quickly. You don't have to sleep with Wesley to get Paris. I will bring her to you tomorrow." Lisa said "However, Fay told me she stopped Wesley going to bed with you after all."

Denyah's mouth stretched opened without making any sound. But she was very much surprised when Lisa told her what Fay said.

"Lisa, it's true that I went to see Wesley on behalf of Paris. But I wouldn't have gone to bed with him. I would rather kill myself. However, I was also glad when Fay had turned up at the right time to prevent me from being raped by him again. I was so foolish to go to him but I was so eager to get Paris. Lisa, I watched Wesley savagely rape Fay in the hallway on the cold wooden floor after drinking a half bottle of whiskey. That could have easily been me" Denyah said.

"So Fay has told you the truth that I was at his house but as I've told you, I only was there to take Paris away from him. That's all. Lisa, that's the God's truth. As I said, I wasn't thinking straight."

"Look Den, I believe you but I have to go now. I'll make arrangements with Richard to bring Paris to you. Oh, about the loan, Richard and I would be so appreciative if you're still willing to lend us the money." Lisa said.

"Lisa, if I'm going too far, stop me please. I'm willing to give you the full amount to pay off your mortgage as a gift to my nephew and the other baby when she's born and take care of Paris." Denyah said.

"Den, you know if I wasn't desperate, I wouldn't have asked you to lend me the money and I haven't asked for money to take an interest in my niece. I love her as I would love my own children. If the bank wasn't on our backs, I wouldn't even bother to ask. But yes Denyah, I accept. I will pay back part of the amount." Lisa said.

"I'm glad you accept. When you bring Paris to me; you let me know how much is left on the house" Denyah said. "And Lisa, the money is really a gift for you. You've been so good to me. And you've treated me like I'm your real sister."

"Thank you Den. I'm your real sister whether you stayed married to Wesley or not. Thank you Den and I love you."

"That's okay. You're a true friend as well as my sister and I love you too Lisa. You have made me feel very happy. Well, we'll see each other tomorrow by God's will. Goodbye Lisa." Denyah said.

"Goodbye Den." Lisa said and hung up. Denyah put the phone down and turned to see Eugene standing behind her.

Eugene hugged her saying "I'm sorry about last night for not coming home. And for the other days, we had to call the doctor in for dad. His heart is playing him up again and I just couldn't run out on him like I didn't care."

"Eugene, I'm sorry that your dad's got worse." Denyah said.

"How was your day sweetheart?" he asked.

"Well, for a start I missed you. Secondly, I went to see Wesley as he asked me to come and fetch Paris as he couldn't cope with her."

"You what, are you going crazy! You could have easily got hurt or met your death" Eugene said outraged.

But for the rest of the day, Eugene, Denyah and Mrs Brown were very happy sharing jokes, food and games.

The following morning Lisa drove Paris to be with Denyah. When they got to Denyah's gate, Lisa sat in the driving seat of her car and had a good look at the house and front garden while Paris sat uncomfortable and anxious and wanted to go into the house to be with Denyah, who she called mother. As Lisa looked back at Paris and saw the frown on her sweet little peach complexion face, Lisa got out of her car, slowly walked to the door and rang the door bell. Eugene answered the door and gave Lisa a lovely smile before he moved to one side and asked her "Come in please."

"Who is it Eugene?" Denyah asked gloomily. Before Eugene could answer Denyah, Paris ran straight into her arms and began to cry. Denyah hugged her, dried her eyes and then thanked Lisa for bringing Paris to her.

"Denyah, I'm afraid what little clothes Paris had are all spoilt thanks to your sister and her father. I bought her a couple of dresses and knickers from a corner shop. Nothing spectacular, well, I have to rush back home before I have my baby in your home. I think I'm in slow labour. My baby's due in about five day's time." Lisa said. "But from last night the pain is on and off like every two hours or less."

"Thank you very much Lisa. And I believe this is for you and my friend Richard, and please don't say one word. Denyah gave Lisa a cheque for half-of-a-million pounds. Lisa stared at the cheque in shock and at the same time screamed out. "Ooh- just one of those labour pains;" she said. Denyah put her arms around Lisa's shoulder and walked her to one of the four seat settees and asked her to lie down while she went to fetch Mrs Brown out of the kitchen to say hello. After ten minutes rest Lisa's pain was gone, Eugene offered to take her home in her car but she told him she would be okay. Then Mrs Brown faced Lisa with smiles. And went and hugged Paris and thanked Lisa for bringing her to her mother. "Poor little thing, she looks as if she were seeing her last days." Mrs Brown said.

"Nice to see you again Mrs Brown and goodbye" Lisa said and then kissed Paris and thanked Denyah for the gift and said good bye to Eugene and left.

"Are you hungry honey?" Mrs Brown asked Paris.

"No, Aunt Lisa gave me lunch. May I have some pop please?" Paris asked.

"Yes. Of course you can have some pop honey" Mrs Brown said, and took her into the kitchen to have a glass of fruit juice.

At dinner and supper, Paris ate all of her food. Mrs Brown was happy to see that. Eugene and Denyah were happy too.

As it was Friday, and the last week of her seven weeks holiday off school, Mrs Brown took Paris shopping for clothes leaving Denyah and Eugene to spend the rest of the afternoon together.

One hour later, Lisa phoned Denyah and thanking her again for the money.

"That's alright Lisa, I'm happy you took it. And I greatly thank you for bringing Paris to me"

"Den you have a beautiful home." Lisa said.

"Lisa, you were here at my home before."

"Yes, I know, but it looks so beautiful. Anyway, how's Paris fitting in?"

"Mom and Paris got to like each other so quickly. She has taken her shopping for clothes." Denyah said.

After Mrs Brown and Paris did their shopping, they took a taxi home. When Denyah saw the clothes Mrs Brown brought for Paris, she looked at Mrs Brown and shook her head joyfully. "I enjoyed shopping with her, and she enjoyed being with me. You're paying me well and I've no one to spend it on. Well, she's as good as my granddaughter. Den, I can't even begin to tell you how happy I am that I'm living here. I love you, Eugene and Paris so much that I don't think I would able to be parted from you. You're my family now." Mrs Brown said.

Paris tried on her five dresses, three skirts, three pairs of jeans, four jumpers, three blouses, four pairs of pyjamas and two pairs of bedroom slippers. She took turn to show Denyah and Eugene what Mrs Brown bought for her and at least two dozen panties of different colours that Denyah hadn't seen.

The smile that was on her pretty little face each time she tried on her clothes filled Mrs Brown's heart delightfully. "She chose them, all I done was paid for them. Tomorrow we'll go shopping for shoes. I bought her some underwear too" Mrs Brown said.

"Thanks mom, you must have spent a fortune. I'll pay you back." Denyah said.

"You'll do no such thing, if I had needed money, I would have asked you. You should have been there to see the happiness on the child's face. She was so happy and that makes me happy too. Now what shall we have for supper?" Mrs Brown asked.

"Chicken and chips for me" Paris said happily fixing her clothes on the hangers.

"We will all have the same." Eugene said and then asked Paris. "Would you like to accompany me to the Kentucky Shop?"

"Yes" Paris said and put the clothes on Denyah's lap saying, "Mom can you please take my clothes up to my room while I go with my dad. And mom, I'll show you my panties my Nan bought me when I get back. Let's go dad."

Denyah and Eugene eyes met in surprise while Mrs Brown lowered her head and seemed well surprised herself. As Paris looked at each of them in turn, she said to Denyah. "You're my mom so Uncle Eugene became my dad and I love him more than my real dad. Mom I don't want to go back to my other dad. I love you too Nan. Am I going back to my other dad mom?" she hugged Denyah asking.

"No honey, you're staying here with us. This is your home now" Denyah told her. Paris hugged Mrs Brown and asked her "Can you be my Nan?"

"Of course my sweet, I'll be your Nan. Now go with your dad and bring us back our supper as your Nan is starving."

Paris held on to Eugene's hand and led him outside to his car while Denyah and Mrs Brown took her clothes up to her room and put them in her wardrobe and her panties and crop vests in her wardrobe drawer.

"I'm sure she will love her room." Mrs Brown said. "What she needs to make her room complete is some dolls"

Half an hour later, Eugene and Paris came back with a bucket of Kentucky fried chicken and chips. After they ate, Denyah saw Paris had her bath before she went to bed as she was looking so tired, and before she dropped off to sleep, she hugged Denyah and said. "Mom, I like my room. It's groovy, much nicer than my old one. I'll like to kiss my Nan and dad before I go to sleep" Paris said. And mom, can I phone my friend Kasha sometime and invite her to our home?"

"Yes of course honey, your friend Kasha can come and see you anytime."

"Mom, I want to kiss my dad and nanny."

"Shall I call them?" Denyah asked.

"Can't I go to them?" Paris asked.

"Of course sweetheart, you can go. I'll wait to tuck you in."

Paris slid downstairs on the landing rail to kiss Eugene and Mrs Brown and then went to the toilet, washed her hands and then to her room. Before she went to bed, she hugged Denyah and kissed her. Denyah dimmed her bedroom lights and left the room. Then as Denyah heard her speaking, she stood behind the door and listened closely. But Paris was saying her prayers softly. Denyah smiled and went downstairs to be with Mrs Brown and Eugene.

"Oh Denyah, I've put the grocery away, we hardly had room for them. Eugene, you have bought enough to last for at least two months. You must have known sweet little Paris would be living here to buy so much cookies and sweets. She's a beautiful girl like her mother" Mrs Brown said.

"I agree" Eugene said.

"Honey, would you like to adopt me as well," Eugene joked.

"So you like her?" Denyah asked Eugene.

"Pity she isn't as old as you and wasn't your daughter. I will divorce you" Eugene joked. Mrs Brown laughed joyously before saying goodnight to Denyah and Eugene and then went to bed. Denyah and Eugene followed later after they'd bathed together.

In the middle of the night, Paris woke up feeling afraid, she went to Denyah and Eugene's room and climbed up in bed between them saying "I can't sleep mommy. Can I sleep with you and dad?"

"Yes of course, sweetheart, you can sleep with us tonight. But you have to get used to your room" Denyah said running her fingers through Paris' hair.

That night Paris slept soundly between Denyah and Eugene and didn't want to wake up until the next morning.

At the breakfast table Mrs Brown asked for Paris.

"She's still sleeping. So I didn't bother to wake her." Denyah said looking half asleep. "She slept half the night with Eugene and me."

"Poor little thing, her room must have felt strange." Mrs Brown said.

While Denyah were having breakfast, Paris ran in to her saying, "I'm so sorry mommy, I wet the bed."

"That's ok sweetheart. Let's take you to the bathroom and have you freshened up then you can have some of Nan's lovely breakfast" Denyah said to Paris and led her upstairs to the bathroom and asked her "Would you like to shower or have a bubble bath."

"A bubble bath," Paris said taking off her pyjamas while Denyah was preparing her bath. Eugene stood at the bottom of the stairs shouting "I'll see you both tonight Den," Paris hurried out of the bathroom to Eugene and kissed him then said, "Goodbye daddy and don't forget my McDonalds Happy Meal."

"I won't honey, go have your bath and kiss mommy for me and I'll see you both later."

"Okay daddy" Paris said and ran upstairs to Denyah, kissed her and said, "That's for you from my dad."

"Well thank you honey" Denyah said then helped Paris in her bath. "Why don't you come in mom," Paris said softly.

"Your bath looks inviting, as much as I would like to join you, I can't because you're a very pretty and big girl. So that means mommy won't be able to fit in the same bath. But we can share the swimming pool tomorrow. Would you like that?" Denyah asked.

"Oh yes mommy. I would."

Denyah shampooed and washed her hair and her back and then helped her to dry her hair before breakfast. It was such a joy to Denyah to see Paris eat all her breakfast and ask for another slice of toast. The telephone started to ring, "Excuse me honey while I go and answer the phone" Denyah whispered to Paris and reached for the kitchen phone. "Hello," she said calmly as Paris was looking at her. "Hello Den, it's me."

"Oh hello Lisa, how are you. Have you had the baby yet?"

"No Den, I don't think she wants to look at my ugly face yet. I'm still having contractions like every hour or a bit less. She's not as quick as Tylo. Maybe she would be ready in the next couple of days. Anyhow, how is my niece settling in now?"

"She's like a magnet to us. You won't believe she's calling Eugene dad and Mrs Brown Nan. Lisa I love you. And I told Eugene I went to see Wesley. He was furious but he forgave me and he's so happy Paris is with us."

"Den, I know Paris would love to live with you. Tell her, her friend Kasha said to call her sometime. And Den, Richard and I cannot thank you enough. We paid off the mortgage and have some money put down for a rainy day. Thank you my friend from the bottom of my heart. That goes for Richard too. Ah, I've just had a contraction. Den, the pain is coming more or less like every twenty minutes. Pray for me aye. I have to go now, I feel like I want to go to the toilet. Bye Den and I'll let you know when the baby's born." Lisa put the phone down. Denyah smiled and hung up then the phone rung again. She stared at the phone before she picked it up. "Hello," she sounded dull and afraid. "Den honey, is that you?" Eugene asked.

Denyah's voice budded out with excitement as she answered. "Of course honey it's me. Please try and come home early so that we can eat together like a real family, we have to make a good impression for Paris's sake, the four of us. Paris is so happy, and thanks for the kiss you gave her to give to me. We love you. And Eugene, please don't make any plans for the weekend. We will be eating out Saturday and we are taking Paris to the cinema Sunday the four of us."

Eugene was absolutely thrilled with Denyah's plan and he agreed not to make anything spoil the two days. Denyah could hear the relief in his voice as he asked her. "Would you like me to bring you anything from McDonalds - it's been demanded by Paris!"

"Just a couple of apple pies for me and mom and don't be too long coming home." Denyah told him and put the phone down.

Seven o'clock in the evening, Eugene came home with a Happy Meal for Paris and four apple pies from McDonald's. Then smiling, he gave Paris a pink velvet covered twelve inch long box. She anxiously undid the ribbon from the box and lifted the lid up to see a beautiful grey kitten. She put the Happy Meal on the chair beside her and carefully took out the kitten and held him to her chest saying "Look Mom, Nan, do you like my kitten dad bought me?" Paris asked them.

"Yes, sweet heart, she's beautiful" Mrs Brown said and looked at Denyah smiling.

"She sure is pretty," Denyah said, and then said to Paris, "Honey, you can play with your kitten after you have eaten. And do wash your hands first. Tomorrow you'll shampoo him."

"Can he sleep in my room with me Mom?" Paris asked.

"Yes, but in his box until we're sure he's very clean." Denyah said.

"Thanks Mom" Paris said smiling and looking at Eugene like he's the best dad in the world. Mrs Brown face looked radiant over Paris's happiness. Denyah's smiled seeing Mrs Brown looking so happy for the first time since her husband has died. Then Mrs Brown said, "Thank you lord to bring this child into this home to make it complete."

After supper, Denyah spoke to Eugene about which school Paris should go to. Then Denyah thought deeply before she said to Eugene "I think Lisa should know we're looking for a school for Paris."

"And don't forget to mention to her you will be seeking your divorce and to get Paris away from Wesley permanently." Eugene said grinning.

The next morning Mrs Brown and Paris bathed the kitten in baby shampoo. Two days later Paris became more settled and slept on her own with her kitten. Denyah was very happy to know she had begun to settle down. Later on that day Denyah gave her a tour around the house. After, she said "Mom I love this house. The winding stairs are very fascinating and I love my room."

"Honey, I'm glad you like it here. How would you like to go to a new school, the one of your choice?"

"I would like to choose my school mom." Paris said then went on to ask "Would my surname be changed to my dad's?"

"No not yet honey, you'll still have the same name as me for now. Now, how about we have our breakfast?" Denyah said smiling. "Oh, your Aunt Lisa told me to let you know your friend Kasha said you must call her sometime. Have you got her phone number?"

"Yes mommy. Can I feed my kitten first, before I phone my friend?" Paris asked showing her light grey sparkling eyes filled with excitement.

"Sure honey, you feed your kitten after. Put your kitten down and then wash your hands and meet me at the breakfast table. Then you can phone your friend Kasha after you have breakfast and fed your kitten. The kitten food is in the cupboard on the bottom shelf."

"Thanks mom. Can't I feed my kitten first?"

"Of course you can honey," Denyah said.

After Paris fed her kitten and washed her hands, she went and had her cornflakes and orange juice and was ready to leave the table when Mrs Brown said, "Do you want to eat some of this delicious looking bacon and scrambled eggs?"

"I'm not hungry Nan." Paris said and went and phone her friend Kasha and to be with her kitten.

"She is a beautiful child just like her mother. Denyah, I love the three of you so much, I can't even thank God enough for giving me such a loving family. By the way Den I believe you did say you were taking Paris shopping to buy her some shoes and she needs some more night clothes."

"Oh yes, would you like to come with us mom?" Denyah asked Mrs Brown. "Sure Den, I would love too - just give me a few minutes to get some clothes on the line. The weather forecast said it would be a lovely day. However, I was just about to leave a note to ask the gardeners if it rained to take the clothes into the washroom for us. Then I suddenly remembered they're not here today. You're a very kind and caring young lady to give Aungus and Sonny the day off without reducing their wages."

"Mom you know me, they don't call me Den for nothing. Aungus and Sonny have family to take care of." Denyah said.

"Let's go Paris. We want to get back quickly. I think you Uncle Ryan and Aunt Meleta will be coming to see you later."

Denyah opened the back door of the car for Paris to get in while Mrs Brown sat in the front seat beside her. On their way to town, Paris fell asleep. "Poor little thing. She must have had a hard night," Mrs Brown said sympathetically.

Denyah got into town and parked her car in a private car park in China Town. After they finish shopping, Denyah paid for parking her car and then drove home. While at home Paris put her shoes, pyjamas, socks away and her two dolls on her bed and played with her kitten after feeding her with milk while Mrs Brown and Denyah were cooking the dinner. Just before the dinner was finished, Meleta and Ryan knocked at the door. Denyah answered the door and said "I thought I gave you both a key."

"Yes, you did, but I left it in my working overall at the hospital." Ryan said. "And I left mine at home." Meleta said. "By the way, has Lisa had her baby yet?"

"Well not yet. But she's having strong contractions she said."

As Paris heard voices, she came charging downstairs and looked hard at Ryan and Meleta smiling. "You must be my lovely niece Paris" Meleta said and lowered her head and kiss her on her cheek.

"Then you must be Aunt Meleta and Uncle Ryan." Paris said then asked "Would you like to see my kitten? My dad bought it for me."

"Yes please" Paris was very happy to show off her kitten. So she took Ryan and Meleta to see her kitten. "She's very pretty like you" Meleta told her, "She sure is." Ryan said looking at Denyah and smiling.

"Have you two eaten yet?" Mrs Brown asked.

"No mother, my wife here starves me so much that I can eat for the five of us." Ryan said smiling.

"Well Ryan, you're in luck. There's more food on the table than all of us can eat so let's go into the kitchen where the nice food is" Mrs Brown said leading the way. After they'd eaten, as usual they moved into the living room where they relaxed with orange juice and cold milk. Then later as Paris was becoming irritated, Ryan asked "Would anyone like to go for a spin around town and then to see where I work."

"Me. Uncle Ryan!" Paris said holding on to his hand.

"Well, Paris answered for all of us. So let's go" Mrs Brown said and Ryan drove them around town and then took them for a tour around the Heartlands Hospital where he works then took them home. Denyah and Mrs Brown thanked him. That night, Ryan and Meleta slept at Denyah's.

Early the following morning just before breakfast Richard phoned Denyah saying "You have a niece born six thirty two this morning weighing at seven pounds eight." Denyah face lit up with joy as she broke the good news to Ryan, Meleta, Mrs Brown and young Paris. Meleta turned and face Ryan and said "Well honey, I think I will need some money to buy a present for the baby - she's only eleven months younger than her brother." Ryan then laughed and said "All the money I have with me is forty pounds."

"Then one of your 'plastic friend' cards will have to do." Meleta said.

"I thought by now you would have had your own" Denyah said looking at Ryan. "She did have her own but spent eight hundred in less than a month practically on nothing, so I took it off her. Give her a year with the card and I'll soon have to come home to you with a begging bowl." Ryan gave Meleta a cheque for a thousand pounds made out to Lisa and said, "This is for the baby." Meleta hugged him saying "Thank you my precious husband." Then she took Denyah on her own and said "Den, I'm so sorry for insulting you that night when I was tipsy. Please don't say anything to Ryan."

"I should, but I won't. You really had hurt my feelings Meleta."

"I realized Den, I'm so sorry. I would never hurt you again like I did. I know now Ryan loves me and is so good to me. Den, I want us to be friends as well as family."

"Meleta, we're that. Now let's go and have a glass of port."

The phone began to ring, Denyah answered. "Hello."

"It's me Cindy. I've heard the good news that Lisa has given birth to a lovely daughter this time and mother and baby are doing very well. We should get together one day and have a drink. Talking about babies, is it true you're having one?"

"Yes, I'm afraid that I am and I'm in my ninth week and Eugene is over the moon. He can't wait to see his first baby."

"I'm sorry to tell you this…" Cindy had a long pause before she whispered over the phone saying, "Eugene has his four year old daughter living with the child's mother's best friend Jade Jenkins but Eugene does not know about the child. I'm helping the child financially. Don't ask me where her mother is as I don't know."

"Cindy how long has you known about the child?"

"The truth is I knew when the mother was pregnant with her. If you can recall I told you she told Eugene the child wasn't his. But she lied. And it's not that mean bitch who tried to fight with you. I really think Eugene should know he has a daughter. Don't you agree Denyah?"

"Yes, of course Cindy, but I won't be telling him. I think you should have told Eugene long ago he has a daughter."

"Believe me Denyah I went to tell Eugene so many times, but each time my mouth stretched open to tell him, I was left dumb struck. Now that I've told you I'll have to tell him."

"So you should Cindy, the sooner the better." Denyah said.

"Please let this be our secret until I tell Eugene." Cindy said.

"Okay, but let it be quick Cindy. " Denyah said.

That evening Cindy phoned Eugene's mobile phone telling him she wanted to see him urgently and then went to see him at his restaurant where he usually ate. "What's so urgent that you wanted to see me Cindy?" he asked her.

Cindy turned and stared at the large aquarium and said "I should have told you before."

"What should you have told me before, is it anything to do with you and Frank?"

"Eugene, I wish it was."

"Then what is so urgent then Cindy?"

"You have a four year old daughter."

"I have what! What's the hell are you telling me. Where's this child."

"Eugene, keep your hair on, you were seeing Chardonnay about seven months after you'd finished with that bitch that was ready to fight Denyah. Your daughter is living with Chardonnay's friend Jade. You were dating Jade weren't you?"

"Yes, I was for a short time."

"Well Eugene, you have a daughter named Jade B. I'm supporting the child because she is yours."

"Well what made you come out of the woodwork to tell me about a child I didn't know I have? Who else know about this beside you and the child minder?"

"Eugene, I won't lie to you. I told Denyah only today and she's the one that told me to tell you. Denyah is a lovely person. She would be a fantastic mother to your daughter. I found out Jade's on drugs and drinking the hard stuff. Please don't look at me like I'm a poisonous snake. I've made a promise to Chardonnay not to tell you or anyone else. But I think you had to know. I'm only sorry to wait until now. If you feel like hitting me, kicking me or making me your enemy I wouldn't blame you."

"Thanks for telling me, but you should have told me long before now. When can I see this child?" Eugene asked.

"Later if you like, would you like me to bring the child to your home, so Denyah could see her too?"

"No, not yet, let me see her first." Eugene said.

"As you wish, you can see her at my place, say six this evening?" Cindy said.

"I'll be there" Eugene said.

Meanwhile Denyah, Mrs Brown, Meleta and Paris went to see Lisa's baby at her home. "Well, how are you my dear and how was giving birth to a second?" Denyah asked.

"I can't say that it was that bad. But I don't think I would be going back down that road in a hurry after having my precious son and daughter. They are almost twins as Taylor is just eleven months older and when Ellie's born he would be just three months older that Ellie and I'm not happy having another child so soon. Believe me Den, she's my second and last" Lisa said.

Denyah smiled.

"Anyway do you all want a drink or anything to eat?" Lisa asked.

"Not for me Lisa, I have just eaten, I don't know about the others" Denyah said and then asked Lisa, "Aren't you happy having two beautiful children?"

"Of course I'm happy to have kids but not as one out one in, I don't want another child" Lisa said.

"You just rest dear. We're okay. Do you want anything before we go?" Mrs Brown asked Lisa.

"No thank you Mrs Brown. Richard's looking after me and the kids' first class. Den, I think Richard would like to have a word with you before you leave." Lisa said.

"Thanks Lisa, I best go and see him then," Denyah said and went to see Richard immediately where he was washing the baby's bottle in the kitchen. "You ask to see me Richard?"

"Oh yes Denyah, Denyah, I wouldn't know where to begin to give you thanks for keeping the roof over our heads especially after taking sides with Wesley. Believe me Denyah I had been really fooled by Wesley."

"That's okay Richard. Wesley would take the clothes off anyone's back with lies and make them believe they are still covered. So don't worry about what has happened. I just want us to remain family without Wesley coming into it. Well you take care of yourself and the family. I'll just go and tell Lisa goodbye before I leave." Richard hugged Denyah and thanked her again. Denyah went to Lisa and kissed her goodbye before she left. Meleta gave the thousand pounds cheque for the baby to Lisa and kissed her. Mrs Brown bought the baby a silver bracelet then left after they said their goodbyes. Paris hugged her Aunt Lisa telling her, "I love you, Uncle Richard and my two baby cousins. And I phoned my friend Kasha. I asked her to come to my birthday party and she said yes."

"I'm happy for you honey." Lisa said looking at Denyah with a nice smile.

"Aunt Lisa, you, Uncle Richard and my two baby Cousins can come too. That's six weeks away."

"Thanks for inviting us honey. I'll let Uncle Richard know." Lisa said.

Paris then kissed her two baby cousins on their little forehead with great care and then her Aunt Lisa before she run into the kitchen and hugged her Uncle Richard and kissed him saying, "I love you Uncle Richard."

Richard was nearly to tears as he looked at Denyah while he hugged Paris and told her, "I love you too honey."

Before Denyah and her family left, they hugged Lisa and said goodbye.

That night Eugene went home to tell Denyah not to be angry with him as he didn't know he had a daughter. While Denyah was sitting in her bedroom alone reading a book, he rested his head on her lap. Tears came to his eyes, he lifted up his head to look up at her and said, "Den, I had to go and see the child and I believed she might be my daughter. I instantly got to like her. She's so lovely. Den you would like her too. Would you like to see her?" Eugene asked her.

"I would love to see her. Now that you know you've a daughter without a mother to take care of her, what are you going to do?" Denyah asked.

"Well, if you'll be her mother - there's no problem for her, I could bring her home. That's of course if you don't mind."

"I would like to take care of her. By the way, what's her name?" Denyah asked.

"Her name is Jade B like her minder. I was told her mother left her with this minder and vanished somewhere. The mother has been into drugs and alcohol for the past two years. Cindy was supporting the child ever since."

"Then you'll have to get her and take care of her from now on. She would be well looked after here. This should be her home as well." Denyah said.

"Thanks sweetheart, you always make me feeling much better." Eugene said.

Ten thirty that night Eugene heard the door bell rang. He opened the door to see Jade the child minder holding little Jade B's hand and a travelling bag. "I brought your daughter home. From when she saw you I can't get her to stop crying. You owe me two years money." Jade the minder said "Her mother named her after me but ended her name with B for baby."

"Would five thousand be enough?" Eugene asked.

"Look Mr Lake, I really don't need your money. But I won't say no to a job in one of your restaurants or hotels. I was an accountant before, but working became difficult after I started looking after Jade B. I'm not asking you for an accountant job, but I can be a waitress since I no longer have Jade B to look after. I would just like to work now to keep my joints flexible and my body in good shape." Jade said.

"Would you like to come in and meet my fiancée?" Eugene asked her.

"Yes, I would like to meet her but not tonight as I have a party to go to. Tell your fiancée good night. Jade B, you be good for daddy. And I'll see you soon." Jade the childminder said.

"I thank you for looking after Jade B. And I want you to go and see Cindy on Monday morning. She'll fix you up with a job. And here, this is for you. Take it." Eugene convinced Jade as she was hesitant about taking the cheque. However, she took the cheque and as she saw it was five thousand pounds, she said "I haven't asked you for money,"

"I know Jade, but I would feel better if you take this small gift from me as a thank you for taking care of my daughter. Jade you can visit her any time and thank you once more" Jade nodded her head, smiled and left. Eugene closed the door and took his daughter Jade B upstairs to Denyah as every one was already in bed. That night Jade B slept with Denyah as Eugene went to help his father catch up on some work as he was recovering from a heart attack and couldn't deal with any strenuous work.

Eugene got home early the following morning to have heard little Jade B wake up crying but as she saw Denyah next to her, she put her tiny hand around Denyah's neck for comfort. Denyah felt her pyjamas soaking wet and she got up and changed her. Eugene moved Jade B into one of the spare bedrooms to sleep being it was mid morning. As she was still crying, Denyah thought she might be hungry. Then as Eugene turned to get out of bed, he kissed Denyah on the face.

"Daddy" Jade B. called as she was trying to reach for the door handle. Denyah picked her up saying, "Honey daddy is in the shower. He'll be with you soon. Come on honey, you had an accident wetting your pyjamas and I changed you." Little Jade B. turned and dropped off to sleep and was the last to wake up at nine o'clock.

While Denyah was giving Jade B her bath, Eugene rushed upstairs calling, "Jade B."

"We're having a bath" Denyah said then she screamed out "Ah," as Jade B flung the wet rag into her face hitting her in the left eye. Eugene quickly entered the bathroom. "What are you two up too, are you fighting?" Eugene asked Jade B and Denyah. Smiling softly he took Jade B out of the bath and wrapping her in a white bath towel and then took her into her room, dressed her and gave her over to Mrs Brown then he went and joined Denyah in her bath where he took her into his arms and was ready to kiss her when Jade B ran back into the bathroom and climbed into the bath with Denyah with her clothes on and crying, "Daddy" As Eugene lips was near to Denyah's lips she moved her head back saying to him "Not in front of Jade B" Eugene smiled then asked, "How did she behave last night?"

"Oh she slept like a log until she wet her pyjamas. And then to my surprise she gave me a warm hug and a loving kiss after I changed her."

"Next she would call you mom." Eugene said in a happy sprit.

"Let's take it, one step at a time aye; I'm so happy for her turning point towards me. But I'm certain she knows the difference between her minder and me. However, having two daughters now, I have become one of the happiest mothers alive." Denyah said as she took Jade B clothes off and took her out of the bath and handed her over to Eugene as he held the towel to dry her. Eugene laid her on the bed to dress her but Jade B had other ideas only wanting to jump on the bed while he and Denyah waited and watched until she was tired? But it was joyful for both Denyah and Eugene as they waited. After a long wait she let Denyah dress her, "You can take her now Eugene." Denyah said. But as Eugene outstretched his hands to take her, she reached out and held on tightly to Denyah's blouse. Eugene smiled and was happy to see how his little daughter had taken a liking to Denyah and that he would be at ease to leave her with Denyah. Eugene raised his eyebrows smiling and said, "I think she sees you as her mother now compared to last night. By the way Den, I think Jade B's minder is a lovely person. I tried to give her a cheque and she refused it and only asked me for a job. I'll ask Cindy to give her a job. With her qualifications, I might even ask dad to give her that accountancy job if it's still available. However, I convinced her to take five thousand. I gave her my telephone number and she gave me hers."

"I think she deserves whatever she takes. You should invite her to your brother Ray and Paula wedding. It might be a little late, but invite her to show her your appreciation." Denyah said to Eugene.

CHAPTER THIRTEEN

The next morning Eugene phoned Jade and asked her if she would like to come to his brother Ray and Paula's wedding in four weeks time. "Well, I don't know Mr Lake. I'm thinking of …Eugene cut in on her conversation then explained to Jade, "I

I know it's late, but it would make me and Jade B very happy to see you at my brothers wedding. With you there, I'm sure Jade B would be very happy."

"Thanks for invited me Mr Lake. I'll be there and thanks again."

"I'm Eugene to you, as I would like us to be friends. And thanks again for looking after Jade B."

"Well, I couldn't let her go into a home. Her mother was my best friend and I'm her Godmother."

"Anyway, I'm still very grateful." Eugene said.

Well, this is four weeks later. And this is Saturday. The day Paula and Ray are be getting married.

Paula happily said, "I have one hour left before I Paula Blakemore became Mrs Paula Lake."

Paula was looking so happy as if she went to Heaven and back down to earth with messages to spread to the world from God. As Denyah was helping her with her dressing, she said to Denyah, "It's so funny how things turned out to be. This should have been your and Eugene's wedding. Anyway, I'm really grateful to you and Eugene to accept me into your family" she then faced Denyah in tears and hugged her saying, "Den, I do love you, you know. And believe me: I'm still sorry that I hurt you."

"No more of that talking Paula, I didn't even remember what you've done. I'm now looking to a decent family life of living together. Now I believe your car has just pulled up by the gate. Wait, before you go, let me hook my borrowed gold chain around your neck" Paula turned for Denyah to hook the chain around her neck and then faced Denyah smiling and kissed her on the cheek before they left in the bride's car with Mrs Brown, Paris and young Jade B to be at the Methodist Church for two o'clock. Paula got married in a full length satin dress trimmed with pearls and sequins with rows of fine lace decorated on the flared skirt, a beautiful fine net with mixture veil and a real diamond Star in the middle of her tiara and white high heeled shoes complete with two dozen scented yellow and white roses in the shape of a heart with letters saying I love you from her husband Raymond.

Her husband wore a lovely grey designer three piece suit with a white striped grey shirt and grey shoes, Eugene, his two other brothers, Patrick, Carl, brothers-in-law Ryan and Curt and friends David, Richard, and Glennis dressed the same as the groom. The eight bridesmaids were dressed in pale yellow full length dresses and white shoes; also the eight pageboys wore light blue suits and black shoes and broad black satin sashes and the young bridesmaids and pageboys marched down the Aisle in pairs holding hands behind the bride and groom. Paula's sister was one of the bridesmaids. Denyah wore a lovely pale blue maternity dress.

The marriage over, Paula showed off her diamond wedding ring to her friends and her family. Her mother and father were so gloriously happy for her. Her sister hugged her and told her "I'm sorry to cheat on you with Barry."

"Well, it's now reached the last part of the world, so let's leave it there. Come on, I'm sure you could give me a real big hug and a sisterly kiss and wish me all the best." Paula said to her sister.

Her sister tears came as they hugged. "Aye, Jude, no tears now. This is our happy day. I love you. How would you like to come and spend a few hours with me next Saturday?"

"I would love that" her sister said smiling between her tears.

"But, if I catch you looking at my husband, I'll poke your eyes out."

"Paula honey, your husband is not my type. He's not rough enough for me. That one standing next to your husband is more my type, do you know him?"

"Yes, he's Doctor Glennis."

"Do you know if he has a girlfriend?"

"For what I heard, yes a permanent one and her name is Kelly and she's a nurse."

"Thanks sis"

"You're very welcome Sis." Paula told her.

After photos were taken of the marriage and the guests, they went to "THE APPLE CORE one of Eugene's restaurants where he gave the guests food, drink and music. Ray showed off his wedding ring to his brothers and friends.

There were at least three hundred guests attended the wedding party and everyone looked happy enjoying themselves. Then suddenly Kalor turned up and went straight to Eugene saying, "You didn't invite me to your brother's wedding but I hope you don't mind me coming."

"Look, my wife and children here and I don't want my wife to know that I know you."

"Eugene, I fully understand. I will be on my best behaviour I promise, but you know I want you. I would give you one million pounds if you want, and would make me happy now and then. I love you Eugene" Kalor said.

"I told you before, I don't love you. I want you to stop bothering me." Eugene said.

"Eugene, only time will tell" Kalor said and went to be with friends.

Eugene walked away to be with his brothers and friends.

Almost at the end of the party Wesley showed up and shouted to the DJ asking him to play the tune 'Tears on my pillow'.

"I haven't got that," the DJ said.

"Well, I've got the CD myself." He said pulling the disc out of inside jacket pocket.

"It's my wife's favourite tune, play it for my loving wife to let her and everyone here know how much I love her. Her name is Denyah Davis. Please request this to my loving wife from her devoted husband, that's me. Then play the CD. Simple as that, this will mean a lot to us."

"Okay" the DJ said and took the CD from Wesley and when the track he was playing finished, he put on Wesley's CD and announced coolly "This song is now dedicated to a lovely wife Denyah Davis from her loving husband Wesley Davis." As it began to play Wesley moved into the crowd and took Denyah's hand by surprise and began to dance proudly with her. As this was happening Eugene was talking to some of guests including Ryan and his brother Patrick. As Wesley forced Denyah to dance with him, she began to shiver with fear that Eugene might see them. Her biggest fear was that Wesley might hurt her if she made a scene. She was very tense and she was trembling nervously - she stopped dancing several times and tried to pull free from him. He looked into her eyes and said, "Stop your shivering darling, I won't hurt you. All I ask is for you and Paris to come home with me tonight where you belong."

"Wesley, I can't, but Paris can come to see you sometimes without Eugene knowing."

"So what are you telling me, that you would have to steal chances to let me see you, my own wife and my daughter? When I'm ready to leave, you fetch my daughter and you better be ready!" Wesley demanded. He then tried to kiss her but she moved her face away. As the song was near the end, Eugene left speaking with Ryan to take Denyah, Mrs Brown and the children home when he saw Denyah and Wesley standing closely. Denyah sighed with relief that Eugene didn't see her earlier dancing with Wesley. Then as Eugene was getting closer, Wesley moved into the dancing crowd and disappeared. Denyah could see Eugene's mother smiling as she looked Eugene in his eyes with content. Denyah crossed the room to her and said to her "You're an evil bitch! You think you've won but I've got you and Wesley jammed in the darkest corner in your little hell."

Twenty minutes later, a kissing couple that were outside the restaurant saw two masked men dumped something big in front of the restaurant. Inquisitively they went to have a look and they saw it was a naked man. The couple asked the man "Are you alright" Then a young dark woman that knew Wesley said "He's a police officer. He's Officer Wesley Davis," then the young woman went on to say, "He's laying face down and saturated in blood from his back passage and between his legs" The man looked deeply at Wesley's naked body and said "He looks like he's been buggered." Then the frightening couple ran in the restaurant and alarmed the other guests. "An officer is lying outside the restaurant gate and seems like he has been meddled with." As the guests looked at the alarmed young black woman with interest, she and her fiancée kept Wesley's name to themselves and only said "my fiancée and I think he has been raped and then dumped."

Within minutes, some of the guests ran out of the restaurant to see Wesley lying naked on the mixed grey marvel and gravel ground with blood covering his bottom and his legs and he seemed to be drunk. Doctors Glennis and Ryan carried him into one of the restaurant rooms and did what they could to make him feel a little comfortable before they dressed him in one of the restaurant overalls. As both doctors were drinking, they radioed in for an ambulance to take Wesley to the hospital so he would get attended to properly. Just before the ambulance arrived, Fay spat in his face and then faced his other mistress Bonnie and told her "You're welcome to the dirty son-of-bitch or a whore of a man, which ever way you take him. I no longer want any part of him as I'm now out of his shitty life for good."

Then daringly Fay faced Wesley and kicked him as hard as she could on his testicles and laughed out heartily saying I hope the pot handle had brake off up your arse. Wesley groaned heavily in pain as his dreamy looking greyish eyes rolled pitifully with his right eye weeping with tears. Then heartlessly, Fay faced Denyah and said, "Sis, your prayer has been answered and you're now free to be with the man you truly love." Smiling, she patted Denyah on her shoulder and said "Smelling the strong odour of semen coming from a dog like Wesley, made my stomach turns." Laughing out aloud she walked away leaving Denyah watching while the two paramedics helping Wesley into the ambulance.

As Meleta wasn't drinking, she acted as a taxi driver for her husband Doctor Ryan to follow behind the ambulance that took Wesley to the Midland hospital been he was so concerned about him even though he'd badly treated his sister Denyah.

After some hours at the hospital, Ryan phoned Denyah and told her Wesley was in great pain and he has been buggered by two men he didn't know. He has also described one of the men to be black and heavy built and seemed to wearing false locks, a bushy moustache and beard. The other person was white and was wearing a red face mask. Denyah burst into laughter as Ryan was reporting to her what Wesley had told him. Denyah laughed loudly down Ryan's ears and said "When he'd raped my dear nurse friend, I bet he laughed all over his devious looking face. What he didn't know was his turn would come. As the saying goes, what goes around comes around. Well, if you think I should feel sorry for a bastard like my ex-husband, I'm not! How does he feel to be buggered? At least they left him with his life and a degrading memory. He didn't give my friend a chance to feel degraded. Instead, the one decent friend I've got to know, he ended her life in the most horrible and degrading way. Not to mention after he'd raped me, he had his two mates in line to take their turn to rape me too, but I thank God they were decent enough not to do it and to trick him into thinking they'd raped me. So you tell me this Ryan. What do you want me to do, cry for him! Well I'll dress up in my red outfit and go and visit him. If you're wondering why the red dress, he had insisted that I should have worn it to Grace's engagement party as I'm one of the biggest whores. So dear brother, if you want us remain as family, please never mention that devils name to me again. Do we understand each other?"

"Absolutely Den, I love you. See you later." Ryan said with a long face and went to check up on Wesley before he went back to the restaurant to face Denyah with a cold look in his eyes. "What!" she asked him as if to say what are you looking at?

He shook his head with the coldest look in his eyes and said "Under that soft spot I didn't realized you had the hardest shell covered by it."

"Are you judging me Ryan for acting on the truth? 'Cause if you are, you have a lot to learn about him" Denyah said calmly. Ryan hugged her around her slender shoulder and kissed her face then said "I'm very sorry sis for wanting you to do what I want. You're right. I shouldn't encourage you to do what you don't want. Truly I'm sorry. Are we friends again?" Ryan asked her.

"How can we not be? Ryan, we're more than friends. We're family if you remember." Denyah said, "Now if you take your giant arms from around my shoulders I have a poisonous dose of medicine to go and pour down my mother-In-law's throat."

Ryan loosened his arms from around her shoulders in wonder and shrugged his shoulders, he smiled then left to mingle amongst some of the guests while Denyah went to Eugene's mother and whispered into her ears, "Too many times you crowned me bitch, and I take off that crown and toss it back on to your head. You see you have everyone fooled including your husband's children. But we know better don't we? I believe Eugene was about eleven when you used to drug him and then seduce him for at least two years until you went on to Patrick who was two years older, not to mention your husbands brother is the father of the only son that you miscarried. An old bitch like you, you were also sleeping with my ex-husband until he became ashamed and told you he couldn't stand the smell of your rancid piss any more. Wesley didn't tell me. But someone did. Should I go now Mrs Lake, I'll let you catch your breath as I realize this potion of medicine is a little too strong for you to swallow all at once. But my dear Mrs Lake, the strongest doses are hung on the highest shelf." Denyah moved her face away and went on to ask her, "I don't have to ask you if you remember your best friend for I'm sure you do. I wonder what Eugene, Ray, Patrick, Carl and Jenny would say or do when they find out who their real mother was and what has happened to her. Oh I even forgot to mention that you were just a home help. So Mrs Lake, when two people know something, it's not a secret any more. So far I think you're the one who is in the middle and I know the real truth about you. Oh and by the way, I'm carrying Eugene's baby.

But I'm not so sure if I should let you anywhere near....I hate incestuous people. What I'm saying, incidentally, is that I think the right word to use is a child molester." Denyah smiled as she moved away, Mrs Lake held her hand and was leading her away from the crowd when Eugene walked over to them and said. "I thought you two had differences." Then Denyah walked over to the DJ, took the microphone and was ready to make a speech. "Every one here, may I have your attention please," Most of the guests faced her with smiles and instantly the hall went silent. She fixed her eyes on Mrs Lake and smiled. When she saw Mrs Lake looking faint and disturbed, she began her speech "I'm Denyah to you that doesn't know me. Forgive me if I said I'm not sorry for what has happened to my ex-husband. That's right! I don't give a damn. In fact I wish he was dead. As some of you already know I was in hospital with burns to my body, it was because of him. He raped me so often and told me he could never make love to me but would take me when he needed to release. I thanked his sister for that day when she found me under a boiling shower unconscious as I was scrubbing the filth off me that he and his two mates had left on me after he called them to rape me by telling them I'm a call girl and left me bounded and gagged. But I thanked God that one of his mates noticed my tears through the blindfold and convinced his other mate I wasn't that sort of person my ex had told them I was. So does anyone still blame me for wanting him dead? Let me see a show of hands - who would blame me for not having any sympathy for my so called ex-husband."

After Denyah didn't see a show of hands, she smiled and said. "Well thank you for not blaming me" Fixing her face serious she passed over the microphone to the DJ then walked away. On her way out of the main door, Mrs Lake went to her and said. "Thank you for not exposing me Denyah."

Denyah smiled, "I bet you almost shit bricks. But don't worry, you behave yourself and I might just let you hold those bricks up your arse. But one more wrong move from you and you really will be shitting those bricks." Mrs Lake walked back to her seat in a corner, smiling broadly out of shame and then her face looked worried throughout the remaining of the evening in thought over what Denyah said to her and who'd told Denyah about her darkest secrets and if Denyah would ever tell Eugene that his mother has committed suicide after she caught her, the woman now known as Mrs. Lake, in bed with his father. The party went on until early morning.

However, Eugene took his family home and went back to his restaurant to be with his brothers and friends. Sometime after most of the guests left, Eugene went into the drink stockroom for a few bottles of Champagne to have a drink with his brothers and friends. Kalor looked at his brothers and friends while moving to the stockroom door. At the rear of the door, she stopped to look at them again. As she saw some were playing blackjack, dominos, and getting down to the last disc, she smiled and as Eugene had left the drink stockroom door opened, she rushed in the room, closed the door and sprang on him and pushed him backward on some of the drink cases. "What the hell do you think you're doing?" Eugene asked her.

"Shut up! I want you" she said. With Eugene holding the three bottles of champagne in his hands, she pushed into him and kissed him. Then with a sudden move, she slipped her hand down his trousers and fondling his penis. With the champagne still in his hands, he slanted his body to push her away. She slapped his face and slipped out of her dress and panties and pushed him against some stocked up drinks cases and lanced her tongue into his mouth. He swayed away, and said "I can't do this" as built up sweat suddenly saturated his forehead.

"If you are worrying someone will see us, don't, as they all seems to be well pissed and those that are not, they are occupied doing their own thing."

"Kalor, this is wrong. Will you put your clothes on and get out of here."

"Who will know? Eugene, I know your married with children and your wife's very beautiful and I know you won't leave her for me, but I love you." Kalor said and kissed him again, took his hand and guided his hands to her vagina. He swallowed deeply and instantly he developed an erection. She turned her back on him and bent forward pressing her bottom against his penis as she took his right hand and sliding upward to her hard breast nipples and guided his left hand hooking her slim waist as she seemed to be desperate for him by the way she was manoeuvring her body movements against his. He closed his eyes thinking of Denyah and his children. But, as Kalor had bent forward and was manoeuvring her lovely body against his penis, he could no longer control his sexual feelings or resist her, so he dropped his trousers and boxers short and angrily he shoved his penis into her and roughly fucked her. After he ejaculated and pulled out of her, she slipped into her shoulder strapped short black dress, faced him with smiles. "You let anyone know about this and it gets to my wife, I will break your fucking neck like a dry twig."

"Eugene, your wife would only find out about us if you tell her."

"Kalor there's no fucking us! And it would never be!" Eugene said. Kalor smiled.

"I'm warning you, you breathe a word about this to anyone, I will kill you."

"Eugene, I will tell no one. I love you too much to lose you now and I want you again." Kalor said.

"There's no again. Or never would be. I want you to leave me alone from here on."

"Eugene, I can't leave you alone. Not now, not ever. I'm sure we can see each other without anyone knowing. I'm a model and I don't want your money or children. At least, not yet, so you have nothing to fear as I protected myself against having kids. All I want from you is a fuck now and then. That's all." She said then kissed his lips and left smiling.

Eugene wiped his lips and pulled his trousers up and rushed to the bathroom, took his trousers off and washed the semen off his penis with soap, before putting on his boxer shorts and his trousers and then returned to the drink stockroom and picked up the three bottles of champagne and went to his brothers and friends looking troubled.

"What's the matter with you brother?" Ray asked him smiling.

"Do I look like anything's the matter with me?"

Ray took him to one side and said. "Brother, you done it again. I saw you whipping that model. Can't you control Mr hot dick, I would not like to be in your place if Den finds out. Are you seeing her again?"

"No, no. I won't. Ray, please keep this between us aye?"

"Eugene my brother, it's not me you should worry about. It's her. When you refuse her, that's where hell will turn over."

"What the hell was I doing to be sucked in by that bitch?" Eugene asked looking at Ray.

"Too late for that my brother, pray Den don't find out, I know she would never forgive you as before" Ray said smiling. "Well brother, it looked like I have to keep my Paula under lock and key."

"Thanks bros, you just know how to make me feel better." Eugene said.

"Eugene, for your own sake I hope Den don't find out. I meant this, bros," Ray said and laughed and walked Eugene back to their friends.

Anyway, Eugene and his brothers and friends stayed at the restaurant until early morning drinking and talking about how many women they scored. As they each took it in turn telling their experience with women, Doctor Glennis said, "When I was fucking a nurse from behind, she farted loud and almost blew my balls off. Eugene, Ryan, Ray, Patrick, David, Carl, Curt, Richard, Austin, Frank, and four of Ray's friends, Dales, Brad, Hilton and Dennis were roaring with laughter.

As the morning was cleared, the men went home to their families. As Eugene got home, he went and had a shower and went to bed with a guilty feeling.

Two days later, Tuesday morning, Wesley was released from the hospital after getting treatment because of the two men that buggered him. The Doctors were satisfied with his recovery and gave him an appointment to see them in six weeks to test him for Aids or other sexual infections. The same morning he was released, he went to Fay mother's home and rang the door bell. Fay opened the door thinking that her mother had returned after shopping. Shockingly she came face to face with Wesley. Quickly she tried to close the door but he wedged the door with his foot. Staring up at him in fright he asked her, "Why you are you looking so frightened now. Have you no more saliva to yank out on me or a pot handle to shove up my arse? A few days back you yanked out so much saliva on me that you almost drowned me. I'm only here to see you, my favourite harlot. Is that so bad that I want to see you?"

"Please Wesley I want no trouble from you. What we had between us is now finished. I just want to be left alone." Fay cried.

"So now you want to be left alone, now you have ruined my marriage? I'll leave you alone when I see you six feet underground. Fay, there's no turning back for me and Denyah. I'll give her the divorce and marry you." Wesley said.

"No, Wesley I don't love you anymore. What I'd felt for you is no longer there."

"Why not, have you another man?" Wesley asked.

"No, and even if I'm seeing someone, it's nothing to do with you. All I want is to see the back of you. Now please go away and leave me alone" Fay said still crying.

"Why should I go away, I was only buggered, I'm still a whole man. I will go now, but I'll be back for you to take you to our home. The same home you drove your sister away from to make room for yourself - aren't you pleased, you see Fay we're two of a kind and we belong to each other" Wesley said with a cunning smile and left. Fay quickly closed the door and poured a large amount of brandy in a glass and swallowed it in one gulp, she then began shivering. She took the empty glass to the kitchen counter when she heard a knock on the door. Very frightened, she stared at the door and stood up still until she heard her mother's voice shouting, "Fay opened the door, I forgot my key." With trembling hands she slowly turned the door latch to open the door but being so frightened that Wesley might be somewhere out there, she stood at the doorway and was looking as far as her eyes could see. "Would you move and let me pass with these two heavy bags and who're you looking for? You look very worried like something is about to happen. I'm going to make some tea you - want some?" her mother asked.

"No mom, I'm going to bed to rest." Fay said.

"Are you feeling sick child?" her mother asked her looking at her very concerned. "No mom, I just feeling tired. I have been working too hard lately. If Wesley phones or called to see me, I'm out."

"Look here Fay! I've warned you to stay away from that Wesley too often and you never listened. So don't drag me in between. You ruined your sister's marriage because you wanted to be with him and now you're running miles away, well, you sorted out you messy problem yourself. One good thing has come out of this and that's Denyah fighting to have little Paris."

Fay looked hard at her mother and went upstairs to dump herself in her bed but couldn't relax as she was thinking the worst of what Wesley might do to her.

At dinner time Fay's mother noticed the tense movement in Fay and that she left nearly all of her food. "Fay you've hardly touched your lunch and now the same with your dinner. What's going on with you and Wesley?"

"Mom, I regret the day I cheated on my sister. I thought I loved him then, but now I hate him so much, I wish him dead" Fay expressed. Her mother got up from the dinner table, "Well, you only have yourself to blame. Like your sisters you could have found yourself a nice and decent young man. Well, its s your fault. As the saying goes, you lie down with dog, you get up with fleas. All I'm asking you for is that you do not bring that evil man into my home. I thank God Denyah has forgiven me for what he made me do to her."

Day after day, Wesley phoned Fay but she refused to answer his call. One Saturday night while she was sitting home, he phoned Fay at least five times in ten minutes Fay's mother became upset and told Fay to either answer the phone or take the phone off the receiver. "Just leave it mom, if we don't answer, he would think no one is at home."

Sunday morning and afternoon the phone continued to ring so constantly that Fay's mother answered.

"Where's Fay" Wesley asked in a bad temper. Fay's mother looked at her.

"Fay is not here and I don't want you to phone here anymore. You want to speak to Fay, wait until you see her" Fay mother said and banged the phone down sounding a loud noise into Wesley's ears. Madly he ripped his phone from the socket and said. "You bitches will pay" he then became frustrated and swallowed a good amount of whiskey from the bottle then angrily tossed the bottle against the wall, it shattered into pieces. He then kicked a broken piece of the bottle onto his and Denyah's marriage photo and broke the glass before he went and put bullets in his gun. Playing with his gun, he mumbled "I lost my wife, my daughter, my reputation, my friends, my sister, and may be my job and all because of that little sick minded slut Fay" Wesley picked up yet another bottle of whiskey that was on the bedroom floor and swallowed nearly a quarter of the whiskey and passed out on the floor with the loaded gun by his side.

That same Sunday night Fay plucked up courage and went to see Wesley. She knocked at his door a couple of times but he didn't answer. Suddenly she remembered she had his key in her car dash board, so she went and got it and opened the door. She walked in and called out his name but there was no reply, she quietly crept up the stairs and went into his bedroom to find him stretched out on his back on the floor. She shook her head in disbelief and kicked him lightly in his side to wake him up. When he didn't react to the first kick, she kicked him a second time to the side of his head. He groaned out a sound and struggled to get on his feet. "You dirty bastard, I came to tell you face to face that I no longer want to see you. Believe me you would be better off with those two faggots like yourself. I couldn't agree more with Denyah, you're nothing but a walking alcohol bottle that's full with germs. If you ever phone my mother's house again, I'll kill you before you kill me. Just like you killed your two mates and Nurse James, It's only a matter of time before they catch you and stop you from hiding behind

DENYAH 197

your badge. Just look at you. You make my stomach feel like I want to throw-up. Wesley, you remember, I never want to see you again." Fay turned and walked away after telling Wesley what was on her mind. Wesley said nothing but grabbed his gun and shot her with the intention to kill her but luckily for her the bullet caught her below her shoulder. Fay managed to stagger outside and then fainted by her car. A young boy about fifteen years old was riding his bicycle and stopped when he saw her fall and asked "Lady are you alright" But as he saw her lying in a pool of blood, he leaned his bicycle against Wesley's fence and asked Fay once more "Are you alright lady?" Thinking that Fay might be drunk and this was why she was staggering and got her injuries by falling. But when he realized she been shot, he phoned for an ambulance on his mobile phone and waited with her until the ambulance arrived. The boy then shouted out, "A woman got shot". In a matter of minutes, outside Wesley's gate was crowded with onlookers. Somehow Wesley managed to stagger by his window and saw a crowd of the people standing outside his gate. As he was drunk, in his eyes the people looked like a swarm of bees. As he staggered and fell in his chair, he remembered he'd fired a bullet at Fay. As he was thinking, he realized the bullet must have caught Fay and that must be the reason why onlookers flocked to his gateway. He then managed to stagger as far as his gate and mumbled "You nosey idle bodies get the hell away from my gate before I have you all arrested" A few onlookers moved away while others stood watching and ignored him especially as they'd smelt alcohol on him and knowing how drunk he was as his face pictured and could barely stand up straight with one of his eyes half closed. As he looked meaningfully at the onlookers, he mumbled. "Get away... move your arses. Go home." Some standby looked at him as he was wobbling all over his yard and fell and face down cutting his left arm and under his chin. He got on his feet and then crawled himself back into his house to finish off a bottle of whiskey. With a little whiskey left in the bottle, he tossed the nearly empty bottle against the glass wall unit shattering the glass doors. A flying piece of glass cut him on his forehead just missing his right eye. As he felt the warmness of blood running down on his face, he wiped the blood with the back of his hand and smearing the blood over his face and then dropped himself in the sofa like a piece of wood log and then dropped of into a deep sleep.

Within fifteen minutes the sound of the ambulance siren was heard coming towards the location. As the Paramedic saw the onlookers, he slowly drove the ambulance and stopped outside Wesley's gate as the onlookers gave way to him. The two paramedics climbed out of the ambulance and rushed over to Fay and examined the bullet wound and saw the bullet was buried deep into the back of her shoulder blade. "Could anyone here tell me what has happened or if you saw anything" the white handsome heavy built six feet paramedic asked with deep concern. "I'm the one that phoned for the ambulance" the young mix raced boy said. "I was riding my bike home when I saw the lady staggering then fall to her knees. I thought she was drunk, but I saw her bleeding, that's when I phoned for an ambulance on my mobile phone."

"Did you see anyone with her or where she came from?" The second slim tall white paramedic asked the boy.

"No sir, I only saw when she staggered and fell. My name's Leon and I' m fifteen years old. When she feels better, will you tell her Leon called the ambulance for her?"

"Sure I will, and Leon, thank you for saving her life." The second paramedic said. Leon smiled triumphantly, took his bike up and rode it home.

After some time, Wesley phoned Lisa and told her someone had broken into his home and trashed his place to pieces. As Lisa had her one year old son and her baby daughter to look after, she asked her husband Richard to go and see what had happened.

Richard went to find out what Wesley was talking about. But as he saw the state of Wesley's house and saw him bleeding, he phoned Lisa on his mobile phone and then reported back to her that her brother's furniture was badly broken up and he had a gash over his left eye that needs to be seen to. Lisa thought for a while before she said to Richard "Well I shouldn't feel sorry for him, but he's my brother and he needs help. Try and get him to come with you. See that his place is locked up before you leave."

Richard persuaded Wesley to leave with him with some clothes. But as Lisa saw his swollen cut forehead, she asked Richard to take him to a hospital to have stitches.

Meanwhile at the Heartlands Accident Hospital, Fay was in a bad way. She became conscious but because she had lost so much blood she looked pale and weak. A doctor went to her and said, "The bullet has rooted deep into the lower shoulder, and we have to take out the bullet before it moves any further, if we don't operate now it might get worse or even prove fatal. Would you like a message passed on to relative or anyone?" the doctor asked.

"My mother, but I doubt if she would be interested." Then Fay said, "I don't wish to see anyone. Just do what you have to do." The doctor looked hard at Fay and said with a quiver in his voice. "Well, I would like you to sign here so we can operate." showing her on the form where to sign in the presence of a nurse.

Before Fay signed the form, she looked at the nurse for attention. The nurse smiled and nodded her head instantly. Fay took the pen from the doctor with shaking hands and signing for her operation. Within minutes of her signing, she was wheeled into the operating room.

Hours later Fay was comfortable in bed.

Lisa phoned Denyah to tell her Wesley shot Fay and she is now in Heartlands Hospital recovering from a bullet wound. Wesley went to the City Hospital to have the cut under his eye attended to and then went back to his sister Lisa's home for a few days.

The following morning Denyah's received a phone call from her mother telling her Fay had been shot yesterday and is now in hospital.

"Mom, I couldn't care a damn about Fay. What's happened to her, she brought it on herself. Let me know about you or Blanch. Goodbye mom."

"Please Denyah," her mom pleaded to her before they hung up. "I know she has done wrong to you, and I'm not happy about it. In fact I'd feel the same way too. But she's family. Our family Denyah, she used to be a lovely daughter and sister to us once. Your husband influenced her, as he'd done to me. Please Den, forgive us all." Tears came into her mother's eyes.

"Ok mom, I'll go and see her, but don't expect me to hug her and kiss her." "Thank you Den and would you mind taking a carton of juice for her?" "Mom......"

"I know Den."

"Yes mom, but as I said, don't expect me to go with open arms. I'll go and see later. Lisa's already told me what ward she's in. Goodbye mom." They both hung up.

Denyah looked at her watch and said "damn, I have twenty minutes to get to the clinic." she raced down a glass of cold milk and said to Aungus and Sonny "we left the back door open and your lunch is on the hot plate. Will you both make sure the back door is locked before you leave? Oh help yourself to what drink you want. And both of you, I'm very pleased with your work, what if you and your families move closer to me. I can't stop to talk now as I would be late for my appointment but I'll speak to both of you later." Denyah told Aungus and Sonny and left with Mrs Brown to go to the antenatal and afterwards she went to visit Fay on the other side in the same hospital. Fay turned her back to Denyah after Denyah said "I thought Wesley was deeply in love with you."

"Why did you come to see me? Don't you know I hate you?" Fay said.

"Not as much as I hate you. I came to have a good laugh and to let you know what I think of you."

"Say what you want and get away from me," Fay said with tears in her eyes. Then Fay went on to say "You never did love Wesley otherwise you wouldn't have had slept with Eugene."

"My dear, you were the one that drove me into Eugene's arms when you took my husband away from me. I was deeply in love with my husband. But you had to take him and his nine year old daughter away from me. However, I got Paris back and I left you with a pile of shit! That's Wesley. You deserve each other. By the way, I believe Wesley found his two male friends more satisfactory than you. I'm sure you won't hold this against me if I tell you I believe him. Incidentally, if I were you, when I get out of here, I would find the deepest and darkest hole and crawl down it and stay there. If I know my ex well enough, the bullet was meant to kill you and do you know why, it's because he found out how much he loves me and how much a little piece of trash you are. Oh, mom convinced me to bring you this drink. I do hope you choke on it." Denyah said and left smiling while Fay sat on her bed speechless.

On the way home, Denyah's smiling brought Mrs Brown to ask "How's your sister?"

"I left her a little shaky" Denyah said.

"Poor thing, that dreadful man almost killed her. Ah, despite his wickedness, I still feel sorry that he has been raped." Mrs Brown said.

"I dread to think how it must've of felt." Denyah said and smiled.

Mrs Brown mumbled. "Of course it must have been horrifying and painful. By the way, someone phoned Eugene to tell him you went to see Wesley at his home and he's very furious and also worried about you. Look Den, I know it's not any business of mine, but I don't think you should see you ex-husband any more or at least be very careful if you are to see him. Just remember Eugene loves you."

"I know he does and I won't be so stupid as to lose him. And about I went to see Wesley, I already told Eugene and he was furious and warned me not to see Wesley again and I won't" Denyah said softly as she faced Mrs Brown smiling. A few minutes away from home Denyah stopped and bought Chinese food. While Denyah parked the car in the garage, Mrs Brown took the food into the kitchen to meet Eugene just about to make sandwiches for the girls. "We've bought some food. Denyah's just putting the car in the garage" Mrs Brown said putting five plates on the table just as Denyah walked in. As she saw the girls, she said "I thought your Dad was going to take you to the pictures."

"He did" Paris said. "But Jade B wasn't feeling well so dad brought us home and put Jade B to bed."

"You carry on eating while I go and have a look at her," Denyah said.

"Eat first, I'm sure she's sleeping," Eugene said and he began to eat but Denyah still went to have a look at her as she was worried. Denyah took her temperature with a thermometer but she seemed to be okay. Denyah left the room and went back to her food.

Much later Jade B woke up and began crying. Paris rushed up the stairs to her and held her hand walking her down the stairs to meet Denyah. Mrs Brown took her into the kitchen and fed her with food she'd cooked before she went to the hospital with Denyah. After, Jade B was happy to play with Paris until Denyah were ready to bath her and put them to bed.

The following morning, Jade B got up feeling so happy that she jumped on Denyah's back for piggy back ride. Denyah wasn't feeling very well but she did her best to make Jade B happy. As Jade B heard Paris calling Denyah mom, she too followed and called Denyah mom as well.

Dinner was ready. Mrs Brown saw the children fed the kitten first and then saw them wash their hands before she seated them down at the table.

"Mom, Jade B and I washed our hands, and mom we love you and Nan" meaning Mrs Brown. As they just finished eating, Eugene walked in with the rain dripping off his raincoat. "Daddy.... Paris called, climbing down from the chairs smiling. Then Jade B followed behind Paris shouting "Daddy, daddy," their pretty faces gleaming with smiles of happiness. As Jade B and Paris held on to each of his hands, he bent down and kissed them and said "Give Dad one minute to get out of these wet clothes" But the children followed behind him to the bathroom where he changed out of his wet clothes and then lifted up Jade B in his arms and gave Paris a piggyback before taking them down into the kitchen to have his supper. Mrs Brown got up saying, "You rest yourself Eugene while I go and heat up your supper and I'm so happy to see your children so very fond of you."

"Thanks Mom, but I had dinner before I came home" Eugene said.

"Okay, maybe later if you're hungry, you supper is in the micro."

"Thanks mom, but I was going to spend the night helping out dad with some work. He seemed to be okay so I came home to my lovely family. Speaking of family, Den, can I have a word with you?"

"Sure," Denyah said and then looked at Mrs Brown in wonder. Mrs Brown merely smiled. Denyah followed behind Eugene into their bedroom and they both sat on the bed. "Denyah, did you go to see your husband again?" Eugene asked softly. Denyah hung her head low and said, "Yes, but only to get him sign the divorce papers."

"Do you still love him?"

"How can you bring yourself to ask me if I love Wesley when you know how much I despise him? Eugene, I wouldn't do anything to hurt you or the children. Believe me. I would rather be dead than to be handled by Wesley again."

"I never want you to go to Wesley's house again, if you do, you might as well forget me and the children. I'm in love with you and I want you to be my wife and mother to my children. Can you understand what I'm telling you?"

"Yes Eugene, I understand and I'm sorry to be such a fool to go to his house." she said as tears built up in her eyes. "I loved you from the very first time I saw you; I was haunted by your love. We belong to each other with two beautiful children and another on its way; I wouldn't jeopardize what we have for a louse like Wesley." Denyah said.

"It's not what happened. It's how it happened." Eugene explained. Denyah shook her head and dried her tears before she went downstairs.

"Is everything alright?" Mrs Brown asked concerned.

"Yes mom, everything is fine" Eugene said before sitting on the soft brown settee. "Maybe I should eat now after having an early lunch."

Mrs Brown said happily. "Don't you go away, I'll be back in a minute with your dinner" Then as she turned she looked back at Denyah and asked her, "Would you like a cup of tea dear or anything?"

"No thanks, you were saying earlier that I had a phone call?"

"Oh yes, a Bernice called while you were having a shower. She said she would call you later. I asked her to leave a message, but she said it's not important."

"Thanks mom," Denyah said, Mrs Brown went and returned with the heated food on a tray and an ice cold bottle of beer and gave it to Eugene. Smiling over the food he said, "Thank you Mom." And he tucked into his lamb chop dinner and afterwards he washed down the food with the cold beer. "I really enjoyed my dinner." he smiled to Denyah. This made Denyah feel so happy that she went to him and kissed him on his cheek. Then Paris and Jade B jumped onto his lap and were playing with his sprouting beard - Mrs Brown started laughing and said "Blessed their little souls."

Denyah phoned Bernice saying, "Mom said you'd phoned."

"Yes, I phoned to ask you if you and Eugene would like to come to a thirty fifth birthday party with me and a couple of friends next Saturday about seven."

"I don't know. Right now I can't give you an answer. I'll have to speak with Eugene first and then get back to you." Denyah said.

"That's cool Den, whatever you decide, let me know will you?"

"Certainly," Denyah said and put the phone down and went to tell Eugene about the invitation. "No way, you've a family to take car of. Besides, you would meet all sort of riff-raff ready to get their dirty ill mannered paws on anyone they feel like. Just tell her no! Simple as that, you want to go out for a meal or to a party I would more than happy to take you. However, I wouldn't want you to take any risks with you being pregnant."

"Eugene, I'll be very careful. The moment I see trouble, I'll be far gone."

"Den, sometimes things doesn't work out the way it should be or the way we want. I can't bear to know anything that's happened to you, so therefore my answered is no. She's your friend and she is very welcome to visit you whenever she likes. I like her very much and I'm happy she's one of your friends." Eugene said.

Denyah was very understanding, and said to Eugene, "Thanks honey for being so frank. I think you maybe right" Smiling she went and sat on his lap then kissed him before hesitating to say, "Honey…"

"Come on out with it" Eugene said looking straight into her eyes.

"Honey, I've recently discovered that I have a half sister on my father's side. She's living in Basseterre St Kitts - her name is Laney Wells. She's thirty five. I would like to get to know her. She's also married and has two daughters. I would really like to meet them soon."

"And may I ask where you gathered this information?" Eugene asked with great concern.

"One of my friends told me she went to a Christening in Manchester and she heard it from my father's brother."

"And you believed your friend?"

"Why shouldn't I, she has nothing to gain from telling me lies. I do have an Uncle living in Manchester. I even got his address from my friend and I've already phoned him. He even told me my other sister mother is black. So honey, would it be ok, if I try and get in touch with her?" Denyah asked nicely.

"Of course you can try to find her but don't put any ideas in her head that you're wealthy."

"That's why I love you so much. I think I will give her a call now. If we're five hours in front, I wonder what's the time is over there?"

Eugene looked on his wrist watch and said "Three minutes after two as the time is now approaching three minutes after seven our time."

"Do you think I should phone now?" Denyah asked.

"Well if you don't phone, you'll never find out if you have a sister on the other side of the world that would like to know you as well."

"Thank honey," Denyah said happily before she went to phone her sister in St Kitts. Looking at the number in her diary, she picked up the handset from and nervously began to dial the numbers and waited anxiously. "Hello," Laney greeted.

"My name's Denyah, I am calling from England. I was told I've a sister on my father's side and was given this number" There was a long pause between them, before Denyah said, "I'm very sorry to have bothered you."

"Please don't hang up. Just give me time to catch my breath. Yes, I think that I might be that missing half sister too. I tried to find you but had no success. Can I ask how you heard of me?" Laney asked.

"Well, I first heard about you from a friend and then from our father's brother. He's the one that gave me your number. That's why I phoned you and now here we are at each end of our phones. Laney, believe me I'm so very happy to find you."

"I feel the same way too. Well can I have your phone number I might give you a call one day" Laney said. Happily, Denyah gave Laney her home phone number as well as her mobile. "Are you crying?" Laney asked Denyah as she heard the sound of her sniffing back snot. Denyah did not answer, and started to cry more tears of joy. Laney started crying too. They both hung on to the phone without saying a word. Then Denyah cleared her throat and said "Laney, I haven't even seen you but I'll like to get to know you. You seem to be very nice."

"Well, you have two nieces Ocelia and Beverly and Paul my husband." Laney said.

"Like me, I have two daughters, Paris and Jade B, a husband Eugene, a brother Ryan and a lovely adopted mother Mrs Brown. We'll have to meet sometime. Laney now that we have found each other, let's keep it this way. Goodbye Laney and give the kids a big hug from my family and me" Denyah said.

"You do the same for me and God bless" Laney put her phone down first. Denyah smiled as she put the phone down and couldn't wait to run into Eugene's arms to tell him the good news.

"I'm happy for you. When are you planning to go and see her or she come and see you? Eugene asked.

"I would really like to take a trip to St Kitts. I heard it's a beautiful place?"

"I would like to come too but dad relies on me. Why don't you go and take the kids and mom with you? Mom can do with a holiday. I could book your passage when ever you like" Eugene said.

That evening Denyah was so happy that she phoned Ryan and told him about Laney and that she wanted him to meet her. Ryan was very happy for her and told her he would indeed be happy to meet her as well. When Denyah hung up the receiver she turned around and looked at Mrs Brown and asked,

"What would you say to a nice holiday in St Kitts?" Mrs Brown looked at her hard and smiled.

"I think the holiday would do you good, cheer you up especially after what you've been through. Just say you'll go with me and if you don't like the place, we can always shorten our holiday. Really, all I want is to see is my sister and her family."

"Oh Denyah, I would be happy to go with you. And I'm very happy you've found your sister. I think I can afford to pay for my passage. Just let me know when you're ready to book" Mrs Brown said.

"I haven't asked you for any money. Besides, I'm asking you to come with me. Eugene would be happy to book our passage and I'll be happy to do the spending and you'll be happy to do the baby sitting sometimes" Denyah joked.

Happiness was Denyah's game for that evening, so she went and searched for a nearly forgotten tape. When she finally found it, she played it. 'I'm searching for you girl a long, long time, now I've found you, you're mine' Denyah was feeling so happy and in high spirits that she pulled up Eugene and Mrs Brown and danced with them both and then with the children.

"I'm so happy for you to know that you have other family elsewhere. I once saw an advertisement of St Kitts. To my surprise it's beautiful. I never thought I would ever see such a place. Well, I must go and get the children some cocoa and get them ready for bed. While I'm in the kitchen, do you want anything?" Mrs Brown asked.

"No mom, I feel like celebrating, do you want a curry?" Denyah asked

"No dear, not tonight, I have to be careful of what I eat when it is late. I'd hate to get heartburn" Mrs Brown replied. "A nice cup of hot milk will do for me."

"And what about you Eugene, do you fancy a curry? "

"No, but if you want a curry, I'll go and get you one."

"It's alright honey, I'll settle for a nice bacon sandwich and a cup of tea."

Mrs Brown made Denyah a bacon sandwich and a cup of tea. "Well, I'm off to the shower and then to bed. So goodnight to both of you, and you won't believe that the children are sleeping. Well, I'll see you two in the morning."

"Goodnight mom." Denyah and Eugene wished her. As Mrs Brown got up stairs she went to have a peep in on Paris and Jade B before she went to shower and went to bed.

After Denyah ate her bacon sandwich, she phoned Bernice telling her, "I'm sorry that I won't be able to come to the party."

"That's okay Den, I myself doesn't feel like going, but I met this lovely white fellow three weeks ago and he invited me, that's why I invited you. Denyah, he's so handsome. His name is Darren. I didn't think I would date a white bloke. But he's exceptional. Denyah he has the most beautiful grey eyes, nice bone structure face, and a well built six feet body. He even owns a workout shop. I told him I went to prison for killing my lover but he said he doesn't want to know the past. You should see his home, very beautiful…. Anyway, he's just walked in. I've to go; I'll call you tomorrow afternoon" Bernice boasted and she and Denyah placed their phones down.

"Honey, you ready to go upstairs now? Denyah asked Eugene.

"Soon as I finish these few papers, just four more then I'm done. You go to bed." Eugene insisted as he lifted up his pen.

Denyah went to have a bath. As she was relaxing, Eugene joined her they made passionate love then went to bed. Sitting up in bed Eugene said to her, "If you really would like to go and see your sister, I think you should be thinking of going soon before you become heavier."

"Okay, now my morning sickness is settled, I would like to go and visit her next month. You said you'll book our passage."

"Have you and the children got passports ready?

"Damn, oh no. Mine's in order but I'll have to get the kids ready. You said Jade gave you Jade B's birth certificate?" Denyah asked. "Yes, you'll find Jade's birth certificate in my blue suit jacket pocket along with Paris's and your passport."

"What would my passport be doing in your suit pocket?" Denyah asked in wonder.

"Don't you remember you asked me to take them out of the kitchen drawer and put them into your dressing table draw, well instead, I've put them in my jacket packet and forgot to put them in your dressing table draw as you asked, well, if you would like to go and see your sister, I think you should get a move on with Jade B's passport."

"Thanks honey" Denyah said then turned on her side and yawned and then fell asleep. Eugene poked her with his fingers lightly in her back a couple of times and had no reactions, he smiled, turned the bed lights off, put his arms around her waist and fell asleep.

As usual at six o'clock Paris and Jade B were the first to get up and they couldn't wait to jump between Denyah and Eugene. Jade B hugged Denyah while Paris was jockeying on Eugene's back before Jade B joined in. After Eugene had enough, he moved downstairs and had a nap in the settee before breakfast.

"I was too tired last night and still I am. I'll be in bed if you should need my service" Eugene joked to Denyah smiling.

"Not anymore sir, I wouldn't want my babies face to dent in with you magic stick." Denyah joked also, but didn't realise Mrs Brown was listening until she heard her burst into laughter. "I best go and tell Aungus and Sonny their breakfast is now on the table" Mrs Brown said.

Later on that day, Meleta and Ryan came to see Denyah, "Where's Eugene?" Ryan asked.

"Upstairs, I suppose." Denyah said "By the way. I thought you two were half way around the world by now. Speaking of which, what's this about you went to Aungus' wife and told her you would like to adopt her grandchildren and she and Aungus could come and live with you. Meleta, that's not the way to approach people. When you asked me to ask Aungus to do some gardening work for you, I didn't know you had other plans for him and his family. Aungus wife was so upset at first, but the children's seems to take a likeness to you and they're asking for you all the time. What really made you ask Aungus and wife to adopt their grandchildren? Has Ryan had anything to do with this?"

"No Denyah, I love those children, and when I saw that their grandmother was struggling to even cut a few slices of bread, the thought came, that's why I asked her and I'm sorry if that's the way she felt. Obviously, I thought I was doing the right thing by lessening the children grandmother's burden, but I guess I was wrong." Meleta said.

"Well with you nearly ready to give birth, I must say you're really brave to have wanted to have the Aungus family to live with you. Well Meleta girl, they've decided to take up your offer and Aungus, his Missus and grandchildren would like to know when you would like them to move in."

"Did Aungus really say they would come and live with Ryan and me?" Meleta asked in disbelief.

"Why don't you go and ask him before he leaves." Meleta smiled widely and went to see Aungus and asked "Did you have words with Denyah about you and the family moving in with Ryan and me?"

"That's if you haven't changed your mind" Aungus said putting his garden fork in the shed.

"Of course I haven't changed my mind. You haven't any idea how happy you've made me feel. Can Ryan and I take the children to our home later, you and the Mrs also, and you don't have to worry about your house, we would see that it is rented out and the money would well looked after for the girls until they become adults."

"You'll do this for us?" Aungus asked looking happy.

"Yes Aungus" Meleta said smiling.

"It's seems like Miss Denyah has to look for a new gardener. Mind you, she treated me first class and like a family."

"Don't you worry Aungus, you will be treated the same, only you wouldn't need to get up until you feel like it. Ryan and I want to take care of you, Mrs Philips and the children's needs. I love those children and my husband and I would be so happy to take care of you all" Meleta said.

"Meleta, I couldn't thank you enough" Aungus said with a gleam in his left eye and his right eye lazily fell closed.

Meleta rushed back to Denyah telling her the happy news that Aungus agreed for him and the family to move in with her and Ryan.

Meanwhile, Ryan was in Eugene's bedroom speaking about Kalor. "Eugene, Ray told me you screwed this model named Kalor. What were you thinking brother?"

"Man she came on to me strong and without warning and naked in the drink stockroom. I couldn't control my biro pen as Den said to me one night. Well I don't have to fill you in with the rest" Eugene said fondly.

"What if Den finds out?" Ryan asked.

"Well, I would just have to take my punishment. But one thing I know, Den would never leave me" Eugene said.

"How can you be so sure mate?" Ryan asked.

"She won't give me up so easily." Eugene said very profoundly.

"That's why you fucking around with any bitches that lift their tales?" Ryan asked

"No, no, no. I will never see her again. And my doing what I did, it was just a fling in the night on account of my weakness and feeling tipsy. Will you keep this between us please, Ryan?" Eugene begged.

"Eugene, don't let Den know that I knew about any of this if she finds out, will you?" Ryan said.

"You can trust me mate." Eugene said.

"Anyway, are you up for a drink later?" Ryan asked.

"Sure Ryan, Ray asked me to come by him later, would you like to come with me?" Eugene asked.

"Sure, I would be okay as I won't be working until tomorrow night." Ryan said

Meleta and Ryan spent the evening at Denyah's and ended up having supper.

That night, Ryan, Meleta, Eugene, Denyah and Mrs Brown helped Aungus and his family to move into Meleta and Ryan's house. The children were very excited and they took Paris and Jade B to see their bedroom. Tommy said to Paris. "I and Chelsea are sharing this room until Aunt Meleta sorts our rooms. But we still have a beautiful furnished double bedroom"

Paris said "Me and my sister Jade B have our own room."

"Well, grandma said, when we get used to the house, Aunt Meleta would let us sleep in our own bedroom soon" Tommy said.

"That's right honey" Meleta said as she watched Tommy and Chelsea choosing their bed even though they were identical and in the same room. Meleta left her two girls and Denyah's two girls jumping on their beds whilst she took Aungus and his wife and show them to their room next to their grandchildren's room. Tears flowed from Mrs Philips eyes when she saw how beautiful their room looked with the built in bathroom and toilet disguised to look like a walk-in closet to suit their needs. The beautifully designed and painted toilet in apple green with a protective door separated from their bedroom was beautiful and showed no evidence that a toilet and bathroom is in the bedroom.

Mrs Philips went and said to Meleta, "Why have you built a bathroom and toilet in the room?"

Meleta smiled and said, "Ryan and I had it built for you and mom, and dad, it's not exactly in your room. We thought it would be a splendid idea as we wouldn't want either of you to have an accident going to the other bathrooms especially at night. Beside, it doesn't even look like a toilet and bathroom in your room. Even if you had said no to living with us, I would have asked you again later. You don't mind me calling you mom?" Meleta asked Mrs Philips.

"Meleta, you calling me mom, it's like a second chance you've given me to own a daughter. Especially when I saw the happiness on my grandchildren's face, I felt like I am not sick at all. Meleta, I guess you know that I'm very sick. Before I'm gone, I would you like you and Ryan to adopt the children fully and give them you and your husband's names. You should have no trouble as their parents have died. Meleta, Aungus and I would be happy to see a solicitor and to give you and Ryan full custody of the children so that you both would have legal rights to be their parents. I'm so happy they have fallen into both your hands. I know you'll also take care of Aungus" his wife said. "And Denyah and her family would be a good family to them. I thank God for people like you. I watched the four children playing so happily together and it made me feel as though my worrying illness I no longer have."

"Mom, please don't you worry over the children or dad, you're now part of our family. Mom, have you ever wanted to go anywhere? Somewhere special," Meleta asked with concern.

"Yes, I always wanted to go to Disney world in Florida but never could afford the fare for the grandchildren, me and my husband Aungus. Miss Denyah, God bless her, she has made living more enjoyable and comfortable for us. Things we couldn't afford to buy for the children, we can now" Mrs Philips said.

While Mrs Philips was pouring her heart out to Meleta, Aungus sat in cool amazement listening and looked so remorsefully pale.

Eugene, Denyah, Mrs Brown and their two girls said goodnight and left.

"Well mom and dad, as you are sitting pretty, would you like me to bring your supper?" Meleta asked Aungus and wife Mrs Philips.

"No Meleta, I will be eating in the dining room with you. Aungus might like to have his here" Mrs Philips said.

"No, we all will eat in the dining room. Just give me a minute to make a call to Sonny." Aungus said. "

"By the way Aungus, would you mind if I call you dad?" Meleta asked.

"Meleta, are you trying to make me cry with happiness? I would be more that happy to be called dad by you" Aungus said showing love.

Meleta followed behind her Mrs Philips, her adopted mom into the dining room and they waited on her adopted dad Aungus until he spoken to Sonny before they started eating. After they had supper, fresh minced fruit and vanilla ice cream followed with fruit juice for the children, coffee for Meleta, mom, and a beer for dad and husband Ryan.

Later on, Ryan and Aungus stated playing games of blackjack while Meleta and was tiding the.

The kitchen and her adopted mother, Aungus' wife was putting the ironed clothes away before they went to bed.

The following morning at breakfast, Ryan was the last to have his as he wasn't hungry. Later when he was ready to eat, Meleta cooked him breakfast. As he was eating, his two adopted daughters, Tommy and Chelsea took his fork from him and ate some scrambled eggs from his plate while he watched them smiling with a heart so content that he offered them more, but Tommy said, "We had our breakfast daddy. But we'd like to have some of yours. " And she and Chelsea laughed then they both hugged Meleta saying. " Mom we love you and daddy, grandma and granddad."

That Sunday morning Ryan went to work for nine thirty and when he came home from work in the evening, Tommy and Chelsea jumped all over him before he washed his hands. "Let dad go and wash his hands honey" he said to them and they followed him to the bathroom and saw him wash his hands. "Honey, dad would like to be on his own for a while" he said to them. They left the bathroom and he urinated and then washed his hands and had a shower and changed before he went down to have supper. Tommy and Chelsea waited on him and halfway through eating his supper, Chelsea took his fork from him and ate some then Tommy did the same. Again Ryan's heart was full with joy. Their grandmother watched them both with smiles.

"Tommy, Chelsea, I think you two should go and have your bath and do your home work or your dad might think I haven't fed you two."

After Tommy helped Ryan eat his supper, Ryan went and made himself a ham sandwich and then washed it down with a can of beer."

"Well, you Miss Tommy, I want you to do your home work" Ryan did most of her homework the night before but she said, "Mommy I already did my home work."

And she hugged Ryan and put her fingers over his mouth to stop him talking. While later, Tommy and Chelsea went and had their bath after some hesitance from Meleta told them too. Tommy thought she was being clever and called her dad Ryan and asking him to bring her up a glass of water. Meleta looked at Ryan and laughed softly and shaking her head as she knew Tommy was pulling a fast one on her dad and that was the only way to get him into her room to help her with her home work. As her grandmother caught on she smiled. Ryan carried the glass of water up to her and pretended to leave but stood by her door with his back turned to her. "Dad, can you help me with the rest of my homework but don't let mom know" She said.

"Tommy, your mom said you can do your homework if you try as they're very easy. You do what you can and I'll come up later and help. We wouldn't want mom to catch us, would we?" Ryan said calmly.

"No dad" Tommy said.

Ryan helped her a little and then left Tommy doing her homework, and as he was coming down the stairs, Meleta was going up to catch him helping Tommy with her home work but they met on the stairs, Meleta laughed, asking. "Did Tommy really want some water?"

Ryan smiled, saying "She must have, or she wouldn't have asked for it."

"Like father, like daughter. Meleta jested up the stairs and went to Tommy and Chelsea's to give them their goodnight kiss. Then as Meleta was leaving, Tommy said, "mom I can do most of my homework. But would you please help me with these two?" As Meleta looked at her smiling, she said "Please mom." Meleta felt so over powered with love and respect from Tommy and Chelsea to have heard them calling her mom and her husband dad even though it was their first night moving in to live with her and her husband Ryan that she faced Tommy smiling then said to her, "okay, I will this time, but you really have to try and do your homework."

While Meleta was helping Tommy with the last mats of her homework, Ryan walked up the stairs quietly and quickly opened the girls' bedroom door to see Meleta helping Tommy with her homework. Ryan smiled shaking his head. Meleta smiled and said. "I'd no choice. She begged me so hard that I couldn't refuse."

After Meleta helped Tommy with her homework, she gave them a cup of warm milk and waited on them until they finished drinking their milk, and see them went to the toilet and said their prayer and tucked them in bed. She then kissed them on their lips before she left the room. On her way out, she asked. "Have you both wash your hands and brush your teeth?"

"Yes mom, we brush our teeth twice. Once when we had our bath and again after we drank our milk" Chelsea said.

"Goodnight honey." Meleta said and dimmed the lights very low.

"Goodnight mom" Tommy and Chelsea said. Meleta looked back at them smiling and closed their door.

Meleta went into the living room to see her husband Ryan and their adopted dad drinking coffee.

"Well, my eyes are closing down so goodnight my dears" her adopted mom wished them.

"Goodnight mom" Meleta and Ryan said.

"I must say goodnight as well, son, daughter." Their adopted dad Aungus said

"Goodnight dad," Meleta and Ryan said.

Aungus took his cup into the kitchen and then went to have his shower and then to bed.

"Are you coming to bed now honey?" Meleta asked Ryan.

"In a few minutes honey" Ryan said and when Meleta went upstairs, he took another beer up with him and had his shower and went to bed. In bed Meleta said to him, "Honey, now that I'm soon to have our baby and with our two daughters, I don't think I want to go back to work?"

"Well sweetheart, it was your choice to continue working. Just remember I ask you to stop working and you said you weren't ready. So when are you thinking of giving up your job?" Ryan asked.

"Well, I'm only eleven weeks pregnant so I would like to carry on working for another three months." Meleta said.

"Do you have to go until that time? Tommy and Chelsea are sufficient to keep you going." Ryan asked.

"I know, but all the same, I would like to go to work until the time I'm six months. Now moms living here, things will be so much easier and the girls are not so little. Oh honey, I would like for you to come with me to parents evening next Thursday evening at six fifteen to Tommy and Chelsea school as you would be working nights." Meleta said.

"Yes, sure I would" Ryan gladly said and he and Meleta went to Tommy and Chelsea school the following Thursday evening to see their work and know how they are in school.

Four weeks later, Meleta and Ryan booked their sick adopted mother into a private hospital where test has been carried out on her after doctors diagnosed she have cancer in her left breast. After another month of treatment, doctor found out it was a twisted muscle, as well as a blood clot in her vein that caused her discharge and also causes her to have spasm and pain and not cancer as suspected.

One of Ryan's surgeon friends took part in the operation on his adopted mother.

After another month, Meleta and her husband Doctor Ryan's adopted mother was fully recovered and she grew in strength again to help take care of her husband and her granddaughters as well as looking forward to their new grandson of Meleta and Ryan's.

As time went on, their adopted mom were even doing most of the cooking and sharing the house work while Meleta goes to work and she would even have a glass of port or sherry occasionally as she couldn't have any before during to her suspected cancer.

Two weeks later, Meleta and Ryan got full custody of the girls and gave them their names of Taylor with their grandparents consent.

As it was getting closer to the school holiday, Ryan booked Meleta, his adopted parents and his two daughters to Disney world Florida then Barbados where they would be spending two weeks at each place in five star hotels.

Two weeks later, Ryan took the family to Barbados for two weeks and then to Disney world Florida where they spent the other two weeks. It was so amazing to know how well Meleta, Ryan, their adopted mom, dad, and the two children enjoyed themselves exploring Florida and the girls had loved it at the Disney world.

The Friday after they got back from their holidays, their adopted mom went down on her knees in the presence of Meleta and Ryan and prayed and cried so that it brought tears in Meleta's eyes.

After Meleta and Ryan's adopted mom got up from off of her knees and looked up to Ryan and Meleta and said, "Meleta, Ryan, I haven't give birth to neither of you, but I couldn't love you more than I do." She then put her arms around their shoulders saying "My beloved adopted children, God has brought me back from the darkest part of the world and into light and place me into your hands, and now you've to put up with one old grumpy mom as me."

Meleta dried her tears laughed heartily then Ryan burst into laughter too. Ryan's laugh was so funny that his adopted dad burst into laughter as well. The laughing became so comical that his adopted mother and the children laughed so much that everyone' laughter had turned into a joke.

Two weeks later the on the Sunday Meleta invited Denyah and her family to dinner. Before dinner, Meleta spoke highly of her adopted family saying "Denyah, I think we have got a lot in common. Like you, I've adopted dad, mom and two daughters and another's on its way soon to be born. Just look at our four girls, my two and your two, they're so happy playing together. Denyah you'll have to bring your children to my house more often. Talking of family, Ryan and me had my mother's house repaired and bought her a new kitchen. As for my cheated sister, she wanted to be a solicitor so Ryan paid for her to go to University.

Well, she and I had laughed after she reminded me of the beating I had given her when I caught her and my boyfriend in my bed. You know what Den, it seemed so funny to me now, but not at that time when I'd actually caught them. The funniest thing is, when my boyfriend ran out the house and jumped the fence naked like a horse over a hurdle. I had to search the fence to see if he had left his balls behind" Meleta said laughing then went on saying "My bitch of a sister sometimes made jokes about him running away and told me she had her eyes on my husband. I warned her if she so much as to look at my husband too hard, I would poke her eyes out. Still, I do love her. She's okay now. Anyway, how about bringing your kids to play with mine sometime Den?"

"Meleta, I don't mind bringing my children to play with yours. You should do the same too sometime" Denyah said.

"I agree with Denyah" Meleta's mom said.

"I second that". Mrs Brown said.

"Well, whatever we agreed on, I have God to thank that we all became one happy and loving family." Meleta's dad said.

"Amen to that" Eugene said. Three hours after dinner, it began to rain and it was approaching eight o'clock, Eugene said "Den I think we should say goodnight and leave as the children have to go to school tomorrow and I have a lot of paper work to finish tonight."

"What would you say to another beer Eugene before you run off?" Ryan asked.

"Thanks, but no mate. It's time I take the children home." Eugene said.

Denyah went and got Mrs Brown, her, and the children's coats and then told her Paris and Jade B kiss their Uncle Ryan, Auntie Meleta and granddad and grandma goodbye. Denyah, Eugene and Mrs Brown wished everyone goodnight and Eugene left with his family holding Paris and Jade B's hands and walking them outside to his car. As he dropped their hands loose to get his key out of his jacket pocket, Paris and Jade B ran back and kissed granddad Aungus and grandma and said to their two Cousins Tommy and Chelsea "bye," Then they ran back to Eugene as he stood in the pouring rain waiting on them while Denyah and Mrs Brown sat in the car waiting.

Meleta and Ryan stood inside their doorway as it was raining heavily. After they saw Eugene and his family drive away, they closed their door. Meleta went to her two daughters and said. "You two upstairs as it's time for your bath and then your cocoa and then to bed!"

"But mom," Tommy said.

"Its late honey and you have to be in school tomorrow. Kiss grandma and granddad goodnight and do as your mom asked." Their dad Ryan said.

"Okay dad" Tommy said sulking and she and her sister Chelsea kissed him and grandparents goodnight. As they both was halfway up the stairs, their adopted mom Meleta told them, I'll be up soon with you cocoa."

After they both had their bath, Meleta took up their cocoa to them, watched them drink it and then told them to go to the toilet while she sat on Chelsea's bed and waited for them. As Tommy and Chelsea returned, she asked them "Have you washed your hands?"

"Yes mommy" Tommy answered then Chelsea followed saying, "I washed my hands too mommy. We always do after we use the toilet."

Meleta smiled as she watched them both climb into bed. She kissed them both on their lips and wished them goodnight as always. As Meleta was leaving, Chelsea asked, "Where's dad mommy? I want him to kiss me goodnight."

"Have you two said your prayers?" Meleta asked.

"Yes mommy. But I want daddy to kiss me goodnight." Chelsea said getting out of bed.

"You stay in bed honey. I'll send your dad to you." Meleta told them.

Meleta went and send Ryan up to the girls. "Dad I love you." Chelsea said.

"I love you both too honey." Ryan said and kissed both Tommy and Chelsea on their foreheads. "Goodnight sweetheart, I love you."

"We love you too daddy." Tommy said.

Ryan smiled and turned the lights low on his way out and then closed the door quietly and then went down stairs to help Meleta tidy the kitchen and the dining room.

"Well, I'm a little tired myself. Good night Ryan." their adopted dad said. And as he got up to leave Meleta said "Good night dad and she kissed him on his cheek.

"Good night my dear." he said to Meleta then he faced Ryan and said, "Goodnight son,"

"Goodnight dad" Ryan replied.

Then Ryan and Meleta's adopted mother looked at Meleta and Ryan and smiled saying, Goodnight my children."

Then as she got up to leave, Meleta and Ryan kissed her cheek and wished her a goodnight" she then followed upstairs behind her husband.

After Ryan and Meleta tidied the rooms and drank their cocoa, they turned off the lights and went and had a joint bath and then to bed.

Meanwhile, as soon as Denyah and her family got home, Paris asked. "Mom, can we go back to Aunty Meleta's to play with Tommy and Chelsea?"

"Of course you can honey," Denyah said. Then told Paris "Look honey, take your sister upstairs. I'll be right up to bathe you both."

"That's alright Den, I will go and see to the children. I feel like an early night as well," Mrs Brown said and she went and set the children's bath and helped them washed themselves before they had warm milk and went to bed. Before they fall asleep, Eugene and Denyah went to their room and kissed them goodnight and dimmed their light after they said their prayers.

Mrs Brown had a quick bath while Eugene and Denyah used different showers and then Denyah retired to bed with hot milk while Eugene a glass of scotch.

The next morning, Eugene and Denyah booked Jade B into the Rainbow nursery school.

Four weeks before Denyah went to see her sister Laney in St Kitts, she went and visited Sonny's wife and also gave Sonny two months off with pay as her garden was in great shape and winter was stepping in. Sonny's wife said to Denyah, "You should take some money from us for rent you know?"

"Mrs Pearson, I bought the house for you and your husband as a gift. I don't need any money from you. The house is yours and your husband's to do with what ever you decide. I will be going to St Kitts next week to visit my family. So you and Sonny take care of each others and your grandchildren. And I'll see you all when I get back. Oh this is for Sonny, an extra month wages and a little extra towards something for the kids." Denyah said.

"Well Miss Denyah, thank you and take care and tell Mrs Brown I'll come and visit her." Mrs Pearson said.

"Oh, just call me Denyah and mom will be going with me and the girls." Denyah told Mrs Pearson.

"She's a very lucky lady. I think we're all lucky to have someone like you to care of us. Oh how I would love to see that little Island. Seeing it on the TV, it looked so beautiful. Well you all have a nice time and kiss your children for me." Mrs Pearson said then hugged and kissed Denyah on her cheek before they said their goodbyes. Sonny wiped his tears dried before he hugged Denyah. "Sonny, I know that you've worked my garden very well and I'm very well satisfied, but I think it's time you spend more time with your grandchildren." Denyah said.

Sonny looked stunned and his wrinkled suddenly showed deeply as he stared into Denyah's face. Then as he stepped back a couple of footsteps he said "What are you trying to tell me Miss Denyah? That I'm too old now to work your garden? And that you want to put me away like an old dog?" Denyah laughed. "You silly fool, I'm treating you like the father I'm so longing for. In fact, I have a very good friend that is looking for a place and a job as she lost her job and also her home and I was thinking she could be nanny for your girls and help you around the house that's if you don't mind. I mean if you and the Mrs would have her. Her name is Bernice she's a very lovely lady. What do you think?" Denyah asked.

"And how would you think I can afford to pay her a wage?" Sonny asked with a stern looked on his face.

"Sonny, I didn't expect you to pay my friend for helping you with your grandchildren. Mrs Pearson is not very well and your grandchildren would need someone to help care for them. Besides, I would like you to take it easy and not working so hard. So what do you say?" Denyah asked.

Eventually Sonny understood what Denyah said to him. He smiled stroking around his lips. "I don't know? Although I like your idea, I'm not really sure as I cannot afford to hire her, nor any one for that matter, even though she might be good companion to the grandchildren and the Missus. What did you say her name is?" Sonny asked interestedly.

Denyah smiled and answered "Her name is Bernice and she's a lovely person. I told you. I think she's around my age thirty four, clear complexion and would fit in well with your grandchildren and your wife. I'm sure your grandchildren and your Mrs Pearson would love her. And don't worry about paying her, Eugene and I would take care of all that. A matter of fact, I would be putting you a cheque into you and Mrs Pearson's account and also some money in investment for your grandchildren until they become the age of eighteen or a bit over. However, just forget what I told you about having my friend as a Nanny. I wouldn't want to put you under any pressure. Well, you take care and I'll see you when I return from St Kitts. But I meant what I said about setting up a trust fun for your girls."

Sonny smiled, raised his black cap off his full grey head and scratched the left side of his head before he said to Denyah "Please wait a minute Miss Denyah, I would like to have your friend Bernice living with us and to help my wife looking after the girls and our little grand son. I think she might make a good Nanny or mother to them. And Miss Denyah, would you mind if I asked you what money you're talking about of putting into our account?" Denyah patted Sonny's right shoulder before saying, "I would be putting fifty thousand pounds into your account for you and the wife to spend on what ever you want and two millions in investment for the girls for when they became eighteen and need further education. And Eugene would be putting Bernice on his payroll. So you see Sonny, you'll have nothing to worry about except your health and to take it easy. I want you and Mrs Pearson to take it easy and enjoy life. Well, should I tell Bernice the good news or would you like to see her and tell her yourself?"

"Miss Denyah, it would be very nice of you to tell her from me that the girls and my wife are waiting to meet her and to have her moving in with us" Sonny's tears dropped heavily on his bosom "then he joked "Who are you really, are you a descendent from heaven or a disciple from the underworld?"

Denyah smile saying, "I do think that it was my devious husband who has made what we've achieved possible for us. Well, my husband thought he had thrown me in the lion's den but God has delivered me out of that den and moved all obstacles out of my way and put me on the road to success. The good lord took me over also and led me in the path of righteousness to meet people like you. And from there, I'm walking tall. Well I shall give Bernice your message tomorrow and I would come and see you all when I get back. Goodbye Sonny my dear friend" Denyah said and hugged him before she left and then phoned Bernice telling her Sonny and his wife would like her living with them and be Nanny to their three grandchildren.

Bernice was delighted with the good news and she got in touch right away with Sonny and his wife and then moved in their home three days later to live with them. Right away, they got to like Bernice very much as Bernice liked them. The grandchildren immediately accept Bernice like their new mother rather than their Nanny. This made Denyah feeling very happy going to St Kitts the following week Saturday early morning.

Bernice was honest to Sonny and his wife by telling them she served time in prison for killing her boyfriend and his girlfriend but by accident as they both were beating her up.

"Well" Mrs Pearson said, "You defended yourself."

She also told Mrs Pearson and Sonny, she were living with her ex boyfriend Darren she fell in love with but he lied to her telling her he wasn't married and she'd believed him until one evening his wife came looking for him and said they were married and she's having his second child -so she left him.

CHAPTER FOURTEEN

The next week Saturday early morning, Eugene droved Denyah, Mrs Brown and their two girls to Gatwick Airport. After he saw them check in and send the luggage through, he bought Denyah, Mrs Brown and himself breakfast while Paris and Jade B had a McDonald's happy meal and milkshake. Sometime later they announced that passenger's for St. Kitts to go through. Eugene kissed Mrs Brown on her cheek, hugged and kissed his children and then a long and loving kiss and hug to wish Denyah goodbye. As he closed his eyes in love, he said "Honey, I would miss you all so much. He then kissed Mrs Brown on her cheek and hugged her again telling her, "I'll miss your cooking and your smile then he kissed his two daughters and as Mrs Brown was waiting for Paris and Jade B, he said to Mrs Brown "Take care and enjoy yourself"

"I think I will" Mrs Brown said.

He again hugged Paris and Jade B and told them "Daddy loves you both. Take care of your mom for daddy."

"We will dad" Paris said and he kissed and hugged Denyah again and said, "Honey, hurry home to me. I'll save myself until you get back."

"You better" Denyah said and she kissed him quickly on his lips then took Jade B's hand into hers while Mrs Brown took Paris's then they went through the area where they gave their passports for checking before they board the plane. After they disappeared and walking through the long entrance, Eugene left and was on his way home. Every passenger for the West Indies was now on the plane and Denyah and her family were in the first class area. As the plane slid away and lifted to the air, Paris and Jade held tightly on to Denyah and Mrs Brown.

The eight hours flight was a little too much for the girls. They slept about five hours going but when they were not sleeping, they sat by the windows and would look at the clouds and told Denyah and Mrs Brown what shape the clouds looked like. Sometimes they said the clouds were shaped like sheep, cushions, or rabbits with short bushy tails.

Denyah had so many admirers that at times she displayed her fingers plainly to show her wedding rings.

Well, Denyah, Mrs Brown and the children landed in St Kitts at twenty-two minutes to four. After they checked in and collected their luggage, they went through to sit in the waiting area. While waiting in the arrivals area, Denyah's eyes moved all over the place looking at all the other people walking through the doors waiting and meeting their loved family or someone. As her eyes flicked past a vending machine she recognised a young brown faced female and a man waiting also to meet an arrival. Her heart started to beat faster with excitement as she recognised the face from the photo it was her sister Laney and her husband Paul. They looked just as their picture. Laney was no taller than five-foot four, very chubby but not unhealthy, her face was very round and her lips were very pout, her skin was very bronzed and her black sun burnt hair that was very curly and frizzy covered her face slightly. Paul her husband was very dark - a typical black islander wearing three-quarter length denim jeans that were frayed at the bottom and some brown buckled sandals. They hugged each other; Paul put their suitcases in the boot of his partly rusted car and set off to his home. As it was Denyah's first time to visit St Kitts, from the airport she admired the breathtaking scenery of the healthy sprouting sugar cane fields, the green healthy surrounding mountains and the beautiful big white painted houses and sheds that looked like shops. As Paul drove in his gate,

Laney said, "Well family, here's where I call my home. It's not very big, but it is big enough to keep the night dew off of our heads."

Mrs Brown smiled as Denyah looked at her. "Well, I'm glad to see you in the flesh." Denyah said and hugged her sister again as they all got out the car and went in the house. Then as she heard her sister Laney asking her husband for money to buy food, Denyah said. "Well, I have to call home to let my husband know we got here safely."

"The phone is in the hall" Laney said.

"It's okay I'll call him on my mobile. Thanks anyway" Denyah said and she called to tell Eugene they are now in St Kitts and they are okay. After Denyah waited for her sister's children to come home from singing lessons she asked Paul to take them to a hotel for a meal. On their way to the hotel, Paul pulled in at the petrol station for petrol. Denyah told him to fill the tank and she paid for the petrol and a drink for all. Then she took her sister, brother-In-law, Mrs Brown, hers and her sister's children to Turtle Beach Hotel for a meal and then Paul gave them a tour around the town in his badly rusted seven seat car. Laney had looked ashamed and hardly said much as Paul pointed out places and told them what buildings they are and tried to describe the people that owned them. After a long and hectic evening, Paul went and bought six bottles of pop and cakes while Laney made arrangements for sleeping. Denyah and her two daughters slept in Laney and Paul's room while Mrs Brown slept with Laney's two children leaving Laney and Paul sleeping on the settee cushions and sheets on the living room floor. After a week went by, Mrs Brown privately said to Denyah, "I don't want to meddle, but your sister seems as if she needs help. Her children are so lovely and her husband seemed well, but I really don't think they can afford much. She could have told you she'd no room but she didn't. Here Den, you take this thousand pounds and give it to her."

"You keep your money mom, I'll look after her," Denyah said.

"I really don't need the money Denyah, you take me to live with you, and I'm very well off. Now where could I spend my money when you giving me everything on my lap. Den, I have three thousand pounds with me. I wouldn't want this much to spend. So please let me share it with her. Giving something back to your family, it would make me happy."

"Ok mom, you can give her when we're ready to go home. Giving her now, she'll think we believe that she cannot afford to look after us and she might take it as an insult. We have to be discreet about what we do" Denyah said smiling. Then as Denyah saw her sister coming towards her and Mrs Brown they stood in silence smiling until her sister broke the silence and said. "We're having fish for supper." Denyah smiled and said "I love fish."

The first Sunday morning Denyah spend with her sister Laney and family, her sisters girls took her and her girls for a walk around the town while they left Mrs Brown in her room resting. Laney thought Mrs Brown was with Denyah and the children' and that her way was clear when she said to her husband Paul, "I have to use the rent money to buy food and the rent has to be paid Wednesday with what we've already owed."

"Well, what do you want me to do? I haven't any money. I'll have to ask the landlord to give me some more time until your sister and her family leave. That's all I can do." Paul said wiping the dripping sweat off his forehead in frustration.

"And what if the Landlord said no, and asked us to leave?" Laney said as she'd looked worried and her eyes covered in tears.

"I don't know, you should have thought about that before you asked your sister here." Paul said raising his voice.

"What are you telling me Paul, are you saying that my sister shouldn't have been here?"

"No Laney honey, I'm happy you get to know your sister and she's a lovely lady. But at the same time, I'm feeling so ashamed for her to come and see the conditions we live in."

After Mrs Brown heard enough, she pretended to clear her throat to make them know she was in the house and letting them think she was sleeping and just got up. Laney knocked on her door, "Come in." Mrs Brown said softly rubbing her eyes and pretended she heard nothing.

"I thought you were with Denyah and the girls." Laney said.

"I would have, but I fell asleep and maybe she didn't want to wake me. However, I'd brought you and the family a small gift as I didn't know what to buy for you and the kids especially what ever I liked, Denyah had already buy it for you. Here, take this. It's just a small change to say thanks for giving us the chance to know you and your family."

Laney took the white envelope and opened it to find one thousand pounds in fifty and twenty pounds note. Her eyes opened wide and her mouth stretched opened as she'd looked shocked. A couple of second after, "she said "Thanks, but I can't take your spending money. Taking this money from you it like you paying me for your keep and lodgings."

"Nonsense, I brought this for you and I have two thousand pounds on me which I could spend if I should see anything I would like to buy. I'll let you into a secret. I live with your sister and she spoilt me rotten. I've a bit of money and can't spend it as she gave me everything I need. So you'll be doing me a favour by spending a little of the money I'm giving you." Mrs Brown said with a nice smile.

"Okay, I really could do with the money. Thanks. I would let Denyah know."

"No, that money is for you to do what you wish, Denyah has nothing to do with what I gave to you. This is between you and me." Mrs Brown said to Laney. Laney thanked Mrs Brown again and kissed her on her cheek. Then looking on the envelope her smile enchanted like a bright light so that Mrs Brown showed her a cheerful smile too. The following Monday morning, Laney went and paid for her months rent and what she'd owed. Then told her husband Paul, Mrs Brown had given her a thousand pounds as a gift.

"Did you say something that caused her to give you that money?" her husband asked her "No Paul, I haven't" Laney said and then goes on, Mrs Brown told me it's a gift from her to us… so I paid the rent and what we'd owed. The truth is. I felt at ease with myself to know that we still have a roof over our heads, for how long, I don't know. But at least clearing the rent, it would keep the Landlord away for sometime. At least until my family is long gone. Besides, Mrs Brown looked as if she could afford what she gave us and believe me Paul, I'm so very grateful to her."

Just then Denyah, her two kids and her sister's two kids walked in while Paul and his wife seemed to be arguing but stopped as Denyah showed. "You two looked so uneasy as though you were in a middle of a conference and I disturbed you. Now, I realize how cramped we are and I was thinking about booking mom, my two children and myself into a hotel near by" Denyah said.

"You'll do no such thing. Yes, I know we're a little cramped but you're my sister and I'm very happy that you're here. I want to get to know you and the other of the family.

As long as we shelter from the night dew we're alright. Beside, you're only here for a short visit. So let's enjoy each others company and I don't want to here anymore about you booking in any hotel" Laney told Denyah as she smiled. I love you and you're all my family."

"I love you too sis, and your family. And my children love to be here. However, would you like to go with me shopping? My treat to you and the kids, speaking of shopping, will you and Paul take me around some nice area and show me where some nice houses are on sale," Denyah said. Mrs Brown looked at her smiling as she caught on what she's up too.

"Sis you've bought us enough. So you don't need to take me shopping. And are you thinking of leaving England to come here to live? Well, if you're thinking so, please don't" Laney said. Denyah smiled.

After breakfast, Laney asked her husband to take Denyah, herself, Mrs Brown and the children for a tour around the Island. After spending four hours touring around the Island, a nice looking big white house for sale in Frigates caught Denyah's eyes. She asked Paul to stop and she had a good look at the house without getting out of the car. "That's one you couldn't afford. These mansions around here ranged from half-a-million to five. Anyway it cost nothing to have a look" Laney said smiling.

"The areas are so beautiful. The houses and mansions are breath taking...and with the sea and palm trees surrounding. Denyah wrote the telephone number without anyone noticing and as Paul drove off, she caught Laney looking back at the mansion. Denyah smiled as Mrs Brown said. "Now, here I would choose to live if I was young and liked to escape from cold England and could afford to buy. But I'm old, used to the cold and the price reach is far beyond me."

After leaving the areas, Denyah took Laney shopping for clothes, shoes, and food for her and her children and gave Paul money to buy clothes for him.

Denyah then brought ice cream for everyone before she asked Paul to take them to a nice hotel for lunch. Paul smile and then drove to the Marriott hotel where she treated them to lunch before they went home. Outside in the yard, Denyah phoned the housing agency to ask about the six bedroom mansion on sale. A woman spoke to her saying. "My name is Melicent Libert. What can I do for you?"

"I'm Denyah Davis. I was driving through Frigates earlier this morning, and I saw this house for sale. I'm interested in buying it." Denyah said giving her the telephone number on the display board.

"Can you please hold the line Mrs Davis while I get the files" Melicent Libert said and she went and got the house sale file and quickly tuned to see the price of the house then called "Mrs Davis,"

"Yes I'm here" Denyah said.

"Mrs Davis, the mansion is five and a half million dollars" Melicent Libert said with a deep sigh.

Denyah went silent for a moment then Melicent Libert said "I believe the price is well beyond your reach. In other words, I don't think you would be able to purchase this mansion but I can show you a couple of smaller two, three and four bedroom houses not far from there."

"Please, Mrs Libert, I'm very much interested in buying that mansion and I would like to have a look at that mansion." Denyah said.

"Will tomorrow suit you Mrs Davis?"

"Tomorrow would be fine Mrs Libert." Denyah said and then went into the house.

"I was wondering where you get to" Laney said.

"Oh, I was speaking on my mobile to someone." Denyah said. Then she began to think hard of how would she go and see the mansion without Laney and Paul knowing. Then after thinking so hard, she came up with a brilliant idea "I know." she mumbled. "I would tell them that I met one of my friends on the same flight to St Kitts and she'll take me to meet her family. Yes! That should work" she thought. Then smiling, she went to Laney and told her "I've a friend that I met on the same flight here and she would like to take me to meet her family tomorrow."

"Okay," Laney said. "I was planning to take you to the beach tomorrow but there's always another day."

Denyah smiled and went into the yard to be by herself and phoned Mrs Libert and explained she did not want her sister to know she's buying the mansion for her and her family. Mrs Libert said "I understand" and she went along with Denyah's plan.

The following morning Mrs Libert called for Denyah ten thirty and took her to have a look at the mansion. Firstly, Mrs Libert said to Denyah, "Mrs Davis, this mansion sits in one and a quarter acre overlooking a salt pond with the sea surrounding and Nevis beyond in the distance. Just look at the fantastic view all around us as we stand here on this balcony with the feeling of the fresh cool mountains and sea breeze hugging our skin. Mrs Davis, let's move inside. There are six bedrooms, a king size, two large, two medium and a single. There's also a walk-in wardrobe, dressing room, each bedroom has its closet. Two toilets up stairs, even a wash one for a quickie wash. Here's a large cubical, a large blue marvel bathroom, two shower rooms, plus a men's lavatory" At this time when Mrs Libert was showing Denyah upstairs rooms, Denyah had a cool smile on her face. "Let's move down stairs," Mrs Libert said, then took the lead with Denyah following behind and entering into the large open plan living room with a beautiful arched door that took them to the roomy dining room with built in cocktail bar, followed by a breakfast area with large tiled blue and white floor and then the kitchen with beautiful blue and white marble tops that sat on about fourteen satin white cupboards including a large double built in fridge freezer and dish washer, a large six burner cooker with double oven, a double sink with a big pantry followed by a laundry room, then a library, play area, one toilet downstairs, a large stockroom with secure lock, a conservatory we call an idle room and double garage and a massive front and back yard with palm trees to explored the beauty of the mansion. Not to mention, lime, avocado, mango, and breadfruit trees. "Well what you think? Mrs Davis?" Mrs Libert asked and goes on to say "There're plenty of yard space for any other buildings and that still leaves plenty of yard room for the children for you to build whatever. There's even a big fish pond, swimming pool and tennis court. Oh and a nice guest house. After this mansion was on the market for eight months, the price was dropped by three hundred thousand dollars. Personally, I think this mansion is well worth the first asking price. Now you could buy it for less, if you really want to buy, I'm afraid the deposit would be one and a half million dollars. And this would left you four mil plus interest to pay."

"I want to buy it for my sister and her family as a gift" Denyah said.

"You sister is very lucky, I do hope she appreciate you Mrs Davis."

"I'm sure she does Mrs Libert."

"Mrs Davis, as I stated I would need to have at least one million five hundred thousand dollars deposit before we could to come to any agreement." Mrs Libert said.

"I would be buying outright Mrs Libert" Denyah told her.

Mrs Libert stood facing Denyah and looking shocked before she asked." Are you a very wealthy Mrs Davis?"

"You could say that. I would have a cheque ready for you tomorrow morning and I would like the deed made out to Mr and Mrs Paul and Laney Wells. Can I ask you to do me one more favour Mrs Libert?" Denyah asked.

"Certainly Mrs Davis, but before the deed can be drawn out, we both will need a solicitor."

"Could you pick me up tomorrow morning as I wouldn't want my sister to suspect what I'm doing? I intended to give the deed to her lest in her thoughts she thinks I would like my nieces to have a better life of living."

"Absolutely, I fully understand Mrs Davis. I'll pick you up about ten in the morning with my solicitors" Mrs Libert said.

After Denyah and Ms Libert had lunch in a nice and clean restaurant, Mrs Libert drove Denyah to her sister's home. Denyah thanked Mrs Libert and Mrs Libert said "I'll come and fetch you about the same time tomorrow morning."

Denyah smiled and walked into the yard to meet her sister Laney and Mrs Brown sitting on chairs in the shade in the back of the yard. As Mrs Brown met Denyah's eyes, Denyah smiled. Mrs Brown got the message Denyah had bought the mansion for her sister. Then Denyah's phone began to ring, she moved away and answered her phone. "Hello"

"Mrs Davis, did I mention to you that I'll come and collect you at ten o'clock?"

"Yes. I think you did. Ten it would be then," Denyah said "And a great thank you or all your help."

That next morning Mrs Libert came for Denyah just a little before ten o' clock and soon they became friends. Mrs Libert gave Denyah a second tour inside and outside the mansion again. "I love it. It's so beautiful and I know my family would love this location. Here's so beautiful and spacious and so breathtaking with beautiful views all around." Denyah said as she looked cool and glamorous.

"Mrs Davis, I know your family would love their home." Mrs Libert said nicely. Mrs Libert then fill four glasses with champagne and gave one each to Denyah, Denyah and her solicitors and she kept one" Thanks you so much Mrs Davis" Mrs Libert said smiling after she received a cheque for the full amount for the mansion.

"Mrs Davis, it was a great pleasure doing business with you."

"Likewise, Mrs Libert, "Denyah said smiling.

Then Mrs Libert placed the deed into a large brown envelope, and handed it to Denyah. Denyah took the deed out and had a good look at the deed making sure it was in order. Smiling contently, Denyah put the deed in the envelope again and sealed the envelope and carefully put it in her handbag. "Thank you again Mrs Libert."

"Mrs Davis, would you please call me Millicent" Mrs Libert told Denyah.

"And I would like you to call me Denyah," Denyah told her.

Denyah also paid her solicitor his asking fee with a cheque and told him many thanks with a warm and friendly hand shake.

Then Denyah asked Mrs Libert "Can I borrow some of your time to follow me to buy furniture for the mansion as it is nicely decorated and freshly painted."

"Yes of course Denyah." Mrs Libert said.

That same morning, Mrs Libert took Denyah to some furniture shops where she helped Denyah choose the furniture for the mansion. Denyah paid for the furniture to suit every room in the mansion and she even chose poster beds with nets to keep the mosquitoes out. The chandeliers for the hall, and all the rooms were exquisite and the same in gold and light blue leaves and side lights were the same. The massive multicoloured rugs for the hall and living room floor looked magnificent on the dark mahogany living room floor and even the highly polished marble light blue and white tiled floor in the wide hall and leading throughout the kitchen and to the back veranda and overlooking Keys, Canaree and so many mooring places. On the hall walls hung four large watercolour painting that looked exquisite to compliment the wide cool hallway.

Within two hours the mansion was fully furnished with two large matching living room rugs to compliment the furniture, curtains and chandeliers. The massive aquarium built into the wall looked attractive with lovely species of fish and living plants. Denyah paid to have the aquarium cleaned and suited for the fish, and sharks, as it is double aquarium. Now the mansion was looking spectacular and was ready to live in. Also to complete the mansion were two brand new cars locked away in the garages one with seven seats and the other five seats and a hired nanny to help Laney with the girls.

Mrs Libert was kind enough to find a nanny for Laney as Denyah asked her to. However, as it was Denyah last day in St Kitts, she took the family and Mrs Libert to a thank you dinner at the Marriott Hotel. Over dinner, Denyah and Mrs Libert exchanged telephone numbers and they promised to remain friends.

Before Mrs Libert and Denyah parted, they both hugged each other warmly and Denyah thanked her greatly and they both made a second promise they'll keep in touch with each other.

The following day at the airport both Denyah's and her sister Laney were in floods of tears. As Denyah had to depart she and Laney hugged each others tightly and never seemed to want to let go until Denyah's flight number was announced. She then hugged Paul, kissed her two nieces and gave Paul the brown envelope and kissed both her niece again and left with Mrs Brown and her two children to aboard the plane. Denyah looking back at her family, she smiled as she waved goodbye and went into the plane in tears.

Paul left the airport and looking so sad that he put the envelope into his jacket pocket to comfort his crying wife. At their home he burst in to tears and then feeling the envelope in wonder when his crying wife said "I've only got to know my sister for a short while and now I miss her so much" Then Paul took the envelope out of his jacket pocket and opened it to find the deed to the mansion they were looking at two weeks ago that Denyah had bought for him and Laney, also the log books for two new cars, four sets of keys to the mansion and for the two cars that were locked up in the garages and even keys for the gate and a cheque for one million pounds made out to both of them. Paul went down on his knees praying with tears of joy and hugging his wife and his children and then gave the envelope to his wife with the contents in it. Anxiously he took his family to see the mansion. Paul turning the key to open the gate, he turned to his wife Laney and said "I'm feeling weak in my knees and nervous in my hands."

"I didn't expect this at all" his wife said. As they went inside and saw their mansion was fully furnished with brand new expensive looking furniture throughout, the children jumped for joy with bright smiles spreads over the little faces, especially when they saw their bedrooms. "Mom can we sleep here tonight," the children asked. "Well, girls we only came to look at the place" her mother told them. "Please mom," they cried. Just then Paul rushed into the mansion looking shocked and raising his eye brows as he said to his wife Laney" She even bought us two brand new cars. Laney darling, I had no idea your sister is a wealthy lady. She must have searched long and hard looking for you. Tomorrow we shall go to the bank and put the money into our account and move into our new home. Laney, we shouldn't have anymore financial worries and we can now afford to send the children to a private school and go into business selling cars. Your sister even gave us a house maid that we will see tomorrow."

Laney went to look at the cars. Seeing the beautiful cars, she put her hands over her mouth in excitement and said. "If my sister could give us this much, she must be filthy stinking rich. Actually, Mrs Brown told me that my sister's very rich and she don't have to rely on her husband for anything. Even though Mrs Brown had already give me a thousand pounds, she gave me two more thousand and she didn't even give me the chance to thank her. Paul, do you think she'd known that we poor?"

"Laney, I don't know, all I know it that we're very rich now and your sister has made this possible for us." Paul said in joyful tears as he looked up to the ceiling saying "Thank-you loving God for family as good as Denyah and Mrs Brown."

CHAPTER FIFTEEN

On flying back to England, Mrs Brown said to Denyah, "I do hope that the money you gave to Paul and your sister doesn't get to Paul's head and cause him to ill treat your sister."

"Why do you say that mom?" Denyah asked.

"Well, giving him great wealth in one day and a beautiful mansion and being he's so handsome with a lovely face enough to attract any women. Ah well, I do hope it doesn't come to that."

"Mom, I don't really think Paul would do anything wrong to Laney, he loves her and the children deeply and he reminds me so much of Eugene. Besides, I've no regrets at pulling my family off the scrap heap." Denyah said.

Mrs Brown took Denyah's hands into hers and said "Den, even though I told you many times that you're a good person, I'm telling you again you're a very good and caring soul. Well honey I'm very tired and I must rest my eyes. Wake me up when we land."

It was a long eight hours flight when Mrs Brown fell asleep. Because she was so tired, she missed out on some of her meals. Paris and Jade B also fell asleep most of the time with their heads on Denyah's lap. At one time a good looking dark skinned man eyed Denyah, Denyah smiled out of politeness. Then as the man stretched his tongue out of his mouth and moistening around his lips with his tongue smiling, his white wife looked him in his face, and noticed his eyes were fixed on Denyah. She slapped his face hard and moved herself to tell Denyah "Keep your eyes off my husband" Denyah looked deeply in her eyes saying "I have no use for you or your husband except to offer both of you a job to clean my toilets as I saw his tongue is long enough to wipe down and around my toilet bowl and you should train him that sexism is discrimination. In other words, he should pick on his class before he lavishes his filthy tongue out of his mouth to offend one that isn't his type. Your husband behaviour is despicable" The wife raised her hands to hit Denyah and dropped her hand to her side when Denyah told her "You even touch me and I'll kick your arse sending you flying out of this plane. Now, I suggest you take yourself to your tapeworm."

During to this time, the young and pretty tanned hostess was watching but wasn't sure what was going on. She went to Denyah and asked "Are you alright Mrs Davis?"

"Yes, I'm okay thank you. My friend only just noticed I was on the same flight and came to say hello. She was just leaving when you showed up."

The hostess smiled and said Mrs Davis, "you have two beautiful daughters."

"Thank you" Denyah said and the hostess asked to be excused and left. Denyah looked up at the standing woman with an expression indicating the question 'are you still here?' was in her mind.

The woman touched Jade B's hand saying to Denyah, "I'm so sorry to have jumped down your throat. My name's Deanne Saunders I don't know why I got jealous when that rat of a husband has treated me so badly. I should have known you are a decent lady and not like his whores. Would you mind me sitting with you for a while?"

"Mrs Saunders, what do you really want of me?" Denyah asked calmly

"Only your friendship, believe me Mrs Davis, I like your honesty, and all I want from you is for us to becomes friends. That's all." Mrs Saunders said smiling. Denyah looked on at her serious for a short time before she sent out a smile.

"Like the hostess said, you really have two beautiful daughters. I, I've none. I was pregnant four months ago but one of my husband whores kicked me in my belly and pushed me hard to the ground outside Marks and Spencer's store. I lost the baby and because of complications, I can never conceive again as my womb was taken from me."

"Oh dear, Mrs Saunders, I'm very sorry" Denyah said sympathetically.

"May I sit with you for a while?" Mrs Saunders asked again.

"Yes of course, please do," as Denyah took Jade B on her lap

Mrs Saunders sat down with Denyah for nearly one hour talking and laughing and so they became friends before Mrs Saunders went back and sat with her husband. "You know what Thomas, Mrs Davis is a nice and decent person. She's nothing like your whores, we have now became friends and I would like you to treat her with respect and keep your filthy tongue in your mouth where it belongs for Mrs Davis is one fine lady you won't get to use your tongue on" Mrs Saunders said to her husband, showing embarrassment.

Long after, when Mrs Brown woke up, Denyah went to Mrs Saunders and her husband. She out stretched her hand to Mr Saunders in friendship and said "I've met your wife and speaking with her, she's a lovely lady. I'm Mrs Davis. It's a pleasure to meet you Sir." Denyah outstretched her hand to him again, saying, "I would really like to get to know you Mr Saunders."

But Mr Saunders sat stunned looking up at Denyah and looking shame. Denyah smiled and leaned forward and kissed him on his forehead and said "Mr Saunders, as of now, I'm friend with your loving wife, I would like us to be friends too,"

Mr Saunders turned and looked at his wife with a long face then he looked up to Denyah with a faint smile before he outstretched his hand to her in friendship. Smiling Denyah gave Mrs Saunders one of her cards with her name and telephone numbers on it and in exchanged Mrs Saunders gave Denyah a hand written note with telephone numbers to her home and her hair saloon and then joked saying "I'm not as famous as you Mrs Davis,"

"Why do you say that?" Denyah asked her.

"Your card is very posh, and that tells me you either famous or wealthy." Mrs Saunders said smiling. As Denyah knew Mrs Saunders was telling the truth, she smiled and then admitted to Mrs Saunders "Yes, I've a little money of my own and my husband owns a few hotels and restaurants."

"I knew it" Mrs Saunders said and goes on to say "I own a hair saloon in Town but I never carry my cards while travelling abroad. When you're ready to have your hair done, give me a call and I'll give you directions - and a free hair do. Take care of my number as I would take care of yours."

"I certainly will Mrs Saunders. Well goodbye to both of you for the time being" Denyah said and turned to leave when Mr Saunders stretched his hand out to her. Smiling, Denyah shook his hand and pecked Mrs Saunders with a quick kiss on her cheek and went back to her seat. By this time Paris and Jade B were awake from their naps and Paris snuggled up under Mrs Brown arm and didn't want to move.

After Denyah has changed Jade B out of her urine clothes, the hostess came round with supper. Again, Paris and Jade B hardly touched their supper. After supper, Denyah settled down to read a book while Mrs Brown and the children completed a puzzle game of Beauty and the Beast.

As the passengers beginning to settled down for the night, Paris starting to cry and complained of a pain in her tummy. Denyah gave her some medicine before taking her to the toilet. Much later she fell asleep with her head on Denyah lap while Jade B was practically sleeping on Mrs Brown. "Den honey, Eugene knew we'll need this room when he booked us first class." Mrs Brown said.

The plane was eventually left in silence as nearly everyone was sleeping and the lights were dimmed. Denyah saw Mrs Brown sleeping before she fell asleep with the opened book rested on her lap.

Five thirty in the morning, everyone was awake by the bright lights followed by hot face flannels that were given to the passengers by the hostess before breakfast. Then, the Captain announced over the mike two more hours flight to England and he wish everyone a very good morning.

At last, the plane landed and the Captain showed up to wish everyone good luck and goodbye when his eyes clashed with Denyah's. He smiled and as he saw Paris and Jade-B and thought it was a fantastic excuse to go to them just to speak with Denyah. As his eyes caught Denyah's wedding ring, he smiled and said "You have adorable children."

"Yes, they are. And thank you for a successful flight." Denyah said and held Jade B and Paris hands with Mrs Brown behind them walking out of the plane to go through the customs departure. After they checked out by the passport department they went through to the luggage department and got their luggage and then paid a porter to take the luggage to Eugene's car. When Eugene saw Denyah, his kids and Mrs Brown, his face lit up like the sun set. He kissed Mrs Brown on her cheek and asked her "Did you have a nice time?"

"Yes Eugene, I had a marvellous time and thanks for the holiday." Mrs Brown said.

Eugene then gave Denyah a long kiss and said to her "I never thought I would miss you and the children so much."

"Me too" Denyah told him. He kissed her again, then smiling, as he lifted up Jade B and kissed her before he sat her into the car and then hugged Paris and kissed her. "Daddy, you should have come with us to see Aunty Laney, Uncle Paul, Ocelia and Beverly. Aunty Laney and Uncle Paul sleep on the floor….." "That's enough Paris." Denyah told her. After some time driving home, Denyah looked back and saw Mrs Brown, Paris and Jade B sleeping. She smiled and told Eugene "I bought a mansion for my sister and gave her one million pounds and a car each for her and Paul." Eugene quickly looked at her before he said "What's money aye?"

"Are you been funny?" Denyah asked him.

"No honey, I'm glad you went and know the truth about your sister and her family, I'm also happy you can afford to give her a decent home. I'll give you half your money back. Say the gift came from the children" Denyah could not believe what she was hearing from Eugene, "I mean what I said to you honey. You tell me how much you spent on everything, and I'll give you back half. As I've stated, the gifts are from the children. Our children including that little nipper you're carrying."

Denyah smiled and said "Thanks honey, but you don't really have to give me any money as I might have to depend on you one day."

Eugene felt her right leg and said "Half I said, half I'll give to you" Then as Denyah moved his hand away from her leg, she noticed he had an erection. She laughed and laughed so much that she woke Mrs Brown up. Eugene looked at her in a funny way then he burst into laughter. "What's the joke" Mrs Brown asked. "Eugene told me he burned every thing he cooked."

Mrs Brown laughed and said. "We'll have to give him cooking lessons." Then she fell asleep again all the way home and only woke up when Denyah call "Mom we're home."

Eugene took the luggage into the dining room. After Denyah and Mrs Brown had looked after Paris and Jade B and fed them, they were so tired that they fell asleep on the settee. Denyah went to have a long hot bubbling bath. Eugene joined her and after making love to her, he said "Honey, you have no idea, how painful I was waiting for this moment."

"I too honey even though I hate to admit it. I really enjoy you and I do love you and I did really miss you when I was in St Kitts."

Denyah and Eugene went to their bedroom and sat on the bed. Denyah gave Eugene two sets of photos and told him. "I took some photos of my sister and her family. And this is the mansion we gave to them." Denyah pointed it out to Eugene.

"Eugene, they're lovely. We must invite them up next summer." Denyah said.

As Denyah and Eugene left their bedroom door open, Mrs Brown walked in and asked "What shall we have for supper?"

"I come downstairs with you mom" Denyah said and went downstairs behind Mrs Brown and into the kitchen to cook supper.

After Eugene saw the photos, he followed downstairs and saw Denyah and Mrs Brown about to start cooking supper. He looked hard at Denyah, and closed his eyes painfully. When Mrs Brown looked on his face, as he closed his eyes and showing a sad expression, Mrs Brown knew it wasn't a good sign. He then opened his eyes to look at Denyah in desperation. Denyah and Mrs Brown looked at him in wonder.

"Den my love, please take a seat. You too mom,"

Denyah and Mrs Brown watched Eugene with interest before they moved into the living room and sat in the curved six seat settee. Tears came in Eugene's eyes as he began to say. "When you were on holiday, Dad passed away on the first week."

Denyah closed her eyes with tears leaking through with both her hands clinching her face. After she opened her eyes and dried her tears and looked at him.

"Why didn't you let us know? We could have come home" she said sadly, hindering Eugene saying more. "Honey, he is family regardless and you should have let mom and me know."

"Den, that's the reason why I hadn't told you. You and mom deserved to be happy on your holiday. Anyway, he was cremated."

"Was it the same complaint that took him out of this world?" Mrs Brown asked sadly.

"Yes mom, I'm afraid it was. But this time, he had a massive heart attack. He went almost immediately as he got to the hospital. " Eugene said.

Denyah shivered remembering her first adopted mother has died from a massive heart attack in the hospital when she was out having dinner. She cried softly while thinking of her adopted mother Mrs Carter. Eugene sat next to her and put his arms around her. Mrs Brown got on her feet and said, "Den honey, I think you should go and rest for an hour or so, you would feel much better when you have. Well, to take my mind off the worst, I better move myself in the kitchen and make myself useful."

"Well, as I said mom, some of your home cooked steam rice with fried fish and sweet corn I would love. I've missed your cooking so much even though I could go to one of my restaurants or hotels for meals. But your cooking has knocked out any other food I've tasted" Eugene said.

"Well thank-you Eugene for the compliment and if that's what you wish for supper will be cooked soon and served."

"Mom, are you sure that you're ready to cook today?" Denyah asked her.

"Of course honey, I need to work off some of my laziness. Well, I better get some fish out the freezer and I'll see you two later. Denyah, I think a message is on the phone for you, I think it was from your brother Ryan. After you speak to him, please go and try to have a nap. The children's father and I would see to them. "

"Thanks mom, I'll phone him right away to let him know we're back safe and well. Before I have my nap" Denyah said.

Denyah phoned Ryan's home but a woman answered the phone. "May I speak to Mr or Mrs Taylor please?"

"I'm sorry that they're not here. Can I take a message and pass it on to Mr Taylor. I'm a friend of theirs. May I ask your name?" the woman asked.

"I'm Denyah, Ryan's sister, can you please tell him I'm home from my holiday," Denyah said but as the woman didn't reply, Denyah said again, "Can you please let them know I tried to phone them last night on my way coming home and got no reply."

"Haven't you heard?" The woman asked.

"Heard what?" Denyah asked.

"A man broke into their home and done a nasty job on his wife, that she almost lost her baby son. Maybe the man thought Mrs Taylor was you as she heard the man called your name and said the bastard you're carrying it should have been Eugene's ex. Mrs Taylor claimed she has never seen the man before. By the way my name's Rona, Mr and Mrs Taylor's neighbour."

"Rona, can you please tell me anything else"? Denyah asked.

"Well the baby born was two weeks premature but he's doing well. As for his mother, she had a few bruises to her arms and face but she's okay. They're at the hospital to see their baby. They phoned to say the baby is off the drip and now feeding from the bottle. Well, thank God for that! I will tell your brother you call. And don't worry too much as the danger has passed. However, Meleta said her attacker was a black man."

"Thank you Rona. Goodbye."

As soon as Denyah put her phone down, she went to Eugene in tears, saying "I've just spoke to Rona, she's a friend of Meleta and she's her next door neighbour, well Rona told me Meleta told her she'd opened her door to a black man she has never seen before. The man stared at her in horror before he pushed her into her house and beat her up so that she almost lost her baby. Why did you hide this from me Eugene? Is there's anything else I should know that you're keeping from me?"

"That's awful. I can imagine what Meleta went through." Mrs Brown said in an angry manner.

"Yes, I know but I didn't want you to get upset on you first hour of your return. I was waiting for the right time to tell you." Eugene said.

Denyah started crying. And because she was crying so much, she developed a strong headache. Mrs Brown gave her two pain killer tablets and some water then advised her to get some rest. Eugene was going to see his mother but changed his mind as Denyah was so very upset. Jade B woke up calling mom but Eugene said, "Mom is sleeping."

"Mommy," Jade B calling and crying. Then Paris woke up asking "Where's mommy dad?"

"Mommy's sleeping honey. I and nanny will look after you."

As Jade B was crying for Denyah, Eugene took her and Paris up to her and said "Honey, they're crying for you."

Jade B climbed up into bed beside Denyah and hugged her saying, "Mommy, I'm hungry."

"Mom, we want a happy meal and milkshake."

Eugene looked at Denyah and smiled saying, "Who's coming with daddy for a happy meal and milkshake?"

"Me, daddy" Paris said jumping on Eugene's back."

"Me daddy" Jade B said happily.

"Come on. Let's go get your happy meals and milkshake" he said to his girls. Then he asked Denyah, "You want anything honey?"

"A couple of nutmeg apple pies for mom and me."

"I'll be right back, come on my two precious" he called Paris and Jade B and walked down the stairs with them holding each others hands and he said to Mrs Brown. "Mom, my two princesses' are taking me to get their happy meals and milkshakes, do you want anything?"

"A couple of apple pies for Den and me."

"Den asked me to bring her the same for both of you."

"Well thank you" Mrs Brown said.

Jade B and Paris took Eugene by his hands and led him to his car. He took them to McDonald's and bought them their happy meals and milkshakes and four apple pies and returned home to meet Denyah in the kitchen helping with the cooking. After he gave Denyah and Mrs Brown their apple pies, he helped himself to a can of beer while Denyah and Mrs Brown had one of their apple pies and a cup of tea until supper was ready.

Meanwhile Denyah phoned her sister Laney. Laney answered "Hello."

"Laney my dear, I'm only letting you know we got home safe and already I miss you and the family. Well kiss the kids for me and tell Paul we're home safe."

"Denyah, I wouldn't know where to begin to thank you. You left me and Paul crying. Den, we love you so much and the girls, well I can't get them to stop saying Aunt Denyah is so malt, meaning you're the best."

"Well, you tell them from me they're the best too and I love them. Laney, I'll phone you soon, Goodbye my loving sister."

"Goodbye Den and kiss the kids for me too and say hello to mother Brown, Eugene and the rest of the family for us. Goodbye sister" And they both put their phone down.

Denyah then phoned Mrs Libert. As Mrs Libert pick her phone up saying. "Hello."

"Millicent it is Denyah here. I called to let you know we got home safely and many thanks for your help towards my sister and me. How would you like a holiday in England sometime?"

"Denyah, I would. Just let me know when you will receive me."

"I will. And Millicent, I would very much like you to keep in touch with my sister as a friend as I would with you. I love you. Well I'll phone you soon and take care."

"You too my friend and goodbye," Mrs Libert said.

Denyah put her phone down and smiled.

"Eugene, I though you were going to see your mother," Mrs Brown said.

"Yes, but with Den not feeling well, I want to be with the girls and help you."

"Eugene, you go and see your mother I think I can manage without you for a while."

"No mom, Den and the girls needs me more. Besides, I won't miss my supper. I've waited too long to taste your cooking. I'll phone to let her know that I won't be coming tonight" Eugene said.

As Denyah was still very shaken up over Meleta and Eugene's dad, she took up her apple pie and tea and went to her room and ate them. After an hour, supper was ready. Paris ran upstairs held her hand and pulled her out of bed saying to her. "Come down to supper mom" her mom went down behind her, and as she saw Eugene eating, she said, "I thought you went to see your mom."

"No, as you were not feeling well, I stayed so that I could help put the children to bed and look after you as mom might be still tired from her flight." Eugene said.

After Denyah finished eating her supper she phoned Ryan.

"Hello" Ryan answered.

"Ryan, it's me. Your sister, I got back two hours ago to hear the bad news. How are Meleta and the baby?"

"Sis, Meleta is recovering mostly from shock. But she's still a little shook up, as for the baby; he's out of danger and doing well. I think he will be coming home in a few days. Sis, I think Meleta wants to sell the house and buy another some where else as she would be always afraid and feeling unsettled."

"Ryan, I think that would be the best. I agreed with her completely as she would be always looking over her shoulder and wondering" Denyah said.

"Now, how are you, mom and the children? And I'm glad to know you all got back safe. Den, can I bring the girls over tomorrow to spend a few days with yours? I thank God the rest of the family were out at this time."

"Ryan why don't all of you come and spend some time here, Meleta can use the cot for the baby and Paris and Jade B would love to have Tommy and Chelsea and your mom would be good company for my mom. We would be good for each other just like old times." Denyah said.

"Okay, I would tell Meleta, have you caught a cold." Ryan asked.

"Why do you asked? Denyah asked.

"Your voice sounded hoarse."

"That's because I was crying when I heard what has happened to Meleta. Where were you at that time?" Denyah asked.

"At work, my neighbour saw a man left the house and she went and saw Meleta bleeding on the floor and called an ambulance then the police came and told me my wife had been beaten up and was taken to the hospital. Den I was so frightened. I thought we would have lost our baby. But I thank God, to give them both back to us." Ryan said.

"Ryan, I'm so sorry" Denyah said. Tears came in her eyes. But as the bad and sad news of Meleta and Eugene's father left her feeling nauseous, she said, "Look Ryan, I would fill you in with everything when I see you. I've brought presents for all of you. By the way, have you seen David lately, I've brought him and his fiancée a gift. Oh, Ryan, here am I talking about presents when my best friend and my nephew almost died."

"Yes Den, David and I had a drink last night in the Fox and Goose. I will see him later at the Social Club. Would you like me to tell him you're back?"

"No thank you Ryan, I'll give him a call tomorrow. Well you take care of yourself and the family and I'll see you all at the week-end." Denyah said.

"Goodbye sis," Ryan said and went on to say "don't take what happened to heart. We'll get over this somehow. Well you be good sis, and give my love to mom and kiss

my nieces for me, will you? I'll give Meleta your message soon as she comes home."
Ryan put the phone down.

The following morning at the breakfast table, Denyah broke down and cried, leaving her breakfast on the table and went into the living room to be on her own. Mrs Brown put her breakfast into the oven and took the girls to feed their kitten. After, the girls washed their hands before they went into the playing area to play with their dolly and after they got fed up playing, they went back into the dining room to be with Denyah. As Mrs Brown felt sorry for Denyah, she sat next to her and asked her. "What's the matter honey?"

Denyah answered "nothing" and she dried her tears.

"Den honey, why can't you tell me what's troubling you. You know you can trust me by now. You treated me like a loving mother and I've treated you like a loving daughter and I don't want you to suffer in silence. I would like to share your pain. Are you still crying over your father-in-law and Meleta?"

Denyah swallowed some coffee and then said tearfully. "When I was living with my ex-husband Wesley, my mother had known my sister Fay was having an affair with him and she didn't tell me. I went home early one day from work due to migraine and caught my sister and my husband in bed. My sister laughed in my face and my husband told me he should have married to my sister instead of me and that I made him sick. I cried to my mother about my sister and my mother pretended to me she didn't know what was going on. To my surprise after my mother had two shots of whiskey, she told me to move out of my own home if I don't like what is going on with my husband and my sister. However, I put up with what he and my sister were doing and I took no notice anymore. I still washed and ironed his clothes, cooked his meals and shared his bed even though I hated to. However, one day I went into town to style my hair and I met his sister Lisa outside a super market waiting on her husband. As her husband was so late in coming to fetch her she suggested that we should go somewhere for a cold drink. Eventually, we ended up in a restaurant where a long time friend of his sister was working. It had turned out that his sister and this friend used to go to the same evening sewing class when they were teenagers. That day in the restaurant after they'd seeing each other after a long time they acted like two happy children and sometimes his sister even forgot I was there, which didn't bother me, for I might have done exactly as her if it was the other way round. Well, his sister and I spend a long time at the restaurant and then went home. Oh that's where Eugene met me. But at that time, I'd no interest in him. Anyway, after I got home Eugene phoned me and my husband answered the phone and then accusing me of having affairs with my boss and Eugene. Countless times he beat me and told me I'm a whore. His sister asked me to go with her to one of her friend engagement party that same night. I asked my husband if I could, and he said yes, after I got dressed he raped me and then made me dress in bright red then told me if anytime I lost my job, he definitely would recommend me for prostitution and then he tossed me out of the house like a piece of maggot meat. I cried walking to his sister's house and dried my eyes before I went into her house. But she noticed my makeup was smeared and she let me use hers and asked me why I was wearing red. I only smiled. Right away, his sister suspected he had something to do with what I was wearing. I begged her to leave things as they were as I was becoming too weak with his beating and too ashamed with his insults. However, I put on a brave smile on my face and went to Joan and Austin's engagement party with his sister. There I met Eugene again and we speak and I had a dance with him. Shockingly, his girlfriend slapped my face and told me to keep my hands off of her man, meaning Eugene. That night I didn't dance with him anymore. Or anyone, I refused to dance and speak with Eugene that night and he asked me to tell him why, but I told him nothing. Then someone must have told him his girlfriend had slapped me and warned me to keep away from him. Then his cousin Cindy told me he used to date her but finished with her when he caught her with one of her brother's friends. So, Eugene finished with her five months ago. Then, there came a friendly face to my rescue when Eugene's woman come to fight me again and told Eugene's ex if she touches me again she would break her to pieces like a dry twig. That friends name is Bernice. Well, Eugene's ex got to find out my telephone number. How, is beyond me. Well, she phoned my husband and told him I and Eugene are lovers. So my husband came and must have seen me dancing with Eugene and then disappeared without me seeing him. The following Sunday morning, he was drinking heavily from a bottle of whiskey before he raped me and then invited his two fellow police officers over. He blindfolded my eyes, gagged my mouth, tied my hands and feet to the bedstead head and foot and sent his friends to rape me. The smell of the whiskey on their breath was disgusting. As I was wriggling out of my bondage, one of his friends must have suspected I wasn't what my husband told them so he convinced his other friend not to do what my husband want them to do as I might give them what their wives wouldn't want. So they left the room and went to him and must have told him they'd finished. He tumbled into our room and said with a heavy tongue during to his heavy drinking. Now you are nothing but a fuck bag to be released into. And he cut me loose and kicked me off the bed onto the floor then sprayed whiskey from his mouth onto me and flamed his cigarette lighter to light me. And then went and told his sister he caught me in his bed with his mates. As his sister knew the animal he is, she came to find out the truth and found me under the boiling shower unconscious and called an ambulance. But worst of all, he spread the lies to my boss, mother, friends, his sister, and Eugene that he caught me in bed with his mates. My mother turned against me, even though she had hated me before. My ex-husbands sister, my boss and Eugene, they all turned away from me. He sent my clothes to my mother's and she gave them away to the Salvation Army. I've lost my job, my friends and my family on the account of my husband's lies. When I was discharged from the hospital, I'd nothing to wear. The only decent friend I had was Nurse James who'd bought me some clothes and took me into her home after feeling sorry for me. And because of that she ended up being raped and murdered in her car going to work one early morning. So were his two mates who'd spared my reputation by not raping me. I was humiliated by the bride of Eugene's cousin and then she asked me to leave her wedding party. But before I left, she gave me a strong dose of her medicine saying the man my husband caught me in bed with was her uncle and that I'm a harlot and it was my fault he's was murdered. As I was leaving, she branded me the dirtiest whore of all time. So you tell me mom, should I run to my mother because she needed help and is now practically living on the street? Mom what would you have done if you were me?" Denyah asked Mrs Brown as she closed her tearful eyes in pain after expressing her hurtful feelings.

"Den honey, it is hard for me to say anything hurtful against your blood mother. But from what you have told me, I would say damn them all to hell for not giving you a chance to defend yourself. Ah, that ex you married once, he's nothing but the scum of the earth. How can he spread these wicked lies about you? And your mother of all people, how can she bring herself to believe that wicket man and not come to you for the truth. They all believed your ex and they all took part in crucifying you. But like Jesus, God has delivered you out of their wicked hands. How could your mother treat you so badly?" Mrs Brown asked angrily as she made a fist out of temper and saying "ah!" with a frowning face.

"Look mom, I think I would go and have a lie down. If I'm not up by seven, please see that the children have their milk an hour before they go to bed." Denyah said to Mrs Brown.

"You go and have your rest honey, and don't worry and you don't have to remind me to look after my grandchildren" Mrs Brown said.

Denyah slowly walked up the stairs and to her bedroom. Yawning from exhaustion and as she was feeling tired she laid across her bed face up with her feet hanging over the edge. Almost dozing off, the phone began to ring - she jumped up looking nervous and seems to be in a daze staring at the phone. As the phone was still ringing and for so long, Mrs Brown opened her door and asked. "Do you want to answer or shall I tell whoever is on the phone that you're sleeping."

"No. Its okay mom" Denyah said and she picked the phone up and covered the mouthpiece with her hand. Mrs Brown smiled and went down stairs to be with the children and leaving her in privacy to talk with the caller.

As Mrs Brown left, Denyah answered the phone saying "Hello."

"Den, it's me Ryan. I'm sure there's nothing to fuss about. I believed you have an appointment for next week Tuesday,"

"Yes, I remember I have an appointment to see Doctor Holden. Why do you ask? Is anything wrong Ryan?" Denyah asked.

"Well I don't think it's serious, we found a trace of sugar in your urine sample but as I told you I'm sure it's not serious as this mostly happens in pregnancy. However, I would like to make sure that everything is okay. I would like you to bring with you a sample of urine as I want to make sure that it's not permanent."

"Look Ryan, I know you're my brother. I would also like to know how you came to have my file in your possession when I'm under Dr. Holden."

"Den, Doctor Holden is on two weeks holiday and I'm standing in for her." Ryan said.

"Didn't you tell her we are now family? Anyway, aren't you supposed to work as a surgeon?" Denyah asked.

"Denyah, we are family, but not blood relative. Beside, I won't be seeing any part of your body. All I want to do is to test a small amount of your urine. That's all."

"Okay, I'll give you that sample but you have to buy mom and me a cup of coffee after."

"Sis, it's a deal and don't blackmail me too often." Ryan said and burst into laughter.

Just then Eugene walked in and kissed Denyah on her forehead while she was on the phone talking to Ryan. He looked spontaneously at her as he took his seat on the bed and waited for her to finish her phone conversation. But Denyah smiled and turned her back on him. Angrily, he stretched out a warning yawn followed by a loud cough to let her know he wanted her attention. But she went on talking and laughing until he stood tall in front her and beckoned her to put the phone down. As she thought he only want her to himself she turned her back on him, but as she faced him again, she saw how troubled he'd looked. So she said "Ryan honey, I'll see you soon and please give my love to Meleta and kiss my little nephew for me."

"Den, remember your appointment is next Tuesday and please don't miss this one as you've already missed the last one." Ryan reminded Denyah.

"Well, I'll see you next Tuesday then." Denyah said and she put the phone down and looked at Eugene to hear him said. "Thank God you were away Den. I can't get what happened to Meleta out of my head. Den, your husband tried to kill Meleta and her baby thinking she was you. Mom told me. "

"Eugene, I don't want to sound disrespectful. You warned me about going to him, yet you've brought him here into our home so many times. I think you should leave him well alone and never bring him here again. You knew how reckless Wesley could be and what he'd done to me. And now you're telling me how poisonous he is? Well I don't want to hear. Only that I'm deeply sorry for what someone nasty had done to Meleta. I know Wesley is a bastard. But doing something like that to Meleta, frankly, this is not Wesley's style."

"Denyah, what he has done to you, he's capable of doing the same and worst to anyone he think would stand in his way."

"Eugene, I'm sorry to disappoint you, but remember your mother is no better than Wesley and what happened to Meleta, she could have had something to do with it."

"Denyah, are you trying to defend your ex? If you are, please don't:" Eugene said. "Anyway, why are you taking his side?"

"There you go again, Eugene, I'm not taking Wesley's side. Nothing would please me more than to see him get what he rightly deserved if he was the one that hurt Meleta and almost caused her baby to die. But the truth is, Eugene, your mother is right down the same path with Wesley." Denyah said.

"What does my mother have to do with your evil ex-husband?" Eugene asked in anger.

"Eugene, your mother hated me so much that she called me a whore and spat on my face months before I let her into our home. She even told me I would regret carrying the little bastard inside me and that she doesn't think it's yours but I said nothing to you or no one. Eugene I'm frightened. So frightened especially when she told me how much my nurse friend begged for her life after she'd been raped. Why has she told me this? All that time I thought Wesley had killed her. I even told the police Wesley murdered her even though he told me he had not raped and murdered her. Now the jigsaw pieces are fitting in the right place" Denyah said as Eugene watched her in wonder.

Eugene couldn't believe what he was hearing from Denyah. He got up from off the bed and stood staring down at her in disbelief as sadness clouded in his eyes.

"Yes Eugene, your mother has boasted to me before about how my nurse friend was murdered. Your mother told me how much Nurse James begged for her life." Denyah began to cry then go on to say "She wants people to think Wesley is the criminal in it all. I agree Wesley is reckless and dangerous to me and his other women, but I do believe your mother is also as guilty as hell and I won't put it past her that she didn't had something to do with my friend's death, and what happed to Meleta. Whoever she hired to kill me, simply thought Meleta was me."

"You don't speak about my mother like that!" Eugene said raising his voice in anger.

"If you don't like to hear what I say, you can get to hell out of my room! And out of my life for that matter. You believe in that bitch of a so false mother so much that even if she has murdered someone in front of you, you wouldn't recognise her evil doing." Denyah said outraged. But trying her hardest not to let him know she knows his mother used to seduce him when he was thirteen.

Anger showed plain on Eugene's face - he slapped Denyah's face very hard so that she screamed out, bringing the children and Mrs Brown running to her to find out what had happened. Mrs Brown knew straight away that Eugene had hit her as she saw his fingerprints left on her face. Paris and Jade B ran into her arms and when Jade B saw tears in her mother's eyes, she tried to wipe it with her little hand and then kissed her on the red spot saying, "I kiss it better mommy" Denyah cuddled the girls and forced a smile while Eugene and Mrs Brown stood and watched. Mrs Brown looked at Eugene, shook her head and left the room in sadness and feeling sorry for Denyah.

"Den, I'm so sorry I hit you. I lost control." Eugene said.

"I think it would be best if you sleep in another room tonight." Denyah said trying to hold back her crying as the children were there. Eugene tried to touch the spot on her face where he'd hit her but she turned her face away. He then tried to pick Jade B up, and she hit his hands and held on tightly on Denyah.

"I love you daddy, but why have you made mommy cry?" Paris asked.

"I'm so sorry sweetheart, I promise, I shall never make your mommy cry again. Daddy was very stupid to hurt your mommy. Will you tell your mommy that I love her very much and I won't make her cry again?" Eugene told the children as he hugged them while in tears.

At this time Denyah had her face turned to the children. Eugene kissed the back of her neck while having the children in his arms. Denyah smiled to assure the children everything was okay again and show them she was happy again. Paris kissed Eugene and then kissed Denyah on their faces and said, "Daddy, please don't make mommy cry again."

Jade B also kissed Eugene and Denyah and followed behind Paris as she left the room behind Paris and went down into the kitchen to be with Mrs Brown. "Nanny, I told daddy not to make mommy cry again." Paris said.

"That's very good of you Paris. I'm sure you daddy sorry to hit your mom. Would you like some ice cream?"

"Yes please Nan," Paris said.

"Yes please Nan." Jade B said.

Mrs Brown gave them ice cream. Then Paris asked, "Can I have some to take up for mom?"

"Of course you can honey" Mrs Brown said and dished out two dishes of ice cream for Denyah and Eugene. Paris and Jade took the ice cream to them. Jade B gave Denyah one of the ice creams, saying "Eat this mommy."

"And this is for you daddy" Paris gave Eugene his.

"Thanks honey" both Denyah and Eugene said to them. Then they left leaving Denyah and Eugene eating their ice cream.

After Eugene ate his ice cream, he tried to make friends with Denyah by having a spoonful of hers, but Denyah was very serious and told him "It will be a long time before I forget you hit me."

Eugene got up and looked hard at Denyah with guilty feelings and left the room feeling sorry.

That night Eugene stayed well away from Denyah but he got on well with Mrs Brown and the children.

The following morning, Paris and Jade B burst into Eugene's and Denyah's room and found Denyah sleeping alone. Denyah looked at the clock and saw the time was two minutes past seven. "Where's daddy?" Paris asked.

"Your dad needs some space, so he's in one of the spare rooms."

"Mommy, did you tell daddy to sleep in the spare room?"

"Honey, why don't you take your sister and go back to bed as it is still early and no school tomorrow." Denyah told Paris.

"Can we come in your bed mommy?" Paris asked.

Denyah throw back her quilt and Paris and Jade B climbed up beside her. Jade B got nearest to Denyah. Paris and Jade B fell asleep. As Denyah couldn't go back to sleep, her thoughts were on Eugene, as when he woke up, he would give her a morning kiss on her face before he showered.

For two nights she didn't let Eugene into her bed. The children noticed and they turned against Eugene telling him, "He's a naughty daddy and mommy don't love him anymore."

As Denyah and Mrs Brown listened, Mrs Brown looked hard at Denyah but said nothing.

That night Eugene did not come home, he slept in one of his hotels he told Mrs Brown.

Mrs Brown and the children got worried that he and Denyah might split up. Especially, when he left a cheque for three million pounds on the dining room table with a note saying, this is my share of the money I said I'll give you from the children. I love you."

When Denyah saw the note and the cheque, she tore the cheque in half and tears came into her eyes as Mrs Brown watched her.

"We want our daddy to come home." Paris cried.

The following evening when Eugene came home to see his two daughters, they ran into their room and closed the door. "Honey, dad came to see you. Please open the door." He asked them nicely.

"Go away daddy, we don't want to see you." Paris said.

"Why is that honey," he asked them.

"You hit mommy." Paris said.

"Paris honey, I'm so very sorry. I would never hit your mommy again." Eugene told them then tears came in his eyes. As Denyah saw the effect of her and Eugene having on their children by not speaking to each other, she knocked on their door and said. "Paris honey it mom. I'm with your dad. Please open the door. We would like to speak to you and your sister."

"Is daddy coming come home to stay?" Paris asked.

"Yes honey, I love your daddy very much." Denyah said and Eugene looked hard at her and smiled. After he whispered to her, "I hope you talking about me."

She smiled and Paris opened her door to see Denyah and Eugene facing each other and smiling. Denyah took Eugene into their room and pretend to hug in him in the presence of their daughters. They smiled holding Denyah and Eugene's hands as they loved to see them happy and together and so both Paris and Jade B ran into his arms and hugged him and then hugged Denyah saying. "Mom, we glad dad came home." Denyah said. "Me too,"

But when the children were not around Denyah wouldn't speak to Eugene and at one time when he touched her, she told him. "Keep well away from me. This was going on for over two weeks behind the girls back. That one time he said to her. "Denyah I love you endlessly, but I can't take anymore of your pretence and the way you're treating me. I was deadly wrong to hit you, but I paid and still I'm paying for that mistake by not been near to you. How much longer are you going to pretend to our children that you and I a loving couple, Den, I don't think that I would be able to keep up with your pretence for much longer, I would move into my parents' home or a room in one of my hotels tomorrow until you're ready to take me back as your husband. I would miss you and the girls very much, but it has to be that way" Eugene said and left in his car with clothes in a travelling bag and a grey and brown suit on its hangers.

"Denyah, I don't want to come between you and Eugene but I think he's right. Honey, please try and forgive him. He loves you and the children very much. You widening the gap between you and him would only end up hating each other. Den, Eugene is a lovely husband and father. Call him and ask him to come home to his family where he belongs. However he asked me to give you this. Four hundred pounds and he said this amount should be your weekly spending money. He also gave me one hundred and said I would get this every week and you must not worry about Sonny and Bernice as they're still on his pay roll. Denyah I really don't need this money. I'm getting a good pension and you're looking after me very well so you add this money to your shopping." Mrs Brown said.

"Thanks mom, but I don't need your money. I don't know what to do. I love him so much but I'm afraid he might hit me again." Denyah said.

"Well sweetheart, I don't think he will ever hit you again. However, all you have to do is to call him and tell him to come home. That's all," Mrs Brown said. "Remember it's not only you that would miss him, just think of the children as well. Don't drive him into another woman's bed. Please put your pride away and tell him to come home to you and his children. Don't let his mother win or any other woman."

Denyah smiled and kissed Mrs Brown on her cheek. "What would I do without you mom?" She said looking at Mrs Brown happily.

"Just phone him" Mrs Brown said smiling.

Denyah looked hard at the phone before she pick it up and phoned Eugene on his mobile phone. "Hello honey" she said calmly.

"Hello Den," he said smiling.

"Honey, the children and I want you to come home. The children miss you so much."

"The children miss me?" He asked smiling broadly.

"Okay honey, I miss you more and I want you to come home tonight."

"Den my love, I'd never move out nor will I. I'm now having dinner at Cindy's. Do you want me to bring you anything?"

"No honey, I've just eaten and your dinner is here."

"I'll be home soon. Does this mean I get my room back in our bed?" Eugene asked smiling.

"Hurry up home and you'll find out" Denyah said looking radiant - Mrs Brown smiled and said. "You see Den, just a phone call brings out the beauty in you and I'm sure the children would love to have their daddy home."

Denyah was so happy that she hung a fresh bath towel over Mrs Brown's hand when Jade B went to her to get dry. "Den, you just relax while I go and put these two beauties to bed and they can see their daddy in the morning."

Two hours later Eugene walked into his and Denyah's bedroom smiling. He kissed Denyah and then went and had a quiet look at the girls before he had his shower and then returned to his and Denyah's bed. In bed they hugged, kissed and make up. At one time they laughed out so loud that Mrs Brown heard them and she smiled as she was feeling happy that they were in the same bed again.

The next day, Eugene took Denyah and Jade B to see Meleta and her baby. He then waited with Denyah until it was time for them to collect Paris from school. On their way to the school, Eugene stopped to buy chicken and chips for their dinner. After collecting Paris, they went home to find a roast beef dinner. Eugene looked at Mrs Brown and smiled holding a carrier bag with the fried chicken and chips. "Oh no," Mrs Brown said, and laughed "Well, since you buy chicken and chips, we might as well have them for tea and put the roast beef in the fridge for tomorrows lunch. Luckily I haven't cooked anything else. I'll get you lot a plate but I will eat mine straight from the paper."

"No mom" Eugene said nicely "We'll eat out of the paper. It would taste much better. After they have eaten, Mrs Brown said "It's the first time I've enjoy a tasty chicken and chips for a long time. Thank you both very much."

"Mom you're right, the chips and chicken were very nice and even the children and I ate it clean." Denyah said.

Mrs Brown rewarded the children with milkshakes while she, Denyah and Eugene had ice cream and coffee. "Now girls go and wash your hands. And Paris, have you brought home any homework?" Denyah asked.

"No mom. My teacher didn't give me any." Parish said. "Oh mom it's P.E Wednesday and I need a new P.E shirt."

"Why's that honey, I bought you three P.E. shorts and shirts a month ago." Denyah said.

"I know mom, I lent one to my friend and I lost one and the other one is stained with ink"

"Well I'm going into town tomorrow I'll get you a couple." Mrs Brown said.

"Thanks." Denyah said. Then Paris kissed Mrs Brown on her cheek. "That reminds me Den, we're running low on fish. Shall I buy some of the usual fish or a salmon?" Mrs Brown asked.

"I've gone off salmon. Just buy ordinary fish and you can take some money from the kitchen drawer."

"Den, just like you, I don't need any money. I will buy the fish as they are always fresh on Tuesdays. And Den, someone has phoned you about some stones. I think they phoned three days ago. They didn't give their name they said you'll know as you'd got in touch with them already."

"Thanks mom. For letting me know." Denyah said, "But I'm not ready to sell any of the stones as they would be for our children's future."

Denyah was ten minutes late for her antenatal appointment so that she missed Dr Ryan her adopted brother. But she was seen by Dr Martin. After her urine was tested for suspected diabetes, she was happy to hear that she was clear and that the trace of sugar was related to her being pregnant. On her way out of the hospital, she bumped into Ryan. They smiled. "So you're late to avoid me." Ryan asked her smiling.

"No I didn't but I'm glad I was late." Denyah laughed.

"Sis, I was the one that delivered our baby." Ryan said.

"That's different, Meleta is your wife" Denyah said smiling.

"Alright sis, I've got the message. Anyway, what was the result of the test?"

"Well my dear brother, I'm so happy to tell you that the result was negative."

"Den, I'm very happy to hear so." Ryan said.

"Would you and the family like to have dinner with us Sunday?" Denyah asked Ryan.

"I would like to. As for the others, I will mention it to them when I get home. If you don't hear from me by Thursday, give me a call." Ryan said.

"Well, mom just went to get us a drink from the machine before we head into the town to buy some fish. Would Meleta like some?"

"No, I don't think she would. In fact, mom bought some only last Saturday. "

"Well I'll see you soon then," Denyah said. Ryan went on the wards to work while Denyah and Mrs Brown went town to do their shopping. The first thing they bought was three sets of P. E outfits for Paris and then some hake and salmon.

The Thursday night Denyah phoned Meleta saying "I met Ryan at the hospital Tuesday and I asked him to ask you if you and the family would like to have dinner with us this Sunday."

"You should have asked me in the first place. You know how forgetful your brother is when it comes to giving me a message." Meleta said.

"Well, what do you say, to you and family coming Sunday for dinner?"

"Yes, of course Den, we'll be happy to have dinner but I think Ryan might be working Sunday until six."

"Well that wouldn't be a problem. He could have his after. Well I let mom know. See you all this Sunday then, and kiss the kids for me." Denyah said.

"That goes for me too. Kiss Paris and Jade B, and tell them Tommy and Chelsea will see them Sunday. Meleta said.

That Sunday it was a very happy scene to see Meleta, Denyah and their family having dinner together. "Only my husband is missing." Meleta said looking at her baby. After dinner, Mrs Brown, Aungus and his wife moved in to the living room to have a chat and relax while Denyah and Meleta went in the conservatory and they chatted about their husband's saying how much they loved them and also they chatted about old times and the misfortune they'd experienced. At one time Denyah told Meleta, her ex was so spiteful to her, that he maliciously took her in her back passage and how she cried begging him to stop but he stopped when he ejaculated. Then the son-of-a-bitch laughed and told me, that what happened to married whores. They should be fucked like the way dogs fucked. I'm still carrying the memory of that scar, that when Eugene is making love to me, I become tense until the end. Meleta, I want so much to relax and enjoy Eugene, but it has become come so difficult."

"Den, you sure are in hell because of your ex. Why don't you get counselling? I'm sure you would feel much better."

"Meleta, I only told you as I think I can trust you, so please don't mention any of this to anyone, especially my brother"

"I promise Den, that I won't say a word to Ryan. But I still think you should get some counselling."

"Meleta, I don't want Eugene to know about this coming from you as I already told him. But whether he believed me or not I don't know."

"Den, Eugene would know the truth only if you or your ex tell him, but you should enjoy your husband especially if you love him. Den, I can help you to find a counsellor and no one has to know."

"Thanks Meleta, I will let you know."

"Den honey, I'll hold you to this. As I said, you should be enjoying your husband as he enjoys you and not to bring him to ask, why are you so nervous. Believe me Den, Eugene would notice your are tense each time he is with you and he might think it is his fault and he might look elsewhere for enjoyment. So, you either get counselling or snap out of that backlash your ex have on you."

Denyah burst into laughter.

"Den, I'm serious."

"I know Meleta, but it's the way you said backlash, it made me laugh."

Meleta laughed saying, "I get what you mean. But I'm still serious Denyah my best friend."

"I believed you're serious and I'll do something about this. Thanks Meleta."

"You're very welcome Den my friend."

Just then rain poured down suddenly and bringing thunder and lightening that Paris and Jade B ran from their playing area with the kitten and their dolls into the conservatory to be with Denyah. Then Meleta's two girls, Tommy and Chelsea ran to her saying, "Mom, Chelsea and I are frightened of the thunder and lightening."

"Honey, you stay with me until the thunder stop." Meleta told them.

Just then Ryan rushed in the house dripping wet from the rain and brushing rain off his hair.

Mrs Brown met him in the hall. "Oh Ryan dear, you need to dry your hair before you catch cold. Eugene is somewhere upstairs."

"Thanks mom" Ryan said and went upstairs to dry the rain out of his hair using a towel and then went to Eugene's room as his door was opened to saw him lying on his back.

"What you doing in bed mate? Waiting on the love of your life to come to you?" Ryan asked.

"No mate, I'd enough of that last night to keep me going until the next month."

As Ryan looked at him and laughed, Eugene said, "I lied, but I'm hoping she would pity me tonight. Anyway, I'd a text on my phone saying to meet her at the usual time at nine next Saturday. Ryan what's going on and why you use my number? If your sister finds out, it's my head on the block. Anyway, who's this woman?" Eugene asked.

"She's a doctor, but nothing between us. I told her I married and have three kids and I'm in love with my wife, but she won't leave me alone. So I gave her your number."

"So this means you have an interest in her. Be careful mate. If Den find out, I'll have to tell the truth." Eugene said.

"Eugene I've been very stupid giving her your phone number. But you're no better than me. What about Kalor, have you scored her again since?"

"No Ryan, I ask her not to phone me again as I've no interest in her. I also hoped she wouldn't." Eugene said.

"Well Ryan, don't tell me you didn't score that doctor?" Eugene said showing a provoking smile.

"I couldn't hold back. Only one time in the sheets closet," Ryan said.

"Well, she's waiting on you to score her a second time. If I were you mate, I would end it before she finds Meleta and tell her. Have you eaten?"

"Not yet, I just got in and mom told me you up here." Ryan said.

"Well, how about going out for a couple of pints after you've eaten?" Eugene said

"You can count on me mate. Well, I'm downstairs eating." Ryan said and as he was leaving,

Eugene said, "Give me a call when you finish."

Ryan went into the kitchen for his dinner as Mrs Brown was taking his dinner into the dining room, "I'll eat here." he said.

As Mrs Brown looked at him, "Really mom, I'll have my dinner here." And he took the food from Mrs Brown and sat at the kitchen table eating.

As Ryan was eating, Meleta went and sat with him. "Honey, why didn't you call me?" she said.

"I didn't want to disturb you." he said.

"Honey, I need my own cheque book and my friendly little card." she said smiling.

"What brings this on, Meleta, I gave you a card before and you almost bankrupted me"

"Well, if that's how you feel, I'm going to find a job."

"Meleta, don't be silly, you've three children to look after. I give you three hundred pounds every week, I paid all the bills and everything else I have paid for, so tell me why do you want a card and a cheque book or going to work?"

"I want my own money. I don't want to have to come to you when I need to buy something. I have to look after mom and dad as well." Meleta said.

"Okay honey, I'll put two million into your account Monday. Would that be enough?" Ryan asked teasing.

"Does this mean my weekly money would be stop?" Meleta asked.

"Of course not, that two million would be for you to use on what ever you like, but it would cost you?" Ryan said.

"You'll have to wait until Ryan junior is at least three months. This doesn't mean you can play your ink pen in any jug that came your way" Meleta said and sat on his knees.

As Ryan knew he had the affair with his woman doctor, he only smiled and hurried down what food he had left, kissed Meleta and shouted up to Eugene saying "I'm ready" Just then their two daughters, Tommy and Chelsea heard him and they ran to him saying "Daddy, we want a kitten like Paris,"

"Ask your mom, she will get you one." he told Tommy.

Tommy turned to Meleta and asked, "Mommy, can me and Chelsea have a kitten? We just want one to share."

As Meleta looked on at Tommy and then at Chelsea then Tommy said, "Daddy said to ask you? Please mommy, please?"

"Okay Tommy. I'll get you a kitten, but you'll have to look after him." Meleta said.

"I will mommy. I will. Grandma will help me."

Eugene came down stairs saying to Ryan, "Let's go."

Ryan kissed his two daughters Tommy and Chelsea. Also Eugene kissed his two daughters, Paris and Jade B and said to Denyah, "I'm going with Ryan to have a pint. We'll be back in a couple of hours."

"Eugene honey, remember Ryan has to take home his family so don't keep him at the pub too long and see that he drink's sensibly."

"Okay Den, but Ryan's not a child." Eugene said then he asked Aungus to come to the pub with him and Ryan but Aungus said "I'll cool it tonight Eugene. I'll go another time."

"Okay pops, you take care" Eugene told Aungus and he and Ryan left in his car to the Hunters Moon pub.

Meanwhile, rain was still pouring down, Mrs Brown and Meleta mom made tea and ham sandwiches for them while the children had cakes, pop and ice cream.

Within an hour Eugene and Ryan came home, "Meleta, get the children ready love," Ryan told her before he faced Meleta's adopted parents Aungus and wife and said "Mom, dad it's time I get you home."

"Well, I'm getting a little tired. So, Mrs Deloris Brown, I'll see you some other time, and thanks so much for cooking us a lovely dinner and looking after us. It will be your turn to come to our home next" Mrs Pearson said.

After Meleta helped her daughters Tommy and Chelsea into their coats she then said to them "Say goodbye to Aunt Denyah and Nana Brown."

Tommy and Chelsea turned and said, "Goodnight Aunt Denyah, Goodnight Nana Brown. And Denyah and Mrs Brown kissed their cheeks and wished them goodnight. Tommy and Chelsea then hugged Paris and Jade B and said "Goodnight Uncle Eugene." before they left.

"Goodnight sweethearts," Eugene told Tommy and Chelsea and wished Meleta and her parent goodnight.

Ryan drove away before Eugene closed the door and went to his bedroom do some paper work.

Meanwhile, as Ryan and his family got home, Meleta phoned Denyah to let them know they got home safely.

As Meleta told Chelsea and Tommy to go and have a quick bath after their grandmother set their bath, they both ran into Ryan's arms and kissed him. "Good night daddy," they wished him and then they went to their granddad and grandma saying, "Goodnight granddad and kissed him on his face and did the same to grandma before they went to have their bath.

After their bath, Meleta took warm milk up to them and waited for them until they drank their milk, "Do you need the toilet?" she asked them.

"No mommy," They answered.

"Well, you both say your prayers and then get in bed honey" Meleta said.

Tommy and Chelsea said their prayer, kiss Meleta and then get in bed saying "Goodnight Mommy."

"Goodnight sweethearts" Meleta told them. After she saw them in bed, she dimmed their lights, walked out their room and went and had a shower and then went to bed.

The next day, Meleta and her family went to Denyah's and spent the day again as it was school holiday, half term October. Mrs Brown left dinner for Ryan. After work, Ryan drove straight to Denyah's and let himself in with his key.

While Ryan was playing a game of blackjack, his lady doctor text Eugene asking for him to meet her at the Social Club. "What are you going to do Ryan?" Eugene asked him looking very concerned.

"I don't want Meleta to know about her, that's for sure" Ryan said.

"Well mate, you'll have to deal with that on your own. Just do us a favour and tell your doctor friend not to text me again. I love my family too much to lose them." Eugene said. "Beside, I have one myself to get rid of."

"I understand mate" Ryan said with guilty feelings and looking worried.

"You want a beer?" Eugene asked him and laughed.

"I wouldn't say no. Eugene, would you like to meet her?"

"Meet who Ryan?" Eugene smiled.

"Doctor Summers. Believe me Eugene. I don't know what I was thinking. I was such a fool letting her lure me into screwing her. If Meleta finds out, I'm so dead."

Meleta went to Ryan and told him it's getting late and the children are nodding off. "Okay honey, get them ready" Ryan said.

Meleta got the children ready and said to her mom and dad "It's getting late and Ryan has to go to work early in the morning."

Meleta told her children to give their Aunty Denyah a kiss, Nanny Brown and Uncle Eugene. Then Meleta, her mom and dad, said goodnight, but Tommy and Chelsea ran upstairs to Paris and fell asleep again on Paris' bed."

"Mom, you get the baby while I go and call Tommy and Chelsea" Meleta said and she went upstairs to Paris and Jade B's room, while her mom went into the lounge and got the carrycot with the baby.

Meleta woke Tommy and Chelsea as they both were sleeping. "Come on honey" she told them.

"Mommy can't we sleep here?" Tommy asked rubbing her eyes.

"Honey, we have nothing to sleep in. And we didn't tell Aunt Denyah we were sleeping here."

"Come on honey, your dad is waiting on us."

"Please mommy, I'm tired" Tommy said.

As Ryan thought Meleta was taking too long, he went to her and asked, "Meleta honey, what taking you so long?"

"I was just about to call you to carry Tommy while I carry Chelsea."

Ryan picked Tommy up and asked Meleta, "What're you feeding her on?"

Meleta smiled and asked "Why?"

'She's breaking my arms" Ryan said.

Meleta then sat Chelsea up and put her shoes on before she carried her downstairs and said good night to Denyah and Mrs Brown before they left.

Mrs Brown gave Paris and Jade B a quick shower and then saw them in bed. "I'm going to fix you both some warm milk." Mrs Brown said and left. But before she warmed the milk, Denyah leaned over the landing and told her both Paris and Jade B are sleeping.

"As I'm in the kitchen, would you and Eugene like some tea or coffee?"

"I'll have some tea please mom and Eugene's drinking brandy." Denyah said.

Mrs Brown made two cups of tea and took Denyah's up and returned to the kitchen to wash the few plates and cups, turned the lights off and went to her room to drink her tea.

Soon as Meleta got home, she phoned Denyah to let her know they got home safely and thanked her and Mrs Brown for an enjoyable evening and for dinner as usual.

"Meleta, thanks for your company yesterday and today. By the way, the old crone had asked me to dinner and asked that I should tell you and Ryan, but as I wasn't interested, I said nothing to you. This was when she had dinner at my home."

"Den, I glad you hadn't told me. And Den, I had to defend myself to get my own money from my husband. So he gave me two million pounds and three hundred weekly for shopping. Mom and dad are getting a pension even though I let the state know I'm rich."

"Well Meleta, they worked all their lives, so they have their right to having their pension."

"Well, I won my rights also to my own money from my husband." Meleta said.

"Good on you girl, at least, you don't have to depend on him for money if you need to buy anything urgently. Oh I bought you all gifts but I've no time to sort them out yet." Denyah said.

"Den, I had to tell him I'm going to look for a job. So that's why he gave me some money. Now he left me wondering why the sudden change, giving me this money. Den, you don't think he's having affair?"

"Meleta, don't be so silly, Ryan loves you and the children too much and I don't think he would do anything like having affairs to ruin his marriage and to lose you and his family."

"Denyah, I don't know, he came home one night smelling strongly of perfume like he was with a woman."

"Just what are you saying Meleta?"

"Eight weeks ago, my husband came home smelling like he was wearing woman's perfume" Meleta said.

"Well did you say anything to him about this?" Denyah asked.

"No, but I noticed he slept with his back turned to me when I always slept in his arms." Meleta said

"Well are you worried?" Denyah asked.

"Not really, if I found out my husband is having affair, I would kill him." Meleta said laughing. "Den, I would never give my husband up to any other women because I love him too much."

"Meleta, Ryan loves you and the children too much to fool with other women." Denyah said. "I know some men are weak to some women. Take Eugene for instance. If I find out he's fooling with any other women, I'll give him another cut but I'll never leave him as I love him too much."

"Den, I know, I know." Meleta said smiling then said, "Den, Ryan Junior is ten weeks now and I haven't had sex with my husband. I'm so afraid to let him--------

"Meleta, not because Ryan's a doctor, he's also a man and he has sexual desire. If you turn away from him, he goes somewhere else.'

"Well what do you mean?" Meleta asked in thought.

"Junior's ten weeks now. Ryan needs you sometime and you know what I meant."

"Of course, I knew what you meant Den, but I still feeling tender inside and I'm so scared to let him------

"Meleta, you can't refuse your husband if he want you and you love him. You can't hide behind how you feeling. As I said, Ryan is a young man and he has sexual needs. If you refuse him, he is bound to turn to other women."

"I would remember that Den." Meleta said.

That night after Meleta showered, she walked in her bedroom wearing her dressing gown wrapped around her. Ryan was in bed sitting and drinking a glass of whiskey. Meleta dropped her dressing-gown at her feet, looked at her baby in his cot and then took the whiskey out of Ryan's hand, took a drink, and shoved him lying on the bed.

"What's the matter with you honey?" he asked her.

"I need you honey and I think it's time I make you feel happy again." she said

"But honey, I'm happy. Put your clothes on and go to sleep." he said.

"Please Ryan honey, I need you. My inside is calling for you my husband and you do not need me? Ryan, are you seeing someone else?"

The glass dropped from Ryan's hand. He took the glass up, put it on the table lamp and lay in bed quietly facing the ceiling. Meleta climb in bed beside him and put her hand down his pyjamas playing with his penis. He jumped and moved her hands telling her "Go to sleep."

"Meleta got angry and hit him in his chest saying, "Tell me Ryan, are you fucking anyone else."

"Honey, keep your voice down before you wake up the whole house."

"You don't want to make love to me, what's going on Ryan?"

"Nothing honey," Ryan said and closed his eyes then hugged her from behind saying, "Honey, I love you."

Meleta faced him saying, "I love you too honey" he then kissed her and fingered her before he carefully took her.

"Thanks honey." Meleta said.

"It's my duty to make you happy honey. And I'm glad we did it." Ryan said.

"Me, too honey. I really enjoy you and I love you with all my heart. Honey would you cheat on me by having another woman?"

"Of course not honey, I love you and the kids too much. Now let's get some sleep before morning clears and remember honey, you're the only woman I would ever want and love. Let's go to sleep honey" Ryan said and kissed Meleta on her lips and held her in his arms. Meleta smiled and fell asleep in his arms.

CHAPTER SIXTEEN

Since Denyah and her sister Laney got to know each other, they took turns to phone each other every week and Denyah would phone Mrs Libert often as well.

Then after six months, Mrs Brown answered the phone saying "Hello."

"Hello Den, it's your sister Laney calling." Laney said.

"Oh hello Laney dear, it's me Mrs Brown. How are you and the family dear?"

"We all are very well. Mother Brown, I and the family can't stop thinking about you and the family. I cried so much after you all left." Laney said.

"Well Laney my dear, I think your sister is taking a nap as she is feeling so tired lately as she's coming to the end of her pregnancy. Just give me a second. I'll go and call her for you if she's awake" Mrs Brown told Laney.

Mrs Brown seated the phone on the phone table and went to see if Denyah was awake. But Denyah was still sleeping. Mrs Brown smiled and got back to Laney saying, "Laney my dear, your sister deep in her sleep. I'm sorry."

"Well Mother Brown, will you tell my sister I called, just to know if you all are okay?"

"Yes, Laney dear, we're okay. And we've heard that you all had plenty of rain in St Kitts to nearly drown half of the population."

"Yes mother, for how its rain, I never thought it would stop. You don't mind me calling you mother?" Laney asked.

"Oh Laney, you made my hair stand on end and I am one of the happiest old ladies to have heard you called me mother. Look my dear, I've sent some money for the kids. You should get it by next week." Mrs Brown said.

"Thank-you, but Mother please not to send me any more money. We really don't need your money now as you and Denyah has given us great wealth. Thanks to you and my sister Denyah has made us millionaires plus two cars and a mansion. We even bought a large shop selling spare parts for any vehicles and bikes. Maybe one day we might open our own hotel or restaurant thanks to you and finding my sister Denyah. Mother, you made us all very happy and the children are so overjoyed that they too are calling you Nanny and would like you to come and visit them again. Mother Brown, we love you. We even take my mother to live with us as she was living alone."

"Laney, I'm very please you have done so. Well, I'll give your sister your message as soon as she's up. Would you please say hello to your mother and Paul and kiss the children for us, well, goodbye honey." Mrs Brown said.

"Goodbye mother." Laney said.

Mrs Brown put her phone down.

Two hours later Laney phoned again. Mrs Brown recognised her phone number and said, "Hello again honey, I told your sister you called. She said I should have woken her. However, I think she's somewhere in the library. I will get her." Mrs Brown said and she went to call Denyah while Laney was at the other end of the phone waiting.

As Mrs Brown was on her way to the library to call Denyah, Denyah was walking towards her. Smiling happily, Mrs Brown said. "Your sister Laney is on the phone waiting to speak to you."

"Thanks mom, I'll speak to her from the dining-room" Denyah said.

"Well, I better go into the living room and hang up the phone then," Mrs Brown said and left Denyah in the dining-room speaking to her sister Laney. After Denyah had a long talk with Laney, she said "Laney, I really have to go now as I just felt another pain." Denyah smiled saying "You know labour pain. I was having the pain every fifteen minutes to twelve minutes. "Ah," Denyah cried out holding under her tummy. I just felt another pain Sis, I do love you but I really have to hang up. Give my love to Paul and kiss my nieces for me and tell how much I love them. Goodbye."

"Ah, the damn pain again" Denyah hung up and cried out bringing Mrs Brown to her. "What's the matter honey? "Another pain and I felt a force down my pelvis."

"How often do you feel the pain honey?" Mrs Brown asked very concerned.

"Mom the pain comes about every ten minute or less," Denyah answered.

"Would you like to go into the hospital now and call Eugene?" Mrs Brown asked.

"No not yet. But I would like to have a quick shower before I go into the hospital. Oh, if I have to go in, don't phone Eugene unless the baby is born. Where're the girls?"

"In their room playing, they had their bath just after they had supper. Do you want me to call your brother or anyone else?"

"No mom. I'll be fine. If I should have to go into the hospital tonight, you'll find my address book in my table lamp drawers. There you'll find Bernice's phone number, she would be happy to help you with the girls" Denyah said.

"I know you have a fondness for Bernice, but don't you think Jade would be more appropriate as she's the one that brought up little Jade B?" Mrs Brown asked,

"I suppose so mom, but as I've already asked Bernice to be Godmother for my baby, I would rather she help you looking after my children. Besides, I like her very much."

"Well honey, I guess you're right" Mrs Brown said.

"Oh no," Denyah held her back and screamed out just before her waters broke. Mrs Brown rushed upstairs to the bathroom cupboard and quickly hauled out three sheets and rushed back into the living room and fixed them under Denyah and then fixed her legs in position for comfort for her to have her baby. As Denyah fidgeting her body and groaning, Mrs Brown said to her. "Relax honey you push when I tell you to" As Mrs Brown teaches Denyah to breathe in and out, Denyah followed her and groaned heavily when the pain hit her. "M mm…" Denyah groaned out as she pressed her lips closed and pushed downward. Mrs Brown wiped sweat off her face and said. "Just relax honey I can see the crown of the baby head. Now push, and again, I have the head in my hand. Honey, I want you to push downward with all your strength." Denyah gave one long push as she groaned and the baby was born. "Lie still honey," Mrs Brown said then she cut the baby cord and cleaned him up before she put the baby into Denyah's arms and said. "Here's you little son. He's red hair like his dad and beautiful like you. She then pressed Denyah's tummy for the after birth to pass out. Den, I'll take the baby to his cot and I'll come and help you up to your bed before I call in your doctor and clean up."

"Mom, I thank you for delivering your grandson. You've done a wonderful job. And I thought you didn't know what you were doing."

Mrs Brown smile saying, "I'll let you into a secret. I'm a retired midwife. I've delivered thousands of babies in my time and now, this one is the treasure of all. I'll be back in a flash." Mrs Brown kissed Denyah's forehead before she cleaned the baby off properly and laid him into his cot. She then returned to help Denyah to her room and she made sure Denyah was alright before she called in the doctor and then went and cleaned the living room where she delivered the baby. Immediately she put the sheets to wash and bury the after birth in a corner spot in the back garden where it would not be disturbed by the gardener or anyone. "I know you just have the baby, but since you hadn't eaten anything all day, how about me making you some cream-of-wheat porridge, something light. Oh I must go and phone the hospital and let them know you've the baby as well as your brother and Eugene. Would you like me to call Lisa and your sister in St Kitts?"

"Yes mom," Denyah said. Then the phone began to ring. Mrs Brown answered the phone. "Hello"

"Mother Brown it me Laney. I call to find out how Denyah is, as when I was talking to her, she'd seemed to be having labour pain."

"Laney dear, you have a lovely nephew and he and mother are doing very well. She had a home delivery as she was too late to go to the hospital. Laney honey, Denyah would call you tomorrow as she having a rest. Tell Paul that he has a nephew and kiss the kids for us, goodbye honey." Mrs Brown said.

"Goodbye Mother Brown and return the kisses to the kids from us" Laney said and hanged up the phone.

Mrs Brown phoned Ryan and told him and Meleta Denyah's had a son born at home at twelve minutes to seven. Both Ryan and Meleta were delighted and told Mrs Brown they would be there tomorrow to see the baby. Mrs Brown then phoned Lisa and told her Denyah's had a baby son born at home. Lisa and Richard were also delighted to have heard the good news and they too promised to go and see the baby. Mrs Brown told Denyah that Lisa, Richards, Meleta and Ryan would come to see the baby soon. Denyah was also very happy and she reminded Mrs Brown to tell Bernice she has had the baby. While Denyah was eating her porridge, Eugene walked into the room and sat on the foot of the bed seeing Denyah eating porridge, "Porridge?" he said "That's what the baby fancied?"

Denyah smiled and asked "Haven't you notice anything?"

"Sure, I noticed you're eating porridge. So that's what I've to eat then?"

"No Eugene, your supper is cooked by mom and now ready to slide down you belly." Then he heard the baby tuning up to cry. He jumped on his feet in shock and stared at the cot and then at Denyah in wonder. "Yes, he's your son. Mom delivered him as I was too late for hospital. As I felt contractions my waters broke and then came the little bundle I was carrying. And to my surprise mom just told me she was a midwife and she delivered thousands of babies in her day. Mom was great. I couldn't wish for a better midwife that God sent to us Eugene. Mom explained to the hospital that my water had broken and left me with no time to get to the hospital and as she is a retired Midwife she delivered the baby. My doctor was well satisfied with mom as she was a retired Midwife and that I was fine. However, a nurse will be sent out to me and the baby the following morning and for the next six days if all goes well." Denyah told Eugene as she looked proudly at her new born baby son.

For six days Nurse Judith looked after Denyah and her baby and on the final day of the six days she took a sample of blood from the baby's heel. As the baby burst out crying, Denyah watched with sorrow. "He's a beautiful baby. Well, if there's anything wrong, we'll get back to you Mrs Davis. But a powerful lung like his, I think he will be okay. Well I have no need to come again but if there's anything you're not sure of please give us a call" Nurse Judith said.

As the nurse way out of the bedroom, Eugene was on his way in. For an instant their eyes met. Denyah has noticed Eugene's smile was more like an inviting smile than a thank-you smile. "I'll see her out" he said and he raced down the stairs behind her but Mrs Brown saw her out and she left in her car. Mrs Brown closed the door and then faced Eugene to see the guilt on his face. Mrs Brown smiled when she saw him looking through the kitchen window. Few minutes later he asked Mrs Brown, "Will she becoming tomorrow?"

Mrs Brown held a straight face as she told him "The best person to ask is Denyah." he said nothing and took a cold beer from the fridge and sat at the kitchen table. Teasing, Mrs Brown said. "She's a pretty looking nurse" he smiled cunningly as he commented "Mi"...Mrs Brown went on "Most mixed races are very attractive. She looks no more then twenty to twenty five. I must say she's slim and tall too. But my Denyah is like a diamond in a class of her own" Eugene got up and went to be with Denyah. Mrs Brown sounded out a happy laugh and carried on with heating up the food for him.

Smartly Eugene took his time to asked Denyah "Would the nurse be here tomorrow?"

"No, I don't think she would as the baby navel cord has dropped and he's healing nicely and she also took a sample of blood form his heel. Poor little thing, She also said if there's any problem with him, the hospital would get in touch with me. Why are you so interested about her coming back?" Denyah asked.

"I'm not really interesting in her I only want to know if my son is okay,"

"Yes Eugene. Our son is okay and if you would like to see that pretty nurse again, you'll have to find her at the hospital. You can start searching by asking for Nurse Judith," Denyah said cool and calm.

"Don't be silly honey, I only in love with my daughters and my son and his mother, and I believe that's you. Besides, where would I find time to play around with other women," Eugene said smiling, before he lay next to Denyah and fell asleep. One hour later, Mrs Brown took Denyah's small amount of supper to her and supper for Eugene. Denyah shook Eugene many times to wake him but he seemed to be very tired and was hard to wake. "Poor fellow, let him sleep. I'll leave his in the oven. Here's the baby feed."

The following day, Monday morning, Eugene took Jade B to Nursery, while Paris went swimming with her white and black school friends Nena and Joleene as her school was closed for the week. When it was time for Eugene to fetch Jade B from the nursery, he fell asleep beside Denyah.

"I'll go and fetch Jade B before the nursery close up with her inside." Mrs Brown said.

"No mom, I'll wake Eugene. He can fetch her today." Denyah said.

"Den, I'll be okay, it's only a throw stone away. We'll be home in a matter of minutes and the fresh air would do me good. Anyway, it's my job to fetch her and she likes me too." Mrs Brown said and went to the nursery to fetch Jade B.

While Denyah was eating lunch, Eugene woke up and stretched upright and said. "I was dead beaten with tiredness. Any left for me?" he asked.

"Mom said yours is in the oven. She has gone to fetch Jade B."

"Why didn't you call me?" he asked.

"We did. But the deep sleep you were in, not even a bull dozer would have woken you" Denyah said.

Eugene heated his lunch and took it up and joined Denyah in eating. As the baby was still sleeping, Denyah didn't wake him. But as soon as Mrs Brown get home, she washed her hands and woke the baby saying "Come on my little prince, it's time for feeding."

Denyah looked at the clock and said "He's lazy like his dad sleeping for nearly six hours."

Mrs Brown fed the baby, winded him and changed his nappy and held him for at least an hour before she put him down into his cot. Jade B went and lay down beside Denyah and fell asleep.

Much later in the evening Wesley phoned, Denyah answered from her bedroom. "Congratulations sweetheart, I honestly though you couldn't have children after we were married for ten years. Oh I almost forgot that you'd miscarriage my baby. However, you take care of that little bastard." Wesley said in a very nasty manner.

Denyah tears came, but before she faced Eugene, she wiped her tears and smiled. "Who was that?" Eugene asked after she kept so quiet.

"Oh, that was the nurse asking if the baby was feeding okay."

"Den, you're not a good liar, you not cut out for lying. I saw you dry your eyes before you face me."

"It was Wesley congratulating me and my baby" Denyah said in thought and looking confused.

"If your ex hurt you or any member of my family, I would swing for him." Eugene said in frustration and hurt.

"Pardon me Eugene. You knew how ruthless Wesley was to me in every way. He beat me up, put all of my family and friends against me because of his vicious lies, murdered my friend and had his friends almost rape me! And still you brought him into our home." Denyah said getting frustrated.

"Take it easy honey, he's just jealous and can't stand the thought of us being happy together. As for my mother, I'll fix her. If she comes to see the baby, watch her very carefully."

"Eugene the truth is. If I don't see your mother, it would be a bonus to me." Denyah said to Eugene before she phoned Ray and Paula telling them she had a baby son. Ray wasn't at home but Paula was delighted to hear and she said to Denyah "As soon as Ray gets home, I would let him know and you'll see us both this Saturday about two o'clock."

"Well, I'll see you then." Denyah said and she rung off to breast feed her baby as she was saturated in milk. After she fed and winded the baby, she phoned her friend Ivy that she got to know in the hospital and told her she has a son. She also phoned her new friends Mrs Libert the estate agent in St. Kitts and Mrs Saunders she'd met on her plane trip coming back home to England. She even asked Mrs Saunders to be one of her son's Godmothers as well having Bernice.

The Saturday afternoon Paula and Ray bought gifts of silver chain and clothes for the baby and lollypops for Paris and Jade B, Paula and Ray spent the rest of the afternoon with Denyah and her family and had dinner with them. Paula spent most of her time holding the baby and looking at Ray in admiration. "Ray, isn't he lovely? Paula said cuddling the baby in her arms.

"Don't you look at me and you can get that baby idea out of that jealous head. You've to get a job first before you thinking of having babies." Ray said.

"Paula, I thought you were having a baby" Mrs Brown said.

"I thought I was, but then my periods came." Paula said with deep sorrow feeling and looking very regretful. She then lifted her head up and looking at Ray "my job is in the home and having babies, our babies, yours and mines."

Eugene smiled. "Come on brother, the Mrs said she want babies and babies she should have. At least you can afford to keep Paula and a couple of kids."

"Look Eugene, I've nothing against kids, but Paula should find a job so she would know the value of money. Of course I've a couple of millions, but if I let her get her hands on it, in a year we'll have nothing." Ray said

Paula went quiet and her face went sad as she asked Denyah if she can speak with her. "Sure." Denyah said and placed the baby into Eugene's arms and took Paula into the kitchen as Mrs Brown and the kids were in the dining having their tea.

"Take a seat Paula." Denyah told her. Paula sat then tears came into her eyes. "What's the matter Paula?" Denyah asked her. Paula smile saying. "Nothing,"

"Come on Paula, no one cries for nothing. Why don't you want to speak to me? Have you and Ray had a fight?" Denyah asked.

"Denyah I think I'm pregnant and he doesn't want a family now. He told me to get a job." Paula said.

"Well, I heard you say your period was late coming and now you thought you were pregnant?"

"Denyah, I'm sorry to have told a lie." Paula said.

"Paula, have you told Ray you're pregnant?" Denyah asked.

"How could I, when you heard him say that he doesn't want a family yet. I'm going to have an abortion. I don't want too, but I've no choice. I'm seven weeks, I believe."

"Paula, don't be silly, I know if you tell Ray he would be over the moon. Ray loves you and I know he would be happy to know he would be a dad. Just tell him as soon as you get home. You'll see I'm right." Denyah said.

Paula smiled and she and Denyah went in the living room to be with Ray and Eugene.

"Where's the baby?" Denyah asked.

"Mom took him to his cot as he was sleeping." Eugene said.

"Well, I better go and give Jade B her medicine before she falls asleep." Denyah said as she turned to leave the room.

"Mom did that too and all three of them are now sleeping." Eugene said.

Denyah looked at Paula and smiled before she took her seat beside her. "Eugene, are there any more cold beers?" Ray asked.

"Some is in the fridge." Eugene said.

Paula filled her glass with brandy and took the glass to her mouth when Ray took the glass off her and said, "I think you've had enough already. I watch you drink three full glasses in less than twenty minutes. I need a clear headed wife and not a walking alcohol bottle."

Paula frowned in temper and slapped Ray in the face as Denyah and Eugene watched in shock. "Since you don't want a family, I might as well drown the little nipper in alcohol. At least, it would save you paying out money for abortion." Paula shouted out in anger.

Ray looked hard at Eugene and then gave a faint grin. "Don't grin at me brother? How come you kept that one so secret?" Eugene said.

"Like you brother, it's the first of my hearing. I'd no idea that I 'm going to be a dad."

"Well, are you happy bros? Eugene asked.

"Happy, I'm more than that. I would be the proudest father that would ever be. Eugene, you remember I told you once that I don't wish to know how much money I have unless I'm married and have a family."

"Yes Ray. I do remember and now you would like to know how much money you have?"

"Yes, I would like to know and I would also would like to have my own bank account in my wife and my name if that's alright with you bros."

"Ray you have forty seven million pounds and I would be happy to put that amount in your and Paula's account tomorrow. You, Patrick, Carl, Jenny and I got the same amount from our grand parents." Eugene said.

"And you ended up with hotels and restaurants." Ray told Eugene.

"That's because I took a gamble and invested my inheritance Ray while you put yours away in a dark corner in the bank. However, you haven't done too badly. With the interest, you could start investing it for your children's future. "Eugene said.

"Well, here's to my lovely wife and my baby." Ray said knocking a bottle of beer against Eugene's bottle. "I'll drink to that" Eugene said and he drank deeply.

"Well, family, it's time I take my precious pregnant wife home." Ray said and got up out of his seat. He said goodnight to Denyah and Eugene and asked them to tell Mrs Brown goodnight from him and Paula. Eugene saw them to their car as Denyah stood at the front door waving and waiting for Eugene as Eugene walked them to their car and stood talking to Ray. But just before Paula got in their car, she walked back to Denyah and gave Denyah a kiss on her left cheek and told her. "Thanks for having me and for listening to me and giving me advice."

"That's okay Paula, and I'm glad you came to me," Denyah said to her.

Paula smiled and she went home with Ray looking very happy.

That same night, Paula phoned Denyah saying. "Den, Ray was so happy that he wanted to carry me into the house. Den, I love him so much. I really thought he didn't want me to have his child."

"And why do you think that Paula?" Denyah asked.

"One of my friends told me he saw him dining in Cindy's restaurant with a white woman and the way they were looking deeply into each others eyes. Den, I thought he didn't want me anymore and Den, I had a fight with his mother so I asked her to leave my house and don't come back. Who does she think she is to call me a black whore and her son is too good for me, I'd really wanted to kick her backside out of my house into the street but Ray was here and he asked me to keep quiet? You want to know what that bitch told his son, that he shouldn't have married me and she was sure that he could have found a fine white lady especially as he's rich. Den, I don't think I would ever want to bless my eyes on that woman again. I don't think Ray likes her very much either. Something about that woman is bothering me. Still, the less I see of that woman, the better. Anyway, that's enough about the dried up prune face bitch. However, you won't believe Ray wants to buy me a diamond ring tomorrow for giving him his first born and each born after, a different but I told him all I wanted is for him to be an honest husband to me as I would be a honest wife to him and a good dad to his children" Denyah laughed and joked "As you were to Eugene."

Paula laughed, "Den my friend, I was very tipsy and I was feeling so ashamed and guilty. Like you, it's a good thing Raymond have a sense of humour. He once joked and asked me if he's a better love maker than Eugene. Den I'd felt so small but he said that was before his time and that he love me. That same day, he asked me to be his wife and

I really love him and I know that he loves me for he said to his mother if she have to come into her home to upset me, he rather her not to come to our house."

"Well, that telling his mother how much he loves you and good on Ray for standing up for you. That woman is a descendant from hell. Anyway Paula, I've to go and feed my baby." Denyah said.

"Denyah before you go, how's was the labour pain?" Paula asked interestedly.

"Well Paula, that's a pain you'll have to experience for yourself. The only thing I could tell you is when I felt the pressure of the baby coming. But I think we experience different pain. I have to go and let my baby express his feed as I'm saturating." Denyah put the phone down and got to the bathroom to wash her breasts before feeding her crying baby.

The Saturday afternoon Eugene's family, Bernice and Claire turned up shortly after each others to see Denyah's baby son. And because for Claire and Bernice it was their first visit to Denyah's house, Denyah showed them around after she fed her baby. "I simply love your bedroom suite. I bet it cost over a couple of grand" Claire said looking at Bernice. "Actually it cost me over three thousands." Denyah said smiling.

"Well I wouldn't be surprised. The five foot bed alone looks as though it's very expensive. Never mind the three door glass wardrobe, dressing table, ottoman, bench, sofa and rug to match. Plus the matching curtains, chandelier, side lights and wall fitted fifty six inches silver TV and stereo Hi-Fi"

Bernice looked at Claire and then eyed Denyah, and said. "Not to mention the corner shelves with those expensive perfumes, aftershaves and the portrait of a lovely old lady that hangs so proudly."

"That lovely lady was my friend, mother and inspiration." Denyah said as her eyes instantly filled with tears. "She's the lady that felt love for me and took me into her home."

"Oh Den." Bernice said. "We never meant to upset you. Mrs Carter was a lovely person and I'm sure you missed her terribly."

"Yes, I do." Denyah said. "Anyway, let's go and eat."

"I'm so sorry to have reminded you." Claire said, "She was a lovely old soul to you."

"Yes she was. Now girls, you both didn't come here to check up on what I've got? Let me show you the other rooms then we go and eat." Denyah told Bernice and Claire as she led the way to Paris room, "This is Paris' - room my first daughter." Then she led them into Jade B's, then Mrs Brown, and then the other three guest's rooms. "Den, you've a beautiful home. You must have won the lottery or the million pounds bingo to have such a lovely home as you said you don't have to depend on Eugene's money." Claire said smiling.

"Now girls, you can always come and stay the odd nights if you like. And no my friends, I haven't won any money. Incidentally, a very special and beloved friend has left all her wealth to me and to my brother Ryan who is Meleta's husband." Denyah told her friends Bernice and Claire. Claire and Bernice looked at each others in surprise then Claire raised her eyebrows as she smiled and showing a little jealousy as she said bluntly to Denyah, "You're one of the luckiest amongst ten millions of us women for you to just walk into a path of wealth and also to have one of the most handsome and super rich husbands. Not to mention a ready made family."

"Claire, I thought you were my friend. I'd no idea my inheritance would upset you this much. And if you're thinking its Eugene's money, don't as I don't have to rely on his money as you heard it from me before. Anyway Claire, you're not badly off yourself as your husband is a film director so girlfriend I don't have anything over you." Denyah said to Claire as she hugged her, while Bernice stared at them and shook her head smiling.

"Well," said Claire, "I should be happy for you and not to be feeling jealous of you like a damn spoil child. But we can exchange husbands." Claire laughed.

"Well, I was just going to invite you and my friend Bernice to spend a few nights but not now" Denyah laughed. Honestly my two friends," said Denyah, "You both would be welcome to come and spend some time with us at any time. Especially when having you girls with me, you always made me laugh and that makes me feeling happy. By the way, Claire, would you do me the honour of standing Godmother to my son?"

"Of course Denyah, I would love to be Godmother to your lovely son." Claire said happily.

"Well Claire, my sons godmothers would be you, Bernice and my two other friends Ivy I met in the hospital when I was admitted a year ago and a friend I got to know on my journey back home. I'd phoned them and asked them and they are delighted and said yes. I'll have my son christened in two months. I'll give you the date. I would ask David and my brother Ryan to be Godfathers. Bernice, would you still like to be Godmother to my son?"

"Denyah my friend, you've asked me even before your son had entered into this world and I told you yes, I would love to. Are you having second thought?" Bernice asked.

"You wish my friend, you wish?" Denyah said before she faced Claire and said, Claire, "this is the lovely Bernice that stood up for me by stopping one of Eugene's rage hogs from biting my head off" Denyah shivered before putting her arms around Bernice and Claire's shoulders and let them downstairs into the dining room where Mrs Brown prepared lunch for them.

"Den, I was there at the party, remember? That's how I came to know our friend here."

Denyah laughed, "Oh yes, of course," Denyah said.

Just before lunch, a knock came on Denyah's door. Mrs Brown answered the door, "Hello Mrs Brown, I came to see the baby?" Eugene's mother said holding a small blue ribbon tied parcel in her hand.

"Please come in Mrs Lake, the baby is in the living room" Mrs Brown said and she led Mrs Lake to the baby where she met Denyah, Bernice, Claire and Denyah's two girls Paris and Jade B. As she saw Jade B for the first time, she looked at her and asked, "Whose child is she?"

"I don't know her mother but her father is Eugene, your son" Denyah said.

"What are you saying Denyah that my son has a daughter right under my nose, and I didn't know about this?"

"Well now you know. If you need to know more about Jade B you'll have to ask her father" Denyah said.

"Well Denyah, I came to see the baby." Mrs Lake said. "Oh this is for the baby, a silver bangle"

As the baby was in his carry cot in the living room she took the baby up. Denyah watched her hard and within five minutes Denyah took her baby from her saying. "It's time for his feed."

Mrs Lake smiled and said "I can feed him if you let me."

"Breast feeding," Denyah said and she took her baby to her bedroom and lays him into his cot bed. Shortly after Denyah joined Bernice and Claire and laughed - then Denyah went into her dining room to sew Mrs Brown and Mrs Lake speaking.

"Mom, is lunch ready? Denyah asked Mrs Brown.

"Yes honey, you can tell Bernice and Claire to come while I put the food on the table. Mrs Lake, Would you like a little lunch?" Mrs Brown asked

"Yes please" Mrs Lake answered.

"Well follow me into the dining area Mrs Lake," Mrs Brown said taking the lead with Mrs Lake following her to met Denyah, Bernice and Claire. "Please take a seat Mrs Lake." Mrs Brown told her. Denyah led Bernice, Claire and her two girls into the kitchen leaving Mrs Lake in the dining room. As they were about to eat, the doorbell rang. Denyah went and answered the door to see Meleta and her adopted mother. "Please come in Mrs Pearson, Meleta. "We were just about to have lunch" Denyah said and she led them to the dining room.

"Where're the girls?" Denyah asked.

"They are with their dad and granddad as their dad is off for a couple of days." Meleta said. "And I'm sorry, I couldn't come before as junior wasn't well."

"I'm sorry. How's he now?"

"He's better Den and he's very greedy. He's drinking eight ounces of milk and pudding."

"That's wonderful." Mrs Brown said.

Mrs Brown put a plate each in front of everyone for them to help themselves to rice, vegetables and salads- fish based with gravy. "Mmm, this food smells delicious. Mrs Brown, I can never get my fish to fry and taste like yours. Thank you for lunch." Mrs Lake said.

"My pleasure Mrs Lake, I hope you enjoy your lunch." Mrs Brown told her.

"I think I will Mrs Brown."

The Paris came to Denyah and said. "Mom, I don't want my lunch. I want daddy to take me and my sister McDonalds."

"Honey, try and eat some lunch then I'll phone your daddy and ask him to take you and your sister McDonald's when he comes home."

"Okay mommy." Paris said.

Mrs Lake looked at Paris and said. "My son is very lucky to have a ready made family." Mrs Brown cleared her throat as Denyah was about to ask Mrs Lake to leave.

Paris ate her lunch, drank her fruit juice and moved from the table. As Jade B hardly ate her lunch, Mrs Brown made her some cornmeal porridge with a pinch of grated nutmeg and milk which she ate totally and seemed to love it.

After every one had eaten lunch, they moved into the living room where they talked and drank what ever they wanted.

Then Meleta's adopted mother said to Mrs Lake, "Sorry I didn't introduce myself earlier, I'm Mrs Pearson."

"I'm Mrs Lake, Eugene's mother I have three other sons and a daughter."

"Lovely to meet you Mrs Lake," Mrs Pearson said.

"Likewise Mrs Pearson," Mrs Lake said.

Mrs Brown took the remaining food and put it on the cooker to cool before it was put into the fridge and then returned and said to everyone. "Well, I will see you later."

Before she left with Jade B to the nursery, Jade B ran to Denyah and kissed her telling her, "I love you mom."

"I love you too honey, mommy see you later. And be good for Nan." Denyah said.

"I will mommy." Jade B said.

Mrs Brown held Jade B by her hand and took her to her Nursery.

Mrs Lake smiled and thanked Denyah for lunch and then said goodbye to all and kissed Denyah on her face and then said to Denyah, "You've beat all of Eugene's girlfriends. Eugene must have loved you even more than me. And now you have his children. I didn't know about Jade B. I should have been the one to have her, but as I said, you are the winner of us all. Well, goodbye my dear," she said and left but as she looked back to wave goodbye to Denyah, Denyah closed the door and laughed.

"Bitch" Mrs Lake said opening her car door, she then got in smiled and drove away. Denyah got back to Claire, Meleta and Bernice and said "That woman has a grudge against me. The less I see of her, the happier I will be."

"Sorry to say Denyah but there's something about that woman making my skin crawl. Besides, she looks evil. Denyah girl, if I were you, when that woman comes here I would pretend I'm not at home." Bernice said. Then went on to say, "Will you give my little precious Godson a kiss from me when he wake, Den, my friend, I love you but I must leave you. I will give you a call, and Den, I'll get his christening clothes."

"Well Bernice, we will go shopping a month from today for our Godson's christening clothes" Claire said and then Claire and Bernice hugged Denyah and kissed Paris then said "Goodbye to Meleta and her mother before they left. Not far behind, Meleta and her mother, Bernice and Claire said "Goodbye" and left. Denyah was looking very happy as she took Paris and her baby son up to her bed- room and lie on her bed with Paris and her baby in her arms sleeping.

A while later after Mrs Brown got back from the Nursery, she took the baby out of Denyah's arms and put him into his cot and left Paris and Denyah to sleep while she went and put the washing on the line as it was a nice and sunny.

Long after Mrs Brown fell asleep on the settee in the living room being she was so tired. But she woke up and went and fetched Jade B from the Nursery.

"Mom thanks you for putting the baby in his cot." Denyah said.

"Den honey, I could see you were very tired." Mrs Brown said.

"Yes mom, I was feeling so tired, that if I was knocked with a brick, I wouldn't have turned. I'm feeling so drained for the past weeks, after I breastfeed him."

"That's maybe because you're not eating well" Mrs Brown said and went on to say." Denyah honey, I've noticed you've only eating a small amount of your meals each time and you have given me the feeling that you were going through antenatal depression."

"Mom, my reason for not eating properly, is because I am always feeling full. Really, I don't know what antenatal depression feels like. I was feeling very happy when I was pregnant and still I am. I would like you to buy some more feeding bottles as I found a trace of blood in my breasts milk and to tell you the truth mom, I'm a little worried that I might hurt him. I told the nurse, she said it's very common for the first couple of weeks. Mind you, the blood's getting paler, but after I breast fed him, I felt drained."

"I understand Den. I think you might need iron tablets. Would you like me to make an appointment for you to see your doctor?" Mrs Brown asked Denyah as she was very concerned.

"No thanks mom, I'll make one tomorrow and I will explain." Denyah said

"Oh, I almost forgot what I came to say, and that is, I really like your friend Bernice. She's a lovely and charming lady. She must have been very provoked to have killed her man friend. Still, I'm glad you asked her to be Godmother to our baby. Yes, I really like her." Mrs Brown said. And it was so sad for her splitting from her fiancée because of his interfering mother and his ex wife. Just Like Mrs Lake, Den, I'd the feeling you were going to ask her to leave that's why I stopped you by clearing my throat. But believe me I don't think I want to see that woman too soon." Mrs Brown said.

"How do you know all this about Bernice and her fiancée's mom?" Denyah asked.

"Den, I got the truth from her after I heard you asked Sonny and his wife to take her in their home as a nanny. Mind you, her last fiancée had really loved her and didn't care about her past, but some of us mothers won't let the past rest. All I said to her was, she's done the right thing to get away from that family. I also wish her well." Mrs Brown said.

"Amen to that mom." Denyah said.

CHAPTER SEVENTEEN

The following Wednesday afternoon, Lisa and Cindy went to see Denyah's Baby. As Lisa chatted with Denyah and Cindy, Denyah asked Lisa when her baby was due. "Not for another five months and a few days. After this baby, Richard would have to be doctored like a tomcat as I won't be having anymore and every year. By that time Rick should be walking." Lisa said.

"Well, my friends, if your husband wants plenty of babies, then plenty babies he shall have." Cindy joked.

"Cindy, shut up! It's time you give Frank a couple." Lisa said.

"I will in a few years. Frank has a nine year old daughter living with his mother."

"Where's the child's mother?" Lisa asked

"She didn't want the child. So his mother had her adopted from an early age of seven weeks." Cindy said.

"Tell me this Cindy, like Eugene like Frank. They're true family." Denyah said, and Cindy burst into laughter. That same day, Jenny, Kelly, Tracy and David went to see Denyah's baby and took gifts of silver bracelets, photo book and clothes for the baby.

The following day, Mrs Saunders went to see the baby. After spending a long time, Ivy called to see the baby. And before Ivy left, she thanked Denyah for helping her get the job with the shop keeper Ella and to live with her.

The Sunday afternoon, Denyah phoned Mr and Mrs Welch and told them she had a son. She also asked them if they would like to see him.

"Yes, Miss Denyah. But we haven't a car to travel." Mrs Welch said.

"Mrs Welch, don't worry, I'll send Eugene to get you both. Just let me know when." Denyah said.

"Would next Saturday afternoon be alright?" Mrs Welch asked.

"Yes Mrs Welch. I would be more than happy to see you and your husband. And thanks for your kindness toward me when I most needed help."

"Miss Denyah, you're a lovely lady and my husband and I were more than glad to help you. But still, I was happier when you left that wicked husband. Well, kiss the baby for us and we'll see you Saturday." Mrs Welch said and hung up.

The Saturday afternoon, Eugene went and fetched Mr and Mrs Welch. After they spend a long time and had dinner, Ryan met them. He too spent a good while and had dinner. Then as it was getting dark, he offered to take Mr and Mrs Welch home and he did. Denyah thanked him. Mr and Mrs Welch thanked him for taking her and her husband home. After he saw them going into their house, he drove himself home and then phoned Denyah telling her how nice it was to invite Mr and Mrs Welch to see the baby.

Seven weeks later the twenty second of November Sunday morning Denyah and Eugene had their baby son named Eugene Carter Junior christened at Methodist Church followed by a family and friends gathering which went on until well after mid Monday morning. Bernice, Claire, Ivy, Mrs Saunders, David, Ryan and Eugene's brother Ray were the Godparents. Denyah told them that she'd named her baby Carter after her late adopted mother. And again she invited Mr and Mrs Welch and their family and also Ella the shopkeeper came with Ivy.

After the Christening party was over, Eugene asked his brother Patrick to take Bernice, and her adopted parents and children to their home. That night Patrick fell in love with Bernice and he asked her out to dinner. But Bernice told him.

"I like you very much but I can't accept your dinner invitation."

"Why can't you?" Patrick asked.

"Must I give you a reason Mr Lake?"

"No. You don't have to tell me if you don't want, but it would put my mind at ease." Patrick said. And hinder me asking you again."

Bernice smiled before she paused then told Patrick, "I have served time in prison for killing my first fiancée and his woman. Plus I recently split from my second fiancée."

"Well," said Patrick "I'm sure you had reasons for what you've done. But this time if you have to leave or kill me, your weapon should be love as I fell deeply in love with you and I couldn't care a damn about the past. Denyah told me you've moved in with Sonny and his wife to look after their grandchildren. Well, that's lovely and decent of you. I would be happy to share in their lives of being a father if you let me. Before you run away from me, can you please let me know if you will have that dinner with me?"

"When would you like me to have dinner?" Bernice asked.

"I would like it to be tonight. But another night would be okay, Bernice will you be my wife?" Patrick asked.

"Patrick, I like you very much. Marry you, your family would hate you especially when they learn that I went to prison for murder. However let's settle for dinner and see what develop aye?" Bernice said "Beside, why would you give up your inheritance to marry someone like me."

"Bernice, you would be married to me and not my family. I would give back every penny if you told me to. But why should I when that slut of a woman caused my natural mother to committed suicide and took what is rightfully ours. I found out six years ago but I said nothing as I wouldn't want my brothers and my sister to know. So please Bernice, would you be my wife?"

Before Bernice gave Patrick her answer tears built up heavily in her eyes. Patrick wiped some of her tears away with his thumbs and then took her into his arms and kissed her gently. "I'll call you tomorrow" he said and saw her into her house before he left in his car smiling joyfully. Bernice closed the door quietly, smiled and went and settled the children in bed before she made all of them some hot milk.

As Bernice sipping her milk, thoughts came to her to call Sonny and his wife dad and mother in the same way as Denyah and Meleta addressed their adopted parents. Smiling, Bernice got up from her seat and kissed Sonny and his wife and said. "I love you both and the children so much."

Sonny and his wife looked up at her from their seats and smiled. Then Sonny's wife asked "What brings you to tell us this Bernice?"

"Mom Pearson, this is how I feel. I do really love you, dad and the children and I want to be a good mother to your grandchildren and I am that daughter to you that you so wanted. I know that I can't take the place of your blood daughter, but all I want is to be second to you both and the children. So can I be that mother and that daughter to the children and to you? This is if this is okay with both of you?"

Tears came into Sonny's eyes. Mrs Pearson got up and hugged Bernice and said, "You're no second best, I love you to be that daughter I so wanted, and for you to be that proud mother for Sonny and my grandchildren. Bernice, I so admire you and I love you."

Tears come into Bernice's eyes as Mrs Pearson hugged her and then kissed her on her cheek. After Bernice sat down, she said, "Mom, dad, Patrick asked me to be his wife."

"What did you say to him?" Mrs Pearson asked.

"I smiled as though he might be joking" Bernice said. "However, he invited me to dinner tomorrow night. What do you think mom? Should I have that dinner with him?"

"Well honey, if you don't go, you'll never know if he was joking or not."

"You know what mom, you're so right. I will phone him and let him know I accept his invitation to dinner."

"That's the spirit dear. The next time you come home and tell me he asked you to marry him, I'm sure he means it and he loves you. Now my dear Bernice, I'm going to have a quick shower and then to bed. Goodnight my dear Bernice."

"Goodnight mom."

"Goodnight Bernice."

"Goodnight dad."

Bernice sat at the kitchen table thinking over Patrick. She smiled and washed the cups before she went and had her shower and then looked in on the children before she went to bed.

Early the next morning Bernice and the children had just got up looking radiant and singing here's comes the bride as she fixed on her head a white window net. The children laughed making their grandmother laugh as well. As Bernice looked at the children and saw their happy smiling faces, she asked them, "Honey, would you like to have a new dad?"

"I would" Starry said lifting the tail of the net on Bernice's head and joining in with Bernice singing here's comes the bride.'

Mrs Pearson shook her head and smiling happily to have seen her grandchildren looking happier than in a long time.

"Bernice, you have no idea how long I've wanted for some one like you to walk into our lives. Thanks for making Sonny and me grandparents. I'm so happy. You're that mother my grandchildren are longing for. My Sonny and I have lost a precious daughter and now the good Lord has replaced her. Bernice we love you and my heart is full of joy to know you're here taking care of us and I watched the children so many times hugging and kissing you as if you're their mother. About that nice Patrick, if you truly loved him, and he ask you to married him, please do before he slips away into the mists of darkness and into some other woman's arms. Eventually, the children would need a father. If and when you are married, you and Patrick could adopt my Sonny as a father and I, as a mother along with our grandchildren with our blessing."

By this time Sonny only listened. He said nothing but smiled as he drained the last of his tea before he got up and took his cup into the kitchen sink and then returned to kiss Bernice on her cheek and said "Good night."

"Goodnight" Bernice answered and smiled.

"So I see you take only your cup into the kitchen." his wife said.

Sonny smiled and said "What is this, mother and daughter has held against me by me taking my cup to the kitchen sink? Well you both better get to bed before morning breaks. As for me, I'm feeling so tired but I must admit, I enjoyed myself last night at Denyah's baby christening, and Bernice, the great Lord bless you and Miss Denyah and I love you both very much. Well goodnight again." he said and left to go to bed.

Mrs Pearson wished Bernice goodnight and she followed upstairs behind her husband Sonny. Bernice turned off the downstairs lights and went and had a shower before going to bed and thinking of Patrick.

The following morning as Denyah settled down to breakfast, Bernice phoned her telling her "Patrick asked me to be his wife but my answer I gave him wasn't a clear yes as I thought he was joking. I've also told him I'd served time in prison for murder but he doesn't seem to care and he asked me out to have dinner with him tonight."

"Well Bernice, what is the problem then? You told him the truth and he doesn't seem to mind. So marry the guy if he's serious. I saw how he was looking at you and I know that's love. Bernice, you're a lovely person and Patrick's a handsome honest guy. Grabbed him and tell him yes, you'll marry him before he walks away. You have a lovely family to take care of now. If you' let Patrick go, you might live to regret that you did. If you have his number give him a call and tell him you accept his proposal and Bernice don't call me again unless you would be telling me you're getting married to him. Or see him again. Well, my breakfast is getting cold as it's waiting for me. Bernice, I'll see you at the week-end. By the way, I have a cake for you. Patrick told me he would be coming to see me later. Would you like him to bring the cake to you?"

"Please Denyah that would be nice. Thank you" Bernice said cheerfully and then put the phone down and began to hum One day at a time sweet Jesus as she twirling herself around and face the mirror smiling saying "I would be soon Mrs Lake." Facing the mirror again, she outstretched her left hand and she visualized wearing her wedding ring on her finger; she said "Patrick my darling, "I love you, and I would make you one of the happiest husbands". She then went had her bath and saw the children had theirs before she went and cooked breakfast. While the children and their grandparents were eating, she went in the living room and phoned Patrick. Patrick answered "Hello."

"Hello Patrick, this is Bernice. "I call to let you know that I won't be able to have dinner with you tonight but I would be happy to dine with you Saturday night if that okay."

"Bernice anytime would be okay as long as you let me take you to dinner. Bernice, I shouldn't be telling you this, but I fell in love with you the moment I saw you."

"Well, goodbye Patrick for now."

"See you Saturday" Patrick said.

Bernice rang off with a gleam in her eye.

That Saturday morning Denyah was up very early as her baby was crying and she couldn't get back to sleep. Much later that morning she cooked breakfast. Mrs Brown was on time to have hers hot just as it was cooked. While Denyah and Mrs Brown were eating, Patrick knocked at the door. As Denyah was getting up, Mrs Brown said to her "You stay in your seat while I go and see who it is" Mrs Brown put her last piece of toast in her mouth and opened the door. "Good morning Mrs Brown."

"Good morning Patrick. Please come in. The coffee is still steaming. Would you like some?"

"Yes please, I can smell toast and bacon. Am I too late for breakfast?" Patrick asked.

"No Patrick there's some left. You come and sit yourself down while I do you a couple of toasts" Mrs Brown said.

Denyah smiled, "You're up very early Patrick. Is everything all right?"

"Sure Denyah, everything's fine. Den, how long have you known Bernice?"

"Over a year, she's a lovely and caring person and I think you'll get on well with her. By the way, I have a cake for her and her family. Would you mind taking it to her?"

"No, not at all, I'll take it to her as soon as I finish my breakfast."

After Patrick finish eating his breakfast, he took the cake to Bernice and spend most of the day with her and her family and had lunch with them. He learned the names of Sonny three years old grandson Kiah and his two granddaughters, Starry five and Passion seven. The two girls were jumping up and down on him like he was a trampoline and little Kiah were trying to prize his lips apart with his fingers. Sonny and his wife watch on with happiness and then told Bernice "That's the man you should marry. He would be a good father to any children. The children love him, just look at their happy little faces. I haven't seen them so happy since their mother walked out on them."

Mrs Pearson caught Patrick's attention so that he asked "Why has their mother walked out on them?"

Said Mrs Pearson tearfully, she got mixed up with some bad company taking hard drugs and then went on to prostitution before she walked out on us to live somewhere in London I was told. Her father and I phoned and write to her countless of times when we found out where she lived but all of our letters were returned unopened and the phone number were no longer in use. We even went to London with the children and spent weeks in different hotels searching for their mother. Well, we found her and she promised to come home with her father and me and her children. She fooled us and ran away to somewhere in Cardiff we've been told. From then I haven't heard or seen my daughter again. Patrick, I really don't know whether she's dead or alive. It is well over two years that the children been without their mother. But I thank the good lord she has left the children with her father and me. I'm not any longer in the best of health. Still, I have a lot to thank the good lord for. Well Patrick, you might as well stay for dinner as it's heavily raining."

"Thank you Mrs Pearson, as much as I would like to stay and have dinner, I really can't as I have to be at the club and I'm already ten minutes late. I'll just go and tell Bernice I'm leaving and to remind her about having dinner somewhere tonight. But I'll be here Sunday for dinner if it's okay."

"Patrick, you would be more than welcome for dinner at any time. Or even to visit. Well, I shall see you this Sunday then."

"You sure will Mrs Pearson. Goodbye then."

"Goodbye Patrick" Mrs Pearson said.

Patrick left and went to find Bernice and the children in the living room watching TV. "Bern, I have to go now as I'm late for my meeting, I'll call for you later about six thirty. I already booked our dinner."

"Can't you miss going to the meeting?" Bernice asked.

"Bern, I wish I could but I really cannot miss this one as it's an important meeting. Mostly it's to do with my father's assets. While I'm here, Bern, will you marry me again?"

"Yes Mr Patrick Lake I'll marry you and thanks for bringing the cake, I'll phone Denyah and thank her. By the way Patrick, would you like to come with me and the girls to Dudley Zoo two weeks on Sunday?"

"Bern, I would love to. Would you be carrying plenty of fried chicken?" he asked.

"No," Bernice laughed and said, "But I hope you would be carrying in your wallet lots of money as the children would want lots of goodies and rides."

"And you Bern, what would you want."

"I only want you Patrick, just you, my family here and our mighty God. You best go to your meeting before I beg you to stay" Bernice told him.

Starry and Passion jumped up all over Patrick again and they only left him when their grandmother called them for their afternoon tea. Patrick then kissed Bernice and then placed a large shaped rose setting sapphire and diamond ring on her married finger and kissed it. "It's so beautiful" Bernice said looking hard at the ring before she said. "This must have cost you thousands."

"What ever it cost, you are worth it and I love you. Bernice would you like to come with me to look for a house sometime this week?"

"But Patrick, I have a home, I'm sure mom and dad won't mind if you move in with us. There are three rooms, the girls in one, Mom and dad in one and you and me and our little Kiah will share the other."

"I think we might be a little too cramped at times. So buying a bigger house, the girls and little Kiah would have their own room. In fact, I think they'll love to have their own room. Mrs Pearson could either sell her house or put it on rent. Why don't you have a word with her and her husband and let me know."

"Okay Patrick, I would ask her but don't be surprised if she says no."

"Just tell her as gentle as could be and I'll see you later when I come to take you to dinner" Patrick said and left.

After Patrick left, Mrs Pearson has noticed the ring on Bernice's finger. She looked hard at the ring and smiled. Bernice had noticed that Mrs Pearson was looking at her engagement ring so she straightened her fingers to her and said smiling "Patrick has asked me to be his wife once more and this time I told him yes. Mom, have I done the right thing by telling him yes? I do love him and I know for sure he loves you, dad and the children as much as he loves me. He even said he'll buy a bigger house so that the children would get their own room. Maybe one with two attics which could be turned in bedrooms for the girls what would you say to that mom?"

"Well, as the girls are growing up, they may one day be happy to have their own bedroom. I must say, I do like him and I know he'll be a good husband and a dad. So when are you thinking of marrying him?" Mrs Pearson asked.

"Well, we haven't set any date as yet. We don't want a big wedding either, just a few friends and my family. That's you and dad and my two girls and my son. Mom, you could put this house to rent for the children's future. I'm not marrying Patrick for his money. I do love him and I think I deserve this chance of happiness for us. Especially having the girls growing up" Bernice expressed her feelings.

"Would you like to have children after you're married?" Mrs Pearson asked interestedly.

"Yes mom. But I wouldn't go to any extreme as we already have two beautiful princesses and a handsome prince, but I won't pretend to you mom, I would like another son if possible and don't worry over the children, they're now Patrick and my daughters and son. You and dad are their grandparents. I love those children and I'll do my best not to let any harm come to either of them" Bernice said proudly and caring.

Mrs Pearson began to cry, "I'm not a healthy person. Each second the good lord breathes breath into me, I gratefully thank him as a bonus. Bernice I'm having treatment for suspected cancer which is now under control after losing my left breast. Five years ago, my doctor had given me just over a year to live, but thanks to the almighty God, I've past five times that figure and now I'm told I could live a normal life if I take my medication and take things easy. Bernice, hearing this news, it's like God has given me a second chance to see my grandchildren grow up and maybe to see a few more from you. Bernice, I love your Patrick as much as my son-in-law."

Bernice embraced Mrs Pearson with joyous feeling. Then their eyes were filled with tears of joy and they settled down to dinner but as Bernice had planned to have dinner tonight with Patrick, she only had a thin slice chicken sandwich. After the children had dinner, Bernice said to them "Your daddy and I will be getting married and we might be moving into a bigger house."

Before Bernice could finish what she was going to say, Starry jumped out of her seat, ran to her arms and shouted "Yes!" The room went silent. Sonny looked at his wife, smiled and then said with joyous eyes, "Bernice, I'm so very happy for you and Patrick. He's a good bloke. And your happiness is our happiness. At least the children would have a name and family that loves them after me and their grandmother are no longer with them" Sonny smiled joyfully again saying, "Yes! How I long for a nice son-in-law to play a game of cards with me and to buy me a half-pint of ale sometimes."

This made Mrs Pearson feel very happy hearing her husband spoke so highly of Patrick. Bernice moved herself from her seat and went and hugged Sonny with a warm kiss and then said, "Dad, Patrick won't make you regret he's your son-in-law. Now how about a small glass of port" Bernice asked her dad.

"Yes please" said Starry.

"Well Starry, I think you'll better off with a glass of soda and then I would want you to do your homework before you go to bed. And Passion you take Kiah up stairs and I'll be up in a sec. to give him his bath. Passion, you and Starry have your bath and don't wet the floor too much and put your dirty clothes in the wash basket."

After Bernice gave Kiah his bath and put him to bed, she phoned Denyah and told her "Patrick has again asked me to be his wife" Denyah was delighted and then said to her "I do hope you say yes."

"Well girlfriend, I was a bit sensitive at first but I told him yes, I'll marry him. Den, you should have seen the happy look on his face and the ring he has given me. However, that's enough of me until I see you. Anyway, how's my Godson?"

"Well Bernice, he's having five ounces of his feed now as well as his breast feeding and he's putting on weight" Denyah said.

"Den, would you like to come and have a meal with me and my family next week-end to celebrate my engagement? I would like to invite Paula, Lisa and Meleta, Jenny and the children and of course, mother Brown. Just us girls, what do you say?" Bernice asked.

"Where would we be having this dinner, at your home or a restaurant?" Denyah asked.

"Here at my home. I was only thinking of the children having somewhere to play. As I said, just us women the men could go to the pub. Are you up for this Den?"

"Bernice, let me get back to you later" Denyah said breastfeeding her baby before she put the phone down.

Later that night Denyah phoned Bernice telling her "I would come but I've to leave the children with mom"

"Why can't you bring the children and Mrs Brown as well, I'm sure she would like to get to know my mom and Meleta's. I'm going to let you into a secret. I would ask Patrick to let us get married on New Years day to begin our life together. As I told Patrick, I just want to get married with my friends and family with no fuss. Denyah, to tell you the truth, I don't think that I would want that mother of his at my wedding. Jenny and his brothers are all right. His mother, she's an evil good for nothing. I even hate to see her." Bernice said giggling over the phone.

"Bernice, I never thought you'd find her dangerous as I have. Well Bernice, Eugene is at home now and I have to go" Denyah said and put the phone down when Eugene walked in and said "Where my favourite girls……..Denyah butted in and said, "Don't forget you have a favourite son as well" Eugene smiled enchantingly as he said, "Boys belong to mothers and girls are daddies favourite."

"So what about me then, am I not your favourite as well?" Denyah asked looking radiant in her jeans, short sleeved black satin low cut blouse and black sandals.

Eugene looked on at her with an affectionate smile before he said joking, "You were once my favourite, but now you're an old foul, but you still looking sparkling fit for another son."

Mrs Brown walked in the room to hear him. She laughed softly before saying "You've to give time to heal you know" Denyah and Eugene looked at each other and burst out into laughter. Mrs Brown put away the baby clothes, laughed and went to give Paris and Jade B's their supper as they told her they were hungry. After she gave Paris and Jade B their supper and cold milk, she fed the kitten.

"Thanks Nan" Paris said.

"That's okay honey."

Mrs Brown washed her hands and prepared the feed for the baby for when he wakes.

Much later Denyah and Eugene ate with Mrs Brown while the Paris and Jade B went and played in their playroom.

Meanwhile, that Saturday evening, Patrick went to get Bernice to take her to dinner. Bernice asked him where they would be having dinner, but he wouldn't tell her, "Wait and you'll see" Bernice smiled then she and Patrick looked in on the children and made sure they were alright and sleeping. Mrs Pearson said to them. "You go and have dinner." And she assured Bernice she listen out for Kiah. Bernice said thanks "Mom I love you." and she kissed Mrs Pearson before she left with Patrick to have dinner. As they walked into the hotel, she said "this hotel is beautiful." He smiled saying, "This is one of Eugene's hotels. 'The Red Rose.'

While they were having lobster dinner and champagne, soft music was playing before a beautiful black singer went on stage to sing (I will always love you) Patrick kissed Bernice under the presence of watchful eyes and then said, "Bern, I love you so much."

"How much do you love me?" Bernice asked joking.

"Honey, my love for you is unlimited."

He then knelt in front of her, took her hands into his and asked her again while onlookers watching them. "Bernice my darling, will you be my beautiful wife?"

Bernice looked at some of the guests with smiles on their faces before she answered "Yes Patrick darling, I would marry you."

There was enormous applause and the singer went and congratulated them saying, "Congratulation to both of you. I wish you both the very best and long and prosperous life with enough healthy children."

"Well thank you" Bernice told the singer.

"You have as beautiful voice as you look" Patrick complimented the singer. And as their eyes mirrored into each others, she smiled and lowered her eyes showing him affectionate love. Patrick smiled politely as Bernice looked hard at him.

The singer left smiling.

"I saw you had an admirer. I think she loves you honey,"

"Bernice, honey, I have no interest in her or anyone else" Patrick said and he kissed her.

Long after as Bernice and Patrick were leaving, the singer slipped one of her card with her home and mobile number into his side jacket pocket without Bernice seeing. "Well, good night to both of you and please come again."

Patrick smiled and left hugging Bernice around her shoulder to his car. He opened the front door of his car for her get in before he sat into the driving seat and closed the door. In the car, she hugged him and he kissed her then he drove away smiling.

That night he slept with her and they made love. Early morning he left before the children and their grandparents got up.

The following week Saturday afternoon, Bernice invited Denyah, Paula, Meleta, Lisa, Tracy, Ivy, Jenny, Claire, Cindy, Kelly and their three adopted mothers and all nine children for dinner, while the husbands went to their local pub. Mrs Brown and Mrs Pearson cooked dinner. Over dinner Bernice showed off her engagement ring saying, "My ring is the best." Denyah smiled feeling happy for Bernice and said to Bernice. "Now that you got Patrick's rock girlfriend, flaunt it."

Mrs Brown smiled saying "You deserved Patrick and what ever goes with him honey"

"I'll drink to that" Tracy said raising her glass of port. Then she said, "may be one day, David might show pity on me and give me one."

"We all would drink to your happiness Bernice" Meleta mother said raising her glass of mineral water.

"To Bernice and Patrick's happiness" Kelly said raising her glass of port.

"To my daughter and her future husband, who will be my son-in-law soon, all the happiness in the world to Bernice and Patrick, may they both have a long and happy life with many more children" Mrs Pearson said as she raised her glass of water. I'm so very lucky Bernice adopted me as her mother."

"Well, we all know we're adopted, so from now, please let's leave out the adopted part, and say daughter, dad and mom" Mrs Brown said nicely.

"I'll drink to that" Mrs Pearson said smiling as she took a drink of her mineral water.

"I'll drink to that too" Mrs Philips said.

"We all would drink to that" Mrs Brown said "and to our family of friendship as we all become one whole family."

After they had dinner, they moved into the living room playing bingo and frustration. Even the mothers. Some hours later, the husbands came, ate and then took their families home as it was quite late and was getting on to eleven o'clock. That same Saturday night, Patrick and Bernice came to an agreement that they would like to get married much sooner rather than wait for another three months. So Bernice and Patrick booked an appointment at the registry office in Broad Street Birmingham City Hall and then got married in two weeks on a Friday morning at ten-thirty.

Eugene, Denyah, Jenny, Curt, Ryan, Meleta, Ray, Paula, Lisa, Richard, Claire, David, Tracy, Glennis, Kelly, Cindy, Frank, the parents, the children and Patrick, Ivy and Mr and Mrs Saunders and Kelly's parents attended Patrick and Bernice's wedding. Eugene gave Patrick away and Bernice's father was her best man. Her mother and her two sisters and her brother were there to witness the marriage of Patrick and her. Everyone's face was looking like a bright morning star except the groom's mother Mrs Lake.

After the marriage was over, everyone moved outside the ground taking pictures. As they did so, all the women kissed Bernice on her cheek and congratulated her except Mrs Lake, her mother-in-law who stood watching with her face fixed as though she'd smell shit. Teasingly, Bernice straightened out her married finger up to her face and smiled.

"Let's see how long it would stay there. Once a murderer, always a murderer;" Mrs Lake said in an aggressive manner.

"You're right there, mother hawk, the only murder I intend to do, is on you. This time I won't be spending a day in a cell," Bernice told her as she looked radiant in her nice cream suit and white high heeled shoes.

"Bernice, my problem is not with you." Mrs Lake said looking steadfast at Denyah with her arms folded and her lips pushed forward.

"Old mother hawk, I'm not only talking for me, but for all of your sons' wives. Now if you would change that old haggard face and put a smile on, I'll let you see your son sometime and you might just get through me to see your son before we set off on our honeymoon" Bernice said to Mrs Lake before she went and joined her husband Patrick and telling everyone they would be having a meal at the Albany hotel four o'clock in the afternoon.

Everyone went home first and then on the evening they all went to the Albany hotel for meals as Bernice and Patrick invited them too. Bernice and Patrick were the last to get to the hotel. As they walked in, the DJ started playing. (You're once, twice, three times a lady.) All eyes were fixed on Bernice and her husband.

Then to Eugene's surprise, Kalor walked up to him and stood before him smiling.

"What are you doing here?" He asked her casting his eyes on Denyah on the other side of the room where she were talking to friends.

"If she's you wife, she's very beautiful" Kalor said.

"Look Kalor, it was a mistake between us. I want you to leave." He said.

"But I just got here. If you're afraid I'll make a scene, don't worry. Here's not the place or the time" Kalor said and walked away and went and sat next to Denyah.

Eugene went and kissed Denyah.

"Your wife's very beautiful Sir" Kalor said to Eugene smiling. She smiled looking at Denyah and said, "Don't the newly wedded couple look lovely?"

"Yes, they are." Denyah said.

"Anyway, it's my pleasure meeting you. I'm Kalor" she said to Denyah, looking at Eugene as he was standing by Ryan and Glennis.

"Nice meeting you Kalor. I'm Denyah."

At this time Eugene had feared the worst that she might tell Denyah about him and her making love so he went and sat between her and Denyah.

Little Kiah ran to Bernice calling "mommy" she picked him up and cuddled him and then kissed him and after passed him over to her husband Patrick.

After Denyah kissed Eugene, he knew Kalor hadn't said anything so he went and make his speech on behalf of his newly wedded brother Patrick and his sister-in-law Bernice. Also Ray, Ryan, David, Glennis, and Carl and Bernice' adopted mother said their speech. Then her real mother, father and two adult sisters made their speeches too. Bernice and her husband Patrick paid for everyone dinner that were at the hotel. When Patrick got the bill for twenty five thousand pounds, Eugene paid the bill.

"What's money aye Eugene?" Denyah teased him.

"Well, you know me" he said and went on to say "I paid from the money you'd refused to take. I saw the torn cheque in the bin. I still want you to have the half I promise to give you from our kids."

Denyah smiled and said. "I would collect when I'm good and ready" By this time, Kalor was also smiling.

After melon and salads served for starters, cream of tomato soup, white rice, buttered lobster with fried onions, steaks and buttered corn, followed by ice cream and crushed fruits. For those that chose, and for others, they had choices of grapefruit, vegetable soup followed by vegetables, lamb, cream potatoes, carrots, shredded cooked cabbage and gravy. Then ice cream or steamed cherry pie with custard or cream. Plenty of best Champagnes, brandy, whiskey, mineral water, apple, orange and pineapple juices were on every table with individual white china bowls packed with cashew nuts, After Eight chocolates, cream crackers, small blocks of cheese and best butter followed by cream coffee, black or tea.

Paula gave Eugene a cheque for twelve thousand pounds and told him, "This is from Ray and me. Half of what you paid."

"What's money," Ray said. "Especially when you have a beautiful wife to spend it for you:" Everyone laughed.

The music was nice and romantic for all to enjoy. Patrick took his new bride Bernice on the dance floor to dance (Forever my darling, my heart will be true.) Everyone sat happily and watched the happy newly wed couple dance. And as the disc ended, he kissed her passionately.

Then as the music was really getting hot and everyone was getting down to the beat, Kalor moved on to dance with Eugene a couple of times but Denyah put it down to pleasure as everyone was enjoying themselves. As Lisa saw a young black good-looking woman dance with her husband three times, so she put her son in his arms and told the woman, "We just had a second son and we're so much in love." her husband smiled and the woman moved on to Ryan but Meleta pulled her husband away and danced with him. The woman went to mingle with others.

As Eugene and Kalor were dancing, she carried her lips to his but he moved his face. Denyah saw her and went and told her, "The next time you come dancing, bring your husband."

"I'm sorry Denyah," she said smiling and looking at Eugene.

"I should think so. Anyway, don't be a doorstop for any men as they wouldn't want to know you when they have their wives with them. You're much too pretty to be shoved aside by men. Even my husband here, if he screwed any women, he has to come home to me. But before he climbed into our bed he would scrub himself like a bitch."

Kalor smiled sheepishly and left to be with Bernice's brother. "Are you married or have any woman?" she asked him.

"No. Would you like to be my woman?" he asked her.

"Well, for the time here." she said.

"My name is Larance." he said.

"Kalor," she said.

"Well Kalor, I like you. Is any chance I can see you again?"

"Yes of course Victor, when I'm not working." she said.

"What work you involved with? Victor asked her.

"I'm a model, a fashion model. I travelled to London twice a week for photo shoot.

"May I ask you what your job is?" she asked him.

"A bus driver, I'm here as my sister got married. Are you serious about letting me seeing you again?" he asked her.

"Well Victor, has anyone told you, you look like Steven Boyd the actor?"

"Well, I had a lot of admires and some people said I look like different actors. But for you, I look like me and I'm yours with no cost." Victor said,

Kalor laughed heartily.

"Don't you like me?" Victor asked.

"Sure, yes. I like you. Here this is one of my cards with my numbers. Call me if you wish. I would really like to get to know you." Kalor told him and kiss him. Eugene saw her and smiled. She went to Eugene and told him. "I'm with the man I think I want to settle with. And our secret is dead and buried as I don't want Victor to know about us. But I still love you and I want to be friends with Larance's family." she then walked to be with Larance and Larance left with her. Eugene felt relief and went to Denyah and his children.

Four o'clock mid morning, everyone left the hotel and leaving Patrick and Bernice with a few of her friends talking. Then they went home later.

For the whole of the following week, Bernice had plenty of visitors mostly family and friends. Victor took Kalor to his sister Bernice and introduced her as his girlfriend. Bernice got to like her and she invited her to her home again and told her she's welcome at anytime.

The following Saturday evening Patrick and Bernice left little Kiah with Paula while they took the girls and their adopted parents to the cinema to see Beauty and the Beast. Then the following week Tuesday Patrick took his wife Bernice and his adopted family to Disney world in Florida for two weeks as Denyah recommended to them they should go as she was there once and told them it's a beautiful place with plenty for the children to see and enjoy. And so they went and spent two enjoyable weeks in a first class hotel in Disney Florida.

On their arrival back at Gatwick Airport in England, Patrick went to collect his car that he'd left for two weeks at Gatwick Airport car park while he left his wife, children and adopted parents waited inside the terminal by their suitcases for his return with the car. After he was gone for sometime, his wife Bernice moved to outside the terminal in the frosty cold winter to wait for him and leaving their children and parents with the suitcases inside the terminal as it was warmer. Bernice paced up and down the gateway minding their suitcases and looking out for her husband to come and fetch them. Lost in her thought, this good looking and tall handsome white Mr Rogers that looked about thirty seven to forty walked up to her and smiled. Then he asked her "Would you like me to give you lift somewhere or help you to get a taxi?"

"Thanks for your help. But I'm waiting for my husband to take us home my children and parents are inside the terminal waiting" Bernice told him.

Mr Rogers looked deeply into Bernice eyes and said "You're a very beautiful lady and so are your children. I saw them go into the building with their grandparents. Your husband's very brave to leave you alone."

"I'm not alone. I wish you would leave me alone and take yourself somewhere else before my husband comes back."

Mr Rogers looked into her face and smiled - joking to her "I don't believe you have a husband. But if you're looking for one, I'm very available and happy to marry you. So will you please tell me the truth, are you really married?" he asked interestedly and teasingly.

"As I told you, my husband has gone to collect his car and he would be here any time now. So would you please kindly leave me alone?"

"Can I see you again?" he asked Bernice seriously.

She replied "I don't think so. I've just married the most handsome husband whom I'm madly in love with."

"Now, I can see by the ring you're wearing. It tells me that your husband may have a few pennies. However, are you living near here?" Mr Rogers asked very interestedly.

Smiling, she said "No, I lived in beautiful Birmingham."

"Well, I think Birmingham's okay. Some of my family live in Birmingham. I've heard the Bull Ring is absolutely beautiful now. I might one day visit the place if you'll be kind enough to show me around. I moved to London just over two years but I'm thinking of moving back to Tyseley in Birmingham. My brother lives there in my house."

Bernice looked straight in to his face and smiled saying "Your best bet is to pitch on someone else" Just then her husband Patrick showed up. "Here comes my husband."

"You're right. Your husband is very handsome. Which of you're wealthy?" he asked with such a teasing smile.

This time Bernice stared at his face in surprise before she answered "That's none of your damn business."

"Please beautiful lady, I never meant to be so formal. But looking at those magnificent jewelleries on your splendid neck, hands and fingers and maybe, who knows what hidden riches you might have beyond that gorgeous body."

"Look whoever you might be don't you have better things to do than to waste your time with someone who doesn't have any interest in you?" Bernice said to Mr Rogers with staring eyes.

Mr Rogers smiled saying "I can see clearly in those exquisite eyes that you're falling in love with me..... He giggled.

Bernice's temper developed showing discomfort before she said to him "As I stated to you, there's only one man in my life and will be. Now if you please leave me alone, I would be so appreciative."

"Here, please take one my cards" Mr Roger said giving the card to Bernice.

"Why would I want one of your cards?" Bernice asked him.

"You never know when you'll need a good lawyer or a friend." he said insisting that Bernice should take one of his named and addressed business cards. As Patrick was walking towards them, she quickly took the card off him and shoved it into her trousers suit jacket pocket so that he would leave. He smiled in her face and walked to his parked car to where his chauffeur was waiting by the side road. He got into the back of his car and sat comfortable and looking at Patrick putting the suitcases in the car boot.

While Patrick was buckling up their two daughters in his car, Bernice took the card out of her pocket and slipped it into a waste bin near to their car outside the airport terminal. As Patrick looked at her, she smiled.

'Well honey, are you getting into the car, as it's time we hit the road?"

Bernice smiled and got into the car with her children. Mr Rogers' chauffeur drove near to Patrick's car and Mr Rogers looked directly into Bernice's eyes smiling.

Old Sonny caught Mr Rogers looking at Bernice, Sonny smiled and shook his head but as Patrick was too busy taking notice of the children to see if they were sitting comfortable he didn't notice Mr Rogers smiling at Bernice.

As Bernice and her mother sat at the back with the children, Bernice took three years old Kiah's on her lap as he was sleeping.

As Patrick drove away slowly, Sonny looked back as Mr Rogers blew his car horn. Bernice waved goodbye and Sonny saw Mr Rogers sent Bernice a blowing kiss. Patrick looked back at Bernice and asked. "New friend?" Mrs Pearson smiled as Bernice said to Patrick "You have nothing to worry about as you're the only man I love and want."

Patrick smiled and said "It's good that I bought this car."

"Very wise of you Patrick, We're very comfortable, any one for a cheese sandwich?" Mrs Pearson asked.

"Yes please" Patrick said.

Mrs Pearson shared the bought sandwiches to her husband Sonny, Patrick, Bernice and herself while the girls had McDonald's burgers and chips and milkshake their grandmother bought for them before they set out.

"Any drink?" Patrick asked.

"Oh yes, of course," Mrs Pearson said, "I bought iced coke for us." she then passed the cans of coke one each. Patrick drank deeply, then belched and said "pardon me."

"Take it easy on the road honey." Bernice told Patrick.

"But honey, I'm only doing forty while most are doing sixty, seventy, eighty and ninety."

No sooner Patrick told Bernice what speed he was doing, than a young driver about twenty to twenty five sped past at high speed in a red Ford sports car doing about one hundred and twenty miles per hour. "Beat that." Patrick said smiling.

"The reckless speed he was in, he drove past us like a puff of forceful wind and disappeared in no time so we couldn't even see him in the long distance. Still, I wish him safe but I wouldn't wish for him to give me a lift" Mrs Pearson said shivering coldly.

"Well, he might be feeling great having a brand new sports car at his young age." her husband Sonny commented.

"I do hope wherever he's going, he would get there in one piece" Mrs Pearson said.

"He's young and a show off." Sonny said.

"Well, I suppose you're right Sonny, but drivers such as he put the wind up me. This is a brand new car as well, but I haven't seen Patrick driving like him."

"Woman, how can he when he have you and the children in the car." Bernice laughed heartily then Patrick joined in the laughing, then Sonny join him in laughing as well and long after Mrs Pearson saw the funny side and she burst into laughter saying "The poor kids, all three of them are sleeping and young Master Lake is snoring."

Patrick smiled excited to have heard the children grandmother proudly said young Master Lake is snoring.

"Patrick, you and Bernice, you both made Sonny and me the happiest grandparents by adopting us and to give the grandchildren your title. I also have to forevermore thank Mrs Denyah to make this possible for Sonny and me. May the truly good lord in heaven forever bless each of you always and protect you. Bernice, you and Mrs Denyah are remarkable and caring ladies. It's so generous of Mrs Denyah to donated four millions pounds from her inheritance to the needy."

"Does my brother give her that much that she had to give charity that much?" Patrick asked.

"No dear, Mrs Denyah has her own money. She has inherited a hefty amount of money from the late Mrs Carter. She has even left the Hot Leg Store to Denyah and many more riches to her and her brother Ryan. So you see Patrick, Denyah doesn't really need your brother's money" Mrs Pearson said calmly.

"Well, I'd no idea Denyah was so powerfully rich. I thought my brother was supporting her. By the way, how come you know so much about her mom?" Patrick asked Mrs Pearson his mother in-law.

"Well- After her and I exchanged words, she told me. She treated us with love and respect as if we're family. So you see Patrick, haven't I the right to love Denyah? Oh and you too, Bernice my dearest. I really do love you. And I'm so joyous that the mighty good and loving God has guided my Sonny in the right direction. Now our grandchildren are well secured thanks to you and Mrs Denyah." Mrs Pearson said. "And you Patrick, my grandchildren's dad."

Patrick smiled brightly like metal. Bernice suddenly called out saying." Oh no, Kiah just soaked me."

"At least we're almost home. Just another half-an-hour then we will be home sweet home." Patrick said.

Driving about another ten minutes, heavy rain began to pour down hard on the windscreen so that it became misty and with the gushing splash rain water against the car make the children laugh especially when they saw cars going fast and splashing the fallen rain against their dad's car. "Dad, why can't you drive faster?" Passion asked. "You dad want us to get home safely honey. He's not a road hog like some drivers. That's why your dad has reduced his speed as he wouldn't want any of us to get hurt." Mrs Pearson said.

"Is that true daddy?" Passion asked.

"Yes honey, your grandma's right. Your dad has to be very careful driving on the motorway and especially taking my two Princesses and my little Prince home." Patrick said to Passion. Then all of a sudden she fell asleep again.

"I do like to be driven in a car when it's raining. It makes me fell relax that I want to sleep. Anyone would like a sweet?" Mrs Pearson asked.

"No thank-you" replied Bernice, Patrick and Sonny.

As Patrick took the bend to drive onto the road to take them to their home, Bernice woke the girls telling them "We are home now honey."

Shortly Patrick drove in his gateway and stopped by their garage door and got out the car, took the suitcases out the car boot, unlocked the garage door and parked the car into the garage before he and Sonny took the suitcases into the living room. Bernice carried little Kiah to his room, swilled his bottom clean before she changed him into his pyjamas and put him to bed as he was sleeping. After she saw Passion and Starry lying on the settees, she had a quick shower to wash Kiah's urine off her then went to help Mrs Pearson cooked dinner. Meanwhile, Passion and Starry fell asleep on the settees as they were so tired from the flight and they could hardly kept their eyes open.

As Patrick saw Mrs Pearson take some lamb chops out of the freezer and Bernice put the vegetables on the counter, He asked, "What are you two doing?"

"We're going to cook something for us" Mrs Pearson said taking a bag of shredded cabbage out of the freezer.

Patrick told her "You put the cabbage back and rest yourself from a long tired journey. We'll order some Chinese-Or K. F. C. Mom?" Patrick asked.

"The truth is, I've eaten too much of those junk foods. I was really looking forward to a nice freshly cooked dinner. Beside it would take me to cook the dinner almost the same time as for he ordered food to arrive. Beside, it's only three thirty and the children had already eaten too much junk food. Moreover, maybe they're not even hungry." Mrs Pearson said.

"Bernice cut in saying," Mom's right, we can do with some freshly cooked food."

"Never argue with the ladies Patrick. They cook, we eat" Sonny said before joining Patrick in a can of cold beer.

One hour later, the lamb chop dinner was cooked and was on the table. Bernice woke Passion and Starry and told them to go wash their hands and come to dinner. She then went and had a look in on Kiah but he was still sleeping. After Patrick had eaten, he said. "I have really enjoyed my dinner. The cabbage and carrots were absolutely tasty. Those kinds of food I didn't like until both of you came into my life. Mom, Bernice, thanks for a nice and tasty meal."

"You're welcome son." Mrs Pearson told him.

"Well, we have only to thank your lovely wife for cooking us a tasty meal as she done most of the cooking while I fell asleep at the kitchen table." Mrs Pearson admitted. Then she went on to say "You have a good wife."

"I know that's why I married her. But don't tell her I said that" Patrick said joking in front of his lovely wife Bernice. Also Bernice joked telling him "I married you so that no other woman can spend your money but me." Patrick laughed then he kissed her lips. Sonny patted him on the shoulder and said, "Son, you have married the right woman."

"Well" said Mrs Pearson, "I'd a feeling the girls wouldn't be hungry after they'd eaten McDonald burgers and chips less than three hours ago. I'm exhausted from my trip and I'm going to tidy myself and then to bed to have a lay down."

"Okay mom" Bernice said and took the uneaten food from the girls, and said "they hardly touched their dinner but they ate their cakes and ice cream clean."

"Well honey, I could have told you they won't eat their food." Patrick said and he opened another cold can of beer and drank deeply and then said, "Pops, I have waited patiently to have a real pint, but this will do until I get to the local. You can't find another tasty beer like the English" Then as he looked at the suitcase sitting on the living room floor, he said to Bernice, "you'll have to leave the suitcases where they are until tomorrow. All I need now is a nap. I better go and join my son."

"Mommy, am I going school tomorrow?" Starry asked rubbing her eyes.

"No honey tomorrow is Sunday and you still have a week holiday. You two go brush your teeth honey and don't forget to put some bubble bath in your bath and don't stay too long in the bath and no water fighting. You'll find towels and your pyjamas in the bathroom cupboard. I'll be up later with your nutmeg milk for both of you,"

Half an hour later, Bernice took warm milk up to the girls but she met them dressed in their pyjamas and in bed sleeping. She fixed their quilt over them, turned the lights off and closed their door softly, then had a look into the bathroom to see how they had left it. She picked their clothes and the bath towel up and put them into the wash basket and smiled after she saw the bathroom was left clean enough. She washed the bath out and put the bubble bath in its place and then run a scented bath for herself and had a long soak.

After, she made a phoned call to Denyah saying "Den, we're at home and we had a lovely time but mom and the kids are flogged out and sleeping."

"Well Bernice, I'm glad you all enjoyed your holiday and are now safely home."

"Well Den, I'm a little tired myself but I'll see you tomorrow."

"Okay Bernice, say hello to all for me. Goodbye then" Denyah said and hung up.

Long after Bernice woke Patrick and said, "P, I think you should have your shower."
Patrick rolled over on his back and asked. "Why, do I smell that bad?"

Bernice laughed, "Don't be silly honey, of course you don't smell, I only thought you would like to freshen up."

"Do you have to disturb my sleep just to tell me have a shower, sweetheart, I'm dog tired. All I need is to sleep. I'll have a shower in the morning. So please, just leave me as I am" Patrick said.

Bernice said nothing more than climbed into bed on the other side with little Kiah between them. Early the following morning Bernice went to make a cup of tea when she heard snoring coming from the living room. She entered the room to see Patrick stretched out on the three seat settee sleeping and snoring like thunder. She smiled and went to make a cup of tea then she went and sat at his feet and tickled the bottom of his feet to wake him up. He drew his feet up and opened his eyes to see her sitting at his feet, "What are you doing downstairs?" she asked him. "I thought you went to the bathroom when I hadn't seen you" Bernice asked.

"I had to find somewhere to sleep and move away from you and your son before he kicked me to death," Patrick said.

"Was his kicks were so powerful honey?" Bernice asked.

"Kiah needs his own room. That's it! I've had many sleepless nights. We're going house hunting. One more month sleeping with him, I might as well buy my coffin" Patrick said.

"Don't say that sweetheart, was Kiah really treating you that bad? Think of it as though he's massaging your back" Bernice said and she found it funny and laughed.

"Honey, I need to have fun with you sometime in bed. But with our son between us, we can't. At least, I can't." Patrick said.

"Okay P, well, if that's the case, we must do what we've to do." Bernice said then she left him to go and phoned Paula saying "We had a great time….. Then after Patrick interrupted her speaking to Paula, she told Paula "I'll drop in to see you later" And she put the phone down to asked Patrick what he'd wanted.

"Be honey, which case have you put my shaver in?"

"Look in your travelling bag and you'll find all your stuff. And Patrick, I would be going to see Denyah and Paula sometime today."

"What about house hunting?" Patrick asked.

"We'll go tomorrow. I promise I'll buy a property news paper on my way to Denyah" Bernice said. Patrick said nothing more but went and gave little Kiah his bath. After breakfast, Bernice went to visit Denyah, Paula, Lisa, Meleta, Vida and Tracy. She gave each of them gifts of perfume. Much later that afternoon, Patrick took Bernice to his family home with gifts for his sister Jenny. Bernice gave her a pair of silver bracelets and a beautiful white silk scarf. Jenny hugged Bernice and said "Thank you. Well how was your honeymoon? And did you all had a good time?" Jenny asked.

"Well our honeymoon went well and the children had a great time. They love Disney world. Well thanks for the coffee. We have to get back to the children." Bernice said and turned to leave when her mother-in-law asked her "Where's my gifts?" Bernice ignored her mother-in-law point blank but when Patrick looked at her she said to him "I would have bought your mother a gun if it could have fired the bullets right down her wicked throat."

Patrick turned his back on his mother and smiled broadly. Jenny burst into laughter then his brother Carl so did Carl's girlfriend Veda before she left the room and ran upstairs into the bathroom and had a good laugh before joining Carl in the living room again. But as Veda watched Mrs Lake, she wanted to laugh again. This time she went in to the kitchen and laughed. Bernice followed behind her and they both burst out laughing. "Bernice, do you want to hear what that old prune face woman said to me? She called me a man eater and then asked Carl if it was only black girls he could date. What's the hell that woman knows about me. Carl is my first man. He met me a virgin. You know what Bernice, that woman gave me the impression that she wanted to bed her sons. And from what I heard, she was a terror for incestuous pleasure." Veda said.

"Look Veda, you take no notice of that evil woman. She said the same about me and I put her in her place. In fact, she said worse about Denyah and Paula."

As you said, maybe she wanted to bed her sons. You and Carl love each other, why don't you get married and get a home of your own away from that cow. Believe me you'll be happier. Oh my telling you to get your own place that reminds me I should have bought a property news paper and I'd completely forgot. Anyway, don't take any notice of that crinkled face bitch but as I said, you and Carl get married. You don't have to go to any great expense. Do as I did. Get married at the registry office. All you need is a couple of witnesses. Speak to Carl. And don't think because you're black she's so against you. She thinks all women are not good enough for her sons. Take Denyah for instance, even though she's white, she still didn't approve of her. Anyway, you have a word with your Carl about what I told you and I'm sorry you missed out not been here for my wedding."

"I'm sorry too Bernice that I missed out on you wedding but I will speak to Carl. About you getting married, I didn't know you would be doing it so soon. Otherwise, I wouldn't have gone to Paris. And Bernice thanks for your advice and the perfume."

"That's ok Veda, I'm glad you went to Paris with your friend. Did you have a good time?"

"Yes, Bernice. We did, Joy's aunt was so nice to us. She treated me swell. When Carl and I get married, Paris is where we will be spending our honeymoon."

"Well Veda, if you want your Carl, you'll have to stand up to that troublesome bitch of a mother of his" Bernice said and she and Veda laughed heartily. By this time Patrick was about to go into the kitchen to tell Bernice he was ready to leave when he heard everything that was said between his wife Bernice and his brother Carl's fiancée Veda. He shook his head smiling before he entered into the kitchen looking a little discomfort. "I'm ready to get home" he said.

"Ok honey, but why the sad face?" Bernice asked.

"Bernice, I've heard what you said about mother. Why do you hate her so much?" Patrick said.

"Patrick, your mother gave me caused to hate her, and believe me what you heard me say is right, I will tell your mother straight to her face, and I have told her worse. Your mother is a nasty dirty bug that I won't let get under my skin. So you see Patrick, what ever you heard me say, it fit your mother from head to toe. And you want to hear something else, the way your mother hates every women her sons loves. She's sending out the impression she want you all for her self. So that means incest. Keep it in the family aye! Patrick you're my husband and I don't think I could love you any more than I love you now. Why should I let your mother speak to me as if I'm rubbish, she looked down on us as if we built out of cow shit and straws!" Bernice said furiously.

Patrick raised his hand to hit Bernice then changed his mind as she widened her eyes at him. "Let's go home" he said then smiled.

Bernice left with him, but on their way home they hardly spoke until they saw a house that they both liked that were up for sale in Broad Street. They stopped at the house and had a good look at each other with smiles. "You know what B honey, everything you said about mother, you may be right. But it still hurts to hear bad things about any mothers no matter what. However, let's forget about her, would you be interested in this house? It seems like a four bedroom. Shall I take the numbers down and phone the agency tomorrow?" Patrick asked.

"Yes, I think we should." Bernice said interestedly and she wrote the phone number down as well and the contact Agency's name. "You know honey, if we get to buy this house, we can build a conservatory at the back or at the front. I really would like to buy this house as it is detached and especially where it is, the area looked so developed and nice. And, if we should have more children, there's plenty of yard space for addition." Bernice said

"Well, we can start here" Patrick joked.

"Start what?" Bernice asked.

"Making babies, what else" Patrick said tickling her under her arms and making laugh.

"Stop it Patrick" she said in vexed mood and crossing her legs tightly knowing he would tickle her between her thighs. Cunningly Patrick smiled and looking in her eyes as he knows she's very ticklish between her thighs. So he tricked her by telling her "Have a look at that man and his look-a-like dog" she fell for his trick and turned to look out through the car window. Smiling, he quickly tickling her between her thighs making her laughed so much, that tears came in her eyes. As he was kissing her with romantic and loving feeling, they attracted a few passers-by looking at them. Some onlookers smiled while others watched in disgust. After a while, Patrick drove away and was heading home. He outstretched his left hand to touch Bernice on her leg when she told him. "If you're on heat, cool your orgasm on the wheel and watch the road" he laughed saying "I'm feeling like having a romantic evening with my beautiful wife but with our son between us, it's impossible. When I want a bit, I don't want to do a quick fit. I would want to enjoy my wife. Honey, the sooner we get a bigger house, the happier for me."

Bernice laughed and said, "Kiah, is the boss of our bed and his dad is getting jealous." Bernice laughed again and whispered softly into his ears, "You'll have to wait until Kiah have his own room then you might just be lucky to score me as many times you want."

Patrick laughed saying "Obviously you're wrong. You wait until I get you home. My pipe needs to be explored as it's now on fire. Seriously B, I was near to hitting you at mothers. I'm sorry I've made that attempt. I love you very much. I shall never raise my hand to hit you again for speaking the truth. But I would like to have some of my fruitful food as soon as I get you home we shall go straight into bed." he smiled as he rested his hand on her leg.

"Patrick, I don't understand what is it you trying to tell me?" Bernice asked him as she'd looking confused.

"I'm telling you I would like to take my beautiful wife to bed soon as we get home and have sex."

"P, the number of time we have had sex, I thought you wouldn't want to see my body until next year" Bernice said.

"B, I'm so longing to be in bed with you, but as I said, with Kiah always between us, I can't get to enjoy you. If we don't buy a bigger home, I may have to look for a lovers spot or into the garage to take you and make passionate love." Patrick said.

"Patrick, have you got white liver?" Bernice asked.

"Why do you asked that B? And what do you mean?" Patrick asked.

"I heard Mom's friend said men with white liver, seems to always want sex."

"What's white liver?" Bernice.

"I don't know Patrick, maybe it's a sexual disease."

"B, we were away for two weeks and we had sex twice." he said.

"That's true honey, but we can't do anything here." she said.

"Neither at home for that matter: I might have to look for a lover's spot somewhere to take you my gorgeous wife as I told you." Patrick said.

"Honey, if you want some of me, it got to be midnight my love. I want you too honey. But I can't help if little Kiah get in the way." Bernice said.

"Well, the garage would do." Patrick said.

Bernice laughed so much, that she patted him on his trousers fly after she saw he had erection. As he guided her hand to his penis, he ejaculated and messed his trousers. Bernice couldn't stop laughing.

"See what you made me do, that could have been a little miss or Master Lake" he said then burst into laughter" B, honey, don't tell anyone about this."

Bernice didn't answer but her laughing caused him to tickle her between her thighs so that she was looking mad as hell and serious. "Promise me you won't tell anyone I ejaculated in my trousers."

Bernice burst into laughter again and couldn't stop until she saw the state of his trousers and told him "soon as you get home, straight under the shower."

"Shit! I have to go and see Eugene after I take you home" he said.

"Patrick, you sounded serious. What's going on?" she asked.

"Nothing that you should worry over, I just want to remind him that we have an appointment with the bank tomorrow morning and then to see someone about a hotel."

"Is Eugene going to buy another hotel?" Bernice asked.

"No honey. I'm going to buy you a hotel for your wedding gift. Oh this is for you from the children."

"What is it.?" Bernice asked anxiously as she happily took the small red velvet box. Smiling, she opened the box to see a beautiful designed lovers knot diamond and sapphire ring and matching bracelet he bought her when they were on holiday. She stared speechless at her gifts before hugging him.

"Take it easy honey, why not wait until we get in bed then you can strangle me with your hug and your love" Patrick said.

"I love you so much you know Patrick," she said joyfully. "But you've given your trousers what you were going to give me." Bernice laughed again and said, "I hope you shower and change before you go to see your brother."

"You don't have to remind me honey, I know you're in love with me and I know that I've to change." he said.

While Bernice was admiring her lovely gifts, Patrick phoned Eugene on his mobile phone saying bros, "I would be coming to see you after I take my Missus home." As Bernice heard him said that, she insisted she should go with him as she'd forgotten to give Denyah an invitation for Paris and Jade B to come to her daughter Passion's eighth birthday party in three week. As Patrick was nearer to Eugene's home, he stopped off there. As soon as Bernice got to Denyah's, she phoned her home. Mrs Pearson answered "Hello,"

"Mom, Patrick and I are at Denyah's and we will be home soon, how's the kids?"

"Honey, don't worry over them. They're alright." Mrs Pearson said and put the phone down. Bernice went to speak to Denyah again.

When Patrick faced Eugene, Eugene eyes fell on the spot he'd messed. He looked into Patrick's eyes, and smiled raising his eyelids on Patrick's fly and pressed his lips in tormented way before he burst into laughter saying, "I saw you had an accident. Couldn't you wait until you got the wife home?"

"Bros if I told you what happened, you won't believe me." Patrick said.

"So where was the missus?" Eugene asked.

"With me, like you, she was in hysterical laughing."

"You should have park up in some dark place and take what is yours." Eugene said.

"You're joking, aren't you?" replied Patrick smiling

Eugene burst into laughter again and stopped when Mrs Brown showed up. Patrick turned sideways with his hands covered over the fly of his trousers before he and Eugene moved into the living room to talk.

Minutes later, Denyah and Bernice went into the kitchen and made ham sandwiches and tea. From the kitchen door, Denyah shouted to Eugene and Patrick. "You two would like a ham sandwich or turkey?"

"Yes please, turkey." Eugene shouted. "And a couple cans of beer and be quick with it" Eugene laughed. Patrick borrowed a pair of Eugene's trousers and he and Eugene sneaked out the house while Denyah and Bernice were making the sandwiches.

Paris went to her mother and said, "Daddy and Uncle Patrick drove off in Uncle Patrick's car"

Denyah smiled as she said to Bernice. "You see what I've got to put up with."

"They're real brothers. Patrick usually leaves the house without telling me. However, I brought Paris and Jade B an invitation to Passion's eighth birthday party. I have already give Meleta and Lisa theirs, and Passion will be taking some to school to give to her friends when she goes back next week" Bernice said.

After it was getting dark, Bernice was ready to go home but Eugene and Patrick hadn't shown up yet. Paris and Jade B kissed their Aunt Bernice and their mother Denyah goodnight before they went to bed.

"Where's mother Brown? "Bernice asked.

"She went to bed early" Denyah told her.

After Denyah settled her baby down in his cot, she and Bernice went into the living room to chat and drank coffee as Bernice waited for Patrick to come from the pub. By this time Eugene and Patrick were on the go searching for hotels that were for sale. While they were driving through Walsall, Eugene's eyes caught a freshly painted hotel that was up for sale in one of the most fast moving areas and the hotel was set in a beautiful location surrounded by shops, computer units and banks. Eugene's eyes were on the hotel as well as the surrounding area. Thinking deeply, he watched Patrick in wonder as his brain was working trying to solve this puzzle of why such a beautiful looking hotel was up for sale and especially as it was set in a fast going area and at this time almost packed with diners.

Patrick glanced at Eugene then asked him "What're you thinking about?" Eugene shook his head smiling, "Nothing" he said. Then said, "Only that I would like to know why's that hotel we just passed is up for sale, especially because it is in a fast going area and looked full with diners."

"Turn the car around bros. I would like to take a look." Patrick said.

Eugene drove about two hundred yards before he made a U turn and drove back to the hotel. As Eugene and Patrick sat in the car and looked at diners going into the hotel they looked at each other in thought, then both left the car and went into the hotel and had a good look around the inside.

"I see what you mean bros" Patrick said and took his pen from his Jacket pocket and jotted down the telephone number on one of Eugene's business card and put it in his jacket pocket.

"Wait a minute" Eugene said, showing the same white painted hotel with the name and telephone number and the hotel's name 'The Bernice Hotel' Patrick smiled and went in thought as he held the card to his eyes level."

"So why are you smiling, and what are you thinking about Patrick?" Eugene asked.

"I give you three chances to guess" Patrick said nodding his head and smiling.

"Oh brother, the son-of-a-gun, is working a fast one on you. You told me you spoke to an Italian geezer last month. Well he sure worked fast and effectively on you brother, I would like to know what his games are. Tell me Patrick, what's going on between you and that geezer. How did he know you're looking to buy a hotel and your wife name's Bernice?"

"Eugene, a woman came to see me and told me, we were adopted and that our father owned hotels and restaurants all over the world. She must have linked me to the geezer after I told her I was interested in buying a hotel. Maybe he knows about us, and he's biding his time to claim us. As you brought this to my attention, how did he know my wife's name? Yes, he might gather information that I want to buy a hotel for my wife and that her name's Bernice. Oh I get it now, I got talking to the woman about buying a hotel for Bernice as a wedding gift, now can you see the picture? Eugene, I heard about this - Mr Frats was the one that sent you the photo of the hotel and the address. He doesn't want to sell me, he wants to hand it to me on a plate" Patrick told Eugene.

Eugene watched Patrick with interest.

"Well, what's wrong with taking a gift from him, at least he might owe us this much and more. Well, he's treating me like a son and I see no harm in taking a small gift off him," said Patrick, " beside, from since I got to know the old brute, he's treating me like family" Patrick smiled.

"How long did you know the old brute as you called him?" Eugene asked interestedly.

"About two months. Why?" Patrick asked.

"How did you get to know him?" Eugene asked.

"Why all these question Eugene? And what are you trying to tell me?" Patrick asked looking into Eugene's eyes.

"You don't see the small print, or you just don't care who you're dealing with. Wake up Patrick. Don't look behind you for the rest of your life in regret. There's something strange about that man." Eugene told Patrick in temper.

"Eugene, I know how hurt you are, but give me a few yards and let me decide for my family and me aye? I know how well you mean. But as you are always there to tell us the does and don'ts, we'll never be able to develop the knowledge to decide for ourselves whether we did right or wrong."

"Well Patrick brother, I had no idea that you felt that way. However, I have to be home to help Denyah with the kids. We will pursue your hotel hunting tomorrow. That's if you need me." Eugene said.

"Okay," Patrick said and he drove Eugene home and watched him opened his iron gate before he drove off. Then, he remembers he'd his Bernice and his trousers at Denyah's. "Shit" he said smiling and turned his car around and went to get his wife and his trousers. He rings the doorbell. Eugene answered the door and stood holding the opened door and smiled. "Why didn't you remind me my missus and my trousers were still here? And I'd to leave your trousers behind."

"Well bros how can you forget the love in your life? About the trousers, keep it. Were you trying to leave her because she didn't ease your pressure earlier? Anyway, I just gave her your trousers." Eugene said.

"What the hell are you going on about bros?" Patrick asked.

"Well, the evidence still on your trousers." Eugene said laughing.

"Well, at least I didn't have to wait on my missus for four months." Patrick said.

"Where did you get this from?" Eugene asked.

"From you brother, you were the one that told me. So you keep my secret and I'll keep yours." Patrick said.

Eugene burst into laughter and walked into the dining room with Patrick by his side. "What time do you two call this, Eugene, I asked you to help me with the children as mom was feeling a bit tired and went to be early."

"Denyah honey, we just went for a pint. You've put the children to bed. So what is your problem honey?"

"Eugene, I need you to be here with us. I need a little help sometime. Mom needs her rest as I think she's working too hard."

"Eugene, Denyah's right. Remember the baby's young and she needed help. As for you my husband Patrick, we should have been home long ago. I might have to put a leash on you Patrick."

Eugene burst out laughing. Patrick kept quiet looking at him.

"Eugene, don't get too happy, you might be put on a leash before Patrick."

"Well Denyah, It's time I went home to my family. I'll call you later in the week." Bernice said and she finished drinking her fruit juice, kissed Denyah goodnight and said goodnight to Eugene and left with Patrick's trousers. On Bernice and Patrick's way home, Bernice kept very quiet and smiled only when Patrick said to her "I love you."

By this time, Eugene was apologizing to Denyah saying, "Den honey, I'm sorry I wasn't here to help with the kids."

"That's okay. Paris was brilliant in helping me. She's getting so much more grown up."

"Do you need anything before we go to bed?"

"No Eugene, Oh will you bring up the feed for the baby, his bottle is on the table."

Eugene washed his hands, grabbed a chicken leg, a can of beer, the baby bottle and turned off the lights before he went up. Denyah woke her baby and fed him then changed his nappy, winded him and held him for at least an hour before he fell asleep and as she was putting him in his cot bed. Eugene asked smiling. "Can I hold my son for few minutes?"

"Of course you can, when you have a shower or a bath." Denyah said.

"Am I not clean enough?" Eugene asked.

"I didn't say that. I don't know where you're coming from." Denyah said.

"Den, I only went to the pub to have a drink." Eugene said.

"Even so, you still have to shower." Denyah said.

Eugene took the baby from Denyah, kisses his little forehead and put him in his cot bed and then pinned Denyah down on the bed and kissed her. "Stop this." Denyah said trying to push him away.

"Den, its nine weeks now since that time when we made love and you were feeling pain as you were not ready."

"I'm still not ready." Denyah told him.

"When will you be ready Den?"

"I don't know. I'm going to bed as I'm tired."

Eugene went and had a shower and went to bed to meet Denyah sleeping. He smiled and turned his back to her.

At this time, Patrick and Bernice were in their house. "Would you like to join me in a bath honey?" Patrick asked Bernice.

"I'll have my bath but not with you honey." Bernice told him.

However, Patrick set a bubbled bath for Bernice and told her he would be having a shower. She believed him and fell once again for his tricks and went into her bath leaving the bathroom door slightly opened. Patrick got undressed outside the bathroom and quickly he got into the bath with Bernice. "What you think you're doing. I haven't remembered inviting you in with me" she said.

"I came in to finish where I left off in my trousers, I still have nearly a full bottle of white honey that is ready to explore in you pot" Patrick said laughing.

"Well, I don't need any of your honey now or later. So wash yourself and get out."

"Please honey, I'll tickle your soft spot," he said laughing.

"Patrick, will you get out my bath?" Bernice said getting up. Patrick pulled her down gently in the bath and was tickling her between her thighs. Laughing so much, she spreads her legs apart. He fixed himself between her thighs and kissed her a few times before she hooked her arms around his neck and gave in to him. After he was well satisfied, he got out leaving her to have a long soak. When she finished her bath, she went and looked on the girls before she joined him and their son Kiah in bed. As Kiah always kicked him, he took him from the bed and put him in his bed cot and moved the bed cot nearer to their bed as the night was cold. That night Patrick tucked Kiah under his cot quilt and that night little Kiah slept like a log until eight in the morning.

That morning, at the breakfast table, Bernice had a glance in last night's evening paper and came across Wesley's name stating he was given one month suspended as he turned up at work well pissed with alcohol. Bernice phoned Denyah to tell her, but as Patrick walked in, she changed her story saying. "Den, I'm inviting us girls out to dinner next Saturday evening. Would you like to come?"

"Bernice, I would like to, but I'm partly breast feeding my baby and my girls are so agitated when I'm not home with them."

"I understand. What if I ordered food and drinks and came to your house?"

"That can work. How many are you thinking of coming,"

"Well, the usual, I would phone Meleta, Lisa, Paula, Tracy, Claire, Cindy, Jenny, Veda, Ivy, Mrs Saunders, Kelly and me. Just us, no men, it's time we have an evening together. The children's grandparents would look after the children."

"Okay Bernice, I wonder what you're up to."

"Den absolutely nothing. So, would three o'clock be okay, I promise to leave at seven as my children will be left at home. So would that time be alright?"

"Yes Bernice, of course it will be alright."

"Thanks Den, I'll tell the girls tomorrow then, and we'll see about three o'clock next Saturday. Goodbye Den."

"Goodbye Bernice'"

Denyah and Bernice both hung up their phones. Bernice kissed her husband and asked him "Where's the Newspaper?" Patrick smiled saying honey, "I completely forgot I had to get one."

"Men," she said looking at her adopted father smiling.

That Tuesday Bernice and Patrick spent the afternoon in bed making love as the children grandparents took the children to see their other grandmother.

Wednesday evening Patrick took Bernice to Denyah again so that Bernice would talk with Denyah. Bernice also reminded Denyah she would like Paris and Jade B to go to her daughter Passion's eight birthday party in three weeks time. She then gave Denyah two tee-shirts one for the Jade B and Paris, aftershave for Eugene and a black silk scarf for Mrs Brown as she'd forgotten to take them their gifts before.

"Den, I've bought tee shirts for Meleta's girls as well and a scarf for her mother and aftershaves for the hubby and dad. Everyone got the same. "

"Thank you so much." Denyah told her.

Then Patrick showed himself telling "B, honey, we can make a round trip to mothers with her gift."

Bernice replied smiling. "I told you before. I would have bought her a gun for her to shoot herself in the mouth. But the retailer was fresh out of bullets." Denyah laughed but Patrick and Eugene were looking deadly serious at first, then, burst out into laughter.

"Seriously B, haven't you bought anything for mom?"

"Yes, Patrick, I bought your mother a scarf."

"That's ok my dear love." Said Patrick. 'At least she won't feel left out."

Saturday afternoon, while Bernice was at Denyah's, Mrs Lake, Jenny and Carl and fiancée Veda walked in the dining room behind Eugene. Bernice and Denyah's eyes met in surprise to see Mrs Lake.

"Bernice reached for her carrier bag and took form it two bottle perfumes, she gave Jenny perfume and aftershave for her and her fiancée' Curt, then she gave Veda perfume, and aftershave she gave to Carl and a brown silk scarf she gave to Mrs Lake her Mother In-Law. Carl, Jenny and Veda thanked Bernice. But Mrs Lake kept quiet and flung her scarf into Denyah's settee without opening the gift box.

"So ungrateful" Veda whispered and followed Denyah and Bernice into the kitchen. "By the way, who invited her?" Bernice asked.

"Oh, I mentioned to Eugene that us, girls will have a slap-up meal and he must have told her. She came with Jenny and Veda." Denyah said.

"Well, that's why she's here." Bernice said.

"Well, there's nothing we can do about her now, except for me to keep my eyes on her with my son" Denyah said with doubt on her mind.

"Would you both like to know what his sour face looking mother of a bitch said to Carl "If only black women he can date, anyway, for what I experience of that woman, I don't even think any of her children like her, I'm sorry I didn't get to know their father as Carl spoke so highly of him. I wish I'd met him."

"Look Veda, you told me this before. Like Denyah and I, take no notice of that evil foul mouthed woman. As you said, she seems as if she wants to bed her sons. You and Carl love each other and that's what matters. She'd said the same about me. Even though our friend Denyah here is white, she'd said worse about her and called her the worst names under the sun. Anyway, I told you this before." Bernice said.

All this time Veda and Bernice were talking, Patrick said, "You two were talking about mother again?"

"Patrick, when are you going to stop listening behind doors, I saw you standing at the door and listening. I told Veda you mother so damn miserable - I gave her a scarf and she just grabbed the box from my hand and toss it on Denyah's settee.

"Well you've said everything you need to say to my mother." Patrick said.

"Not everything my sweet husband Patrick as the best is yet to come to your ears. However, I just told Veda you're going to buy us a new home. And you're so lucky to always hear us talking so nicely of your evil mother. I believe this is twice you've heard us. Honey, have you nothing else to do than to always stand at doorways listening to hear us speaking so nicely of your mom? I think you should really be put on a leash." Bernice said after she threw her arms around his neck and kissed him.

"Honey, don't push your luck. If you're looking for a good spanking, you're working towards it" Patrick said to Bernice.

"You won't hit me honey, will you?" Bernice asked giggling.

"You behave and I won't." Patrick said giggling too.

"Are you still buying me the hotel?" Bernice asked looking rather disinterested.

"Yep- the hotel would be a wedding present from the kids and me. So it is to the bank Monday morning" Patrick said. Bernice smiled. "Oh here honey, I almost forget to give you this. It's from me this time" Patrick said then smiling he took out of his dark blue shirt pocket a brown velvet box and passed it on to Bernice while Veda and Denyah watched with interest. Bernice looked at him before she looked at Veda and Denyah. Then smiling she opened the box to find a matching set of beautiful pale blue diamond ring, bracelets and necklace that was set on a double bar of Sapphire and Diamond. "Where are the earrings?" Veda asked Patrick. Patrick smiled looking at Bernice while Bernice looked at him. "Oh," he said feeling in his pocket then taking out a same similar small box and gave it to his Bernice smiling, he faced Veda,

"Thanks for reminding me." Patrick said cunningly.

Bernice said to him, "I was going to play a game with you tonight, but as you were ready to cheat me, I don't think I'll bother. But I must thank my children as soon as I get home"

Veda smiled into Patrick's face saying. "You'd wanted to give this one to your mistress, didn't you?"

"I wouldn't want to share my life with any other women. My loving wife is sufficient." Patrick said happily.

"That's what you men always say until you get caught." Denyah said joking.

Bernice gave her husband a quick kiss on his lips and said joking. "Don't expect anything else tonight."

"And here's me thinking when I get you home, we will have a very special second honeymoon." Patrick said.

Bernice got up from her chair and hugged him with a long kiss. As she parted from him he said "Take it easy honey, I'm sure you can wait until you get me in bed, then you can strangle me with kisses and hugs. "I love you so much Pat" she said looking deeply into his bright blue eyes.

"You don't have to remind me honey, I know how much you love me." he said.

After Eugene and Patrick ate, they both went looking for hotels and houses once more. As Eugene and Patrick driving through Edgbaston looking for hotels and houses on sale, they came upon a beautiful white painted hotel. They stopped and went into the hotel and asked questions about the hotel. Interestedly, Patrick was extremely surprised with the price. And again the cheapness of the hotel has raises doubt into Eugene's mind. And again, Patrick sunk into wondering if it was coincidence or if the hotel belonged to Frats as well as the one they saw in Walsall and if it was a set-up by Mr Frats to get close to Patrick and Eugene. However, whatever it was, Patrick had made his mind up and he'd decided he wanted to buy this one on Hagely Road Edgbaston. As Eugene silence came to Patrick's notice, Patrick quickly faced him and said anxiously "bros, I have to snap this one up before someone beats me to it."

"Patrick, I know you would like to buy a hotel, but please not this one" Sadly Patrick asked Eugene "why not this one."

" Eugene replied doubtfully, "the thought remains with me that the price is so well below what it should be, and this worries me and has left me with even stronger doubts as to why the price are well below market value. Sorry to say, I believed something's not measuring right. But it's up to you bro on whatever you decide. Which ever way, I would be with you all the way" Eugene said to Patrick.

CHAPTER EIGHTEEN

Four days later, Patrick had a phone call from the hotel manager in Walsall asking him if he still wants to buy the hotel. "Well yes, I'm interested. But please let me get back to you yah," Patrick told him.

"Of course Mr Lake, but please don't take too long." Mr Frats said.

"Not at all Mr Frats…." Patrick said.

"Well, I've sent you a list of nineteen hotels and twenty six restaurants around the Birmingham area. I hope one of them would be to your liking." Mr Frats replied.

"Thank you Mr Frats, I do like one that I saw in Hagely Road. Soon as I talk to the Mrs, I would get back to you. Say sometime tomorrow?" Patrick said.

"Tomorrow is fine." Mr Frats said.

"Well goodbye Mr Frats." Said Patrick and rang off. Then as he seated himself down into the settee and feeling happy, the thought of what Eugene told him races through his mind over the price of the hotel and, as to why Mr Frats wanted to sell him any of his hotels and especially well below the market value. He smiled, "Well Mr Frats, what fast one are you trying pull on me mate?" Patrick asked.

Then he sunk deep into thought as he was wondering how Mr Frats knew him and his name, and that he want to buy a hotel or a restaurant, and why has he sent photos to him about these hotels. Once again as Patrick sat thinking, he said to himself, "Mr Frats, whatever you're up to, "I shall find out mate."

As Patrick was so eager to find out what Mr Frats was up to, and how he knew Patrick was interested in buying a hotel, Patrick hired a private investigator to find out about this Mr Frats.

That night Patrick told his adopted dad he's thinking of buying Bernice a hotel as a gift from the children.

"Are you sure about this? Patrick, what has worked brilliantly for your brother, might not for you. I would invest in properties if I was you, but of course, I'm not you, or would I ever fall in that position. Son, I'm only giving you advice. Still, it's up to you in the end." Sonny told Patrick.

Patrick smiled looking deeply into Sonny's eyes and also in deep thought knowing his adopted dad opinion made sense. "But dad, I still would like to buy the hotel for my wife, the mother of our children. The hotel would be a gift from our children. If the hotel was not successful, we can sell and put the money in trust for the children."

"We, Patrick, you said we. I have, nor want, any part in this."

"Come on dad, I understand what you said, but this hotel is coming from our kids, I think their mother would be over the moon."

"Yes Patrick my son, how is Bernice feeling about you and the children buying her a hotel?"

"Well, she told me she wasn't interested. And she doesn't know why I'm buying her a hotel."

"There you are. So, I rest my case." Sonny said.

Still, Patrick was determined to buy a hotel for his wife for a Wedding gift no matter the cost. He told himself that he didn't want to think over anything else but to buy that hotel whatever the price. After much thinking, he phoned Eugene saying "bros, I thought over both hotels and I've decided that the one on Hagley Road is my choice. Would you come with me tomorrow morning, let's say about eleven."

"Sure, bro, you want to pick me up, or, shall I come and get you." Eugene asked him.

"I'll pick you up" Patrick said. Then as Eugene rang off, Patrick phoned Mr Frats and told him, "Thanks for reducing the price of the hotel. My mind is set on the one in Hagely Road."

"Well Mr Lake, I'm happy that you've made a wise choice. I ate in all my hotels, but that one is where I choose mostly to have my meals and to meditate. However, I'm so looking forward to meet you in person." Mr Frats said.

"Likewise: Mr Frats. Well goodbye for now Mr Frats." Patrick said.

"Mr Lake before you ring off, may I ask you the name of that hotel?" Mr Frats asked.

"I'm not sure, my brother and I were driving through and I just happened to have a glimpse of the hotel and I like it. If I'm buying that hotel I would like to know why you selling the hotel this cheap and as its sets in a fast going location and seemed to be an exquisite hotel and it have surrounded by pubs, factories and clubs."

"Mr Lake, is the hotel white washed on the outside with black window wash surroundings?" Mr Frats asked.

"Yes Mr Frats. I think so, why do you ask?" Patrick said.

"No reason. Well, I shall see you tomorrow. And thanks for letting me taking up some of your time. Mr Frats." Patrick said.

"Thank-you, Mr Lake, tomorrow then, goodbye Mr Lake."

Patrick put his phone on the receiver and smiled as he was looking and feeling pleased within himself.

His adopted dad looked at him, smiled and shook his head.

When Bernice saw the smirk on his face, she asked, "Patrick, have you scored one of your lady friends last night?"

"What mischievous thoughts you have in that head of yours. Honey, as I've told you so often you are and would be the only woman in my life."

"So you said Patrick, so you said" Bernice said and smiled.

Eleven o'clock the following morning, Patrick was on time to pick Eugene up, as he was getting out of his car, he saw Eugene walking towards him. He ejected a disc he had playing in his car (I'm in love with you girl) Eugene got in his car and he drove away. On their way to see Mr Frats, Eugene asked Patrick, "Are you sure you want to work in a hotel?" Eugene asked.

"Eugene, I'm buying the hotel for my wife." Patrick said.

"If I'd heard rightly, Bernice told you she wasn't interested in any hotels or restaurants, so why are you insisting on buying her a hotel. Just what are you up too bros, are you having an affair, and want to use this hotel for an escape to set up your love nest?" Eugene asked.

"Eugene, why do you thinking so ill of me, I would never cheat on my wife." Patrick said and went on to say "I'm wearing my married ring and I don't want any woman to laugh in my wife face and telling her I'm sleeping with them."

Eugene giggled.

"What about you Eugene, would you cheat on Den again?" Patrick asked.

"Patrick, there's only one woman in my life and that's the same one that have my kids. Speaking of kids, would you like any of your own?" Eugene asked Patrick as guilt written all over his face. Then as Patrick stared into Eugene's face, Eugene asked him. "Would you like to have children?"

"Absolutely, but if it won't to be, then I'll satisfied whatever the outcome." Patrick said happily. Then he said "Eugene, I was seeing someone about five years ago, well we broke up after I caught her kissing a man, she phoned me a few times and told me she wanted to get back with me, but I threatened if she phoned me again, I would not responsible for what I would do to her but the truth was, I didn't meant her any harm. I'd just want her to leave me alone as I didn't think I could have trusted her again."

"Did you love her?" Eugene asked.

"Yes Eugene, I did love her, but that's all in the past. I'm now deeply in love with my wife and the kids. Sure brother, I would like a kid or two of my own, but as I said, if it won't to be, well that's it. But I wouldn't want to have any kids outside my marriage." Patrick said.

"That's the way to think bros." Eugene said smirking.

"Anyway, what's this I heard about you cutting two chicks while living with the love of your life? I know of one of them that our brother married which Den knows about. Well, I'm happy for you to tell me about the other one. Lucky for you, things work out in your favour, but did you have to go and screw another one? Eugene Brother you playing with fire. Just pray Den don't find out about the other one." Patrick said.

"What are you talking about bros?" Eugene asked under his cunning smile.

"I'm talking about my cunning brother Eugene and Kalor, this brother that's sitting next to me" Patrick said smiling.

Eugene turned away his face and laughed.

"You can laugh now, but a few weeks ago you were sweating thinking Ryan would tell Den. Bros, you're one lucky bastard." Patrick said and burst into laughter then Eugene laughed too, saying, "you know what bros, we really might be bastards."

They both laughed happily again as they mirrored into each others eyes like lovers. "Well, it's time we go to find out what hold the mighty old fart has on us and just what he's after." Eugene said.

Patrick looked on his wristwatch and said, "Yep- its time we find out."

Patrick stopped his car near Mr Frats' office. Both he and Eugene got out their car and walked inside the hotel in silence and smiles.

Then Eugene and Patrick looked on their wrist watches again and both watches show five to eleven. They walked into the hotel and gave their names at the inquiry desk. They then were taken into a posh waiting room not knowing that it was Mr. Frats they were going to see as the male receptionist gave impression that they there to find out about the hotel they'd wanted to buy. From the waiting room, a very young and beautiful slim and tall dark complexioned secretary with short cropped and wavy brown hair escorted them to Mr Frats' office door and knocked at the door. As Patrick and Eugene waited behind her, she knocked on the door softly again as she had no reply from the first knocking and seemingly Mr Frats hadn't heard the first and second time knocking, she knocked a little harder on his door a third time. "Come in" he answered.

The secretary opened the door, looked back at Eugene and Patrick and smiled before she escorted them both into his room. "Thank-you Miss Barns." Mr Frats said smiling to his secretary but she stood transfixed looking at Eugene with such a stunning smile then said warmly, "You both are the most handsome men I have seen in months." Patrick and Eugene smiled at her complimenting them.

"That would be all Miss Barns. Thank you." Mr Frats said smiling.

As the secretary turned and stood watching Patrick and then Eugene with an inviting smile, Mr Frats said. "You are no longer needed here Miss Barns."

The secretary had seemed stunned as she took turns looking in Eugene and Patrick's eyes with such a crafty smile and then at Mr Frats as if she had being asked by Mr Frats to choose Patrick or Eugene.

"Miss Barns, will you please leave us." Mr Frats told her as he beckoned her to leave by clearing his throat and making signals with his hand telling her to leave.

But as she was so fascinated by Eugene and Patrick blue eyes and lovely texture of their light tanned skin, she ignored what Mr Frats said to her, and said, "If I get the chance to date you, I would have both of you. Your eyes and skin alone"--- Mr Frats made a croaking sound clearing his throat again and she turned and looked at him smiling then faced Patrick and showing him a welcoming smile as Eugene had had his eyes fixed on a silver framed photo that stands on Mr Frats mahogany desk of a slim beautiful redhead tanned skin young lady that looks like she had blue greyish sparkling eyes which complimented her beautiful rosy high cheeks on the most exquisite face with a smile like blazing fire - and he didn't know she was their mother.

As the secretary was leaving, both Eugene and Patrick's eyes following her until she walked out of the office and closed the door behind her. Eugene smiled showing his likeness for her. Mr Frats smiled saying, "Will you two would like to take a seat please?"

Eugene and Patrick took their seats smiling.

Mr Frats twirled his chair facing them with a smile showing happiness and at the same time, his eyes showing a clearly picture of tenseness and an expression of embarrassment. Patrick looked him in his eyes and smiled. Then Mr Frats smiled showing sadness - as he took turn looking hard into Eugene and Patrick's faces, sadness on his face changed to contentment and happiness. He then paused pressing his palm over his mouth and his bright grey eyes looked tense and yet still joyful. As Eugene and Patrick waited patiently for him to talk, Eugene took the photo off Mr Frats' desk and studied his beautiful mother although he had no idea she was their biological mother. As Mr Frats looked at him it brought back to him the boy's mother's smile. Mr Frats turned his face away then wiping tears from his eyes he faced Eugene and spoke "I know you are both wondering why you were asked to come here. Well first, sending you photos of the hotels and the fake prices, I thought you would be interested and it would bring you here, as well as the invitation card I sent to you." Mr Frats then paused briefly before a smile came on his face as his eight fingers tips covered his lips and under his mixture of grey and red short bearded chin and his two thumbs firmly pressed behind his ears with his head held upright and his eyes moving, taking turns looking at Patrick and Eugene. As he was still smiling, he took turns looking deeply into Eugene's and Patrick's faces again but as though he was studying them. But as he caught Eugene's eyes focused on his mother's photo, he said, smiling, "I miss her very much."

"She's very beautiful" Eugene said in thought she's his daughter.

"She sure was" Mr Frats said and he took the photo from Eugene and turned the photo faced down and then looked at both Eugene and Patrick with moistened eyes.

"Well sir, my brother and I would like to know why we are here and what is your game by wanting to sell us one of your hotels well below the market value?" Eugene asked.

Mr Frats smiled as tears come from his eyes. He pulled a white handkerchief out of his jacket pocket and wiped his tears dry, he then smiled saying as he fixed his eyes on Eugene "I noticed you have the same colour beard like I had when I was in my youth."

he smiled again with contentment, and, instead of giving Eugene an answer as to his asking question he looked away and kept silent.

Patrick got on his feet and asked Mr Frats "Why would you be selling us a hotel well below the market value? Are you so urgently in need of money?"

"Oh no, Mr Lake, nothing like that- money at least is not my problem. Let's say, I'm giving you a heavy discount." Mr Frats said.

"And why would you want to do this Mr Frats?" Patrick asked very inquisitively.

"Well, I have more hotels and restaurants that I can manage, and I would like to sell a few now as I'm getting on in age and slowing down in strength." Mr Frats said and closed his eyes in desperation and love for his sons and a daughter Jenny.

"I understand that part. But what I don't understand is, why you ask us here and why do you want to dump your hotels on us at a giveaway price?" Patrick asked in frustration, while Eugene listened.

"The truth is, boys, you didn't find me, I found you. I heard you both were looking for hotels some months ago, and, gathering some information about you, I thought I had struck gold after knowing who your adopted parents are. I was happy when your photos were given to me along with some interesting information as I have just stated. I've done some investigating with help from a friend and of course, I came up trumps. Eugene, I met you two months ago in Denyah's Hotel I believed you've named that hotel after your wife. Well, while I was dining alone, you came to me and asked me if I was alright and we chatted mostly of hotels and restaurants. I don't know if you can recall that time. However, you invited yourself to my table and we had a glass of champagne together. The champagne you've chose, is my favourite as I told you and we had a good laugh. I'd felt so alive and wanted at that moment."

"Naturally, how could I forget when I caught you staring at me, that I'd invited myself at your table to ask you if you okay. About the champagne, why should you refuse when you offered it after all, why should I let one hundred and twenty five pounds bottle worth of champagne go to waste? After all you paid for it."

"Eugene is this coincidence that we like the same brand Champagne and lamb marinated in fresh garlic and ginger sauce and crisp roasted, and also how we were attracted to each other? Isn't this telling you something? If I told you I'm your father, you might have plunged the knife you were eating with straight through my heart. Or, have me thrown out of your hotel on my head. Eugene, it wasn't because I'd wanted to eat in your hotel, but because I'd heard the hotel is yours and I was so wanted to get to know you." Mr Frats said then he closed his eyes painfully and opened his eyes to reveal tears of joy. After he blew his nose, he said, "Patrick, Eugene, I'm your natural father and you were the first born Patrick, Eugene followed you, then Raymond, Carlton, your sister was last but I didn't know her name as your mother had left me in limbo before she was born. But I can prove she was about four months pregnant. Well Eugene, this fine lady in this photo your eyes were fastened on, she was your mother. I expected it would not be easy for you five of our children to embrace me. But believe me sons, I had not run out on any of you. In fact, I was left feeling so devastated when I turned up to be with you my children and then learnt your step-father had moved out wit your mother and all of you leaving no address. After searching so long and hard and finding you, and proving you are my children, it was like a heavy iron mask slipped off me."

As Eugene watched Mr Frats, his temper rose as he faced his brother Patrick and said "Shit smells are overtaking my breathing in here. Patrick, are you going to let us get out of this shit hole?"

Patrick looked at Mr Frats, who shook his head vibrantly. Then, as they turned to leave, Mr Frats asked "How's Carlton, Raymond and my precious Jenny? And Patrick, have you still got that harmonica. Your grandfather gave it to you when you were just eight months after you fell in love with it. You know what Patrick you didn't even know how to blow it"

Shocked, Eugene stopped walking and faced Mr Frats and asking "What the fuck are you talking about?"

Mr Frats smiled. Eugene landed a heavy punch on his face knocking him out of his recline black chair onto the floor. Mr Frats eventually held on to his desk for support as he struggled up on his feet after taking sometime. As he was staggering to reach his chair, he pitched forward and in amazement he almost fell to the floor again but Patrick caught him and helped him in his chair. "Are you alright? Patrick asked him.

"Mr Frats looked up at Patrick and smiled saying, "I think so." he then took out of his pocked a handkerchief and wiped the dripping blood from his busted lips.

Patrick faced Eugene and asked him. "Do you have to hit him?"

"Are you coming or not?" Eugene asked Patrick in his angry mood as he turned and walking toward the door.

Patrick turned to Mr Frats and asked "Are you sure you okay?"

"Yes, I am okay. I think so. Your brother has my father's temper. I knew it would come to this one day, but I didn't prepare for this lashing out so suddenly. However, that's how it goes sometime between fathers and sons. Believe me I would win in the end but my blow will be with words." Mr Frats said and smiled.

Patrick showed Mr Frats a smile and left with Eugene in thought that he did remember having a harmonica up to the age of four.

As Eugene and Patrick stood by their car, Patrick face showed confusion. "What's the matter with you now?" Eugene asked him.

"Eugene, I remember I did have a harmonica and I remembered mom took it from me and put it in dad's tool box after she told me I was making too much noise."

After Eugene remembered the harmonica, he leaned forward on his car door, closed his eyes and shed tears. He then faced Patrick and said. "You're not taking the old fart seriously are you?"

"Eugene, I don't know what the hell to believe and take serious. All he'd said, I have proves him right so far. Let's leave it at this and get away from here. I don't think I would want to buy any hotel or restaurant anymore."

Eugene and Patrick got into their car, Eugene started the engine and turned it off and looked on the building. "Now what Eugene, have you forget to tell the old man to fuck off?"

"Patrick, I'm sorry I hit him. I really am."

"I'm not the one you should apologise to." Patrick told Eugene. Eugene got out their car, Patrick got out after him. Eugene confronted Patrick with guilty look and said. "I'm feeling really guilty for hitting him."

"So you should Eugene. Hitting an old man like him made me wondered if your brains is in your head."

"I have to go to him and apologise for hitting him." Eugene said.

"Are you sure you want to do this?" Patrick asked.

"Yes Patrick, I'm sure although he's the arsehole of the century."

Patrick smiled "Well, I'll come with you." he said.

"Why? Do you think I would hit him again?" Eugene asked

"No. But I know the temper you have." Patrick said.

"Okay, let's get back to the rat then," said Eugene. And he and Patrick went back to Mr Frats. Eugene apologised to him. "I'm sorry to hit you. I should have left before it came to hitting you. I'm sorry."

"Your apology is accepted." Said Mr Frats and stretched his hand out in friendship for a handshake from Eugene.

After a moment of hesitance from Eugene, he managed to shake Mr Frat's hand with mixed feelings. Patrick sighed with relief and shook Mr Frats' hand and reassuring him with a smile that everything would be okay.

"I know you are driving, but would you both join me in a small drink of scotch? However, if you say no, I would understand as it would be wise, never to drink while driving." Mr Frats admitted.

As Patrick looked at Eugene with a begging smile, Eugene said "Why not? After all, I'm not paying for it."

Then a giggling laugh came from Mr Frats while he was pouring scotch in three glasses. He passed one each to Eugene, Patrick and kept one. He then faced Eugene but as he looked hard in Eugene's face, his smiled was widened but Eugene held a straight face.

"Thanks" Patrick said, while Eugene remained silent pausing, holding the glass still with a straight face.

Mr Frats sipped some of his scotch while Eugene watched him.

"Cheers mate." Patrick said to Mr Frats raising his glass before he swallowed some of his scotch, but still Eugene held on to his glass standing while Patrick took his seat.

"Now Mr Frats." said Patrick. "I'm willing to hear how you become my dad."

"As I said, I have searched long and hard to find my family. You're my family." Mr Frats said.

"Just cut the crap and tell us why you're so eager to claim us as your sons." Patrick said fuming.

"Patrick, let's get away from this man. If he thinks he could win us over with a mouthful of scotch, and a shabby hotel, he should think again!" Eugene said and banged down the glass with the untouched scotch on his desk so hard that the glass shattered.

Mr Frats looked up at Eugene and smiled but as he saw Eugene walked to the door, he quickly got up and said. "Wait, please hear me out Eugene."

Eugene stood facing the door while Patrick was still sitting.

"Please Eugene," Mr Frats said. Eugene turned facing him and asked. "What do you want from us?"

"Please, all I'm asking of you is to please hear me out then if you don't want to see me or know me, I'll keep my distance."

"Okay," Eugene said and he walked away from the door and took his seat to listen to what Mr Frats had to say.

Mr Frats looked at both Eugene and Patrick as he was smiling. He began saying, "I was a simple every day clothes salesman calling from door to door. I called at your mother's door one Friday morning around ten-thirty. After ringing her doorbell for so long and didn't get an answer, I walked away, then I heard a voice shouting from over the opened window saying "Aye salesman," I turned and looked and there was your mother looking down on me from her bedroom window. I walked back to her door and there was your mother standing at her front door wearing a pair of white shorts and crop top and she was bare footed with a stern smile also some curling rollers in the front of her hair. "Did you ring my doorbell?" she asked smoking a cigarette and puffing the smoke in my face.

"Yes," I said, "only to ask you if you would like to buy something."

"What are you selling?" she asked. I opened my suitcase and showed her what I was selling. "I'm feeling so hot." she said, turning up her crop top shorter to fix like a bra. "I would call back another time." I told her after I became embarrassed. She took from my case a sets of three panties and she said, "I would buy this set of panties, but only if you'll help me in one" as I was feeling so embarrassed already, I didn't know if I should smile or walk away leaving her with the panties she was holding. During that time, I was sweating buckets. She laughed saying, "I was only joking" she then went on to asked. "Would you be bashful if your wife had asked you to help her in a pair?"

"I'm not married." I told her. "Neither me." she said showing instant radiance on her face indicating she likes me, as she said frankly. "I like this red one."

"Aye," I said. She smiled and looking hard into my eyes then said, "I like this set of panties with the red one but I have no money now."

"Keep them" I told her. It's a welcoming gift. The next time I call, you'll have to pay for what you want" I told her and closed my case while she was holding the sets of panties and smiling. As I turned to leave, she asked me to wait a second and she went somewhere inside and then returned smiling and said thank you."

I smiled and as I turn to leave again, she slipped a note in my hand saying, "don't throw it away before you had a look, it is my telephone number, if you would call again, I, might have some money to buy some more panties. Or if you should change your mind and would like to help me in a pair of them, just knock on my door and I'll let you in." I smiled and left with thoughts that she might be crazy. But the more I though of her, the more I was visualising her and getting to like her. Few week later, while selling on her street I tried to avoid her but not for long. She was like a magnet drawing me to her. As I lay in bed one Saturday night thinking of her, I reached for her phone number and I phoned her. The magnet in her voice seems to tell me she was waiting for my call. We began to meet secretly of course, and after a while, we couldn't care who saw us as we were so much in love. We didn't get married but we had four boys born to us. We didn't live together as it had seemed difficult and shameful in some ways. I did ask her many times to be my wife but she refused every time. Her reason for not marrying me, I didn't know. I had no idea she was planning to take you boys away without my knowing. She asked me for money - I had no idea how much she' wanted but I gave her five hundred pounds and told her if she want more, just ask. Well I had an injured foot for seven weeks due to a car accident. I kept phoning her for three weeks and got no reply. After another four weeks, I phoned her again in thought I've given her the time she needed to accept my proposal of marrying me but as before I hadn't any reply. Even though my foot was bothering me I forced myself and went and look for her and you boys but her neighbours told me she's no longer living at that address. However, I still was trying to find her, I left messages with neighbours and her Landlord but I was unsuccessful finding out where she was living. All I was told she took you boys and left in the dead of night. I'd searched everywhere for you boys but I couldn't reach you. I asked her Landlady to tell me where she moved too, her Landlady said she moved out not telling her and left no address. I even asked some of her friends if they have her new address, each one said no. I myself done some searching to find her and had no success. After searching for years and not finding her or any of you, I gave up. Then after ten years, I saw in the newspaper your mother has married a High Court Judge, Mr Lemoore Lake and how happy she was. I cried in silence without telling anyone the truth about you boys as I didn't want to hurt any of you and put you through the fire of hell as I have been. So, I left all up to the good lord as I truly thought the day would come when the truth will be revealed to you my children. After fifteen years of your mother's marriage, I got married but divorced two years later without having anymore children. Then to my surprise, after I bought my first restaurant I though I saw your mother walking into my restaurant, but as I approached her I knew she wasn't your mother. However, I had a phone call from her saying she's living in Bromsgrove. I didn't know where in Bromsgrove as she hadn't given me her address. I phoned her with the number she'd given me but again, each time I phoned her it has turned out that she was calling from a phone kiosk. I did get to see your mother in the end but she was dying from a heavy overdose of tablets in a private Hospital. Oh, I had a doctor friend working in that hospital. I had told her about you my boys. In case you're wondering. I found out she was four months pregnant with Jenny when she ran out on me, you see sons, it was hard and still is to come to terms with what had happened but I had to keep strong as I knew one day you my children would appear and learn the truth. Well that mother and father you thought you had were not your parents. They stole you from us, your real mother and I, as for you Eugene my son, I was told by their house maid that that woman has done dreadful things to you and then moved on to you Patrick. I could not go anywhere with what I heard, as I had no evidence and I had to be extremely careful about not destroying the bonds I thought may have developed between you or segregated any of you by having you putting into care. As I said, your pretend father was a High Court Judge and he was well known. My hands were completely tied. I've also learned that he couldn't have children I didn't know his reason and I didn't ask why as he wasn't important to me. You were and still are and I would like to be that father to you if you let me." Mr Frats cried. "Oh Eugene, you boys should be okay as your inheritance came from my father your grandfather. He was a brilliant architect in buildings and boats. Sadly he passed away twelve years ago. He was eighty four years old."

Eugene and Patrick eyes met in surprise and, in believing everything Mr Frats had told them. When Patrick saw Eugene's face showed an expression of doubt over Mr Frats told them, Patrick brought himself to asking Mr Frats. "What dreadful things are you talking about?"

Mr Frats looked deeply into Eugene and Patrick's eyes in tears and snot before he said. "One of your mother's friends said after that bitch you're calling mother gave your mother some tablets for her headache, your mother hadn't stopped vomited and that she was rushed into the hospital but died two days later from poisoning." Eugene closed his eyes in pain and tightened his fists as he breathed out heavily.

"I knew you would be very hurt sons after hearing this. But it has hurt me more to know that I could not be there with any of you to protect you from that evil monster of a pretend woman that made you all call her mother and seduced you both at the age of thirteen and twelve after she dosed your cocoa with drugs. I'm so sorry to have I tell you in this, but I can't hide the truth from you any longer" Mr Frats said and broke down crying harder.

After Eugene and Patrick listened with interest and hurtful feelings, Patrick said, "No, no- I don't believe you." Tears came into his eyes as Eugene stared up at the ceiling and trying hard to hold back his tears.

"Okay, I have cuttings from newspapers stating after the wicked pretend mother claimed you lot, she took no time to marry the Judge. She was just a housemaid and conned her way into your mother's bed even before your natural mother had passed away. She and that man took you over. Eugene I confronted the bitch over drugging you and Patrick before seducing you, she threatened me she would take me to court for slander. Even though I had money and was willing to fight her in court with every penny and up to my dying breath, I had been told by a top class solicitor not to drag you in court with this humiliating scandal for even if it is true, I would only damage your young life by letting the world know. So I apologised to her as I care so much about all of you and besides, as I said, I had no proof and I couldn't go to court with hearsay. I have been beaten up by two men I didn't know and I had eight stitches below my left jaw and I was told keep well away from that bitch, or else I would be a dead man. Most of all, I was prepared to give my life for any one of you. Eugene, Patrick, I have tried desperately hard to gain access to you but that was impossible. I couldn't beat the judge on any grounds. I'd no claim on none of you as you were not carrying my name and I wasn't married to your mother. See, look at my forehead, I'm still carried the scars form the beating over twenty years ago. I've already told you how your mother died. Then one of her friend decided to come forward and gave evidence, she was murdered in car crash. Police thoroughly checked out the car and claimed that the brake had been tampered with. Here take a look at your birth certificates. The housemaid mother has given them to me without telling me her reason. I offered her money but she said it's a present from her. I held these birth certificates for twenty years. She told me they were copied. I believe your false mother has no idea that I have these in my possession. My name and your biological mother's name are on these five birth certificates. She changed your names from Frats to Lake. I'm so sorry your mother and I never got married. However, your mother died and it's time we claimed each other and go forward. Eugene, a daughter of your mother's friend named Pamela claimed she saw that bitch you called mother seducing you. After she told a friend, that friend hadn't heard or seen Pamela or her mother again. Maybe they both were threatened too and left leaving no trace or like your mother, and your mother's friend, they might have been murdered and buried somewhere, or left England."

After Patrick and Eugene saw their mother's and Mr Frats' name on their Birth Certificates bearing the names of Andrea Dangrey and Malic Frats, Patrick remained dumb struck before he became semi-fainted and fell on the floor. Eugene brought him around with some water on his face from the flower vase.

"What happen?" he asked.

"You had a shock and fainted" Eugene told him.

They both took their seat again and looked at each other in bemusement then tears of disbelief as if they were lost in a world of tight webs.

"Sons, I didn't want to drop this information on you so heavily" Mr Frats said looking like he was looking at something that only he could see.

"Don't say another fucking word. Just don't." Eugene said as tears rolled down his face.

After the news has left Patrick and Eugene feeling sickened and shaken, Patrick managed to say "Well, I'll be damned. Okay, are you Asian or Italian? Our mother was white. My wife's black. Do you like black women?" Patrick asked him feeling bitterly hurt.

Mr Frats answered, "So what son if your wife's black. My father was Asian and my mother was Italian. They both died in a car accident along with my sister who was the driver. When can I meet your wife or any member of the family? Mr Frats asked anxiously after he dried his tears."

"Why? To see how black my wife is?" Patrick said.

"No, I don't care if she is as black as the bottom of my pot. I would like a chance to get to know my family. That's all I'm asking of you."

"Come on Patrick let's get the hell out of here. If he wants a ready made family, he'll have to buy else where" Eugene said pushing Patrick out the door.

"What's the matter with you brother? You're acting impulsively. Maybe what he said about us might not even be true." Patrick said.

"Patrick, you weren't even listening to what that creep been saying, he said our mother seduced us when we were boys of thirteen and twelve." Eugene said angrily.

"Eugene, I have listened to him with interest and I can't see any point in him telling lies. I think I believe him and I intend to find out the truth and nothing but the truth." Patrick said pacing the floor.

"Where would you start from?" Eugene asked Patrick.

"I don't know, but as I said, I intend to find out the truth starting with mother, that cow even if it takes me the rest of my remaining life." Patrick said and he put the card with the telephone number and address Mr Frats gave to him in his jacket pocket and then poured a large scotch and raced it down to his belly. Eugene wasn't at all interested to keep his card after what he'd heard from Mr Frats, so he angrily tore the card up and tossed the pieces into Mr Frats' face and he left. "I'm sorry" Patrick said to Mr Frats.

"I'm sorry too Patrick. Your brother took it very hard." Mr Frats said.

Patrick showed a faint smile to Mr Frats and left shortly behind Eugene. Before they get into their car, Patrick looked hard at Eugene, shook his head and gave Eugene a warm friendly touch on his shoulder then got into the driver seat. Eugene then got in and Patrick drove away. All the way home, they hadn't said one word to each other except they were looking at each other coldly. As Eugene drove Patrick to his home, Patrick broke the silence as he flung the car door open and said, "Bros, I'm sorry" Eugene turned his face to the other side avoiding looking at Patrick. Then as Patrick got out of the car, Eugene drove off at high speed with his car wheel screeching. Patrick shook his head with morbid feelings.

Bernice met Patrick by the gate and asked, "What the matter with Eugene to drive off like that?"

"Let me catch my breath aye honey?" Patrick told Bernice.

"Sure Patrick honey," Bernice said as she took Patrick's hands into hers while they were walking into their house.

Meanwhile, Eugene got home but didn't wish to see Denyah just in case she saw the tense pattern on his face and ask him what wrong. He went into the library and sat in thought for at least an hour before he faced his family. Patrick phoned Eugene and telling him, "You can bring me my car tomorrow Eugene," Eugene banged the phone down. Patrick patted his right ear as the sound of the phone crashing down had penetrated into his ear. Eugene moved to the drinks bar and poured himself some brandy and swallowed it all in one go then went and lie on his bed.

A few minutes later, Simon, Patrick's friend called and asked Patrick, What the matter with Eugene?"

"Why do you ask?" Patrick asked.

"I saw him driving like he was on a racing track. The speed he turned on New Hall Street I thought his car would overturned. Patrick, he scared me. I wondered if he was high and on drugs. I followed behind him in fear that he might injure or kill himself but before he went home, he stopped at his local pub and had a couple of pints and two shots of whiskeys. However, after he left the pub, I followed behind him without out him knowing but he got home safely." Simon said.

"Thanks Simon," Patrick said.

"Well you take care as I just come to let you know." Simon said.

By this time Bernice was listening to Simon telling Patrick about Eugene. After Simon left, Bernice asked Patrick "Why didn't you invite your brother in and invite Simon at our wedding?"

"I'm sorry sweetheart, even if I had asked Eugene in, the state he was in, he wouldn't have come in and Simon was away in America working when we got married." Patrick told Bernice.

"Patrick, what have you done or said to upset your brother?" Bernice asked.

"Nothing, absolutely nothing, and please Bernice stopped looking at me like I've just murdered him."

"Well, you must have done something wrong to cause him to be so upset that he didn't even bother to stop to say hello to me or any member of our family."

"Bernice, Eugene and I went looking for a hotel for you and we both had a shock that caused him to be furious. To my surprise we'd just learnt about our real parents and the mother and father we were calling our parents, well they aren't. Mr Frats has claimed that we're his children including Ray, Carl and Jenny. I am the eldest he said, I was nine years older than Jenny who's the last of us. Eugene followed me then Ray and Carlton. He left me in wonder as he has us framed out in the right order. He further said, he was doing some investigating on us, but lost track when our mother disappeared with us and leaving no trace. I didn't think I would bring myself to believe him. But I do. Bernice, he gave us every proof about our true mother" Patrick began to cry. Bernice hugged him to comfort him as she said "Patrick darling, I'm so sorry" Then she asked him. "Will you see Mr Frats again?"

"I don't know, after what he told us, I really don't know. All I'd wanted was to buy you a hotel and not a lecture"

"Honey, all I ever wanted is a family and you gave me that. I don't want any hotel now or ever, and I'm not forcing you to see Mr Frats. But wouldn't you like to see him again? Or if he should ask to see you, would you refuse him?"

"As I said, I don't know. Bernice, that man told Eugene and me that that woman we're calling mom has seduced Eugene and me when Eugene was twelve and me thirteen. And that she was my mother's maid and she had affairs with our mother's husband. Also she'd poisoned our mother with an overdose of tablets. Our mother died in a private hospital. Bernice, that bitch fooled us all this time - tricking us into calling her mom. And as well as the son-of-a-bitch we called dad, was no better than her. Mr Frats even told Eugene and me that one of my real mother's friends saw the bitch seducing Eugene after she drugged his cocoa and that she saw her do this twice. That bitch use to go to Eugene and my room and have her way with us. However, after the housemaid confronted her saying she would make sure the welfare knows about her seducing Eugene, she threatened the housemaid and had her beaten up. From that day the house-maid disappeared and no one heard from her or seen her again. Well, I think a Mr Jay had known what went on between the bitch and my brother from the time my brother was twelve years old. Now Eugene's thirty five years old. Speaking of Mr Jay, I was told he was also beaten up nineteen years ago and had half of his manhood hacked off and then he was dumped at the border of Handsworth Cemetery bleeding and police claimed a man that was on his way to work for his six o' clock shift found him. Anyway, the rest was up to his wife. Also the house-maid died in a car accident. Her car brakes had been tampered with police claimed. But funny enough, no one had been charge with any of these murders or attempted murders. Not even up to this day even though this had happened twenty years ago. B, our inheritance was left to us by our grandfather Frats. This we just also learnt. Not even the dad we use to call dad knew we'd this amount of money. Our grandfather was an architect designing mansions and boats."

Patrick broke down crying with his head on Bernice's lap like a baby.

"Patrick, I realized how painful it is for you and the others, especially for Eugene." Bernice said running her fingers through Patrick's hair. Then she went on saying, "I didn't want to say anything, but since you told me this, I should warn you that Denyah knew about what the evil bitch had done to Eugene for some time. I think her ex-husband had told her. Honey, what your fake mother done was appalling and damn well disgusting. How on earth, could a mature woman looked at a boy of thirteen and twelve and seduce you and Eugene. Pat, honey, I know how shameful and disgusted you must have felt. But Wesley knew about all her meddling with Eugene. Wesley was also having affairs with the evil bitch for four years until her friend Angelina told her if she don't end her affair with Wesley, she would tell Denyah and also she would tell the Judge, meaning your deceitful dad, well she took her friends advice and she did end the affair with Wesley. Angelina told me this before I got to know you. I didn't know Denyah then. I don't think Denyah had known her ex-husband was having affairs with Mrs Lake until a few months ago. Forgive me, let me correct this, I mean the wicked bitch! Your mother was the real Mrs Lake. Now it all adds up as to why that bitch hated Denyah so much." Bernice told Patrick. And as Patrick looked up at Bernice, she lowered her lips to his and kissed him.

"What do you mean by mom hating Denyah?" Patrick asked.

"Patrick, you haven't been listening to one thing I said. It was Wesley that told Denyah in confidence that you all call mother seduced Eugene. I don't think he knew about you. But, after your mom was riding Denyah's back so hard, Denyah threatened her, if she doesn't stop interfering into her and Eugene's life, she would tell Eugene and then go to the newspaper about her seducing Eugene when he was twelve years old. Denyah also told her she has written a letter that would get into police hands if anything should happen to her.

Well, Denyah method has worked. And you mom backed away from Denyah. Denyah also told me in confidence, that's why I couldn't tell you until now. Denyah has treated me like a loved sister and there's no way, I would have ever betrayed her. Not even for you my darling, even though I'm deeply in love with you. All I wish for was for her not to tell Eugene that Wesley was having an affair with the evil deceitful dangerous woman you all thought was your mother. I do hope Denyah doesn't tell Eugene about Wesley and her. Denyah also knows she seduced you. Patrick. What that wicked bitch did to you and Eugene were cruel." Bernice said sadly and she hugged Patrick and said.

"As for you my love, we would bypass what she's done to you. However, I understand she only played with you, but seduced Eugene."

"I don't want to hear about what you just told me ever again! And as Eugene, Denyah would know how to deal with him." Patrick said and looking upset.

Bernice smiled then said "I guest you're right honey. And as she went to hug him, he moved away and said "Right now I just want to be on my own." Bernice moved into the living room and left him in the dining room. He reached for a bottle of red rum and drank a full glass and filled the glass again and closed and opened his eyes in disgust before drinking the glass of rum again and then smashed the glass on the partition bringing Bernice out to him. "Honey, take it easy." Bernice said and took the bottle of rum into the bar and hover the pieces of glass then looked at him and smiled. "Bern has why she done this to us?" Patrick asked.

"Honey, she had no respect for any of you. She's cold and heartless." Bernice said and sat beside him. He kissed her and said, "Bern honey, I do love you."

"I know you do and I love you too. Let's go and have lunch." Bernice told him.

Meanwhile, as Eugene got home, Denyah noticed how upset he was. She fixed him some scotch on with ice and massaged his neck and shoulder to relax him while he sat on their bed. He looked up at her smiling without saying one word and in turn she said nothing except kiss his lips and smiled before they had lunch.

CHAPTER NINETEEN

Two weeks later on the Saturday evening, Mr Frats called at Patrick's home to see him but at this time Patrick was at the Hunters Moon in Ward End drinking with his brothers Ray, Eugene, friend David and his brother- in-law Ryan.

"Well Mr Frats, I'm sorry my husband is not at home." Bernice told him.

"Well would you tell him Mr Frats called to see him?" Mr Frats said.

"I could, but it would be nice if you can wait a little while. I'm sure he won't be too long as he promised to take me to see a friend at about two 'o' clock." Bernice said.

"Thank-you, I do hope that I'm not intruding." Mr Frats said.

Bernice smiled saying "Of course not. Besides, I have come to know we're family. And, I would be very happy if you would have lunch with us."

Mr Frats smiled and said gladly. "It would be an honour to have lunch with the family."

"Well, I think you should come in and meet the children and their grandparents." Bernice told him and led him through the dining room to meet the children eating.

"They're beautiful children." He said smiling.

"They sure are. This is Poshion. She would be eight in two weeks. Starry just turn six. And son Kiah is three." Bernice introduced the children .and their grandparents Mr and Mrs Pearson. Denyah full another plate with food for him. And the children laughed to have seeing him eating so well that Starry asked him, "Are you very hungry?"

"Yes, I'm very hungry." He said and smiled.

After Mr Frats had lunch and then waited for at least another hour, he said to Bernice it was time for me to leave as Patrick hadn't come home. Well thank you for lunch. Please tell Patrick I would call again."

As Mr Frats stand up to leave, Bernice looked at the clock and said, "I wonder where my husband has got too. He should have been here by now or at least an hour ago."

"Anyway, I should have phoned to let him know I was coming. Thanks again for looking after me. If ever I should need another cook, I'll know where to come." Mr Frats said smiling.

Bernice smiled also and showed Mr Frats out. Then as she walked with him to her gate, he said calmly, "Would you kiss the kids for me and said goodbye to your parents for me as they were not at present when I was leaving."

Bernice smiled saying, "They are my adopted family. The children parents had died by motorbike accident. As Patrick and I have more than we need and the children love us as we loved them, we took the opportunity to care for them along with their grandparents. But Patrick and I are expecting our first baby. And I would return your goodbye to them." Bernice said looking radiant and in high sprit. Then she went on saying, "Patrick doesn't know I'm going to have his baby yet, as I only found out a couple of hours ago after I tested to see if I was pregnant."

'I'm very happy for you both." Mr Frats said smiling. "Oh the children fit well within you and Patrick."

Bernice laughed, "Oh, I see what you mean. I'm black, Patrick's white and the children between. And that makes them half breed. I believed that's a compliment to us. Thank you so much to remind me."

"Oh my dear, I hadn't meant to sound so profoundly rude, or to insult you with my thoughtless behaviour. I'm very sorry if I offended you. Would you please forgive me, please," Mr Frats said nicely with a sincere and friendly smile.

Bernice smiled and asked curiously, "Mr Frats, have you any children?"

"I did, at least I thought I had four sons and a daughter. But now I'm not too sure if I would accept by them." Mr Frats said sadly showing a pleasant smile.

"Well have you any other children besides Patrick and his brothers. Mr Frats?" Bernice asked out of curiosity.

"No, I haven't. After my wife miscarried with her first child, she was unfortunate of not to conceive again. We ended up divorce." Mr Frats said in deep sadness.

Oh, I'm very sorry I asked." Bernice said. "However, time will heal for the boys to come to you."

"Bernice, I hope you're right." Mr Frats said.

Meanwhile, just hang on and be patient dad. Patrick and Eugene would soon fall at you feet. " Bernice said.

Mr Frats laughed happily. "That's okay, Eugene's the one I have to work on but I usually regain what I lost." He said smiling and hugged Bernice then he went on to say "However, I have to go now as I have to be somewhere to take care of some business. Would you please tell your husband to give me a call, he has my number. And Bernice, I honestly wish you were my daughter."

Bernice smiled, "I will certainly tell him to call you." She said and walked with Mr Frats outside her gate and to his car. But before Mr Frats left, she gave him a quick hug telling him. "You take care."

"Thanks you my dear," he said and left in his car looking very delightful. Bernice walked into her house to see her mother sitting in the settee with Kiah sitting next to her. Kiah jumped out of the settee and ran into her arms calling mom. She kissed him as her mother watched her with a suspicious smile and with the intentions of asking her a question.

"Now what is it mom? Why are you looking at me as if I'm guilty of something?"

'What made you think I want to ask you anything?" her mother asked.

"Mom, seeing the look and smile on your face, is telling me you've a question to ask me."

"Bernice honey, I can see the resemblance between Mr Frats and the boys. So he must have told Eugene and Patrick the truth that he's their father. The boys are very good looking with olive skin. And especial Eugene and Raymond looked so much like him. What I don't understand, why some children should be the pig in the middle and get squashed or being pushed to one side on the account of others mistake which is no fault of the children's. Doesn't the other part of the family realise how hurt children would be when they find out the truth of whose they belong to? No wonder Eugene drove off in rage after he dropped Patrick off. Anyway Bernice why are you smiling so happily," her mom said.

Bernice sighed with relief and happiness and then said, "I'm six or seven weeks pregnant and that means you and Dad will be grandparents a fourth time. Patrick doesn't know as yet, but I'm sure he will be over the moon when I tell him."

Mrs Pearson smile, "Honey, I'm so happy. We should wish for another brother for Kiah to play with. Are you feeling okay honey?"

"I'm feeling fine Mom."

"Well, I think I should go and take in the washing as the weather looks like it is going to rain." Mrs Pearson said and went to get the washing but before she took the washing into the house, she looked up to the sky as tears build up in her eyes as she spoke, "Dear good and loving God, I thank-you greatly to lead my husband in the right path, so that he has guide our grandchildren and myself in the same path. As for my loving daughter Bernice, please let no harm come to her and make her strong, comfortable always and keep us all together in a bonded loving way and shower us with love my faithful and merciful God. Thank-you again" As tears came into her eyes, she looked to the sky again and dried her eyes before she took the basket of clothes into the laundry room and then into the kitchen to see Bernice pouring red wine into a glass. "You're not going to drink that much?" she asked,

"I just fancy some." Bernice told her.

"I think some white milk would be better or a glass of iced lemonade" Mrs Pearson said.

"I agree Mom, but I only fancy some wine. And please don't look at me so hard. Just let me drink this and I promise you that I'll never drink another drop while I'm pregnant."

"Okay Bernice, go on then," Mrs Pearson said and smile.

"Thanks mom and not a word to Patrick about my pregnancy or the wine,"

Two hours later, Patrick left Eugene at the pub and went home to meet Bernice sitting at the table and drinking red wine.

"I see you drinking. What are you celebrating and what for dinner?" he asked, Mrs Pearson got up from her seat and into the kitchen and brought him his hot roasted chicken dinner and put it on the table in front him and said, you meant what for supper.? "

"I'm sorry mom I miss dinner."

"You haven't missed dinner Patrick. You only miss the time. You're eating your dinner." Mrs Pearson said.

Passion laughed, "Daddy you should come home early, you and Uncle Eugene always at the pub."

"That's what you hear your mother say?"

"No daddy, you always told mommy you have to meet Uncle Eugene at the pub."

His mother-in-law looked at him and smiled.

It's nearly five hours since we had dinner and you were not around" Bernice said.

"I'm sorry I'm late coming home honey, I was with the lads and I got carried away playing darts. Just let me eat as I'm starving." he said and pulled off one of the chicken leg and bit it ravenously. Bernice looked hard at him as the children laughed and Passion said "Dad, you should wash your hands."

Bernice looked hard at him again, "What?" he asked smiling,

"Passion's right, you should wash your hands before you eat." Bernice told him smiling as he looked into her eyes.

Bernice shook her head then said "You're setting a good example to the kids by not washing your hands and your table manners are rude and unpleasant. By the way, Mr Frats came to see you earlier. He said to phone him. He sounded seriously desperate to speak to you about some sort of a hotel. Patrick honey, why you so interested in buying hotels all of a sudden and after I told you I'm not interested. I have my hands full with the three kids and another is making a coming into our lives. If I had wanted to go on working, I wouldn't have quit my job. So you can forget buying any hotel."

"Bernice honey, I was buying a hotel for you for your wedding gift. I'm so much in love with you" Then Patrick suddenly got what Bernice told him about she's going to have a baby. He stared at her in surprised before he asked, "We're going to have another baby?"

"Well, that's what I said Patrick honey. If you don't want another child, I can always go to the scrap heap you know?"

"Honey, you try to get rid of my baby and I'll get rid of you. Come here honey, this is calls for a celebration. Honey, I'm in love with you so much." Patrick said

"I'm in love with you too honey. That's why I married you. I don't need hotels or expensive gifts from you to prove that you love me. I just want you to be a good and loving husband and father as I would be a loving wife and mother to you and our children."

Mrs Pearson cleared her throat to get attention. Silence restored immediately "Well, the food is on the table. Should we eat before everything on this table turns into jelly and stone?" Mrs Pearson said as they had a light lunch.

Mr Pearson said a table prayer before they eat.

At this time, Denyah and her family were having roast leg of lamb, cream and roast potatoes, mixed vegetables followed by ice cream and apple crumble. Also their brother Ray and his family were having roast beef dinner.

After Bernice and her family had eaten, she reminded Patrick that he should phone Mr Frats. Patrick went into the living room and phoned him. After, he got back to Bernice and said "I phoned him and everything is okay."

During bedtime, Patrick faced Bernice smiling and said "Honey, have I heard you correctly that you're having our baby?"

"Yes honey, that's what I said. I would let the rest of the family know tomorrow. I would invite all to lunch."

"Tomorrow is Sunday." Patrick said.

"I know honey," Bernice said.

The Sunday morning Bernice phoned Denyah, Meleta, Paula, Lisa, Veda, Jenny and Tracy. Patrick said to Bernice, "What's this, all lady friends you invited to lunch, what about us men?"

"Honey, you take the men to your second home the pub and celebrate."

Aungus laughed saying. "Son, you can't argue with the women. We'll just have to gate crash for food."

Two 'o'clock on the Sunday afternoon Bernice's friends and their children arrive for lunch. After lunch Bernice persuaded them to spend the rest of the evening and she told her friends to phone their husbands and asked them to come.

The wives phoned their husbands and invited them to Bernice's home. That Sunday was turned out to be very enjoyable with plenty good food, drinks and music and everyone was having a good time. Much later in the evening, Mr Frats called again to see Patrick as he thought it might be a good time. Patrick refused to see him but Bernice convinced him telling him Mr Frats is more of gentleman than Mr Lake was.

Patrick said nothing but looked at Bernice. "You can look at me all you want, but just search your heart for an answer and you'll come up with just how you his children were robbed of parenthood. He was robbed in the same way honey. And it wasn't easy for him either."

Patrick nodded.

"Honey, just hear what he has to say then tell him you're no longer interesting in buying any hotels. But be nice."

"Okay Bernice, I will speak to him then after, I wish he would leave us alone."

Patrick met Mr Frats outside the door, "You asked me to phone you, which I did. I'm no longer wanted to buy any hotel or anything else. So would you please leave me alone from here onward?"

"Patrick I only want to know you better. Is that so wrong?" Mr Frats asked.

"Look Mr Frats, All I need from you is to leave me and my family alone. I had one dad and I don't need another. Beside, I'm very busy entertaining my family and friends. If only the hotel you came to speak to me about, as I told you, I've change my mind and I'm sorry you came here for nothing."

"I understand what you said Patrick, I came to tell you that I was out of order to tell you I'm your dad even though I've told you the truth. I'm sorry and I won't be bothering you again or any member of the family for that matter." Mr Frats said but looking pale and remorseful. He then turned to leave as tears fill his eyes.

"Wait. Please wait." Patrick asked him. Mr Frats stood nervously with his back turned as pull out of his jacket pocket a handkerchief and dried his eyes before he faced Patrick. "Are you really our dad?"

"Yes Patrick. I'm your dad as well as Eugene, Raymond, Carlton. As for your sister Jenny, I'm not sure but she could be my daughter too. After your mother went into hiding with you all, I didn't know where to find any of you. I've searched long and hard for years, months and days without success. I have realized that none of you need what I have as I knew all five of you are well off with money my father has inherited you. But I do need you all. The five of you-Patrick, I have proof you are all my biological children and proof that wicked false woman molested your brother Eugene which you and Eugene saw a few days ago in my office. I'm sorry for you my son, if that's not enough to convince you. Well I came here for nothing. As for your brother Eugene, he is as stubborn as his grandfather, my father. Poor me,"

"Poor all of us that think that woman were our mother." Patrick said.

Just then Eugene walked over to Mr Frats and Patrick. "I saw both of you were talking before I walked over to you. Don't stop on the account of me. However, what is he doing here?" Eugene asked Patrick.

"Mr Frats is here on business" Patrick said smiling behind his guilty feeling. Eugene then faced Mr Frats and said "Why don't you get the hell out of our lives and leave us alone."

"Eugene leave him be! He's here because I have invited him." Patrick said.

"Well, it's time I take my family and myself home. You want a second father, you're welcome to him, but just don't come running to me when things get beyond you."

"Eugene, I think you're so unreasonable. I didn't think that I would bring myself to speak to you in this way, but I do believe Mr Frats told us the truth."

"What truth Patrick? That the man we just met, he's our dad?"

"Yes Eugene, I do believed he's my dad, as well as yours, Ray and Carl and even Jenny"

"And what about the dad that brought us up Patrick? And who gave us everything we have."

"Eugene, he gave us nothing but lies and returned what he stole from us. Our wealth came from our dad's dad. This daddy, not the lied and cheating one we used to call dad. However, he also had a duty, a duty to see that we were okay after he stole us from our real dad. And as to that wife of his, she murdered our true mother. Thanks to this man that you addressed him as. Without him I wouldn't have known the truth. Eugene, I

don't know about you, but for me, now I found my true dad, the hell I should lose him
again. I want to get to know him. I also wouldn't want you and me to be enemies. I love
you brother and I'm also asking you to help me close in on this case."

"Patrick brother, you follow your heart. Forget the dad we had, but I can't."

"Eugene, our true dad has showed us proof. He seems to be a very honest. He
knows we don't need anything from him, so why should he came looking for us and tell
us he's our dad if it's not true."

"Patrick, it is pointless talking to you. I have to go now." Eugene said and he left
with his family. At home, Denyah watched him swill down four large shots of whiskey in
less than half-an- hour. "Eugene, what's wrong?" she asked him looking worried over
him.

"Nothing, just leave me alone." he said angrily.

"I would when you tell what is wrong that is causing you to drink so heavily."
Denyah told him.

He carried another glass of whiskey to his lips. Denyah knock the glass out of his
hand as she looked hard at him. Very aggressively he pushed her away but she managed
to keep her balance and said, "Eugene, I've watched you turned from a gentle person to
a savage animal. Your behaviour is reminding me of ex-husband. And to tell you the
truth, I don't think I want you to be around us while you're behaving in this way."

"I'm sorry Den, he said with tears in his eyes then he went on to say "Mr Frats told
Patrick and me that he's the dad of me, Patrick, Ray, Carl and maybe Jenny."

Denyah intervened saying "Maybe he has told you the truth. He might be thirty nine
years late with the news, but why should he be bothering any of you if it's not true."
Denyah closed her eyes painfully before she sat on his lap and say "Eugene honey, Mr
Frats is father to all five of you. I was told by my mother that one of your mother's
friends Mrs Ramsey told her that your mother was early pregnant with Jenny when she
ran out on Mr Frats and went to and live with Judge Lake somewhere where your true
dad wouldn't find you all. You boys were very young then, and didn't understand what
was going on as your true mother and dad didn't live together. You were three then, two
years older than Ray then Carl followed. Patrick was nearly four years old. I only knew
about this, two weeks ago. However, your true father had left England and went to live
somewhere in Spain for twenty years before he returned to England again and settled
somewhere in Dudley before he moved on Mere Street in Manchester. Mr Frats is a
good father. He has never given up searching for any of you. Now he's found you, why
do you want to shut him out? Do you really hate him so much Eugene? I believe he's
your father and all of you are his children. After Mr Frats settled in Dudley for four
years, he moved to Manchester and lived there for thirteen years and now he's back in
Birmingham as he wanted to be near all of you.

As you were children, Mr Frats also learned that your true mother was poisoned by
overdose tablets and died days later. Somehow, he found out about you boys and where
you were but he couldn't do anything because he was afraid or too ashamed to drag you
all through the mud. And because he loves you all so much, he left all five of you where
you were. Mr Lake was a decent person, but the cheating wife of his, she's very wicked.
Still, he should have told you the truth that he's not the father of any of you. That
woman stole all of you away from your biological father and your mother. Eugene, bad
things had happened to you when you were twelve. Wesley showed the photos of her
seducing you, hoping I would leave you and run back to him. I told him I'd fallen in love
with you and I still am. I love you so much Eugene but as I said, I wouldn't want to be

around you and watching you turning into a savage and tear yourself apart. What has happened to that handsome gentle man I fell in love with? What would I tell my children in ten years or later if we separated, that their father was a lovely and kind father but I left him because he had turned into a vicious animal, honey, I don't want that. I would like us to grow old and still in love. Take a hard long look at yourself in a mirror and then you might be able to come up trumps whether Mr Lake was or Mr Frats is your father. As for me, I know which one. Also for you, it would be easy as you only have to take a DNA test from the one that is living."

Eugene broke down crying and said, "Why didn't he fight for us when we most needed him."

"Because he was afraid he might never see any of you again if he had lost the case. And besides, how could he fight a high court judge when he had nothing to fight the judge with. So you see Eugene, I'm on Mr Frats' side even though I could have got on well with Mr Lake. Incidentally, do you think if Mr Frats didn't love and care about you all, would he have bothered about any of you, knowing that you all are well off because of his dad, remember he wants nothing from any of you but to be the father that he so longs to be. Please Eugene, for the sake of your brothers and our children, try and not to let ignorance come between you and your true father. Go to your father honey, as he has cleared the way for you. I'm sure you wouldn't love your adopted father any less. I wish my father had come looking for me when I needed him and even now. You and your brothers are so lucky you get to know your father. As for me, I might never get the chance to know my father." Denyah said.

After Eugene listened to Denyah, he broke down crying and then went to see his brother Patrick.

Later that evening, Fay went to see Denyah. At first Denyah refused to see her. Then after Mrs Brown pleaded with Denyah, she met Fay by the door. "Why have you come here Fay?" Denyah asked her

Fay looked on at her showing in her eyes pity and said "I'm so sorry for the terrible things I have done to you. And I'm asking you to forgive me. But my reason for being here is because of our mother and our sister Blanch. They both need your help. I'm not here for me. If you kick me away from your door, I deserve it. But please help them both for the love of God. Mother tried many times to phone you but I threatened her if she does, I would leave home. Mother cried bitterly over you. She so wanted to tell you how sorry she were for the way she'd treated you."

This brought back bad feelings to Denyah that her eyes fill with tears. Fay broke down crying.

"Okay Fay you can come in." Denyah told her.

As Fay walked in, Mrs Brown rushed into the kitchen and brought her a hot cup of milk. "Drink this," Mrs Brown told her. "It will relax you" Fay took the milk with a smile and sat down as Denyah told her too.

"Drink you milk Fay." Mrs Brown told her while she stood over Fay.

After Fay finished drinking her milk, Mrs Brown took the cup and said, "I'm glad you've the decency to come to your sister and ask for help. At this time Denyah was sitting in the living room breastfeeding her ten week old baby son.

Fay's yawning was telling Mrs Brown that she were hungry or tired. Mrs Brown asked her "When was the last time you've eaten?"

Faith barely smiled as she said. "I'd a couple of toast this morning."

"Poor child, come with me into the kitchen and I'll fix you something to eat."

Fay followed behind Mrs Brown into the kitchen and she sat waiting until Mrs Brown heated up some food for her. "Thanks." she said and she began to eat. Mrs Brown left her eating and went to Denyah telling her "I remembered what you told me about how mean she was to you. But don't fight evil with evil," Just then Fay walked up to Denyah and smooth her right palm of her hand over the baby's head. Denyah looked up at her and shifted her baby on the other side of her breast to avoid her touching her baby again. Mrs Brown looked at Denyah with sad eyes and Denyah smiled and then passed her baby to Fay. Fay glowed as she looked very happy. Mrs Brown smiled and left Fay holding the baby. Fay spent nearly an hour helping Mrs Brown ironing sheets and clothes and playing frustration with Paris and Jade B. Denyah gave her two hundred pounds to buy food for her mother and Blanch and asked her to keep in touch.

After Fay left, Mrs Brown said to Denyah "As I said, I know they all treated you wrongly but I'm glad she came and asked for help. And my heart is pleased that you did not turn her away."

Meanwhile Eugene and Patrick went to find Mr Frats at his home, they chatted, played blackjack and had a couple shots of Jack Daniels and laughed. After Mr Frats beat Eugene five to one and Patrick seven to two playing blackjack, the three of them had a hearty laugh. "Old man, you must teach me to master that game soon." Eugene told him. "Me too," Patrick said, and looked at the time on his wrist watch and said, "Well old man, I must say good night and be off home before the missus chains the door." Mr Frats laughed heartily. Eugene and Patrick got on their feet and were ready to leave. Mr Frats outstretched his hands for a handshake. Eugene smiled and hugged him instead. Patrick smiled and also hugged him too. He then saw Eugene and Patrick out. Eugene said, "Dad I'm sorry to have doubted you. Would you like to join us for drink tomorrow evening?"

"Sure- sure, I would love to." Mr Frats said smiling.

"Patrick and I would call for you about seven. Well good night dad." Eugene said.

"Good night sons."

Eugene and Patrick got in their car and Mr Frats closed his door smiling and got ready for bed. The following evening Eugene, Patrick and Mr Frats went and had a drink in the Crown and Cushion pub.

Two week later Denyah went to visit her mother. They both cried and hugged each other. A little while after her mother said. "Den, I'm so sorry and ashamed of what I've done to you" As her mother was going on to say more, Denyah said "Mom, please don't say any more. Wesley had us ripping out one another's throat and I know what you've done to me, it was to do with Wesley. You should have asked me if I was unfaithful. And I would have said no, as it was the truth. But I realized you were as weak as the rest of us. Wesley has put you against me as he has done with the others. You did what you believed was right as he had us all under his evil claws. We all suffered by him. If I could forgive him, I could forgive you. I'm so sorry to know you're sick. I have to go now. Tell Blanch I'm sorry I didn't get to see her, but she has my address and the girls would like to see her again. Here, this is for you and Blanch."

"What is it?" her mother asked.

"There's a thousand pounds. I would come and see you again. I would like to speak to Fay about a job and Blanch about staying on at school for another year and then to University when she leaves school. Blanch told me she would like to study to be a solicitor or an actress. I would like to help her to achieve her goal. I would be happy to pay for her studies." Denyah said.

"Would you do that for us?" Denyah mother asked.

"Mother, I love my family and I would do the best for any of you and I thank God that he is given us a second chance."

"Denyah, I'm so happy you gave us a second chance in spite of what we'd done to you." her mother said and burst out crying. Denyah hugged her mother to assure her that she loved her.

"You don't have to look after us. I have done you so much wrong." her mother said.

"Mother, would you please stop crying. For all the wrongs my ex husband has done to us, he's already paying heavily and he still would. For I know there is a loving and living God that has now rooted out hate and injects the very best in us. I am very wealthy now. I have a handsome baby son with a loving partner, two adopted daughters and an adopted mother and brother. I also got you back mother and the sister who had despised me because of my wicked ex, as well my other lovely sister Blanch and as I went to St.Kitts to meet my other sister and her family. So Mother, we must bury the past and go forward. I haven't stopped loving any of you. And I will not! We should be stronger together now. Neither Wesley or anyone else can divide us again but God." Denyah said.

Shortly after Denyah left, Fay walked in with enough groceries for at least two weeks.

"Denyah were here." her mother told Fay.

"Yes. I know. I saw her car turn the corner. I should ask her to buy me a car as my hands are hurting from the carrying these bags." Fay said smiling. Then her eyes caught the edge of the money in the half opened white envelope. She picked the envelope up off the table, bent the edge back and saw the amount of money. "Did you ask her for this mom?"

"No Fay, she gave it to me. She said you could have a job in one of Eugene's restaurants or hotels if you want."

"No mother, tell her I don't want another job. Looking after you is more than enough. I know she means well for us, but I would tell her when I see her I can't take any job as I'm looking after you." Fay said then picked the envelope up and gave it to her mother saying, "Here is your money. You best put it somewhere safe until Monday - I will go and pay the rent and whatever else we owe and there would be about seven hundred left." her mother nodded her head and took the envelope with the money.

When Denyah got home, she spoke to Mrs Brown of the untidy condition her mother and sisters lived. "The carpet's very tatty and filthy and Blanch bed and the furniture looked like they're ready for the bonfire."

Two weeks later, she bought her mother and her sisters Fay and Blanch a beautiful three bedroom house two streets away from where Bernice and her family lived.

Denyah had their house beautifully furnished. Her mother cried and Blanch hugged Denyah and told her "I love you. Fay watched Denyah impetuously and said "You know me" Denyah grinned slightly and drifted off to say goodbye to her mother. Before Denyah got into her car, Fay fled out of the house and caught up with a wide grin on her face. "Can I do anything for you Fay?" Denyah asked her.

"Well yes, I know we're not close at the moment, but I was meaning to ask you if you could loan me some money."

"Why don't you ask Wesley, he might still have some of my forty eight thousand pounds he stole from me?" Denyah said.

"Den however I've also learnt my lesson. In other words, I almost paid with my life for my cheating on you. And to say, I would have deserved it. Den, I never thought I would beg for you to forgive me. But, please do forgive me. And about the loan, please forget I asked you. Kiss my nieces and my baby nephew for me. As for Mrs Brown, she's a lovely mom. Give her my love." Fay said and went into her house.

Denyah got into her car and thought for a while before she went and knocked at the door, Fay answered the door, "Have you forget something?" Fay asked her.

"Yes Fay, I forgot to thank you for pushing me out of the door. If you were not there, heaven knows what Wesley might have done to me. In spite of what you did to me, I never thought I would bring myself to thank you either. Thank-you Fay, this is for you. It's not a loan. I want you to have it as a gift from your nieces and your nephew."

As Fay refused to take the cheque, Denyah, said, "Okay, it's a loan, you pay me back when you marry that rich handsome man." Denyah laughed then asked "How would you like to baby sit for me sometime?" Fay smiled. Then her smiled turned into laughter that Denyah had to laugh as well. Fay then took the cheque and looked hard on it, "Den, I haven't asked you for this." she said.

"I know. You haven't told me how much you want. I've also know if you didn't need the money, you wouldn't have asked me." Denyah said.

"This is too much. I only want to buy a car - second hand." Fay said.

"Why would you buy second-hand to give you dozens of problems, when you can buy a brand new car and change it every year problem free. Besides, if you have to take your nieces to the zoo, you will need a reliable car." Denyah said.

"Den, you're so right. But would you trust me with your children after what I did to you?"

"Fay, I think I can now trust you with my life. We both were too weak to fight Wesley, but as we're now free of him, I don't see why we can't bypass the past and go forward as loving and caring sisters."

"Thanks, Den, but even if I buy a new car I won't be spending a hundred thousand pounds" Fay said and hugged Denyah in tears as she said "thanks again."

Denyah smiled, then Fay explained to her saying "Den, I have to take care of mother and Blanch that is why I can't take the waitress job. I'm sure Eugene will find someone to work in his restaurants or his hotels."

"I understand" Denyah said and left in her car while Fay watched and waved goodbye before she went into her house to cook their dinner.

The following Saturday afternoon, Denyah took the children and Mrs Brown to see her mother. As her mother didn't expect them, she didn't prepare anything for them. "Why didn't you phone to let me know you were bringing the children and Mrs Brown to see me? I would have prepared something for the children to eat."

"Mom, I fed the girls before we came."

"What about you, have you eaten?" Mrs Brown asked concerned.

"Yes, a couple of cream crackers and a slice of cheese about an hour ago."

"Well, we brought enough lunch for three. I hope you like roast chicken, rice and sweet potatoes." Mrs Brown said.

"Well, I would be grateful for mine now as I'm starving." Denyah's natural mother said. Mrs Brown gave her a plate of food and dished out two more plates for Fay and Blanch and left their food covered on the cooker.

"I don't even think I have a drink to give to my grandchildren." Denyah's natural mother said.

"Don't worry mom, we brought some goodies for them as I thought you might not have what they want." Denyah said.

After Denyah, Mrs Brown and her children spent a long time with Denyah's natural mother, Denyah told her it's time she took the children home as the night was getting very dark and bringing in chilliness . Then as Mrs Brown was helping the children with their coats on, a knock came on the door. Denyah answered the door to a middle aged white woman. She looked at Denyah and said. "I only want to know if Mrs Holliday is alright - I always have a look in on her when Blanch and Fay are not at home."

"Oh I'm Denyah her daughter and we were just getting ready to leave. But I am sure she would be okay as I'll see her in bed before we left."

"Well, Denyah I should leave - nowadays we can't trust anyone especially the druggies that don't care who they rip apart to fulfil their needs for a fix. Well, goodnight Denyah. And let your mother know I came to see her will you. And I'm pleased you were here as she shouldn't put too much strain on her lame knee as she's always complaining how painful her knee is. Oh I'm Brenda Archer your mother's next door neighbour."

"Well goodnight Mrs Archer and thank you very much to help take care of mother. She's very lucky to have a friend and neighbour like you." Denyah said.

"Well goodnight and say goodnight to you mother from me, and tell her I will pop in and see her tomorrow." Mrs Archer said and left.

Denyah closed the door and went to tell her mother. "Mrs Archer had come to see if you were okay, but when I told her I'm your daughter, she said she'll pop in tomorrow."

Denyah mother said. "Mrs Archer is so nice to me."

"Well mother, I'm sorry we have to leave as the children are getting tired and the baby won't settle until he's in his cot."

"Mrs Brown, Thank you for helping me with my bath and for the food."

"Well Mrs Holliday would you be alright when we leave?" Mrs Brown asked.

"Yes Mrs Brown I would just like to go to the toilet and then to bed."

"Would you like a cup of tea before we leave?"

"Just a glass of water please," Mrs Holliday said.

Mrs Brown fetched Denyah's mother a tall glass of water and saw her in bed and Denyah and her girls kissed her mother before she dimmed her mother's bedroom lights and asked "Mother will you be okay after we leave?"

"Yes, of course Den, Blanch will be here soon, she's doing a part time job at weekends and she usually get home just after nine. Thanks for coming and to bring my grandchildren and Mrs Brown. She's like a true mom to you." Denyah's true mother said.

"Yes, she is." Denyah said.

"Well good night Janice and I'll come again to see you soon and do take it easy on that knee as you just had the operation." Mrs Brown said.

"Goodnight Mrs Brown. And thank you so much for coming" Denyah mom said.

The children kissed their grandmother goodnight again and Denyah put her baby son into her mothers' arms. She kissed the baby on his forehead and said "Nan loves you and your sisters very much." she then passed the baby to Denyah and said, "Denyah I always have headaches. However, thanks for the food, it's very tasty and I really enjoy eating every bit except the bones." she smiled.

"I'm glad. You should come and spend sometime with your grandchildren." Mrs Brown told her.

"Yes I must." Denyah mother said. Denyah and her girls kissed her again before they left and Denyah promised her she would take her to a private doctor to see about her headache.

One hour later, Fay and Blanch went home to find the dinner that Mrs Brown had left for them. "Mom, I see you managed to cook, where did you get sweet potatoes from?" Blanch asked.

"I did not cook the food you've just eaten, Mrs Brown and your sister Denyah brought it for us. You should see the baby. He's beautiful." her mother said.

"I saw him mother and he's so lovely." Fay said.

"I would go and see him tomorrow." Blanch said. And the next day Blanch went to see the baby. "He's beautiful just like mom said." Blanch said.

Two weeks later, Denyah booked her mother into a private clinic where she would be having tests for her constant headaches and pain in her hips. After the doctors found what was wrong, she had the best treatment given to her after Denyah paid for her left hip operation. After her mother was going on five weeks in the hospital, she was regaining full health except she would still have light migraines but her knee and hip were healing nicely.

The doctor told Denyah, "Your mother's headache was due to developing blood pressure which was due to stress." The doctor's pause and smiled, then went on to say. "With your mother knee and hip problem being solved and getting treatment, I don't think she would be worrying too much now and her headache will eventually cure. However, she's okay and she would be discharged next Thursday. Mrs Davis, I would like you to keep your eye on her for the first three weeks. Would you see that she only walks with the frame we will be lending her until she can balance using a walking stick for support? However, I think she needs some one to stay with her when going to the toilet for at least two weeks. Then after six weeks she should be able to take short distance walking with her walking stick in and outside the house as far as the yard. The operation has left her hip with two pins connected to her bones for at least three to four months. The walking stick is to help take the pressure off her knee and hip so that her bones will be strengthened and heal nicely. As for her migraine, it should be lessened and then completely cured as I explained to you earlier."

After ten weeks, Denyah mom was walking much stronger and her migraine were completely cured as the doctor's said.

Every week end, Eugene and Patrick would take Mr Frats to have a pint. And three months later, Eugene went to see Mr Frats at his home and ended up having dinner with him. Over dinner, as they spoke, they both were in tears of joy and laughter as they were having a father and son meal together and said they loved each other. Mr Frats was so happy that he kissed Eugene on his forehead and said "You are the stubborn son like my father. And you're also that missing link that I've so long wanted to complete the family. I knew why none of you want anything from me as my father had shared his wealth amongst you after I told him he has four grandsons and a granddaughter. He started me off with one restaurant and now I have eighty-four hotels and sixty seven restaurants here, Italy, and in America. I have no other family but the five of you. I would be so grateful if each of you would take a small gift of ten millions and one of my hotels or restaurants each to welcome me as your father. You're the only children God has blessed me with. There's no other children, and there's no one else who can I leave my entire wealth too but the five of you and my grandchildren. Eugene, like me and your great grand father, I see you're in the same business. We have something in common. But one of my sons might follow in my father's footsteps and go in the building business."

After Eugene listened to his long lost dad with interest, Eugene embarrassed him and said, "Well pops, it's time I went home. I will see you soon."

Mr Frats got up the same time as Eugene, and they shook hands. He then watched Eugene drive away before he walked in to his mansion smiling like he had just won the world cup. As Eugene got home, he went to Denyah and said, "Honey, I had dinner with the dad I almost cast away. He's a gentleman."

Denyah hugged him and said "I'm so happy you went and saw him."

"Den, he invited all of us, his family to a get together dinner next Saturday evening. He said we're his family. He even wanted us to invite our friends."

The next Saturday evening, Eugene and the others of his family as well his friends were dining with Mr Frats in one of his hotels - "The Savers Hotel". Mr Frats' cook put on a spread of different food. The soft music complimented the occasion. The hotel was looking spectacular with cream and lemon beautiful chairs and matching tables cloths with flowers laid on every table. And with high giant vases spaced out and sitting along the long and wide hotel room in corners beside large tall palm trees standing in large white buckets, giant exquisite patterned rugs covered large sections on the hotel floor and large framed pictures of his parents and grandparents and older family of the Frats hung proudly in the centre on the high partition on the four sides of the partition that complimented the beautiful painted white hotel. There was also a very large white magnificent see-through crystal boat set in a section of the partition facing the diners. When light up, it looks magnificently beautiful displaying three dimensions of multicoloured lights to entice customers. The see-through scenery of the fifty two inches ship was a master piece in its own class and seems to be looking like it was sailing in clear deep blue sea. This handmade ship was spectacular to look at with the setting of sunrise in the background over the rich green mountain and the three wide streams of water falls running from the mountain into the deep blue sea gliding gently towards the ship. Mr Frats claimed his father had designed the ship. As Eugene and the others admiring the Frats family pictures, Mr Frats said. "Those faces, goes back more than two hundred years of four generations. Soon, I will tell you boys who they are. But some of them I hadn't the chance to get to know them. Now we must feed our faces."

After every one had eaten, Mr Frats got up and said "I gratefully thank all of you for coming and to make me feel very happy and important. I do hope that I will not offend anyone by giving you a thank-you gift." Pausing, Mr Frats had looked nearly to tears as he breathe slowly out and said, "Please don't slap me down for what I'm about to do."

"Look here Dad Frats, if I didn't like you, I wouldn't be here. You're okay, and to prove that I do like you, I would leave your son Raymond and marry you" Paula said joking and with inspiration.

Mr Frats laughed heartily so did everyone else. "Now would you please tell us what you about to say," Paula said.

Just then the children started running and playing through the hotel with smiles and making noises. Mr Frats watched them with cheerful smiles for some times before he turned to face his adult family and friends and said, yesterday I had nothing and now I have everything. From his jacket pocket he took a set of blue envelopes and held them proudly in his hands. Still wearing his happy smile, he gave one envelope to Denyah, Bernice, Veda, Paula, Meleta, Lisa, Fay, Kelly, Ivy and Tracy, Cindy, Claire and then hugged Jenny.

They opened the envelope to find a thank-you card and an invitation to attend his sixty-seven birthday in the coming five weeks at his home.

After Paula had a couple of gin and tonics, she pulled Mr Frats out of his seat to dance with him. After Mr Frats had one dance with her, he said, "Paula I must rest now. I thank you for a most enjoyable evening."

But Paula thought he was making excuses to get away from her. So she shouted to him, "I do hope you like me in my black skin, for that's all you shall see me in."

Mr Frats laughed heartily and took his seat and dried the sweat off his face, he laughed out heartily again and so much that tears came in his joyful eyes. Then he said to Paula, "I wouldn't want to see you in any other." All looked at Paula laughing as she was comical and had a great sense of humour. Her husband Ray danced with her and then kissed her in the presence of everyone and announced "I love her with all my heart" But as she was looking tipsy and knocking back gin and tonic, Ray told her no more drinking but she insisted she should drink more if she wanted, Ray took her by herself and warned her not to have anymore strong drinks.

She pulled away and said, "I drink if I want" Ray slapped her face and threatened her, "You drink anymore drop and I'll take you home and give her a good hiding." She put her arms around his neck saying. "Honey, I'm sorry." for the rest of the evening she drank soft drinks mostly fruit juice.

Eugene smiled strongly.

"You can dry that smile off your face." Denyah told him.

The party was well over and Mr Frats thanked them all to make him feeling happy on that special evening.

"This is one time, I shall never forget." Mr Frats said and the children kissed him on his

face and everyone wished him good night and his sons Eugene, Patrick, Ray, Carl and daughter Jenny hugged him goodnight and his daughter-in laws kissed him on his face before they went home.

The following Saturday Paula invited Mr Frats to dinner and he accepted gladly and attended. He again met everyone including the grandchildren. By this time, Mr Frats knew everyone and by name. Bernice and Paula announced to him that he would be gaining another two grandchildren. He went to Bernice and Paula and kissed them both on their cheeks. As Paula was so barefaced, she said to him "It wouldn't harm you to give your little grand a peck pushing forward her pregnant tummy. As everyone applauded, Mr Frats smiled and Paula pushed forward her pregnant tummy to him insisting he has to kiss her baby. Mr Frats then looked at Paula in surprise and said bashfully, "Now I got to know all of you my lovely family, and I wouldn't want us to separate ever!"

"Well, if you don't kiss your son's son, when he's born I would tell him you refused to kiss him." Paula said to Mr Frats.

Then Eugene and Raymond said "Go on dad. Kiss your grandson and makes his mother happy."

Mr Frats looked hard at Eugene and Ray before he kissed Paula's tummy quickly and then said shyly as his face turned red as beetroot, "It wouldn't be fair not kissing Bernice's," Everyone laughed and Bernice let him kiss her tummy too. Again, that evening was a blessing for him as he'd enjoyed himself so much.

That early night Eugene drove him home in his car, while Patrick followed behind in their dad's Mercedes.

After Eugene and Patrick saw him home, and knew he was all right, they left.

One month later Eugene, Patrick, Raymond, Carl and Jenny added their father's name Frats to make their names double-barrelled. Even though their step-parents had cheated them out of their rightful names, they decided that they should keep his name Lake out of respect for him.

The news of Mr Frats and his reunion with his long lost four grown-up sons and a daughter spread like wild fire - Denyah had to explain to her adopted brother Ryan that Eugene has added Frats to his name and that made her and Eugene's baby son Carter Lake-Frats Junior.

After Eugene added Frats to his name and then asked his deceiving stepmother. "Are you my mother?" She lowered her head and murmured and said "Of course, I'm your mother,"

As Eugene looked hard in her face, she turned and walked away towards the kitchen. "Eugene." she shouted.

"My true mother crumbled in her grave poisoned by you!"

"What was that all about?" Jenny asked Eugene.

"Ask that blood sucking bitch! Let her tell you how strong the tablets were when she dosed our mother to be with the next deceiving bastard that we were calling dad."

"He's dead. So let sleeping dogs lie." Jenny said feeling annoyed.

"Jenny, I won't expect you to understand any of this. But I shan't forget what that evil woman had done to my mother, nor will I ever forgive her for what I heard she'd done to me. I wondered if that man we were calling dad had known that our mother was murdered by this evil bitch!" Eugene said.

Jenny was dumb-struck with her mouth wide open by what Eugene said that she just stood and looked at him. "I'm not the one you should look at. Look at that evil bitch and count how much wicked streams you can see on her wrinkled ugly face" Eugene told Jenny.

Even though Jenny heard what Eugene had said, she couldn't bring herself to believe he was telling the truth. After Jenny heard the dreadful news about her real mother and her deceitful stepmother, she had looking drained and painful as it was too much for her to take in all of a sudden. In hurting feelings, she faced Eugene and said, "I think you should leave!"

Eugene kissed her on her right cheek and said, "I think you're right. The foul smell coming from her is beginning to choke me! If you should need me, give me a call or you can reach me at my home" Eugene then walked to the front door to leave when his deceiving mother Mrs Lake held on to him saying, "I brought you up to what you are. I love you."

Eugene pushed her down on her back saying, "Keep your filthy hands off me. I'm not twelve anymore. You touch me again and I will slaughter you like a pig. You explain to my little sister here how and why you murdered our mother and how old I was when you seduced me and how many times after drugging my cocoa." Jenny looked at her deceitful mom in disbelief and then cried before she went to her room and lock herself in. After she stopped crying, she packed some clothes and drove herself to Eugene and Denyah's home where she spent three weeks.

After the three weeks Jenny spent with Eugene and Denyah, the suspense was burdening her. She went home and asked her fake mother "Is their any truth in what my brother said three weeks ago?"

Her mother cried, as she lowered her head and her face showed guilt and shameful as she mumbled, "I did it to him twice only. I was drunk. Forgive me."

"Were you drunk as well when you had Denyah's ex-husband, or you only done it to him twice too and sorry?"

"Jenny, that was before Denyah's time. I ended the affair when I met your father."

"You get away from me! I despise you for murdering my mother and for taking advantage of my brother when he was only a boy of twelve. How could you be so cruel and heartless to fuck my twelve year old brother after you drugged him? Just look at you - You sick minded bitch! You make my stomach want to heave to vomit. And you know what! You should leave this house before I do what my brother has failed to do. Now I know why you despised Denyah so much because she took Eugene from you that you were fucking under duress. I bet you thought your wicked doing would never come to light. Get you fucking arse out of my home and stay out! You're not welcome here any more. I will hate you for ever!" Jenny said.

Mrs Lake tried to hug her, but she attacked Mrs Lake viciously by strangling her around the throat with her hands and only loosened her hands from around her throat when she saw her knees buckled and her eyes were blinking rapidly. Breathlessly Mrs Lake fell hard knocking the wooden floor. She looked down at Mrs Lake with hate, stepped over her and went to her room and left Mrs Lake struggling to get up. After Mrs Lake fought so hard to get up she fell face down as she went dizzy. After dragging herself to the foot of the stairs she grabbed the railing and held on picking herself up. She was panting for breath. She was straightened her self up and slowly walked up the two flights of stairs when her hands slipped off the rails making her fall and rolled to the bottom of the stairs and banged the left side of her head against the rail post. She cried out to Jenny but because Jenny was crying she did not hear her call. Immediately Mrs Lake developed a nasty bump on the side of her forehead and a gash on her right shin. As Jenny heard her crying, she rushed out of her room, looked down at her smiling. Hopelessly and painfully Mrs Lake looked up at her with begging eyes.

"Why should I help a murdering bitch such as you," Jenny shouted to her then went back into her room, sat on her bed shaking her head vigorously and crying. After some time, she made three attempts at dialling a few numbers to phone Eugene and her fiancée's Curt but banged the phone down and staring at it and then paced the floor for five minutes. She went to the phone again, stretched to pick the phone up but never did. After a moment of thought, she went down stairs to Mrs Lake and saw her chin was bleeding. She stood over her and smiling before she helped her to a seat and said, "Pity you still alive."

"Jenny you don't mean that" Mrs Lake said catching the dripping blood in her hand. Jenny turned her back on her.

"Please Jenny, I need your help."

"I would help to murder you in the same way you murdered my mother! But don't worry. You'll get what coming to you without me dirtying my hands. If its one wicked bitch I hate it's you! "

"Jenny, would you leave me to bleed to death, I'm suffering."

"Why don't you fucking die," Jenny told her and then faced her to see a bump on the left side of her forehead as big as a golf ball and looking fierce. Jenny beginning to shiver with fear and then slowly walked to Mrs Lake and dumped a white bath towel on her lap. Mrs Lake held the towel on her cut before Jenny struggled to help her in her car and she took her to the accident hospital. As there were only a few patients waiting to be seen, she spotted Kelly and Kelly took them into a small room and told them she would go and find a doctor. But as Nurse Kelly saw the bump, she said, "That's a nasty bump. Mrs Lake. Would you like to come with me please?" Jenny and Mrs Lake followed behind Nurse Kelly where she took them in a small room that contained a single bed and a trolley with a pack of tissues and a silver bowl contained cotton buds. Nurse Kelly gave Jenny a medical form to fill in on behalf of Mrs Lake. Jenny stated Mrs Lake and wrote on the form Mrs Lake was drunk that's why she got the bump on her head. Jenny then gave the filled in form to the nurse Kelly. "Thank you" Nurse Kelly said placed the form on the trolley for the doctor. As Kelly was leaving to go and take the filled in form from another patient, she said to Jenny "I'll be right back" A few minutes later she returned with a pretty young black female - Doctor Bracher. Nurse Kelly picked Jenny's filled in form up and gave it to Doctor Bracher. After Doctor Bracher read the statement she passed it back to Nurse Kelly then Doctor Bracher said to Jenny and her mother. "We might have to drain the waste out of the bump."

"She fell down the stairs and bumped her head." Jenny said.

But as Doctor Bracher examined the bump on Mrs Lake's forehead, she replied. "My goodness, you have got a nasty bump." After Doctor Bracher felt the bump, she asked, "Have you been drinking Mrs Lake?"

"She was drunk from evil and she fell." Jenny said with a straight face.

Doctor Bracher looked at Jenny and smiled, as she thought Jenny call alcohol evil. After she attended to the bump, she said to Jenny, "I'm Doctor Bracher."

"Yes, your names on your badge." Jenny said.

"Well, I would like your mother to take one of these tablets four times a day for six days to clear the blood clot and I'm sure your mother will be okay in a week or two. Doctor Bracher then gave Jenny some tables and told her. "Well good bye Mrs Lake, if after two weeks you're still in pain, I would like to see you. But I'm sure you will be fine. Goodbye Mrs Lake and daughter,"

"Goodbye doctor." Jenny said.

"Doctor Bracher left.

As Jenny and her fake mother walked to the out patient door, a black woman said to them, "You were lucky coming when almost everyone has gone. I was here waiting for nearly three hours before a doctor saw me. Now I have to pay twice the fare. Anyway, my taxi has arrived. You want to put an ice pack on that bump to help take down the swelling as it is very swollen and badly impacted with bad blood. It should have been lanced to drain the bruised blood. Still I guess the doctors know what they are doing." The woman left in a taxi.

Two days later, Mrs Lake went to see her doctor complaining of severe headache and neck pain. After she told her doctor she fell and her doctor saw the blood bruised bump, she sent her back to the hospital with a written letter stating the bump should have been lanced and drained. After a thorough check at the hospital, the bump was lanced and cleaned before she was discharged with an appointment to see Doctor Marsh the following week Wednesday morning at ten thirty. But before Mrs Lake left the hospital, she was given a five day dose of tablets to prevent infection.

"Please Miss Lake, see that your mother take her tablets as prescribed." said Doctor Marsh. "Thanks doctor, I'll see that the evil bitch takes an overdose." Jenny said under her breath. Even though Jenny hated her mother, she still cared for her until she was well again. But in spite of their living together, Jenny kept her at a distance. However, as Mrs Lake noticed Jenny refused to eat from her, she said "Jenny dear, I would never hurt you. I love you."

Its now nine weeks since Denyah's baby son was born and Eugene's ex girlfriend phone Denyah. "Hello" Denyah answered. "Who's this? Denyah asked."

"Never mind who I am. I'm trying to save your baby."

"From whom or what," Denyah asked.

"You stupid bitch, Why don't you listen to me, I once told you I would like to kill you, but I've by passed all that hate and jealousness I had towards you. All I care about is Eugene's baby. I would like you to take me serious. I once loved Eugene, but I realised I'd to cut him loose and moved on. That bitch of your mother-in-law is planning to hurt your baby. Possible kill him. I heard her said once someone killed a baby by planting a needle in the crown of a baby head. That woman frightened me. I can't give you my name, but for the sake of your son, please take me serious. That woman is wicked and she would do anything to split you and Eugene. She paid a man by the name of Robert Jay three thousand pounds to rape and kill your Nurse friend and she also had Officers Tom and Finch killed and then blackmailed Robert Jay into going to the police and tell them he saw your ex fighting with his police mates earlier before their bodies were discovered in their cars. That bitch aim to frame your ex for the murders of your nurse friend and his two mates. She also vouched she won't rest until she see your ex locked up for life for telling you and his friends he had sex with her. Denyah your ex was taken in and questioned but as the police found no way he was linked to any of the murders he was released without charge. Denyah your ex might be a wicked bastard, but I don't think he murdered Nurse James or his colleagues. These murders I think have something to do with evil Mrs Lake. That evil bitch had them killed and wanted to pin their murders on your ex for telling you he had sex with her as I have stated. His police friends also knew. That's why she had them killed and tried to frame your ex for their murders and had Robert Jay beaten up and threatened him she would have his wife killed if he doesn't tell the police your ex beat him up. I confronted her with vital information that she paid Robert Jay to murder Nurse James and your ex's friends. But she doesn't know who I am as I attacked her by phoning. Denyah, have you seen the midday news on TV?"

"No. I hardly have time to look after my children, much less to sit around the TV and listen to News" Denyah said with mixed feeling as her thought clearly focussed on Eugene's ex flame that slapped her in the toilet.

As Denyah breathe out in lamentation, the caller said, "Well, I wish you'd listen to the six thirty new this morning and the mid-day. Robert Jay's body were discovered by his wife early this morning. Police claimed he was covered in petrol and set alight after he was knocked out unconscious after he'd stabbed himself as police claimed it self conflicted. Denyah, Robert Jay came to see me late yesterday and he appears to be very agitated and frightened. He also gave me a tape saying if anything should happened to him, I must give it to the police. Well I made a copy before I handed the tape to the police but after they listened to the tape, I was told the tape was blank. I know the police were lying after they found out Mrs Lake was a Judges wife. I would give you proof that that evil bitch paid to have your friend raped and killed as she thought your friend would harbour Eugene to be with you. Denyah, when Robert Jay broke down and cried in his mom's house, I watched him gulp down over a half bottle of whiskey straight. I told him to go to the police with what he told me, but he said they wouldn't believe him as Mrs Lake is Judge Lake's wife."

"However, whoever you might be, thanks for telling me." Denyah said to the caller. Then she asked her, "How did you come to have my phone number?"

"Does it matter, look Denyah, my reason for not telling you who I am, is because I am on probation for selling drugs and lying on oath, besides, I might be killed before I see my daughter fostered in a decent home. If Mrs Lake knows I give you this information, God knows what she would do to me. Not that I care any more as my time for living is limited as I have an incurable infection, but I have to protect the rest of my family, and especially, leaving a seven year old daughter behind. Denyah, her father is," the caller said with a croak in her voice then said "never mind. But, I am ill and I'm afraid that I haven't much time left and that my illness will certainly take me away form my daughter" The caller began to cry softly.

"I understand. But as you said, what had happened to you and Eugene, was long before my time. "Where's your little girl?" Denyah asked.

"Denyah, I had nothing to do with Eugene, he's not the father of my child" the caller asked.

"Well, it's none of my business what you did or do. But with a child to consider, I fully understand why you wish to hide your identity."

The caller burst out crying and blew her nose.

"Why are you crying," Denyah asked her.

"Denyah, I was having flings with Eugene, but I cheated on him with Patrick and got pregnant. I told no one Patrick's my daughter's father. I had served six months in prison four years ago for possessing drugs and being drunk and disorderly. At this time, my daughter was three and living with my brother and his woman. I'm not the one that slapped you."

"So where's this child?" Denyah asked.

"She's with my brother's girlfriend. She was with them since I went to prison."

"Why didn't you tell her father about her?"

"I've tried so many times, but when I heard he got married, I didn't want to cause any trouble."

"Well don't you think the child has the right to know her father?" Denyah asked her mother.

"Yes Denyah, I suppose so, but how could I tell him now. Would you think he's going to believe me after seven years?" Little Miah's mother said crying softly.

"What are you trying to tell me, I should go to Patrick with this information saying he has a seven years old daughter when I don't even know your name or your child's?"

"Okay, my daughter name is Miah. That's all I can tell you for now. But seriously, what I told you about your Nurse friend it's true." the caller said.

"Well, I would like to see justice done for my friend, but with you not identifying yourself I would have to leave it up to the police to solve my friends murder whenever. Well, goodbye and please don't phone my number again unless you tell me who you are." Denyah said and put the phone down.

After Denyah thought for a few minutes, she phoned Patrick. Patrick answered. "Patrick, its Denyah. Are you free to talk?"

Patrick looked to see if anyone was near him, but as he saw the family watching TV in the living room, he then asked Denyah to hang up and he went into the dining room and phoned Denyah on his mobile phone "Okay, I'm listening."

"Patrick, I had a phone call from a caller, stating she was seeing Eugene for a short time when she cheated with you for five months while Eugene was away" Patrick laughed softly before Denyah could finish speaking to him. Denyah took his laughing as a yes. "Well," Denyah said, "I understand you are the father of her seven years old daughter Miah" Patrick almost choked on the news.

"Are you still there Patrick?" Denyah asked him as he went dead silent.

"Yes, I'm here" he answered after swallowing his saliva then replied softly. "Yes, I was having a little thing going with Natasha when she was a waitress in one of Eugene's restaurants. After some time, she left and I didn't see her again. I had no idea she was having my baby. Have you seen her or the child?"

"No Patrick, all she said over the phone was the child is yours - I wouldn't doubt her. She wasn't pregnant when Eugene left and went to Canada on business. She said, Eugene was her first then you until long after sometime she started dating you but left her job when she found out she was pregnant and that she'd told you."

"Will you hear from her again?" Patrick asked Denyah.

"I told her not to phone my number unless she tells me her name." Denyah said.

"Well, I wouldn't know where to find her or the child. I would like to tell Bernice about the child if I am sure the child is mine and know where she is." Patrick said.

"Well that is up to you to search for her if you really would like to find her." Denyah said.

"Denyah, please don't say anything to Bernice about this until I get to the bottom of this, about the child."

"Patrick, it's nothing to do with me. But for the sake of the child, please try and find her before she becomes much older and gets herself into trouble."

"Thanks Denyah, I'll do my best."

"Well, I see you then."

"Bye Den,"

Patrick walked away in though and looking downhearted over the child. As he faced his wife Bernice, she saw nervousness carved on his saddened face. She moved away from her children and her parents and took his hand leading him into the kitchen and asked him "What is the matter honey?"

Patrick wiped some sweat from around his forehead and lips as tears instantly came in his eyes that he said. "Honey, I just spoke to Denyah about me having a seven years old daughter. B honey, what am I going to do, and where was this child all this time?"

"Firstly you should take off the dull looking face and put your smiling bright one on. Secondly, you should go in search to find your daughter. And thirdly, you should bring her home to her family or make sure you support her if she's yours."

"B, she's not living with her mother. She's with her mother's brother and his girlfriend."

"Patrick, I think the quicker you go and find you daughter, the better it would be for her and for you." Bernice said hugging him and showing him with a nice smile.

Patrick kissed her and said, "Honey, what would I do without you." he smiled and went to his children and said to them, "I love you." He hugged the three of his adopted children as the children's grandmother and grandfather saw tenseness on his face they watched him with concern and wondered.

He faced the children's grandparents and said, "Mom, dad, I only just find out I have a seven year old daughter somewhere out there and I have to find her. We have to find her and bring her home to be with us her family," Bernice said.

"Yes of course Patrick, you should go and look for your daughter and bring her home." Mrs Pearson said.

"Yes mom. Thanks." he said and closed and opened his eyes in desperation.

"The missus speak for me son." Aungus said with an assuring smile."

As Patrick turned to walk back to be with his wife, the door bell starting to ring, Bernice answered the door to see Eugene smiling. "Come in Eugene, Patrick is in the living room." Bernice said and moved aside to let Eugene through. As Patrick saw Eugene, he kissed Bernice's cheek and walked Eugene into the hall. "Just let me get my wallet." he said walking up stairs but Eugene followed upstairs behind him into his room. Patrick picked his wallet up and looked into his wallet to see how much money he had. As he had more than enough, he zipped his wallet and put it into his breast coat pocket and as he turned to leave his room, Eugene grinned in his face. Patrick said nothing, but he knew Denyah told him he has a daughter.

However, after they came downstairs, they both went into the living room. Passion got up from her seat and ran into Patrick's arms saying. "Daddy, I love you, and you too Uncle Eugene."

"I love you too honey," Eugene said and she kissed her uncle Eugene on his face.

"Hey honey, doesn't daddy get his kiss?" Patrick asked.

Passion smiled and kissed her daddy Patrick on his lips, then, Starry kissed him on his face and as Kiah was sleeping, he kissed him on his forehead. Eugene said good night and he and Patrick left to go to the pub have a drink.

On their way to the pub, Eugene asked him, "What's this about you have a daughter with the chick I was dating?"

As Patrick didn't reply, Eugene laughed.

"Hasn't Den filled you in with the information?"

"Well," she told me she believed you have a seven year old daughter and you told her I was dating her mother until I left to Canada and then you took over. Den said this as a joke. So what are you going to do bros?" Eugene asked.

"To find my daughter," Patrick said.

Eugene laughed.

"I'm very serious bros. I believed I have a daughter somewhere out there. And I have to find her but I wouldn't know where to start." Patrick said.

"Anyway, can you be sure she's your daughter?" Eugene asked

"Well, Denyah phoned and told me. This is why I have to find her and know the truth?" Patrick said.

"I wonder why they told Den of the child and not you in the first place." Eugene said.

"Well, Denyah told me a caller called, I mean phoned her - telling her, our deceitful mother paid this man name Robert Jay to murder Nurse James and that Wesley had nothing to do with the murders of his two mates. Eugene, Denyah said, this caller said she has proof from Robert Jay he refused to do what that so called mother of ours asked but after she confronted him about your fake dad had sex with him in her bed, he done what she wanted and they had him beaten up and his manhood hacked off and was left bleeding for dead at the border of Witton cemetery. He left a confession letter stating everything and then he committed suicide."

"Well how my wife's come to know this caller?" Eugene asked.

"She doesn't, Eugene, the caller might be Natasha."

As Eugene heard Natasha's name called, he turned and looked at Patrick with a smile and surprise before he said, "So tell me brother, you were the one carry on where I left off? Well lucky you, you have that child which should have been mine. Well done brother, like brother, like brother, as the saying goes. I hope you would be as lucky as me finding your daughter. I bet she's a pretty darling. Anyway, well done brother, you've knocked your balls in the centre of the hole." Eugene said then let out a hearty laugh.

By this time, Patrick was looking pretty serious before Eugene said. "However, look at my little Jade B. How she turned out to be a lighted candle, bright and pretty. I really was in love with her mother. But some things are not meant to be. Now my Denyah was there budding out for me and if I try to love her anymore I couldn't as I'm deeply in love with her. Now she's the mother of my children. Mind you, I'd fell in love with her the moment I set my eyes on her. Just like your Bernice. I'm sure you fell in love with her. She's beautiful in every aspect. I really do like her, as a sister-in-law."

"Eugene, I bet my daughters pretty. Most mixed raced children are very beautiful." Patrick said. Then went on to say, "You won't hold this against me to love Natasha, would you?"

"Patrick, I wasn't really dating her, I must have scored her twice. I won't lie to you. I like her a lot but I'd no time to be serious with any women after the three women I'd trusted deceived me. But now, there's only one woman I want to go to bed with and wake up looking in her smiling face every morning and that's my Denyah."

That night Denyah told Eugene what the caller told her about the child and about her been sent to prison for possessing drugs and lied on oath. "She also told me your evil mother has a hold over Wesley as she knew Wesley was sleeping with a Marlo's wife and Marlo is one very dangerous man that would kill without a blink. Anyway, Wesley knew your pretend mother had his two mates and my Nurse friend murdered but said nothing, both Wesley and her are two of a kind. You pretend mother has murdered your true mom. And she got away with it and then claimed you all are her children.

Wesley is the only one that can prove your false mom murdered your true mom by overdosing her with tablets twenty years ago. Wesley told me he was sleeping with her from when he was eighteen and even when she was married to the Judge. You know who I mean. Eugene honey, we have to watch that wicked bitch and not to let her anywhere near our son or any of the children. Don't bother to thank me honey" Denyah told Eugene as she looked pleasing with herself.

Three days later, the caller phoned Denyah again. "Hello," Denyah answered.

"Denyah, you told me not to call you unless I give you my name, well I'm Natasha, I don't know you, but no way would I let Eugene's bitch of a fake mother hurt his son. She was the one that drove me away and threatened me if I said anything to Patrick about his child and that I would regret that I did. I was scared and I kept silent and went into prostitution and selling drugs and as a result of it all I got what I didn't want. Anyway, one of my friend's mothers saw the wicked bitch inject poison in the back of their true mother's head after dosing her with pills. My friends' mother said, Wesley saw her give Eugene's mom an injection but had no idea the injection was fatal but after your mother was admitted to hospital she died a few days later. Wesley said nothing as he didn't realize what the wicked bitch had done to your mother. From then, Wesley was knocking off your false mother. I suspected that before Wesley and you got married. However, that old deceiving bitch seemed to get away with her wicked doings! I would like to see her and Wesley locked up for the rest of their life.

Denyah wasn't at all impressed by the news of her ex and Mrs Lake after Natasha told her. But Denyah hearing this again from Natasha as before from Wesley, it sounded so morbid that she said, "Look Natasha, about your daughter, why don't you get in touch with her father, I'm sure if the child is his, you won't have any trouble in him taking the child?" Denyah told Natasha.

"I don't think he would want to know after seven years." Natasha said

"Natasha, I speak to Patrick about his daughter, and he so wanted to meet her. So why don't you phone him and arrange to meet him somewhere. I would be happy to give you his mobile phone number." Denyah told her

"How can I, when he's happily married and has other children?" Natasha said.

"Natasha, his wife is a lovely and understanding person. She would love to know her husband's daughter. If you don't want to speak to Patrick, I'm sure his wife would like to here from you about the child. Would you like me to speak to her?" Denyah asked Natasha.

"Will she Denyah?" Natasha asked.

"Yes, Natasha. I will speak to her, but I still think, the father's the right one you should speak to." Denyah said.

"I guess you're right, but I'm feeling so weak these days. Denyah, I'm sick, really sick. And I need to find a good home for my girl."

"I'm sorry about your illness Natasha this is why you should tell her father. He might be able to help you find a good doctor," Denyah told Natasha.

"Denyah, I caught something few years ago after I had my baby. What I caught no one can cure, not even the doctor. This is why I have to keep well away from the world. I can't work any more or provide properly for my little girl as I caught what I have by using dirty needles, or, by having sexual intercourse with the wrong man. This is why I only want to see my girl settle into a nice home then I would happily crawl under a rock and die peacefully."

"Natasha, you sound as though you illness is very serious."

"Yes Denyah, I'm dying slowly. And I don't want my baby girl to be with my brother and his woman as they heading the same direction as I. I don't want my baby to handle dirty needles."

"Well, you should let me give you the child's father's number or tell me where you wanted to meet him." Denyah said.

"No Denyah, I have the child sent to you. Say Sunday ten o'clock?"

"Okay Natasha, would you like some money?" Denyah asked her sympathetically.

"No. I don't need any money. All I need is for my child to know her father and to have a good home. That's all." Natasha said crying.

Denyah was feeling very scared and sorry for Natasha and thought she must be dying with Aids. The news had left Denyah nervous and so shaken that she was shivering and tears came in her eyes. After she spoke to Natasha, she dried her tears before she went to Eugene and Mrs Brown in tears again, but before she speak to them, she turned her face away quickly and dried her eyes. Mrs Brown suspected something was wrong, but she asked nothing as Eugene was there. But as men don't usually notice a woman's problem, he didn't detect the seriousness of Denyah's movement. No more than he said to her, "Denyah honey, I should go and join my son in a nap as I am feeling dog tired." Eugene said and went to bed. Denyah faced Mrs Brown and told what she been told by the caller.

"Did she give her name?" Mrs Brown asked.

"Not at first mom, but she sounded serious. Then she called me again and told me her name is Natasha."

"You'll have to tell Eugene."

"Well yes, I did and then again her name after he confronted me telling me Patrick had told him about the child Patrick didn't know he had. Natasha also told me Wesley hadn't murdered his two mates and that it was Mrs Lake murdered Eugene's mom, and Mrs Lake had paid a Robert Jay to have Nurse James murdered and that she has a written statement from Robert Jay to proved he'd raped and murdered Nurse James on account of Mrs Lake blackmailing him as she knew he was selling cocaine and that he used to work for the Judge as his driver and that he was Judge Lake's bitch. She'd caught them in bed in a spare room. So as Mr Jay didn't want his wife to know, he'd done what she wanted to her to keep quiet. The evil deceitful bitch had Wesley and Mr Jay just where she wanted them. But how can I go to Eugene with this? I don't want to drag up the past even though I would like that woman sent to prison. And I don't want Eugene to say I'm a troublemaker either. Nor would I want him to hate me as he's already accused me of hating her. Beside, he once asked me, why am I defending Wesley? He said it seemed as if I'm protecting the bastard or I still love him."

"Well we have to be vigilant about that 'retched woman getting near our baby" Mrs Brown said.

The following day, Eugene went to see how Mrs Lake was getting on after that fall. She told him that she had to go to the hospital. "How's the head?" Eugene asked her out of pity.

"Well, I'm not feeling too badly now. Well, how is the family and especially my grandson?" she asked.

"We're good! My son is not your grandson. Where's Jenny?"

"She went to see a friend about an hour ago but if you care to wait I could rustle you up something to eat."

"I'll phone Jenny later. Well I have to get home." Eugene said.

"Wait just a minute. I bought something for the baby." she went to the dining room and brought out a carrier bag and gave Eugene saying, "I bought my grandson a St. Christopher silver chain for the baby and two tins of baby milk."

"The baby doesn't need anything." Eugene told her and refused to take what she was giving him.

"Please, Eugene, since I bought them already please take the bag. I'm so sorry for all the bitterness I've caused to you and to everyone." she said and burst out crying.

"I would take them to Denyah, but don't be too surprised if you heard she threw them in the bin" Eugene said and he took the carrier bag without thanking her. As she tried to kiss his face, he twisted away and walked out the door leaving the door wide open and he got in his car and drove off. When he got home, he met Denyah and Mrs Brown sitting and watching TV in the lounge. He smiled then said, "Good evening."

"Good evening son" Mrs Brown answered. "Would you like to have your supper now?"

"Yes please mom, but let me wash my hands first and have a look on the children." Eugene said. And he marched upstairs into the bathroom and washed his hands before he went and saw his three children sleeping. Smiling he marched downstairs again to have his supper. After he'd eaten he gave Denyah the carrier bag with two tins of baby milk and the silver chain saying. "The old hog sent them for the baby. I didn't want to take them, but, as she was in tears and begging me to, I took them as I don't think she'll harm our baby."

Denyah said nothing but looked Eugene extremely hard in the face.

"Den, I felt the same as you, I don't care for her to buy gifts for any member of my family."

"Well, I suppose she wants to get back in your life. But, I've to stay well clear away from her as she's hated me from the beginning, and I don't see why she should like me now."

"Well as you said Den, I will take no more gifts from her. Now where's my coming home kiss?" he asked smiling as Mrs Brown left to go and fetched his supper.

Denyah looked on at him and as he took her in his arms, Mrs Brown showed up with his supper. He moved his lips away from Denyah's and smiled.

"Don't mind me." Mrs Brown said smiling. "I'm now on my way to feed the kitten."

"Mom, you'll have to let Paris take responsibility to feed her kitten" Denyah said after Eugene ate his supper, he took the lead up to their bedroom with Denyah following behind to go and breast feed her baby as her breast milk was spouting and the baby was crying. Eugene picked the baby up while Denyah went to the bathroom to wash her breast. Shortly she returned and took the baby, as the baby fixed his little mouth over her nipple, he took in milk then let go. Eugene sampled some of the spouting milk and said, "Its warm and sweet." he smiled and rolled over on the middle of the bed and said, "You can have some of mine later, only it's much richer and energizing to the body. By the way, our baby is going on thirteen weeks, when you think you'll be okay to give me another son?"

"Well as mom said, "You have to give me time to heal and that is at least another three months time?" Denyah said.

"You're joking aren't you? Right now I'm suffering." Eugene said.

"And I'm still feeling sore." Denyah said.

"Well, you don't mind if I release my burning pipe on some gorgeous woman like you?" Eugene asked.

"Dear - you do that and I get to know and you'll pay the full penalty." Denyah said.

"I'm only joking honey. One woman for me, and that's you honey. You're the only one I would want to have all my children. I love you so much honey. You want some tea, as I'm going to make some?" Eugene asked.

"I wouldn't say no. And bring me a slice of cake and don't bother mom to do it. It's time you looked after me." Denyah said.

"I have honey, you're feeding him and I'm willing to give you a second son."

Then as Mrs Brown was on her way to her room and heard Eugene asked Denyah if she wants some tea, she went back into the kitchen and made two mugs of tea and cut two slices of cake. As she was going up, Eugene's going down.

"Here's you tea and cake that I heard Den asked you for when I was on my way to my room."

"Thanks mom. You're an angel" Eugene told Mrs Brown and took the tray and walked in to his room smiling. "I told you not to bother mom."

"He didn't bother me honey, I heard him asking you while on my way to my room. So, I went into the kitchen and made my precious Den her tea. You too son, well good night and I'll see you both in the morning."

"Good night mom."

"From me too," Eugene said.

After Denyah fed her baby and changed his nappy, she had her tea and cake and a little later, she had her bath and settled down in bed while Eugene went to have a quick look on Paris and Jade B. He fixed Jade B's quilt over her as she'd kicked it halfway down her leg and went to see Patrick.

As soon as Eugene was gone, Denyah put the two tins of milk into the garbage bin. And busted the silver chain in half and also tossed it into the bin. "There's where you belong with the bitch that sent you." Denyah said smiling

That night when Denyah saw Eugene's erection she gave in to him.

CHAPTER TWENTY

One week later Mr Frat invited friends to his hotel to have dinner. That Saturday night the hotel was crowded with friends and diners. Mr Frats announced happily and proudly to the crowd. "I'm so overjoyed to be accepted by my four sons Patrick, Eugene, Raymond, Carlton and daughter Jenny at last." His eyes filled with tears as he shouted happily in his hotel to the diners, "I'm wearing the crown I thought I would never again regain after thirty four years. Free dinner and champagne for everyone for tonight."

The diners looked on at him whispering to each others in wonder. Some asked what has come over him to give free dinners and champagne. Others thought he must be going senile or, he'd good reason to celebrate. "Whatever his reason, this is my night to eat well, drink and enjoy myself." a Mr Lincoln said for all to hear. Then Mr Frats made an announcement to the diners saying "I have two newly born grandchildren, one a son and a daughter. This is why I'm wearing my invisible crown that I alone can feel. None of my family is present here at this moment but us my friends. Therefore, it is now my pleasure that I should make arrangements to celebrate my newly born grandson of one my four sons - Eugene - and my other three sons, Patrick Raymond, Carlton, and daughter Jenny. I'm hoping I would get the chance to know my children well, as well as all of my other loved grandchildren, their lovely mothers and the other members of my family that I thought I would never regain. Well my friends, I would like for all of you to come here and celebrate with my family and myself on a very special occasion one month from now - Saturday evening here." Mr Frats smiled "with a generous invite to all."

The following Saturday afternoon before Mr Frats' party, he went to see Patrick and he chattered with Bernice and Patrick, saying to them, "I would like get to know all of my family and to invite all of us to a celebration meal three weeks Saturday at my hotel. The Pearls Hotel, in fact, I would very much like for all my family to be there with me to celebrate a very special evening and to let the world know I regained back the most precious gift of its kind, getting back my long lost family again. I'm feeling like I'm floating on a feather bed going to heaven. Patrick, I would like for you to pass a message on to family and friends. I would be so grateful."

"Dad, I hate the idea for you to claim some of the family you've never got the chance to meet as yet," Patrick said.

"Well, I think it would be okay for the family to get to know me better. So I believe this would be my chance for all my family to know who I am." Mr Frats said smiling.

"Well Mr Frats, I think the others of the family would love to meet you." Bernice said.

"Well, I thank you Bernice greatly." Mr Frats said. Bernice got up out of her seat and said. "Well Mr Frats and husband, I have to leave you and get into the dining room to set the table for lunch" Bernice then moved herself into the dining room and set the table. After, she went to tell her husband Patrick and Mr Frats. "Lunch is ready" Mr Frats and her Patrick went to the bathroom and washed their hands and then to the dining room to have lunch with the rest of the family.

Long after lunch, Mr Frats said to Bernice "Thank you for a nice tasty lunch." He smiled then said. "Goodbye" to all and he kissed the grandchildren on their forehead before he left. Patrick walked out behind him and they walked chatting to his parked car by the gate and faced each other. "Dad, I am happy we get the chance to know each other" Patrick said. Then as Mr Frats opened his car door, Patrick said. "Dad, thank you for coming up with this idea to surprise my wife with her birthday party."

"Are you sure about this son?" Mr Frats asked.

"Well after thinking long and hard about the idea of a surprise party for my missus, I think it's an excellent gift to her." Patrick said.

"Well, Patrick, don't forget to let the family and friends know they're invited three weeks Saturday evening at the Pearls Hotel at six 'o' clock to celebrate the reunion of our long-lost family. Well you know the hotel." Mr Frats said, and then went on to say "I would also like to celebrate Denyah and Bernice's newly born babies and also Bernice's birthday as her birthday would be the Monday two days after. Son, please try and not to let Bernice know what we intend for her. "

"Dad, I also have to thank my missus for her thoughtful advice by telling me I should be happy you accept us as your family and to make us officially Frats. However, I really have to be careful not to let Eugene know we would be celebrating my missus' birthday with you dad."

"Well," Mr Frats said, "I won't be breathing a word about this to anyone. But son, I think it would be a brilliant idea to celebrate your beautiful wife's birthday to the world to let her know how much you love her."

"I agree dad. But as you said, she mustn't know or catch on to what we're going to do, otherwise we wouldn't see her at the reunion." Patrick said.

"Well son, you say goodbye to my family from me again and I'll see you soon." Patrick smiled and shook hands with his dad before he saw him left in his car and blew his car horn. Patrick waved goodbye then went into his house to meet Bernice clearing the table. He helped her take the remaining plates into the kitchen and then took her in his arms and kissed her and said "thanks honey for being so thoughtful and a loving wife and mother and especially for encouraging me to welcome my natural dad in our family."

Three weeks later that Saturday evening, when Bernice and her family arrived at the Pearl hotel, the hotel was full with the Frats family, friends and diners. Much later as Bernice saw so many people flocking into the hotel, she asked Patrick to take her and her family home as the time was going on to seven forty. "But we haven't had dinner yet." Patrick told her. Then he went on saying, "it would be rude to have left so early as if you don't want to mix."

"Patrick, will you please take me and my family home, you can come back if you like." Bernice said.

"At least, let me go and tell Den and Eugene I'm going to take you and the family home." Patrick said to Bernice.

"Look honey, after you take us home, you can come back if you want as I told you." Bernice said.

Patrick left and went to Denyah and Eugene. After he spoke to them saying, "Dad's looking so happy," he returned to Bernice, and said, "B, honey, I'll get our family ready then we go home" But at this time Patrick was prolonging time asking some of the guests. "Are you enjoying your self?"

It was now eight 'o' clock and Mr Frats went on stage and said. "I would like all here to have a nice time as I'm celebrating my beautiful new born grandson and my acceptance into my long lost family that I though I would never have."

Paula took the mike phone from Mr Frats, and said to the guests. "May I have your attention please?" At this time everyone finish eating, and they went silence and turned and watched Paula with interest. "Please everyone, please full your glass with what ever, as there's champagne, brandy, rum, gin, whiskey, vodka and so many others. Well, is everyone has a full glass. Well, let's raise our glass Daddy Frats, our newly born baby son of Denyah and to Bernice's and my forthcoming babies" Paula laughed happily before she announced "Bernice, I know you might murder me after" and she sang (Happy Birth day to Bernice) in reggae with the steel band. After Paula sung, everyone congratulated her on her smooth velvet voice, and also everyone wished Mr Frats well. And a warm welcome of congratulation to Denyah and Eugene on the birth of her newly born son Junior Carter Lake Frats and also the future coming of Bernice and Patrick's, Paula and Raymond's babies that will be born in spring in the new year and a very happy birthday to Bernice.

As Bernice sat in surprise and stunned with tears in her eyes, Patrick and Mr Frats were more surprised that Paula had done what they were thinking to announce Bernice's birthday. Patrick kissed Paula on her cheek saying "Thanks" then he moved on to take Bernice's right hands into his to help her out of her seat and kissed her in front of everyone "B, I am so much in love with you." he said proudly, then led her on the dance floor and dance with her to the steel band playing, I love you because your understanding' by Jim Reeves.

Then everyone wished her "Happy Birthday" again. After a while she felt so happy when Patrick stood by her and said, "B, my darling, I'm one of the proudest, happiest of husbands and fathers. I love you so much that I had the pleasure to get you this lovely gift." Smiling, he took her hand into his and slipped on a diamond ring above her married ring and then hooked a double band matching bracelet on her wrist and kissed her. Again he said, "B, I love you and if I'm to love you anymore, I don't know how." Bernice was in tears as the Steel Band played 'we were waltzing together to a dreamy melody.' And, the biggest gift to her, husband, and her family, is when little Miah's aunt placed Miah's hand in hers Patrick's hands and said, "This is your dad and you new mom." Bernice lifted up Miah and kissed her before she cried with joy then she took Miah and seated her beside her children and told them, "Miah is your new sister. She was living away but she has come home to us her family" she's a beautiful little girl." Mrs Pearson said and hugged Miah and then said, "Thank-you sweet loving God to bring home our precious baby." Patrick was the happiest father of that night - he showed Miah proudly to all of the guests and said, 'This our third daughter" he then showed off his other two daughters, Passion, Starry and his son Kiah and said "I'm truly blessed with four lovely children, with another on it's way, a beautiful wife, loving mom and two handsome Dads. Aren't I'm the luckiest of all men? Not forgetting three handsome brothers Eugene, Raymond, Carlton a beautiful sister Jenny and my brother's wives and their children and some trusted friends. Thank for listening to me."

Eugene, Raymond, Carlton, Jenny, his adopted parents and daddy Mr Frats all stood by his side. After Patrick made his brilliant speech, Eugene patted him on his shoulder and said, "Bros, I must hand it to you, you've left me felling very proud. I'm so happy you're my brother" All applauded what Eugene said before he walked back to Denyah smiling. At this time dark slim and tall, Miah's mother stood far in the background and unnoticed outside the doorway wearing dark glasses, ginger coloured head wig and dressed in black jeans and dark blue long sleeved shirt. After she saw her daughter being welcomed by her father and the family and running and playing with her sisters, cousins and other children's, she left in tears of joy feeling very happy and left in the taxi she came in.

Just before Patrick took his beautiful wife under the soft multi-coloured lights to dance, he asked little Miah's aunt her name and he made out a ten thousand pounds cheque and gave it to her with a thousand. "Thank you." And asked her and Miah's uncle to stay and enjoy the evening. But they both said "Thanks for the money" and they left. As Patrick was feeling on top of the world, he took his wife Bernice on the dance floor again and they danced to the reggae tune of the Steel Band (One day at a time sweet Jesus) Eugene also took Denyah on the dance floor. In fact, every one was on the dance floor getting down to the beat even the children.

At one time when Patrick and Bernice were dancing, her eyes caught Mr Rogers watching her and he eyed her smiling. She tried not to look at him and she buried her face in her husband's bosom. After that dance Veda went to Bernice and said, "I see you have an admirer and very handsome he's too." Veda smiled. "Oh he's Mr Rogers I met him at the airport on my way back." Bernice said. By this time Mr Rogers was standing in a near corner drinking scotch and watched her dancing a waltz with her husband 'I would always love you.' After a long night of celebrating, Bernice told her husband "It's time I take the children and mom home as the children are getting agitated and they're tired and the time was approaching mid morning."

Patrick respectfully asked for everyone's attention and then announced to the guests "The family gratefully thank each of you for coming to help us to share in the celebration of my lovely wife's birthday, my sister-in-law Denyah and my brother Eugene's newly born son and my added daughter Miah and also in a few months a new born son to my dear friend Ryan and her beautiful wife Meleta. And also I must wish my sister-in-law Paula and my young brother Carlton all the best in the future for them to have a healthy baby. And last but not least, my lovely long-lost and now found dad Mr Frats. Please come up here daddy Frats and father-in-law Aungus." Patrick said.

Mr Frats gladly and proudly went and stood shoulder to shoulder beside Patrick. Then Patrick said, "Come on up brothers and stand beside me and Dad once more."

Again, his brothers Carlton, Raymond, Eugene and sister Jenny they went on stage and stood beside their brother Patrick, Aungus and Mr Frats with the cameras taking photos of them. The guests had looking very happy this time and applauded Patrick and they wish Mr Frats and family well.

By this time most of guests were looking darn tired or drunk. Then the DJ announced this would be the last dance and it's now mid-morning." The band began to play (I want to wake up with you".) Surprisingly, the handsome Mr Guy Roger took Bernice on the dance floor while her husband went and mingled with some of the guests. "How did you find me and what are you doing here? Bernice asked him.

He smiled saying "I got your address from your suitcase. And I'm here after I made a few investigations. I was told you would be here to celebrate your birthday. Well, I'm also here because I fell in love with you and I was invited."

"Well, I think you're here for the wrong reason. I only love my husband and no other man" Bernice said looking directly at her husband Patrick as he stood with some of the guests in conversation.

As Mr Guy Rogers saw Patrick back turned to him and everyone was looking flagged out and was drooping, Mr Rogers tried to take his chance to kiss Bernice but she quickly moved her face and told him, "Are you so stupid that you don't care who sees you kissing me, beside, I don't even know your name."

"I am Mrs Denyah Davis' solicitor. I took over from my father before the late Mrs Carter died and my father was her personal solicitor for many years and is now retired from any association. However, if you were interested, you would have known my name is Guy Rogers as it was on the card I'd given you at the airport."

"Well Mr Rogers, I wasn't at all interested in you and as I told you, I love my husband deeply. I've also served time in prison because I killed a boyfriend and his woman. I told my husband before he married me. He didn't care as he still made me his wife. He could have married any women as he's handsome and wealthy but he chose me. So do you think it would be fair for me to have affairs with other men?"

"Well, I'm not any other men, I'm me, and I do love you and I'm sure you had reason for what you done and you've paid. I may not be as wealthy as your husband but I think my love is stronger. I've a few millions and my business is growing strong."

"Mr Rogers, I'm a very happy married wife and a mother to my four children and this one inside me. In fact, this room is filled with so many beautiful unmarried women. I'm sure you'll find one that would say yes to you."

"But, I love only you, and I want you" he said.

Bernice stopped dancing with him and then went and joined her husband. "This is my lovely wife Bernice" Patrick told his three men friends. His friends warmly greeted Bernice and gave her gifts they'd brought and said, "We're sorry to be a little late for the beginning. But we have had a lovely time. Bernice looked on at them and thought they were gay, not least because of the black mixed lace shirts they both wore, but as they saw the way Bernice looked at them, one of then said. "We two are brothers. I am Kalvin, my brother Eagan. We like to dress alike. Oh and this is Tyrone, our workmate." said Kalvin one of the two brothers.

"Well, I'm very glad meeting the three of you, but I came to ask my husband to take us home as the children are ready for bed."

Patrick looked at his wrist watch and then said to his mates, "Would you excuse me as I must take the family home and I'll see you later at the usual place."

"You take your family home mate. It's well past their bedtime." Tyrone said,

Patrick then took his family home and after he drove himself back to make sure Mr Frats was okay.

"I'm so proud of you all, and thanks for giving me a very happy time." Mr Frats said.

"That's ok dad. I had a lovely time too." Patrick said.

Mr Guy Rogers walked up to Denyah and touched her neck, Denyah looked back and saw him smiling, "Oh hello Mr Rogers, it's nice meeting you again."

"Please call me Guy. As I'm now your personal solicitor, I think, as from now we might be seeing each other more often as I would be spending some time working in the city of Birmingham."

"Mr Rogers, I mean Guy, I was wondering with you so young, how come you were working for mom, Mrs Carter." Denyah asked.

"Oh, I see what you mean. My father was Mr and Mrs Carters' personal solicitor for years before I was born. I also trained to become like my father, so three years before the death of your mother, I took over from my father as he's now retired and travelling around the world. I have two other brothers Jason and Melvin. They are actors and now living and working in the States."

"Well now that I understand, I would be happy to share a cup of tea with you sometime. And Guy many thanks for a well done job." Denyah said to Mr Rogers.

"And many thanks Denyah and to keep me on your payroll." Mr Rogers said.

"Guy, what is forty thousand pounds per year between friends." Denyah said.

"I didn't ask you to double my payment. But I'm very grateful." Mr Rogers said.

"I know. Well Gus, if I go broke, I can always come to you with my begging bowl." Denyah said.

"Denyah, I don't think you'll ever get to that stage. In fact, you'll never go broke in a million years." Mr Rogers said.

"Well, Goodbye Guy," Denyah said.

"Goodbye Denyah." Mr Rogers said and went and mingled amongst the guests.

One hour later Patrick phoned Bernice and asked, "Are you okay honey?"

"Yes, I'm okay, but I'll be happy to have you next to me:" and she hung up. Patrick smiled and went and had a couple of drinks with his brothers and friends. Meleta phoned her husband Ryan and told him to come home and she hung up before he could answer.

While Patrick was having a good time with his friends drinking, Guy Rogers phoned Bernice, "Who's this?" Bernice asked, half asleep.

"It's me. Guy Rogers please don't put the phone down. Will you have dinner with me next Friday night at eight o'clock?" he asked.

"Mr Rogers, how many times must I tell you I'm a very happy married woman?" Bernice said.

"Please Bernice, just have this dinner with me, and I would never ask you again." Mr Rogers begged.

"Okay, Mr Rogers, I'll see how I feel tomorrow. I'll give you a call?" Bernice said.

"And Bernice, please call me Guy." Mr Rogers said.

Mr Guy Rogers was glad when Patrick couldn't drive himself home as he was drunk, so Mr Rogers was happy to give Patrick a lift home. After he saw Patrick to his door, he was leaving. But Patrick invited him into his home. His eyes were wandering around the living room with interest looking at the beautiful furniture and displayed lovely large ornaments. As Bernice heard laughing, she wrapped a housecoat over her pyjamas and went down to see Guy and her husband, drinking, chatting and laughing. Shockingly, she looked hard at Guy before she thanked him for bringing her husband home.

"That's okay. The condition he's in, I couldn't let him drive." Mr Rogers said. "But he and Eugene saw their father safely home first before he got like this."

"Well, thank you again. I think I could manage to look after my husband from here. Goodbye Guy." Bernice said.

"I'm happy to bring him home." Mr Rogers said.

"Thanks again. Goodbye Guy."

"I was hoping for a thank-you kiss." Mr Rogers whispered to her.

"Guy, I love my husband very much. There's no way I would jeopardise my marriage." Bernice said.

"Bernice, I do love you and I wouldn't give up on you this easily." Mr Rogers said.

"Goodbye Guy." Bernice said.

Guy smiled and as he knew Patrick was drunk and flat out on the sofa, he pulled Bernice into him and kissed her. She pulled away and slapped his face. "Would you please leave?" she told him angrily.

Barefacedly, he took her in his arms and kissed her again before he left smiling. And again, Bernice slapped his face and closed the door with a bang waking up Miah. Mr Rogers smiled feeling the spot where she slapped him before he left in his car.

The next morning, Bernice phoned Denyah's Sister Fay and asked her, "How would you like to have dinner with a very rich handsome lawyer?" Fay laughed over the phone and said "You having me on aren't you?"

"Would I make a fool out of you? If you think so, you don't know me at all. Look Fay, I met him at the Airport and I can't get rid of him even though I told him I'm not interested and I'm a happily married with children. He won't take no for an answer, so I would like you to help me get rid of him by having that dinner with him."

"I don't think he would fall for me. Beside, I've nothing suitable to wear."

"Fay honey that is the least of your problems, we go shopping Tuesday. After I finish with you, you would look like you just stepped off the cat walk."

"Bernice I don't know….."

"Look, he's not a bad looking bloke. If you don't want to have dinner with him, I would ask some one else. His name's Guy Rogers, and as I said, he's a good looking bloke. You will like him. "

"All right Bernice, I'll have dinner with him."

"Thank Fay, I would arrange everything and let you know what to do. I will see you Tuesday morning, about ten thirty. Oh and I'll make an appointment with my hair dresser for Friday morning for you."

"Bernice, are you sure about this? What I mean, do you love the bloke and you want to play me to prolong time? If so, I would understand. Just put me on the right track."

"Fay, as I told you, I would get someone else, if you don't want to do this."

"Oh what have I got to lose? Bernice, I'll see you on Tuesday. I can do with a changing of clothes." Fay said.

Meanwhile, to every call Guy made to Bernice, she answered and spoke to him nicely making him feeling confident and happy. Tuesday Bernice and Fay went shopping for clothes, shoes, perfume and make-up. And, Friday morning, Bernice took Fay to her hair dresser and she had her hair styled and her nails manicured. Later the Friday, Bernice asked her husband if she could go out and have dinner with Fay. He didn't like the idea, especially the way Fay had treated Denyah but he said, "okay"

"Are you sure honey?" Bernice asked him.

"I just want for you to be happy. Beside, you need a little pleasure now and then. I'll help mom look after the children."

"But honey, I'm very happy. You, the children, mom, dad and my lovely friends made me very happy, and you gaining our long lost daughter Miah, I couldn't be happier. "

"Well, I love you and I'm sure I could trust you honey." Patrick said.

"Thanks honey, remember you're the only husband I want to father my children."

"And you're the only mother I want to bear my children. Now would I get a kiss?"

"No honey, you were a very naughty husband coming home drunk last night that Mr Guy Rogers had to bring you home. So you lose your kiss. Maybe, I will show pity on you some other time and peck you a kiss if you come home sober for at least two months." Bernice told her husband and smiled.

"There's where you're wrong my dear wife. You belong to me, and I'll take my kiss anytime." Patrick said nicely and smiling as he took her in his arms and planted a passionate kiss on her lips. At this time, Passion was watching them with her hands covered her mouth and trying to be silent from giggling. She stood out of sight and tried to be silent, listening, but when she heard her dad said to her mother, "Mr Stiffy wanted to release himself as it's almost five weeks he'd been blocked and he's really suffering." As he took her mom's hands to his erection she yelped out and giggled. Bernice moved away quickly leaving her husband standing with his back turned to Poshion. Bernice went up to her room, closed her door and had a hearty laugh.

When he lost his erection, he faced Pashion and asked. "Have you done your home work?"

"Not all my home work dad, I came to ask mom to help me with my maths." she said holding her maths book and her pencil.

"Well, your mom is upstairs, you best go and ask her." he said.

Soon as Passion left to go upstairs to Bernice, Patrick couldn't help himself laughing out as he looked down on himself and said, "Mr honey stick, you'll have to be patient and learn to control yourself until the Miss give you the go a head." He put his jacket on and shouted from the bottom of the stairs saying "B, honey, I'm going to have a pint."

Bernice shouted down to him "Don't come back drunk or you'll be sleeping in the shed or the garage."

Patrick smiled.

"You go and have your pint Patrick." Mrs Pearson said.

"Thanks mom. I'll be home early. Are you coming dad?"

'No, Patrick, not tonight. I'd had enough last night to serve me for the next two weeks. Thanks all the same." Aungus said. Patrick left in his car.

Meanwhile Bernice was helping her daughter Pashion with her homework when her mom went to her and asked. "Would you like some cocoa honey?"

"Yes, please mom and some milk for Pashion." Bernice said then she told Pashion. "As for you honey, it's time you went to bed as you have school tomorrow. When you Grand brings you milk and you finish drinking it, I want you to go to bed"

"Well, I won't let your milk get too hot" her Grand said.

"Grand, tomorrow is a teacher training day. Mom's helping me with my homework for Tuesday as I remember and I'm not tired" Pashion said.

"Honey, now your homework finished, why don't you drink your milk and go to bed"

"Mommy, I'm not tired,"

"Pashion it's now five past nine. So go and join your sisters in bed now young lady." Bernice told her.

"In the same bed mom," Pashion asked.

"Only if your bed is wet honey," Bernice told her.

"Mom Miah's sleeping in my space." Pashion said.

"Honey, you're a big girl now that's why you have your own bed. Miah took over your bed and sleeping with your sister Starry now that she came home to live with us. So you'll have to sleep in the single bed until we move into a bigger house and get your own room." Bernice told her Pashion. "So honey, you have to seep in the single bed for now until we get a bigger house."

"I love her mommy and I'm glad she came to live with us" Pashion said.

As she was lying on Bernice's bed, her grandmother took her hand saying. "Come along Miss Madam. It's time you went to bed and let you mother rest. Your two sisters are half way around the globe dreaming by now."

"Goodnight mom," Passion said and as she was leaving behind her grandmother Bernice said, "So no kiss for mom tonight."

"I'm sorry mom" she then went and hugged Bernice and gave her a quick kiss her on the face.

"Thanks honey, am I been punished for sending you to bed?" Bernice asked.

"No mom. I love you and dad, grandma, granddad, my baby sisters Miah and Starry and my little brother Kiah, Aunty Denyah, Aunty Meleta, Aunty Lisa and Aunty Jenny, Uncle Eugene, Uncle Ryan, Uncle Ray, Uncle Carlton and my other Uncles Richard, Curt, David, Glennis and all my cousins and my new granddaddy Frats" Pashion then hugged her mother Bernice tightly and gave her a nice kiss on her lips saying. "Mom I love you." she said rubbing her eyes.

"I love you too. Honey, you can stay up late when you not going to school the following day when you have you weeks holiday." Bernice said.

"Goodnight Mom. Goodnight Grand. I'll go and kiss Granddad goodnight."

"Your granddad has gone to bed honey. I would kiss him goodnight for you." her Grandmother told her.

Pashion kissed her mom and her Grandma again and went to the toilet, washed her hands before she went in her room and to bed. A little while after, her Grandma looked in on them and found her sleeping. Her grandma smiled, fixed her quilt over her, dimmed her light, and looked on Miah and Starry as they shared the double bed. As they all were deep in sleep, she turned the ceiling lights off, dimmed the sidelights, closed their room door very quietly and went to her and her husband's room. But as she and Bernice could not sleep, she went and made her and Bernice some more cocoa. "Here honey, I bought this bottle up for Kiah. It's hot and by the time he gets up it would be warm. Drink your cocoa honey," Mrs Pearson said to Bernice. Then as she heard Kiah crying, she turned to take him out of his cot bed but he fell asleep again.

"It okay mom, you go to bed. I'll look after him." Bernice said.

"Are you sure honey, it's no trouble me feeding him you know," Mrs Pearson said.

"Mom you go to bed." Bernice said.

"Well goodnight honey." Mrs Pearson said.

"Goodnight mom." Bernice said.

Bernice took Kiah out of his cot bed, bathed his little bottom as he was soaked, put his nappy on, gave him his milk and held him on her lap for about an hour before he fell asleep. She puts him in her cot bed covered him up to his chest then she went to her bed. As she was on the blink of falling off to sleep, she heard her dad appeared to be up now as she heard him going down the stairs. "Dad," she called. "Yes honey, I just going to make myself a sandwich as I'm feeling hungry. Do you want anything?"

"No thank you dad." Bernice said. Her dad smiled and went into the kitchen to make a sandwich when Patrick walked in and head straight to the kitchen and as he saw his adopted stepfather washing his hands before making his sandwich. "Sonny, I can do with one of those as I'm starving." Patrick said.

"Well son, we have cheese, ham, roast turkey or corned beef?" Sonny said.

"Roast turkey laced with a little sweet chilli dipping sauce." Patrick said.

Sonny smiled and made roast turkey sandwiches for the two of them. Then he said to Patrick. "Son, you put on what chilli sauce you want."

Patrick spread chilli sauce over the turkey sandwich while Sonny had his plain. After they ate their sandwiches they turned the kitchen lights off and moved into the dining room with a can of beer and drank while playing two games of blackjack before they went to bed.

HYACINTH BROWN

The following morning Patrick went to look for a bigger house. He saw a nice looking detached house for sale in Patters Grove, Tyseley. He went home and told Bernice and the following day he called the house agent and bought the five bedroom house in Tyseley about forty five minutes drive from Denyah's. Bernice was very happy. She told Denyah and her other friends Patrick has bought a new five bedroom house for her and the family.

That same Friday evening Bernice called at Fay mother's house to see Fay. Blanch answered the door "Come in Mrs Lake." she said.

"Blanch you could call me Bernice as we're partly family."

Blanch, smiled as she said "Bernice, you're looking lovely. I would love to have a bracelet like yours when I can afford it."

Bernice took her diamond bracelet off of her wrists and hooked it around Blanch's wrist and said "It's now yours. If you should need anything, I would like to help." Bernice said. Blanch nodded her head and went to Fay and told her, "Bernice is downstairs waiting and would like to see you." Then Blanch asked Bernice, "Is this the bracelet your husband gave you?" Bernice smiled saying "No honey."

A few minutes later Fay walked down stairs looking glamorous. "Fay. Where were you hiding your beauty girl? You looked absolutely stunning. I bet every diner's head would turn to look at you" Bernice said. "Shall we go and make the husband's wives get jealous?"

"Well, I'm all yours and I'm ready!" Fay said then pecked her mother with a quick kiss on her face. "Fay, you look lovely. Both of you have a good time" her mother told them.

"We sure will," Fay said and she and Bernice left in Bernice's car. At this time, Blanch were seriously admiring her diamond bracelet on her wrist. Meanwhile, as Bernice and Fay walked into the Ibis hotel, all head turned to watched them and the smell of their perfume filled the room. Mr Rogers got up out of his seat and went to meet them and escorted them to his table. He fixed their chairs in turn for them to sit and then he requested a waiter to bring a bottle of best iced champagne. The waiter went and then returned with champagne on ice and served their glasses then rested the bottle in the bucket of ice on their table. Fay sipped her champagne like a lady as she smiled. Mr Rogers' eyes were playing on both Fay and Bernice. Bernice smiled and then asked to be excused. Mr Rogers got up in respect and sat down when Bernice left the table and went to the ladies.

Fay was looking deeply nervous - Mr Rogers noticed and smiled. "Fay, please try and relax. You'll find me a gentle person when you get to know me." he said calmly.

Fay smiled and he topped her glass up with more champagne. As Bernice had planned for him to fall in love with Fay, she took at least ten minutes standing in the ladies.

As time went on Fay carried her lips to his as she saw Bernice approaching.

At this time his back was turned so that he couldn't see Bernice coming. Fay took her lips away and smiled. As temptation was building up within him, he carried his lips to Fay's and was having a long kiss with his eyes closed. He then opened his eyes, to see Bernice in the mirror standing and looking at them.

"I can explain." he said wiping his lips with his handkerchief.

"You don't need to explain anything to me. I'm a very happy married mother and you're a lovely single handsome man. My friend is also single. So kissing each other, it's none of my business. Now my friends, let's have a good time to remember." Bernice said showing her most beautiful smile.

In turn Fay asked to be excused and she went to the ladies.

"Who is she?" Mr Rogers asked.

"Would you like to meet her again?" Bernice asked him.

"I would of course, but I only love you as you know," Mr Rogers said.

"Guy, I like you a lot, but I'm in love with my husband and I've no intention of leaving him and I would fight the woman that tried to take him away from me." Bernice said happily.

"Well, at least you are the one that turned me down. So, I would be happy for second best if you would introduce me properly to your friend." he said.

Bernice was overjoyed to have heard him said that, so as Fay returned to the table, Bernice introduced Fay and Mr Rogers to each other by saying, "Fay, this is my friend Guy Rogers and Guy this is my friend Fay." Now would you both excuse me while I go and make a call to find out if my children are all right?" Bernice said asked to be excused.

Mr Rogers stood up in respect to see Bernice leave the table to go to the ladies where she phoned her husband Patrick and told him to hire a taxi as she had the car and to come to the Ibis hotel and accompany her.

Patrick took a taxi and he was with his wife in a quick time for him to have dinner with her, Fay and Mr Rogers. While they were in conversation, soft love music played and Bernice watched Fay sunk in Guy's arms and kissing him. Bernice smiled happily to know Guy was falling in love with Fay. After a while, when Guy got Bernice on her own, he said "Bernice of all the women I got close to, you're a cut above all. I had wanted you so much. I do love you Bernice. But as I said, I would have to accept second best as I know you planned it this way. Still, the very best has come out of it as I think I'm falling in love with your friend Fay. Mind you, I don't love her half as much as I love you, but I guess I might get to love her eventually. Bernice, I would have given up my life for you. However, can we still be good friends?" he asked,

"Naturally, the best," Bernice said and kissed his cheek before she went home with her husband and left Fay with him.

That night Fay phone Bernice and told her "Guy has asked me to dinner next week-end and I told him yes. Bernice, I owe you part of myself sweetheart, and I'll never forget you as long as I live. You gave me my man, and I would turn myself into a good wife if he married me. And Bernice, I promise you, you would be my first babies Godmother. I love you honey."

"Just don't you go and spoil your luck by moving in on him too fast." Bernice said.

"Bernice, you know me, I would be taking one step at a time, right to the end." Fay said in high spirit and laughed.

One week later, Fay had dinner with Guy at the Ibis hotel. Over dinner, Guy took her left hand into his and asked, "Fay, will you be my wife?"

"Are you proposing to me?" Fay asked him as she looked on at him with wondering eyes and his mouth open and waiting for her answer.

As she did not answer, he asked her again. "Fay, would you be my beautiful wife?"

"Are you sure you want to marry me?" Fay asked him in wonder.

"Yes Fay, I'm sure. How about you, would you like me to be your husband? "

"Yes Guy, I would marry you now if it were possible. Guy, I fell in love with you the moment I saw you." Fay said and then threw her arms around his neck hugging him tightly.

The following day Fay went and told Denyah that she has fallen in love with Guy Rogers. He's a solicitor. And that she met him because of Bernice.

Denyah was happy for Fay and warned her if she's serious about this Mr Guy Rogers, she should be truthful by telling him her past before he heard it from someone else. "By the way, he's my solicitor and he's a nice person."

Naturally, Fay was afraid to lose Mr Rogers if she told him about her and her sister's husband, he might not want her. Fay cried and promised Denyah she would tell him before their love life goes any further.

"I think you would be doing the right thing. If Guy Rogers really loves you, he would understand and bypass the past. If you don't tell him and he finds out, you wouldn't see him for dust as he would not be able to trust you. So the sooner you tell him, the better your mind would be at ease. Fay, I will be right behind you if you should need me. But as I told you, if you would like to know whether or not he would like to spend the rest of his life with you, please tell him about Wesley."

"Okay Denyah, I suppose you're right. I would tell him Saturday night when he calls to take me to dinner." Fay said then tears filled her eyes.

Meanwhile, Bernice told Denyah how she came to meet Guy Rogers and her reason for asking Fay for her help to get away from him. Denyah laughed then told Bernice, "I'm happy for Fay as she seemed to be in love with him." Then Denyah went on to say "I told her to tell him the truth about her and my ex-husband. Bernice, do you think I went too far by telling her to tell him? He's my solicitor but I don't want him to know me and Fay are sisters and to do her a favour because he's on my payroll. If he wants Fay after she tells him, he shows he either loves her or he has feelings for her."

"No, you did not go too far, and yes, I agreed with you Den, if she tells him and he doesn't want to see her again, he doesn't love her, or, have sufficient any interest. If he loves her, what happened between her and your ex would be a thing of the past. Yes, Den, I think she should tell him." Bernice agreed with Denyah.

The Saturday over dinner, Fay built up courage and told Mr Rogers about her and Wesley. "Who is Wesley," he asked not looking interested.

"He was my sister's ex-husband. I'm so ashamed of what I've done. However, he slugged a bullet in the back of my left shoulder for not sleeping with him anymore and while I was in the hospital and thought I was dying slowly from the bullet wound, my sister, his wife, came and gave me a right mouthful for which I didn't blame her. I cried bitterly of course, not about the bullet but for the bad deed I've done to my sister. Believe me Guy I could not see I was hurting my sister at that time. She forgave me and no way will I hurt anyone like that again. "

After Guy listened to Fay, he smiled and said, "No one is perfect. And I'm glad you told me. I would be happy to marry you if you want me."

Fay tears slid down her face. Mr Rogers dried her tears with his handkerchief and took her left hand and slipped on a diamond engagement ring on her marriage finger and kissed it. "Now you would soon be Mrs Guy Rogers." he said smiling. After dinner, he took Fay home and kissed her and saw her into her home and as she closed her door he left smiling.

After that Saturday night, they saw each other almost every night for two weeks before he asked her to move in with him. Fay was scared at first, but her mother told her when opportunity knocks at her door, grab it if she really wants. So, Fay moved in with him and within three weeks they planned to get married the following eight weeks Saturday at St Paul's Church.

On the fourth week, Fay invited Denyah, Bernice and her women friends to a night out for dinner on the Saturday night. But Denyah refused to accept her invitation to dinner.

"Den honey, she's your sister and you have forgiven her. You go to that dinner and I'll look after the children. It's time you enjoyed yourself a little. Fay needs you beside her, and Carter Junior is nearly four months now." Mrs Brown said.

"Mom, what would I do without you-I'll phone her to let her know I accept her invitation for dinner." Denyah said after Mrs Brown spoke to her.

Saturday night Denyah, Bernice, Lisa, Veda, Tracy, Meleta, Paula, Jenny, Claire, Cindy, Kelly, Kalor and Denyah's two friends Ivy she met in hospital and Mrs Saunders she got to know on the plane and Fay. As they were fifteen of them, the waiter joined two tables together. Each of them ordered food of their choice and they each sampled one another's food happily like children. As they drank four bottles of champagne and a bottle Jack Daniels whiskey between them, they were feeling merry, Paula opened the happy conversation, by saying, "I was cheating on my friend Denyah with her husband and she has forgiven me. Den, I love you."

"Denyah, is that true?" Veda asked.

"Well, if she said so, it must be true" Denyah said. All of them laughed.

"Well, when I give myself to my Ray for the first time, it hurt like hell so that I screamed out" Paula said laughing.

"How can it hurt Paula when you weren't a virgin?" Vida said.

"That's because, he'd missed and he went straight up my arse." Paula said laughing - then they all laughed. Then Paula drank more champagne and said,

"Denyah welcomed me with open arms into her home and I repaid the compliment by sleeping with her husband. Denyah, I owe you plenty for letting me off nicely and to top it all, you help me to get the man I truly love and adore." Paula said again.

Veda said, "I'm still a virgin. I think, mind you- Carl and I almost do it, but I told him not until we're married. He respected my principle and he backed away." As they all had their eyes fixed on Veda she burst out laughing and said, "I've lied for the first time. I gave myself to Carl - it felt like a knife slotted inside me. I groaned and bore the pain but now, I can't get enough of him as I always enjoyed him. Honestly, I was a virgin and that's the truth. Now my friends, I rest my case." Veda said and every one burst into laughter.

Then all eyes were on Tracy as she was sitting next to Veda. Tracy said, "Like you Veda, I was a virgin when I gave in to my David. At first it was so painful like a knife penetrating into me that I bit him on his arm. I cried out as I felt pain, then as he saw blood, he said, "Why didn't you tell me you were a virgin but he still never stop poking hard up me and grinning like a Cheshire cat until he comes and flapped his head between my breasts. The second time was almost the same, but after that I was enjoying him." all laughed again.

"Your turn Jenny" Paula said laughing. "Well said Jenny, "I'm the same as Tracy, at first it hurt and burned like fuck" …………..

"That what it was Jenny a fuck" Paula said laughing to the tilt of her voice, while her friends stopped laughing and watched her as well as the diners. "Come on girls, where's your sense of humour. We're here to have a damn good time. And we're one family I would say" Paula said.

"That's why you went to bed with Dens fiancée?" Meleta said. Everyone tried to kept serious but they laughed when Paula said, "Well, two brothers were in love with my friend Den here, I sampled the two and both were very romantic. Well as I told all of you, Den had felt sorry me, and she gave Ray to me and Ray I would love until my dying day."

"Good for you Paula. I couldn't put it better myself." Denyah said smiling.

"Come on Den, how was your first time?" Tracy asked

"Well, it was a long time ago. I was also a virgin when I got married. It was very painful at first, but the pain disappeared about the fourth time leaving pleasant enjoyable and romantic feelings to every time I was having sex. Then as bad things happening between my husband and me, enjoyable sex became a thing of the past. Well, I am enjoying my Eugene now. But I have to wait until my periods finish in about four days time. I fancy him right now but I won't enjoy him as I'm in red blood land." Denyah said. Every one laughed again.

"Me as well," Clara said, "but not periods. My husband would have to wait for some time as he planted a seed into me and most time I'm feeling sick. Mind you, I did give in to him two nights a go, and it hurt my breasts as he rested on them, so I had to push him off me. He spouted nearly on my face but tonight hurt or no hurt, I want him as soon as I get home. I love him so much. So, little darling, you'll just have to move aside in mom's tummy as mommy wants you're daddy tonight." Clara said patting her tummy. Laughter came from them again. Then Clara went on to say. "Well, after I had my baby and he was five weeks old, I had sex with my husband and it was the sweetest fuck I had even though I was still sore. But, oh my, even when he come, I had wanted more but he turned his back and started snoring" Laughter sounded again from them.

Then Bernice said again. "Well, my husband is the third men I had. I killed the first one like I would have killed a fly as he was a fly and he and his other woman were beating me up after I found out he was cheating on me with her. As she came at me to hit me with her high heeled shoes, I pushed her, she slipped and fell and hit her head on his doorstep. He pulled me into his kitchen and was beating me so bad that I stabbed him with one of his knives. He died two days later. I paid for both of them in prison. I told Patrick, he didn't give a damn. He married me and we have four beautiful children and another coming. I love him with all my heart. And the second man that was in my life was a mommy's boy so I left him after he lied to me saying he was single and all this time he was married and his wife was pregnant. Now I'm so in love with my prince Patrick."

"Bernice, honey, you're a good person." Denyah said. "And what you done was self-defence" No one laughed but they agreed with Denyah.

"I'm Lisa, Richard was and is the only man I have or want. I was also a virgin and I believed us women felt love pain at first. When I first saw Richard dick, it frightened me as it was hard and stretched about nine to ten inches long and fat. I tried to run but he grabbed me and made tender love to me by giving me an inch at his every move and as he was coming, oh boy, he must have thought he was poking the ground and the force he went in into me, I thought his dick had broke off and left in me as I saw stars. Now, I'm the one who's grabbing him and it served me right to get pregnant again after my first baby only ten months old. Anytime I see his dick he sets me on heat so when he walks into our bedroom naked, I quickly put on my dark glasses so that I can hardly see my sugar stick. As the saying goes, what the eyes don't see the heart will never grieve." Loud laughter came from them again that the diners looking at them. But they couldn't care a damn.

"Lisa, you're glutton for punishment. Anyway, they said any other child slips out easily after the first born, but for me, I don't think I would want to go down that road too quickly again" Denyah said.

"Well, I guess its now my turn" Meleta said laughing. "My Ryan married me because he loves me and I love him. I wasn't a virgin when he met me but I was tight. Very tight that he asked me, if I was a virgin. Meleta laughed. My first boyfriend cheated on me with my sister, to make a long story short, I caught my sister in my bed on top of my man and I wiped her arse until she begged me not to beat her anymore. As for the son-of–a bitch of a boyfriend, I landed one of my dad's beers to his head chopping him and as I was going to land a second, he ran out the house naked and over the fence he jumped like a horse would jumping over the hurdle. All I could have seen was his balls flapping behind him and oh boy, the way he jumped over the fence with his balls flinging behind him. I had to look in the fence to see if he left his balls behind" There was a such a loud laughing came from them that a nice waitress went to them and said, "I like diners like you that make this hotel comes alive" the waitress then left smiling.

"Well friends, I am Debra Saunders and I got to know this lovely Denyah on the plane coming home. As my husband was watching her so hard with his tongue hung out of his mouth like he was catching flies, I wrongly accused my friend Denyah of flirting with my deceiving bitch of a husband. But my, oh my, was I wrong. Then as I approached my friend here with my insults, she promised to kick me out of the plane. Then as I found out she's not one of my husband's type of a bitches, I apologised to her and took my seat like a sheep dog beside the dog of my husband. Then my friend Den here came and sat beside me after I spend about an hour sitting with her and to my surprised she kissed me and the dog of a husband on our faces. I was so surprised that tears come into my eyes when you left me. Den I love you as I love myself. However, I married three times. My first husband left me for a school girl and then wanted to come back to me. He was the one that scored me when I was a virgin. And believed me his cock was like it had a double head. As for his balls, they were like two big egg plants. I'd felt sorrier for the school girl than for me. I was getting beating from him both ways, from his cock and his balls and when he comes, he groaned like a flipping lion. My second husband, his cock could have nearly measured up to a donkey. I'd to run from him otherwise by now I would be pissing myself as he would leave my pussy like a running top. Now with this husband I have now, I don't like to have sex with him when he's pissed as he couldn't care witch hole he enters so long as he get his fuck. " A hearty laughed was bellowed out again as Debra Saunders told her story.

Cindy began to tell her story "Frank is my first and I hope he would be my last as I was a virgin. I felt pain, but it was worth it for he's the love of my life and he always sucks my nipples when we are having sex - he will lift himself up off me and gracefully I would see his cock slipped in and out and in and out until he's ready to explode and then he would really give me a feel for his money and then paw! He really sent his pistol up me and shot his load messing all over my legs and bottom and then grinned in my face and rolled off me saying don't wake me till I gather another load to shoot up into that honey pot and then I heard him snoring like thunder. Cindy yelped in laughter and the others.

"As all eyes stared on Kalor she smiled. "Oh no," she said looking at Denyah. "Well come on Kalor, tell us your love story." Denyah said. Kalor giggled, "Well Kalor, you heard ours, now we like to hear yours" Paula said. Kalor giggled again and said "Well, firstly, I think I was too young and naïve when I had sex with the man I thought I'd fell in love with. As he was easing his dick into me, the pain was crucial so that I cried softly and eased to the pain but as he was coming he rooted into me like he was digging a hole and he was in a hurry. He burst my pussy bleeding and left me in horrible pain that I'd never wanted to have sex ever again. I got to hate him even more as it had turned out that he wasn't the face I was enjoy looking at. But to achieve my model career, each time we had sex, I closed my eyes and chew chewing gum otherwise I would feel sick even though he was good-looking and well built, tall and dark. Then I fell in love with a nice guy but his cock could have also measure up to at least ten inches with a round ball head. But, I had run from him like wild fire as I know having sex again, I would bleed and felt hurt as before. But as he was the one to help me to further my modelling career, I made my mind up and let him have sex with me and many times until I was enjoying him. Well my friend married him and she told me, she would anointed his cock with Vaseline before she let him have sex as his cock is too big and when he's ejaculating he dribbled on her face and groaned like a bitch in pain till he finished and rolled off her. And she said she can swim about a mile on his semen the amount he would leave on her. Anyway, as my modelling career took off and he said I still owe him a body wine up. Then the man I'd fell in love with, he had the perfect cock but I finished with him as I caught him having sex with another one of my friends on my settee. And for almost three months I didn't had sex and I was willing to say goodbye to all men until three weeks ago I met one of the most handsome blue eyed man and when I approached him, he refused me. So, I bet him he would give into me. You know what he told me, he rather poke his dick into a bottle. But I know my time would come when he won't resist me. Well, he couldn't refused me after I stripped myself naked in front of him and bent forward and manoeuvring towards his cock until it became hard. The next thing happened he dropped his trousers and rushed into me from behind. And believe me I did enjoy him as I love him. Actually he said he could never have sex with me again and that we could never be lovers as he loves his wife too much. Well, after getting to know his wife, and she's so lovely, I left him alone as I wouldn't want to bust up his home. But now I'm going out with Larance - Bernice's brother. Bernice, I would never cheat on your brother ever cause I love him and what I did, it was before his time. Bernice your brother really made me felt good when we're having sex, he's so gentle right up to the end of our intercourse and I love to be with him and his dick suited me and I enjoy him every time that I even take a turn on top. " Kalor said.

"There was a loud laughing from the fifteen of them. Then Bernice told her, "I'm happy for you Kalor and I hope my brother marries you."

As time went on, Fay pulled Denyah out of her seat and danced with her to (I'm in love with you girl.) After the fifteen of them drank seven bottles of champagne and other mixture of drinks, Fay showed off her Diamond engagement ring.

"Well, Lisa said, Denyah my dearest loving friend, I was saving the best for last. I know you would thank me for this, but first, how much do you love me?"

"Lisa, I wouldn't know how to love you any more. So please don't put me under the spotlight." Denyah said.

"Come on Lisa, what you and Den used to get up to." Meleta asked interestedly.

"That you'll have to find out all by your self," Lisa said feeling high.

"Well, girlfriends, I would like the thirteen of you to witness, as from now, my best friend Denyah as well as my ex-sister-in-law is no longer married to my rat of a brother. Den, here's your freedom, your proof of divorce. I stole it from my brother while cleaning his bedroom, signed and sealed under his pillow. Don't say I haven't given you your freedom back" Lisa said and hugged Denyah.

Denyah was so shocked even though she was feeling tipsy, she cried for joy as she hugged Lisa. "Take it easy honey I don't want to give you a crushed niece or nephew." Lisa said.

"Aye Den honey, stop crying, I thought you wanted to marry the man you love. Here's your chance to be his loving wife. You best hold on tightly to your freedom. My brother had this for the past two months signed and sealed under his pillar. Now you can get married whenever you like. Honey, good luck and don't forget to invite us, especially me." Lisa said and laughed.

"Well girls, it's time we get home to our loving family. Are any of you too drunk to drive? I am, so I am calling my husband to take me home." Lisa said.

"We all will phone our husbands to come and get us." Paula said feeling merry.

Fay asked for the bill so she could pay. Bernice tipped the waitress fifty pounds and so did Denyah and Fay. Fay laughed saying, "Yesterday I had nothing. "Tonight I'm marrying a very handsome very well off Solicitor. Thanks to my good friend Bernice. And Den honey, I can now pay you back the loan and I thank you for giving me advice and for putting up with a bitch like me. I love you. I love all of you here my friends. Den I'm going to pay you every penny back."

"You keep it Fay as a wedding gift." Denyah told her.

"Well, thank you sister." Fay said.

Each of them phoned their husbands to come and take them home. Patrick and Eugene had a lift with Ryan as Denyah and Bernice drove their own cars to the hotel.

As they waited for their husbands to come and fetch them, the manager said "Girls I've enjoyed your company. Please come again soon." he then went on saying, "It's the first time I had so many beautiful and full of life ladies dining in here and at one time. Fay paid the full bill of seven hundred and forty two pounds with gold credit card Mr Rogers gave to her.

The husbands went to the hotel and took their wives home. At home, Denyah was all over Eugene kissing him all over his face and neck as she was feeling tipsy. "Den honey, take it easy. You know that I love you." Eugene told her.

"Honey, I really do love you and I want you. I want another baby now." she said.

"Den honey, I love you very much. But you're drunk and I won't take advantage of you. I would like more children but not this way. Now please go to bed." Eugene told her and then undressed her and as he saw she was having her periods, he cleaned her legs with warm water using a flannel before he push a tampax up her and dressed her in pyjamas and then put her to bed. As his baby son began to cry, he took him out of his cot bed, fed him, changed him and held him until he dropped off to sleep then he kissed him on his little forehead saying "Daddy loves you." and he put him down gently in his cot bed.

The following morning, Denyah was feeling so sick that she couldn't even cope with her children. Eugene and Mrs Brown looked after the children. Later in the afternoon, Eugene asked her, "How you feeling honey?"

"Oh darling, it's the last time for me drinking. How did I get into my pyjamas honey?" she asked him trying to get out of bed.

"I put them on you after I cleaned you." Eugene said.

"I can't remember any of this. Did you put a tampax on me too?" Denyah asked.

"I had too. Den, you were so pissed up and messy. I was expecting you to have a good time and not come home drunk. Junior's just a baby and he needs a sober mother." Eugene said.

"Honey, as I told you, it was my first and last time I will get drunk."

"You have that in one sweetheart. You ready for something to eat?" Eugene asked.

"Not yet honey, I'm still feeling sick and weak. How's my babies honey, I should have put them first. I wished I hadn't drunk so much champagne. Oh honey, can you pass me a couple of paracetamol out of my handbag as I have a splitting headache." Denyah said.

Eugene reached for her handbag and took the paracetamol out and gave a couple to her and some water. As he was putting the handbag down, she said "Would you mind passing me my diary, I need to phone my sister Laney to know how they are getting on."

As Eugene was searching for her diary, he came across the envelope addressed to Wesley. He looked hard at Denyah and holding the envelope.

"What's the matter honey?" she asked him.

"What's this? Why is it addressed to Wesley and is now in your possession?"

"Eugene, what are you talking about?"

"I'm talking about this letter. Are you having second thought about us?"

"Eugene, I love you." she said. Then she suddenly remembered Lisa gave her a signed divorce statement that her ex-husband had signed and wanted to keep. "Oh my God, Eugene, that is to prove I've got my divorce. Wesley has finally given me my divorce. You're holding it in you hand."

Eugene quickly pulled the documents out the envelope and looked at it with interest. Smiling, he went and sat on the bed and holding Denyah's hand, "Honey." he say happily, "You know what this means to us?"

"We can get married as soon as I declare my divorce. I would like for you and mom to follow me to court to prove I'm single again. You wouldn't need to sign as Lisa and Richard have signed."

"Den, would you marry me?"

"This minute, my darling," Denyah said.

Just then Mrs Brown knocked on the door, "Come in mom." Eugene said.

"Den honey, would you like a little supper. You hadn't had any breakfast, lunch, nor dinner and you'll have to eat as you're breastfeeding Junior as well."

The phone started ringing. Mrs Brown answered the phone in Denyah's room. "Hello"

"Mother Brown it's me Fay, can I speak to Denyah please?"

"Of course honey," Mrs Brown said and she passed the phone to Denyah saying, "It's Fay."

"Hello Fay." Denyah said with her eyes half closed.

"Den, how's your head honey, mine feels as if I'm carrying a sack of potatoes. I was drunk a few times, but never in history have I felt like this. However, Guy and I set the date to get married next month the third week Saturday. Den, your divorce has come through, mom gave me the letter as the one you have is Wesley's. I opened it thinking that it was a letter came for me as I didn't look at the name. I'm sorry. Aye, we could get hitched at the same time."

"Will you please hold on to that piece of precious paper for me, how's mom and Blanch?"

"They're doing well, oh Den I will be able to take care of Blanch through University as I will be starting to work next month after I'm married. I got a job as a secretary to work with my husband."

"What about mom? I though you said you have to take care of her when I asked Eugene to give you a job."

"Yes Denyah, my reason was because I didn't want to meet up with Wesley or his kind. Anyway, it's time I take on a ladies role. Mom is getting better, but I would be able to hire a helper to look after her. Den, all the wrong I've done to you, I truly regret." Fay said.

"Forget it Fay, just don't let Blanch down in any way. However, how would you and Guy like to spend your honeymoon in St.Kitts to see your other half sister Laney and her family, they're absolutely lovely. I had a hell of a time." Denyah said.

"Den, I think I will take you up on that offer. I will tell Guy. Den, I do love you. And thanks for helping me to be a better woman." Fay said.

"Goodbye Fay." Denyah said and put the phone down.

Mrs Brown took Denyah supper to her. "Here honey, eat up while Junior's sleeping. The girls and their dad are having theirs, would you like some ice cream, apple crumble or trifle?"

"Oh mom, neither. I still felt like I'm drowning in a tub of champagne.

"That will teach you, don't take what you can't handle" Mrs Brown said and laughed.

"I'll take you advice mom. And thanks for looking after us."

"That's what moms are for honey, to take the very best care of their family. That's good. I saw you ate all your supper. Oh dear, you're soaked. When was the last time you breast feed Junior?"

"Yesterday, before I went and got drunk," Denyah said laughing.

"Well, would you like to feed him? He's due for feeding. I will give him his nightly bath after the girls have theirs. By the way, Den, I'm so happy you would be taking Blanch and your mother to live with us."

"I was, but Fay has decided to take care of them both now she's in a better position. That's what she told me, I would still do my part to see Blanch in Uni. This is her last year in school, and she decided she wanted to go to university, to study be a doctor or a Solicitor"

"Den, you're so good to everyone. I know for sure you wouldn't have left your husband if he'd treated you right. But thank God he drives you in the right hands. Well, I'm going to set the children's bath."

"Thanks mom."

"Den, you don't have to thank me. Honey, I'm their grandmother and it's part of my duty to see them okay" Then the phones start ringing. Mrs Brown picked the phone up and answered "Hello."

"Hello mother Brown, "Oh hello Laney. Your sister's here" Mrs Brown said and passed the phone on to Denyah telling her "Give my love to her and her family."

Denyah smiled and said "Hello sis,"

"Hello Den my darling, we're over here and very well and so happy thanks to the Good Lord that reached your heart to find us. The girls can't stop talking about their Aunt Denyah and Nanny Brown. Paul is doing more than well. A thousand thanks from us to you and the family. Would you like me to send anything?"

"No honey, I have all I need including you and my family. Well honey, give Paul and the kids a big hug from me and the family. Remember to call me if you need me. Oh the baby is doing well. Goodbye my dear sister." Denyah said.

"Goodbye sister Den and also give my family a big hug from us. I won't forget to call you. I owe you a call." Laney said.

"And I owe you too Laney honey. Kiss Paul and the kids for us and give your mother our love" Denyah said and put the phone down.

One week later on Sunday afternoon, Mr Frats had all his family to dinner; again he was looking so joyous that his face lit up like a blazing fire and especially when Patrick called him dad.

As Mr Frats was admiring his grandchildren playing and running all over his enormous living room, his face glowed with happiness. He looked well contented and especially when little Kiah climbed up to his chest and was playing with his silver grey beard. As the children was making too much noise running and jumping over his settees and furniture, Denyah asked them to be a little quiet and she tried to stop running,

Mr Frats said "Leave them be," as he was smirking all over his face. "My heart couldn't be any fuller with happiness seeing my grandchildren helping to smash-up some of their profit" he laughed, as Denyah smiled out of politeness just to please him.

After a long evening, everyone told him goodbye. His sons Patrick, Eugene, Ray, Carl, shook his hand and daughter Jenny and the daughters-in-laws and grand- children hugged and kissed him on his cheek before they left.

In bed that night, Eugene was thinking about his newly discovered father. Eugene thought he must be so lonely and all alone in his eight bedroom house.

When Denyah saw the gloomy expression on Eugene's face, she asked him "What are you thinking about now? Is it one of you lady friends?"

"Den, you're the only woman I have and would ever want in my life."

"So why do you look so sad then honey?" she asked him.

"Oh nothing, go to sleep Denyah." Eugene told her.

As Denyah saw the worried expression on Eugene's face, she faced him and hugged him saying. "Honey you face tells me something's bothering you."

"I'm okay honey," you go to sleep" he said and kissed her. As she felt warm emotional feelings towards him, she slipped out of her pyjamas and encouraged him to make love to her. As they were having sexual intercourse, he knew she wasn't quite ready from the fixation of her face and her fidgety movement. "Honey, why have you encouraged me when you were not ready? Eugene said.

"Why do you say that?" Denyah asked him.

"I realized by the tenseness of face you weren't ready for me. I'm hurting you honey?" Eugene said.

"A little, but I wanted you. I must admit I'm still feeling tender inside, maybe a little sore." Denyah said.

After Eugene reached his climax he pulled out showing blood on his penis, with a little blood seeping out on the sheets and on Denyah's legs "Have I hurt you much honey?" Eugene asked her.

"A little," she said smiling. "But I'm feeling so happy I was so longing for you."

"Den, I was thinking of dad living alone in such big house and it worried me that if things should go wrong and no one is there to help him, it might be fatal before help could reach him. It must be so lonely at nights for him." Eugene said.

"Well, why don't you have a word with Veda and Carl? They might be willing to stay with him sometimes. I'm going to tidy myself. Would you mind change the sheets for us honey?" Denyah asked Eugene then she gave two clean sheets and took the soiled one and put them into the washed basket and then had a quick shower and returned to her room to see her bed was done. She climbed into bed and under the quilt while Eugene went to the bathroom and had a quick shower and returned to bed with two cups of coffee for her and him.

As Eugene was twisting and turning and couldn't sleep, he woke Denyah and told her that he was sorry for leaving his dad Frats on his own and in such a big house. Tears came into his eyes.

Denyah understood and said, "Carl and Veda can keep his company some times as I told you as Jenny and her boyfriend are always together at home. I'm sure Veda would prefer to be living with your dad than to be staying at your devious false mother's house. Can't you see Eugene, instead of Carl and Veda buying their home, they could move in with him. I'm sure your dad would be happy about that." Denyah said.

"Denyah honey, you just hit the nail right on the head. I would speak to dad tomorrow and then to Carl and Veda. Incidentally, dad asked us again to come to Sunday lunch. I would like you to asked Meleta Ryan, Lisa and Richard, David and Tracy. To me, they are family. Patrick, Ray and Carl will be there with their family." Eugene said.

"Eugene, I'm so happy that you boys eventually accepted your true dad and made him part of your family." Denyah said.

"Den, take a look at what he gave me. I told him I don't need his money. And yet he shoved a ten million pounds cheque in my shirt pocket then told me he has one each for my brothers. I really don't want anything from him, but he was so persistent and wouldn't take no for an answer. However, I would donate this money to hospitals across the country in memory of your late friend Nurse James and mother Carter."

"Oh Eugene, that's marvellous. Thank you very much. Giving you this money, he wants to try and make up for the past even it was not his fault." Denyah said.

"But why force his money unto me, even though I told him I didn't need his money" Eugene said.

"Eugene, he knew that. And I am not at all surprised with him wanting to share his wealth to the five of you. Oh, my sister phoned to say they're doing very well" Denyah said.

"Which sister," Eugene asked.

"Laney, you know, the one in St Kitts, aye, you looked so far away. What's the matter now honey?"

"Den, I don't know what that man is after." Eugene said.

"Eugene, for the love of God, he just wants to be a good father to the five of you. Just remember you were stolen from him by a very powerful step-father. I understand you have a right to feel that he's bribing you to love him as a father. But I do think he only wants to make up with you. It's no fault of yours or his that he wasn't around to take care of any of you. Eugene, he had no chance to be with any of you. So please, would you give him that chance to get to know you better? I'm sure the others don't feel pressured as you. Your dad simple loves you all even though you all have grownup. Is he so wrong to love you?" Denyah asked Eugene. "Please Eugene don't do as Mr Lake does, make your long lost father feel that warm glow from you."

Eugene made no reply.

"Can we get some sleep now?" Denyah asked. He faced Denyah in bed, hugged her in his arms and fell asleep.

CHAPTER TWENTY ONE

The following morning while Denyah and her family were having breakfast, Mrs Brown answered the ringing telephone saying, "You have the nerve of the devil" Denyah looked on at Mrs Brown in wonder holding a slice of toast to her mouth. "Yes he's here. And if Eugene uses his senses, he will keep well away from you. Wesley, you're a wicked serpent. My Den is so happy now and I want you to leave us alone." Mrs Brown told Wesley and then gave the phone to Eugene.

Before Eugene spoke to Wesley, he looked at Denyah in wonder then said. "Yes, what can I do for you?"

"Well, I want to congratulate you on your son even now he's older. You're more lucky than me mate to score her. Oh, I almost forgot that I want to speak to you about the dominos you asked me to get for you"

"Look mate, Denyah is now my wife and please don't call this number again. About the dominos, you can forget it!" Eugene told Wesley and put the phone down on the receiver. The phone rang again. Eugene answered.

"Look mate, I know when to cut loose, I have the dominos for you, I'm courting again and I would like to remain friends with you as I'm asking you to let me see Paris sometime. I want nothing more to do with Denyah."

"Okay, I'll take your word as a friend." Eugene said.

By then Mrs Brown had left the kitchen leaving Denyah eating her breakfast.

As Eugene sat down at the table, he smiled.

"Eugene, why are you so tightly up that devious bastards arse, Wesley is using you to get to me. He has lost my sister Fay, his mistress Bonnie and God knows who-else including his only sister Lisa."

"Den, you're so naive, he's simple buying me a set of dominoes of my request and I would like you to fetch them for me and please don't look at me like I'm a criminal. Wesley knew when to cut his losses. It's over a year since you left him and he can't harm you anymore."

"Eugene, I don't want to see Wesley again. He's the one person on God's earth I really should keep away from. As I said, Wesley is playing you for a fool. He's very dangerous and you should keep well away from him too." Denyah told Eugene.

Eugene moved away from the table looking vexed. He turned and faced Denyah saying, "Are you going to get the dominoes from him or not!"

Denyah burst into tears staring at him and said "If you so want to drive me back into that poisonous good for nothings arms, you're going about it in the right way. But if when I go to fetch your damn dominoes you're so eager for, and anything goes wrong, I hope you will be able to live with it and to tell our children you forced me to do what I didn't want."

Eugene said nothing but left to go with his brothers Patrick and Ray to see their dad Mr Frats at his hotel.

Denyah felt saddened and hurt for the rest of the day and hardly ate her dinner.

"Den honey, has that vicious ex-husband upset you?" Mrs Brown asked.

"Not more than Eugene mom. Sometimes, I wondered why I bother with men."

Late that evening Eugene came home. He hardly said anything to Denyah. Mrs Brown didn't like it when Denyah and Eugene were not speaking. She felt so uneasy to see Denyah unhappy. However, she heated Eugene's supper and then said to him, "Son, I hate to see you and Den so unhappy."

"I've eaten at the hotel. Thanks mom. I should have let you know before."

"That's okay son, I should have asked you first."

"Goodnight mom." Eugene said.

"Goodnight son." Mrs Brown answered.

As Eugene came home tipsy he went to bed with his clothes on and fell asleep. Denyah took his clothes off leaving him in his boxer shorts.

Early the next morning, Jade B climbed up in bed next to her dad. Paris followed her and as she saw him sleeping in his boxer shorts she asked her mommy. "Why is daddy sleeping in his boxer shorts and not in his pyjamas?"

"Your dad was very tired honey, so he fell asleep before he put his pyjamas on. Anyway, since you two are up, I better get you in the bath before your baby brother wakes."

"Mom, I'm still tired, can I sleep with you and dad?" Paris asked.

Well, of course you can." Denyah said, but before Paris could climb up beside her dad, Jade B wedged herself between her dad and Denyah. Denyah got out of bed and left them lying beside their dad and went and had her shower then as she returned to her room to see them playing horses on their dad's back and making laughing noises.

Mrs Brown went to them saying "Come on young ladies, I've set your bath and your breakfast is almost ready. Den, I think you could do with some more sleep. I would see to the children and then I will bring your breakfast and our baby feed up to you." Mrs Brown told Denyah.

"No need to do that mom, I'm not really tired. You go and have your breakfast while I see to the girls while our son is still sleeping." Denyah said.

As Denyah left the room, Mrs Brown said to her on the stairways, "Den sweetheart, you can put me in my place by telling me to mind my business. However, I couldn't help myself from hearing Eugene asking you to collect something from your ex-husband. Well, I think Eugene isn't thinking clearly. I also think you going to that devious ex-husband's house, would be a very bad mistake. I don't care much for you going there but it's up to you." Mrs Brown left Denyah looking sad and disturbed so that when she was setting the plates, two of them slipped out of her hand and smashed. Shaking her head, she spoke to herself saying, "Please God, let Eugene see through that wicked Wesley and what it is doing to him and our lovely Den," Mrs Brown then wiped tears from her eyes before Denyah and the children sat at the table for breakfast.

Denyah saw the smashed plates on the breakfast area floor to one side in the corner, but said nothing. "Oh I had an accident with two plates slipping from my hands." Mrs Brown said.

"Have you hurt yourself mom?" Denyah asked her,

"No, oh no, but losing two it spoil the set."

"Mom, they're not important, you are, and I'm happy to know that you are okay. So don't worry over what can be replaced mom."

"Den, I'm so worried over you and I really don't feel happy at the thought of you going to Wesley's house ever, Eugene shouldn't send you to him for anything as that louse can't be trusted."

Denyah said nothing, but her eyes showing fear. Mrs Brown vaguely smiled and then left leaving Denyah, Paris and Jade B in the breakfast area having their breakfast before Eugene joined them.

Mrs Brown was worrying about Denyah going to Wesley so much it brought on her migraine like she had experienced three years ago. And because she was worrying so deeply over Denyah, she went to her room and cried secretly. After Mrs Brown spent a long time in her room, she went to the bathroom and washed her face before she went into the kitchen and faced Denyah and Eugene. She wasn't at all feeling happy, but she put on a cheerful face. Later on, Eugene phoned Patrick and told him Mr Frats would like all of his family and friends to have dinner at his home the following Sunday.

"Well dad, I would let the family know." Patrick said, "I would pass on the message to the rest of the family, including Lisa, Meleta, Tracy and their husbands. Well dad, you will be going away on business for the following two weeks, which is why you want us to have dinner with you before you go."

"Yes son, I would be going to Turkey to sort out some business." Mr Frats said.

Patrick went to see Eugene and told him, "Dad wants us to have dinner with him Saturday."

"Patrick, since you get to know this geezer, you have tied your apron string to his. Are you sure we're not pressuring him too much?" Eugene asked.

"I don't think so," Patrick said. Anyway, he asked me to pass this message on to you, Ray and Carl. I wonder what that man is up too, He's acting very strange. By the way, don't forget to let our friend's know they're invited to dinner next Saturday.

"Patrick, you said you were taking the family to the pictures on Saturday. Are you still going?" Eugene asked.

"No. Not if we have to go and have dinner with dad" Patrick said then goes on

"Anyway, from when he came in our lives, he has invited us out to more dinners than I had at home. Eugene, I wonder just what he's really up to this time. By the way, I have a message for you from an admirer. The pretty lady that kissed you last night,"

"Patrick, Den's the only one woman in my life, and I intend to keep it that way. Any others would have to go through her to get to me." Eugene said.

"Ok, Eugene, I believe you. But what should I tell her when I see her?"

"Believe me or not Patrick, Den is the love of my life. Tell her I'm not interested and I'm a family man with children." Eugene said.

Patrick laughed saying. "Okay brother,"

"Patrick, why don't you have her?" Eugene told him.

"Like you brother, I can't afford to lose my family." Patrick said.

Two days later, Eugene went to Cardiff, Chelsea and Spain in the same week on business and took food stock in his hotels and restaurants. Every night of the week he phoned Denyah to ask if she and the family were alright and as he got to meet a few of her mother's family in Spain including one of her mother's sisters, Rona. Eugene was more than happy when Rona invited him to corned beef and salad lunch on a sunny Wednesday afternoon. Over lunch Eugene and his Aunt Rona chatted mostly about his mother. "Your mother was very beautiful and I used to get jealous of her. She would have all the boys carrying her school books while I trod behind her carrying mine. "Yes Eugene, your mother was the prettiest in our class. In fact, she was the prettiest in the whole school. She was vivacious and after she left school, she gave up the chance to be a pharmacist and went to England. After four years, mom died, she attended her funeral. She then went back to England. We took turns phoning each other but one day I phoned her and I was told by her landlord she moved, I'd not heard from her again. Well, you're very handsome. Tell me Eugene, how many children did you're mother have? I only have one daughter,"

"She has five of us, four lads myself included and a daughter. We are all married now and I have three kids, my eldest brother Patrick has three girls and a son and another on its way. My young brother Raymond is soon to have one and my youngest brother Carl has none at the moment. I'm the second son and youngest of all is Jenny. She's engaged. Well thanks for lunch and I would like for us to meet again Aunt Rona"

"Well goodbye Eugene, I hope the next time you call you'll meet my daughter Irene. She's in Paris on a design course. Goodbye Eugene and give my love to all."

Eugene waved goodbye to his Aunt Rona and left in his hired car to his hotel.

Back home in England Patrick also did Eugene the favour and told all concerned that Mr Frats has invited them to dinner on Saturday evening.

Three days later, Eugene returned home and told Denyah all about his mother's family and his mother's sister Rona that he met in Spain and as well as some of his family that are living in Italy. Denyah wasn't in the least interested as she wasn't happy going to her ex-husband. But, because she was so in love with Eugene, she smiled and said, "I'm happy you met some of your family." But she had in her back of her head, I would do what Eugene wants no matter how much she hated to because of her love for him.

The Saturday came when the family met up at Mr Frats to have dinner. Every couple sat next to their partners around the special thirty two seats oblong dark rich looking mahogany table with their children sitting next to them. As Mr Frats looked on them all, a bright smile came on his face. Then, just before dinner was served, Mr Frats stood up and blessed the food in his Italian language and said how much he was in love with their mother and then translated into English. But as only Denyah and Eugene understood the Italian language Eugene spoke in Italian. "That is a nice speech. And we all must thank our long lost old fart of a dad."

Denyah looked hard at Eugene and said in Italian language, "Eugene honey, sit down and shut up!" The family looked at Denyah and Eugene in wonder and interest before Mr Frats smiled and said "Thank you son. I agreed that I was a long lost old fart and now I'm found with my lovely family."

All the family burst into laughter.

As Eugene looked at his dad, he felt love for him more deeply than before. Then as Eugene was trying to explain to his brothers, Denyah and his sister Jenny that his father's speech was about his natural mother, Denyah said "I know and I understand he had loved her and still does." Then as Mr Frats heard Denyah said to him in the Italian language "I'm sure she knows you did love her."

"With my whole heart, mind, body and soul" Mr Frats said looking very happy. All looked at Denyah and then at Mr Frats. Mr Frats smiled and left his seat and kissed Denyah on her forehead and then said in English, "I will treasure every moment of time I spent with you my loving family. I love you all very deeply and I thank the good and merciful God whom has blessed me with a second chance to restore my precious family back to me. Thank you my merciful God and thank you my precious family" Mr Frats then looked up at the ceiling before he said happily, "Family, let's eat" But this time his grey eyes glittered with happiness. He put his arms around Eugene and Patrick's shoulders then walking them away from the table to the far side in the room, spoke to them a little about their mother before they returned to the table and took their seats. Mr Frats looked at Ray, Carl and Jenny with smiles and love.

Just before they had eaten, every one raised their glass in honour of their mother and father Mr Frats. "The next time we have dinner it would be in the hotel so that every family and friends would come and enjoy themselves." Mr Frats said.

"About my true mother," Carl said, "I would have liked to know her and, I surely miss her" Carl tears dropped heavily on his lap and he moved into the living room. His fiancée Veda followed behind and hugged him and comforted him then Mr Frats followed behind them.

"Carl my young son, I'm so sorry to speak of your mother and to spoil everything when we are supposed to be happy together at this special moment instead of me being careful of what I said, I've dug the past up and I made you so unhappy. I'm sorry. Please forgive me and try to enjoy what's left of the evening. Veda, I thank you for your compassion. I saw just how much you love my son and I love you." Mr Frats said and then he walked Veda and Carl to the table again and after he saw them sat, he smiled and said "I love you." And as he made to leave, Paula held his hand and told him, "You're my stepfather. And I insist you should sit down with us your family and eat with us." Every one laughed including Carl.

"Paula, would you please try and use the correct words, by saying father-in-law and not stepfather," Meleta said.

"Well, what ever, I love you daddy Frats." Paula said.

Everyone laughed and seemed to be very happy again.

After dinner and much later on the evening, Paula though it would be a good idea to turn the evening into a party, so she played some of Mr Frats CDs mostly love songs to cheer up the place and she even played some reggae. After Mr Frats had a few scotches, he had them listening to him and called them by name as he said "Patrick, Eugene, Raymond, Carlton, Jenny. And I am very happy to be a second dad to the five of you. I thought I would die a lonely old man, but I have a lot to thank the good Lord for. You're my children, as I have told you before, I was married long after when I knew I couldn't have your mother again, but I'd divorced as I couldn't love her as I'd loved your mother. I thank God profoundly that I found all of you that were taken away from me. And I'm really very happy. Before you leave nothing would make me happier, than for all of you to spend this coming Christmas with me."

Paula again said "Daddy Frats, it would be an honour to spend Christmas with you in your Mansion or your big house. So this means Ray and I would be sleeping Christmas-eve night with you which is just nine weeks away?"

"Paula, it would be an honour." Mr Frats said and smiled. "Well we have nine weeks left before Christmas. " Mr Frats said and I would like for us all to spend Christmas together."

Paula again answered, "Daddy Frats, me and my husband Ray would be very happy to wake up with you Christmas morning and serve you your breakfast."

Mr Frats smiled and then said, "I would be very happy for all here, and the grandchildren to wake me with pleasant noises Christmas morning."

"So shall it be." Eugene said, looking into Denyah's eyes.

"We all agree Patrick said, so did David and his fiancée, Ray and Meleta, Lisa and Richard, and the rest of their family. After an enjoyable day, Carl and Veda spent the night at Mr Frats. The Sunday morning, Carl and Veda went home and had a bath, packed their pyjamas and a change of clothes for them to spend a few days with Mr

Frats. They spent the Sunday and Monday with Mr Frats. And the Tuesday afternoon, they all went and spent the day with Mr Frats again.

Again, Mr Frat's face showed he was extremely happy and excited when Eugene and Patrick and their family showed up. As Mr Frats and children were playing and running up and down his long corridor his face lit up like a ten year old joyous boy. After an hour or so, he asked the children to excuse him while he went to speak to Carl and Veda before they leave to go home. Denyah went to one of his bedrooms to breast feed and change her baby.

"Dad, it's getting late, and I'll like to take Veda home as she on early morning."

"I understand son, will I see you soon?" Mr Frats asked Carl.

"Yes of course dad, you'll see me later tonight." Carl said.

"Well goodnight to you and Veda for now." Mr Frats said.

"And to you Mr Frats" Veda said and she left with Carl to take her home but Carl went back and slept that night.

Eugene and Patrick and their family wished him goodnight and left happily as Carl was there.

The following evening, Patrick, Eugene and Ray went to Mr Frats and they spent a couple of hours with him. Veda cooked supper. After they ate, Veda was playing some discs while Mr Frats and Carl were playing blackjack. As it was getting late, Carl said, "Well dad, I hate to leave you, but as last night, I have to take Veda home for her to get some sleep as she's still on early morning shift."

Veda hugged Mr Frats and said goodbye then moved to her and Carl's car. As Carl wished his dad goodnight he joined Veda in the car. He started his car and faced Mr Frats to see his face showed sadness. Even though Mr Frats tried to hide his feelings and faked a smile, tears came into his eyes. Carl looked away and rested his forehead on the steering wheel in thought as Mr Frats sadly walked to his door, waved good bye and walked into his house and closed the door.

"Carl honey, I think your dad's crying," Veda whispered. Carl pretended not to hear or take any notice of Veda as tears came into his eyes. As Veda was about to speak again, he stopped her by saying loudly. "Shit- shit- shit. Veda, I hate to leave him this way now I got to know him and like him. What do you think we should do?" Carl asked and wiped his tears.

"We should ask him if he want us to move in with him." Veda said.

"Yes honey, that's what we should do - and get married." Carl said and kissed Veda then turned the key in the ignition starting his car and smiling.

Mr Frats slightly moved the lace to have a look at Carl and Veda but Veda saw him and she waved goodbye smiling. Mr Frats opened his door and walked out and stood behind his gate and smile. Carl smile to him, blew his car horn and drove away. Veda looked back at him saying. "Poor old dad," Carl looked at her and as he was driving slowly away from the mansion's gate. Mr Frats barely raise his hand to wave goodbye.

"Carl, he looked like he's really missing us already. I think we should spend a few weeks with him. Then we should ask him if he would like us to move in with him to keep him company. Yes, we should tell him the next time we see him." Veda said smoothly with sorrowful feelings for him.

"Veda honey, let's not be in a hurry aye, as I just thought he mightn't even want us around him twenty-four-hours of the day. Remember he used to be on his own for years" Carl said smiling.

"Carl, your dad is knocking on. He needs someone to be with him. And, you and I should be the ones to move in with him as we will be soon married. I do really like him. And I would like to help take care of him." Veda said.

"Okay Veda, let's spend a few weeks with him before we make any decisions on moving in with him. Now I got to know him, I like the old geezer too. But we don't want him to think we're with him for what he has." Carl said.

"You know what honey? You're absolutely right." Veda asked. "I absolutely agree with you honey that we should take it slowly and see if the old man wants us to live with him. You know what honey?" Veda said.

"What Veda?" Carl asked.

"I love you with my whole heart." Veda said.

"I love you with my whole heart too Veda." Carl said.

Each Sunday of the month, Mr Frats' four sons took turns and invite him to have lunch and dinner. As Jenny, Carl and Veda were living in the same house, Veda would do the cooking as Jenny wasn't a good cook.

One Friday evening, Mr Frats invited Eugene and Patrick to a favourite hotel to have dinner.

Over dinner, Eugene said, "Dad, this is a brilliant restaurant and the food taste brilliant"

"That's why I asked you both here. I like it here as I like to escape from people who know me. Come on, have some more champagne both of you."

"Dad, I have to be sober when I get home." Eugene said then he went on, "Dad, you have so many hotels and restaurants all over the place and abroad, so why do you eat here on a regular basis in someone else's restaurant?"

"As I told you, to escape from some of the people that I don't wish to see some of the times, besides, it's a test to sample someone else's cooking. However, I'm enjoying being with both of you."

After Patrick and Eugene left, Mr Frats told a Mr Meah, "Eugene and Patrick are my sons and they should never know the restaurant is mine-at least not yet."

"I understand Mr Frats. You can count on me" Mr Meah said.

One week, Saturday evening four days before Christmas Eve, Mr Frats had his entire family at his home for dinner. After dinner, Mr Frats played happily with his grandchildren. He joked, "I'm no longer a workaholic in my hotels or restaurants. Gaining my entire family has induced me not to work so hard. I can now take it easy," he smiled and said.

Then laughing again, he asked his family to excuse him as he got up and went to each of his employees and gave each of them a sealed envelope and after joined his family again with a nice smile.

As Eugene looked at him, he said, "It's time I treated my workers with more respect and small gifts now and again as well as raising their salaries. I couldn't wish for better employees. They work extremely hard and they're very sincere, so it's time I treated them with dignity.

While Mr Frats was standing, Eugene looked up from his seat and smiling but looking confused over Mr Frats.

Just then one of Mr Frats' employees came to Mr Frats and asked" Mr Frats, are you felling well?"

Mr Frats replied smiling, "I couldn't be feeling happier. In fact I'm feeling so great that I could leap from here into the hands of God."

Eugene's eyes met with Mr Frats' employees and he asked the employee. "What' going on mate?"

"Mr Frats had given me money I thought I shouldn't have."

"No my friend, I gave you that money because you very well deserved it" Mr Frats said.

"You enjoy what he gives you mate. I'm sure you well deserved it. By the way, I'm Eugene, his son."

"My goodness, I'm very please to meet you, I'd no idea he had a son and to that a very handsome young one."

"Well, it's four sons and one daughter. We were living with other parents." "Well, it's so pleasing to meet you Mr Frats." the cook said.

"I'm Eugene to you sir."

"Well, the pleasure is all mines Eugene. And I'm very glad to know you." the cook said. Then he turned to look at the rest of Mr Frats' family and said. "I'm glad to have met all of you" Then the cook faced Mr Frats saying, "Your family are very lovely and it's very much a pleasure to know them."

"Thank you Daniel." Mr Frats said to the cook.

The cook smiled before he went into the kitchen in smiles and wonder.

Four week later, Mr Frats happily told most of his staffs he was no longer a single man and that he has four grown sons and a daughter. Most of his staffs looked on at him like he was going senile, but after he explained to his staff, they were so happy for him that they wished him well.

One week before Christmas, he gave his two hundred and thirty four staff in his different hotels and restaurants one thousand pounds each in their pay packet. One of his young cooks opened his pay packet and saw a cheque for one thousand nine hundred and twenty pounds. He stared nervously at the cheque and jumped for joy. Then thinking for a moment, he took his pay packet to Mr Frats telling him, "You have paid me a thousand pounds too much" Mr Frats rested his hand on the young cook shoulder, smiled and said, "You're very honest and I think you will get far. I haven't paid you too much. You all have worked hard so I think you deserved a little treat. Mr Frats smile and said to the cook, "Simon, like young Daniel I have watched you both working on many occasions, and you both please me. However, how would you like to be manager in one of my restaurants?"

The young Simon looked hard in Mr Frats' face and asked, "Me Sir? I know nothing about management. Thanks all the same."

"Simon, with your intelligence, it would come easy to you. I watch you directing some of the cooks. My son Eugene would be willing to teach you what you need to know, and I know you would be good at your job."

"Thank you sir, was it because I came to you about you paying me too much?" Simon asked.

"Partly," Mr Frats said. "But my main reason, you have got potential, and I was told you have created three new tasty menus that became very popular with customers. Simon, I've sampled all three menus and I can proudly tell you they become my favourites. So please Simon, I would like for you come and see me after the holiday. I would like to talk to you about going on a management course. And, I won't take no for an answer. I' would see you after the holiday." Mr Frats said.

"Mr Frats?"

"Yes young Simon,"

"Thank you Sir. You can count on me not to let you down" Simon said.

"I know you won't my young friend. You've already boosted profits up with your new dishes" Mr Frats told Simon as watched Patrick leaving in his car.

Simon smiled. Mr Frats left and went to see his son Patrick at his home before he went to one of his hotels, The Red Mullet, and then one of restaurants asking the managers to pass messages on to his staffs that the thousand pounds in their pay-packets was a Christmas gift and bonus. Mr Frats then explained to them, "All pay-packets had an explanatory slip except these ones, for some reason. Thank you."

The managers thanked Mr Frats and then told their staffs the extra money was a Christmas gift from Mr Frats.

"Leroy, isn't Mr Frats generous this year giving us a thousand pounds compared to the hundred pounds he usually gives us at Christmas?"

"Yes Viola, this year he must have made a vast profit to give this much. Well, I thank him and I'm using mine on a holiday to Miami next year."

"Well, we should still receive a profit share accordingly to sales." Leroy said.

"What I want to know, is, Mr Frats' sense is leaving him to give us a hefty bonus?" Viola asked.

"Viola shut up. And enjoy spending the cash." Leroy said.

"Don't worry Leroy, I will." Viola said. And as she saw Patrick and Mr Frats she faced Patrick saying "What a handsome man."

Patrick smiled.

"Mr, if you are looking for a quick fix, just calls on me." Viola said.

Patrick looked at her smiling. Then a middle aged man said. "She's young and very good looking."

Patrick smiled while Mr Frats kept a straight face.

"Mr, you know what they said, the blacker the berries, sweeter the juice." Viola said.

Patrick walked away smiling and then left with Mr Frats and went to his home. As he and Mr Frats were drinking brandy, Mr Frats said, "Patrick, I've asked the entire family last week to spend Christmas with me."

"Yes, I know. The family went shopping and they'll be coming later." Patrick said.

"Good." Mr Frats said.

"Well Pops, thanks for the drink and I think I should go home as we have to be here later. Should we eat at home or when we get here?" Patrick Asked.

"Here of course, so don't be too late and please reminds the others. Dinner would be serve at seven but I would be happy for all to get here at least five o'clock as I would like the children to have dinner early."

"Well I would let them know." Patrick said and touched Mr Frats on his shoulder and left. As Mr Frats saw him drove away, he smiled and went to his house maid and said. "My family would be here later and I would like you to join us in having dinner."

"Well thank you sir." She said and carries on with folding the sheets.

Five thirty, the family starting to arrive and at six o'clock all the family arrived at the Gold Leaf Hotel where they would have dinner and spend Christmas and the Boxing Day. Every one took some clothes to change off in and they were shown to their rooms before dinner. Bed cots were provided for the babies in their mothers' room.

Christmas morning, it was joyful opening gifts Mr Frats had given to them. As the children were running around, Denyah asked Paris to be quiet but Mr Frats said, "No one else is here but us. I have closed this hotel to all customers as I wanted my first Christmas with my family to be very special. So let my grandchildren to enjoy themselves." He said.

Veda show off her diamond gifted bracelet and Mr Frats laughed happily before saying, "You all got diamonds bracelets, only in different design. And the men each got gold pen. Well the children got dolls and cars for the grandsons."

His house maid unwrap her gift to find a lovely matching thick gold chain and earrings. Young Simon and his fiancée Cathleen were also invited by Mr Frats as they great cooks and Simon were also gifted with a gold pen and Cathleen a diamond bracelet.

Simon and Eugene had done all the cooking and everyone enjoyed their meals as they cooked exotic and very tasty food. Denyah and Mrs Brown were very much surprised and pleasing with Eugene after pleases their appetite with a nicely cooked and tasty fresh salmon and cream potatoes supper with freshly steamed vegetables.

"Well Eugene, this Christmas Eve supper I shall never forget - the taste! You should be cooking at home more often." Mrs Brown said.

Every one was so delighted and happily praising Eugene and Simon for nicely cooked and tasty dinner.

Christmas morning, Eugene, Mr Frats, and Simon cooked breakfast. Again the breakfast was nice with plenty to eat.

Lunch was light with ham, cheese salads and spaghetti laced with minced seasoned chicken for the children's and dinner was great with turkey, roast lamb, roast beef, rice, roast and creamed potatoes, sprouts, carrots Yorkshire puddings and plenty of rich gravy followed by Christmas pudding, trifle and ice-cream and to compliment the meal was rich red wine, Champagnes, soda and milk for the kids. After dinner, the children were so happy running and playing in the hotel hall. The grandmothers asked the children to stop running but Mr Frats said, "Let them enjoy themselves. This is why we're here just us family."

After an enjoyable Christmas day, everyone retired to their rooms. Mid morning Boxing Day Eugene went for a shower and then went to bed.

"Where are you coming from?" Denyah asked.

"I went to have a shower as I couldn't sleep" Eugene said and he climbed in bed behind her and hugged her. Paris and Jade B slept in the other bed in Denyah's room while the baby slept in one of the hotel cots in the same room. Mrs Brown slept in a single room. So everyone slept in their rooms with husbands and their children.

Boxing Day morning, over breakfast, Mr Frats gave, Denyah, Lisa, Veda, Meleta, Bernice, and Fay a blue scented envelope each, and told them. "Will you please open your envelopes when you go to your rooms and I don't want to hear a word from any of you about what is in them," he then turned and faced Paula, saying, "You've taken twenty five years off my age by making me feeling important, young and making me feeling so alive. I've no favourite here, but, I can't help controlling my feelings towards you. Paula, I wish you were my daughter. But still, you're very close to me by being my daughter-in-law and I couldn't love you any more than I do now. In fact, I couldn't love any of you more that I do now" he then gave Paula one of the same envelopes. Paula was the first to hug and kiss him with her usual friendly ways and laughter then cheekily saying. "Thank you daddy Frats".

"Well, thank-you Paula for your warm hug." he said. Then he went on to say, "My four sons, and daughter Jenny, we should get together and talk over lunch. Oh, I must not forget the mothers-in-law," he hugged and gave the three adopted mothers-in-law each an envelope. Eugene's, Patrick's, and Raymond's, adopted mom and said, "I couldn't wish for better mother-in-laws as well as friends.

You became my family and I love you." he told them and then kissed all his ten grandchildren on his face.

Boxing Day morning, before breakfast, his daughters-in-law flocked together and opened their envelopes to find a cheque for one million pounds and the mothers In-law each got five thousand and he gave his personal cook Simon fiancée Cathleen a cheque for ten thousand pounds and a big thank you.

Cathleen thanked him then tears came into her eyes as she didn't expect her gift and great wealth.

Denyah told Eugene, "All I was expected from your dad was a thank-you for coming and a happy Christmas kiss on her cheek."

Meleta, Paula, Lisa, Veda, Bernice, Fay, Cindy and Denyah had their private meeting over the money Mr Frats had given to them.

"He must be filthy rich to give us so much." Veda said.

"Denyah, I know you don't need yours, as your filthy rich already." Paula said.

"So are you Paula, what do you really know about me? Has Eugene told you how rich I am?"

"Den, I'm sorry, I've a big mouth and it would land me in big trouble one day. Eugene and me, was a hell of a mistake. We both were drunk and I'm now married to the man I really loved. I don't want us to be enemies. I like you very much Denyah. And, all I want from you is your friendship. However, we're become practically family since we are married to blood brothers." Paula said and she kissed Denyah's face.

As Lisa saw Paula kiss Denyah, she said "Den, I saw Paula kiss you, what was that all about?" she asked.

"Oh nothing, you know Paula, she's very festive." Denyah said.

"By the way Den; I wasn't looking for Mr. Frats to give me anything but goodbye. I should be the one to thank him for an enjoyable time. But instead, he left me so speechless that I couldn't bring myself to tell or to show my husband the cheque yet. Den all I was expecting of him, was a thanking you for coming and a goodbye."

"Lisa, you had a sudden surprise. Mr Frats can afford to give us what he gave us. I'm sure he won't miss what he's given us. So honey, pinch yourself and wake up to spending some of that money and enjoy your life with that lovely husband and your son and plus another one on the way." Denyah said.

"Den from one sweet bitch to another, I think you're right. Thanks honey to have me as one of your family as well as a friend." Lisa said.

"Sweet bitch Lisa, I wouldn't have you any other way" Denyah said feeling very happy.

Just then Paula walked up to Denyah and Lisa smiling and then said. "Aye girls, I just saw one of daddy Frats bank statements he had on his dressing table and you won't believe he has so much dough. No wonder he can afford to give us a million pounds each. Denyah, I give you three guesses to tell me how much money you think our daddy Frats has?"

"Paula, I don't wish to know and you should not meddle with what people have." Denyah told her.

"Paula, Den's right." Lisa supported Denyah.

"Denyah, I accidentally saw one of his bank statements. I didn't mean to pry." Paula said.

"Why were you in his room?" Denyah asked Paula.

She replied, "I happened to carry some ironed clothes to his room as he asked me to. This is when I saw one of his bank statements resting on his chest table showing over three billion pounds. I should keep my mouth shout but I guess telling the two of you, it wouldn't go any further." Paula said.

"You're so right Paula, it won't go any further because what you told me and Lisa, it would stay here. I don't want you to even tell your husband about this. And most of all, I don't want Mr Frats to find out you're advertised his business."

"I understand and thanks, Den," Paula said.

Meanwhile, just after supper on Boxing Day, Mrs Brown told Denyah that she wanted to send her gift of five thousand pounds her sister Laney's daughters. "Are you sure you want to do this mom?" Denyah asked her.

"Of course I want to, Den your sister might be in need of the money more than me. Education books are very costly. Besides, what can I buy, that you haven't given me. You don't need my money. So it's best I exchange it for another cheque and send it to your sister. The money could go towards the children's education."

"Okay mom, you're a good caring and loving mother to her and to me. I'm going to transfer the millions with the five thousand in her account that should secure her and my nieces for life even though I've already made them wealthy. I would like to know they have a comfortable life." Denyah said.

"I know they would. She has a wonderful and caring husband." Mrs Brown said.

Then just before Mr Frats family and friends were ready to leave, Mr Frats showed his daughter Jenny the deed to one of his hotels 'Green Stone hotel,' and told her, "I will put your name on this deed. It will be fully yours when you can manage it. Meanwhile, as I understand you are unemployed, I'm willing to have you working in your given hotel. It will bring you an income and I'm sure the others employees would treat you the same as everyone else. I also suggest you should take a course in management as well as cooking, so that you would know when the customers complained how to deal with their problem and put it right. I have asked your brother Carl and his fiancée Veda, to move in with me. Well they said they would in the next couple of weeks. Jenny, I was told you're courting a young man called Curt. I hope I will get the chance to meet him very soon. Well about your brother Carl and his fiancée Veda, I hope they would like to live here as I'm looking forward to their company. Jenny you can't imagine how happy all of you made me feel. Now Patrick, Eugene, Raymond, Carl and you, my precious Jenny, I'm going to divide my entire fortune between the five of you. I would like to do this before I'm too frail or die. My employees, should each received one hundred thousand each as a handsome gift and be kept on in employment even when I retire or should I kick the bucket. Eugene, you're the stubborn one and Patrick, I believed you're the eldest. It would be soon when I would hand over to the four of you lads, my entire empire. And so, I would have to speak to my solicitor, Mr Guy Rogers. I think he would serve you well as he has to me. You should get on well with him as I do. I have his number and I would give him a call sometime."

"Dad, we don't need Guy Rogers. We have our own Solicitor Muriel Lewis. Beside, us brothers would be fair to each other." Patrick said.

"Sure, I have my own. Owen Longford." Eugene said.

"I know that son, but it is best we do everything the right way." Mr Frats said. Then he went on to say, "I have five of you, Jenny got her share, less of course, because I think her husband should provide for her. However, she would be well off for the rest of her life with her share of one hundred and fifty millions and one of my hotels and a restaurant. As for you boys, you have to provide for your family. So, each of you would receive ten of my hotels and four restaurants. The remainder I would keep in work for my grandchildren's future. I'm sorry sons, since Guy Rogers my solicitor, I can't cut him out. Even if I wanted too, he's my right hand ever since he took over from his retired father."

"I'm sorry dad, I guess you're right. We respect your decision" Ray said then Patrick, Eugene and Carl agreed with Ray and Mr Frats. After they agreed with Mr Frats that he should keep Guy Rogers on as his solicitor they looked hard at each other before the four of them looked Mr Frats in his eyes and said "Yes dad, he's a good bloke." Eugene said.

Then Ray said, "Dad, you give our sister that much money at one time she would spend like there's no tomorrow as she's already a millionaire."

"I totally agreed with you Ray." Patrick said.

"Oh don't worry about money, she's young, let her spend until she learns the value of money. With what she has, she will only be using part of her interest. However, what's the use of saving money that would accumulate more and have it sitting in some dark corner in the bank. I got that from my dad. Life is too short and life should be enjoyable with the blessing from God the maker and our provider but we should give a little to the needy. I have given so much too the less fortunate. We only have an expanded life of maybe eighty years if we're lucky and I'm now heading to be that. So boys, cheer up and show me those pearly white teeth and the sparkles in those handsome blue eyes. However, I am the one that's very lucky to have found you my children - quite well and living."

"But really dad, why have you given our sister so much at one time." Patrick asked again.

Mr Frats laughed then he hugged Patrick saying "Son, Jenny got nothing compare to the four of you my sons. There will be over eight billion pounds between the four of you plus hotels and restaurants, bonds and shares that is why I should call in my Solicitor as well as your solicitors of choice. Mr Guy Rogers is mine now as his father was before him for over forty years and we became faithful friends as Guy Rogers is now. I can trust him as I trust myself. And if I'm rightly remembered, Eugene, I believed your missus told me told me she has Mr Rogers as her Solicitor as well. All I want of you boys is to see that I wouldn't forget to eat or have my medication if I should come to that. Oh, I have a housemaid that works three days a week. But now I have a daughter-in-law that would cut my nails if needed, and a son to help me get showered or see me alright in my Jacuzzi and out. My house maid I will keep on and I would like to give her a million as she was my faithful and trusted maid as well as a good friend to me."

Patrick laughed, "I know what you meant Patrick, but you're wrong. She used to set my bath now and then along with the other house work." Mr Frats said smiling.

"Sure dad, "That's what I meant. And cooling the old burning pipe aye dad?" Patrick asked laughing.

"Now Patrick," Mr Frats said and laughed. "I must confess, yes---- I had some fun with her but there was nothing serious between us as she was an ex married woman. However, I'm sure she and Veda would get on well as she's a lovely lady." Mr Frats burst into laughter and walked off with his hands around Carl and Ray's shoulder while Eugene and Patrick walked behind them smiling.

Eugene took Patrick to be on their own and told him, "I had no idea that this dote were so powerfully rich and cares about us so much."

"If he started out selling clothes only, and he became so successful, well? Anyway, look at you Eugene, you have a head for business and you followed right in his footsteps. As they said, like father, like son. As for me, maybe I followed in my mother's, handsome and successful with the women. Seriously bros, I think that dote is our true dad and we should give him full respect as he truly deserves."

"You know what Patrick, you're absolutely right. After all, he's giving us his entire fortune that he thinks he owes us. How could I not give him respect? However, if he wants to give me a one off payment why I shouldn't I am grateful. But the truth is. I'm not sure if I should take his money." Eugene said to Patrick.

"Well brother, it left to you to refuse what he gives you. But as for me, I will donate some to charity. My wife's grandmother died in a home and one of her sister also died in a children's home when she was four with pneumonia. I'm sure my wife would agree with me." Patrick said.

"Patrick, Bernice is a good wife. I remembered, meeting her for the very first time at Austin and Joan's engagement party, she threatened an old flame I used to date to leave Denyah alone. I like and respect her." Eugene told Patrick.

"Yes, I know what you're saying as I was there but hadn't met Denyah or Bernice at that time. Bernice now is my wife and she is very truthful and straight forward. This is why I love her so much, but mostly for her honesty that is why I can't afford to have affairs as I love her and I don't want to hurt my children. Besides, I wouldn't want any woman laugh in her face and telling her I'm sleeping with them." Patrick said.

"Well, if I know you well, I'm sure Bernice is the only wife you would have in your life." Eugene said smirking.

"What's that suppose to mean?" Patrick asked.

"Nothing brother, nothing," Eugene said smiling.

"Well dad got some fine scotch and I need a drink. You want some?" Patrick asked Eugene.

"Why not, "Eugene said and he and Patrick had a couple of drinks with Mr Frats, Ray and Carl while they were playing dominoes.

As nights closed in, Eugene said good night and he was the first to leave then Patrick and Ray, leaving Carl. "Well dad, would you like me to stay the night?" Carl asked him.

"I would be happy and grateful. But if you rather have to be with Veda, I would understand." Mr Frats said.

"Well I was going to fetch her and return. What about your housemaid, isn't she sleeping here tonight?" Carl asked.

"Yes of course, this is her home as she has lived here for seventeen years. Page has never been married again after her husband divorced her. This is why I would like you to keep her on. That's of course if you should move in."

"Dad, can I ask you a personal question?"

"Carl, my answer is no as I have a feeling I know what you are going to ask." Mr Frats said and laughed and then went on to say. "Carl, I had married once, but I found out I didn't love her, so I divorced her. Your mother was the only woman I fell deeply in love with. When you ready to leave, you should take the house key. Here, you may keep this as you would need to let your self in as I might be in bed when you get back. And do have one cut for Veda"

Carl hugged Mr Frats and told him, "I would be gone only for a little while and Veda and I would be here soon" he left Mr Frats sitting and drinking scotch whiskey and within a half hour, he and Veda let themselves into his home with the key and with their overnight bags with clothes. By this time Mr Frats was speaking to someone over the phone. As he heard Veda and Carl laugh, he turned to look at them and as his eyes clashed with their overnight bags, he smiled. "Well, thank you for your time speaking to me Mr Larance and goodbye."

Mr Frats put his phone down and looked at Veda and Carl smiling.

"Goodnight dad Frats," Veda wished him.

"Goodnight Veda. And thanks for your company. I really appreciated you and Carl coming." Mr Frats said.

"Dad Frats, how would you like to have Carl and I move in with you?" Veda asked.

Mr Frats smiled. "I would love that." he said.

Veda looked hard at Mr Frats before she said. "Well that's settled. Carl and I would like to make your home our official home starting from tonight."

"Yes Veda, I would like for you and my son Carl to move in with me as it would be one day you and Carl would be the owner."

Veda kissed Mr Frats on his forehead and said, "Yes, yes, yes! I would like to live here. But I would need a car."

Mr Frats remembered he had another set of spare keys to his mansion, garage and gate. He went to his bedroom and took the spare keys from his chest of drawers and marched downstairs and gave the set of keys to Veda saying, "These keys are yours now and you'll find a new car in our garage and here's the key to the car. I'll have the logbook change into your name."

"You mean I could move in now and have the car?" Veda asked happily.

"It's up to you Veda. You can have the car or you can buy one. The car is only four months bought. And yes, this house is partly yours now."

"Dad Frats, you don't know how happy I am to get out of that cow's way. I'll be happy to move in permanently tomorrow and thank you." Veda said smiling happily.

"Well, goodnight kids, I must go and have a quick shower and retire to my bed."

Mr Frats said and left Veda and Carl into the dining room. Veda eyes opened wide looking at the massive fitted kitchen and what it contained. "I would like it here she said looking happily at Carl.

"Yes, honey. I think we can get use to living in this big and beautiful house." Veda said, then left the kitchen to go and look at all the rooms except Mr Frats and Penny the housemaid's room.

Veda hugged Carl saying, "Honey, just look at the exquisite furniture." she then led Carl into the kitchen again and opened the large double door fridge freezer in excitement and her eyes lift opened wide saying. "Oh Carl honey, these utensils are beautiful and wow, I love this kitchen. Carl honey, there're so much food here to cook.

Lets get married as quickly as possible, and honey, I would like for us to have a daughter first and then a son." Veda said.

"Don't tell me you're jealous of not been married and having children? Come here honey," Carl said and he pulled Veda into his arms and as he was about to kiss her, Page showed herself and smiled then looked at Veda and Carl and said, "Don't mind me honey, I just come to make a cuppa and then I'm out of here and to bed."

Carl went to the bar to help himself to a drink. While Veda stay with Page and asking her, "Wouldn't you have like to get married again?"

"No honey, not now. I was a very long time ago, but after my husband divorced me to be his younger woman, I move in here as Mr Frats had felt sorry for me as I had no where else to live. And I'm here for the past seven teen years I think working for Mr Frats." Page said.

"My father-in-law told me you live here. Have he ever made a past at you?"

"Good heavens, No Veda. He hasn't. He might have had his pleasure else where. But it wasn't my business."

"Sorry to get deep in your life." Veda said.

"That's okay, However, I'm happy to know you and his son Carl would be moving in, I suppose I would have to find a place to live."

"Why Page, don't you like me?" Veda asked.

"Of course I like you Veda, but I wouldn't want to tread on you and your husbands shadows"

Veda laughed, "Come on Page. I was hoping to call you mom as my mom has died almost nine years ago." Veda said.

Page turned to look at Veda in surprise then said, "I'm so sorry about your mom."

"Got you Page, my mother is not really dead, she left me when I was two years old with my grandmother and fled somewhere in America with the lover of her life. This was twenty two ago. I'm now twenty four." Veda said.

"Your mother left you when you were just two years old?" Page asked.

"You got it in one Page." Veda said.

"How awful," Page said.

"Well Page, I have survived after been put into a children home because my grandmother took ill and couldn't manage. Poor Grand, she did not live to see me grow up. Page I would like for you to be my mother."

Page smiled and said, "Veda, I would be happy to be your mother but would you like a white-----

"Page what you were going to tell me? I'm sorry I should never have asked you to be my mother." Veda said.

Page hugged Veda.

"Well Page, let's not bring colour into it. I could pass as your daughter. What you say?"

"Veda, I really like to be your mother. Yes, I would like be your mother very much. Would you like some tea?"

"Yes please mother. Veda said and laughed. Page laughed too. "Well mother Page we would share the house work. Yes, we'll do everything to together. I would like us to get on well and I would like you to get to know Carlton and the rest of the family as well. The family children are absolutely adorable. And when Carl and are married, we would like to have children. I hope you don't mind me calling you mom or mother. I'll let you into a secret, my fiancée's brothers' wives. Denyah and Bernice have adopted parents and children. Oh Denyah have a new son with one of Mr Frats' sons - Eugene - and two adopted daughters, one by her ex-husband and the other daughter is by Eugene from his ex girlfriend. Also Bernice is now pregnant by her husband Patrick another of Mr Frats' son, and he and Bernice share two adopted daughters and a son. These grandchildren are Bernice adopted parents. But as I said, they're beautiful children."

"I got to know all the family and they seemed to be nice people." Page said and their children are beautiful as you stated."

"Yes Page- I meant mom, they are beautiful – All the children and their mothers."

"Well here's your tea, goodnight honey and I'll see you in the morning." Page said

"Goodbye mom, have a goodnight sleep and when Carlton and I move in permanent, you shall move into a bedroom nearer to us." Veda told Page.

Carl whispered to Veda's saying, "You're being so thoughtful to want dad's housemaid to be your mom and you don't lose any time wanting to change things."

"Carl, I missed not having a mother. So what so wrong to claim someone I really like to be that mother I'm so longing to have. Page seems a nice mother and with us getting married soon, we will need her. So what do you say honey about Page being my mother?"

"Nothing honey, I just want you to be happy. I suppose Page would make a good mother. We would need her to be our children's Nan." Carl said.

"Honestly Carl, I'm beginning to feel lost in this mansion. Do you like it here Carl?"

"Yes of course, I like it here. Veda honey, give yourself time, and you'll soon be happy living here."

"You know what Carl, we're the youngest and hasn't our own house yet and with Jenny's fiancée Curt coming to see her regularly, and especially that foulmouthed old dried up prune of a wicked bitch of a stepmother of yours always stabbing me with her eagle eyes, we might as well live here with your dad and my new-found mom." Veda said.

Carl laughed.

"Veda, your suggestion is marvellous and dad would be so happy to have us for companions." Carl said.

However, Carl and Veda finally moved in with Mr Frats four days after Boxing Day.

The Tuesday evening Mr Frats thought Veda and Carl were joking at first, but when he saw their suitcases, he was very delighted and he put on one of his dancing performance that he made Carl, Veda and Page laughed. None of the other family was there at this time. But as Veda and Carl saw the gleam in his eyes and happiness carved in his face, they were happy for him. Page face lit up with excitement as Veda pulled her up out of her seat to dance. "Well, Veda my dear, I think I should say good night and go to bed."

The following day Patrick, Eugene and Ray went to visit Mr Frats and met Veda cooking lunch with Page. Carl said to Eugene, Ray and Patrick, "Veda and I moved in permanent with dad."

"I'm happy for the old fellow. At least, I won't have to worry over him." Patrick said.

"You brothers would like some lunch?" Page asked.

"No thank you Page, I have to get home to have mine." Eugene said then he said to Carl. "I thought you and Veda were only spending some time with the old man."

"We were at first, but Veda and I decided to move in with him as Page only working here part-time as well as sleeping. Shouldn't we move in with him?" "Actually Carl, I'm happy you and Veda moved in to keep the old man company" Eugene said.

"I have some lunch." Ray said and took his seat at the table.

Eugene looked into Ray's eyes and said, "Anywhere you go you walk with you gut."

Ray laughed saying, "I could sick up what my gut doesn't want but you would have to get treatment for that uncontrollable dick you can't keep in your trousers."

Patrick laughed and asked "What's the hell is going on between you two."

"Just a little joke between us brothers," Ray said.

Eugene smiled and said to Carl, "You and Veda moving here, this has pleased me." "This goes for me too." Ray and Patrick said. "We all are very happy Carl, you and Veda moved in and thanks" Mr Frats said showing his four sons a bright smile.

Before Eugene and Patrick left Ray having lunch, Mr Frats said to them joking, "Any of you can collect your card for free food in any of my hotels or restaurants which would soon become yours."

Eugene and Patrick laughed and left feeling happy to know their father would be more than alright now that their youngest brother and his fiancée were living with their dad and to know Page the housemaid become family as Veda adopted her for her mom and Carl liked her being Veda's mom.

Veda phoned Denyah, Bernice, Paula and Jenny and told them, she has made Page her adopted mom. The four of them were very please and Bernice said to Veda "Denyah told me and I'm really happy for you. I would like my adopted mom and my blood mother to get to know Page better as she always disappeared while they were there."

"Well, as now, my mother Page would be visible as she's now my family." Veda told Bernice.

That night before Denyah went to bed, she told Eugene, "I'm sorry I have to tell you that I won't be going to my ex's house for any dominoes. Every time I think of going to his house, I'm beginning to feel sick and degraded."

Eugene became annoyed and said. "Denyah, I don't want to hear any more of your stupid talk. For goodness sake, the man has moved on and so should you. If you don't mind, I would like to get some sleep. I can see you can't trust yourself." Eugene said and turned his back on Denyah.

"Eugene, you not being fair, I'm only proving to myself and to you Wesley can't be trusted. He's devious and would always be, and I really don't want to be anywhere near to him. You're right, Wesley has moved on - to be more cunning and dangerous. Open your eyes Eugene and wake up to see what that cunning snake is doing to us. Wesley is jealous of you that I'm with you and not him. Do you really think Wesley wants to befriend you? He has envied you Eugene and he's our enemy. You send me to him and you'll regret it. Please Eugene. Think of our children even if you don't think much of me. Our son is only a baby and feeding mostly from my breasts."

Eugene said nothing, even though it was late, he got out of bed, got dressed and left the house in such furious mood and didn't even bother to close the front door.

Mrs Brown was making hot chocolate as she couldn't get to sleep. She saw Eugene leave the house and leave the front door wide open. As Mrs Brown saw him leave in his car, she shook her head frowning and then closed the door but left the chain off.

As Denyah's door was open, Mrs Brown stood by her door holding the two cups of tea, "Honey, are you okay?"

"I think so mom." Mrs Brown moved to Denyah and gave her a cup of tea. Denyah sipped her tea then tear came into her eyes. "Honey, would you like to tell me anything?" Denyah shook her head and rested her head on Mrs Brown's shoulder in sadness. "Den honey, I saw Eugene left the house and leave the door open and this tells me something's not right." Mrs Brown said.

"Mom, Eugene is not speaking to me. He still insists I should go to Wesley to get a set of dominoes. Mom, I fear Wesley, but I would go only to please Eugene."

Denyah tears fell heavily as Mrs Brown looked in her face and shook her head. Denyah put her tea on her side table and went under her quilt cover. Mrs Brown left feeling sad and upset to see Denyah so unhappy that tears came in Mrs Brown's eyes. As Mrs Brown heard noise coming from Paris and Jade B, she went into their room to see them running around. "Sweethearts, it's time you two get into bed. Mrs Brown told them but took them to the toilet to urinate then she saw them wash their hands and saw them in their room again and then tucked them into bed, kissed them on their foreheads, dimmed the lights and left. As she closed their door softly, she heard Paris saying her prayer. She waited at Paris's door until she was quiet and in bed to go into their room again and to know they were all right. She fixed their covers over them and kissed them on their foreheads, saying "Bless your little souls." She dimmed their lights and whispered. "Goodnight sweet little angels." Then she left and leaving their door slightly opened as she remembered the girls like their door to be left slight opened.

That night Mrs Brown didn't sleep well as she was thinking of why on earth should Eugene wanted send Denyah back to her ex's husband's house. All through that night Mrs Brown was thinking if Denyah went to Wesley's house, he might hurt her badly or possibly she might be killed.

Early the next morning, Denyah hardly touched her breakfast. Moving herself from the table, she said "Mom, if anything bad should happened to me while I'm with Wesley; I would like you to stay and have full control over my children to bring them up especially Paris for what ever time you have left. I have written a letter and left it in my safe. You should find the key in my dressing table drawers in my diary."

"Den honey, don't you say that! Nothing would happen to you. But still I don't like you going to that wicket ex husband."

"Well, I might as well get it over with and go to Wesley for the dominoes for Eugene what ever the outcome." Denyah said.

Late that evening, she went upstairs looking at her baby son sleeping in his cot bed. She leaned over him, looked hard on him and kissed his tiny fingers and touched his little forehead lightly then went to Paris, Jade B and Mrs Brown and kissed them on the faces. "Would you like me to go instead?" Mrs Brown asked her.

"No mom I have to do this myself otherwise I wouldn't hear the last of it from Eugene." "Denyah said and turned to leave.

"Den, before you go, have you put the money into your sister's account as you said you would? I hate to ask you at a time like this, but it's important," Mrs Brown said.

"Yes Mom, I have transferred two millions as well as the five thousand you gave me to give her into her account yesterday and I would like you to keep in touch with her should I not return alive."

"Den you'll be fine" Mrs Brown said. "And please don't speak as if you won't see your sister again, or any of us for that matter."

Denyah left in her car crying. On her way, she phoned Eugene on his mobile but as he forgot his phone in his car, he couldn't receive her message. But as he sat having dinner in one of his restaurants 'Wings-Of-Dove,' he felt his pocket for his phone then said, "Blast! Why did I leave my phone in the car as he thought about Denyah going to her ex-husband on the cause of him and thought seriously of what Denyah said to him that Wesley is jealous of him and her being happy together?. He left his unfinished supper and raced to his parked car to get his phone. As he checked for messages, he came up with a message from Denyah telling him, "I've gone to get your frigging dominoes that might cost me getting rap or even cost my life."

"Damn," he said as he thought he saw what looked like a shadow of a man passed over him that he shivered coldly and left him feeling sickened. But as he looked up above his head, he noticed a tree branch from the tree was blowing in the strong wind and shaped like a man. And it was also dark and raining the branch had fooled him. Tears came instantly in his eyes and he phone Denyah immediately but as he got no answer, he closed his phone and while putting the phone in his jacket pocket it slipped out of his hand and smashed. He got in his car and sat at the wheel with his head resting against the wheel and in deep in thought over Denyah and his children. He lifted his head up with thoughts of Denyah's on his mind. Smiling, he looked out his car window to see a slim and tall woman standing by his car looking in on him. The woman spoke but as he couldn't hear what she said, he wound down the window a little and looked at her. "Mr Lake, are you okay?" She woman asked.

Nodding his head, he answered, "yes, yes thank you, I'm fine."

"I'm sorry to disturb you, but watching you like you were day dreaming and distance away, I had to waken you." She smiled and then left.

Eugene sunk into thinking again trying hard to remember his mother as he'd vaguely remembered her but seeing her photo on Mr Frats' desk it had brought strong memory of the way he knew her when he was three years old. As he closed his eyes in sadness, tears slide down his face. He then opened his eyes and wiped his tears dry and thought of the slim woman he'd spoken too. The more he think of her, the stronger he could see his mother's face transfix onto the woman's face. He slapped his face lightly and shook his head telling himself, "snap out of that dark mind Eugene and face the real world." He shivered coldly, then said. "Mom, are you trying tell me something about my Denyah, or about us." He looked away in the far distance before driving away.

At this time a Mrs Jay phone Denyah at her home. Mrs Brown answered. "Hello, can I help you. I'm Denyah's mother."

"Can I speak to Mrs Denyah Lake please? My name is Mrs Jay." Mrs Jay said.

"I'm sorry Mrs Jay, Denyah just left." Mrs Brown said.

"Do you mind if I ask where she leave to go to?" Mrs Jay asked.

"I don't know for sure?" Mrs Brown said.

"Mrs Brown, it's very important for both Mrs Lake and for me. I'm Mrs Jay as I just told you. I would like to help Mrs Lake as her ex-husband might be planning the worst for her. I saw him bought cyanide from a super drugstore and as he was getting in his car, he was showing a man a small package and I heard him tell the man "It's for some one special   He was also fidgeting with a gun and at one point I heard him called Denyah."

"Oh my God, she's gone to collect a set of dominoes from him." Mrs Brown told Mrs Jay.

"Mrs Jay put her phone in her hand bag and sped over to Wesley's house in her car like she was on fire. By this time Mrs Brown was calling, "Mrs Jay, hello, hello-" but as Mrs Brown got no answer, she phoned Eugene on his mobile phone but as his phone had dropped and smashed so he couldn't receive Mrs Brown's message. Mrs Brown phoned the police telling them Denyah might be in trouble and she's at her ex-husbands house giving Wesley's name but not his address as she didn't know.

"Mrs Brown, can we have the address where Mrs Davis went to please," the policeman asked.

"I don't know his address or his telephone number." Mrs Brown said panicking. "But he's a police."

The police officer looked at his college in surprised as he heard Mrs Brown said he's a police. But before he could ask anymore question, Mrs Brown hung up her phone sadly.

At this time, Denyah was at Wesley's house ringing his doorbell. Before he answered the door, he swallowed whiskey from the bottle with squinting eyes and looking agitated. But as he saw Denyah he smiled like he'd won the lottery. He moved inside saying, "Come in my sweet wife." Denyah moved inside the hall leaving the door opened. He closed the door before holding her right hand and holding the whiskey bottle in his left hand and tried the kiss her but she slapped his face and pulled away from him and moved into the living room in tears.

By this time, Eugene phoned Denyah on his other mobile phone and as Denyah was going to answer, Wesley grabbed her mobile phone from her hand and threw it against the wall unit and smashed it and shattered the wall unit glass. "You still my fucking wife even though we're not living together. How do you think I feel knowing you sleeping in that fucking idiots arms every night and me slurping whiskey out of bottle because I can't sleep after thinking over you and my daughter? Honey, I made a hell of a mistake treating you so badly. There's no other woman I could love as I love you." He said and began crying.

"Wesley, I don't love you anymore but I can let Paris visit you." Denyah said.

Wesley slapped her face hard knocking her down and saying, "You had to miscarry my child but you can give that fucking idiot a healthy bastard. You killed my baby and I'm going to make you pay even thought I love you."

"Please Wesley, we can be friends and we can share Paris." Denyah cried.

"I don't want you as a friend. I want you back in my home as my wife and beside me in our bed every night. "Wesley shouted.

At this time, Eugene and two police cars were on their way to Wesley's house after Mrs Jay phoned the police. But by then Mrs Jay got to Wesley's house before them and rang the door bell. Wesley opened the door and as he saw Mrs Jay, his eyes immediately stretched widely showing hate and anger with an evil grin on his face. Then as he looked hard in Mrs Jay's face, he said to her, "Get the fuck away off my premises before I blast you straight to hell."

He kicked his door flying shut into Mrs Jay's face and went to Denyah smiling and said, "You can forget going back to that bastard. Tomorrow I shall get my daughter and your little bastard." He then looked on at Denyah with one eye closed and a grin before he showed her their married photos and said, "Just look at us darling. We were very happy together and we can be still happy when you come home to me."

"Wesley, I could never live with you again." Denyah said.

Wesley grinned, "I would never let you go back to that idiot of a man. We were married for better or for worst and I owned you. All of you: I shall never give you a divorce." He said.

"Why don't you ask Bonnie or Fay to move in with you, I'm sure they still love you?"

"Denyah, you don't fucking get it, do you? I only want you my wife and my daughter and maybe that little bastard. If you be a good wife," he said and smiled. Then said, "Come on honey, it has seemed that I was about four hundred miles away from you and Paris. The only two loves of my life." Wesley said then held her hand and led her to the settee and said "Have a seat honey."

Denyah tries playing it safe and cunningly she sat down, smiled and pecked his face with a quick kiss and asking him, when was the last time you eat a healthy meal?"

Wesley seemed shocked by her asking, and said, "Never mind. Did your damn foolish man sent you here for his dominoes?"

"Wesley I won't lie to you, I past all the hate I was carrying towards you. I'm here because I wanted to know how you're getting on and that I would like for Paris to spend some time with you, as I realized you didn't deliberately set out to hurt me but you were angry. I know how much you loved me. I also realized how jealous you were towards me." Denyah told him.

Wesley laughed for a good second and said, "Don't kid your self."

"Okay, Wesley, I'm here for a set of dominos for Eugene that you promised to him."

Wesley didn't answer but sank in thoughts and seemed to be in a tangle with a full moon night of nightmares. Denyah moved towards the door as Mrs Jay knocked at the door again. He followed her and stood facing her saying, "Den, I love you, you know," then as he tried to kiss her, she pushed him hard enough rocking him unbalanced that he almost fell.

"You stay away from me." Denyah told him. He frowned at her. "Wesley, I'm here because of Eugene and partly because I felt pity for you and hoping we can be come friends on the account of our daughter." Denyah said but was lying through her teeth about becoming friends.

He looked on at her in a devoted desire before he said, "I'm willing to give up drinking and women when you come home to me and anything else you don't like my dearest darling." He then took her right hand and led her into the living room and said. "Please sit down my darling." Nervously, she took her seat then she began trembling out of fear. He slipped her shoes off and began massaging her feet saying "You remembered how you used to laugh when I was playing with your toes and tickled the sole of your feet?"

Denyah quince and closed her eyes for a second.

Mrs Jay was beating down his front door with hard knocking. But stop and went to stand by her car and waited for the police to arrive.

At this time, Denyah was shivering in disgust when he kissed her feet before he said. Ignore the fucking fat bitch and please try and relax. Why are you trembling? Do you thing I would swallow you, or hurt anymore?"

"No, you can't hurt me anymore than you already have. I think I'm coming down with the flu caused me to trembled." Denyah said trying to soften him.

"Would you like a couple of aspirins honey?" He asked her.

"Yes please." Denyah said pretending and want him to leave her so she could run out the house.

"Come with me." He told and her and helped her up out of her seat by holding her right hand.

As she was following behind him, fear took her face over and she beginning to sweat of not knowing what he would do next. She tried pulling her hand out of his, but he held her hand firmly and smiled looking back at her. As he led her as far as the lounge door, he stopped and looked at her again and said. "Come on my precious, follow me?" He showed her one of his cunning smiles before he put his arms around her shoulder and led her into the kitchen. Poured her a glass of water from a bottle he took out of the fridge. "Now my sweet, from since you left me, I'd never been the same as you can see. I admitted I'm a little under nourished only because I can't eat properly because I'm pining bitterly for you to come home. Honey, please try and relax. I wouldn't take you unless you're ready. I would be a loving husband and a good father to you and Paris from now on. Oh, God, I still love you so damn much!" He closed his eyes painfully before opening them and smiled.

Denyah looked painfully hard at him as she was shaking from fear of him. "Take you aspirins honey then maybe I would let us go to bed and rest for a while." Again Denyah looked at him with hatred in her eyes and then tossed the aspirins in the bin when he wasn't watching and pretend drinking some water then rested the glass on the sink unit when he watched her. After, he guided her into the dining room with his hands covered her eyes as he was walking behind her. He then said to her, "Honey, what you're about to see, I done this for us. You and me, I'm sure you would agree with me," he said as he stopped walking and took his hands away from her eyes. And as she saw Eugene pretend mom Mrs Lake sitting in one of the single chair and looking like she's sleeping, she asked him "What is Madam Cheat are doing here?"

"Oh don't worry about her. She is stone cold and out of this world. Anyway, let's talk about us. You wouldn't know just how long I have waited for this moment. I still in love with you- you know, when I had you, I treated you rotten as I was so jealous of you and didn't know how to love you even though I loved you. Will you forgive me my darling? I hate to admit how much I love you and miss you. But it's true. Den, you told the truth about my jealousness and possessiveness towards you. But one thing I'm sure about, I wouldn't know how to stop loving you."

"Wesley, I'm here only to collect the damn dominoes for Eugene, just let me have them then I would be out of your stinking life."

"So you didn't come to be with me, Denyah, I had wanted us to spend Christmas together - you our daughter and me. Still, I should be grateful for this moment. Oh, the dominoes your fiancée sent you for, there's none. He's so stupid. So fucking blind and stupid to send you back into my arms. Still, I should grateful."

"What do you mean?" She asked him.

"He sent you back into my arms where you belong." He said. "How thoughtful of him,"

"Please Wesley if you really want me, I would go home get some clothes and come back to you. Please don't hurt me anymore."

"Den my darling do you think I would ever hurt you again? I married you because I was in love with you and I still am!" He said as he closed his eyes feeling power of love towards her.

Her shivering was showing enormously before tears came into her eyes. He fell on his knees at her feet saying "Sweetheart, I love you so much that my heart is hurting so much to know that each night you lie in that idiots arms and not mine. As I've have told you I done you many wrongs out of jealousy, by having whores in our bed. But that was because I was so jealous of you and didn't know how to treat you and let my foolish head ruled me. But not anymore, please forgive me my love. I can never send you back to that idiot fiancée. Now, please let us dance together to our song as we use too, I bought this CD specially, for us. Would you like some brandy before we dance? Its good French brandy." He said smiling.

Denyah didn't answer but cried. "Its useless crying my darling, no one can hear you. And as for that deaf and stone cold bitch sitting over there, she can't even breathe." Wesley said and gulped down plenty of brandy from the bottle. "Now," he said. "This is our own Christmas party even though its four days past, so, let's dance!" She pulled away from him.

"Now why do you do that? The calmer you be the better," he told her and gripped her firmly around her slim waist saying "This is our record my precious. And he began smothering her lips and face with wet intoxicated kisses all over her face and neck - she scratched his face with her long finger nails and pushed him away and almost sending him to the floor but he gained his balance and charged into her and slapped her face hard. She slapped him back and he slapped her face again so hard that she staggered and fell to the floor. He looked down on her saying "Never raise you hand at me again. You're lucky this time I didn't hurt you, but the next time you raise your hand at me, I'll hurt you real bad. Not because I will want too, but because you have disrespect me." Denyah raised herself up and stared hatefully at him. "I know you hate me for now darling but your love would grow stronger for me than ever." He said then put the CD into the playing system to play (Stand by your man) then as she got on her feet, he pulled her closed to him and forcing her to dance. Crying, she said. "Wesley, why are you doing this to me?"

He laughed at her saying, "Denyah, my sweet love, you know that I am always in love with you from the beginning of the time we met and now if you must end your love for me, we will have die together as it should be.! Here drink this, my precious and please don't fight me anymore as this it's now our destiny to be parted from this world and into the next. Now my sweet love, before our breath has left us, I must confess to you that I lied to you about my two mates I beat them both but I didn't kill them neither did I rape and kill your Nurse friend. Not that I wasn't tempted to do her in for her trying to take you away from me. The one that had your friend raped and murdered is that stoned hearted dead bitch of a false mother-in-law there on our chair. She had some man by the name of something Jay done in your friend. However, she can't tell us the truth now as the evil bitch is dead. I think she has had a heart attack I recognised the pain and death the other two bastards I'd set you up with, I wish I had the pleasure of slitting their throats my self. But as I already told you, I did not kill any of them and that's the truth! As for that bitch there in the settee, she had murdered your fiancée's mother to get her husband. So you see my darling, she can't seducing your little bastard when he becomes thirteen as she'd done to his stupid dad when he was thirteen. I didn't want her to have anything to do with my daughter either. That bitch had hated you because you took her lover from her. She was the first to seduce your idiot fiancée and had murdered his real mother and took her husband as I told you. So I made sure she wouldn't seduce your bastard son by not calling in the doctor. Aren't you happy Den my love?" he asked laughing like he was going crazy. Oh Den, I used to screw her too until she pissed herself under me then I decided not to screw her anymore. For that I'm sorry too."

"Please Wesley, let me go and get the children and bring them here, we could be a happy family again. I would tell Eugene I don't want to be with him anymore and I would not tell anyone what you did to that wicked bitch. We can call in the police and tell them she fainted and die."

"Denyah I know you believe I kill her."

"Wesley I don't doubt you when you said you had nothing to do with her been dead. This is why I'm asking you to let us call in a doctor."

"Denyah if you're trying to trick me to get out of here, it won't work. He said and he looked at her smiling. She tried to trick him into letting her out of the house. But he was so dangerous and cunning. He laughed at her saying, "I didn't touch the bitch! She just flop her head to one side and drop dead like a fish out of water."

He then looked hard in her face and asked her, "Are you trying to make a fool out of me?" Denyah turned her face away. He then went on to say, "I don't believe you love me anymore. However, my love for you is growing stronger and this is still our dance. So let's dance to this beautiful song. It has been a long time since we danced."

As he held his gun in one had around her shoulder, she forced herself to dance with him. He then tried to put whiskey in her mouth but she knocked the glass out of his hand. "I don't want to drink." She said. He poured whiskey into the glass again and took it to her lips telling her, "Drink! It doesn't matter if you don't want. It's what I want you to do and that is to drink and be happy. So drink! Now drink!" He demanding her and after said "I would drink after you. You would go to sleep in no time. Just a little cramp and pain you will feel. Just drink my love and we'll be together for ever. Oh I should tell you what the drink contains. Just a strong dose of cyanide, it works so fast that you would hardly feel any pain." He said laughing as he was lying about cyanide in the whiskey. He then carried the glass with the whiskey to her lips again and telling her, "open your mouth and drink! We'll both drink together. Just a little pain then it would be all over for us, you and me" His eyes looked demented and cold. He poured from the bottle more whiskey into the glass and demanded her to "Drink!" as he was trying to prise her lips opened with the rim of the glass she need him to his groin. He crossed one leg over the other for a moment before he straightened himself up and carried the glass to her lips again. But as before she pressed her lips more tightly and the harder he tried to prise her lips apart, the more she tightened her lips then pushed him away. He became furiously and pulled her to him and hit her across her face with the back of his hand and was very insisted she should drink the whiskey. "Open your blasted mouth!" he teased her holding the glass to her lips. Energetically she punched him in his faced and knocked the bottle from his hand and scratched his face with her long finger nails. While he was patting his stinging face, blood was seeping through. She kicked him on his testicles. He dropped to the floor on his knees with his hand between his legs with blood dripping from his scratched face. As it was impossible for Denyah to get away, she stood in fright and watching him and was wondering what would be his next move on her. After the pain wears off, he wiped blood off his face with hand and drank some whiskey and as he was getting up, he lost his balanced and fell backward on the floor but still holding the gun but the bottle of whiskey rolled away and the whiskey running out.

As he then managed to staggered up and picked the bottle up and grumbled. "There's still enough cyanide whiskey left to kill a horse. And even if none had left, I only have to kill you with my bare hands. Remember I'm a police officer and I do what I want and get away with it. So pay attention to me honey and quickly. "He grumbled as his tongue was becoming heavy to talk plainly after drinking too much whiskey.

Mrs Jay exhaled deeply and left her car and went and stood at the door calling, "Denyah," and trying to look through the kitchen window. When she had no response, she kicked the front door wide opened. Denyah ran into her and she pushed her behind her and kicked the gun out Wesley's hand and fisted him to the floor and said to Denyah," you have luck as a cat. I understand his sister and your sister saved you from him twice. He's nothing more than one maggot in a lump of shit. Anyway Denyah I'm Robert Jay's wife. Also forgive me if I don't call you Mrs Davis, as I don't think his name suited you. My husband's dead because of him. And, as for that Mrs Lake, she's a deceiving manipulating bitch! It's time the police know about the bitch and your evil husband."

At this time, Denyah eyes filled with tears as she watched Mrs Jay standing over Wesley and holding her gun on him.

As Denyah was leaning against the wall unit in the living room, and shivering she went into a state of shock before she fainted and fell.

As Mrs Jay was trying to bring Denyah around by patting her face, she happened to see Mrs Lake sitting slanting into the chair with her mouth opened and her tongue partly hung out of her mouth. As she watched Mrs Lake hard, she knew she was dead. She faced Wesley holding his gun on him and said. "You're going down for all the murders including my husband even though the coroner claimed he'd killed himself. You also going down for that bitch you have murdered, even though she deserved to be." Angrily Mrs Jay ranged his gun at Wesley's head and said, "I ought to give you one of you own bullet straight through your fucking wicked head and blow your fucking rotten brain out so that it would plaster all over your floor, but why should I make it easy for you. You cheap low down good-for-nothing lousy cop that preys on your beautiful wife. Nothing would please me more to see your arse rotten in jail for the rest of your life and serve the male prisoners like a bitch."

"Are you alright?" Mrs Jay asked.

"I think so Denyah said.

"Thank you." Denyah said.

"I slapped topped you face lightly to bring around as fell and you were unconscious. You don't know me. But that wicked bitch, your ex has murdered had my best friends mother and also Eugene's mother murdered twenty years ago. And I wouldn't put it pass her that hadn't had something to do with your nurse friend's death. However, after she blackmailed my husband by forcing him to rape and murdered one of Eugene's mother' friend's, and told police my husband done it, my husband killed himself. As for this lump of stale shit here, he doesn't deserve to wear a police uniform. Anyway, coming back about my husband, when I got home from work one Tuesday afternoon, I found my husband's body in my back garden and looked like a burned log of wood with his razor stuck in his belly. Police claimed he took his own life as they proved it was self inflicted before he set himself a light. I didn't know he was that weak. Neither did I know he was in trouble."

"I'm so sorry to hear this." Denyah said.

"My husband was Judge Lakes chauffeur for thirty three years and before Eugene's mother was murdered. My husband told me one night he was taking Judge Lake to Spoon and Bowl Social Club where Judge Lake would meet some friends. Then on the way to the club the Judge suddenly remembered he'd left his wallet on his dressing table. However, my husband drove him home for him to go and get his wallet but instead of the Judge going in, he sent my husband to get his wallet. Anyway, my husband said he knocked at the door and got no reply at first, then as he turned to go and tell the Judge he couldn't get an answer after knocking on the door, the housemaid opened the door. He told the maid the Judge forgot his wallet and that he sent him to get it. The maid told him to go and knock at Mrs Lake bedroom door as she was having her tea. He went up to Mrs Lake and knocked on her bedroom door. He said as he didn't get any answer he knocked at her bedroom door a couple of times but still had no reply. Well, as the door was ajar he said he thought the bitch went to the bathroom. So he pushed the door opened to go and get Judge Lake's wallet when he saw the bitch Mrs Lake with Eugene's penis in her mouth. He told me he punched her away Eugene and told her Judge Lake would have to know what she had done. He said he was feeling sickened and disgusted from the shock of seeing what she'd done. As she left the room, he tried to speak to Eugene but he found Eugene had been well drugged. He said he took Eugene to his room but hadn't told him what he saw. That was so fucking sickening and disgusting he said he told the bitch. But she threatened him she would tell the Judge he raped her when he came to get his wallet if he tells anyone what she'd done to Eugene. My husband said he told no one what he saw. Your ex also knew that old bitch used to drug Eugene and seduce him. Eugene was the one she'd love but she seduced Patrick also. My husband said. I begged my husband to tell the judge no matter the cost, but he told me he was scared to tell him but the maid knows as she saw her one Sunday morning playing with Eugene's penis while he was sleeping but didn't had any idea he was drugged. My husband was scared all right, of the old dried up prune faced bitch Mrs Lake. She had my husband badly beaten up after he caught her with Patrick one time on the library floor. Like she'd drugged Eugene, so she'd done to Patrick. Only Patrick was fifteen, two years older than Eugene. My husband told her he would go to the news papers after he'd quit his job. Well, she sent two men to the local pub on Saturday night where my husband was drinking with friends. One of the men sat in their car while the other one went into the pub and whispered in my husband's ears telling him he was wanted outside. My husband left the pub with the man although he didn't know him. However, the two men had him beaten up, and hacked off half of his penis, drove him to the border of Handsworth Cemetery gate and dumped him there to bleed to death. If it wasn't for a man who was on his way' in the early morning, to work and found him stretched out on the gravel ground bleeding and groaning and called the ambulance, my husband would have died. However, he spent three weeks in the hospital. After he was discharged from the hospital, I'd to nurse him for another four weeks like he was a baby by bathing, plastering cream and bandaging what was left of my husband's penis. Denyah, I shouldn't be telling you this, but to make my husband feeling like a man again, I let him used his finger on me. I despised your ex-husband and that dead bitch so much to have left my husband with only a stump to dribble his urine out of. He couldn't make love to me again. I supported him to go on living by make him a promise I would never be unfaithful with men as long as we're together. I loved my husband. But after he was murdered or he'd taken his life as I've been told by the coroner and police, I've kept my promise to my husband and I have never dated another man even though my husband had died. My husband was white but I loved him to bits. It is well over a year since they took my husband away from me. Now I've to live with the horrible horror of what he told me about Eugene and Patrick of what their bitch of a fake mother had done to them. But you know what Denyah? You deceiving mother-in-law hadn't thought her day would come. And what has made me so joyous about her getting what she deserved. It's by the hand of her deceitful bastard lover Wesley. I'm sorry to speak so profoundly, but I hate to be a hypocrite. Well, we all knew about the old saying, what goes around comes around. Well that leaves your ex-husband to face up to the murders of his college friends, Tom Bailey, Finch Lomott and your nurse friend. As for that deceiving bitch of your mother-in-law your husband murdered, she deserved what she got and as for this son-of-a bitch Wesley, he deserves to rot in prison even though he didn't murder your nurse friend. If my husband hadn't cleared him, I'm sure he would have been charged with their murders as he won't be able to prove he didn't murder them. I gave the police a signed statement my husband had left in his letter case stating Mr Ferlance Rice had raped and murdered Nurse James. Ferlance Rice was been beaten up badly and then murdered in his flat three months ago. Police claimed he was stabbed in his throat and he bled to death and he was also drunk. Ferlance had never drunk alcohol since I knew him. But I think he was murdered like my husband. Denyah, I honestly thought my husband had raped and murdered your friend but thank God I was wrong. Well, as for Eugene's real mother, I'm glad her children knew the truth about her. I'm so happy my husband told me the truth of the good Mrs Lake. I also thanked my husband to have passed on information to the police stating the bitch was only a housemaid before she murdered Eugene's mom by overdosing her with tablets. I supposed the written statement had swept to the bottom of the river as they claimed my husband was a drug taker, liar and he wasn't trust worthy. I'm also happy that my husband told no one that that evil bitch of a fake mother used to seduced Eugene and Patrick after drugging them. But the truth remained she did really seduce both boys. And I believed my husband as he cried so much over them. I opened the envelope my husband had hidden in the back of our wardrobe and I read the letter that said Mrs Lake seduced Eugene and Patrick and she was having an affair with your ex-husband as well as Sergeant Fisher. Denyah, I know my husband told the truth. Ah, this is all behind me." Mrs Jay smiled.

"Mrs Jay, have you told anyone about this?"

"No Denyah, I only just told you. As I said, I found two letters, I gave the police one stating Logan Mathew murdered Eugene's mother and not Larance Rice as police thought. The other letter I destroyed it as it had mentioned Eugene and Patrick's name. I'd found that letter when I was cleaning out my flat to put it on the market. I apologise for my husband for not going to Mr Lake with the truth but I now I know it's better for the boys him not knowing and making living bad for them."

Mrs Jay your husband had had his reasons not to tell Mr Lake and I'm glad he didn't" Denyah said. "Otherwise, God knows what would have happened to Patrick and Eugene if their name went publicly" Denyah said.

"Well, my husband loved those children like his own" Mrs Jay said and he used to gave them donkey ride on his back sometimes."

Mrs Jay, I'm so very sorry about your husband and for what you both went through. I know what fear means. If I can help you with anything at all, I would like for you to call on me." Denyah said sympathetically.

"I'm sorry about your Nurse Friend too, and I'll be fine. Well, as your ex-husband, I knew her time would come and you know what Denyah? I'm happy she was murdered by his hands, now she would go to her grave without confessing to the murder of

Eugene's mother and having her lover tampered with my friend mother's car's brake that killed her. Well as I said, your husband is responsible for all the murders as he'd knew the truth and said nothing.. If I said I'm sorry for him, I would be lying. Oh those two shits that had beaten my husband so badly before he killed himself, they both died in a car accident a year after my husband killed himself. Maybe you don't recall about them as they were not of any interest you at that time and you were so young but it was all over the TV news and news papers." Mrs Jay told Denyah.

Denyah nodded her head in understanding before she phoned the police from Wesley's house and reported to them saying, her husband Wesley just murdered Mrs Lake in his house. Very soon three police cars speeding down to Wesley's house sounding sirens followed by an ambulance.

Denyah let the nine police in the house- two of them were female. Shortly the ambulance arrived and stopped in front of Wesley's gate. Two tall and well built and handsome looking paramedics got out and rushed into Wesley's house as the door was left opened then a short plump white doctor about five foot two inches tall, very grey around the sides of his front and top, and bald headed with thick dark brown freckles covered the front of his bald head, chubby unshaved face and wearing thick rimmed black framed glasses, and dressed in a well creased grey suit. He rushed into Wesley's house carrying a medicine case. Denyah led him into the dining room to see her ex-husband covered in blood and Mrs Lake sitting upright in the settee dead and her head slightly leant on the right side.

"My husband told me he poisoned her." Denyah told the police as two of them stood silently behind the Doctor.

The investigating officer and the Doctor looked at each other in astonishment before the Doctor felt the right side of Mrs. Lakes neck for a pulse and before he expectorated a light cough out and then announced to the police, "I'm afraid Mrs Lake is no longer with us."

The young black handsome police officer took a statement from Wesley but he told them he'd no clue what his wife was talking about.

Then Officer Dickson stepped forward and asked Wesley. "Can you tell us how you got your wound and why Mrs Lake ended up in your chair dead?"

Wesley said, "I was shot by my wife- the fucking big bitch of a lesbian. And as for the dead bitch she just flapped her head on the side and dead. I haven't touched her."

As Officer Dickson looked Denyah in her eyes, Denyah said to the Officer Dickson, "He's my ex and he's also a police and a murderer."

"Well Officer Davis, Mrs Lake is dead and now sitting up in your three seat settee. Would you mind telling us how she got there and also how you got gunshot wound? And please Mr Davis, the truth this time" Officer Dickson said. Wesley hissed his teeth before he walked a couple of steps away and looked hard at Denyah and said to Officer Dickson. "When you find out you let me know. However, I don't wish to answer any fucking question without my lawyer. Now get the hell out of my house and take the dead damn bitch with you."

An Officer Jefferson came forward and asked Denyah "Can you prove your husband is responsible for Mrs Lake's death?"

"Denyah replied tearfully, I came to collect some dominoes for my fiancée and my ex-husband told me he poisoned Mrs Lake by forcing her to drink poisoned whiskey."

"Did you shoot your husband Mrs Davis?" Officer Jefferson asked.

"No Officer, I did not shoot my husband. But I wish I did" Denyah said.

"I shot him with his gun Officer. He was forcing Mrs Davis to drink some of whiskey he'd give to Mrs Lake. I had to stop him by shooting him. I'm Mrs Edna Jay."

Officer Dickson asked Denyah. "Is there any truth in what Mrs Jay said Mrs Davis?"

"Yes officer, my husband's a police officer and I've suffered under his hands so many times. But I guess now he won't be able to hide behind his badge anymore" Denyah said crying.

"Officer, Mrs Davis is telling you the truth and it's time she went home to her family. She had nothing to do with Mr Davis bad running blood. I told you I had to shoot him to stop him from killing her." Mrs Jay said.

"I see nothings happened to Mrs Davis" Officer Dickson said as the other Officers watched and listened.

"That is because he was trying to poison her with cyanide. You'll find cyanide mixed with the whiskey he was going to force down his wives throat Officer" Mrs Jay said dominatingly.

"Officer, Mrs Jay is telling you the truth. I'm willing to give you a signed statement that my ex and Mrs Lake murdered a Nurse James and Officers Tom Bailey and Finch Lomott. I gathered this information from my ex-husband before he was trying to poison me with cyanide whiskey" Denyah told the police, lying as she wanted so much to hurt Wesley.

Then Mrs Jay said, "Officer, I have suffered deep pain and I was longing for this day to revenge my husband's murder but I only wounded Mr Davis to stop him killing his wife and I swear Mrs Davis had nothing to do with the shooting of his ex-husband. If you should charge anyone for wounding Mr Davis, you should charge me."

"Officers I have proof my ex-husband had a grudge which led him to murder that cold hearted bitch" Denyah said unremorsefully as the Officers looked at each others in thought. Then Denyah whispered into Wesley's ears and told him, "It's now your destiny to have your rotten arse in prison where you should have been a very long time ago."

One of the officers put the bottle with the whiskey that was left into a plastic bag with two glasses that contained a very small amount of whiskey and then sealed the bag and handed it over to another Officer who carried the bag to one of their cars.

"Mrs Davis, you should go home to your family where you belong" Mrs Jay told Denyah again while one of the Officers ejected the CD from playing 'Forever, my darling' and then read Wesley his right and put him in handcuffs.

Then the investigating Officer said to Wesley, "Officer Davis, I'm sorry that it has come to this" he walked away leaving Officer Jefferson standing by Wesley.

Then Officer Jefferson touched Wesley on his shoulder and said "Officer Davis. I'm really sorry we had to put you in handcuffs" As Wesley was bleeding and was in pain, the Paramedic helped him into the ambulance and attended to his wounds and as the ambulance drove away, a police car took the lead until the ambulance got to the hospital with a second police car behind the ambulance.

Meanwhile, two porters carried Mrs Lake's body into a different ambulance and left with the Doctor behind. Police left Denyah in the house with plenty of onlookers flocking outside Wesley's gate in the cul-de-sac.

Denyah made a phone call to Lisa, Wesley's sister, telling her, "Your brother is going to prison for the rest of his life for the murders of his two mates and Mrs Lake who is now stone dead - police and the Doctor took her body from his house ten minutes ago. Your brother has poisoned her with whiskey and cyanide."

The news had left Lisa in silence so that Denyah had to ask, "Are you still there Lisa?"

Lisa swallowed deeply and tears flooded her eyes as she was trying to holding back her crying.

"Denyah," Lisa croaked on her saliva saying, "I always had a strong feeling that my brother had murdered Nurse James. He is lucky Fay told the police him shoot her was an accident but I can't see him getting out of killing your friend.

"Lisa, he had nothing to do with my friend Nurse James murder. A Mrs Jay gave police a signed statement that Mrs Lake paid to have my friend killed and then had the killer murdered. Now the cold hearted bitch is dead, I suppose justice is somehow met. But I gather police claimed the killer that killed my Nurse friend had taken his own life"

"Denyah, where's Wesley?"

"Lisa, the police took him away in an ambulance as he had been shot."

"Denyah, I know my brother is damn right wicked, but he's my second brother, and I don't know how to stop loving him or what went wrong that he turned out this way. But, thanks for letting me know" Lisa said. Then as Denyah heard her burst out crying, Denyah put the phone down. Lisa ran into her husband arms crying and told him "Wesley has been charged with Mrs Lake's murder. Denyah phoned to tell me" she told her husband.

"Then you should help him to get a Lawyer" Richard told Lisa.

"Richard, hiring a good lawyer would take money,"

"Lisa you have money now, you can afford to help your brother with a good lawyer thanks to Denyah and Mr Frats. Lisa honey, whether you brother may be guilty or not, he's also flesh and blood. You'll have to let his mother and brother knows right away." Richard said.

"Oh Richard, phoning my mother and telling her, might take her to an early grave as she only came out of the hospital with heart surgery a month ago. Richard what am I going to do? What about poor Paris. What will she think of her father after hearing he is a murderer"

"Would you like me to phone Keith?" Richard asked

"What did you say?" Lisa asked him crying and felt distraught.

"Lisa, I'm talking about you first brother that is living in Canada. We'll leave your mother out of it for now, but she'll have to know."

"Yes of course Richard, would you mind driving me to see Denyah?"

"Lisa honey, I don't think this is the right time as I'm sure Denyah must be in shock herself" Richard said calmly.

Lisa looked hard at her husband before she went to her bedroom and left him sitting in the kitchen washing their baby Rick's bottles. From her bedroom, she phoned Denyah in spite of her husband telling her not to trouble Denyah at the moment.

However, Eugene answered Lisa's phone call, but when Eugene answered "Hello." Lisa burst into crying then asked Eugene. "What the hell was the matter with you to send my friend to her evil husband for your convenience? I know you were an idiot to send Denyah back into my brother's arms. How low can an idiot like you go to stoop to my brother's level! Had you forgotten the lies he fed to us about the woman you love and what he had done to her at Joan's wedding? Don't you realize how much Wesley despised you knowing you have his wife and daughter the two people he most loved, Eugene hear this from me, my brother only starting drinking heavy since Denyah left him and knew she won't come back to him. Eugene, you left me in thought wondering if you really love Denyah as you said you do! Are you so much hungry for a set of red dominoes that almost cost my dearest friend her life? Eugene, what the hell were you thinking? She has just given birth to your son. It appears to me as if you want her out of your life. If it wasn't for a Mrs Jay to be there and to rescue her, we would have lost her. Eugene, is there's another woman you wanted beside Denyah and you regretted having my friend?"

"Lisa, --------"

Lisa banged the phone down in temper and went downstairs and sat beside her husband Richard and trembled with fear over hearing her brother Wesley was going to murder Denyah which is her best friend. Richard hugged Lisa to comfort her before he made her a cup of tea saying "drink this honey, I'll go and see to our son. And don't worry too much and make yourself sick as you might upset the baby you're carrying."

"Richard honey, Wesley bought back the past to me by lying about how he catch Denyah in bed with his mates when it is who'd set up his mates to have sex with her. Oh Richard why has my brother turned out be so evil?" Lisa began crying again.

"Look honey, you're upsetting yourself, please try not too aye, honey think of our son and the one you're carrying. Please stop crying. Wesley brought this on himself. Why don't you go and have a lie down as Rick's sleeping" Richard said and kissed Lisa's on her forehead.

"What about supper. It's nearly time to start cooking." Lisa said.

"Honey, don't worry. I can cope with the cooking and with our son Rick" Richard told Lisa and hugged her in supporting her up the stairs and into their room. "I think you need a nap" Richard told her.

"All I need is a strong drink to settle my mind" Lisa said to her husband.

"Look Lisa honey, please go to bed" her husband said to her peeling the quilt backward. Lisa looked hard at her husband then he told her again, "Get in bed honey." she hugged him tightly and said, "Richard honey, I love you so much."

"I know honey, now you go to bed and rest."

Lisa climbed into bed and her husband spread the quilt up to her bosom and kissed her on the lips, eyed her, slightly opened the window to let in fresh air before he left. Outside the room he closed the door softly behind him. As their son Rick was just put down to sleep. Richard looked at the door smiling and then went started cooking supper.

Meanwhile at the hospital, Wesley said to the woman police officer "I'm bleeding and in pain."

"Well you're at the hospital now. And I'm sure the doctors will do their best to keep you alive."

"Where's my wife, isn't she here?" he rudely asked the W.P.C as he looked pale and distant and his eyes rolling almost to a closing point.

"Officer Davis, I understand, you're no longer married. Beside, if help hadn't reach your ex wife in time, you would have killed her like you've killed Mrs Lake. Officer Davis, are you aware you're under arrest for the murders of Mrs Lake and two of your fellow Officers Tom Bailey and Finch Lomott?"

"I need a Solicitor. I know my rights. And I'm an Officer like you, Offer Webster. I should be treated with respect. "

"Officer Davis, I know you know your rights. But, some of us ended up on the wrong side. Like you Officer Davis. And as you're claiming respect, you gave that up when you murdered your fellow Officers. What makes you think you would have got away with what you've done. Is it because you're an Officer that's why you thought you would have got away with these murders? Or, you thought you were untouchable. Well Officer Davis, you of all people should have known that the Law never closes any murder cases until justice is met. However, as you're undergoing surgery, there would be an Officer guarding you when you get back from surgery and at all times. Good bye Officer Davis. Oh by the way, when you are strong enough, you will be moving to a cell until your case is tried."

Wesley looked hard at the W.P.C and said, "Get the hell out of sight before I hold you in contempt for harassing an Officer."

"Officer Davis, you been a loser and you still will be. The one I am sorry for is your ex wife. But I'm sure she's very happy now with the husband you have driven her to. So I was told. The W.P.C. sounded her teeth in disgusted manner before she said, "you're a bad and horrible man" Then two male nurses one of mixed race, the other black and two white female Doctors came and wheeled Wesley into the surgery.

Meanwhile, Denyah hugged Mrs Jay crying and said. "Thank you for giving me back my life,"

"Mrs Denyah, it's time you get home to your family."

"Please take one of my card it bears my address and both my home and mobile numbers, if ever you should need me or even to say a friendly word." Denyah said to Mrs Jay.

Mrs Jay took the card from Denyah and thanked her as she smiled.

Denyah smiled between tears and hugged Mrs Jay again saying, "I thank you with all my heart and I shall never forget you as long as I live. I do hope you would call on me soon, as you have my address and my number."

Mrs Jay touched Denyah on her right arm and said "I sure will. Give my love to your lovely family for me."

Denyah nodded her head and walked to her car, when she saw her fiancée Eugene and her brother Ryan come out of Ryan's car. She leaned against her car crying. Ryan went to her and hugged her then asked her what happened. Then Eugene went to her as she was crying so much. Mrs Jay said to Ryan and Eugene her ex-husband was trying to force her to drink whiskey that he'd laced with cyanide. "But I thank God I got to her in time to prevent him forcing some down her throat. I had to shoot him with his gun but I should have given him a straight bullet in his evil heart. Then again, it would have been too easy taking him away from justice for the murders he'd committed."

Both Ryan and Eugene thanked Mrs Jay for saving Denyah's life.

But as Eugene and Ryan were listening to some onlookers, Denyah got in her car and drove away still crying and in shock. And because of her uncontrollable crying, she lost control of her car and nearly crashed into the back of another car. The sharpness of putting on her car brakes caused her to jerk forward and hitting her forehead on the steering wheel as her car stopped instantly bringing the car behind her to a screeching halt and almost hitting her car. The woman that was sitting in the car behind told the driver "I saw her head jerk forward after she stopped her car suddenly."

The young white handsome blond short hair male driver got out of his car leaving his mixed raced young pretty wife in his car and he went and asking Denyah "Are you alright lady?"

Denyah lifted her head, but the young driver suspected Denyah was lightly knocked unconscious as he saw a cut over her left eye and blood dripping on her lap.

"Lady, you banged you forehead on the steering wheel. Would you like me to call anyone or a taxi?" Denyah stared at the driver in somewhat of a trance then shook her head and drove away. The driver shook his head with pity and went into his car and drove away.

"Is she okay?" His wife asked as he got into the driving seat. "She must be if she took off naturally" he answered smiling.

"Well," said his wife, "the way she stopped, she was either in thought or well drugged up with booze or maybe high on drugs. Mark. She'd looked frightened as if she was running away from someone. She also looked a very decent lady that caused me to wonder what could be wrong" the driver's wife said.

"Well Lila, she's gone. And what ever wrong with her, it's no business of ours" he said with straight face.

"You men are so inconsiderate. I watched her and I knew something was wrong" His wife said.

"Well, she was bleeding a little. What ever else is the matter, she's long gone and neither you nor I might find out. Still, I hope whatever is her problem, it won't be more than she can handle" he smiled as he lightly slapped his wife's leg, and went on saying, "anyway, we have our own problem. Do you love me?"

"Mark, I married you because I love you. And you can wipe that smutty smile off you face as I'm in Cherry Red Island. And you know what I mean. Anyway, why you asked me if I love you?"

"No reason" he said and rested his hand on her legs.

"Mark, whatever you after, you'll have to release yourself some other way as I won't be able to give you whatever you want until cherry red is normal again."

"So this means I can look else where?" her husband asked.

"You just try it mate" said his wife.

"I'm just joking honey. I'm sure Mr powerful could wait for the next few days without getting cocky" he laughed.

She laughed also.

Meanwhile, as Denyah was on her way home, Ryan was driving at full speed so that he caught up with her just before she turned on her road for home. Ryan blew his car horn to get her attention but she took no notice as she was crying. Ryan sped past her and stopped at a distance in front of her car. He and Eugene got out and ran to her car as she drove near to the kerb and stopped and was sitting at the steering wheel sobbing, Eugene got in her car and hugged her and told her "Please move over honey" But instead of her moving over, she hooked her arms around his neck and hugged him tightly.

After a short moment, he dried her eyes with one of his handkerchief and said, "What the hell had come over me to send you to that animal and nearly caused you your death" Eugene said with tearful eyes.

"Take us home honey to our family" Denyah said shivering.

He grinned and dried his tears and drove Denyah home while Ryan drove his car behind them.

Meanwhile, Lisa phoned Meleta and told her Wesley tried to kill Denyah.

Meleta then phoned Denyah, but Denyah refused to take any calls until Mrs Brown told her. "It's Meleta."

Denyah took the phone from Mrs Brown and said "Hello Meleta"

"Den honey, I heard that son-of–gun tried to kill you. Are you alright?"

"Well, I'm still shaking a little. But I'll be okay." Denyah said.

"Would it be okay for me to come and see you tomorrow?" Meleta asked.

"Of course Meleta, I won't be going anywhere for a long time now. Beside, I can do with my family support. Will you kiss the kids for me?"

"Sure Den, you kiss yours for me. And will you tell Ryan, on his way home, to buy mom and me two fish and chips. Well Den honey, take care and we would see you tomorrow."

"Goodbye Meleta," Denyah said and hung up. And as she was walking to go into the kitchen, she stumbled and nearly fell but Mrs Brown was quick enough and grabbed hold of her and helped her to a seat and asked her, "Are you feeling alright honey?"

"Everything went so dismal. And my head has felt light" Denyah told her.

"That's because you were crying so much honey that it left you light headed. God knows what would have happened to me and the children if that wicked ex-husband had got his way with you. Ah, I knew that Wesley set out to hurt you and it would have been Eugene's fault" Mrs Brown said.

Just then Eugene and Ryan walked into the living room. Mrs Brown slapped Eugene's face and said, "You fool, I hope you will always remember this night."

Eugene felt the spot on his face where Mrs Brown slapped him and said "Mom, I deserved that. Why couldn't I see what Wesley was doing to us?"

"I'm sorry son, but we could have lost our Denyah and our children would have suffered without their mother."

"Mom, I made a very big mistake. I would never leave her side again or let her out of my sight in that way. Oh God! I love her so much. Why haven't I seen through that wicked ex of hers, and why was I so damn naive not to have seen what he was doing to Denyah and me. I almost drive the woman I'm so much in love with to her death" Eugene said then knelt at Denyah's head and kissed her lips and asked her, "Honey, will you forgive me?"

"I love you Eugene. Promise me," Denyah said.

"Anything honey" Replied Eugene.

"Don't bring any dominos into our home." Denyah said.

"I promise, I will never play another dominoes game in our home." Eugene said seriously and showing tears, "I'm very sorry Den." Eugene said.

"Honey, I don't want you to give up playing dominos as I know it's one of your favourite games. But just keep them out of our home" Denyah told him.

"I respect what you say honey." Eugene said.

"Are you feeling okay now sis?" Ryan asked Denyah also in tears.

"Yes Ryan, I'm feeling much better now I'm with my family. By the way, Meleta phoned to say, on your way home stop at the fish and chips shop and buy her and mom two fish and chips."

"Well sis, since you're okay, I better go and get mom and the missus their fish and chips. I'll come and see you tomorrow then. Well family. Good night."

"See you tomorrow mate?" Eugene told Ryan. And he closed the door after he saw Ryan drove away.

Denyah smiled as Eugene sat next to her. "Are you hungry honey?" he asked her

"A little," Denyah said.

"Would you like some fish and chips?" he asked

"I wouldn't say no." Denyah said.

"Mom would you like some?" Eugene asked.

"Yes please son" Mrs Brown said Then Mrs Brown faced Denyah and asked her. "Would you like me to set you a scented bath?"

"Please mom. Are the children okay?"

"Of course honey. I don't think they had missed you at the time you went out. But I thank the good Lord he brought you back home to us safe and well."

Eugene left in his car to go and buy the fish and chips. Denyah went to have her bath and almost fell asleep in the bath if Mrs Brown hadn't knocked on the door and said. "Honey, it's time you got out before your bath gets cold and you get cramp." Denyah was startled hearing the knocked on the bathroom door. She got out, dried off and dressed in a pair of pale blue satin pyjamas and went and had a look in on the children and kissed their foreheads before she went into the living room with Mrs Brown and waited for Eugene to come home with their fish and chips. Ten minutes after Eugene went to the fish and chips shop, Mrs Brown said, "Denyah, honey, I knew God would send you back to us your family" Then she dropped on her knees in prayer saying, "Dear God, I have faith in you all of my live and I still am. You're the most highest and almightiest. I thank you greatly to give me back my most kind and loving daughter." Mrs Brown then burst out crying. Denyah knelt beside her and hugged her.

As they both got up, they heard the front door opened and then shut.

"Well, here's your fish and chips Mrs Frats, and mom." Eugene said.

"Haven't you bought any for you?" Denyah asked.

"No, all I need is a strong drink and to spend the rest of my life with you my family." he said as he picked a few chips from Denyah's.

"You can have some of mine, as I won't eat all this." Denyah told him.

"Believe me honey, I don't want anymore. I'll see you when you come to bed. Good night mom." Eugene said.

"Good night son." Mrs Brown answered.

Eugene went and had a shower and then as always, he had a looked in on his two daughters and as they were sleeping, he kissed them on their foreheads and left their room quietly and went to his and Denyah's bedroom. Seeing his baby son sleeping, he kissed his right hand four fingers and touched his son's hand. Smiling, he said softly over his son. "Daddy loves you son."

That night he made love to Denyah and told her, "I love you so much."

The following evening Eugene met Ryan at their local Pub. Over a pint he said to Ryan, "I'm going to ask Den to marry me" Eugene said to Ryan.

Ryan was happy to have heard him said that even though he was feeling so hurt over what happened to his sister Denyah, he looked hard at Eugene and asked him. "What the hell were you thinking of to send my sister to her ex" As Eugene didn't answer, Ryan said, "Eugene my sister almost got killed, and for what? A fool's game of domino you haven't got?"

"Believe me Ryan. I thought Wesley was honest. I believed he'd moved on from loving Den. Obviously, I was wrong. Ryan, I love Den, if he had killed her, I would have fucking swung for the son-of-a–bitch! I would break his fucking neck like a dry twig. And after, I wouldn't care one fuck what the law done to me as I wouldn't want to go on living without my Den" Eugene said as tears filled his eyes.

"I know you do love my sister. But you can't be vexed with me for speaking out for her? And what about the children, have you stop to think if Den was hurt or killed what would have happened to them? I suppose not"

"Mom would look after them." Eugene said.

"Eugene, mom is not so young." Ryan said.

"You're right Ryan my friend. But what the hell was I really thinking about to have driven the woman I'm so much in love with back into that savage's arms to be killed. What would I have told my children if their mother were murdered on the account of my damn selfishness because of a set of dominoes - I now realize the son-of-a-bitch was playing the fools games with me to hurt sweet Denyah, Ryan my friend, I don't think I would want to see another domino again."

Ryan was listening to Eugene with sad feelings. He faced Eugene and said. "I'm sorry I pounced on you mate, but I had to as I love my sister so much."

"Still, Ryan, I can't say I blame you for protecting her. However, no hard feeling mate, I deserved whatever you dish out to me as I should have used my dumb nut and been more cautious. I want Den to be my wife" Eugene said proudly.

Ryan smiled and said, "I want you to be her husband, and for us to be family" And he and Eugene shook hands in friendship.

Eugene then called Denyah on his mobile phone in the presence of Ryan and asked, "Den honey, would you marry me."

Denyah smiled hugging his pillow as she replied "I'll marry you this minute honey. On your way home bring us a priest" she laughed and said happily "Yes, Eugene, I would marry you. But I would like my friends and family to be at my wedding including my sister Laney and her family and a very special friend, Millicent Libert a housing agent I became friendly with in St Kitts and another friend I got to know on the plane on my return home."

"Yes of course honey, you can invite the whole world as long as you marry me." Eugene told Denyah proudly and looking happy.

Eugene turned and asked Ryan in smile, "May I marry your sister?"

Ryan laughed blissfully and said, "If she would have you my friend. And as long as I would be the best man."

"Sure, you would" Eugene said laughing then he and Ryan left the pub and drove to Denyah. As Denyah was in bed, Ryan went to her and asked "Are you alright?"

"Sure bros. I'm fine. Are you?"

"Yes sis, I am, now that I know you're okay."

"Yes I'm okay. By the way, Eugene phoned and asked me if I'll marry him. And I said yes, I will."

"I'm happy for you sis. Just let me know when the date is set."

"Yes of course bros, you and mom would be the first to know as you would have to give me to him and if he doesn't treat me right mom would take me away. Have you seen Eugene tonight?"

"I was with him when he phoned and asked you if you'll marry him. He's standing outside the door with a bright smile on his face. Well I must get home to my other set of family before they send out a search party to find me. I shall see you all at the week-end. Will you tell mom I was here?"

"I certainly will." Denyah said.

"I'll let myself out. Good night mate." Ryan said.

"See you at the week-end mate" Eugene said. And as Ryan turned off the lights on his way out, Eugene had a quick shower and went to bed, kissed Denyah and fell a sleep in a matter of minutes.

The following day Denyah hugged Mrs Brown and Ryan and said, "Thanks for been here for me."

Meanwhile, two Police Officers called to see Denyah and told her "Mrs Jay has provided us with insufficient evidence towards you ex-husband but still we are strongly convinced he had nothing to do with the murders of Officers Tom Bailey and Finch Lomott but we're not sure about Mrs Lake. However, he would be held until we're completely satisfied he had nothing to do with their murders. Of course he has denied murdering any of them and we have nothing on him so far. However, he's still at the hospital where he had surgery and now under police guard until he's taken into custody."

Then a second policeman asked, "Mrs Davis, would you like to file a complaint on your ex-husband for trying to murder you?"

"No Officer, as much as I would like to, he has already charged with three murders"

"Well, it's up to you Mrs Davis. Without your statement, we can't charge him with attempting to murder on you. Oh the glass we took for test, it contained sugar and not cyanide. Even so, three murders hang over him."

"That's right Officer. I think the three murders he's charged with, my attempting murder won't make much difference. I'm sorry but even though I wanted to see him suffer, I can't give evidence against him. I will have to live with my guilt of keeping quiet towards him for the sake of our daughters."

"I understand Mrs Davis. I'm sorry to know a once-good Officer such as him has turned out to be on the wrong side of the law. Goodbye Mrs Davis."

"Goodbye Officers."

While Denyah was speaking to two officers, the oldest one was asking the questions and doing all the speaking while the younger officer remained silent with a smiling face throughout the fifteen minutes interrogation. Then as a third officer showed up, the young officer asked Denyah, "Would you be willing to give evidence that your husband Mr Davis has tried to murder you?"

"Office, I'm sorry, but I'm going to refuse giving evidence against Wesley" I meant Mr Davis." Denyah said.

"Well Mrs Davis, we can't force you to give evidence" the Officer said smiling like it was a relief. The officers left.

The following day Lisa went to Wesley's house which was three streets away from hers. She let herself into his house as always with her given key. As she entered into the living room, her eyes fixed on the dried patch of blood on the wooden floor. She shivered coldly before washing the blood off the floor. While throwing the blooded water down the toilet, she cried. "Oh Wesley, what has made you turn out to be a devil." she dried her eyes, blew her nostrils and tidied all over the house. She then packed four pairs of Wesley's pyjamas suits, shower gel, toothbrush, paste, mouthwash, slippers, electric shaver, aftershave and a comb, three bath towels, flannels and six pairs of boxer shorts. Later that night Richard took them to the hospital and gave them to Wesley along with bottles of juice and fruits telling him, "Lisa couldn't come as she has to take care of Rick and being she's pregnant she's not feeling well and it was too late and chilly to take Rick out but she said you'll see her tomorrow. Is anything you would like her to bring?" Richard asked Wesley.

"My wife and daughter, can she bring them? For they're all I need right now."

"Wesley, you're asking for the impossible. I won't expect you to forget your daughter, or give her up, but you should try and forget Denyah. She's now living with Eugene and she has his child."

"Don't you think I don't fucking know that? She's all I want. Thanks for bringing these to me, but you can leave now."

"Wesley, be sensible------------

"You still here" Wesley cut Richard short from saying what he had to say.

"Well, good luck mate and I'll see you sometime" Richard said and left.

Outside Wesley's door, Richard shook his head as he looked seriously hard on the door and walked out of the hospital to go get to his parked car when he bumped into a very pretty black woman and almost knocked her over. "I'm sorry. I should look where I'm going?" Richard said.

The woman smiled saying, "I'm Doctor Milburn and it's alright, I should look where I'm walking as well" she laughed.

Richard laughed too."

"Are you one of us?" she asked.

"Us," Richard asked showing a nice smiled.

"I meant a doctor?" she asked showing him an inviting smile.

"No, oh no, I came to see my brother-in-law."

She laughed saying "Well, it's nice meeting you Mr......

"My name's Richard."

"I'm Penny, Penny Milburn. Well goodbye Richard," she said and walked away leaving him standing. As she walked a short distance, she looked back at Richard smiling. Richard smiled and she shook her head and walked off then he turned facing her and fluted out a loud whistle at her blowing his fingers for her to hear. Smiling broadly, she slowed her walking and closed her eyes as she'd instantly felt love towards him. With her back turned and with some distance between her and Richard, Richard blew her a second whistle. She looked back at him in smiles and walked off again. Richard smiled looking at her in thought then before she walked in the hospital he trotted after her catching her up and touched her shoulder. Smiling she faced him. "Have you forgotten something Richard?" she asked him.

Richard smiled, "I would like for us to be friends."

"I'll like that Mr Richard." she said and turned to walk away.

"I'm just Richard." Richard said smiling.

"Richard would you like us to have a drink together some time?" she asked.

"I would be looking forward to that sometime." Richard said.

Doctor Penny gave Richard one of her cards with her telephone number. She then walked into the hospital smiling while Richard went into his car. As he looked at her telephone number, he smiled and said, "Richard, what have you done? Well, having a drink with a pretty doctor wouldn't hurt. Would it Richard?" he asked himself and then answered. "No mate. Having a drink with a pretty doctor wouldn't hurt." he then put the card in his jacket pocket and drove away smiling to his home. As he got home, he took the card out of his pocket and told Lisa with guilty feelings, "I met Doctor Penny and I think she's taking care of Wesley. She gave me one of her cards that had her telephone number. She said if I need to know about Wesley, she's the one to ask." As Lisa looked in his eyes, he kept a straight face and then smiled when he walked out the living room into the kitchen and made two cups of tea and took one to Lisa.

"Thanks" Lisa said. Then says "Well honey, I hope that's all she wanted from you. Anyway, how did you leave my brother?" Lisa asked Richard.

"Alright, He will be okay honey." Richard said.

"What do you mean honey, is he alright? Hasn't he give you a message to give to me or asked for anything?" Lisa asked

All he asked for is Denyah and Paris. I'm through with him. He's your brother Lisa and I won't stop you seeing him." Richard said.

"Richard, where's all this building up from? Of course it would be unfair of you stopping me from seeing my brother. You have your family and I wouldn't dare ask you not to see any of them." Lisa said. Then she went on to ask Richard, "Are you sure you're not falling for that Doctor Penny?"

"Don't be silly honey. I only have enough strength for you. However, I don't need her card as I won't be having any more interest in your brother" Richard said and tore Doctor Penny's card into half.

"Richard, because you tore the card doesn't convince me you're not interested in her. If I find out you're having affair, I'll screw you into the earth so that only me can reach you. Honey, how seriously hurt is my brother?" Lisa asked.

"His foot and arm are in casts and he looked drained and haggard. I can take you to see him tomorrow if you like." Richard said.

"Okay, I left your supper in the micro. Would you like me to heat it for you?"

"Yes please honey." Lisa said.

Lisa heated Richard's supper and took it to him in the living room as he was watching TV.

The following afternoon, Lisa went to see her brother Wesley in the hospital. She tried talking to him, but he said nothing but rolled his eyes and looked at her as she was putting the goods away in his locker that Richard had taken to him the day before. As she did so, Wesley said, "I still love my Denyah."

Lisa looked at the handcuffs on his hands and said, "There's a policeman sitting outside your door" she said, trying to ignore him talking about Denyah.

"Let the bastard sit and count every visitor that passes as he has nothing better to do." he said.

"Wesley, Richard and I will find you a solicitor."

"I don't need your help. All I need is my wife and my daughter."

"Wesley, you're my brother and I'm only trying to help you. Three murders hang over you. You would need a good and fighting Solicitor. Wesley, you're in the worst way, what has driven you to commit these murders? Wesley, you said you want your wife. Remember, you tossed her to the dogs, and you had me and my husband fooled with your lies about her and every one else that we almost flung the same wife you now want into a burning hell. Wesley, she wants nothing to do with you now. I would also be through with you if you weren't my brother. Saying so, I don't even know who you are any more! You're responsible for your own doing. I phoned our brother Greg and told him what you've done but I'm keeping mother out of this for the time being as I don't think she could stand the strain hearing about you right now as she recently came out of a heart operation. Greg would be coming to see you soon." Lisa told Wesley.

"How's my daughter?" Wesley asked trying to ignore what Lisa said. Then said to Lisa, "The next time you're coming to see me would you bring my daughter to see me?"

"Wesley, I won't be coming to see you again and you've given your daughter to her mother nine years ago. Paris would be happier not knowing that you were going to murder her mother and that you've murdered three people. Eugene is a better father to her than you'll ever be. She's calling Eugene daddy. Wesley, you're now out of her life for good. Would you want her to carry the evil burden that now rest on you that you'd rape her mother so often and that you're a murderer? Well I don't think it would be fair on her, so leave her alone Wesley."

"Lisa you wouldn't understand. I'm still in love with my wife. After losing her, I couldn't bear the thought of her in another man's bed. I was so jealous of her that I couldn't trace where I was going and doing wrong. I had wanted to end our lives together." Wesley told his sister Lisa as tears flooded his eyes.

"And what about Paris, the daughter you want me to bring to you. Did you stop to think about her and how would she have cope if you'd murdered her mother? Wesley when you leave here, straight to a cell you would be going until your case is tried" Lisa told her brother Wesley.

"Do you think that I don't fucking know that, that's why I want to see my daughter to tell her the house would be hers."

"Now tell me brother, what will Paris do with that house. It's best you sell the house and donated the money to charity. I know for sure Paris wouldn't want your money. And if you know what is good for you, you would leave her alone. She never one time ask about you since she left you. And if you don't really want her to hate you for the rest of her life, I think you should leave her alone. Goodbye Wesley." Lisa said as she got up out of her seat.

"Fuck off" Wesley said rudely staring up to the ceiling lying on his back as his leg and hand were in casts and his left hand shackled to the bedstead head.

As Lisa walked out of the room, the police held the door opened and had a quick peep in on Wesley and said goodbye to Lisa before he closed the door to Wesley's room and took his seat again drinking a cup of coffee he had just taken from one of the nurses.

Before Lisa went home she went to see Denyah. As she and Denyah hugged, tears came in her eyes as she asked Den. "How are you?"

"Well, you know me? Always bouncing back from the dark side into light;" Denyah said then she asked Lisa "Would you like something to drink?"

"Well, I wouldn't say no to a cup of tea. How's the children."

"They're very well thank-you but they're in bed." Denyah said.

"Den, before you say anything, I'm so sorry for what my brother tried to do to you and what he has put you through."

"Lisa, I should have been more cautious. Don't feel bad. I know what Wesley is as he was my husband, and I still went to him. I wouldn't even blame Eugene. I should be stronger and told Eugene to fetch his dominoes himself. What was I proving? My children almost lost their mother. However, how my nephew and Richard and that little nipper you're carrying?"

"Den, they're very well and I'm feeling great at the moment. But I'm not coming from home. I went to see my evil my brother, but that the last time he would see me. I'm through with him."

"Well Lisa, that is up to you. He's your brother and I wouldn't hold a grudge against you for his evil doing. Or, if you're looking after him." Denyah said understandingly.

"What went so wrong with him that causes him to act like a wild cat towards you, and to make him a murderer? My other brothers are so different." Lisa cried.

"Lisa my friend, you don't need to explain to me about Wesley. He was my husband and I did love him, but he killed the love I had for him and also the little respect I had left for him on behalf of our daughter. Well, that's enough about him. Would you like some more tea and something to eat?" Denyah asked Lisa.

"Yes please Den, I'm feeling a little hungry." Lisa said.

Mrs Brown went and made ham and cheese sandwiches and coffee for everyone.

"Den. I heard your sister and her family came to visit you." Lisa asked.

"Oh yes, they arrived this afternoon about three o'clock. I was going to let you know. Lisa you'll like her, she's so adorable." Denyah said.

Lisa phoned Richard from Denyah's and told him she's at Denyah's and asked him if their son was okay?"

"Don't worry Li, I bathed him fed him and he's now sleeping. Will you say hello to Den and Mrs Brown for me?" Richard asked.

"Sure honey, anyway, Dens sister and her family came to visit Den but they're out with Eugene. Honey, I'll be home soon and if Rick cry for his teething, will you rub some teething gel on his gums and give him a teaspoonful of Calpol. Den gave me a bottle of Johnnie Walker whiskey to give to you." Lisa said.

After Richard went silent, Lisa said, "It's from Denyah's sister Laney and husband?"

"Would you thank them for me please honey?" Richard said.

"Yes I will. See you when I get home." Lisa rang off and finishing drinking her coffee. Another she spend another ten minutes, she drove herself home to meet Richard and son in bed.

"He was crying honey and I did what you asked and he fell asleep beside me." Richard said.

Lisa gave Richard the whiskey and asked him, "Why are you in bed so early?"

"I was a little tired and lying with Rick, I fell asleep. Anyway, I have a busy day tomorrow and I had to be somewhere with Eugene" Richard said.

"Oh," Lisa said.

"Honey, I have to go to work early in the morning. Would you drop the sterilizing tablets in the baby sterilizer, I washed and put the bottles in the bucket" Richard told Lisa.

After Lisa sterilized her son's bottle she made tea for her and Richard. She then turned the lights off from downstairs, joined her Richard in their bedroom drinking tea and eating a bacon sandwich. After supper, Lisa went and had her shower and joined Richard in bed.

Meanwhile, Eugene opened his front door with his key as he didn't want to wake the children by knocking on the door. He let Denyah's sister, Laney, and her two girls in the house then he followed to see Mrs Brown in the dining room drinking coffee. "Mom, I have to get back to the Social club to get Paul as I'd left him with my brothers and told him I'll be back to fetch him" Eugene told Mrs Brown and left to go to the Social club. By this time Denyah was in bed after breastfeeding her baby son as she'd felt tired.

"And here's me thinking, you're just on time for some hot coffee. Mrs Brown said to Laney and Eugene before he went to fetch Paul. "Thanks mom, but, I have to rush away" Eugene said and left.

"None for me, thank you mother Brown" Laney said, "Eugene had given us a big meal" Then Laney said to her two daughters, "As for you girls, kiss mother Brown goodnight and go the bathroom before you go to bed."

"Yes mom" they said and they kissed Mrs Brown on her cheek before they went upstairs to the toilet. Then Laney asked Brown "Where's Den?"

"She went to bed honey as she said she was feeling tired" Mrs Brown said.

After sometime, Ryan went home and told Meleta Denyah's sister and her family came to visit Denyah. Meleta phoned Denyah, but Mrs Brown told her Denyah was sleeping. "Mom would you tell her I called." Meleta said.

"Sure honey, I would tell her first thing in the morning" Mrs Brown said.

"Mom I'm so happy she's okay" Meleta said in tears and feeling sad and mixture of happiness.

"I am so happy to have my Den home." Mrs Brown said inhaling deeply.

"Mom would you please give my love to Laney and her family and I will come and see them all tomorrow."

"Okay Meleta honey, we'll see you tomorrow." Mrs Brown said.

After Mrs Brown hung up the phone, Denyah's sister Fay and her fiancée' Guy rang the doorbell. Mrs Brown answered the door to see Fay and Guy. "Come in Fay and Mr Rogers" Mrs Brown said as she moved from the door to let them in, "Mom, you don't mind me calling you that would you?"

"Not at all Fay and you too Mr Rogers you can call me mom if you like," Mrs Brown told Mr Rogers.

"Well, Mother Brown as I'm family it's only fair of you to call me Guy" Mr Rogers said.

"Well Guy, Fay, I just made plenty of hot coffee and sandwiches if you would like some?"

"Well the truth is mom, Fay and I have just eaten. Fay is here to see her sisters, Denyah and Laney. Especially Denyah as we haven't been to see her since we heard what happened" Guy said.

"Well she went to bed as she was feeling tired. However, she is alright. Fay, I would tell her you and Guy came to see her." Mrs Brown said.

"Well will you tell her I would call to see her tomorrow lunchtime," Fay said.

"I will and would you like me to leave lunch for you?" Mrs Brown asked Fay.

"You better," Fay said smiling.

Mrs Brown laughed. Fay took a ham sandwich and bit it ravenously. Guy looked at her smiling and shook his head saying. "I might have to work around the clock to feed you"

"I'm still a little hungry, besides, mom sandwiches looked so tempting. You sure you don't want one honey?" Fay asked Mr Rogers.

"No Fay, I'm tightly packed having a four course meal and almost a bottle of champagne. Well, lets go honey, we come back to see Denyah soon" Mr Rogers said.

"Okay Guy" Mrs Brown said and as Guy faced the door to leave, Fay grabbed another ham sandwich and smiled and as she and Mr Rogers were on their way out,

Eugene and Paul were on their way in. Fay and Mr Rogers got back into the house to say hello to Paul.

"Hello Paul, how was your trip?" Fay asked.

"Not bad at all," Paul said.

"Well, I'm Fay one of Laney's sisters and you will soon meet another younger sister Blanch. Fay embraced Paul and kissed him, while Eugene and Mr Rogers watched and then Mr Rogers shook Paul's hand telling him and Eugene, "I'll see you both tomorrow"

"Well family, I'll be back tomorrow to meet my sister Laney and my nieces as they're in bed. And Paul, I'm so glad to meet you." Fay said.

"Likewise Fay." Paul said.

Fay and Mr Rogers left the house and ran into their car as it starting to rain as Fay sat brushing the rain out of her hair, she said, "Guy, I love you."

"I love you too honey" Mr Rogers said and he kissed her and told her again, "I love you so much" he then drove way with Fay's hand resting on his knee.

Ten minutes later Mr Rogers and Fay got home.

Eugene and Paul said good night to their brothers and friends and left as everyone were leaving. As soon as Eugene and Paul got home, Paul said to Eugene, "Well Eugene thanks for a nice evening, but as I'm so tired, I must join my wife in dream land. Goodnight mother Brown."

"Goodnight Paul."

"Me too goodnight mom and I will go to bed." Eugene said.

"Goodnight son. I'll be up soon." Mrs Brown said.

Eugene went to have his shower and then to bed. Paul had his shower in a different shower and then joined his wife Laney.

As Eugene couldn't sleep and he was feeling hungry, he went into the kitchen and ate a couple of ham sandwiches and a can of beer and then took a coffee tray off Mrs Brown and said, "Mom, you go and have a rest" Mrs Brown watched him and smiled as she said, "I can do with some."

Eugene watched her as she slowly climbing the stairs until she had disappeared. Then he tidied the rooms, the kitchen, took out the bin and turned off the lights before he joined Denyah in bed.

Early the following morning when Mrs Brown went down stairs to do the cleaning, she was very much surprised to have seen everywhere spectacularly clean and tidy. Shaking her partly greyed head she smiled pleasingly and then sat at the table relaxing and drinking a cup of tea before everyone got up. As it was very early, she prepared the feed for the baby and put the bottle of milk in the bottle warmer to keep it warm until the baby was ready to feed.

Eugene was up early too. As he met Mrs Brown ready to cook breakfast he took over and said, "Mom you should take it easy. You sit in any room while I take over and cook breakfast."

"Are you not going to work today son?" Mrs Brown asked Eugene.

"No mom, I'm my own boss, besides, I won't be missed and I would like to spend sometime with my family and with Denyah's family. I owe it to Den after what she's been through. Now for breakfast, we have bacon, sausages, eggs, fried bread, tomatoes, waffle, tomatoes and beans."

"Son, you sure you don't need my help?"

"Mom, I used to be a chef before I became boss, and I still have the knack of cooking. So please relax mom. As they said, too many cooks spoil the broth."

Mrs Brown took Eugene's advice and went and had a lie in the living room on the sofa.

Eugene cooked all the breakfast and left in under the hot grill then set the large table to make it looked inviting and beautiful with white fresh roses set on a pale blue table cloth with a long strip of white satin spread in the centre of the table cloth. Everyone was up then, and it was an impressive morning to have seen the dining room looking so beautiful. Denyah looked at Eugene, smiled and shook her head. "I did this for you honey." he whispered in her ears. Everyone took their seat. Eugene filled the table with breakfast including sweet potato pancake and fried plantains. Everyone plated their breakfast. Laney and Paul ate well while their girls had waffles, sausage and beans.

"Well Eugene, I'm so happy that we all here enjoyed your cooking." Mrs Brown said.

"I wish my husband could cook like you Eugene. The only thing my husband could cook is water and he still would burn the pot." Laney said.

"Is he such a bad cook honey? " Mrs Brown asked Laney laughing.

"Well, he buttered bread nicely." Laney said. Everyone laughed.

"Well it's time I take my girls to school and nursery" Eugene said as he got up from the table. Mrs Brown and Laney cleared the table and Mrs Brown put the dishes in the dishwasher to wash.

Denyah woke her baby up and fed him. Afterwards she winded him and changed him and put him down in his bed cot as he was sleeping. Paris and Jade B kissed her, their Aunt Laney and Mrs Brown before they left with their dad Eugene to go to school and nursery. Shortly later, Eugene returned with a tin of sweets for Laney two girls.

"Thank you Uncle Eugene," they both said.

When the baby woke, Eugene bathed the baby and dressed him while Denyah sat with her sister Laney in the conservatory looking at family album.

As the baby was crying and moving his head into Eugene's bosom for feeding, he took the baby to Denyah and said, "Daddy milk is not mature as yet. Your mom has plenty to fill a bucket" Eugene said and smiled as Laney looked up at him smiling. Denyah passed the baby to Laney and she quickly went and washed her breasts and returned to feed her crying baby.

While she was feeding the baby, her other breasts was spouting. Eugene looked at her and smiled deeply as he'd tasted her milk before. She laughed. And as she said, "Your dad," Eugene shook his head meaning don't tell Laney he'd tasted her milk. Denyah understood and said, "Would you tell mom to put some fish to thaw out?"

"I was taking us to a hotel meal." Eugene said smiling.

"Thank you honey," Denyah said.

Eugene left Denyah feeding the baby and Laney looking at the family album and photos of Denyah and Ryan taken with the late Mrs Carter and some with Mrs Brown. While Denyah were breast feeding her baby and looking on his face, she though deeply of what has happened to her and almost left her baby motherless, tears streaming down her face. "Honey, what's the matter?" Laney asked

"I don't know, all I know is I love you so much and the rest of my family."

"I love you too honey" Laney said

Eugene again cooked lunch and then went and got Jade B. And hour later he went fetched Paris from school. After speaking to Mrs Brown, he said, "Mom, I had no idea women's work was so hard."

Mrs Brown smiled and said, "When you having pleasure with other women, think of our sweet Den and your children."

"Mom, Den is the only woman in my life and would be. I love her too much to mess with other women" Eugene said lying through his teeth.

"I'm glad to hear you say that Eugene." Mrs Brown said.

"I though we would be skipping lunch and have dinner" Mrs Brown said.

"I only cook a light lunch as we would be eating out tonight." Eugene said.

Ten minutes after Eugene prepared lunch. Fay came to see her sisters Laney and Denyah and had lunch. "I came to see you last night but both of you were in bed. Anyway Laney, how was you trip?"

"Well, the flying was long but it was enjoyable and as for the girls they slept half the way. Yes, it was okay and I'm so glad sister Den gave us the chance to come and see the rest of the family. You and Blanch should take a trip to St Kitts."

"Guy and I will soon after we're married." Fay said. Then Fay asked Denyah "Are you okay Den?"

"Yes- sure, I'm okay. Thanks for asking." Denyah said.

That day Blanch called to see her sisters Laney, Denyah and family, and spent the day with them.

One week later, Fay took Laney and her two girls shopping for clothes and shoes to wear at Denyah's wedding while Eugene and Patrick took Paul to the men's shop to buy him a suit, shirt and shoes. Eugene paid for everything Paul had bought.

The following week before Denyah and Eugene got married Eugene and his brother Patrick took Laney and her family to see many places in Birmingham, London, Scotland, Wales and Liverpool and Manchester to meet some family from her fathers' side. Laney and her family were so appreciative to Eugene and Patrick and especially to have seen Buckingham Palace and the changing of the guard and so many beautiful places that Eugene pointed out to them and named. After a long and interesting week outside Birmingham, Eugene took them to Walsall and Wolverhampton for a day on his way home from those far away places and took them to McDonald's and bought food for them including his girls and apple pies for Denyah and Mrs Brown.

The following day Thursday, Denyah and Bernice drove Laney and her two daughters around and show them some of the most beautiful places in Birmingham. Fay, Veda and Paula also took Laney and her two daughters to the Bull Ring Market and other places in around the City. When Laney daughters saw so many different fish in the Bull Ring market, they said, "Mommy, there's more fish here than we have in St Kitts."

"But our fish is much nicer and fresher." Laney said.

As they exploring the indoor market Laney bought gifts and clothes for family and friends in St Kitts.

After Laney and her family spent two week with her sister Denyah and family, Eugene and Patrick went to the airport the Sunday morning to get Denyah's friend Mrs Millicent Libert. At the airport Eugene and Patrick recognised her by her wearing black trousers and blue long-sleeved shirt as she had stated. As Eugene and Patrick saw her, they went to her and asked, "Are you Millicent Libert?"

"Yes" she answered and smiled. Patrick paid a porter to carry her suitcase and bag to their car. Patrick drove home as Eugene had driven to the airport. Two hours later they got home. Denyah hugged Millicent telling her, "It's nice to see you again" Denyah showed her to the room where she would be sleeping. Mrs Brown made sandwiches for everyone as they would be having dinner later at one of Eugene's hotels.

That Sunday evening, Eugene took everyone to White Lily Hotel for dinner.

The following Monday, everyone went to see Millicent and had lunch at Denyah's.

That Monday it made two weeks Laney her husband and two daughters spent with Denyah and family. The third week Denyah and Eugene got married the Saturday morning eleven thirty at the Town Registry Office. Later that afternoon family and friends went to the party at Denyah and her husband's home. Mrs Brown was extremely happy for both Denyah and Eugene to have got married. Amongst the guests, was Mrs Jay, no one had recognised her but Denyah and Denyah hadn't told anyone who she was. Mrs Jay stayed in the background. Denyah smiled and went to her and hugged her saying "come and meet my family."

Mrs Jay smiled nicely as she raised her glass of champagne to the family and said "Denyah, I wish you and your family a long and very happy life."

Then just as Mrs Jay wished Denyah all the best, Clair, Joan and Austin showed up and knocked at the door. Denyah met them at the door, and said, "Come in, you're very welcome."

Joan looked at Denyah then tears came into her eyes. Denyah smiled and told her, "I hope your tears mean happiness for me."

Then as Joan said to Denyah "I'm so sorry" Denyah hooked her arm around her shoulder and said, "I'm so glad you came. Now my friends are complete as before. Now let's dry those beautiful eyes and go and join the others."

"I bought you a friendship bangle as I knew you have everything" Joan said smiling but looking shameful.

"Now I have everything I need. Meaning you my friend and I hope we can lay the past down behind us and visit each other as before." Denyah said.

"Den, you wouldn't know how much this means to me hearing those words. I love you Den" Joan said.

"I never stop loving you Joan. Anyway, would you hook your beautiful gift around my wrists please?" Denyah asked her

"Sure Den," Joan said barely smiling and nervously as her hands were shaking while she was hooking the gold bangle around Denyah' left wrist.

Denyah joked saying, "Oh my wrist, a bump just came up."

Joan fixed her face seriously. So serious that Denyah laughed saying. "I got my own back on you honey."

Joan burst into laughter and said. "You wait. Just you wait Den my friend." Then Denyah walked her to meet her sister Laney, husband and their two nieces, and her friend Millicent. Then Denyah told Laney, Paul and Millicent. "This is one of my good friends Joan and her husband Austin standing by Eugene."

"Nice to meet you Joan, your husband is very handsome." Laney told her.

"Likewise Laney, you have two beautiful daughters and a very handsome husband. I'm so very glad to meet you" Joan said looking much happier. "And you too Millicent."

"I'm also glad to know you too Joan." Millicent said.

Fay, Cindy and Clara were going around topping up every ones glass with champagne or what every drink they wanted. Even though there was at least a hundred of all type of alcoholic drinks sitting on a long table with plenty of nice food and snacks for the children.

As the party was nearing the end Veda announced this song is dedicated to the new bride and groom and us lovers. She then placed the disc to play (That Night We Met)

sung by Judy Bulger. Eugene took Denyah on the dance floor then everyone joined in the dance. At the end of the dance, Eugene gave Denyah a long sentimental kiss and then announced proudly and happily "I will love my wife to the end of my time." he kissed Denyah again. Everyone applauded them. Then Mrs Jay shouted, "This is the happiest time of your life honey. Enjoy every moment of it. Your nurse friend would of been so happy to have seen you if she was here."

David's face went sad, but as his Tracy was holding his hand, he forced a fake grin.

Then Mrs Jay asked Veda to play the tape a second time (If I could turn back the time I'll do it for you) "this is for your friend honey. Nurse James and your other adopted mom Mrs Carter." Then as Veda placed the tape in the Stereo System then announced: "This song is dedicated to two loved departed friends of Mrs Denyah Frats. The late Miss Louise James who was viciously taken away from us because of her kindness and a very kind and precious old lady that went peacefully with a heart attack."

Denyah burst in tears. Eugene comforted her, dried her tears with his fingers then took her hand to dance when David went and took her away from Eugene and began dancing with her.

Eugene touched David shoulder and said "I understand." Eugene took Denyah's sister Laney and danced with her. Then Fay took her bother-in-law Paul on the dance floor and dance with him, Mr Rogers danced with Tracy.

After the disc finished playing and another was playing, Mrs Jay took Denyah on the dance floor while Eugene and everyone stood in somewhat of a trance and watched silently as Denyah and Mrs Jay were dancing. As the disc had finished, Mrs Jay planted a long and somewhat of a loving caring and friendly kiss on Denyah's forehead and said. "You became special to me and I love you."

Tears come into David's eyes while listening to the music. Tracy hugged him and said, "We can never forget our Louise. But I'm your fiancée now." She said. He smiled.

Then Denyah played the disc. 'Oh What -A -Joy to have someone by my side:' This time Denyah took Eugene, Mrs Jay ,Mrs Brown, Lisa, Meleta, Ryan, Bernice, Veda, Paula, Jenny, her sisters Blanch, Fay, Laney and Laney husband Paul, Mr Frats, Cindy, Joan, Clair, Ryan, Ivy, Mrs Saunders, Millicent and everyone else joined hands together to formed a ring with Mrs Jay dancing in the middle of the ring. Then Denyah was playing a game asking everyone to guest who Mrs Jay was. Everyone had a go at guessing but came up with the wrong answer. Denyah told them "Mrs Jay was the kindest lady that saved my life when my ex was trying to kill me."

Mrs Brown, Eugene and Ryan hugged and thanked Mrs Jay saying "Thank you for giving me my daughter back." Mrs Brown said and kissed Mrs Jay on her face.

Then Eugene said, "And thanks for my wife and my children's mother."

Ryan hugged Mrs Jay and said. "Thank you for giving me my sister again."

"God had given her back to you. I was only working as a messenger." Mrs Jay said to them.

And as they danced to Oh what a Joy to have someone by my side, almost every woman was in tears as they held on to their husbands. That scene was very emotional even though it was a wedding party. Laney hugged Denyah and Mrs Brown and said to them, "You both are my joy. Thanks for everything and the money you both put into our account, we set up trust funds for the girls. Thank you with every blood that's in my body."

Then Paula said, "This is another lover's disc, so grab your husband girls." Paula then played the disc (Save the last dance for me) Then Kalor and Victor, Bernice's brother showed up. Victor went to the drink bar to get drinks for him and Kalor. Eugene went to Kalor and asked her. "What the hell are you doing here?"

"Don't worry. I came with my man Victor. As you don't want your wife to know about us, so I wouldn't want my man to find out." Kalor told him. Ray looked at Eugene and smiled.

Eugene crossed the room to Ray and told him "You say anything to my wife or anyone and I'll snap you fucking neck like a dry twig."

"Bros, my mouth is sealed. But Ryan's the one you should warn." Ray said.

"Ryan's safe and I'm sure he won't say anything to hurt Den." Eugene said and went and danced with Denyah.

"I shall never forget this day." Meleta's step-mom said as her real mother was standing by her side.

"I don't think any of us will ever forget." Bernice's adopted mom said.

Mrs Brown lifted her glass of mineral water and said "To all of us here and especially to Mrs Jay - who God gave the power to send Den back to us." Mrs Brown cried out as she realized if it wasn't for Mrs Jay, her Denyah wouldn't be around for any of them to be dancing at her wedding party. Mrs Brown blew her nose in her handkerchief and made her speech saying, "Mrs Jay, God bless you where ever you go. May the good and gracious God keep you from harm at all times. Mrs Jay." Mrs Brown said smiling and sipped her mineral water. Then all raised their glasses again saying "To Mrs Jay," by this time, Mrs Jay was standing in the far corner of the room and nearest the wall unit and smiling.

"Well this is the final dance." Paula said, "So grab your partner as this song is now dedicated to our long lost and now found father-in-law Mr Frats as well as our new family Paul, Laney and their daughters and Denyah's new friends Millicent and Mrs Saunders. Paula then set the CD to play (You Both My Eyes). As Ray was walking towards his wife Paula to take her on the dance floor, she took Mr Frats on the dance floor. Denyah, Bernice, Meleta and Jenny, Lisa, Veda, Laney and Fay each took turns dancing with Mr Frats during the playing of the one song. At the end of that CD, Mr Frats said, "I thanked all of you my family and friends. I hadn't thought I would ever get this chance to be with you or enjoyed myself so much. Well family and friends a big thank-you all of you."

Mr Frats then took his seat next to Mrs Brown and said, "I couldn't wish for a better and a more loving and caring family. I love my family as I believe they care similarly for me. If I was thirty years back in time, I'll fight my son Eugene for Denyah. She's so beautiful" Mr Frats said and smiled. Doctor Penny looked at him and smiled. "Well they're all beautiful. But Denyah's the first to take my name. I'm feeling so fortunately honoured" he faced Page his housemaid and said, leaving Doctor Penny standing on her own.

Bernice looked at Denyah's wedding ring and said. "You not wearing a ring, you're wearing a rock. It's so beautiful."

"So is yours my friend." Denyah said to Bernice.

"Well, it is my turn to get married next sis, "Fay said to Denyah holding on tightly to her fiancée's hand.

Mrs Jay kissed Denyah on her forehead, wished her all the happiness in the world, smiled and left. Denyah had looked confused as she watched her walking out of the front door. Denyah went after her calling, "Mrs Jay." Mrs Jay stopped walking and turned and faced her.

"Mrs Jay. If you should need anything or my help, please call on me. My home would be always open to you."

"I'll keep that in mind, but I would be okay Denyah my dear. By the way, Natasha's little girl Miah, I'm very happy she's with her family that love her. She seems to be very happy. Her mother appears to me to love her very much."

"Yes Mrs Jay, her mother loves her and she will be the best mother to Miah." Denyah said.

"Miah's other mother is very ill and now living in a private home. I paid her bills and the house I put on the market, the money would be for her keep and for her burial. Denyah my dear, I would be joining my sister in Miami next week and I don't really need the money. It is also best I don't reveal which home Miah's mother is staying in. When Miah is old enough and she asks about her mother, will you tell her mother went away and left her with her father, as I wouldn't want her to find out her mother died from aids. "

"Mrs Jay, are you sure Natasha is dying from aids?"

"Yes Denyah, I saw her last month. She's really looked skin and bone in the last few weeks. She's my best friend and I've promised her that I wouldn't say which home she's in"

"Then let me give you some money?" Denyah said to Mrs Jay.

"Den honey, I have more than I'll ever need. Thanks all the same. But I have over four hundred thousand pounds and as I told you I put my flat on the market so that some of the money would go to care for Miah's mother and to bury her. The remaining will go to the home she's in - I have no children. I would send you a card soon as I settled in Miami."

Denyah hugged Mrs Jay and said "Goodbye and please get in touch."

"I'll send you a card." Mrs Jay said and she reached in her hand bag and took out a perfume, sprayed some on Denyah and then gave it to her saying, "each time you use it I would be with you" A lump of mixed sadness and joy came in Denyah's throat as she'd scented the fragrance in Wesley's house. Then Denyah asked "Mrs Jay, how did you know I was at my ex's house, and in trouble?"

"The truth is, Natasha told me she saw you heading towards your ex's house so I phone your house with a number Natasha given me, I phoned your mom asking her to give me your mobile number so to speak to you or to tell me where your ex-husband lived, but she had refused to tell me until I told her I was trying to save your life, so she told me you went to your ex's. That's why I was there and I was glad to be there at the right time. However, Natasha is little Miah's mother which you now know. I believe Patrick is the father of little Miah. Natasha gave her Uncle Miah's birth certificate that has your husband's brother name on it - Patrick Lee Lake. Well, as you already know her mother is dying from aids, I had booked Natasha into a private home last week. I don't know how much time she has left to live. But she's in a pretty bad way. This is why I'm asking you not to tell anyone about her. She's my niece and my friend as well. Natasha's mother doesn't want to know her or her grandchild. Well, as I knew Miah's father can afford to support her, I begged her mother to give Miah to her father. Miah is not affected by her mother's illness as her mother was okay until two years ago when she caught the aids virus by using dirty needles or sexual intercourse. Which way she caught the virus, I don't know."

"Mrs Jay, you were the one that rescued me from my ex-husband and I'll do anything to make Miah happy. But she would be well loved and look after by her new family. And thanks again for saving my life. I shall never forget you. It was you came to my rescue. Am I wrong?"

"No Denyah, you're not wrong. I was the one. I know you ex-husband, and he's a corrupt cop and would hurt you badly as he's very jealous of your happiness being with Eugene. Take care of yourself and your lovely family and kiss Miah for her mother and me." Mrs Jay said.

"I will Mrs Jay." Denyah said.

"Thanks." Mrs Jay said.

"At least let me take you lunch tomorrow," Denyah told Mrs Jay.

Mrs Jay replied smiling, "I'm sorry. I would be leaving very early in the morning to get to the airport for seven thirty. Denyah, you take care as the stumbling block is now out of your way. Oh by the way, do you know of anyone that needs a car, as I won't need the car anymore. And do you mind me leaving the car in your drive way with the log book. I'll be more than happy for you to give the car to someone of your choice. It's brand new just five months old. I didn't know I would be leaving so soon to Miami." Mrs Jay hugged Denyah and kissed her on her right cheek.

Denyah watched as Mrs Jay left in her car. Mrs Jay wound down her car window, looked back at Denyah then said "Goodbye, sweetheart."

Denyah went into her house smiling to see everyone was getting ready to leave. They all kissed her and said they had a hell of a time. As Mrs Brown eyes looked as if they were closing from exhaustion Denyah said, "Mom, it's time you went to bed. I had a look in on all the kids and they're sound a sleep."

"I must say, little Master Eugene must have known his parents got married to behave so well. As you said, it's time for my bed." Mrs Brown said and she struggled up to the bathroom and then to her bed. Mr Guy Rogers and Fay took Denyah's natural mother and sister Blanch home. Denyah mother phoned her and said "Den honey, I was too ashamed to make a speech as I took Wesley's word and drove you away."

"Mom, that's all behind us now. So let's live for each other aye. How would you like to have the baby next Tuesday morning while I go to my doctor for examination?" Denyah asked her mom.

"Why honey, are you feeling sick?" her mom asked.

"No mother, I was bleeding heavily when the baby was six weeks and I've to be there to know if everything is okay. So would you and Fay look after the baby until mom and I get back?" Denyah asked again.

"Of course honey, would you like Fay to come and get him? Or would you like us to come to your house and look after him?"

"Which ever is best for you mom,"

"I'll ask Fay to bring me over. What time would you like me to be there?"

"About ten Tuesday morning," Denyah said.

"Okay honey and thanks for trusting me again."

"Mom I have to feed the baby. And of course I trust you. I will see you Tuesday."

After Denyah fed her baby, she went to have a quick shower and then flagged out in Eugene arms sleeping.

Early the following morning, Eugene and Paul cleaned the living room, dining room and the kitchen spectacularly again. When Eugene went to take the rubbish out and saw the car in the driveway, he went to Denyah and said, "Den honey, There's a new car parked in our drive way with the door opened and a set of keys and logbook on the front seat."

"Mrs Jay asked me if I know of anyone that would have it as she's moving to Miami to be with her sister."

"Have you offered her money?"

"Yes. But she refused. And told me she's not too badly off."

Eugene smiled before he said, "How about giving it to Blanch, as she just passed her test."

"What would I do without you honey?" Denyah asked.

"Come here," Eugene said and took her in his arms and kissed her.

Mrs Brown and Laney went to do the cleaning and they were very surprised to have seen the rooms and the kitchen so clean. "Paul and Eugene had done the cleaning and even cooked breakfast" Denyah told them. Laney's two girls and Denyah's girls helped themselves to some of the wedding cake - Denyah and Laney laughed to have seen them stuffing the cake in their mouth. Laney moved the cake out of their way and told her daughters, "I expected better from you girls as you're old enough to know right from wrong and to ask."

"That goes to you too Paris." Denyah told her.

"Mom we were hungry and dad saw us and he did not say anything. I'm sorry mom." Paris said

"That's okay honey. Go and have your bath and take your sister with you. See she brushes her teeth. Your clothes are on your bed and after please come and have your breakfast."

"Okay mom." Paris said and she said to Jade B, "Jade B, you come with me." Jade B followed behind her and Mrs Brown helped Jade B with her bath and helped dressing her and sent her and Paris down to breakfast.

In the evening, Eugene took Laney's husband Paul to his local pub where they met his brothers and friends to have a drink. As Eugene had got married he treated the lads.

"I'm through with drink for the day," Doctor Glennis said as he was beginning to get pissed. He found a seat in the corner of the pub and rested there after he phoned his fiancée Kelly and told her he loved her.

Patrick called Eugene to play dominoes. "Brother, I never want to see any dominoes ever again. Sending my wife to her ex for a set almost cost her life." Eugene said.

"When was this bros?" Patrick asked interestedly.

"Last week" Eugene said, and as he felt hurt, he walked away in tears.

The following Friday Wesley and Lisa's brother Greg landed at Manchester Airport from Canada. He took the coach to Birmingham coach station and then a taxi to his sister Lisa's. He paid the taxi driver with a five pounds tip. "Thanks mate." He said before he left the taxi with his travel bags. "And thank you sir." The driver said and drove away. Greg knocked at Lisa's door. Richard looked on the wall clock to see twenty past three and then at Lisa asking, "You expecting anyone honey?"

"No, not as far as I know." Lisa said. "And I don't wish to see that brother of mine in a hurry."

The knock came on the door again. "You best answer the door honey?" Lisa told her Richard.

Richard left his dinner and went and answered the door. In a sort of a trance he stood at the door looking at Greg.

Greg smiled and said, "Richard my brother-in-law, don't tell me you forget how I look?"

Richard smiled and still stalled at the door and said, "Good heavens, why didn't you let us know you were coming. I would have come and get you."

"Does this mean I can't come in?"

"Of course you can my friend," Richard moved to one side to let Greg in then closed the door saying, "I'm just a little surprised seeing you standing at my door. Your sister is upstairs. Lisa, Greg is here" Richard shouted up to Lisa. Then shook Greg's hand and asked him, "You want some food?"

"Well, I wouldn't say no as it was sometime since I've eaten. But I can really do with a cold beer."

Lisa rushed down the stairs and hugged Greg. "Am I glad to see you? Why didn't you let us know you were coming? Richard would have come and got you" Lisa said.

"Well, after I got the coach from Manchester to Birmingham coach station then I took a taxi here. I had to be here after you phone me about our brother. Tell me this sis, what had come over our brother to treat Denyah as he had. She was a good wife to him. I was once jealous of him when I saw him with her. The bad always get the good ones. Anyway, when is visiting time?"

"I think seven to eight. I will take you to see him. But you must eat first then tell me about my nieces and Cathy" Lisa said, and heated some food and put it on the table in front her brother Greg. Greg began to eat and Richard put a cold can of beer aside of his plate and a bottle of whiskey. Greg looked at him and smile. "Cheers mate" Richard said and pulled the ring pull on the can and swallow deeply. After Greg emptied his plate, he said "thanks sis, I needed that food" he then drank from his can of beer and swallowed deeply and belched saying "Pardon me. I'd so longed for a pint of English beer."

"So tell me Greg, how things at home?"

"My dear sister, Nardia is nineteen and passes out to be solicitor, and Carina; she just took her first step on the cat walk as a model. Her mother tried talking her out of being a model, but she just won't back down."

"So, they both are doing well?" Lisa asked.

"Yes, I think so. But I have to get back by next week to finish a job as I need the money to buy Nardia a car as she has to travel so often. Well, Richard, I bought you a couple of bottles of Kessler whiskey and one for Denyah as I remembered how much you like the taste. Anyway, how's Den?"

"Oh she's much happier now she's out of our brother's life. And her husband Eugene is so good to her and loves her. You can see her later when we get back from the hospital" Lisa said. Then showed Greg to his room and phoned Denyah telling her Greg come to see Wesley.

"Well tell him, don't forget to come and visit us." Denyah said.

"Den my friend. I wouldn't hear the last from him if he hasn't seen you. Anyway, he said your Goddaughter is a solicitor now and Carina just starting out working on the cat walk and their mother is keeping well."

"Well, I'm glad to hear." Denyah said.

"Well Den, I'm getting ready to take him to see his no good brother, so, we'll drop in to see you on our way back."

"Okay Lisa. I'll see you then." Denyah said and put her phone down.

Lisa asked Greg "Are you ready to visit our deranged brother?"

"Ready as can be Lisa," Greg said.

"Well let's go and be out of his face quickly." Lisa said. And turned and said to Richard. "I've made two fresh feeds. If he doesn't wake within the next hour, will you wake him, feed him and change him honey."

"Sure honey, you say hello for me."

"Sure I will." Lisa said and she and Greg left in her car. When they got to the hospital, Lisa parked up and she and Greg signed the visiting book and the time and then went to see their brother Wesley.

At Wesley's room door, the police knew Lisa and let them in. "So, what bring you here brother? Don't tell me, my malicious sister had to let you know I'm here, does she?" Wesley asked.

"Yes. But only because she cares about you." Greg said.

Lisa left her two brothers Greg and Wesley talking.

"Wesley, if you don't want to see me, no love lost brother, I'll just leave."

"No, no, say what you have to say and get lost." Wesley told Greg.

"I'm happy to see you too, brother. Anyway, what's going on with you, brother?" Greg asked.

"Do I look worried?" Wesley asked.

"Wesley, I cared about you, this is why I'm here. So are you going to tell me what happened or shall I leave."

"Okay, here's my life story brother Greg." They said I murdered three people. Two of which was my colleagues, and the other one was a nurse my ex wife was living with. They claim I raped her before I murdered her. You know what brother, the funniest part of all this, I can't remember, because I was stone drunk. The first part of my life, I was sleeping with my wife's sister and even though my wife found out, I couldn't care a damn. Anyway, everything backfired on me. The bitch of my wife's sister, shoved up my arse one of my pot handles. I shit on my bed pulling the pot handle of my arse when I got sober. I had to call in my doctor. After two weeks, I can still feel up my arse tender when I take a shit. Then I been buggered by two faggots when I was drunk and then they tossed me naked in front my wife's lovers hotel. Now my wife I truly loved is sleeping in his arms and my child is calling him dad."

"Well Wesley, who fault is this? Denyah would have been with you if you had treated her with love and respect. Remember, I was living here when you was having affairs and you used to beat her and yet she stayed with you and treated you right. I even remembered asking her how long would she put up with your beating, and you know what she told me, until you put her six feet under. Brother, she was the lady for you, but you were so damn stupid and so blind that you couldn't see the goodness in her." As Greg looked at Wesley, he burst out into laughter. Then he asked Wesley, "Well, who shot you?"

"Some old bitch. I don't know."

Just then Lisa came back and opened Wesley's door and walked in. "So where you got too"? Wesley asked.

"To have a cup of coffee, to give you and Greg some space to talk. Are you feeling better? Would you like some money to get a paper or anything?" Lisa asked.

"Do I look as I suited for the scrap heap yet?" Wesley asked then said, "No, I don't need your damn money. All I need is my wife and my daughter. Now you both can move out of my face and stay out." Wesley said.

"Wesley, I know you don't mean that." Greg said.

"I'm sorry brother, I'm really glad to see you and thank you for coming. When are you flying out?" Wesley asked.

"Well, I have a full week. I'll be seeing you again. You take care, brother"

"You too and take my love back home." Wesley said.

Greg smiled and left behind Lisa thinking of what Wesley told him. Walking out of the hospital, Greg asked Lisa. "How often our brother got drunk?"

"Well, from since he was sure Denyah wasn't coming back to him. Why do you ask?"

"Something he said. Lisa, I don't think Wesley murdered those people as they claimed."

"So, what now Greg, what has Wesley told you to convince he's not a murderer."

"Lisa sis, I have to stay and help him prove he didn't murder anyone one. I don't want our mother to know about this. At least not yet," Greg said.

"Greg, I agree with you. Mother must not know. Well, if you think Wesley is innocent, do what you will to help him. I will have a word with Eugene. It might be tough convincing him to help Wesley, but I'll ask him all the same."

"Who's Eugene?" Greg asked.

"Denyah's husband," Lisa answered.

"Are you sure he would want to help Wesley?" Greg asked.

"Eugene is a decent bloke. If he thinks Wesley is innocent he would help even though Wesley tried to hurt Den."

CHAPTER TWENTY TWO

From the hospital, Lisa took Greg to see Denyah. They were both happy to see each other. Then Greg gave her a litre bottle of Kessler whiskey he brought for her from Canada. "Thank you very much" Denyah told him. They then hugged and chatted over coffee and roast turkey, ham and grated cheese sandwiches. Eugene, his brother Patrick, Denyah brother-in-law's Paul, and brother Ryan walked in.

"Eugene, I'd like you to meet Greg, Wesley and Lisa's brother. He flew in from Canada today to see Wesley."

Greg stood up and outstretched his hand to Eugene. Eugene smiled and shook his hand saying "good to meet you mate." Then Greg took turns to shake, Patrick, Paul and Ryan's hands.

"Well where have you left your family Paul?" Denyah asked.

"Oh, she the girls and Millicent are with Bernice. Bernice said she'll drop them off later as our girls are playing with her girls." Paul said.

Paris heard Eugene's voice and run from upstairs to him saying, "Dad, have you bought us McDonald's?"

"Oh yes of course honey, would I ever forget to buy my favourite girls McDonald's. You go and look on the kitchen table honey. Where's your sister?"

"She's sleeping." Paris answered and before she went to get her Mc Donald's" Denyah said, "Paris honey, say hello to Uncle Greg. He's your daddy's brother."

"Daddy, you have another brother?" said Eugene.

"Paris honey, Uncle Greg is your daddy Wesley's brother. He came from Canada today to see your daddy and us." Denyah supported Eugene.

"I don't love my daddy anymore, he treated you badly mommy. I love daddy Eugene. He's nice to you mommy."

Greg and Denyah's eyes met, Denyah's smiled and Greg signalled a twisted lips smiling. "Well anyone for a drink?" Eugene asked.

"A cold beer would be appreciated." Greg said.

Eugene looked on his watch, "Well lads we have two hours to get to the local. Greg, are you coming with us?"

"Sure, I would like too." Greg said and got up. Paris kissed his face and said, "I love you too Uncle Greg" and she went into the kitchen for her Mc Donald's and milkshake.

"How long would you be staying Greg?" Lisa asked.

"Sis, I'll be back when they bring me." Grey said.

"Lisa, don't worry, we'll bring him home to you. You go when you're ready." Eugene said. Then the five of them left in Eugene's car to the Red Lion pub. After a few pints, Greg and Eugene got talking mostly about Denyah and how badly she was treated by Wesley.

"Well Lisa told me everything including when she was scalded and I admit to you, I felt so ashamed to own him as my brother, but as the saying goes, you can choose your friends, you can't choose your family. He's rotten but he's my brother and I love him. I listened to my little Niece say her father's bad and that makes me feel sad. But Eugene, I went to the hospital to see him. He gave me some lip before he told me he don't remember killing anyone as he was always drunk."

"And you believe him Greg?" Eugene asked.

"At first no, but I asked Lisa if he was always drunk, Lisa said he's a walking whiskey bottle. He admitted he was so jealous of Denyah that he wanted his mate to have sex with her so that you would leave her and she would come back to him. That he said he'd done. But as for raping and killing, he doesn't remember any of that."

"Greg, you seemed to be a good bloke and I'm going to help you to clear your brother's name as I think he might be innocent. But after, I wash my hands of him. I would speak to a Mr. Flemming's brother tomorrow - I remember Mrs Jay mentioned Flemming might have something to do with Officers Bailey and Lomott's death and blaming it on her husband and only Flemming's brother knows the truth." Eugene said.

"Thanks Eugene, would you like me to come with you when you go to see this man?" Greg asked.

"Well, yes I would like you to come. If anyone can clear your brother, Flemming's brother is the one person. I'll call for you tomorrow as he would b in the Horse and Plough. He's there twenty four hours begging for drink. You can have dinner with us. That's of course, if Lisa wouldn't mind."

"I'll speak to her. I'm sure she won't." Greg said.

"Good. I'll pick you up about three o'clock." Eugene said.

"Thanks mate." Greg said.

"Don't thank me yet mate, but I'll do my best." Eugene said.

At this time when Eugene and Greg were talking, Paul, Ryan and Patrick were playing darts. Ryan paid for all the drinks. After two hours drinking, Eugene phoned Denyah and asked her if Lisa was still there. "No honey, she left over an hour as she had to go home to her husband and children." Denyah said.

"Thanks honey, I'm on my way taking Greg to her and then home to you sweetheart. Keep my side of the bed warm for me. I love you. I'll see you soon."

"Okay Eugene." Denyah said.

Eugene took Greg to Lisa after speaking to Flemming's brother and then he went home. Bernice took Laney and her girls to Denyah while Millicent spent the night sleeping at Bernice's. Patrick and Ryan went home in their own car. Paul said goodnight to Eugene and he went to bed. Eugene went to bed just after. As he met Denyah awake, he asked her smiling, "Honey, are you ready to give me another son?"

"You're drunk! Go to sleep." she told him.

"I might be a bit tipsy, but Mr Pipe here is over flowing and in pain and also he's ready to burst." Eugene joked.

"Well, I suggest you go to the toilet and release yourself." Denyah said.

He then starting tickling her between her thighs and making her laugh softly, but trying her hardest not to make a loud noise to disturb anyone.

"Go to sleep Eugene." she said laughing softly.

"Not until I get my night cap." he said as he was kissing her on her lips and moving down to her vagina kissing her all over until she felt a warm sentimental feeling and gave in to him then he rolled over and fell asleep. She looked in his face, she smiled, shook her head and went and had a quick shower and went to bed. In the morning, before he got out of bed, he poked into her from behind. She jumped and asked him, "What do you think you're doing?"

"Do I have to ask my wife if I can have fun with her?" Eugene asked

"I'm your wife and not your sex pot" Denyah said.

"So you want me to go elsewhere, if so, that can easily be arranged and then you'll be wondering why my husband doesn't want me anymore. You'll soon at my knees begging me to score you" Eugene said laughing.

"That's what you think." Denyah. said.

"That's what I know honey." Eugene said. "Anyway, Junior would like a little brother" Eugene said.

Later that morning, everyone was up. Mrs Brown and Laney cooked breakfast. After they ate, Mrs Brown loaded the used dishes, glass and cups into the dishwasher and turned on the washer. As she walk past the phone to go and get ready to go to church the phone starting to ring. She walked back and picked the phone up and answered "Hello, good morning"

"Good morning mother Brown. I was wondering if I should invite the family to a celebration dinner as this is Laney and her family, and Millicent's, last Sunday here. What do you think mom? Should I invite the family to dinner?" Bernice asked

"Honey that would be nice," Mrs Brown said.

Later the Sunday morning Bernice took Millicent to Denyah's. "Where's Denyah?" she asked Mrs Brown.

"Well Bernice, she's in the library, would you like to see her?"

"Oh mother Brown, I meant everybody to come to my home for dinner on Friday."

"Well, Bernice, I don't know as Denyah has invited Wesley's brother's Greg to dinner."

Mother Brown, there would be more that enough for everyone. In fact, I will phone all the family and make it a special day." Bernice said.

"In that case, would you like me to roast a chicken or a leg of lamb?"

"Mother Brown, all I would be asking of you, is to pass my message on and I'll be looking forward to share a happy meal with you all my family and friends."

"Well thank you Bernice, I will pass on your message to all here. And thank you. Wouldn't you want to see Den?"

"Oh, I won't bother her, goodbye mother Brown."

"Thanks for inviting us and I'll let Den and the other of the family knows" Mrs Brown said.

'I'll see you soon mother Brown." Bernice said and left. Millicent went to her room and had a lie down.

"Well," Denyah said, "I hope Greg doesn't think I'm trying to avoid him by going to Bernice for dinner mind and not inviting him to my home for dinner as I'd promised."

After Bernice phoned and passed on the message to Mrs Brown to let Denyah know that she has invited all the family to dinner the Sunday, Mrs Brown gave Denyah Bernice's message then said, "I think she invited all the family including Lisa's. But you'll still have to let Greg know what is going on as you had invited him to dinner. However, Bernice said she has already invited Lisa and her family. Also she has invited Mr and Mrs Welch, oh and the shopkeeper and Ivy. Den, I would never stop telling you that you're the best to ask Ivy to move in with the shop keeper." Mrs Brown said.

"Mom, I don't know if we should have dinner at Bernice's as I would really like to have Greg for dinner as I don't want him to feel bad about me."

"Honey, Greg won't, I summed him up, and he seems to be so much different from his brother Wesley" Mrs Brown said. "Besides, if we all have dinner at Bernice's it would be so joyful with family and friends."

Denyah smiled and said, "What would I do without mom?"

"Plenty honey, plenty." Mrs Brown said and laughed. "Well I must go and get ready for church." she said.

"Let me know when you're ready mom." Eugene said. "I'll drop you."

"I'll be okay son. I can do with the exercise."

"Not today mom, I heard Laney, Millicent and all the kids are going to church with you"

"And what about you and Paul," Mrs Brown joked.

"Well, I have to be somewhere soon." Eugene said laughing.

When Mrs Brown, Mrs Millicent, Laney and the children were ready, Eugene asked Paul to go with him. He used the seven seat car and took them and dropped them at the Methodist church gate. "Are you coming in daddy?" Jade B asked."

"No honey, but daddy will be back to fetch all of you."

"Well, you can come and get us in an hour and fifteen minutes." Mrs Brown said

Eugene kissed, Jade B, saying "You be good for Nan."

"I will daddy."

I'll see you later honey" Eugene said.

"We'll see you later too daddy" the Laney girls told their dad. And as they were walking towards the church door, Eugene drove away. He stopped some distance away and phone Denyah asking her, for Mrs Jay's phone number.

"Why," she asked.

"I just want to ask her something." Eugene said.

Denyah gave him Mrs Jay's phone number and her address.

"Thanks honey." he said and then drove to Mrs Jay's and rang her door bell. Mrs Jay answered the door and looked up at Eugene in surprise and then asked, "What brings you here Mr Frat's. Or should I say, Mr Lake?"

"Well, you call me whatever you wish. But I'm here to find out something. I hope you can help me if you can." Eugene said.

"Well, you better come in then," Mrs Jay said and she moved inside for Eugene to walk in but before he went in, he said to Mrs Jay, "My brother-in-law is in the car?"

"Well it depends on what you want. So you should go and ask him in." Mrs Jay said.

Eugene smiled and went to Paul asking him "Would you like to come in."

"I'll be okay mate. I'll wait in the car." Paul said.

'I'll try not to be long." Eugene said and went back to Mrs Jay. As he was about to ring the door bell again even though the door was left opened, Mrs Jay said. "Come right in Mr Frats." Eugene walked in. "What would you like to ask me Mr Frats?"

Eugene smiled, "Well, you might call me a fool after what my wife ex had done to her, but I'm here only to find out the truth this is of course if you know and can tell me."

"Mr Frats, I guest you're hear to find out something. I will tell you whatever if I know and you're very lucky to meet me as my plane is postponed. Well, what would you like to know?' Mrs Jay asked.

"Well Wesley's brother came from Canada yesterday to see him after their sister let him know about him murdering his two mates and my wife's nurse friend."

"Oh I see, well the truth is Mr Frats, I don't think Wesley murdered any of them. Before my husband was murdered or killed himself as the police said, he told me- Mrs Jay stopped talking and then came a long deep breathing from her followed by a watchful silence as she looked into Eugene's eyes before she went on to say, "Mr Frats are you sure you want to hear what I have to tell you and to help that wicked rat?'

"Mrs Jay, I would like to know the truth even if it hurts. I don't know why I'm helping him, but no matter how bad someone is we should still do what's right no matter the cost, and I'm afraid, I'm depending on you for your help if you can."

"Mr Frat's you're a decent man. Some other won't give an eye wink."

"I know Mrs Jay but I'm me." Eugene said

"Well Mr Frat's, Wesley didn't murder those people. Although I would like to see him go down, I can't hide the truth after you came to me and ask the truth. Wesley was stone drunk for days drowning his sorrowful arse in bottles of whisky. Your mother was responsible for those murders. She paid to have them killed by a Mr. Flemming, and then after had Mr Flemming murdered to shut him up as he knew all that went on. Mr Flemming was the same man she'd hired twenty two years ago to kill a man named Picard but he had killed Picard brother instead thinking he was Picard as he was sleeping in Picard's bed that Sunday morning. Picard had migrated to somewhere and may be well and alive. Flemming's brother also escaped to somewhere unknown as well." Mrs Jay said.

"Yes, I saw his brother and he told me." Eugene said.

"Well Flemming confessed to my husband before he fled into hiding and not even his brother knows where he is. My husband was murdered. Yes, Mr Frats, Wesley was having an affair with the old bitch of your fake mother. Sorry to say so. And then when Picard saw her blow jobbing you, she knew she had to have him out of the way. She used to seduce you and Patrick, but I supposed you knew about that. Well, I'm sorry the old bitch wasn't alive to confess to you and Patrick for what she done. But I guess she'd paid for her crime the other way. I don't feel sorry for that wicked woman. Here's the tape my husband left. You might find what you're looking for that might clear Wesley. As I said, you're one of the best. Well, I would be going to Miami next week. Mr Frats, you're very lucky to see me as my flight would have been this morning but postponed until next Saturday. I'm going to Miami to be with my sister for at least six months and then if I like it there, I be staying longer as I have a visa. Oh well, who knows, anyway you say hello to Denyah for me and all the best with helping that good for nothing ex of his. Well, goodbye Mr Frats."

"Goodbye, Mrs Jay. And thank you very much and I hope you'll have an enjoyable flight on your way to Miami."

"Well thank you Mr Frats," Mrs Jay said and saw Eugene out and closed her door. Eugene looked at the tape, and put it in his jacket pocket and got in his car. In his car he played the tape and heard Nurse James's voice crying and begging for her life and a man's telling her he'd been paid by Mrs Lake to kill her and the two officers and Wesley would be blamed for their murders.

Tears came into Eugene's eyes as he heard his deceitful mother's name linked to the murders. He took the tape to the police and told the police his mother was responsible for these murders. "Well Mr Lake, we had a report from the coroner stating your mother has died from a massive heart attack caused by sudden shock."

"So she wasn't murdered then?" Eugene asked looking no more interested than to say oh well, the bitch's death has paid for all the wickedness she'd done.

"Mr Lake did you hear what I said. Your mother has died from a massive heart attack." the doctor said as the police looked at him.

"So she wasn't murdered?" Eugene asked,

"No Mr Lake. However, we will forward to you a full report. And thanks for the tape which we would have our urgent attention and quickly." The police said.

"Well goodbye Officer. And I expect quick results about Mrs Davis." Eugene said and went to pick up his family from church. After he took them home, he took Paul with him and went and saw Greg. He told Greg, Lisa and Richard that he went to see Mrs Jay and that Wesley is innocent of all murders and that his mother, Mrs Lake, had paid to have Nurse and Wesley's mates murdered along with his real mother. Everything about my fake mother was stinking, she's seduced me, and she murdered my mother, Denyah's friend and framed Wesley. Shit:" Eugene said, "I should have demanded a receipt for the tape from the Police Officer."

"Eugene phoned Mrs Jay and explained. "Don't worry Mr Frats, I have at least three copies and they're yours if you want." Mrs Jay said.

"Thanks Mrs Jay. You're a life saver. I owe you a lot." Eugene said

"Just take the best care of Denyah and her family aye, and have a look in on Miah now and then for me." Mrs Jay said

"Bet your life I will. I will." Eugene said with a lovely smile. After he spoken to Mrs Jay, he took his seat and continue telling Greg "Well, it's up to you now to root some sense into that brother's head of yours. I tried my best to clear his name. I have done the donkey's part and now I have to get home to my family."

Richard got up and hugged Eugene saying "Thanks mate, even though he and I can't see eye to eye, you don't know how happy I am he didn't commit those murders. Well thanks again mate. I always knew you were not that useless." Lisa laughed so did Greg, Paul and then Eugene. Greg got up and shook Eugene's hand, saying "Thank you my friend. You take the family. Greg, you encourage your brother to take a trip to Canada."

"Well, as for me, I hope to take a trip over sometime next year to see how business getting. So I will sure look you up. Well goodbye my friends." Eugene said. Paul said goodbye and he and Eugene left and drove home.

At home Denyah told Eugene and Paul they would be having dinner at Bernice's.

"Okay honey, what time?" Eugene asked

"Three o'clock." Denyah said

Two thirty on the Sunday afternoon, Eugene took the family to Bernice's home, Then Meleta and her family arrived, then Lisa's and hers, Fay, Jenny, Paula, Veda, Carl, Mr Frats their dad, Jenny and her mother, David and his fiancée Tracy, and Doctor Glennis, Bernice's brother Victor and his girlfriend Kalor. That Sunday dinner time, Bernice had a full house. After dinner, the men went to the pub to have a drink while the women and children were playing frustrations, card games and children playing with the dolls house.

After the ladies got tired playing cards and frustration, they tided Bernice's home. Her massive living room was looking beautiful again. Bernice and Millicent became good friends. And Bernice invited her to spend two days with her and her family as she only had a week left before she went back to St Kitts.

The Monday Eugene and Greg went to see Wesley at the hospital. Greg went to see him first while Eugene waited outside his door. "Well, I see they took the shackles off you and the police have been removed from your door." Greg said

Wesley smiled asking Greg "What did you do for them to move the shackles from my hands?"

"Well brother, you only have to thank the one man you might hate."

"And who that might be?" Wesley asked

"Eugene. He found out his mother was behind the murders and rape you were framed for. You didn't kill her either. She died from a severe heart attack. Brother, you're home free. How would you like to come and spend some time with us in Canada when you're ready of course?"

"Did you ask Eugene to help me?"

"Yes, after I spoke to you last night and you said, you didn't remember murdering anyone, I thought deeply before I asked Eugene for help. Well, as I see it, he was the only one I thought you might have a good chance with and I was right. Would you like to see him?"

"Why would I want to see him, he took my wife and child."

"Brother, you gave them to him. I saw Paris and she's a happy and beautiful child. If you give her respect and leave her you might share in her life again. Eugene is a good father to her. I saw love from her towards him. You were the one that played the fool and the loser brother. Well, as I'm no longer sorry for you, I left Eugene outside the door waiting. I don't want him to think I'm the same as you, so I think it's time I get back to him. Well goodbye brother and take care." Greg said and as he turned to leave, Wesley said, "wait a minute brother." Greg faced him.

"Greg, I really appreciate you come here. Thanks for caring. Send Eugene in,"

As Greg stared sternly at Wesley, he said. "Please Greg I would like to thank him."

Greg smiled, and went and told Eugene "Wesley would like to thank you".

Eugene looked at Greg, "Wesley would like to have a word." Greg said again.

Eugene walked in his room and stood watching Wesley. "Eugene, I didn't think I would bring myself to say thanks to you. But I honestly, I thank you from the bottom of my heart for looking after my daughter and now me. I won't be able to pay you, but you're a real gentleman. And thanks again. Can I ask you to do me a favour?"

"Sure, if I can." Eugene said.

"I know I treated Bonnie badly, but would you please look her up and ask her to come and see me? I would be so grateful." Wesley said.

"Okay Wesley, I see what I can do" Eugene said

"Eugene I gratefully thank you and please kiss Paris for me." Wesley further outstretched his hand to Eugene. Eugene hesitated at first then shook his hand and said to him, "Take care of your self."

Eugene walked to the door and turned and looked at him and said, "I wouldn't stop you from seeing Paris."

Wesley nodded his head smiling.

Eugene left, as he and Greg walked out of the hospital, they had nurses, female doctors and other women watching them. They drove to Bernice and had a very good time. After it was getting dark, everyone said goodbye to each and went home.

"I had a lovely time," Mrs Libert told Denyah. "Thanks for giving me a great trip over.'

Mrs Libert looked hard at Eugene, but he warned her off saying,

"There's only one woman he wanted in her life and that's Denyah."

That week Tuesday, Bernice came for Mrs Libert to spend two more days with her and her family. The Thursday, Bernice and Veda took Mrs Libert to town and bought her a few gifts.

Saturday very early morning, before Eugene and Patrick took Mrs Libert, Laney and her family to the airport for their ten thirty flight, Laney and Denyah were in floods of tears as they hugged. Laney's two girls hugged Denyah and said, "We love you Aunty Denyah."

"I love you both too honey" Denyah said

Laney hugged Mrs Brown and said, "I love you mother Brown. And we'll miss you so much."

"Well, take care honey and soon as you get home, will you phone and let us know?" Mrs Brown told Laney.

"I will mother Brown. I will. And thanks again for treating us so nicely."

Mrs Millicent hugged Mrs Brown and said "Thanks again for treating me well. I phone soon as I get home."

As Denyah's children were sleeping, Laney and Mrs Libert asked Denyah to kiss her children for them.

Eugene looked on his watch and said, "Well family I don't want to rush you, but it's time we set out. You got everything including your passport?" he asked.

"Yes, I've mine." Millicent said then asked, "Laney, have you got your passport?"

"Yes Millicent I have our passports, all four of them."

Meanwhile, Eugene, Patrick and Paul carried the suitcases to the car boot. While Laney, her two daughters and Millicent stood by the car. Denyah and Mrs Brown watched from the doorway, Laney and Millicent planted a long goodbye kiss on Denyah's and Mrs Brown cheeks and got in the car. Paul hugged Denyah and Mrs Brown and said, "Thanks for a lovely time and for being such lovely family as you are" he then got in the car and sat next to his two daughters while Laney sat with Millicent. Eugene drove away and Laney, Millicent, Paul and their two daughters waved goodbye. As the car drove out of the gateway, Mrs Brown closed the door. "Would you like some tea honey?" Mrs Brown asked Denyah.

"Yes please mom," Denyah said and she sat at the table and waited for Mrs Brown to make her tea. After Mrs Brown made their teas, she and Mrs Brown took their tea upstairs with them and went back to bed.

All the way to the airport, Laney's two girls were sleeping and only woke when Laney shook them and told them "We have to go and get something to eat before we get on the plane."

Eugene hired a porter to take the suitcases to the check-in and he and Paul put the suitcases on the scale. Everything was okay. The suitcases were labelled and went through then Eugene took them and bought breakfast for Laney, Mrs Millicent, Paul, Patrick and himself and bought McDonalds for Laney's two daughters.

Sometime after as their flight was announced, Laney and her two daughters kiss Eugene and Patrick on their faces. Paul shook their hands and said "Thanks mate for looking after us."

Mrs Libert kissed Eugene on his face saying "Thanks for your kindness towards me. Would you please kiss Denyah and the kids for me when you get home?"

"I will and you take care." Eugene told her.

Mrs Libert then hugged Patrick and kissed him passionately shoving her tongue into his mouth. By this time Eugene was watching them. Then before Millicent left, she whispered to Patrick, "You should take a trip to St Kitts." She then left behind Laney and her family and walked through the passenger's area to go and board the plane. But before they disappeared out of sight, they turned and waved goodbye. Eugene and

Patrick waved back and watched until they disappeared. "Well brother, its home time for us." Eugene said.

As he and Patrick were on their way out of the airport, they had lots of women admirers smiling invitingly at them. As they got into their car, Eugene looked at his wrist watch and saw the time was eleven minutes to eleven, he phoned Denyah on his mobile phone telling her, "well honey, your family boarded the plane, and Patrick and I are on our way home."

"Thanks honey and please drive carefully home as it's heavily raining. I love you honey," Denyah told him.

"I love you too honey and will be home soon." Eugene said.

And as he drove going to the airport, Patrick took his turn driving home. But before they got home, Eugene asked him. "Have you screwed her?"

"Screwed who?" Patrick asked smiling.

"Come on Bros don't play the innocent with me. I saw you two were tongue lashing."

"Okay, yes I did but I felt nothing for her. Look I don't want this get back to Bernice."

"Well, who's going to tell her, you?" Eugene asked him.

"Eugene, I'm very serious, I didn't want too, but you should know when a man's drunk and feeling sweet and a woman come on to him what will happen. Bernice was sleeping and I was roasting. I had to take her. Anyway, it's not like I'll see her again."

"Did you enjoy her?" Eugene asked laughing.

"Well yes. Naturally, she'd wanted service and I gave it to her. It's a one off brother." Patrick said.

"Well just hope she doesn't phone you often or tell anyone and it get back to the missus. Oh brother, I wouldn't like to be in your shoes if Bernice find out." Patrick smiled brightly and said. "I hope I haven't plant a little one."

"I hope so brother, I truly hope so. Eugene said and he and Patrick got home, they had coffee and then Patrick took his car from Denyah's forecourt and drove home and went to sleep. Eugene went to have a nap as well.

Later that day, Eugene went to see Bonnie. "What are you doing here Mr Lake?"

"Please call me Eugene."

"Well Eugene, what bring you here? And what you want with me?" Bonnie asked.

"I went to see Wesley yesterday, he asked me to come and see you and told you he would like you to come to the hospital and see him. Do you know which ward he is in?" Eugene asked.

"Yes, Lisa told me." Bonnie said

"Do you love him?" Eugene asked

"Yes Eugene I still love him" Bonnie said

"Well I think he still loves you too." Eugene said.

"Okay, I'll go and see him. I don't suppose you can lend me ten pounds?" Bonnie asked.

Eugene took his wallet of his inside jacket pocket and gave Bonnie at least two hundred pounds as he knew she had no money. "Thanks Eugene I'll pay you back."

"You keep the money. Just go and see Wesley soon will you?" Eugene said.

"Eugene, why are you so good to him in spite of what he's done?" Bonnie asked.

"Well we get a little crazy sometimes so that we can't control ourselves. Well I took his wife and daughter from him and he had reason to hate me. However, he has realized now Denyah is my wife. If you love him and want him you go to him." Eugene said.

"Eugene, did he really ask for me to come to him?" Bonnie asked

"Yes Bonnie and just for the record, he did not rape or murder anyone. My mother had set him up. He' a free man and his jobs safe:" I was told.

That evening Bonnie went to see Wesley. She took him fruits and juice. "Bonnie, I'm so sorry about the way I'd treated you. I was under too much strain. If you don't want to see me again I understand. But believe me or not, I still love you."

"I never stop loving you Wesley" Bonnie said.

"Where are you living now?" Wesley asked.

"With my friend as I have nowhere else to live." Bonne said.

"Would you like to move in with me?" Wesley asked.

"Wesley, I would be so happy." Bonnie said.

Wesley gave Bonnie his house key and asked her. "Will you marry me?' He asked Bonnie.

"Yes Wesley, I will marry you." Bonnie said happily.

After a while and when Bonnie was ready to leave, she kissed Wesley on his lips but he gave her a romantic kiss and told her, I do really love you." he said.

"I'll see you tomorrow honey. Do you need me to bring you anything?" Bonnie asked him.

"Just you honey, just you." Wesley said.

The Monday before Greg flew out to his home in Canada, he went to see Wesley.

Wesley told him about Bonnie and he would like to marry her soon. Greg was happy for him and told him, he and Bonnie should take a trip out to his home in Canada.

"I'll speak to her." Wesley said.

"Well you do that. And let me know. Well, all the best brother and please keep out of trouble. When would you think you'll be home?" Greg asked him.

"Sometime next week, I think" Wesley said looking happy.

"Would you be alright?" Greg asked him.

"Sure brother, I have Bonnie to look after m:" he said happily.

"Well you treat her right brother" Greg told him.

"I will. Oh Eugene told me I can see my daughter." Wesley said.

"Wesley, Eugene is okay. Try not to upset him and you'll get on well with him. He even told me, he would give you a job if you want. But he also said your police job is safe. Well you take care of you and Bonnie and I'll call you when you're at home" Greg told Wesley and shook hand with him before he left. Outside the door, he met Bonnie. "Are you Wesley's brother?" she asked him.

"Yes, I am." Greg said smiling

"Well, I'm Bonnie and Wesley's woman."

"I'm Greg, well Bonnie, it is nice knowing you. I told Wesley to take a trip out to Canada and bring you with him."

"I would like that very much Greg. And thank you."

"Well goodbye Bonnie and take care of yourself and my brother for me"

"I will and have a nice flight home."

"Thanks Bonnie."

Bonnie went in to see Wesley while Richard waited in the car park for Greg to take him home. Greg then went and said his goodbyes to Denyah and her family. As Denyah heard him telling Eugene he's hard for cash, Denyah gave him a cheque for one hundred thousand pounds and told him "that is to help my Goddaughter Nardia and Carina and give my love to Cathy from us." Denyah said.

"I will Denyah and you take care. Goodbye."

That afternoon, Richard took Greg to the airport and waited until his flight was announced. Greg shook Richard's hand and thanked him for looking after him. As Richard saw him walking through the departure area to go and board his plane, Richard left. From Manchester it took him over an hour to get home. That afternoon, Richard went to see Eugene and then he, Eugene, Patrick, Ryan, Ray, Carl, David, Guy Rogers, Glennis, Victor, Mr Frats, Sonny and Aungus went to have a drink at their local.

One month later, Fay and Guy Rogers got married in the Methodist Church. And after, the wedding reception was held in one of Mr Frats' hotels. So many people had attended. Denyah's friend Ivy and Mrs Saunders were amongst the guests. Even though Bonnie and Wesley weren't invited, they both turned up and also Doctor Penny that Richard was shocked to see but as Doctor Penny was dancing with him, he said to her. "Nothing can happen between us as I love my wife and my son and she's having another child."

"I understand but we can be friends." she said.

"Well this would be okay with me." Richard said and after the dance finished he danced with his wife Lisa.

Wesley wished Fay all the best and announced to everyone that the next wedding would be mine and Bonnie's. But at the same time his eyes were fastened on Denyah and looked like his eyes clouded with tears.

Eugene raised his glass of champagne and wished him and Bonnie well. Then everyone wishes the married couples well.

Denyah took Paris to Wesley and told Paris to say hello to her father. But as he got talking to Paris, she hugged him. Then Jade B hugged him also. Wesley then said to Denyah, "I'm so sorry and very ashamed for all the wrongs I've done to you and to everyone."

"You were very jealous and selfish, but I can see now you've grown up and changed and I would like us to be friends."

"I would like that." he said.

Bonnie hugged Denyah and said "Thanks for all you and Eugene have done for Wesley and I shall take good care of him. And thanks to let me share in my daughter's life."

The music was heavy and every one was swinging away happily and getting down to the disco beat with plenty to eat and drink. The seven tier sponge wedding cake was looking spectacular in light pink, blue and white icing. Wesley was very well behaved and he was very careful of what he drank.

At the party he told Eugene he got back his job in the force, Eugene was happy for him and told him," if at any time you decide to change your job, come and look me up" But Wesley said "I love being a cop and thank you my friend to help me getting my job back and to make me a better man."

Denyah walked over to Wesley and Eugene and hugged Eugene while Bonnie held Wesley's hand and told him "I love you." Then she asked Eugene for a job in one of his hotels or restaurants. Eugene looked at Denyah. "Well" Denyah said, "If you can help her out, please do."

"Thanks Denyah. Wesley doesn't know how lucky he is to have people like us." Bonnie said.

Denyah smiled. "Come on let's go and have a drink."

Bonnie smiled and proudly walked over to the bar with Denyah. Fay walked over to the

Bar and said to Bonnie. "Good luck with Wesley. You too deserved each other."

"Thanks Fay. But at least I didn't sleep with my sister's husband. " Bonnie said to Fay.

Fay looked at Denyah. "Now Fay and said, "You asked for that my dear."

"Well, Good luck to us all." Denyah said and then as save the last dance for me was playing Eugene took Denyah on the dance floor and Wesley took Bonnie and as Richard saw Doctor Penny was walking over to him, he went and took Lisa on the dance floor while Eugene's friend Herman took Doctor Penny on the dance floor. Curt and Jenny and everyone had their partners and after that dance was finished, Fay announced to all, "I and my husband will be spending our honeymoon in St Kitts." Fay and Guy's wedding day was a day out of this world for all to enjoy and the music was great with plenty food and drinks

Eugene took Denyah in his arms and kissed her as Guy kissed Fay. Paula slapped Ray's face as she saw him kissing one of his old flames. Eugene laughed, hugging Denyah.

After that dance was finished, Doctor Penny went and said to Richard, "I'm here because of you."

"I'm sorry my friend but I'm so in love with my wife and we have two kids between us"

Then as she saw Eugene, she smiled. Eugene walked over to Denyah and kissed her. "Who's he." Doctor Penny asked.

She's his wife and I don't think you would get half a chance with him as he's so in love with his wife" Ryan said and smiled and went to be with Meleta and his children.

That night while Denyah and Eugene were making love, Jade burst into their room and asked. "Daddy what're you doing to mommy?"

"I was only rolling over your mommy to get off the bed honey." Eugene said and laughed and rolled off Denyah. Jade B found her self between them and playing with Denyah's long hair and Eugene burst into laughter, then Denyah.

The End

www.ingramcontent.com/pod-product-compliance
Lightning Source LLC
Chambersburg PA
CBHW060810030726
47503CB00002B/431